26/12/2015

John

Praying — as ever —
and thanking the Lord for you —
for your 82nd on St. Stephen's
Day.

Pax et Bonum

Jll CGollaghy

Saint Johnny

Owen Dudley Edwards is an Honorary Fellow in the School of History at the University of Edinburgh, where he has taught from 1968. In keeping with that University's treasured tradition of 'generalism', he is very much a polymath.

Dudley Edwards' natural brio and mastery of words confer on his most scholarly contributions a spirit of entertainment. He was born in Dublin and educated at Belvedere College and UCD. He has been acknowledged as 'a distinguished Irish scholar and man of letters, whose pan-Celtic spirit comprehends a Welsh name, a university post in Scotland and several important books on Irish history.' He is a regular contributor and reviewer for radio, television and the press. His books include *The Quest for Sherlock Holmes: A Biographical Study of Arthur Conan Doyle*; *Mind of an Activist: James Connolly*; *P.G Wodehouse: A Critical and Historical Study*; *Macaulay*; *Burke and Hare*; *Hare and Burke* (play); *Éamon de Valera*; *British Children's Fiction in the Second World War*; *How David Cameron Saved Scotland* and *Scotland's Waterloo*.

For Brother John with every kind wish

Saint Johnny

A Study in Historical Imagination

Owen Dudley Edwards

GRACE NOTE PUBLICATIONS

Saint Johnny
This edition published 2015 by
Grace Note Publications C.I.C.
Grange of Locherlour,
Ochtertyre, PH7 4JS,
Scotland

books@gracenotereading.co.uk
www.gracenotepublications.co.uk
ISBN 978-1-907676-68-0

First published in 2015
Copyright © Owen Dudley Edwards 2015

Owen Dudley Edwards has asserted his right under the Copyright, Designs and
Patents Act 1988 to be identified as the author of this work.

A catalogue record for this book is available from the British Library

Front cover drawing 'John' by Timothy Neat, 2013 (pen and ink)

Typeset and design by Grace Note Publications

Pardon, O Saint John Divine, That I change a word of thee
None the less, aid thou me!
— *Francis Thompson*

There was some one thing that was too great for God
to show us when He walked on Earth; and I have
sometimes fancied that it was His mirth

— *G. K. Chesterton, Orthodoxy (1908)*

For our Grandchildren

Owen, Rosie, Sophie and Max

CONTENTS

CHAPTER 1: Andrew   1

CHAPTER 2: James   11

CHAPTER 3: Mary   23

CHAPTER 4: Nathaniel   37

CHAPTER 5: Matthew, Shimon, Jim, Thady   50

CHAPTER 6: Miriam   67

CHAPTER 7: John the Baptizer   88

CHAPTER 8: Peter   113

CHAPTER 9: Judas   132

CHAPTER 10: Tiberius   154

CHAPTER 11: Deianera and Deiphobos   171

CHAPTER 12: Mary, Martha, Lazarus   191

CHAPTER 13: Philip   223

CHAPTER 14: Annas   246

CHAPTER 15: Nicodemus   269

CHAPTER 16: Eucharist   291

CHAPTER 17: Pontius Pilate   312

CHAPTER 18: Barabbas   337

CHAPTER 19: Mary Magdalen   360

CHAPTER 20: Daddy-Joe   387

CHAPTER 21: Thomas   406

CHAPTER 22: Polycarp   440

ACKNOWLEDGEMENTS   453

NE

ANDREW

In the beginning was the Word

Johnny always saw the story like that, right from where it began, and never put it any other way. It meant many more things when he was old, maybe, though from the first nothing could go deeper inside him than what he saw and heard. He knew more later, he would never see or hear more than that beginning. The beginning was everything.

Everything before the beginning was nothing, Johnny might think, except where it was part of the beginning, and Johnny was clever enough to know he didn't know how much was. But from where he stood, the beginning began for him with Andrew. Except that at that time Johnny didn't call him Andrew, and wouldn't until Johnny began to think in Greek. At that time Andrew was Aaron, Aaron bar-Jonah, Johnny's people worshipped in Hebrew, and Johnny thought and spoke in Aramaic.

Johnny was ten, strong enough for it. He may have been tall for his age but his work in the fishing-boats put him among older boys and men, so he thought of himself as small. He was quick with his hands, and they were still small enough to untangle nets and mend them more rapidly than grown-up fishermen were normally able to do. That was one reason for starting young on the boats.

The sea was the Sea of Galilee, and to Johnny at that time it was the only real sea in the world, whatever stories people might tell about the

1

voyages of Noah or Moses or Jonah. For one thing it was like a deep bowl of blue, capped by the lighter blue in the sky – or darker blue when the boat was becalmed and the fishermen were out after dark. For another, there was a strange mist around it, as if the water was drawn into cloud and the cloud came back to the water, filling and fulfilling one another, for ever and ever.

Johnny knew perfectly well that many people on the sea lived some distance from it, though he lived near at hand, with his father Zebedee, and his mother Salome, and his brother James. Some of the fisherfolk lived in Capernaum, like big Shimon bar-Jonah, or Peter, as Johnny learned to think of him later. Shimon was married, and widowed too, losing his wife and his child at the moment of birth. His wife's mother had come to live with them during that birth which became two deaths, and she stayed there afterwards. Shimon was so helpless without his wife, peering silently around him as if he had put her somewhere he was unable to recall. His brother Andrew stayed there too, when he stayed anywhere, but he had been down the Jordan listening to a holy man, whom he called a prophet. Johnny enjoyed listening to stories about the prophet, chiefly because his name was the same as Johnny's.

Even in talking about boats, Andrew made it an adventure. That was all right by Johnny, who still relished the touch of danger when a boat with him on board stood out to sea and a wind arose. His father Zebedee and the others had long ago lost any romance in their work, and Shimon was as pedestrian as the rest, if not more so. He always liked everything clear, which meant that it was often dull by the time he had finished with it. But Andrew had a strange habit of cocking his head to one side, as if he heard winds and sea from far away, breaking against long shores. Andrew was slighter than Peter, and Johnny often forgot that he was actually taller, until he would raise his head upright with a sparkling eye and a slightly grim smile, as though something which he had expected was about to happen. Johnny never asked him if it meant anything, and Andrew didn't make mysteries, or rather he talked about mysteries in a down-to-earth way. Curiously enough, it didn't make them less exciting. Nobody else talked about them at all.

The new prophet, John, sounded romantic when Andrew first mentioned him. Johnny had a vision of Elijah, or some follower of his like Elisha, thundering away regardless of the real thunder behind him. But Andrew gave no encouragement to dreams like that. He knew all about John, who was the child of a very old father, the priest Zacharias, and his wife Elisabeth, both of them now dead. 'And that', said Andrew, 'is more than we are told about Elijah, whose father is unknown.' 'Or Melchizadek', said Johnny brightly. 'Melchizadek was a priest and a king', said Andrew firmly. 'Elijah was a prophet. So is John.' Andrew was talking to Johnny because when he spoke to the others about John they smiled politely and worried about fish, silently or, as in Shimon's case, out loud. Johnny was a good listener, and always had been, since his mother first started telling him the old stories. Johnny thought he remembered them all. He certainly tried.

'Have you seen him making dead little boys come alive?' asked Johnny.

'Like Elijah and Elisha? No', said Andrew. 'I suppose he could.'

'Did you ask him if he could?'

Andrew grinned. It was one of the things that made it easier for Johnny to talk to him.

'He's not the kind of person you'd ask something like that, or much of anything.'

'I don't see why not. We Jews' – Johnny liked saying that, squaring his shoulders – 'We Jews like asking questions.'

'And why shouldn't we? But John is a prophet! You don't ask questions of prophets.'

'*Has thou found me, O mine enemy*?' remembered Johnny from the story of Naboth's vineyard.

Andrew laughed. 'King Ahab knew perfectly well Elijah had found him. It was a way of giving him best.'

'Do you think they liked each other?' It meant a lot to Johnny that people should like one another. It meant fewer noisy arguments, sometimes.

'Probably. That's one of the sadder things about it. But anyhow John is my friend, not my enemy, although I certainly like him very much and I hope he would like me.'

'Would he like me?'

'I suppose so. You couldn't expect him to notice you much.'

'I could make him notice me' said Johnny decisively.

Andrew shuddered, remembering some of Johnny's methods of drawing

3

himself to the attention of indifferent adults. 'Then he probably wouldn't like you. People don't want to be bothered with children when they are busy. John the prophet is always busy.'

'Priests have time to stop and talk to children.'

'He isn't a priest. His father was, but he died when John was quite young.'

'How old is he now?'

'About thirty. Young for a prophet.'

'Thirty is old. Samuel was younger.'

'Samuel lived in the Temple which fed him. This man has had to make his own way. He lives around the Jordan, away from cities.'

'What does he talk to you about?'

'He doesn't. He preaches.'

'Does he take a long time to preach?'

'That's the funny part. He doesn't. He cries out two or three sentences. Then he says nothing, which gives you time to think about what he has been saying.'

'Are all prophets like that?'

'Well, we don't really know. There hasn't been one since Malachi, at the time when Nehemiah came back from Babylon, and rebuilt the wall. We know what they said, but we don't know how they said it. The stories make preachers go on, but they may have said what they had to say over several days.'

'Most grown-ups say what they have to say over several days', said Johnny gloomily. 'Then they say it again.'

Andrew hardly listened to Johnny. If anything, he seemed to be still listening to John.

'Some pompous city slicker who clearly had come down to laugh at him and show off in front of his pals shouted at him, asking who he thought gave him authority to prophesy. And John answered him, saying

'"My father told me to go before the face of the Lord to prepare his ways, to tell the people how they might win forgiveness for their sins through God's tender mercy, and that God has visited us like dawn coming down from the sky to give light to people still in the dark and in death's shadow and to guide our footsteps in the path of peace."'

'Thought you said his father died when he was a kid.'

'Yes, but he seemed to be quite sure he remembered what his father had said to him. In fact the city slicker shouted back "how old were you when your old man said that?" and John said "I was newly-born". That finished the city slicker, there was no sense in arguing with an answer like that. John doesn't waste time.'

'I suppose his father must have told him again when he was a bit older.'

'I suppose so. One of the men around him told me an odd story about that. He said that John's father had been struck dumb before John was born and was only able to speak after the birth when John's mother had said he was to be called John and the neighbours had said they shouldn't call him that, none of their people had been called that, and Zachary wrote "His name is John" and found he could speak again.' Andrew grinned again. 'It looks as if God likes the name John.'

'Of course he does', said Johnny reverently.

Andrew smiled, and then frowned slightly. 'John doesn't think *he* is the person most pleasing to God. He says there is somebody else who is to appear, and that he himself is not worthy to unloose the shoe of that person.'

'What is that person to be called?' asked Johnny, a little jealously, a little hopefully.

'He hasn't said yet', said Andrew. 'But John says he is here, whoever he is, so we may know soon.'

'What does John look like?'

'He wears camel's hair, and has a girdle around him. He's barefoot, since he has to go into the Jordan often.'

'Why?'

'Well, when people tell him they are sorry for having sinned and will try not to sin any more, he brings them into the river and pours water on them. It isn't deep.'

'No', said Johnny, who had played in the Jordan with other children when he was younger. 'And it is friendly. It's *our* river, and it tells us so.'

'It sometimes welcomes other folk. It washed Naaman the Syrian and cured him of leprosy at the command of Elisha.'

'I hope he freed the little slave-girl from here who first told him of Elisha.

It must be awful to be a slave in a land of false gods.'

'As opposed to here where we are merely chattels in our own land under the rule of believers in false gods', said Andrew acidly. Then he shook his head in warning. 'Don't you start talking like that, Johnny. You'd be in trouble, and your family with you.'

'*I* know how to keep in with the Romans', said Johnny scornfully. 'They tell me how they conquered Gaul. And Egypt. And each other. You haven't told me what John looks like, just what he wears.'

'Or doesn't wear. He certainly isn't clothed in soft garments, that's for sure. There is something odd about what he looks like. He takes no pains to make himself handsome, but he is naturally handsome, rich, cascading black hair, tied back but well washed, in the distance like bunches of grapes and curling, a strong, red mouth all the more striking because his skin is white. And that means he can't have been out of doors much before he started preaching. You're very brown, and so am I. He's about thirty, what was he doing so long indoors?' Andrew curved his arm over his head, scratching his skull.

'He may have been ill', reflected Johnny.

'And he may have spent a long time studying', brooded Andrew. He nodded. 'Priest's son. Going over writings in his father's house after his father died.'

'He must have done it for a long time.'

'He must. Well, he needed to know what he would be talking about.'

'Prophets are supposed to talk about what God has told them to say.'

'That's no reason for them to be avoid study.' Andrew seemed to look accusingly at Johnny, who had certainly avoided as much study as he could. But this was an old reproach and Johnny was ready for it now.

'No use looking at me. I'm not going to be a prophet.'

Andrew laughed. 'Yes, that would be a miracle.'

Johnny had a flicker of irritation. There was no need for Andrew to be quite so quick in agreement. Still, prophets were uncomfortable people.

But Andrew didn't seem to think so, because the next time he talked to Johnny (which is to say, the next time he found nobody to talk to but Johnny) he told him that he had become a disciple of John.

'What', demanded Johnny, 'is a disciple?'

'It means someone who wants to be taught by someone else, not just by

6

anyone but a very special someone else.'

'What on earth do you want to be taught for?' asked Johnny. You don't have to learn verses and laws. You're a grown-up.'

Andrew was patient. 'It means you have found someone whose way of talking answers things that have puzzled you and whose way of life wins your respect.'

Johnny was uneasy. 'Not like a Roman soldier? There are some kids around here who think Roman soldiers are the biggest fish in the sea, or would be if only they were Jews. It would be a fine thing if we had a country of Jews acting like Roman soldiers – I *don't* think' he added hastily, having learned some time ago by painful experience that grown-ups often took literally what he had fondly intended for sarcasm.

Andrew dismissed the Romans. 'I mean holy men, wise men, good men, people better than you – and me.' Andrew was one of the few grown-ups who freely admitted he might be no better than Johnny. Johnny was sure he knew many who were no better, but he had found it advisable not to point them out. He could, and did, like Andrew. He liked him enough to find another cause of anxiety.

'Does this mean you'll be going away from here?'

'I don't think so. Not yet, anyway. John stays at the Jordan, meeting large numbers who come from city and country to see him. I suppose I can help directing them when I'm there.

'Directing them to what?'

'Directing them to come up to him, confess their sins and be baptized, washed in water and blessed in God's name.'

Johnny shivered. He was used to the thought of cold water and lived most of his life half in it, but he found it enough trouble to avoid the results of sins of which grown-ups accused him, without inviting further punitive measures by accusing himself. 'Have you been baptized?'

'Certainly', said Andrew.

'And what did you tell the people?'

'Nothing. I told John. Nobody else gets to listen to a person confessing to John including you', added Andrew hastily seeing an obvious question forming on Johnny's lips.

So Johnny dropped the idea of getting Andrew to tell what sins he thought he had committed, especially since Johnny was sure he knew persons with many more sins than Andrew, notably sins of bullying people smaller than themselves. 'Did you make friends with any other disciplines?'

'Disciples. Not very easily. Everyone is a bit shy after confessing. And listening to John makes you feel you have been turned inside out and shaken by a great storm at sea. There was one chap I got on with. He's rather nervous, and a bit over-educated. Not from near here, from Kerioth. Judas, his name is. Judas Iscariot. His father's named Shimon. He seemed stand- offish at first and I thought he might be a snob, but it turned out he's fed up with city slickers and their crawling to Romans while sneering at their fellow-Jews. No, I like Judas.'

Johnny had more respect for Andrew's likes and dislikes than he would accord to those of most grown-ups but he rather disliked the sound of Judas. A man from elsewhere might draw Andrew elsewhere. Of course John the Baptizer was much more likely to have that effect if he began to travel and take his schoolchildren with him (Johnny grinned to himself) but John the Baptizer was less a person than a great natural force. If you followed a prophet nobody knew where he might tell you to go. (Johnny hoped he wouldn't tell Andrew to go anywhere since quite apart from liking Andrew nobody else seemed likely to talk about things as interesting. But if he did, that was that.)

And Johnny stayed away from people who seemed over-educated. They usually reminded grown-ups that Johnny was under-educated.

Andrew drifted away from talk of Judas and went back to talking of John. 'He keeps on talking about this other person who is to come, who baptizes not with water but the holy spirit.'

'How can he do that?' asked Johnny.

'I suppose we'll find out', said Andrew. 'Somehow I think we may find out soon. He may be a very frightening person. John talks about the axe being laid to the root and trees which give no fruit being thrown into the fire. John told the Sadducees and Pharisees to bring fruit suitable for repentence.'

'For his dinner?' asked Johnny, thinking it sounded a bit mercenary. He had heard of holy men whose demands for proof of the goodness of their audience were satisfied when their own pangs of hunger had been satisfied.

'No, of course not', said Andrew irritably. 'He meant they had to show

8

their being sorry for their sins was real, not just the fashionable way to talk to prophets.'

'The way for a Sadducee to be sorry is to stop being a Sadducee', grinned Johnny who had been told that Sadducees believed that when you were dead you were done for. 'But if Sadducees are wrong, are Pharisees right?'

'John says they are too pleased with themselves for being right, and that because you believe in life for ever and ever doesn't mean you deserve it. He says the one who is to come will purge his floor, take wheat into his barn, and burn up chaff with fire that never ends.'

'What floor?' asked Johnny. 'Anyhow we don't have much to do with wheat apart from eating what it makes. What about fish?'

'Oh, Johnny' said Andrew sadly, 'I did think *you* at least wouldn't be always bringing the conversation around to fish.'

Johnny tried to look as if he could turn the talk back from fish, but in fact it stayed there because his father Zebedee and elder brother James were yelling from the lake for him to get back to cleaning the fish they had recently caught, and Andrew found himself with a similar if slightly more polite conversation with his own brother along the same lines.

Nevertheless Johnny looked forward to bearing more about John, which made it all the more surprising the next week when Andrew returned to the Jordan and came back to the lake to tell Johnny that he had met the new person and had now become *his* disciple. So had Judas. Johnny wondered what John had thought of this. Andrew reflected.

'I think he wanted us to', he said at last.

'Why should he want to lose you?' asked Johnny.

'Because our new Master is someone he knows is greater than himself. He said so when the new Master appeared. He didn't want to baptize him, and said he himself should be baptized by him. But the new Master insisted on being baptized.' Andrew hesitated.

'Then what?' pressed Johnny.

'I'll tell you some other time' said Andrew, and to Johnny's disgust turned towards James and Shimon and drew them away. The talk seemed to be about fish, but Johnny wondered if it stayed that way as they drew out of earshot. If this new Master meant Andrew was going to talk to the others instead of to Johnny, Johnny wished Andrew had stayed with John.

He became more morose over the next few days when Andrew's talks with James and Shimon continued, and all three remained proof against all his efforts to find out why they were keeping things to themselves and what the things were. Johnny took professional pride in knowing secrets before almost anyone else and the new secret seemed both insulting and threatening.

And then, one afternoon, while Johnny was sitting in his father's boat unravelling a particularly ugly knot in a net, he looked up and saw a man walking on the shore. The man was walking with Andrew, who was smiling, and with Shimon, who seemed much excited. Then the man stopped, raised his head, and looked at Johnny.

The man was tall, taller than Andrew, and bore his head upright His eyes were brown, dancing rather than sombre. His hair was dark and curly, trimmed neatly without pretension. His nose was big, hooked and confident. His lips were rich, full and frequently smiling, drawn back from regular white teeth: although now they were pursed almost in a silent whistle. His shoulders were powerful and athletic, the arms muscular, the hands – Johnny would come to know later – showing the calluses of a carpenter. His body was covered by garments showing a solicitous mother rather than a concerned wearer. His legs were long and lean, tapering into strong, powerful feet.

Johnny barely saw those things. He looked in reply. Afterwards he hardly remembered what happened next but in fact he seemed to fly, leaping over the side of the boat, crashing on water and then shingle, cutting himself open on a cruel shell, hurtling breakneck across sea and shore, faster and faster, as though every life he loved depended on it, ultimately tumbling into the man's arms. There he could only gasp without a breath left in his lungs.

The strong arms continued to hold him, lifting him slightly off the ground, firm and certain in their grasp. At last the man said:

'No word?'

And Johnny managed to falter out a syllable:

'Word!'

And the man said:

'That will do very well. I will be your Word.'

10

TWO

JAMES

And the Word was with God

He was 'Word' to Johnny from the day they met. In a way it was a pet-name, such as any child might have for any grown-up it liked. The other disciples called Word 'Master' or 'Rabbi'. Johnny's name for him caused a little trouble initially, especially when James arrived. James was the older son of Zebedee, in his early twenties, and entrusted with many responsibilities by his father, which should have taken up enough of his time to prevent his keeping an eye on Johnny. But Johnny had never been able to convince James of that. At whatever cost to his patience, concentration, tactics and strategy he was forever gallantly exhausting himself in the arduous task of finding out what Johnny was doing and stopping him from doing it. It often seemed to Johnny that he did it so frequently that his other work must suffer severely in consequence but James's altruism in the matter was incessant.

Now he came down from the boat where Johnny had been working under his eye. He was exceedingly respectful to Word, all the more because his own progress from the boat was moderate in pace and dignified in manner. He was greatly concerned that Johnny should be such a nuisance as to take up Word's time. Word said mildly that he wasn't taking up his time. James was concerned then that Johnny's injury to himself on the way to Word would soil Word's garments by impure issue of blood. Johnny looked down to where blood was flowing and felt pain there for the first time but the next moment Word's hand passed over his lower leg while

11

the other arm still held him, and the pain and the blood were gone. Word simply said that there was no blood flowing.

James looked, and there was none. There was none on Word's hand or on his garments either. Johnny himself had never felt better, though he had not the slightest desire to leave the hold of Word's arm. It was a protective arm. Johnny felt in no need of protection from James, to whom he could usually give as good as he got while the argument remained verbal. But the protection of Word's arm seemed to strengthen Johnny against all the world.

James then apologised to Word for Johnny, for the informality of the situation, and for himself. He explained that he wanted to become a disciple of Word, but he would have to get Johnny back to the boat first. Johnny said he was going to become a discipline too, and stood up for himself in all senses. James said that discipline was right and that Johnny didn't get enough of it, but that what he said was disciple, and how could Johnny become one if he couldn't even remember or pronounce it. Johnny said that he had met Word before James had, with all the logic of a child making its claim to something also demanded by another child. James said that Johnny was silly and that Word had been very gracious but that the time for playing games was over. Johnny said he knew that perfectly well and the silliest game was James trying to be Johnny's mother. James said that if Word were not here he would teach manners to Johnny. Johnny said with perfect truth that he hadn't been able to do it yet. Their next sentences were more or less incomprehensible because both were speaking at once, each one growing louder, Johnny higher, James deeper. Shimon made some effort to quieten them, which proved hopeless as usual. Andrew knew better. Word watched them, a little like a doctor looking at two sick children whom he was seeing for the first time. He seemed ready to them shout themselves to a standstill. Both of them were conscious of his presence, and therefore James did not try to hit Johnny, and Johnny did not try to kick or bite James. At last Word spoke, finding a space in the shouting.

'Sons of Thunder!'

His voice was very gentle.

James and Johnny looked at him. Word spoke again.

'What did Elijah experience on the mountain?' Johnny was quicker off the mark than James.

'A great and strong wind which rent the mountains, and broke the rocks in pieces.'

'And after the wind an earthquake', picked up James.

'And after the earthquake a fire', triumphed Johnny.

'And after the fire a still small voice' murmured Word 'Little children, love one another.' James looked at Johnny. Johnny looked at James. For the first time in his life, James held out his hand to Johnny in a handshake such as grownups give. Johnny took his hand nervously, and then burst into tears and threw himself into James's arms. James hugged Johnny rather awkwardly, and then said to Word:

'When you tell us to follow you, may Johnny come too?' Word inclined his head gravely.

'Johnny will come too.'

Johnny said nothing, but he slipped his right hand into Word's left, and Word gave Johnny's hand a very slight pressure. After that when they were sitting down or standing in a group, it was understood that Johnny would always be on Word's left hand. When the others had gone away Johnny would face Word, as he did this time. Andrew remarked as he was going: 'Johnny would like one of your parables, Master'. Naturally Johnny wanted to know what a parallel was, and Word explained that his stories were called parables, although they might also be called parallels because they were meant to help explain things which resembled the subject of the story.

'For instance', said Word, 'there was once a boy called Johnny. ...'

Johnny never told anyone else the rest of that story, but when it was finished he kept his eyes on the ground for a minute or two before looking back at Word. It wasn't very easy to talk. Eventually he managed to get out

'Sorry, Word'. Word smiled, but not with all his mouth. Then he ran his hand through Johnny's hair and said 'Thank you, Johnny', and Johnny felt happier than he had ever known.

But for Johnny to become a disciple meant more work for Word than accepting the homage of Andrew and Judas (it turned out Judas would not be able to travel with Word until later, since first of all he had to settle things up in his own place). Word would make a parable for whole-heartedness such as saying that to follow him was like leaving the dead to bury the dead, but he never said that it was like ten-year-old boys running away from home without permission. Zebedee and Salome needed to know much more about him. They knew some things already, which Johnny did not. For instance soon after Word called him – and Johnny always knew that was what had happened – Johnny was asking him where they were going next and Word said something about going to Nazareth. Johnny liked to repeat what he thought were grown-ups' witticisms (usually clichés) in order to sound as old as James, so he brightly responded 'Can anything good come out of Nazareth?'

And Word answered mildly 'I did'.

Johnny went scarlet, but Word simply laughed and rumpled Johnny's hair.

'You may like Nazareth well enough, Johnny', he said.

'Of course', said Johnny, wanting to eradicate his foolishness as quickly as possible. 'It must be a very wonderful place, you being born in it.'

'No, I wasn't born in it. My mother and my earth- father had to go to Bethlehem and I was born there.'

Johnny blinked. What was an earth-father? Word would have to tell him later. But not now. It didn't seem tactful, for one thing. 'When did you leave Bethlehem? Did you like it?'

'I have no human memory of it. We left when I was a couple of weeks old, lived in Egypt for a few years and went back to Nazareth where Daddy-Joe, my earth-father, was a carpenter, and trained me to become one too.'

'You learned to cut down trees and saw wood?'

'I learned to cut down and saw, yes, but also to respect trees and value their wood. These things are not here just to act as our servants and victims. If we are to work with them properly, we must love them. The same is true of anything that grows or lives.'

'Even fish?'

'Very much even fish.'

Word showed what he meant while staying beside the sea (somehow Zebedee's insistence on looking him over became an invitation to stay with them as long as he was there). It had been agreed that while they were staying by the lakeside, Andrew and Shimon, James and Johnny would make the biggest catches of fish they could to finance Shimon's family when the brothers had gone with Word, and to leave Zebedee some compensation for the loss of James's – and Johnny's – labour. But having made a great point of fishing right through one night, and getting nothing, when Word came down to the lakeside the following day Shimon was ready to contradict anyone, Andrew was itching to go on his travels again, and James and Johnny were exhausted by their efforts not to fight with one another. Word simply climbed into the boat of Shimon and Andrew and asked them to take it a little off shore. And he talked to the people who came milling around on the waterside. Johnny sat entranced, listening to the endless stories and things to think about. James sat still, only leaving his place to move Johnny so that Johnny could lean against him instead of tiring his back. Shimon leaned against an oar, his mouth slightly open. Andrew relaxed, occasionally nodding his head in sympathy with some point of Word's, or at the end of a story. Zebedee smiled, as though he took almost a father's pride in Word's – brilliance? no, because Word was never flashy or smart or exotic, simply clear and straightforward and slipping in touches of comfortable, quiet humour. Johnny thought one of the most wonderful things about Word was the way he made grown- ups remember how much they liked stories for children, and then showed them how useful the stories could be in explaining things.

When Word had finished speaking and the crowd at the water's edge, having stood enraptured for several minutes, moved slowly away, Word told Shimon and Andrew to launch the boats into the centre of the lake and catch fish. Shimon assured him there was nothing to be caught but sent the boat on its way while he spoke. Zebedee and his sons followed. Probably Shimon was the only one of them who was not expecting what followed, although all of them were staggered by its extent. Fish were everywhere, leaping and jumping, gliding and flying, twisting and turning, dancing and pirouetting. Fish were in Shimon's and Andrew's nets, in Zebedee's nets, over and into the boats, cluttering up the seats and lining the bottoms. Fish swarmed over Shimon, dropped on the shoulders of Andrew, and fell into the hands of Word who quickly and secretly slid them back into the water. The nets were breaking, the boats were sinking, the men were staggering, and Johnny was so helpless with laughter that he was the most useless person there. On the one hand no fisherman had ever had so abundant a joke ever played on him as Word had played on Shimon, on the other, they had magnificently solved the problem providing for the families of Shimon, Andrew, James and Johnny when they took to the road. Word said something nobody heard, and suddenly nets were mended (to Johnny's great relief) and boats were navigable, and the excess of fish in the boat somehow got itself back into the water and swam away. But what followed almost eclipsed the miracle. Shimon stood up in the boat, shaking, half-naked, hairy, wild-eyed, yet with more dignity than anyone had ever seen in him. He turned to Word, indeed he turned on Word, and said in a voice of fear and reverence:

'Go! Go away! The only thing I know about is fish, and you have shown me I know nothing about fish. If your power over my fish is so great, you must be immeasurably more powerful than me. I am not fit to associate with you. I am a man of sin, and wrong, and evil!'

Johnny was not laughing now. The others muttered their agreement, but hardly audibly. Word leaned across to Shimon, stood up like a landsman but not with a landsman's awkwardness, and hugged him. 'Shimon! Shimon! A miracle which makes a follower repudiate the miracle-worker is the best of miracles! I will never see a more honourable acknowledgment. Your greatness of mind will catch many fish, but the fish will be men. Your repudiation of me promises me that I can rely on you. You are the firm ground, you are the strong Foundation, you are the rock. You are Peter!'

Shimon looked at him bemusedly. 'I am Peter!' Andrew put an arm around him. Peter shivered slightly. Word nodded and sat down again. The boats turned back to the shore.

Johnny didn't see this as a beginning in the way that he felt he himself had not really begun until he saw Word – or rather until Word saw him or still more rather until Word looked at him. Nor did he see Peter as a different person from Shimon. But he did see Peter as someone more than the Shimon he had known and laughed at. It was as if Word had discovered a part of Peter that none of them, including Peter, had ever known to exist. There was plenty of the old Shimon to find in Peter, still.

The other person who was profoundly moved by the fish that came and went was Zebedee. He had heard enough about Word from James and Andrew not to be startled: that is to say, he heard of Word's wisdom, and to Zebedee wisdom could make miracles, if the wise man had pondered wisdom long enough. If anything Johnny might have made him more

16

sceptical about Word, since Johnny would not have been in the least surprised if Word had stopped the sun in the heavens like his namesake, Joshua, and Johnny talked as if they might expect Word to do it, any day. What impressed Zebedee most of all was Word's laughter. He made fun of himself, and while his words were to be taken seriously he undercut any deference to himself. He obviously preferred Johnny making him his best friend than making him someone to be given long faces and whiny noses. And obviously Johnny held him in respect, a respect born of adoration.

It had happened suddenly, but prophets affected young people suddenly. It couldn't be thought of as fraternal: Johnny would have died rather than speak to Word as he used to speak to James, although Zebedee was impressed by James and Johnny hardly fighting at all since they met Word. Zebedee was amused at himself for thinking of Word as Word: nobody ever called him that except Johnny – Zebedee naturally called him Rabbi, partly because he liked getting Word's opinion on sacred texts that perplexed him – but it made sense to think of Word as Johnny's friend as well as Zebedee's Rabbi and James's Master. Zebedee got James by himself later in the big fish day, as Johnny called it, sometimes in allusion to the endless fish, sometimes in allusion to Peter.

Zebedee and James were used to dry talk: it made sense, Zebedee said, since their business kept them long enough in the wet. This time he cocked an eyebrow at James and said 'Too many fish for a fisherman? Shimon seemed to think so.'

'We'd better call him Peter, father.'

'Maybe that was his last thought as Shimon.'

'Maybe. He'll take the road with the Master, now.'

'And you?'

'And me.' James paused, and added 'And Johnny.'

Zebedee sighed, and said: 'You're a good fisherman, James.'

James coloured slightly. Compliments were rare in their business. 'I'm glad you think so.'

Zebedee laughed. 'I know so. You have patience with fish, more than you have with men. You would have had to learn patience with men to inherit the business.' Zebedee commanded several boats, and several fishermen.

James said sadly 'I'm sorry about the business'.

Zebedee shrugged. 'I'm not, not after what happened today. I was sorry to think you wouldn't have it. But the Rabbi is better than any business. I'll sell it, when I want to, and hold the money for you and Johnny. I hope your mother will approve. She likes the Rabbi, but she is even more ambitious for you two than I was.'

James smiled. 'Perhaps we should leave it to Johnny to talk her round. It's worked before.' But it wasn't Johnny, it was Peter, who came to Zebedee's house in tears and torment, announcing that his mother-in-law was about to die. Salome was by his side back to Capernaum as quickly as it took to tell her husband and sons to stay where they were, they would only be in the way and they were to look after the Rabbi. But Word, riding on a donkey, had drawn abreast of her donkey before she was out of sight of her home, and rode alongside her, remarking in answer to her customary and fairly accurate generalisations about the uselessness of men that he had learned a lot of women's wisdom from his mother. This kept them going until Capernaum, since Salome had an authoritative command of folk remedies, of most of which Word spoke with respect. Peter was too upset to listen, and his donkey kept poor pace with them. But when they reached Peter's house Word went in to his mother-in-law before Salome had undone her various packages of nature cures. Salome entered the bedroom to find the patient on her feet announcing her intention of getting the evening meal. Salome was by now very fond of Word to the point, like Zebedee, that she looked on him as an honorary son, but she certainly had no intention of passing a man's medical work without the closest of scrutiny. It was not a doctrine she needed to explain or defend: it was axiomatic with most women, leaving it discretionary as to how far they expounded it. Peter's mother-in-law normally could be trusted to give full support to any such argument, with innumerable examples of the shortcomimgs of Peter.

But as to what Word had done, she was adamant. Before he had entered her room, she was practically gasping her last, bathed in perspiration, her skin like fire, her tongue cloven to her mouth like dry leather. Word had simply taken her by the hand, after which she never felt better in her life. When Peter arrived, he first kissed his mother-in-law with the gratitude of someone who had never expected her to be alive to receive him, and then he said to Word 'I should have known because of the fish'.

Johnny got the whole story from Peter the following day, but found his own mother virtually dead on her feet since no sooner had the gossips of Capernaum heard of the miraculous cure than they were down to Peter's house with every sick man or woman in the town, and Salome was working far into the night arranging the arrivals, answering questions, providing space, providing water, providing food if Word thought someone he had cured needed immediate feeding, and making sure that Peter's mother-in-law was not overdoing it in her necessity for hospitality. Word was in favour of her making the evening meal for her family, since it increased her confidence in her cure, but he was as implacable as Salome against her doing much else. They managed to get some food into him before the front of the house took on hospital conditions. The worst part of it was the lunatics, whom Word had first to silence and then to exorcise, but Peter had the sense to keep most of that from Johnny, beyond telling him that various people whom he knew to have been mad were now sane, thanks to the Master. Peter might not be as good as Andrew in talking to boys, but in some ways he remembered better what it had been to be a boy, and the nightmares which the sight and sound of insanity could induce. And these had been no ordinary dafties, even when they had been known to Peter for as much as ten years. The sight and sound of the Master had driven them into violent paroxysms, and their language was worse than could be heard from tax-gatherers or Roman soldiers. All was well when the Master had done his work, and with final yells, blasphemies and four-letter filth the evil spirits vanished for ever from those they had tormented. But there was no sense in making Johnny imagine what it must have been like.

It did mean that Johnny was unprepared for the sight and sound of the demons whom in his turn he would witness Word driving out. But he was better to see and hear them than to get a hair-curling story at second hand.

When Salome had recovered, Zebedee and James thought it was time to get her permission for the boys to follow Word on the road. But by that time the number of Word's disciples turned out to have risen from four to six. When Word has come back from Capernaum he has gone for a stroll with Andrew, and inevitably, Johnny, and Andrew recognised an old acquaintance who, like Peter and himself, had been born in Bethsaida, not far from Capernaum on the seashore. In fact they heard him before they saw him, singing as he usually was. Andrew had been fumbling with an introduction to Word when Word simply looked at Philip and said 'Follow me'. If Andrew was faintly surprised Johnny was not, but he had a mild pang of jealousy which he thought he had concealed until he saw Word frowning slightly at him. Johnny nodded: Word would know he was sorry. But then Philip turned up at Zebedee's house next day with a friend called Nathaniel bar-Tholomeas. As it happened Nat arrived in a condition of the utmost scepticism – it turned out later that he had promptly asked Phil how anything good could come out of Nazareth – and this time Word did not simply call him. He hailed him as someone he already knew for an honest man. Nat raised a civil eyebrow, and asked how he knew him. Word looked at him with a smile in which love and laughter were well mixed, and said he had seen Nat when he was under the fig tree. Nat stood stock still, whitening in disbelief: whatever Word had meant it was clear he knew the most private and most precious thoughts Nat had ever felt. Johnny realised that: what he only understood later was that it wasn't a matter of thought-reading, it was Word's respect for the way Nat's mind had reasoned and the faith it silently spoke. What shook Nat even more was that Word clearly saw his natural demeanour of scepticism was the effect of deep faith. Philip had an inkling of it, but there was only one way a stranger could have known it.

'Rabbi', said Nat, 'you are the Son of God.'

Johnny looked at him with pleasure. It was nice to see that some grown-ups could have intelligence. But even he was startled when Nat went on to say that Word was the King of Israel. There hadn't been one since King Herod, the present tetrarch's father, and Johnny wasn't sure it was altogether a compliment. But Word was clearly touched. 'Because I said I saw you under the fig-tree, you believe? You will see stranger things, you will see heaven open and the angels of God ascending and descending upon the Son of Man.' And Word laughed. Nat kissed Word's hand, and so did the slightly bewildered Philip. Johnny followed them into the house and brought out wine and cakes for them all, knowing this was what Word wanted him to do. He was less ready to do it on his own account. Here were more grown-ups to ignore and resent him, and while he knew his place in Word's love was secure and unending, going on the journey ahead of them seemed less fun than he had been expecting. Simon was much friendlier since he had become Peter, and Johnny had no more fear of James. But here were two people he did not know, and they seemed to have ways of reaching Word not easy for him to understand. Johnny thought it might be useful to fix his own position more clearly.

So when his mother asked him if he really wanted to go away with Word, he said that of course he did, but would she ask Word to keep him and James as the most important of his followers. What Salome actually said was, would Word be sure always to keep control of Johnny and keep him close at hand, and make sure James had an eye on him when Word was called away teaching and healing, and of course Word assured her that he would. But when Johnny brightly told the others that this meant James and he would be the most important people among the disciples, Peter was hurt by him, Andrew was disappointed in him, Phil and Nat looked mildly disgusted with him. James had known his mother was going to speak to Word to give permission for the journey and took it that this was the way in which agreement had been reached. It got mixed up with Johnny's automatic place on Word's left hand, which was in fact a place where Word could control Johnny, not where Johnny could control anyone else. If James sat on Word's right – and he was much more likely to sit on Johnny's left – that was also for the purpose of keeping an eye on Johnny. But there was a touch of stateliness about James which he meant for conscientiousness but which might look as if he thought he was the most important person apart from Word. James and Johnny came from a family of more wealth than any of the others, so far as anyone knew. It rankled, and from time to time over the next few months any sign of conceit on James's part might be put down by Peter, Andrew, Phil or Nat to this reaching for power, and they did mention it to the other six followers whom Word would recruit. It meant that Word sometimes kept James and Johnny aside with him when he went places by himself, for fear of acrimony breaking out with the others, and he would take Peter as well, since Peter would always need reassurance and leaving him behind would make him worse. It meant that if there was an obvious leader among the six, and later among the twelve, it was Andrew. Word would leave him in charge automatically.

Word did try to dispel the ill-feeling by asking James and Johnny could they drink of the cup of which he himself would drink. Johnny of course said he would, and so, with more bewilderment, did James. Word said sadly that they would, and that when he had been killed James would be the first to follow him into martyrdom. Johnny hardly heard this, and could make no sense of it: someone as close to God as Word could not possibly die, Johnny was sure, and what Word was doing was telling them to be brave, for certainly Johnny realised some people did not like Word, such as spiritless Sadducees and self-righteous Pharisees. Johnny realised some people might try to hurt Word and James and himself, but Word would cure any damage they might do to any of them. He thought James seemed to take it all too seriously, gulping a little, giving Word a wan smile, and bowing his head in sad agreement.

Word put his arms around James, and then turned to the others, saying:

'All this business of who rules whom is what the Romans do, and it is something we should never infect ourselves with. First of all, nobody on earth can lay down who is to be where in Heaven. Secondly, the only people who are great among you are those who serve you. Peter's mother-in-law is the greatest person in his house. James's and Johnny's mother is the greatest in theirs. I am not here to be served, I am here to serve, I am the servant who wants to save you all and your people and to do that I will not only serve but give my life to ransom all people.'

Johnny had been listening to all of this with uncomprehending interest, and when Word spoke of giving his life, Johnny was sure he meant that he would live out his life helping and loving everyone else. In any case Johnny was likely to remember the next bit.

'And Johnny –'

'Yes, Word?'

'That means you will be making sure everyone has what they need in eating and sleeping before eating yourself. If you come on this journey, you are the servant of us all. I, of course, will be your servant.'

'But it's you whom I want to serve, Word', expostulated Johnny.

'And that's how you'll do it best', said Word. 'You will never be the leader.'

'Very well, Word', said Johnny, as usual wishing he had kept his mouth shut.

'On the other hand', smiled Word, 'there will never be anyone like Johnny.' And as he laughed, Johnny laughed too, and so did the others, more slowly.

HREE

MARY

And the word was God

Johnny never knew at what point he realised that Word was God. Looking back, he could remember no time when he thought he wasn't. The first moment, when he practically flew into Word's arms, he certainly thought of Word as from God, by God, with God – it was all the same thing – which was easy. Words synonymous with Word were Love and Beauty and Truth and Grace and Wisdom. It was true that God was not the thing in his mind when he thought of Word – which from the time he first saw him was almost the whole time. God was remote, known only to the very old and learned, best expressed by a name so sacred that nobody knew what it was. Johnny knew that God had taken his fellow-Jews out of the land of Egypt which was why they celebrated Passover, and Johnny knew that God became angry with Johnny's people and permitted them to be defeated and driven as prisoners into slavery in Babylon and Persia, and allowed them to return when Nehemiah rebuilt the Wall, but let then struggle under overlords like the persecuting Antiochus and the extortionate Augustus. Johnny also knew that God would send a Messiah who would redeem his people, although it was some time before it occurred to him that Word was the Messiah. The proof had come in an odd way. Johnny had once excused himself to Word when they were walking together, and said that he had to urinate, and Word said so did he, and they found a secret place, and Johnny remarked that he had been circumcised when he was born and he supposed Word had been circumcised when he was in Bethlehem, and Word said he had been, in Jerusalem, but in fact had been born without a foreskin. And Johnny said that the Messiah would be born without a foreskin. And Word said 'Or was born without one', and smiled in that funny, crooked half-smile of his that Johnny loved. And Johnny, perfectly naturally, fell on his knees before Word, but Word simply caught him up in his arms and kissed him, and put him down again and they walked on together with Johnnie's right hand in Word's left as usually did. Word told Johnny that when Mary and Daddy-Joe took him to the Temple to be circumcised and the priest Simeon saw that Word had no foreskin he hailed him as the Messiah, and said his own Time for peaceful death had come for he has been promised he would see the Messiah before he died.

Did this mean that Word was God? Johnny seems to have concluded firmly that he was, without any recollection of thinking it out. It may have been hastened by some fear that the Messiah would be killed, and the thought that if the Messiah were God he would not be killed, because of course God could not die. This meant that any reference made by Word to his own death was simply a story or a way of talking, and not something that would happen. Just to make sure, Johnny once asked Word when they were alone, 'You are God, aren't you?' and Word laughed and said 'Yes', and that time Johnny answered by jumping up on Word to catch arms around his neck and kissing him. He knew all the old stories about the burning bush, and Moses taking off his shoes because God's presence made it holy ground, yet with Word the important thing wasn't to worship but to love. Anyhow, Word would have told him if he was doing something wrong, and in fact all Word seemed to want was that Johnny hold his hand, which was all Johnny wanted, most of the time anyway. Other people made a difference, of course, because Word had to give up time to them, and Johnny might sulk or show off, which was no way to behave in the presence of God, as Johnny would say apologetically to Word when they were alone again, but Word, while hoping Johnny would stop being silly, remarked that everyone behaved badly in the presence of God whether they could see him or not. Word liked Johnny to say he was sorry when he ought to say it, but he did not want Johnny despising or hating himself. 'There is only one Johnny', he would say, 'so we'll have to do the best we can with the one we have', and maybe twist the front of Johnny's hair into a curl, grinning at him. Johnny, who was quite good at pulling faces, usually pulled one back.

Certainly Johnny was thinking of Word as God long before anyone else was. People often went into long discussions about Holy Writings when speaking to Word, although Word gave them short answers. The shortness was not impatience or rudeness: it was giving them something about which to think without cluttering it up. Yet these discussions did not work their way into realisations that Word was God, and Word didn't seem to want them to, only that people would make it easier for themselves to think. The two people Johnny would really remember for saluting Word as God were Peter, whom nobody would mistake for an intellectual, and Martha, who always made it clear that the intellectual in her family was her sister Mary.

After that real enquirers into theology like Andrew or Martha's Mary found themselves startled to realise that this was what they themselves believed but hadn't realised they did, or so it seemed to Johnny looking at them. But there were several weeks before anyone except Johnny seemed to know, and Johnny realised how appalled people would be if they heard him saying any such thing, and so he didn't say it. He was beginning to wonder if James had realised it when Peter eventually spoke out, but he had never liked to ask James. They got on better after Word told them their business was to love one another, but if James did not believe Word was God, he would be absolutely horrified to have Johnny say it, and embarrassed at how it might make Word feel. So Johnny knew what he himself believed and left it to the grown-ups to decide for themselves in their own time.

Believing that Word was God also meant that Johnny was less inclined to give himself airs as being a friend of someone important. Everyone could see Word, and so in early days Johnny might swagger because Word wanted his company for its own sake, which nobody else did, unless they lacked a better audience. But to be a friend of God wasn't something anyone could see, except, as Word said, there were thousands of people who were very good friends of God without knowing it. It was clear that Andrew, Nat, Phil and James all believed in Word as what Nat had called 'the Son of God', and Peter didn't know what Word was but thought whatever it was it was Godsent, and so all worked their way to seeing Word as the Messiah. But that did not mean Word was God, and Johnny could only reflect (as he had so many times before) that grown-ups spent a lot of time making things difficult for themselves. Afterwards Johnny learned other people had known that Word was God before Johnny was even born. Word's mother Mary was one, and she told Johnny when first they were alone together that Daddy-Joe had known, and so did her cousin Elizabeth whose son was John the Baptizer, and John the Baptizer himself and his father Zachary, and perhaps Simeon and an old lady in the Temple during Mary's purification after Word's birth. But Mary was the only one Johnny would ever really meet although she talked about them all so vividly that Johnny could swear he had met them, and in a way he would meet Daddy-Joe.

Johnny did meet Word's mother quite soon after Word saved Peter's mother-in-law because both mother and son had been invited to a wedding at Khiber Qana and Word said he must bring his disciples, and the people of the wedding apparently told Word that he could bring anyone so long as he brought himself. Johnny had been looking forward to meeting Word's mother, but it was a shock when he saw her. He had never seen anyone so like anyone else as Word's mother looked like Word. Word's was not a woman's face, and Mary's was not a man's face: he was strong where she was delicate. You expected parents to look like children, but this was beyond anything Johnny had ever seen. He was so much taken aback that he hardly knew what she said, and he stammered eventually 'I'm a friend of your son', and Mary laughed a rich gurgling laugh, and said 'I've never met anyone so good at making friends with children as my son! The two getting married today were children whom he befriended when he had grown up, and I think he introduced them to each other. So watch out, Johnny!' Word said that Johnny probably had some time yet before he thought of that, and Johnny told himself he would never think of it, because it would hardly be proper for a disciple to marry, so he was a little taken aback when Word added 'but here is Philip, who may make a very handsome husband', and laughed as Philip went scarlet, and then quickly added to his mother 'and here is Shimon whom I name Peter, and like yourself, Mother, he'll find this a time of sadness as well as happiness, for he too has lost his beloved partner', and the two of them

26

held their hands out to Peter, leaving Johnny wondering yet again at the perfect counterparts, the richness of the black hair, the natural dark curls, the finely curved noses, the dancing brown eyes, the rich, red lips, the strong bodies – and the height, for while Mary was several inches smaller than her son, she was taller than almost any other woman there.

Anyhow Johnny was quite clear as to what he had to do now, because while the wedding was a wealthy affair, with the ruler of the feast snapping out orders, and many servants jumping to attention whenever he spoke, there was work enough for a polite boy. Johnny began by conducting Mary to a couch, and Word went with her, and Johnny, being smaller than the rest of them, was quick on his feet to get places near Word for Peter, Andrew, James, Phil and Nat, so that when the appropriate steward came round he could assign the seats automatically to them with the great air of a genius solving a difficulty which had perplexed multitudes. Johnny had some small space to which he could retreat when his services were not wanted, but he made sure that his services were well and truly wanted, as people waited for someone to meet their needs and Johnny was in the gap long before the ruler's and steward's minions were at hand. Word was looking at this performance with affectionate amusement but was quickly drawn away as ceremonies demanded him. Johnny liked the smashing of the glass, but naturally his favourite moments would be when Word was called on to speak a blessing, and then later to make a speech, or, as he put it in a joke exclusively for Johnny, to say a word. The blessing was so beautiful that Johnny thought for a moment that it might be worth getting married if only Word blessed you like that. It was as though Johnny could see goodness itself wafting from Word around bride and groom and holding them in what seemed a solid cloud, if there could be such a thing, and then behind them smaller solid clouds, all of them smaller than Johnny and some tiny, stood very close, looking both separate from bride and groom and part of them. And then the clouds vanished, Word became silent, Johnny blinked and the wedding went ahead. Johnny wondered if anyone else could see what he had seen, but nobody had the look of having seen anything unusual, although many looked as though they had loved what they had heard. And then Johnny turned back and saw Mary. One other person had seen what Johnny had seen.

When the wedding-feast was on, the speeches made their way, some good, some bad, some boring, Johnny scurrying around making sure everyone's glass was full long before wine waiters noticed. Word gave a wonderful speech with the faintly serious note that sometimes underlay his jokes, but keeping the audience rolling with laughter as he solemnly stressed the duties of husbands to obey their wives. He went into considerable detail about it, and his language rippled itself between parody of speeches so often given telling wives to be subject to their husbands and little reminders that however hilarious Word meant what he said. Johnny had by now put the fleeting thought of marriage well out of his mind, but if its ghost lingered, this prospect easily put it to flight. But in any case he was hard at work with his pitchers, and vessels, and fine earthenware, and it was not until an hour after Word had spoken that, looking for the next vessel to refill the one he was carrying, Johnny couldn't find one. He had been outside the door, giving wine to beggars standing outside, and taking a little while as the word of unexpected munificence got around, but he had finished his last beggar just as he finished his last pitcher. He struggled back to Mary, who took one look at his face, which she had been intending to tell to feed itself. 'I can't find any more wine', said Johnny, and Mary, quickly looking around at the eyebrows of guests beginning to rise and the feet of waiters beginning to stop, half-stood so that she could move fast but not noticeably, and Johnny slipped behind her like a dutiful shadow. Mary reached Word, who was talking mildly enough to a stout Sadducee, and the Sadducee was as usual denying the existence of miracles, and Word was playfully interpreting the Sadducee's logic to show that it might imply what he was trying to deny, but doing it so pleasantly that the Sadducee was growing less combative by the minute. Mary whispered from the side of her mouth to Word 'they have no wine', and Word, looking at the Sadducee, said 'not now' or something like it, meaning that he didn't want to flatten the stout Sadducee with a miracle collapsing his argument, especially as the Sadducee was murmuring benevolently 'I'm only waiting for someone to prove there can be miracles'. To Johnny's surprise Mary said not a word of disagreement with Word, but merely walked over to the group of servants who were by now huddling defensively around the empty wine-jars, nodded at Word and said 'do whatever he tells you' and went back to her seat. Johnny noticed that the servants at least realised the women knew what was happening and were best to rely on, although the men were officially in command. Word waited until the Sadducee had repeated himself three times about only waiting for the proof of miracles, and briefly excused himself, apparently walking out as though on his way to relieve himself, but in fact paused in front of the same servants to whom Mary had just spoken and said 'Fill the waterpots with water' in a quiet voice of such authority that every servant moved at once to fill the pots to the brim. Apart from anything else Word's blessing and his speech had been sufficient to win him respect among the listening servants, by this stage jaundiced enough with wedding-speeches to value good ones in the rare event of hearing them. Word went out of the room in the usual way, washed his hands on his return and walked back towards the Sadducee, pausing as he reached the servants to say 'Draw out now, and bring what you pour to the governor of the feast'. Johnny couldn't hear this, but he had been on the watch for Word, and saw his gestures. So Johnny picked up one of the waterpots and followed the servants to the ruler of the feast in time to see him take a brief swig, blink open his eyes wide, spit, take another swig, swallow it, take a third swig, slurp it round his mouth and draw it luxuriantly round his throat, and say in a voice of utter disbelief to the bridegroom 'the usual thing is to start the proceedings with the good wine, don't you know, but you don't seem to hold with that, I've never tasted anything as good as this, you've kept the best till now, not that most of them will have the palates to appreciate what you've giving them', and Johnny slid back to Word and filled his beaker and the stout Sadducee's beaker, and the stout Sadducee took a swig, followed it up by another sufficient to choke him, spluttered his way into some form of coherence and said to Word, 'Now here's a miracle, if you like!' 'What is?' asked Word. 'They've kept the best wine to the last!' 'I'm glad you think so', murmured Word, 'Johnny, you must now sit down and have something to eat, you have served well, but leave it to the servants now.' Johnny was about to say that he wanted to look at other responses to the miraculous wine but he caught Word's eye and that, of course, was that. When he rejoined Mary she made room for him: he was a little startled to see she was shaking with laughter. When Word came back to her, Mary said 'You're a good boy', and Word said 'fortunately not as good as Johnny', and they both laughed, and Johnny might have been a little upset and puzzled, but Mary put her arms around him and he hugged her back.

Johnny wondered whether he should tell Word if the food where to run out before Johnny had had enough, but somehow it didn't seem to. When Johnny went up at the end to thank the ruler of the feast, the ruler assured him it had been a pleasure, except that the words in the sentence seemed to run backwards.

Mary asked Johnny to come back with Word to Nazareth for a few days after this, and Word said it would do Johnny and Nat some good to see Nazareth for themselves, after which they would be coming out of Nazareth and would thus be superior authorities on whether anything good could come out of the place, and Johnny looked at Nat, and Nat looked at Johnny, and both of them thanked Mary, and off they went. While they were in Nazareth Johnny went down to the well for water quite a few times: he well was dark and deep and looked as if it might have had many secrets, but Johnny could not imagine anyone telling secrets near it because the place was always surrounded by gossips who were forever asking everyone about anything. They all wanted to know where Johnny had come from, and why, and what was a well-to-do fisherman's son doing in the company of a carpenter who was, they agreed, a very good carpenter – the best one in Nazareth, many said – but who had retired from business at the age of 30 and why on earth would anyone do that unless he was demented or religious or both, and was it true that he was taking up wholesale fishing and what did he know about fishing anyway, or was it true that he was turning vintner, and were the people who said he had healed them lunatics or cranks, didn't everyone know that Galilee was full of chronic malingerers and hypochondriacs, now if he could produce cures for hypochondria he would be doing well, it seemed to be going round like an infectious disease. When Johnny succeeded in tearing himself away he was concerned enough to ask Word back at Mary's house whether he could cure hypochondria, and Word replied gravely that he could not. Then Johnny gave up trying to pretend he knew what the word meant, but at the same time he said that nothing was impossible to God, and Word said one could not cure what did not exist, which was what hypochondria was.

Mary remarked that a lot of people could probably kill themselves from hypochondria all the same, which puzzled Johnny until Word said that people who spent all their time fussing about themselves were not really living since living had to be for other people if it was real. Johnny wondered if all the gossips at the well were living for other people, and Word explained that they were mostly thinking about what to say about other people rather than finding out about them. But he agreed with Johnny that the old well was a holy place, since so many people had gone there to help others, and Mary said that Word must have been to it every day for nearly thirty years to get water for Daddy-Joe and herself, and it must have taught him a great deal about human nature. Johnny doubted if anyone could pray there, and Nat thought they might if they looked into the well, and Mary laughed and said there certainly was no place in Nazareth less likely for angels to frequent as she doubted if they could hear themselves speak. Word grinned at her, Johnny could make little of what she had said but remembered it later, but Nat went a little white and stammered and said 'so it wasn't there!' Mary smiled and shook her head, and Word said that when he had talked of Nat being able to see the angels moving up and down some day it was most unlikely to be at the well in Nazareth. On the other hand Johnny enjoyed meeting neighbours who showed them furniture made by Word and older work made by Daddy-Joe and Word talked about the problems of skilled carpentry and managed to make it much more interesting than Johnny would have thought possible. But everything fell to pieces on the Sabbath when they went to the synagogue, Johnny feeling proud of the new yarmulka Word had given him, and enjoying saying the prayers with Word. And then someone handed Word a scroll.

Johnny's dark eyes lit up and he leaned forward. Word would read, and Johnny knew no music more wonderful than Word reading the holy words. Word would speak, and while Johnny might not understand everything he said, Johnny would agree with every word. Johnny half-noticed that the men in the congregation were leaning as attentively as himself, but he hardly noticed that Nat had picked up the strong, knob-headed staff he had rather oddly chosen to carry that morning. Some whispers reached him, and he frowned: occasionally badly-behaved people whispered in synagogue – Johnny tried to forget that he had, once or twice, and if he could not quite forget it at least he told himself that he had been *much* younger – nothing they said was clear to Johnny, it simply sounded like bad-tempered snakes. Word opened the scroll, and the words of Isaiah rang out:

'The Spirit of the Lord is upon me: because the Lord hath anointed me to preach good tidings unto the meek; he hath sent me to bind up the brokenhearted, to proclaim liberty to the captives, and the opening of the prison to them that are bound.'

It was never clear where Word began to speak rather than to read, what he read and what he said seeming seamless: 'and recovering of sight to the blind, and to set at liberty them that are bruised.' But now be handed the scroll back to the priest, and sat down, pausing for a moment, and then began speaking, very quietly:

'This day is this scripture fulfilled in your ears. Ye will surely say unto me this proverb Physician, heal thyself: whatsoever we have heard done in Capernaum, do also here in thy country.' This brought uneasy shrinking, and Johnny diagnosed that it was in the minds of many.

'Verily I say unto you: no prophet is accepted in his own country.' Johnny's eyes darted from face to face, and saw them hardening. 'But I tell you of a truth, many widows were in Israel in the days of Elijah, when the heaven was shut up three years and six months, when great famine was throughout all the land; but unto none of them was Elijah sent, save unto Sarepta, a city of Sidon, unto a woman who was a widow. And many lepers were in Israel in the time of Elisha the prophet; and none of them was cleansed, saving Naaman the Syrian.' In a flash Johnny saw what Word was explaining, that God was God for everyone and not simply for Johnny and his fellow-Jews. He had the same tincture of jealousy he had when Word adopted yet another disciple, or even when Word seemed to be what Johnny thought over-long with some other child. Word was showing him that these feelings were wrong, silly nonsense, so when Johnny got them, he kicked them out of his mind as fast as he could, and now he told himself that it was just like Word to give himself to everyone instead of his own people in Galilee and here even more in Nazareth, which must be the dearest place in the world to him. And then in the silence that had followed Word, Johnny heard grunts, and cries, and men began to jump up from their seats, and some of them nearest to Word managed to get their hands on him, and were hustling him to the door with shouts to take Word and throw him down Jebel Qafza, which Word had pointed out to Johnny as the great hill on which Nazareth was built,

350 feet higher than the Sea of Galilee. Johnny jumped to his feet, but immediately Nat swung him up under his arm and pushed towards the door, hard, for the crowd around them were also trying to close around Word. And when they reached the door, the people at the head of the crowd were pushing and shoving Word nearer the edge of the cliff. Johnny managed to scramble out of Nat's hold, although he had to fight to do it, but as soon as he landed on the ground and was picking himself up to fight his way to where Word was, Nat swung his staff, and Johnny knew nothing else until he woke up on a couch in Mary's house with a headache worse than he had ever known, and Nat was looking at him apologetically, and Mary's cool hand was on his forehead, and Word was walking through the door as though he had just been out on a long walk, and, taking in the group walked up to Johnny and put his hand on the back of Johnny's head, and the headache was gone. And Word said:

'Good work, Nat. Mother, I'm afraid we must leave Nazareth. Salome and Zebedee will give you shelter. Don't pack more than we can carry. Ask Didymus next door to take possession of the house and what it holds and sell it for the best price he can get and give you what he gets apart from his commission.' He smiled and said: 'Tell him I said he was to have the carpenter's equipment since he liked to play with it when Daddy-Joe was training me. He isn't a carpenter, but he will enjoy playing with it. Say it's my gift to him.'

'He didn't go to the synagogue', said Mary, 'because as you said I asked him to stay here with me and pray instead of going. He didn't know why.'

'He would have tried to fight for me if he had been there, the way Johnny wanted to', said Word 'and we can't have that. They're still looking for me at the cliff, but they'll be back here. They won't hurt you, Mother, or Didymus but they will wreck the house if Didymus isn't in it and can say it is his, so meet us a mile down the road to Khirbel-Qana. Eat as you pack, everyone.'

Word threw his arms around Mary, who hugged him back. Mary went next door.

The few days since he met Word had made a great difference to Johnny. A month ago he would have been objecting like fury to all this, to Nat for knocking him out, to Word for praising Nat for doing it, to everyone for not fighting with somebody, somewhere, because Word had been insulted, manhandled, and threatened with death. As it was he waited until Word and Nat handed him bread and extra olives and some fruit, thanked them, and put his extra clothes and shoes in a sling. When he did speak, his first question surprised even him: 'Why Didymus?'

'Oh, you mean, because it means "twin"?' said Word. 'He was the boy next door, he liked me, and he used to do everything that I did.'

'*Everything*?' asked Johnny, startled.

Word grinned, sharing the private joke with Johnny as Johnny wanted. Nat didn't fully know Word was God, yet. 'Well, not quite everything. But I wasn't working miracles. He used to work hard at trying to become a carpenter when his parents wanted him to become a lawyer. Oh, and in Heaven's name don't call him Didymus. It's a pet name for use by me, Mother and a few others. He won't want to be called a twin and then have to explain that he wasn't one, only a copycat. Besides, he's his own man, and doesn't really copy me any more. If he can't work miracles he will probably be pretty good at cross-examining them.'

'Have you seen him on this visit?' Johnny couldn't remember a time in Nazareth when Word had not been among them.

'When you were asleep on the first night, a bit tired after your journey. He came in but didn't wake you. He wanted to know what evidence I had for assuming you could be one of my disciples.'

'Cheek!' snarled Johnny indignantly.

'I think I managed to convince him.'

'How?'

'Never you mind. And you know well enough that the arguments of boys who were friends together do not depend on grown-up forms of logic.'

'That's true', said Nat. 'Philip and I were boys together, and there was no logic when he to persuaded me to come and see you.'

'Or when I came to you', remembered Johnny.

'Have we everything?' asked Word. The others said that they had, and Word had reached the door. when it swung open. Word jumped back, and Johnny realised that he could not be sure the people who had been trying to kill him hadn't come back to the house. But it was Mary, with a short, dark, contentious-looking fellow behind her, not looking in the least like Word, apart from the way he kept his hair and beard. Johnny suddenly realised he had never discovered Didymus's real name, but Word simply said: 'Johnny, this is my oldest friend, Thomas.'

Thomas shook hands with Johnny, quite formally, looked him over and turned back to Word. 'If he's going, I'm going too. I'm bigger than he is, for one thing,'

'Well, perhaps' judged Word, solemnly.

'And I don't want to stay here if you're not coming back', affirmed Thomas.

'Afraid of the girls, without me?' asked Word, solicitously.

'Guessed it in one', nodded Thomas.

'But he's going to stay here and sell the houses', said Mary. 'He can join you in Capernaun at the end of next week'.

'We won't get the best prices for the houses at short notice' said Thomas.

'It doesn't matter' agreed Word.

'So I'll come with you now', said Mary, 'and I'm taking little enough. Thomas, you know the things made by Daddy-Joe that I most valued: bring them next week with your own on a cart.'

'But we'll take the donkey now', said Word, 'for Mother to travel.'

'Like old times', said Mary.

They left Thomas behind them in Mary's house. As they walked away, Johnny wondered whether neighbours would inform against them to the people who wanted to kill Word. Johnny wasn't frightened, because Word was God and nobody could kill him, but he wondered if there would be a fight, and if so he would stay well away from Nat and give a good account of himself. But what happened was strange. Nobody whom they saw seemed to know they were there. Near the edge of the town some children, playing a game, ran right at them, and yet somehow went through them without touching anybody or apparently seeing anybody. Word walked on, leading the donkey, with Nat and Johnny behind them. At one point Johnny asked 'are there no other friends of yours in Nazareth?'

They were close to their last look at the town at that point, and Word paused and looked back.

'I thought there were', he said at last. 'I discovered today that I was wrong.'

'Or relatives?' asked Johnny.

'I had no other children', said Mary. 'Daddy-Joe had four sons and two

35

daughters by his first wife, but they had all grown up when we married. I think all of them are in Jerusalem now. Their mother died when the youngest was as old as twenty. I don't think they approved of me.'

'Or of me', smiled Word.

'Cousin Elizabeth and her husband, Cousin Zachary are long gone. Which reminds me, son. Any news of your cousin John?'

'I heard about it just before I reached the synagogue', said Word. 'Herod Antipas has arrested him.'

'For saying that Herod ought not to have formed an adulterous relationship with his brother Philip's wife?' asked Nat.

'Apparently', said Word. 'Probably put up to it by the woman, Herodias.'

'Where is he held prisoner?' asked Johnny.

'Machaerus, not far from Jerusalem, held in the fortress itself. A very bad place, Johnny, bad for prisoners and worse for their captors. Herod and Herodias have imprisoned themselves by imprisoning John. And now, before we walk on, I have one thing to do.'

Word looked back at Nazareth. Then he held up his hand. Johnny wondered if he was going to curse it, but in fact Word spoke only in blessing, pleading that punishment not fall on the town, whose people did not know what they were doing. As Johnny looked up at him, he saw that Word's face was covered by tears. Mary wept a little too. The boy, the men, and the woman on the donkey went on down the road.

OUR

NATHANIEL

The same was in the beginning with God

The four walked in silence, Word's right hand on the donkey, sometimes straying back to his Mother's arm, Word's left hand in Johnny's right, Nat on Mary's right, and for a long time they did not speak. Then Word sighed, and said:

'It is the fate of our people. The Gentiles speak of the wandering Jew. But wherever we have gone, we can never forget the homeland.'

'If I forget thee, O Jerusalem, may my right hand forget her cunning', quoted Johnny, more in misery than in satisfaction at having found the right text.

'If I forget thee, O Nazareth,' murmured Mary

'To say goodbye to one's place is to die a little', said Nat, 'and a small town holds the heartstrings often as much as one's entire country.'

'Did you know this was going to happen?' asked Johnny of Word, forgetting for a minute that Nat didn't know that Word was God. Word glanced over at Nat for a moment, and then said:

'Well, I certainly didn't want it to happen. To know something will happen is not to will it. I knew I would be cast out, I did not know that some of the people who would try to kill me were men whom I once knew to be my friends. They probably thought they were doing good in destroying a blasphemer, or maybe that they would save me by destroying some devil within me even at the cost of my life. That isn't how devils are cast out, to kill is evil, God's purpose can never be fulfilled by killing. But many people possessed by devils have been killed by good, foolish relatives and friends.'

'Did your mother know?'

Mary's voice seemed to draw on a strange, unknown sea of sorrow: 'I had been told what would happen to my son, and to be exiled from his own town was an obvious tragedy before us. Neighbours had talked of John with disapproval, and it was not difficult to know that behind my back they would be saying the same things of my boy.'

'But they must be proud of John now that his courage has made Herod imprison him for telling the truth', insisted Johnny.

'There probably will be little pride in him. When he first began to denounce Herod's incestuous adultery with Herodias, several people came right up to me at the well and said it was disgraceful for a good Jew to insult our own tetrarch.'

'Not to speak of insulting our tetrarch's wife', murmured Nat, 'and insulting our tetrarch's brother's wife.'

Mary said thoughtfully. 'I think a lot of it comes from fear of the Romans. Herod is a Roman official.'

'But so is his brother Philip', interrupted Johnny, 'tetrarch of Ituraea and of Trachonitis.'

'Roman morality is essentially administrative', remarked Nat, 'if people's family scandals don't get in the way of their keeping order and collecting taxes, the Romans are unlikely to interfere. They have enough family scandals of their own.'

'That may be part of the problem', said Mary thoughtfully. 'People might be afraid that if John denounced the tetrarch, he might then denounce the emperor.'

'Why?' asked Johnny. 'Has he run away with his brother's wife?'

'He has done many things which would merit denunciation', said Word.

'And you're as well off without knowledge of them', affirmed Mary.

'The Emperor Tiberius is not a Jew, and so John would not rebuke him for breaking Jewish commandments', added Nat.

'But plenty of people were too worried to realise that', continued Mary, 'and they feared that John would bring the governor Pontius Pilate and his Roman soldiers down on them.'

'He wouldn't interfere because of Herod?' asked Johnny.

'He doesn't like Herod', explained Word.

'Why not?'

'Herod is a Jew. Pilate doesn't like Jews.' Nat laughed.

'No, not even good ones?' asked Johnny.

'No, not even good ones? He got rid of several high priests.'

'Some of them quite good ones', added Word, a little quizzically.

They kept talking of John and Herod, since Nat saw, and Johnny began to see, that almost any allusion to Nazareth was bound to hurt Mary and Word. But Nat thought of the beginning of the conversation with Johnny's belief that Word could foresee. He had made up his own mind about Word's being the Messiah and it was to be expected that the Messiah was a prophet with a prophet's powers of foresight. He had hailed Word as the Son of God. Was it even remotely possible that Word was something more? Nat did not answer his own question yet, but he realised that whatever the answer was, Johnny knew it. And Nat had thought enough about God to realise that Johnny was the obvious person to know it.

Nat reflected on Johnny's square jaw, and firm chin, and knew Johnny would never knowingly tell what he knew. So he shrugged his shoulders and walked on. He would find out in the future and there was no point in making everyone miserable by premature questions.

Of course Mary knew too. Well, women usually did know things quicker than men did. And tragedy was linked with what she knew. It was a warm day, but for a moment Nathaniel shivered.

The ground beneath their feet was hard, dry, brittle. Johnny resented it mildly, in loyal contrast to the sea-shore he loved so well. He seemed to notice obstacles under foot making the way more cumbersome: he hardly noticed any when beside the Sea of Galilee. At length he said, 'Tell us a story, Word.'

Word obediently began a story.

'Once upon a time there was a King.'

'A good King?' asked Johnny.

'Perhaps not', reflected Word, 'but whether good or bad, he was a just King. One day he began to look into his accounts, and see what was owed to him by his administrators, tax-gatherers, publicans, and whatnot.'

Johnny giggled, having a sudden vision of a pompous Roman official hearing himself described as a whatnot. Word smiled, silently sharing the cause of the giggle, and went on:

'And one of them was brought before him who turned out to owe ten thousand talents. I suppose the King may have been indolent, or fighting wars, or making journeys far afield, and so had let this fellow go without receiving tributes due for a long time.'

Word said this rather rapidly, seeing Johnny was about to ask how the money owing to the King had been allowed to grow as big as that in the first place. Having circumvented Johnny for the moment, he continued:

'The man clearly had concluded that the King was never going to ask for his money, and had simply spent it on himself, having a high old time, gambling, and roistering, and eating and drinking the most expensive foods – and wines.'

'Had he grown fat?' demanded Johnny.

'Yes, very, and very lazy. He would never have taken a journey like we are making.' Johnny looked virtuous, caught Word's eye, and hastily looked ordinary again. 'He would have had to be carried, on a gorgeous palanquin, by sweating slaves. The more he ate, the more the slaves sweated. Now the more airs he gave himself, and indulgence he showed himself, the more he had to pay, and by the time the King asked for the money, there wasn't any. So the King commanded that his house, property, goods, slaves, children, wife and himself should all be sold to restore what the man owed. And the man flung himself on the ground and wept at the thought of the wife and children, whom he had rather neglected, should be sold into slavery.'

'I imagine he was really crying at being sold into slavery himself', reflected Johnny.

'I imagine so', nodded Word. 'But the King was touched, released him, and said he could forget about the sum owing.'

'Bang went ten thousand talents.'

'So it might seem. The King had been deeply moved with compassion. Anyhow, out from the King's palace went the man, and the first person he saw was a minor Royal official who had borrowed a hundred pence from him and had never paid it back. If the major official had seen the minor official before being arrested himself, the hundred pence would have been useless to him in trying to pay the King, but now, when he was under no pressure to pay anything he laid hands on his debtor, took him by the throat, and said "Pay me what you owe".'

'Probably he was charging usurious interest', said Johnny.

'Probably. Anyhow, the poor debtor threw himself down at his creditor's feet, beseeching him, probably crying in his turn, saying "Have patience with me, and I will pay it all back to you." And he would not: he had him thrown into prison until the debt was paid, and of course the poor minor official would never be able to earn enough money while in prison, and would be dismissed for not continuing to work at his own job, and while the other Royal officials were usually ready enough to keep their eyes on what money they could get and asked few questions and made fewer reproaches against each other, this was too much, and several of them told the King.'

'They might have felt themselves in danger of the man's brutality if he ever got power over them, and with a clean slate from the King he was well on his way to doing so', agreed Johnny.

'Quite so. Anyhow the King called the cruel official to him and said, "You wicked servant, I forgave you all your debt, because you begged me for mercy, and ought not you have had such pity on your fellow-servant just as I had on you?" And he handed him over to the most barbarous prison in his land and made him remain there until the ten thousand talents were paid, and there the prison guards were the most brutal money could buy, and there the wicked servant remained.'

'And serve him right', said Johnny, roundly.

'So also my heavenly Father will do to everyone who does not forgive others for anything they have done to them or taken from them or owe to them.' Word suddenly was grim.

'But our heavenly Father isn't like that King, neglecting his work and making things go wrong and maybe getting wealth from places his armies had conquered where the inhabitants were brutally taxed?' Since Johnny was actually thinking of Word when he thought of his heavenly Father, he felt himself entitled to speak with confidence.

'No, he isn't, Johnny, except in this matter of insisting that if we humans are to have his divine mercy, we must earn it by always being merciful to others.'

Johnny was a little taken aback by being suddenly put on the same level as Word, but he realised that since Word was a man as well as God, he talked to men from the standpoint of men when he could. It was easier for Johnny to do this than it would have been for Nat, because Johnny was still a child and children can understand these things better than grown-ups. God becoming man was a little like a child dressing up as a grown-up while playing a game.

Word went on speaking. 'And for now, Johnny, I want you to forgive the people of Nazareth, my own town.'

Johnny was oddly defensive. 'I hate them, Word, I hate them for what they wanted to do to you, but you can't say I've got to forgive them, because after all they never did any harm to me.'

Word was patient. 'Johnny, do you love me?'

'You know I do.' The 'you' was a little strong, since Johnny was always conscious that Word knew everything.

'You love me more than yourself.' Word made it as a statement, and Johnny answered as a simple fact.

'I do. I always will.'

'I know, and believe me, I'm grateful. But if you love me more than yourself, then an injury to me, or an injury intended for me, is a greater injury to you than an injury to you would be.' Word was deadly serious, yet laughing as he tripped out the repetitive sentence.

'Hold on', said Johnny. 'You mean that when someone tries to hurt you I will hate them more than if they try to hurt me?'

'Isn't that so?'

Johnny had never thought of it like that, but –

'Yes, it is so. I hate being hurt, but I'd prefer it to your being hurt, not that you could be hurt.'

'May be I could be. We'll see. But if I mean so much more to you than you do, at any rate where being hurt is concerned, then for you to forgive people who wanted to kill me is even more important than forgiving anyone who wanted to kill you.'

Johnny looked at Word in amazement. 'All right. I forgive them. But I hate them.'

'You may not hate them, Johnny. You may not hate anyone. And apart from anything else, those people who wanted to kill me did not know what they were doing, and probably thought they were doing right. You *must* forgive them, really forgive them'.

Johnny stopped, and so did the others, even the donkey. The donkey had an instinct for stopping where he ought to stop, so he had been named Balaam. Johnny looked murderous for a minute: as a matter of fact his mind was tearing into action against the mob who wanted to murder Word, punching, kicking, biting. His teeth clenched, his jaw muscles flexed.

Then he looked up at Word, his eyes glistened, and he said quietly 'Very well, Word, I forgive them.'

'You don't hate them.'

Johnny felt his throat constrict. Then he got it out.

'I don't hate them. But don't ask me to love them.'

'I won't. At least not yet. But *I* must love them.'

'And so must I', said Mary, as Balaam began to move again.

Nat said nothing. But from then on he looked at Johnny with a new respect, and the feeling that the boy and his brother were pushing themselves forward for high status began to subside. Word gave Johnny a quick kiss on the forehead and they walked on.

They stayed that night in Khibet Qana, with the parents of the bridegroom whose hospitality Johnny had dispensed and Word had distended. When Johnny got Word alone, he asked him a question which had been puzzling him.

'Word, since I know you are God, what do I do about praying? How can I pray to you?'

'You should not pray to me, Johnny, any more than you do to any created person, because like you I was created when I was made flesh. Pray to our heavenly father, yours and mine, for so he is, although he and I are one, pray to him in heaven, so that nobody will think you are praying to a being on earth. Like this.' Word dropped his head, and Johnny dropped his. 'Our Father, who are in Heaven, may your name be blessed, may your kingdom come and may what you want be done here on earth just as it is in heaven. Give us this day our bread for the day, and forgive us for the wrongs we have done just as we forgive any wrongs done to us. Do not let us go where temptation is greater than we can resist, but save us from all that is evil, for yours, and yours only, are the kingdom, the power and the glory, for ever and ever, Amen. Try saying that, Johnny, we'll do it sentence by sentence.'

It was a beautiful evening. They had walked a little way from the house where they were staying.

The sky had a strange red colour which seemed oddly reflected on the ground. Word's shadow, and Johnny's smaller shadow, stretched away from them. Johnny had little difficulty remembering the words. If asked, he would have said he had only to think of Word, and he knew the words. He did ask what 'Amen' meant, and Word said it meant 'Be it so'. Then Johnny wondered:

'But how can you seem to say that you might have done wrongs, since being God you can't.'

And Word said:

'When I took on this work of being a man, I set aside the right to imply I was better than anyone else.'

And Johnny said:

'But you are.' They smiled at one another, Word put a hand on Johnny's shoulder and they walked back inside the house. Just before they entered Johnny said:

'The bread you spoke of, is that just what we eat and drink?' Word said:

'No, it's also the bread of heaven, and being the bread of heaven it's me. You are asking God to give you me every day.'

'I want nothing more than that', said Johnny, 'and neither does anyone else, if they've any sense.'

'They don't know that yet, Johnny. We have to tell them. And it means travelling a long way, all the more since I no longer have a home town.'

'My home will always be yours. And your mother's. She'll stay with my parents.'

'And with you, Johnny, in due time.'

'And you', insisted Johnny.

For answer Word simply ruffled Johnny's hair.

As soon as they were back in Capernaum beside the sea, crowds began to follow Word, who took them up a nearby mountain, and preached. It was at this point that Johnny learned he himself had more work to do than being a willing servant, especially since his willing service might require Word to work more miracles, or so Word put it. The youngest has a vital role to play in Jewish ceremony, and Word used to say that he had come to enlarge the old Jewish traditions, not to deny them. So in the middle of the sermon Word turned to Johnny, as he had warned him he would, and after telling the people to pray by themselves instead of trying to become famous as pious posturers in public Word said that the words in which to speak to God were what Johnny would speak. Word was standing near a little rock, which he helped Johnny to climb, and when standing on it Johnny's head was a few inches higher than Word's.

And Johnny's young voice, strong and sweet, rang out in the morning air over the great crowd. Word had told him not to shout, and not to worry about whether his own natural tones would carry the words. An afterwards Word helped Johnny off the rock, and Johnny sat down at Word's feet, where not many people could see him among Andrew and Peter, James, Phil, Nat – and Thomas, who had finally caught up with them. And Word went on with the sermon.

Johnny had listened to many sermons in the past, and had listened carefully, chiefly because he had a gift for mimicry, and many a worshipper, severely bored by a preacher, found great relief in subsequently listening to Johnny. His instinct was automatic, his motives as much in quest of popularity as the average preacher, and his technique painstaking and inspired. He knew the measure of condescension his target had applied, and sprinkled his caricature with its derisive echo. He lit on absurd analogy with the cruelty of a hawk sighting its prey, implacably zooming home with claws and beak sinking in. He might ignore actual deficiencies in speech and concentrate on minor follies if the preacher had been obviously if ludicrously genuine, but anything that betrayed hypocrisy he met by total war. He could transform any artificiality of manner into blatant ham acting by the slightest of touches, and where he suspected his victim had exploited the innocence of his audience his mockery virtually skinned him inch by inch. In theory his parents and James should long ago have knocked it out of him: the trouble was, that as soon as they listened they found themselves helpless with laughter. His parents simply enjoyed his performances after feeble remonstrances in the early stages, and even James, pulling back his robe from his arm the better to swipe Johnny, found his strength deserting him as Johnny's latest shaft struck home and James's unwilling laughter found itself almost drowning the rest of the audience. Johnny had no objection to extending his repertoire, and many a public official or even a Roman officer would have writhed had

45

he heard the second edition of his pomposities released by Johnny to an expectant crowd as soon as he had departed. Johnny had natural linguistic ability, and lit readily upon Roman botches of Aramaic, or Herodian mishmash of official Latin: and many a genteel Greek-spouting traveller was subsequently reduced to farmyard cries and crows.

Johnny worshipped Word. Johnny would certainly have died rather than sully Word's discourse by caricature. Admittedly Word was very nearly his only exception, although Peter's genuineness would usually keep Jonnny's ridicule firmly locked up behind closed lips. Otherwise he used his gifts rarely, and largely for entertainment, when he had grown up, but on one occasion Paul fell into his usual mistake of implying to the surviving disciples that he, Paul, who had never known Word, understood him better than anyone else (as, now and then, he did, but not as often as he imagined): and Johnny listened to him, dead-pan, and then, as Paul said repentantly later, 'he withstood me to my face', and did so in Paul's own words, exhortations, warnings, infallibilities, perfectly mirrored with the most elegant of twists reducing them to wonderful nonsense. Paul told his friend Barnabas later that it was the worst shock he had in his life other than being struck blind by the vision of his Saviour on the road to Damascus. It was the more devastating since Paul did not share the Galileans' knowledge of Johnny's gift, and the thing burst on him from the stocky ex-fisherman whom he knew to be the youngest of the apostles and vaguely assumed to be the least important. Johnny would later be a valuable ally for Paul in welcoming non-Jews to become followers of Christ, but from that moment Paul always looked on Johnny with a very slight tincture of fear. After being brought before Nero, when Paul showed not the slightest trace of fear, someone asked him was he afraid of anyone, and without a moment's hesitation he replied 'John'.

So Johnny heard the sermon Word spoke on the mountain listening with the passion of love and the aesthetics of criticism. It would never have occurred to him that he was judging Word, and however conceited he might be about his own entertainment value he would have looked on any such pretension with horror. But unconsciously he was judging Word's sermon, instinctively noting again and again how it quietly moved through its work shunning tricks and contrivances except such as made the most direct road to his hearers. Word began with what Johnny recognised as poetry, turning the word 'blessed' again and again in one direction and another. It was so like Word to begin by showing in so many ways how so many people were blessed, and Johnny almost physically sensed the fall of the blessings around them, little grains of manna in the wilderness, running streams to refresh deer, calm sea water after storm. Yet the very peace of the opening turned the world upside down. Word said that the poor were blessed in spirit, that theirs was the kingdom of heaven: and in that first declaration he overturned all the ambitions and snobberies and complacencies of a world which at bottom judged everything on whether people looked and sounded rich and proud and powerful. He defied the conventions even more spectacularly. The meek were blessed and would inherit the earth: Johnny knew that those who ruled the earth justified their title by having won it in war, and that those who had opposed them in vain insisted they would defeat the present rulers by war some day. And here was Word, denying the right of anyone to rule or own anywhere in the earth, unless they were meek and gentle. He told those who mourn that they would be comforted, and the merciful that they would receive mercy, which meant there would be no comfort for the pitiless, the hard-bitten tough guys. He told those hungry and thirsty for justice that they would get it. He told the pure in heart that they would see God; that meant that those always discovering alleged impurities in any victims they could find, would not see God since their minds stank with the impurities they imagined. He told the peacemakers that they would be called children of God; that denounced both the Romans who declared that their armies made peace and their emperor was God, and their opponents who demanded war against the Romans in the name of the Jewish God. Finally, he told everyone that when they were persecuted for believing, supporting and speaking what was right, and when they were reviled and denounced and injured and lied against, because they were followers of him, Word, then their reward would be great in heaven and then its kingdom would be theirs. Johnny listened happily: Word was showing how silly it was to escape love. And wonderful he looked as he showed it, the rich, dark sheen of his hair, the dark, brown skin, the mastery of his curved nose and full, dark beard, the whiteness of his teeth flashing as his red lips drew back from them when he lightened his words and brought laughter to the crowd. Crowds loved Word's laughter, so unlike almost all preachers they had ever heard before, and Johnny, master of laughter against a sermon, relished laughing inside one. There was no man like Word. There was no God like Word either. There was no God but Word, infallible, inimitable, invulnerable.

Word made the crowd laugh at itself, again and again. 'You are the salt of the earth', he assured the crowd, and Johnny could see the men preening themselves and the women less ostentatiously bowing their heads in appreciation, and when they had digested the compliment fully, Word beamed at them and asked 'But if the salt has lost its savour, with what shall we salt the salt?' His voice quivered with mischief, and his hearers found themselves laughing at the trap into which he had walked them. 'You are the light of the world'– and Johnny could see them trying to work out how light might prove to be dark. But Word was not playing the same trick twice (and anyway, as he told Johnny, light could not in itself become darkness for darkness could not surround light, and could not understand it, which meant that sin was stupid). 'You do not put light underneath an empty measuring-cup: you put it in a candlestick to light the whole house. And so let people see the good things you do, and by doing them you sing the glory of your Father in heaven: You have people who know how to measure goodness according to the letter of the law, the scribes, and people who know how to proclaim goodness according to the way they tell you they keep it, the Pharisees. They are the official limit of goodness?' They waited for it. He shook his head. 'You have to show a greater goodness than the official limit. You've been told not to kill: I tell you not to be angry with one another, and calling your brother a fool puts you in danger of the destroying fire of hell.' Johnny thought uneasily of one or two of his richer insults hurled at James in times past.

'You've been told only to swear truly, and fulfil what you swear, but I tell you, don't swear at all. For what can you swear by?' They looked at him doubtfully. He spread his arms wide, hands open. 'You can't swear by heaven, for that is God's throne – not yours. You can't swear by earth, for that is his footstool.' Automatically the entire audience looked downward apprehensively. 'You can't swear by Jerusalem, for that is the city of the great King.' Very nice, thought Johnny, they know there is no great king in Jerusalem, not even a nasty pretender like Herod the Great whose son the Romans wouldn't let become a King. He's reminding them of the great

King David, who skew the giant Goliath when he was about Johnny's age.

Clearly the crowd began to think of what they owned, and Johnny in thought jammed his chin on his fist (briefly clenched while he mentally slew Goliath), and the jolt reminded him that at least his head was his. But Word had read his mind, and, by the look of their faces, the mind of the crowd. 'You cannot swear by your head, because you can't create one hair of it black or white.' Word threw back his black locks and laughed, to cascades of echo from the crowd.

He did not need to remark that dyeing and painting hair was not making it, and they read the joke in his mind and enjoyed it with him. Suddenly swearing was left empty and meaningless: Word had laughed it away. 'Say yes when you mean yes, no when you mean no, anything more than that comes from evil.' Johnny looked up at a sky which looked an honest blue back at him.

But now Word became solemn, almost hard. He took the old cry that said an eye should be the penalty for the person taking an eye, or a tooth for a tooth. Johnny could see that Word was not ready to live with that. 'If someone strikes you on the cheek, turn your other cheek to him.' Johnny thought sadly of many good fights now condemned in retrospect. 'If someone takes away your coat by law, give him your cloak, if he makes you walk a mile, walk two, give to anyone who asks you, lend to people who want to borrow from you. And'– with a little chill down his spine Johnny knew what was coming now – 'it's not simply a matter of loving your neighbour and hating your enemy, you must love your enemy, bless any who curse you, do good to any who hate you, pray for people who tell lies against you, injure you, hurt you. If you limit your loving to people who love you, does that make you any better than tax-collectors or corrupt officials?' He laughed again.

And then he told them how to pray, and brought Johnny to the top of the rock. And Johnny knew Word had made him the leader of the crowd for that one moment, because he was the least important person in it. He liked that.

IVE

MATTHEW, SHIMON, JIM, THADY

All things were made by him

But when Johnny slid up beside Word after the crowd dispersed at the end of the sermon he found a less important being in his place and was faintly annoyed by it, since it was a fox. He made to drive it away, but the fox sneered at him, or so he decided it meant by opening its jaws, and Word, noting his disapproval, murmured 'Pearls cannot equal the whiteness of its teeth', and the fox grinned, and licked Word's finger before it ran off. It paused for a second beside Johnny, who somewhat gingerly patted it in a contrite farewell. 'My fault', reflected Word, as they walked on. 'A perfectly well-meaning scribe announced he would follow me and lodge wherever I was going, and I remarked that foxes have holes, and the birds of the air have nests but the Son of Man hath not where to lay his head, since after Nazareth I am a vagrant. The fox may have thought that in the circumstances it was only fair to offer me hospitality.' Johnny looked at Word speechlessly, and Word continued 'and a couple of birds showed signs of landing on my head so that I didn't know whether they were offering me their nest or decided I was their nest. We all parted friends, and I'm glad you decided not to be jealous of the fox.'

'Well', said Johnny, a little more firm now that the fox had trotted off, with an occasional, apparently amused, backward glance, 'the children in the fiery furnace in Babylon told the fowls of the air and the beasts and cattle to praise and exalt you above all for ever'.

'I think they were a little older than you, Johnny, but then we are all children and the more we realise it the better. Do you know their names?'

'Azarias, Mishael and Ananias', said Johnny proudly after a moment: naturally he knew their hymn better than he knew their names.

'And nothing would induce you to call them Shadrach, Meschach and Abednego?' smiled Word.

'Well, you could induce me of course', said Johnny, 'but I hope you won't. It seems like collaborating with the Babylonians who imprisoned them and tried to force them to blaspheme against you. Taking away people's names steals in a meaner way than any thief.'

'Poor Shimon Peter!' murmured Word.

'Word, you know I wasn't talking about you!' Johnny wheeled round and looked at Word indignantly.

'Just talking to me', nodded Word.

'You gave him that name, so it's all right.'

'Nebuchadnezzar or whoever his empire authorised gave those three their Babylonian names. What's the difference? Shimon didn't ask to be called Peter.'

Johnny looked mutinous. Word watched him with interest. Another bird flew past, crying. Then Johnny brightened:

'Shimon Peter wanted to become part of your disciples. Daniel and the three in the furnace didn't want to be taken prisoner and dragged all the way to Babylon. Whether you are free to accept a name makes all the difference.'

'Shimon Peter may have thought he had to take the name I gave him if I was going to admit him to my disciples.' Word smiled.

'Yes, but he was accepting the name given because he wanted to follow you. It began with his choice.'

'I agree, even if his way of making his choice was to tell me to go away. But how did you make your choice, Johnny?'

'I saw you' remembered Johnny, 'and I ran over to you.'

'Why?'

'Because you looked at me.'

'And you could have said no?'

'I never gave no a chance when I started runnlng but when I fell and cut myself running to you I suppose I could have stopped. But stopping didn't make any sense. I had to go to you. But you didn't give me a name.'

'No, you gave me one. And I had to decide to take it, which I saw as part of the task of taking you.'

'The task?' Johnny sounded slightly hurt.

'Or the fun of taking you. Same thing, really. Any good task is fun. But either of us could have said no.'

'It feels even better to think we said yes and could have said no.'

'It does. And now we must find the others, who have been talking to some people who think they want to say yes. Race you down to the seashore.'

They ran, but stayed level with one another. Word didn't seen to be holding himself back, but Johnny could never draw much ahead of him or fall much behind him. Johnny worried slightly that Word would return to a walking pace when other people could see them, but he kept up the good run and reached the others at the same time as Johnny only with rather more breath, James looked a trifle disapproving, but Word caught his eye and he turned away smiling. Andrew took charge as usual, introducing four men who had been talking to them:

'This is Matthew. He's – 'Andrew coughed, and Johnny realised he was embarrassed. 'He's a publican.'

'Was.' Matthew looked a sharp-eyed calculator.

'He wants to give it up and follow you'. Johnny thought he had never seen Andrew show such distaste, all the more obviously as he was trying to conceal it. Johnny himself was more curious than anything else. He had, of course, never met a publican before, and didn't think he had ever seen one long enough to know what he might be. Matthew turned glittering eyes on Andrew with what looked like a generous return for his distaste. Then he turned to Word, made a sketchy bow, and said 'You are the Messiah of whom the prophets and sacred writings have spoken. I have checked against the texts, what you have been doing and saying, and you qualify under every head.' He paused, and continued with a shade more cordiality and even humanity. 'I was a little worried about the fact that Isaiah stated that Behold, a virgin shall conceive – Your mother is a virgin, I take it?'

'Yes', said Word, whose mouth seemed a little grim, Johnny thought, but as always he looked at Word's eyes and to his astonishment saw that they were brimming with merriment.

'That's essential', nodded Matthew. 'Check. Virgin, right. Meets specifications. ... Isaiah then says she will bear a son.' He had been counting off on his fingers and looking at them, but now he looked at Word and nodded. 'All right on that score. But it then says she will call his name Immanuel. That's not your name? Your official name, anyway. You are called Jesus, which is Josiah, which qualifies you under the saying of the man of God to Jeroboam when Jeroboam stood by the altar to burn incense that Behold, a child shall be born unto the house of David, Josiah by name. You are of the house of David –'

'Yes', said Word, perhaps a shade wearily, Johnny thought, 'David begat Solomon.'

'Of her that had been the wife of Uriah', said Matthew severely.

'Bathsheba', said Word quietly.

'Yes, Bathsheba. Very deplorable, the whole thing, but we're not responsible for the faults of our ancestors.'

'We have enough to do to worry about our own', agreed Word.

Matthew looked a little startled. 'Well, you don't, you're not supposed to have faults. I hope you don't, or I'm making a big mistake.'

'I think you won't find much difficulty in meeting people who feel I have a lot of faults', said Word demurely.

'Yes, but they're the wrong people. Pharisees and so on. Anyhow they wouldn't talk to me. Pharisees don't like publicans. They're good, we're bad. They are conscious of their faith and works. We know we're sinners. At least, I do, and I'm anything to go by, my colleagues must. God have mercy on me, at least I can say that, and the Pharisees are not entitled to prevent my saying it.'

'No', said Word, 'and God bless you for saying it', and as he looked at Matthew his lips turned that half-smile, a little crooked, that Johnny was coming to know so well. 'You won't mind if I quote you sometime? Not by name.'

'Oh, no, I don't mind certainly not. Don't worry about my name, anyway. My name's perfectly good, among publicans and tax-gatherers in general. Not anyone else, of course. Why, I expect to be quoting you, quite a lot, one way or another. But as I was saying, David began Solomon.'

'Yes, I'm sure we all agree on that point', said Word solemnly.

'And Solomon begat Roboam. And Roboam begat Abia. And Abia begat Asa. And Asa begat Josophat...'

Johnny had switched off and was mildly wondering what Word's hair would have looked like if the birds had nested in it. Pleasant and warm for the little birds when they had been hatched. Word would have caught any that fell off and put them back. The mother bird would be grateful and would sing him beautiful songs. It would have to be a singing-bird, of course, and one – or rather two – which had not been captured by the bird-catchers for the tetrarch or the emperor or some other nasty brute who rolled in tax-money and imprisoned birds, beasts and John the Baptizer. And –

'– and Eliud begat Eleazar. And Eleazar begat Matthan. And Matthan begat Jacob. And Jacob begat Joseph –'

'– and his eleven brothers', said Johnny, to show he had been listening.

'Did your father have eleven brothers?' asked Matthew to Word, surprised.

'No', said Word wearily. 'Johnny is thinking of the boy with the technicolour dreamcoat.'

'Oh, no, that's much earlier', said Matthew, 'and that Joseph did not beget your ancestors, but rather Judah or Judas his brother, the same who told his brethren to sell Joseph to the Ishmaelites, was your ancestor.'

'As you said, we can't be responsible for the faults of our ancestors', interposed Andrew, with a touch of irony in his voice. Johnny was glad to see he wasn't the only one anxious to tune out. One thing was puzzling him anyway, and since he had interrupted Matthew already he felt he might as well do it again.

'Since your mother is a virgin, Word, why does it matter who Daddy-Joe is descended from?'

'My mother was also descended from David', said Word, and added hastily before Matthew could start on her intervening ancestors 'she called me Immanuel when she used to sing me to sleep as a baby.' He sang softly:

'Oh come, oh come, Imma-a-anuel

And rescue captive Is-ra-a-el.'

'Splendid!' Matthew suddenly stopped fussing. 'Most satisfactory. The man of God at the altar of Jeroboam got it quite right. She called your name Immanuel. Even though she had given you another name. Very satisfactory. Everything tots up. Even the imperial accountants couldn't fault that. Or the imperial auditors. A perfect balance-sheet. Congratulations.' He beamed. Then a thought struck him, and he fell on his knees. 'Master', he said, in a completely different tone of voice.

Word raised him up. 'Thank you, Matthew. And thank you for responding to my call.'

'Your call?' Matthew seemed bewildered.

'Yes, you were sitting at the receipt of custom and I saw you and told you to follow me.' Matthew looked at him in amazement.

'I called you under your own name.'

'My own name?'

'It's Levi, isn't it?' Matthew nodded. 'And that was why you suddenly began to check the verses of the sacred writings.'

'I knew I could not stay where I was', said Matthew. 'But it was a voice within me.'

'Oh, that was Levi', said Word. 'You had buried Levi inside Matthew long, long ago.'

Matthew looked as though he had just received an entirely unexpected present (or tax-offering, thought Johnny maliciously), and he also looked as if he were about to cry. Word simply looked at him, the half-smile smaller, yet softer. Then Matthew squared his shoulders, checked his writing instruments and scrolls, and took a place beside Thomas, who drew back involuntarily and then nodded and silently took Matthew's hand. Word turned to the next man being brought forward by Andrew. But when Johnny and he were alone afterwards, Word said 'Some day, Johnny, I think you may write something about me, but do you mind not working your way back through my ancestors, or my mother's, or Daddy-Joe's? It takes rather a long time.'

Johnny said promptly 'I'll begin by saying you are Word and always were and were with God and were God.'

'That will do well', said Word, 'but wait until other people have written about me.'

'I'll have to', said Johnny, 'come to think of it, I can't write or read.'

'Very well, Johnny, I'll teach you', said Word. 'We'll do a little each day.'

So when we are talking about the rest of the days Johnny spent with Word, we must allow for somewhere between fifteen minutes and an hour which they spent together daily writing and reading. They began with Hebrew, and added some Aramaic since it was easiest to study the language they spoke, and then Word started Johnny on Greek, remarking that he might need it some day. They even did a little Latin. Word was so good a teacher that Johnny looked forward to each lesson, and used what time he could for practice. And since it was a very happy learning time, there is no story to tell about it. All we have to do is to remember that it was happening each day, and it built another bond between them.

But when Matthew had finished his inquisition – for the moment – the second of Andrew's four approached Word, announcing he was Shimon (which made Johnny feel relieved that their existing Shimon was now Peter, since life was quite complicated enough as it was). The new Shimon had a square set to his shoulders, a nice if rather fixed smile, and a tilt to his chin challenging the mount from which they had recently climbed down. He took great care to draw Word aside from where they could be overheard. This hardly recommended him to his prospective new friends: Andrew looked contemptuous, Peter indignant, James disapproving, Philip inquisitive, Nathaniel suspicious, Thomas doubtful, and Matthew as if Shimon was clearly not the full balance-sheet. Johnny was his deepest failure, since the result was that Johnny pointedly walked out of earshot, then out of eyeshot and so worked his way round right behind Shimon where he could hear and see all he wanted. For a moment he thought Word was going to send him away. Word's eye rested on Johnny slightly severely but as soon as it became clear there was nothing that was going to be said about Shimon's personal life, Word's jaw muscles relaxed and the slight lowering of his mouth on the extreme left meant Johnny could stay. By this stage Shimon was so excited by his own message that he would probably have been oblivious if Johnny had worked his way back into eyeshot. The first words caught by Johnny were:

'And I don't need to tell you this is of the utmost importance.'

'Quite', said Word.

'Pontius Pilate would give his eye-teeth to know about it.'

'Indeed?' asked Word.

'It's the biggest thing in our time.'

'Really?' wondered Word.

'Nothing even begins to touch it.'

'Nothing?' echoed Word.

'Nothing. It's the works. It's the top. It's the business. We're going to save the country.'

'How?' inquired Word.

'Well, I don't need to tell you that no people in history have suffered more than we have. In the name of God and of the dead generations from which she receives her old tradition of nationhood, Judea, through us, summons her children to her flag – 'Her what?' raised Word's eyebrow. 'It's a code, a new idea, it'll come in later. – and strikes for her freedom. Having organized and trained her manhood through her secret revolutionary organisation, the Jewish Zealot Brotherhood, and through her open synagogues, having patiently perfected her discipline, having waited for the right moment to reveal itself, she now seizes that moment, and, supported by her exiled children across the Mediterranean and by gallant allies in Rome, but relying in the first on her own strength, she strikes in full confidence of victory. We declare the right of the people of Judaea to the ownership of Judaea, and to the unfettered control of Jewish destinies, to be sovereign and indefeasible. The long usurpation of that right by a foreign people and government have not extinguished the right, nor can it ever be extinguished except by the destruction of the Jewish people. In every generation the Jewish people have asserted their right to national freedom and sovereignty; six times during the past three hundred years they have asserted it in arms. Standing on that fundamental right and again asserting it in arms in the face of the world, we hereby proclaim Judaea as an independent sovereign state, and we pledge our lives and the lives of our comrades-in-arms to the cause of its freedom, of its welfare, and of its exaltation among nations.'

This, thought Johnny, is worse that the begats. 'Judaea is entitled to, and hereby claims, the allegiance of every Jew.'

At least other people's ancestors can't bully you. Or can they, Johnny thought gloomily, remembering the six times in three hundred years. That would be Judas Machabeus for one, but Johnny was hard pressed to work out who Shimon meant by the others. Gideon and Samson and such leaders were long before King David, who lived more than a thousand years before Johnny.

'What are you going to do to the Romans?' asked Word, as if he had been asking a neighbour about his vines. Johnny expected some impressive if empty claims, but he was hardly anticipating Shimon's next:

'When in the course of human events it becomes necessary for one people to dissolve the political bands which have connected them with another, and to assume among the powers of the earth the separate and equal station to which the laws... God call them...'

Johnny had wiggled himself on his side behind Shimon. Initially he had hoped he might store up enough verbiage to give himself another popular imitation, but no audience could possibly stand this. His body confirmed his analysis by drifting into sleep. He woke up suddenly to find Shimon apparently instructing Word about his funeral arrangements:

'... when Judaea takes its place about the nations of the world then, and not till then, let mine epitaph be written.'

'You are', said Word thoughtfully, 'three speeches in search of an historian.'

'But that's it', said Shimon triumphantly, 'if I can get you giving speeches like that, instead of this daft stuff about forgiving your enemies, we'll get the whole country moving. The crowds love you, it doesn't matter what you're saying.'

Johnny at the back could scarcely see Word wince, but he saw his fists clench and his elbows constrict to his sides.

'We're building up support in Jerusalem. There are good leaders there, like Barabbas and Dismas, and Brian.'

'Doing what?'

'We've got to build up a war-chest, so they're out robbing wherever they can.'

'Patriotism is the first refuge of a scoundrel?'

'That's not fair. It's true Barabbas has had to kill quite a lot of people to get their money, but it's their fault for not handing it over to the Zealots.'

'And who are your gallant allies in Rome?'

'A-a-a-h!' Shimon sighed luxuriously. 'You'll never believe it, but we have support in the very highest places.'

'I didn't know there were any Jews in the highest places.'

'There aren't. But young Gaius Julius Caesar Germanicus thinks he is one. He's Tiberius's great-nephew whom they call Caligula.'

'He thinks he's a Jew? Why?'

'He has heard prophesies about a Messiah, and has decided it's him.'

'And you are going to free Judaea with the aid of a teenage voluptuary trying to become Roman Emperor?'

Shimon said sulkily 'Well, the Messiah has to be somebody.'

Johnny was delighted to see Word struggling to hold his smile within a decently small space. He succeeded, agreeing 'Yes, the Messiah has to be somebody.'

'Of course it isn't Caligula.'

Word nodded his head thoughtfully. 'I think you may have a point there.'

'But if Caligula thinks it is, and will help us along –!' Word breathed hard. 'Did you ever hear the story –' Johnny settled his body comfortably.

'– of the sheep who preferred a wolf to their own shepherd?' Shimon the Zealot looked bewildered. 'No.'

'There isn't much of a story', said Word tersely. 'The wolf ate them up.' Johnny thought it rather unfair of Word to cut the story short.

Shimon seemed rather taken aback as well.

'But why did they follow him?'

'Oh, I thought you'd know that bit. The wolf explained that he was the super-sheep, the sheep of sheep, the sheep whose sheepishness outsheeped all other sheep, and since shepherds didn't belong to the same order of creation as sheep, sheep were better without shepherds.'

'Any other reason?' Shimon was beginning to hunger for refutation, Johnny thought. Probably quite a nice chap, if you only knew him.

'What can wolves give sheep?' invited Word.

'Training, maybe. We can learn from our enemies how to defeat them.'

'What effect do wolves have on sheep?'

'Well, Death, I suppose, but they can train us to turn their weapons of Death on them?'

'And the Romans will politely wait to see how well you are learning to kill them? Cannot you see that those who rule by Death will always have more Death to bring than their imitators can supply.'

'A sling in a child's hand can kill a giant if it strikes his head.' Johnny imagined it again in his mind.

'Goliath was the Philistine champion. The Romans are far too clever to set up champions. Maybe you can help the next Emperor to succeed a little quicker. If you do he will not proclaim himself champion. As Messiah he will demand that his statue be placed in the Temple.'

Over ten years later Johnny, like the rest of the horror-stricken Jewish people, heard that the Emperor Caligula had indeed given that blasphemous order, but Caligula was murdered by the Romans before the statue could be erected.

Word was patient. 'You see, Death is their weapon. It can never be ours. God did not create Death; Death is the child of Sin. Death is evil. So thou shall not kill. Killing can never serve God, whether you kill the child in the womb, or the old man at the tomb.'

Shimon cried 'But does not God want us to drive the Romans out?' Word shrugged. 'You cannot drive the Romans out by becoming new Romans. If you make the last Roman Emperor die, the killer inherits his kingdom of Death. Even your thefts are Roman. Who is on the coins you steal?'

'Caesar', said Shimon uneasily.

'So what you want is more Roman wealth to be called Judaean.'

'It takes money to free a country.'

'Money will always enslave a country.'

'Why don't you tell the people not to pay taxes?' It was almost Shimon's last protest.

'While the people rule themselves with Caesar's coins, Caesar can take the tax. Render therefore to Caesar the things that are Caesar's, and to God, God's.'

'So you will not free the Jews.'

'On the contrary, Shimon, that is exactly what I want us to do. But not by playing Roman games. All that will do is to drive you into shedding Jewish blood. Barabbas's victims are not likely to be Romans.'

'No', admitted Shimon.

'A smart man, Barabbas', nodded Word.

'He is very popular in Jerusalem.' But Shimon seemed less proud of it now. Word threw an arm around his shoulder, and they walked back towards the others. Johnny discreetly wandered back by the long way.

By the time he rejoined the others, Shimon had been reconciled to Peter, who now was delighted to welcome another Shimon, and one who like himself was going to do the opposite of what he had proclaimed.

Meanwhile Andrew had produced Jim. Johnny looked doubtfully at this rival for his brother's name, but relaxed on seeing that Jim was smaller than James, less dignified, less authoritative, less entitled to be treated as a natural commander. However much Johnny had had reason to deplore James's authoritarianism, he would permit nobody else to question his right to express it apart from Word, of course. On the other hand, Jim looked as if he might be fun. He didn't seem to want to draw Word away from the others, so Johnny could eavesdrop more or less legally.

Jim grinned at Word. 'Jim is short for Shem', he said, 'as James is jokey for Jacob.'

'So I've heard', agreed Word. 'Are you anxious to put things right with the past, or dreaming of the future?'

'I'm looking at the right here and now', said Jim 'It takes me all my time and I wouldn't be here if I knew what to do about it.'

'Can you tell stories?' asked Word.

'Like you tell?'

'That kind.'

Jim looked uncertain, then shook his head like a dog, ending with it pushed as far back from his throat as it would go. He was lean, and his Adam's apple was a bit obvious most times. Now it seemed to be wobbling by itself as if it was calling the rest of him into action.

'Once upon a time there was a man who looked in the mirror. He looked himself up and down, turned himself round, raised up his hands, smoothed his garments this way and that, tried what he looked like sitting down, tried what he looked like lying down, got up again, smoothed his clothes afresh, tried a few faces, worked out which one he thought looked most impressive, held that, and in the end walked away. But as the day went on he completely forgot what he had meant to look like, he forgot what way he decided was the best to make himself look like what he wanted to look like, and finally he forgot what he actually looked like.'

'That's a good story', said Word thoughtfully.

'Well, it's really a riddle', said Jim, nonetheless grateful. 'I'm better at riddles than proper stories.'

'Maybe I am too', sympathised Word. 'Where is the riddle?'

'What is this man like?'

Johnny was deciding he liked Jim's grin.

Word was deciding to answer Jim without politely pretending not to know the answer at first.

'He is like a man who hears the word of God, but does nothing about it.'

Jim pursed his lips, drew them into a circle, and relaxed them into a smile.

'You're the one, all right', he nodded, whatever he meant by it. He went on:

'And the word of God is about freedom, right?'

'The word of God is about freedom.'

Johnny was waiting for Jim to start cursing the Romans, but he only added:

'The law of liberty.'

'The law of liberty.' Word bowed his head.

'Interesting about that mirror', continued Jim. 'You might say that its lack of a third dimension is faith without good works, only a beautiful picture.'

'In a beautiful golden frame', agreed Word.

'A person who has faith and does nothing with it is like one who receives a talent and buries it in the ground instead of enabling it to increase', mused Jim.

'You are a good story-teller', said Word, 'and I will use that story.'

'Many thanks.'

Johnny was inclined to think that Jim's stories had some growing to do, but Word would know what to do with them. At the same time Johnny wondered what exactly Jim meant by good works. Miracles? But nobody could work miracles except Word, and Word did not need faith in God, since he was God, and the good works he did came from love.

Meanwhile Word asked Jim for another story.

'That sermon of yours', brooded Jim, 'beginning that the poor in spirit were blessed. So it follows that the rich are lower than the poor. Like this –

'There was once a flower in the grass which rose luxuriant and magnificent over the heads of all the grasses and flung its exuberant beauty towards the sun. But the sun grew warmer and warmer, and hotter and hotter, and its heat dried up the moisture from the grass, and the flower fell off its stem, and its beauty was gone and itself as nothing. And so the rich man will vanish to be forgotten.'

'You are a very good story-teller', said Word. 'If my word falls into the earth and yields such fruit, I have indeed been fortunate.'

'As it is nurtured away from the burning heat of the sun –' put in Johnny, who really had been listening this time and wanted to show it.

'– and the fowls of the air have not devoured it', improvised Jim.

'– and it has not fallen on stony ground', smiled Word.

'Even our duty to love our neighbour as ourselves becomes fawning on the rich while the poor are left to be scorned.' And Jim tightened his lips.

'And so doing becomes so teaching, and those whose actions teach respect for the rich over the poor, shall be least in the kingdom of Heaven', nodded Word.

'And being guilty of this breaking of God's law in this one way are guilty of breaking it all', said Jim. Johnny surprised himself by coming in 'and if the rich man sees someone else poor and does nothing to help them, how can he say he loves God?'

'That's what we mean by good works, Johnny' said Word, and Johnny was used by now to Word reading his mind.

'Saying you believe in God and doing nothing for others is no better than the devils who fear God and do what they can to kill men', agreed Jim. 'What good is your faith in God if you do nothing for people who are cold and starving? It is like a dead body whose spirit is gone.'

'They are the hollow men', agreed Word.

'Help us not to become like them, Word', said Johnny, hardly noticing that now he was praying to Word. 'Help us not to defer to them', and Jim automatically followed Johnny in the prayer.

'And you must help me to rescue them', smiled Word. 'The hardest task may be to bring love back to a rich man's heart.'

They nodded to each other, Word and Jim, and Johnny was wondering whether he should nod too, when Jim said, not quite soft enough to stop Johnny hearing, 'Why the boy?', which was a pity as it cut short Johnny's rising flower of respect for him. Word looked Jim hard in the eye and said:

'You have seen that I am come to dissolve the chains that keep rich and poor apart. I am also come to dissolve the chains that keep old and young apart. Watch that you do not forget your youth, Jim.'

Johnny tried to look anonymous, and failed.

Jim strolled over to Philip, having noticed Philip was one of the few disciples who had shown much interest in his talk with Word. Andrew brought forward the last of his four men, saying 'And this is Judas'.

'We already have one Judas', smiled Word, 'he will be joining us shortly.' Johnny had forgotten about the Judas who had been a follower of John the Baptizer and then turned to Word. Once again, he found himself not liking the thought of that Judas.

Word cocked his head to one side. 'How about Thaddeus? It's a perfectly satisfactory version of the name. Thady for short.'

Thady nodded, thus adopting the name. 'Fine by me. They used to call me Jude, my brother especially.'

'Your brother?'

'You've just been talking to him.' Word glanced from Thady to Jim and back, and Jim grinned. Johnny couldn't see much resemblance between them, Jim seeming so vital, vigorous, vehement, Thady much more passive, almost fatalistic.

'Do you agree with him about the rich and the injustice of our oiling up to them?' The absurdity of Word oiling up to anyone made Johnny choke. Word turned a sardonic eye on him.

'Certainly. But I also dislike success very much. Nothing fails like success.' Thady smiled, with less fun in his smile than Jim.

'And nothing succeeds like failure.' Word looked solicitous, with a very faint spark in his eye. 'I hope that doesn't depress you unduly, Thady.'

'You are the man I want', said Thady happily, and strode off to join Shimon the ex-Zealot, who had been listening to their conversation with some wonder. From Shimon's new point of view it made sense which his old viewpoint would have denied. Word began to walk towards the lake, and Johnny as usual attached himself to Word's left hand. Word was walking ahead of the others to give them time to get to know each other better, and Johnny had to make rapid progress. When they were out of earshot, Johnny asked:

'Is Shimon a Zealot because he is a Jew?'

'Shimon is a Zealot because he isn't a Jew.'

'What is he?'

'He's a Canaanite. People suppose that he was born in Kafr Qana. and he may have been. But he is of the blood of the older people, who lived

64

here before Moses brought the children of Israel back, and whom Joshua conquered.'

'So why does that make him a Zealot?'

'If you have people telling you that you are no good, and none of your ancestors are any good or ever have been, you may decide the easy way to answer that is to prove you are better than the people who run you down, and since the only judgment they give is from themselves, say you work harder for the cause of the true judgment than they do. A Zealot sounds like a more patriotic Jew than anyone else. So Shimon began to say he was a Zealot and soon began to think he was a Zealot. But he won't need that any more.'

'Why not?'

'Because none of those who follow me have a higher place than any other.'

'But I thought you have come for the children of Israel alone.'

'Did you, Johnny?' Word sounded regretful. 'Watch this.'

As Word spoke, a prominent Roman dignitary walked up to him, demanding imperiously:

'Come down to my house in Capernaum and heal my son, now! He's dying, I tell you! Come at once!'

Word said stonily 'It cannot be done unless you believe that I can do it. And you won't believe until you see signs and wonders.'

Johnny thought the nobleman was about to strike Word and was quickly deciding where to bite him when the nobleman's face creased, and he wailed like Johnny remembered Jeremiah had prophesied of Rachel:

'O Lord – my Lord – come down before my son dies! My son! My only son! What Father can be silent when his son is about to die?'

Word suddenly drew back his head, bowed it, as though he was answering someone else, and said in the gentlest voice Johnny had ever heard him use:

'Go back. Your son will live.'

The wealthy, ostentatious noble Roman looked into Word's eyes, gulped, kissed Word's hand and fled away.

'He believes', said Word quietly, 'and he is entitled to the love of him in whom he believes. If you should ever see him again, ask any servant who accompanies him at what hour did his master's son recover, and he will name this one. And he isn't a Jew.'

'I saw that', murmured Johnny, flickering a grin but still caught up in the storm of the Roman's grief and the calm that followed his surrender.

'And as long as you live keep it between us that Shimon is not a Jew, there's a good Johnny.'

'Promise. Word, when you told Jim you came to dissolve the chains keeping young from old, I know you have followers among grown-ups, you have to, you're one yourself – '

'But you very magnanimously don't hold that against me', nodded Word.

Johnny swung Word's hand violently to and fro, and then kissed it. 'But you don't have friends who are very old?'

'The best friend I ever had was an old man who died a few months ago', said Word softly.

It took Johnny a moment or two to get it, and then he said 'You mean –'

'Quite right, Johnny. Of course it was Daddy-Joe.'

SIX

MIRIAM

And without him was made nothing that was made

And a few more days afterward, there was Judas, and Johnny got off on the wrong foot with him from the start. It really wasn't Judas's fault, even Johnny admitted that whenever he thought about it later, but it didn't make him like Judas any better. In any case Johnny still wasn't used to the demons, and they would unsettle anyone. Johnny had now seen Word expel many demons from poor people they had invaded and afflicted, and maybe it was good, as always, to see Word's power, and to glory in its triumph over things so despicable and base – and vomit-worthy, Johnny felt, having nearly vomited at his first sight of one tearing its way out of one of its victims on Word's command. Not that he had seen it, really, but the expression on the face of a sufferer just before the demon was driven out probably gave some idea of a thing like that, and Johnny had never seen anything more hateful. He made no bones about it, he had been truly frightened that first time, and inched his way closer to Word. And Word's face had been sterner than Johnny had ever seen it, and more disdainful, and more commanding. Johnny talked to Word about it very quickly, since Word had known that the thing had brought Johnny out in goose-pimples, and Word turned aside with Johnny after he had comforted the man he had healed who was now sitting up and smiling. In fact neither Johnny nor Word had had to say very much: Johnny just needed Word's love, and Word knew.

So Johnny was suitably horrified when walking through Capernaum on an errand he turned into a wider street and there in front of everyone was a man he had never seen before almost fussily instructing a demon to vacate a victim, and to do so in the name of Jesus Christ. Johnny stood frozen to the ground as the youth possessed by the demon screamed Christ back. Johnny had heard that before, certainly: in the synagogue of this very town, when he had been with Word soon after their first meeting, and sooner after their first demon; a man properly clothed, yarmulka on his head, suddenly began to scream 'Why do you interfere with us, Jesus of Nazareth? Have you come to destroy us? I know who you are, you are God's Holy One.' The congregation had been shocked and naturally upset by the disturbance, although Johnny's chief reaction was one of amazement that the devil in the man could speak the names of God and Word. Word simply said to the demon, curtly, as if addressing an old and detested acquaintance: 'Shut up! Get out of him'; and the demon, yelling his way out of the man's body, hurled it on the ground making a particularly foul stink, after which the yelling went very quickly out of earshot. Johnny remembered how Word picked up the man, ran his hand over the shoulder and hip which had hit the ground most violently, put his other arm over the shoulder and the man's whimpers died as he clung to Word. Word told the reader of scripture he was sorry for the interruption and the ruler of the synagogue thanked Word before asking the lector to continue. The exorcised man stayed with Word, Johnny, Andrew, James and Peter until they left the synagogue, and they took him to his home. Word told the man's sister he would never be afflicted again, and her amazement and gratitude said as much as her grey hair over a young, tear-stained face. But Word had been in control of that miracle from the moment he first spoke to the demon. Here now was someone unknown to Johnny making free with Word's name, inciting the demon to start cursing Word, as he was doing, in picturesque language, some of it unknown to Johnny despite his days among fishermen losing their patience with fish and with him.

The exorcist seemed sufficiently sure of himself not to lose command, and Johnny, however hostile and alarmed, admitted that. Unfortunately the exorcist, when excited, stuttered, and the unclean spirit was yelling blasphemies while the exorcist struggled to tell him to get out of his victim in th-th-th-th-the n-n-n-name of J-J-J-J-Jesus K-K-K-K-Christ so that Johnny to his own surprise found himself irritably shouting in the name of Jesus Christ leave that man's body and never return! and as a Son of Thunder his bellow filled the entire street. The demon screamed again, flung his victim down, and with what Johnny took to be his final filthy but incomprehensible curse, stank his way out of the body and out of earshot. Johnny felt a little shaken, and more than a little staggered, never having worked a miracle – or half a miracle – before, and muttered underneath his breath 'thanks, Word' having had Word in the centre of his mind while pronouncing the crucial words. The other exorcist (Johnny was pleased to think the word 'other') looked at Johnny a bit resentfully and said 'Th-th-thanks, but I'd have m-m-m-managed myself' and Johnny said 'Y-y-y-yes?' which was rude, and the man said 'K-k-k-k-conceited little b-b-b-b-bastard' and walked away. The sun glinted on his hair, and Johnny somewhat abstractedly noted the hair was red, which was quite unusual around those parts. Meanwhile Johnny thought he had better pat the victim's shoulders as he had seen Word do, but the victim gave him a nasty look and asked if he was trying to steal his purse, so Johnny left in disgust, rather hurriedly, it clearly being no time to explain to the man that he, Johnny, and not the stutterer, had got rid of his demon, especially since the man didn't seem to realise he had had a demon, though no doubt some of the onlookers would tell him. Johnny didn't worry about getting the credit, which he would have wanted for any heroic achievement before he met Word: Word would know what he had done, and how well he had done it, although, thought Johnny uneasily, Word would not be pleased that Johnny had stuttered at the stutterer. It did not occur to Johnny to conceal such a thing from Word. He knew he would always tell Word anything wrong he had done, quite apart from knowing that Word would know it. It was funny that the two things – him telling Word and Word knowing it anyway – didn't cancel each other out, but they didn't.

What happened next made Johnny forget about the stuttering exorcist, since as he hurried along a couple of side-streets, and then back to one in greater use by Capernaum's 2000-odd inhabitants he met Miriam again. He had seen her for the first time only a couple of days previously. Word and all the disciples had started across the sea in one of Zebedee's boats, and Word, who had been healing and exorcising and telling stories all day, lay down and slept, and a nasty sea got going rapidly, with waves lashing the sides of the craft and spilling over. The wind grew louder and more venomous, and James sent Johnny half way up the mast to check the strength of the sail fastening. There was little out of the ordinary in this, and Johnny told himself he had been up many a mast – or at least up this mast – many times in many worse seas. He liked battling the wind, and the taste of the flying sea-foam, and the general sensation of being in a good fight in which he could play as valiant a part as any grown-up. He had always been proud of James's confidence in him from the first time James had told him to check the knots, admittedly in calm weather, and Johnny had never been mistaken on that chore. It never occurred to him as odd that James was fussy about Johnny's safety only when they were on dry land: as fisherboys the sea was their environment. But when Johnny got down from the mast this time, it was to realise that while James, Andrew and Peter simply saw this as yet another storm, part of their lives' routine, even if they were giving those lives up to follow Word, the other seven were looking very worried. Phil and Nat as boys growing up in Bethsaida must have known the sea of Galilee well enough, but it was not their livelihoods as it was Andrew's and Peter's and Zebedee's sons'. Of course fisherfolk were drowned in the sea of Galilee as they were drowned anywhere else when freak storms struck, but Johnny knew as well as James and Peter and Andrew that that was the price you might one day have to pay and if your turn was going to come you paid that price without whining. So as Johnny slid down the mast, maybe with a faint sigh of relief since that wind really did not like him, even as he licked the salt spray from his lips with relish, he heard Thady announcing with what seemed some satisfaction that they were doomed, and Thomas asking if the boat would hold together, and Matthew inquiring whether they had invested much to keep it seaworthy, and Jim remarking that it was no wonder you had shipwrecks when the makers' anxiety to make money led them to underpay their workers who skimped their work in revenge, and Peter with his usual tact asking them if they were frightened. Johnny watched the landlubbers with mild derision and then asked James, sarcastically, whether he should wake Word and ask him to still the storm, and to his surprise James said irritably, that he had better. So Johnny somewhat regretfully made his way to the hinder part of the boat, to find Word sleeping peacefully on a pillow regardless of how wet it was getting, and kissed Word's left eyelid which promptly opened, and Johnny explained the landsmen were frightened, and as Word got up and walked forward with what Johnny thought were good sea-legs, Philip bawled plaintively 'Master, are you not concerned that we are about to die?' and Word shouted back 'A man born to be hanged will never be drowned', but Johnny didn't hear that. Johnny was hardly surprised when Word in a much quieter voice, yet audible to Johnny this time, said into the wind while looking at the sea 'Peace, be still', and wind and sea simply cut out. James smiled, having also expected it, and so did Andrew, and Peter was beaming wide enough to drink all the water in the boat, but the landsmen were still blinking and shivering, and Word cocked his head on one side and asked why they were afraid, and hadn't they enough faith to know Word would look after them, and Philip asked Nathaniel who was Word that the wind and sea did his bidding, and Nat said wryly that he was beginning to find out. Johnny was a little puzzled at that, since he had thought Nat was likely to be the first of the grown-ups to tumble to it that Word was God, but he realised that the fishermen, none of them particularly frightened, had all more or less expected Word would command the sea if the sea if the sea needed commanding, while the landsmen still could not quite convince themselves that it was possible although they had seen it happen. Johnny amused himself by singing a sea-chanty in their hearing as the boat neared the far shore,

> For the raging seas did roar
> And the stormy winds did blow
> And we poor sailors clinging to the mast,
> And the landlubbers lying down
> Below, below, below,
> And the landlubbers lying down below!

Word might say the song was unkind to the landsmen, but Johnny was all set to explain that he was being very kind, really, since the fishermen on board hadn't been clinging to anything apart from his own lawful, mast-climbing, knot-inspecting duties. But all Word did say was that, speaking as the only landlubber who had actually been lying down below during the height of the storm, he thought it was very unkind of Johnny to make fun of him. A few weeks ago this might have dismayed Johnny, but now it simply set him into a cascade of giggles at the thought of Word as a layabout landlubber.

And then there were the pigs. The boat had anchored in the country of the Gadarenes. Johnny had often seen them on his own side of the sea, and had landed there once or twice himself, usually if Zebedee's boat had been swept out of its course for one reason or another, but he found the Gadarenes rather remote and taciturn and maybe a bit shy, and the place seemed more hostile, being part of the Province of Syria under direct Roman rule. As soon as James and Johnny had tied up the boat, Word led them all ashore, very firm in his direction although none of them knew what he meant or where he was going or why he wanted to go there, and after a long walk, suddenly Word said there he is, as though he had been having a conversation with someone, and, before Johnny could make sense of that, a man with no clothes apart from bits of chains on his wrists and his ankles came yelling up to them, bleeding from all sorts of cuts and abrasions where he had hurt himself probably by falling violently over stones, for now he came bounding up, taking fantastic risks to cover ground and making wildly suicidal jumps, and when he reached them Johnny realised that, mad as he clearly was, he had been making for Word all the time.

Johnny, holding Word's left hand as usual, must have radiated the tension in his own muscles through to the hand of Word, all the more as Johnny's left hand was making a fist to defend Word if need be, and Andrew, James and Peter were closing in around Word (the others were still a bit frail, and Matthew and Thomas still looking a trifle green under the brown of their skins). But the man hurled himself at Word's feet, and to Johnny's amazement he could see what looked like love trying to shine its way out of the tortured eyes, while the face was racked with convulsions and the horrible, dirty, naked limbs were thrown on each other, twisting and wrestling. Johnny actually sensed that there was more than one demon in the man because fighting seemed to be taking place inside the wretched body. Word was already glaring at the man or rather, as Johnny realised, the dirty devils inside him, and in a voice crackling with anger he told them to get out of him. And then something happened unlike any other time Johnny saw Word exorcising. First several voices fighting against each other could be made out roughly saying the same thing, speaking Word's name and asking why he had come to interfere with them, and hailing him as the son of the most high God. And it seemed to Johnny that there was almost a sound of reverence in the way they addressed Word, more than the angry deference he had associated with such demons. Word in a milder but still very firm voice asked what is your name?, and the voices replied, this time in a rather ragged chorus, 'Our name is Legion, for we are many' and begged him not to send them back to hell. Word actually seemed sorry for them and asked where did they want to go, and they asked him to let them go into the pigs dotted above them on the mountain-side, and Johnny oddly found himself agreeing with the demons that it was the best place for them, since the demons were unclean and so were the pigs, whose flesh was forbidden to Johnny and all other Jews and was only eaten by Greek civilians & Roman soldiers and such people (and Johnny thought, as he often had, how depraved these conquerors of his country were). Word evidently agreed as well, telling the demons to enter the pigs, and then the pigs went mad, and thundered down the mountain straight for the calm sea before them. There was a high cliff at the point where they went over, fifty or sixty of them, screaming violently if incomprehensibly, and a succession of splashings came as each pig hit the water. The other disciples turned away after the pigs had disappeared, but Johnny ran over to the cliff and looked down. To his amazement he saw what seemed every single pig swimming forcefully and wholeheartedly for the opposite shore. It was clear that there was nothing demented about them now: they were sensibly getting as far away from the Gadarene coast as they could, and as they swam out of sight there was every sign that they would make it. Word was talking to the man, when Johnny got back: the man's eyes were happy and sane, his wrists and ankles were free of the shackles he had otherwise torn to bits in his mad fits, and his cuts were healed as usual with anyone in Word's company. Word simply said out of the corner of his mouth 'pigs all right?' as Johnny got back, and Johnny said 'yes, they are swimming hard for the far off coast and they'll make it,' and Word, still audible only to Johnny said 'Good!' The man had got hold of some clothes, among which Johnny recognised garments of Peter's and Andrew's, and a belt that had belonged to James. It was made of durable, well-meshed cords, and James valued it and Johnny thought it looked well on him, though of course he had never said so to James. Word had evidently asked them to help clothe the man who was no doubt embarrassed at being naked once he was sane enough to be embarrassed, and if Johnny knew anything about it, Peter with his usual generosity once enlisted had been half-denuding himself until Andrew restrained him and added a garment of his own, and then others contributed. The man would have to do without shoes until later, and his madness had presumably hardened his feet over months and maybe years of running across hard surfaces and sharp stones. The man wanted to go with them, but Word had told him to tell the people he met what had happened, in hopes it might make them think of the need to drive evil out of themselves, and he would be alone to do it, because when the Gadarenes who saw what had taken place came up to Word the first thing they did was to ask him, very politely, to please go away. Johnny could not bring himself to resent their doing it: he could see terror in the herdsmen's eyes as to what form of livestock Word would next send jumping into the sea, most of it fattened for Romans. So they returned to the fishing-boat, and the sea was calm, and Matthew and Thomas began to look brown again, and Shimon the ex-Zealot was noticing that there was no sign of storm on the horizon while reminding everyone he had not been frightened. Johnny was about to ask if Shimon's yells of terror during the storm had been merely cheers because the thunder and lightning looked so pretty, but he caught Word's eye and kept quiet. When they got time to themselves Word thanked Johnny for it, remarking that one of the hardest times to keep quiet is when you have thought of something funny, but he didn't need to remind Johnny that they had to be careful about Shimon, who was still thinking his way into a world where you couldn't kill anyone however much you thought they deserved it. (He did need to remind Johnny, of course, and they both knew it.)

Johnny always derived great pleasure from the way Word would explain things as though they were the same age – or maybe putting Word at eleven, since Johnny was ten, or putting Johnny at 29 since Word was 30 – but just then he said: 'I never thought I could get so much fun thinking about things I can't understand.'

'You do understand them, but you do it without words.'

'Only with Word.'

'Exactly. Not a bad way.'

'The best way.'

'Thank you, Johnny, but don't be surprised if people don't understand you if you say that. You see, we became friends while you are a boy. The result is that you may find you don't use words the same way as other grown-ups when you grow up. And so they may not understand you.'

'Because I'll be too difficult for them?'

'No, because you'll be too easy for them. When people grow up they forget to think easily. They are always trying to make things difficult for themselves. That's why my disciples will have to have a leader who is easy to understand – and, as you know, it won't be you.'

'Andrew?'

'Andrew is much too intelligent and much too enquiring to be a leader. He takes charge well, but for a leader when I am not there you want – ?'

'Peter!'

'Quite right, Johnny. Peter. Now, keep your eyes open about that, and your mouth – ?'

'Shut.'

'Shut.' Word nodded approvingly.

'Word, when did you discover you could command the demons?'

'When I discovered I had to, if I was to be of any use here.'

'How did that happen?'

Word reflected. ' Daddy-Joe had been ill for some time before he died. I wanted to cure him but he told me very firmly I must not, that it had to take its course, and that I ought not to use any divine power until my work in the world had begun.'

'You mean you did nothing that showed you were God?'

'Nothing. Except that I knew what certain scriptures meant and certain happenings, and sometimes, when I was about your age, I showed I did, not always at the best of times, as I realise now.'

'Go on.'

'Daddy-Joe died, and I told Mother I would stay and look after her. But she said we had enough money saved for her to keep going, and it was my job now to do God's work among men. She told me to talk with my cousin John the Baptizer. So I did. He started me right away, even telling two of his own disciples that I was greater than he was and they should follow me – which they did, though I had to send them back, each to his own people, until I was ready to start work with them. One was Andrew, as you know.'

'And the other was Judas.'

'You remember hearing his name? Yes, that's the one. He should be here soon.'

'But where do the demons come into it?'

'Cousin John advised me to retreat.'

'What did he mean?'

'He has a nice turn of humour, though he didn't use it much in his preachments. He hates killing as much as I do, so he said that where soldiers begin a campaign with an advance, I should begin mine with a retreat. Go away from everyone, walk and live in the wilderness for some days, think, pray, fast.'

'Fast?'

'It is a way of praying. Digestion keeps your mind on yourself, if you're not careful. Fasting can help you to distance yourself from wanting always to coddle yourself. Of course if you simply spend all your fast in counting the minutes till it's over, you may not do yourself much good.'

'Did you take water?'

'Certainly. In our climate you lose your wits without water very quickly. And nobody is much use to themselves or anyone else if they live without water for more than three days.'

'How long were you without food?'

'Several days. I don't remember, naturally.'

'Forty?' asked Johnny brightly.

'It's a nice, round number. Anyhow, it ended when the spirit of supreme evil appeared before me.' Word stopped, like a man remembering a serpent in his path. Johnny felt the blood drain from his own face.

'What did he look like?'

'Johnny, thank God you don't know.'

'Did he know who you were? His demons do.'

'It's a good question, Johnny, because I don't think he did – or rather, *it* did, because It isn't a he, or a she. He and she mean beings made by God. This thing has not been made, as we know creation anyway.'

'Why does it exist?'

'Because men have willed It into existence. If you say no to God, you declare your support for a thing that does not exist, a denial, a rejection,

76

above all a hatred. I don't want you to brood about it, and when your time comes to tell your story I don't want you to talk about It, either the thing I saw in the desert or those other things I exorcise from people's bodies although the day will come when you will exorcise them too.'

'Other people will tell your story and tell about them.'

'Let them. Not you. Don't ask why.'

Of course Johnny had just been about to ask why. He gulped.

'Oh, all right', said Word. 'It is best this way, after all.' He put his hands on Johnny's shoulders. 'Apart from my mother, you are the being I love most on this earth. That *thing* is the utter opposite of all love. So I don't want you to write about it, or to tell anyone who takes down your story about it.'

Johnny nodded. He could not speak.

Word smiled, wanly. He ran his hand from Johnny's neck to the crown of his head, and went on talking.

'It came before me. It knew I had been fasting, and made the obvious move that to show I was the Son of God I should make the stones of the wilderness into bread to feed myself. I suppose it thought I was some creature with miraculous but not divine powers. Since I am the Son of God, as a Man mortal but as God one with the Father, it wasn't possible that I could ever have obeyed the *thing*. Anyhow I told It that man does not live by bread only –'

' – but by every word which proceeds out of the mouth of God', finished Johnny, who might not know the entire Torah by heart but who could repeat a remarkable lot of it.

'Thanks, Johnny. Thinking back, it's almost as if you were there, giving me the love and support I wanted.'

'But you didn't need it', said Johnny, complimented but bewildered.

'God does not need Man's love but is very happy to get it. And Man – and I am Man also – needs as much love as he can get.'

'What did it do?'

'Took me up to our holy city of Jerusalem, placed me on the pinnacle of the Temple and told me if I was the Son of God to cast myself down, for it was written "He hath given charge to his angels concerning thee, to watch over thee wheresoever thou goest; they will hold thee up with their hands lest thou shouldst chance to trip on a stone".'

'But that was written by the Psalmist!' shouted Johnny excitedly, 'it's by David!'

'It's actually *about* David. It's by Jonathan. Some of the Psalms are by David, some by Jonathan, and some by other people, and this one is a promise of faithful friendship, and a prayer to God for David's protection.'

'Did the *thing* know that?'

'You would imagine It might, but it is probably incapable of understanding perfect love. It knows all about exploiting imperfect love, love that does not go far enough but recoils in selfishness on its abuser. And as my experience shows, It knows how to take the word of God and twist it to its use. I suppose that It knew I was descended from David, although It may have thought my descent was through Daddy-Joe and It forgot about Mother, a big mistake on its part, and It thought I would be flattered to be addressed in words of David, whether by him or about him.'

'And you told It?'

'I stayed with the Torah. "Ye shall not tempt the Lord your God."'

'That was telling him, Word!'

'That was telling *It* Johnny.'

'It's a wonder It didn't throw you down from the pinnacle.'

'It might have some hopes of my getting dizzy, but if I had been thrown down I would have been borne by angels, which would have meant that *It* had spoken truth, a thing impossible for It in ultimate terms, if you follow me.'

'I don't,' said Johnny, 'but go on, and I'll follow you to the ends of the earth.'

Word laughed happily. 'You rascal! Thank God for you and your nonsense. You are the breath of God against that *thing*.'

Johnny smiled, and held on to Word's left hand.

'Then what?'

'Then It took me to the highest mountain in the world.'

'Where is that?'

'It's part of our continent, Asia, but it's three thousand miles east of here. But he made it seem as though all the kingdoms of the world could be seen from it, and all their glory.'

'Do they all owe allegiance to Caesar?'

'Caesar is unknown to most of them. Anyhow It offered them all to me if falling down I would adore It. I said it was written "Thou shalt adore the Lord thy God and him only shalt thou serve."'

'The cheek of it!' spat Johnny, inadequately but with sufficient vehemence.

'I don't think that was the first time It had made that particular offer', said Word thoughtfully. 'And I suspect it wasn't an offer that has always been refused.'

Johnny followed him well enough that time, and shuddered. 'So that's what you think of the Roman Empire!'

'I am an appropriate leader for Shimon the Zealot', smiled Word. 'A kingdom built on fear and hatred is all that the *thing* can provide.'

'What happened then?'

'It vanished, thanks be to God.'

'Leaving you on the mountain?'

'The angels took me back. A much more agreeable form of transport.'

'No travel-sickness', agreed Johnny, thinking of the landlubbers.

'Those poor fellows! Johnny, remember it's your duty to be kind to those – I mean, to us landlubbers.'

It was very shortly after the boat's landfall near Bethsaida when one of the rulers of a local synagogue named Jairus ran up to Word, begging him to heal his daughter who was either dying or dead.

It wasn't particularly like the Roman who got Word to cure his son when Word and Johnny were talking after Word had admitted the last four of the disciples (for Judas had been one of the first two, although Johnny had never seen him yet). That had been condescending bluster by a potentate facing Word, whom the Roman saw an alien man and culture, but his desperation very quickly cracked through his normal defences and offences. This father Jairus was flesh of Johnny's flesh and bone of his bone (and Word's too, he supposed, a little doubtfully since Word was also so much else). Jairus actually spoke to Word in Hebrew which meant that he thought Word was someone from the depths of sacred tradition. Johnny suppose Jairus could not think Word was God: it was becoming clear grown-ups didn't have that kind of intelligence and what had been easy for Johnny to discover was too great a leap for most of them, at least for a long time. Maybe foxes and birds really did know it, as well as Johnny: do animals know their creator instinctively? Johnny wondered. But if Jairus didn't think Word was God, he clearly thought Word was from God, and he told him of the girl's illness with a frankness and detail as if they had known each other all their lives. It was as if the Hebrew language made them brothers in God's eyes. Jairus was obviously a very devoted father, but he was also a man in love with his religion, and he deferred to Word much as he would have deferred to one of the few people who had studied the Scriptures deeper than Jairus. Johnny might not have digested all of this immediately but he put it into place easily enough when he thought about it later. Also, Jairus said something really nice about Johnny: he said he thought Word could understand what it was like to be a father. Word smiled, sympathetically, called Andrew and told him to look after the others, and asked James and Peter to follow Jairus and himself, and Johnny.

A strange thing happened as they were on their way to Jairus's house. A crowd had as usual been following Word, and almost leaning on himself and Jairus as if to pick up special blessings by eavesdropping on their talk which was all very well, thought Johnny, if the listeners-in were that good at Hebrew. Johnny wasn't bad at it, and was getting better under Word's teaching, but there was still much Hebrew he could repeat without being able to understand, and more he could neither repeat nor understand.

He had made reasonable sense of Word's talk with Jairus, especially as it was in short, sharp sentences apart from initial compliments and salutations. And they had not been long. Two scholars take much shorter time to know that each other is a scholar and to convey their mutual respect, than it takes two gentlemen to recognise one another as gentlemen, or at least to admit it. But as the crowd pressed around Word and Jairus, Word suddenly stopped and said 'someone touched me'. Peter promptly pointed out that they had all been touching him, and that bodies were leaning on him left and right, some of them well known to him, such as Peter himself (who probably had the biggest feet in any crowd, thought Johnny, uncharitably), and some not well known, but all of them near his arms and his feet, and left to himself, Peter could prolong the obvious to distraction, and Word cut in saying 'Somebody touched me: I can tell that power has gone out from me.' This fascinated Johnny, showing as it did how quick Word was to know some things, and what were the limits of his knowledge of others: someone less attentive to Jairus might well have seen who touched him, and someone without Word's power would not be able to deduce that someone had touched him. When Johnny asked Word about it later, Word laughed and said 'To leave one's godhead and take human flesh isn't in order to cheat at Blind Man's Buff.' Anyhow, Word – and therefore Jairus also – turned and looked into the crowd, and a woman who was in fact worming her way away from them and out of the crowd stopped, and burst into tears, and fell on her knees, and said 'Master' (as Peter had been calling Word while telling him there were many people touching him), and said that she had an issue of blood (at which the crowd thinned rapidly and many people hurried away to purify themselves and even Peter looked a little worried) and that she had been suffering from it for twelve years, and that she spent every penny she had on doctors who took the money but could do nothing for her, and if anything she was worse after the doctors than before she found them, and she thought if she touched the hem of Word's cloak it would cure her, and she began crying even more while telling Word that it had. Peter, sorry for her and perhaps thinking her flow of blood might have polluted Word, said that was very sensible of her because now Word would not be polluted. Jairus, who might be expected to know more than Peter about pollution and the need for purification afterwards, simply wanted to keep moving to get Word to see his daughter. Word said 'Daughter' (at which the flow of tears dried up as fast as she said the blood had) 'your faith has cured you, go in peace, you will never suffer from your illness again. You have done well', and with his love ringing in her ears, he turned onward with Jairus.

But as they walked forward towards Jairus's house, someone came running, wailing 'she's dead!, she's dead!, come home, Jairus, and bury your daughter, the Rabbi with you can do nothing, she's dead!, you were from home when she died, oh, she is dead!' Jairus staggered, and would have fallen, but Peter caught him with a swift reaction – he was unusually quick in reaction when not distracted by speech, and it was the falling man that spurred him to aid, not the wailing messenger – and James threw an arm around Jairus's waist, and Word turned on Jairus and said in a clipped, clear voice 'Do not be afraid. Only believe, and she will recover', and Jairus, choking back tears, hugged Word and actually laughed, a fast croak but still a laugh, and said 'if you can heal your daughter, you can heal mine', and Word kissed him and said 'she will be my daughter also.' They made the best time they could, although the wailing messenger continued his wailing somewhere between sorrow and duty. At Jairus's house the tidings had brought neighbours from far and wide, minstrels were already at their work, and the cries and lamentations were enough to bring Word from Heaven if he hadn't already been on earth, or so Johnny felt. Jairus broke through to the side of his wife, saying the Master said all would be well, and Word said firmly that the girl was not dead, only sleeping, and wiseacres told him he was out of his mind, and Peter was about to object when Word twirled him towards the girl's room, his other hand drawing Jairus and his wife after him. James followed with Johnny, having no intention of exposing Johnny to a potentially hostile crowd, or the crowd to an even more potentially hostile Johnny. Once inside the room, Johnny looked at the couch where a twelve-year-old girl was lying with her mouth open neck and her skin yellow-white. Word dropped Peter's neck and Jairus's arm, and walked straight towards the body, put in his right hand in hers and said *'Talitha cumi'*, which Johnny knew meant, 'Maiden, arise!' At once the girl sat up, smiled the widest smile Johnny had ever seen on a child's face, then drew her lips together in a mock-serious purse, then jumped down and, dropping Word's hand, hugged her parents together. And Word sent Peter and James out of the room, told Jairus to give his daughter something to eat before she left it, and bade Johnny follow Jairus to bring the bread and olives back to the girl, whom Jairus's wife told him was named Miriam. Peter shouted over the noise of the minstrels that the girl was well, probably without being understood, but the noise he made howled down the other noises, and Jairus's firm assurance that the child was fully recovered had to be believed. Johnny came in to Miriam's room with food, avoiding some mourner complaining that it polluted food to take it to a corpse. While Johnny was giving her the food, and to his own surprise taking some trouble to serve it – it certainly was his greatest civility to any girl up to that date – Word was saying firmly in Hebrew to Miriam's mother, 'remember, *she has not died*, and contradict anyone who says she was raised from the dead' and when the mother answered in slightly halting Hebrew that Word ought to get the credit for his miracle and that the more people knew what a holy man he was, the better, Word smiled and said that it was essential for *Miriam's sake* that she not be turned into a freak to be pointed at by endless children and be perpetually cross-questioned on what it was like to be dead. Word asked Miriam how she felt, and Miriam threw her arms around his neck and hugged him bearishly, and then he left her to talk to Johnny while he walked through the public rooms, telling the ex-mourners that the child had been ill and was now well, that was all. Johnny asked Word afterwards if it wasn't a lie to say she had not died, but Word merely smiled and said that he was entitled to know whether she was dead or not in his capacities as God and man, and when Johnny persisted, pulled his nose and kissed him.

So when to his pleasure Johnny met Miriam in Capernaum some days later, after losing the strange exorcist, he put himself on guard to keep Miriam's death safely out of sight under the cover of Miriam's illness, and was suitably dischuffed when she greeted him affectionately as the nice boy who brought her food when she had stopped being dead.

'Sh!', said Johnny, horrified. 'You weren't dead, you were only ill!'

And he looked nervously about him, but nobody was paying attention to the chatter of two children.

'I suppose', said Miriam, sounding irritatingly like Word, 'I'm entitled to know whether I was dead or not in my capacity as corpse and maiden.'

'Yes', hissed Johnny, 'but Word said it would be bad for you to have people saying you were dead and asking you all about it every day.' 'What did you call him?' demanded Miriam.

'Word', said Johnny.

'But everyone else calls him Rabbi or Master?'

'Word is my name for him. He likes it.'

'Hm. He is God, isn't he?'

Johnny had been expecting to hear this from someone else for many days, but he had never anticipated that the first person would be a girl scarcely older than himself. He struggled for utterance. Miriam looked at him kindly, and said:

'Yes, I thought you wouldn't lie about something like that. You'd only lie about unimportant things, like whether I was dead or not.'

'You weren't dead', roared Johnny indignantly. 'Word said you weren't.'

'And since he raised me from the dead he ought to know. I will say for you men, you always know how to have your bread and olives and eat them too, and somebody else's as well, if you can manage it.'

Johnny was rather pleased about her calling him a man until she saw he was, and she hastily added 'and half-men as well, of course.'

Johnny was about to explode and then saw she was laughing at him, and promptly said 'then we half-men only eat half-loaves, leaving the rest for little girls who were famished from being dead.'

'Well, I was dead, and I can tell you that dying isn't a bit nice. You should try it sometime.'

'I will not', shouted Johnny, before he realised what he was saying. She looked at him oddly.

'Maybe you won't either. If you don't, you have better sense than I thought. It's awful.'

'How do you mean?'

'You feel a paralysing weakness, as if your bones have turned to a nasty, putrescent jelly, and you have eaten something really horrible, and you feel a clammy sweat – I'd been desperately hot, with the fever, but now I had the supreme discomfort of knowing I had been very hot and actually feeling very cold, and my tongue seemed to cling to the roots of my throat, and my body kind of dissolved.'

'And then nothing?'

'You do believe I died, you *do*, you *do*, you *do*!'

' I *dont*!'

'Do.'

'*DON'T!*'

'DO! Anyhow, shut up while I tell you about it', and she hurried on while Johnny had been inflating his lungs for a really thunderous DON'T!

'I felt as if my brain was on fire and it split in two, and one part was falling to bits, and the other half was looking at it as like a congregation in the synagogue listening to a really bad preacher.'

'Well, that doesn't sound in the least dead to me!', hooted Johnny, recovering himself.

Miriam ignored him for the moment. 'Then there really was nothing. And then I saw him, your friend, Word, God or whatever you call him, just a head and shoulders and arms, and he didn't have any covering, and he looked at me as if he was about to tell me to go for a message or say a prayer or read something, but friendly more than bossy, and I heard a voice inside my head saying "Talitha cumi" and felt a hand coming into mine, and the voice was the sweetest I had ever known, and the hand was so cool – not cold but cool – and I felt a splendid shivery cool all over me and felt better than I ever have in my life and when opened my eyes there he was just as he had been when I was dead except now he wore garments and he seemed smaller, somehow, and so did the rest of you, and YOU were smallest of all!'

Johnny grinned at her. 'You weren't dead.'

'I didn't feel any of that pounding you do when you stop and listen for it. I couldn't see anything, not even the two ghostly noses you see.'

'What was the last thing you heard before you heard Word's voice?'

'Somebody playing a musical instrument very badly and somebody else screaming that somebody was dead.'

'That was you they were talking about. And you weren't dead then and you weren't dead afterwards.'

'Was.'

'Wasn't.'

'WAS!'

'WASN'T – I mean, weren't!'

'Silly boy doesn't know proper Aramaic!'

'Silly boy does – ' Johnny hastily realised he would only walk himself from one trap into another when arguing with this girl. But he liked her, very much, and he was sure Word would like her too. So he asked: 'Will you come back with me and see Word?'

'Yes, I thought you'd need some help from somewhere soon enough. I'd love to see him. I've only half thanked him. You owe a lot to someone when he stops you being dead.'

'What are you doing in Capernaum anyway?' Johnny avoided the D-word this time.

'Staying with my aunt and uncle. Mother and Father wanted to get me away from all the people asking me what it was like to be dead.' She looked severely at Johnny. 'Fat chance.'

'Word won't be asking you that.'

'Word knows – or, as I'd prefer to say, God knows.'

They made their way through the town, telling each other what they thought of it, and appreciating each other's judgments whenever they forgot to be rude. When they got into the room in Peter's house where Word was staying they found the usual babel of voices, with Word looking a little tired, and James disdainful, and the rest arguing as to which of them was the most important, and Johnny could see that it was the same row that had followed from the others thinking James and himself were pushing for the top places, and he blushed to think of how stupid he had been about it. James had been utterly indifferent to such questions since he had been told that he would be the first disciple to be killed: for him that, now, was honour enough. Johnny did not know that, but he was glad James was outside the dispute as he himself was. Anyhow Thomas was now putting the question to Word directly, and Matthew seemed about to enumerate everyone's virtue and honour status and as Johnny and Miriam entered the room Word stood up, walked towards them, and picked up Miriam who had fallen on one knee before him and kissed his hand. Word held Miriam up over the heads of them all, straining his shoulder-blades, while she smiled, nervously. Word's eyes gleamed as she looked down on them safe in his hands, and he said in hard tones 'This is the greatest of you' and swung her down, and gave her a seat beside him. Miriam couldn't resist stealing a triumphant look at Johnny, but slightly to her surprise Johnny was looking absolutely delighted, his mouth parted in a huge grin, teeth flashing and chin jutting cheerfully forward, so she grinned back at him. And James beamed at her, and it was about time he gave his smile muscles some exercise, thought Johnny, and Peter scratched his head and nodded like a goodhumoured bear. The others, none of whom had seen her before, seemed rather more disconcerted. And Word said:

'Amen I say to you, unless you be converted and become as little children, you shall not enter the kingdom of heaven.'

Peter was quite excited about this, and it was from this moment that he began to make friends with Johnny, and even ask his advice. Johnny would find a good mate in Peter, although sometimes a bit old for Johnny, in a way Word never was.

Word went on:

'Whosoever will humble himself as this little child, he is the greater in the kingdom of heaven. And he that shall receive one such little child in my name, receives me.' And Miriam put her arms around his neck and kissed him. The rest stood in silence. Eventually Johnny remembered the strange exorcist and said 'Word, there was a strange man in the town casting out devils in your name. Wasn't that wrong?'

Word said patiently 'You should not forbid such actions' which was nice of him since he knew nobody would have taken the slightest notice of Johnny if he did. Word continued: 'There is no man who shall do a miracle in my name that can lightly speak evil of me. For he that is not against us is with us.'

And, as he spoke, Johnny out of the corner of his eye saw a man with red hair entering the room, and, turning, he realised it was the strange exorcist.

Word stood up, kissed the red-haired man, and said quietly 'Welcome, Judas.'

EVEN

JOHN THE BAPTIZER

In him was life

'What is that b-b-brat d-d-doing here?' demanded Judas.

'Brat yourself!' said Miriam indignantly.

'I don't m-m-mean you', said Judas, 'I m-m-m-mean him!', pointing at Johnny.

'I know you mean him!' said Miriam scornfully 'and nobody calls him a brat except me, when I'm around.'

'And Word', said Johnny, quite extraordinarily touched by her championship.

'And G – , all right, and Word.' Miriam was not so much accepting Johnny's leadership as taking direction from Word, who had looked into her eyes as Johnny spoke. Word flashed a grin at her, and then turned round to Judas, laying an arm on his shoulder and saying, very gently:

'Open your mouth, Judas!' and when Judas did, Word blew into it, and Judas, blinking, said in a milder voice:

'I said, what is that brat doing here?'

He didn't seem to realise Word had cured him of his stutter, thought Johnny, who by this time needed no further proof that the cure was real and permanent. But Andrew was already crossing over to Judas and was greeting him warmly, and asking had he any news of John the Baptizer whom Johnny knew was still in prison. Word took each child by the hand, Johnny with his left as always, Miriam with his right, and walked them over to the front door at which he picked up Miriam again and kissed her, and did the same for Johnny, perhaps to stress their equality before him, and told Johnny to see Miriam to her aunt's house, and Miriam to see Johnny got there all right and was firmly directed back, and that she should give Word's love to her parents and that he looked forward to seeing her again soon. Then with one more smile from parted lips and the blessing from his eyes, the door was closed and the children were walking down the street. Then Miriam spoke, after a few minutes:

'Is he always like that?'

'Judas? I've only met him once before.'

'No, silly. Judas isn't worth bothering about. God – Word, you call him.'

'How do you mean, like that?'

'Making you feel he is the most wonderful human being you have ever seen in your life and you want to be with him for ever and ever.'

'Yes', said Johnny simply.

'No wonder he had to come down to earth and redeem it when it's a world where you can go through the land with him and I can't.'

'Redeem it –?'

'Win it back to him.' She was impatient.

'You make it seem like buying it back after it has been out on loan, pawned, or something.'

'Well, it's been pawned to Caesar, for one.'

'And they tell us we got civilisation in exchange for it', agreed Johnny gloomily.

'And to Herod the tetrarch and the rest of them.'

'What did we get from *him*?'

'More civilisation. We should be dying of a surfeit of it soon, if Herod doesn't die of a surfeit of everything else first.' Miriam sounded highly authoritative.

'What might he die of a surfeit of?'

'Never you mind. Things nice little boys shouldn't know about.'

'I'm not a nice little boy!'

'Tell me something I don't know. And I dare say that Judas would agree with you. What did you do to him anyhow, and what does God want with him?'

Johnny considered it for a moment. 'Andrew was the first to tell me about him. They were disciples of John the Baptizer.'

'Who's he, when he's at home?'

'He isn't at home, and probably won't be, ever again, by the look of things. He told Herod he ought not to be living in con – con – '

'Maybe Judas's stutter is catching, and you caught it when Word, as you call God, blew it out of his mouth.'

So she had realised that too. But then she was one of Word's miracles herself, so she had a right to know. Anyhow Johnny wanted the missing term more than another argument. Eventually he got it out.

'Con – cubinage.'

'And incest, if he had his facts straight.'

'He did. That was why they imprisoned him.'

'They?'

'Herod and Herodias. She wanted his head off.'

'Well, she would, wouldn't she?'

'He's Word's cousin, and he baptized Word.'

'Why did *he* need baptizing?'

'Because he wants to live a human being's life and do what a human being ought to do.'

Miriam whistled, daring Johnny to reprove her for indelicacy, and having done so to no response eyed Johnny directly but not belligerently.

'You know that's gigantic, Johnny. To come down from his level to ours! That's one very big jump!'

'I suppose so', said Johnny. ' Mind you, it wasn't too big: he didn't become a Gentile or a Samaritan or even a Judaean. He became a Galilean! After all, that's something.'

'My dear Johnny' – after all, she was two years older than him – 'it's nothing at all, compared to the gulf between God and man. Consider the intellect of God against that of man. He couldn't have gone lower. He didn't even compromise and settle for becoming a woman! Our intellects are so much superior to men's!'

Johnny went as red as a jug of wine that has been well watered, until he saw she was laughing at him. Then he chuckled. 'But he could hardly have any influence if he did: after all, Miriam, women are so unfairly belittled that God himself would probably find it too hard to convince men of his importance. You know how petty men are!'

90

'Well done, Johnny. You have buried me, horse and foot, in the Red Sea. Still, we do run the world, you know, all the more because men think we don't. Think of your mother! Think of his! I haven't met either of them, but I'll wager there are very few things they want which they don't get. And he knows it. You'll find his most important work will be with women. He has his disciples as a front organisation – how many of you are there?'

You! She really didn't miss much. 'Twelve', said Johnny, trying to look modest, and failing.

'A nice, round number. A good hatch of chickens. Mind you, it's a better one than any other I've heard of. Do you know why?'

'No.' Why did he always have to seem so dumb before this girl?

'You. That's the clue to his being such a remarkable man, so remarkable that he's God. If there's one group of people who are despised more than women, it's children. And yet it's crazy. Children are the future! Give me a child of ten years of age and the future is mine! Maybe in a few thousand years there will be one or two other people clever enough to see that. But only God can see it now. Has he taught you to read and write? I'll wager he has.'

Johnny had surrendered, Red Sea or no Red Sea. 'He has – or rather he's doing it now.'

'He'll want you to write his story.'

'Only when other people have written it.'

'The last speaker makes the best speech.' She paused, and then continued:

'I wonder why you?' She looked at Johnny, curiously rather than unkindly.

'Because I love him.'

She nodded. 'Yes, and that answer explains why you are the person he needs. Well, you can be proud of yourself. You are unique in human history.'

Johnny liked that, but he didn't want too much being made of it. 'What about Samuel?'

Miriam considered. 'It is a lovely story, and I agree it's proof that God likes children, if nobody else does. But God never became man during his friendship with Samuel, although it's the best friendship I know of. 'Do you remember how they hated kings?'

'Herod – shmerod!' agreed Johnny.

'Not that Herod is a king, this one is only a tetrarch, tetrarch – shmetrarch, in fact. Although because of his horrible father all sorts of people still think of this one as a king when they're not thinking, and most of the time, most men aren't. You'll find those others who write about your Word before you do will call Herod a king. You'll have to get things right.'

'I'll try', said Johnny, feeling very small.

'I hope I'll be around to tell you where you're wrong. Oh, yes, I can read. After all, I'm Jairus's daughter, and you may have noticed that I've got a very loving father.'

'He nearly fainted when he was told you were dead.' Johnny saw her eye beginning to light up and added hastily:

'What a good thing you weren't!'

She was no taller than he was, but it didn't stop her catching him by the top of his head and gently shaking him from side to side by his hair.

'Naughty Johnny! You should never go back to arguments you've lost. Besides' – forestalling him as he was about to insist on having actually won – 'go back to John the Baptizer and tell me more about him. I don't understand him, and yet he seems a crucial figure in the story.'

'I don't altogether understand either, but I heard a little from Andrew, and more from Word.'

'Andrew?'

'The tall fisherman who came across to greet Judas just before we left. He and Judas were disciples of John before they followed Word. Apparently John told them they should follow Word, and so they did.' Miriam was thoughtful. 'Well, that does explain Judas. He's a gift-horse who can't be looked in the mouth.'

'But I thought we've just seen Word doing that?'

Miriam was about to explode and then found it was her turn to realise she had met a joker. She made another grab for the top of his hair, clearly with a view to swinging his head by it rather harder, but Johnny managed to pull himself away from her avenging hand.

'Little boys should leave the making of jokes to their elders and betters!'

'That's what my brother James is always saying.'

'If he is, that may account for you. Big boys are usually the explanation of why little boys behave badly. Go back again to the Baptizer. I want to get this right.' They were walking through the market now, and Johnny had to move rapidly to avoid an importunate rugmaker, almost certainly Armenian.

'He was Word's cousin, but Word hadn't seen much of him in recent years until he came to the Jordan where John was baptising. Maybe John came to Word's house when Word's earth-father died.' Johnny told her what he had heard from Andrew about John.

'Anything more since then?'

'Andrew told me what actually happened when Word came to John's bit of the Jordan. John looked at him – remember they were cousins and may have seen one another quite recently – and as Word was approaching, John said "Behold him who takes away the sin of the world. This is he of whom I said 'He who will come after me is placed higher than me because he was before me.'"

'That must have confused a lot of them – I mean a lot of the men', added Miriam hastily.

'I don't think there were many women there. Andrew went on, remembering John saying about Word,

'"And I knew him not."'

'Meaning he hadn't thought of him as anything special when they met as young cousins.'

'I suppose so. You don't think of your own cousin as being God.'

'Not mine.' Miriam made a face.

'Not mine either.' Johnny reciprocated. 'John went on to say that he baptized with water so that Word would be known to all Israel. He said that whoever told him to do that said "The person on whom you will see the Spirit descending from Heaven like a dove and remaining on him is he who will baptise not with water but with the Holy Spirit.'"

'Who told him all of that?'

'Maybe *his* father before he died. After the old man was cured of being dumb which he was when he gave consent that his son be called John' (Johnny smirked, and Miriam kicked him unobtrusively), 'he seems to have known quite a bit about what was going to happen. Anyhow John said that it would be the Son of God whom he would witness like that, and when Word arrived he did, calling him the Lamb of God, so maybe John did see the Spirit coming down on Word, but Andrew didn't see it so

93

I suppose neither did Judas.'

'You wouldn't expect Judas to see much.'

'If he couldn't find something wrong about it.' Johnny was sticking Judas with his own feelings, Johnny having thought it wrong that Judas should exorcise devils in Word's name without being one of the gang. Actually Judas had disliked Johnny for his bad manners, and resented his exorcism only because Judas thought he could have completed his work without Johnny barging in.

'Do you know what John thought about Word afterwards?' Miriam stopped outside her aunt's door, keeping the conversation going without admitting she didn't want it to stop.

'I have never seen him, but Andrew kept in touch, bringing messages for Word, and he said that when people tried to make John jealous of Word by saying Word was drawing bigger crowds than he was, John said a wonderful thing. He said he was like the best man at a wedding, who rejoices because of the bridegroom's voice.'

'You don't mean Word is going to get married?' Miriam sounded shocked, she hardly knew why.

'Oh, no.' Johnny had no doubts on that score. 'He gets on with women very well, and in some ways relies on them more than on men, except for – 'Johnny searched her face for ridicule. It might have been hidden there, but Miriam didn't want to upset him now, as they were parting. She simply smiled very kindly:

'Except for you.'

Johnny was overjoyed, but shrugged unconvincingly.

'Well, there are lots of things a ten-year-old can't do, I suppose.'

'But you won't admit having found any', murmured Miriam before she could stop herself.

'No, but Word has', grinned Johnny. 'This is your aunt's house?'

'She lets my uncle live there too', said Miriam demurely. She grabbed Johnny by the shoulders and kissed him on the forehead. He hugged her. They said 'Shalom' to each other more or less simultaneously, and Johnny walked away, turning back at the corner to look at the house and happily seeing Miriam as well, waving at him before she went indoors.

Johnny trotted back to the house where he had left Word. He really liked Miriam, but he did not like being away from Word, even for an hour.

Not that he worried about Word leaving him, to get married or anything else. He began to run over what Andrew had said that last time, more than he had told Miriam. John the Baptizer had answered his tempters:

> You heard me say I was not the Christ, but was sent before him. It is the bridegroom who wins the bride, but the bridegroom's friend standing and hearing him make his vows rejoices at the groom's voice: and this my joy is fulfilled.
>
> He must become greater, I must become smaller. He who comes from above is above all: he who comes from the earth is earthly, and speaks of the earth.
>
> He who comes from heaven is above all, and no man receives all he has to testify. He who accepts his witness as far as he can understand it, has declared once for all that God cannot lie, since the words spoken by him whom God has sent are God's own words.

Johnny's memory was excellent and under Word's teaching was getting better as he understood more and more about what he had learned by heart, but he did not fully understand this, and it seemed to be saying that nobody would fully understand it. He was happy in knowing that it was Word who spoke God's own words. Johnny knew the story of the Tower of Babel, saying that one language became many to prevent men thinking they were gods: now words would unite in Word, who was God. It increased his wish to improve his reading and writing and speaking in Hebrew and Greek as well as Aramaic: even Latin, maybe, in spite of the Roman soldiers. Know the many languages so that they may become the one. Of course it couldn't be done without Word to teach you.

How had Andrew's memory of John the Baptizer's words finished?

> The gift that God makes of his Spirit has no limits. The Father loves his Son and has given everything into his hands.
> He who believes in that Son has everlasting life.

Johnny skipped back to Peter's house with additional zest. Funny how these prophets kept talking about believing in Word, when the most important thing of all was to love him. Johnny could no more disbelieve in Word than in his own existence, but loving made you a giant.

Loving also meant that Johnny had to slip in quietly. He knew he could rely on Word to have calmed Judas down or shut him up, even if Word would have an eye to roll at Johnny for having upset Judas in the first place. But it wasn't a moment for showing off or for arguing back. And it became clear as Johnny slid down at Word's feet, slipping his hand into Word's left, squeezing it surreptitiously and then trying to make himself smaller, that the twelve of them were gravely concerned. It seemed that Judas had been in touch with his old Master, John the Baptizer, now lodged by Herod in the prison of Machaerus near the Dead Sea, far to the south, but this seemed to have been elicited slowly because by the time Johnny got back, Philip, as usual the questioner, was asking:

'How did you get in?'

'I didn't get in', said Judas, a bit evasively (or so thought the critical Johnny), 'but I met two of my old mates who did.'

'Did I know them?' asked Andrew.

'No', said Judas, rather quickly, Johnny felt.

'How did *they* get in?' inquired Nat, who sometimes took Philip's questions to their next stage.

'Well, they had influence, greased palms, you know, and that sort of thing', hinted Judas. 'You can usually count on a lot of corruption in these courts.'

'I dare say you can', murmured James, with what Johnny was pleased to notice had some stress on 'you'. Matthew was more audible:

'How did they get the money to grease the palms? How much did they need?'

'Well, they didn't invite me to audit their accounts', said Judas acidly. 'What was important was what they reported John as saying!'

'Which you swallowed', said Thomas, disparagingly.

'I wasn't going to put them to the torture, was I?' snapped Judas. 'I had to accept what they were saying, didn't I?'

'Who knows how far they had compromised with Herod's oppressive regime?' demanded Shimon, the ex-Zealot, not so very 'ex' at this point, reflected Johnny.

'What were their names, anyway?' Philip pushed the question. And at this point it became embarrassingly clear that Judas could not give the names, either because he had forgotten them, or had never properly heard them. Or because they didn't exist?, wondered Johnny.

Ultimately Peter broke into Judas's self-contradictions and half-recollections. 'I don't understand this very well.'

'I don't expect miracles', sneered Judas.

'Well, you should, around here', muttered Johnny, and Word reprovingly squeezed the back of his neck. Andrew, up to now friendlier to Judas than the rest, fired up as he always did if someone seemed to ridicule his brother.

'There's no need for that, Judas. It's a perfectly reasonable reaction. As a matter of fact I think we could all learn a lesson from Peter in honesty since he asks the questions the rest of us are too conceited to admit we can't answer.'

'I'm sorry, I'm sorry', said Judas, trying to ingratiate himself since turning attention to Peter's stupidity didn't divert attention from the thin parts of his story.

'Tell us again', said James. 'Johnny didn't hear it the first time. He was looking after Jairus's daughter.'

'Was that Jairus's daughter?' asked Philip with interest. 'She seemed a very jolly soul. Your resurrection of her was a perfect cure, Master.'

Word smiled. 'Thanks, Philip. She did most of the cure herself, with faith, hope and love. As I said, she is the greatest of you.'

'She is indeed', murmured Johnny, audibly only to Word.

Judas was uninterested in Jairus's daughter which homologated her views on him, reflected Johnny, enjoying himself rolling the big word around in his mind. Judas started up again:

'Well, to make a long story short' (and Thomas, for one, looked as though Judas had finally admitted it was a story) 'the report I received at Machaerus was that John the Baptizer wanted to know if the Master, that is to say *our* Master' (and Johnny was not the only one to wince at his intrusion) 'is he that is to come or should we look for another?' Remembering what Andrew had told him John had said, Johnny didn't believe for a moment that this had come from John, and by the look on Andrew's face neither did he. Peter put it plain:

'But why should he? Wasn't he the person who said the Master was the Messiah sent from God in the first place?'

'It's a prophet's privilege to change his mind', insisted Judas. 'Look at Jonah, for instance.'

Johnny looked at Jonah, and wondered if Judas thought conditions in Machaerus resembled those inside the whale. Bad and all as Herod was, there can't have been anything like all that ingestion of water and every kind of rotting fish stinking all the way up the whale's spout not to speak of the utter loneliness. John the Baptizer at least had guards who weren't starving him to death. Did Jonah recycle the whale's lunch? Johnny began, invisibly he hoped, to internalise a giggle about this and realised that Word's hand, still on the back of his neck, seemed to radiate a similar entertainment.

'What I want to know' demanded Judas 'is what I am to tell John's disciples.'

When you remember who they were, thought Johnny nastily. Word answered, sounding a little tired:

'Tell them the eyes of the blind are opened and the ears of the deaf are unstopped, the lame man leaps like a hart, and the tongue of the dumb sings, waters break out in the wilderness, and streams in the desert, and the parched ground has become a pool and the thirsty land gushes springs of water, and in the habitation of dragons where each lay are reeds and rushes.'

Johnny supposed that the last bit was metaphorical which seemed a pity, as he would like to have gone dragon-hunting with Word. But he knew perfectly well that Word's words declared the fulfilment of a prophecy by Isaiah, and he wondered that the other eleven did not see what it meant. The previous words of the prophecy are 'Be strong, and fear not: behold, your God will come with a vengeance, even God with a recompence: he will come and save you'. *When* would they realise what was so obvious to Johnny and Miriam that Word was God? Johnny looked at them: at first no real change in the faces of any, certainly not among the brightest, Andrew, Philip, Nathaniel. He caught his breath: James was not looking different, and yet there was an expression on his face which Johnny remembered from times when James knew something he was refusing to tell Johnny. But beyond James, a face almost unable to conceal reactions was gazing at Word with staring eyes and dropping jaw, and very clear worship: *Peter*! Johnny caught his breath. The one most like a child, and James the one most concerned with a child. There would be no point in asking them, they would not admit that Johnny had known first what they knew now, better wait until they came out with it. James would hold his peace, beyond a private word he may have already had with Word, Peter would let something slip before them all, sooner or later, and then they would all be in the secret. Johnny had enjoyed being the first to know, but now he felt he would be glad of the company. Miriam had made him see that. But now Word was speaking again, and as he spoke he stood up, and Johnny realized that while sharing his hidden laughter about Jonah with Johnny there was a new grief on Word. He began, Johnny supposed, by speaking to Judas and maybe Andrew also, but it quickly enveloped them all, and Johnny would hear him tell crowds more or less the same thing in the next few days:

'What did you expect to see when you went out into the wilderness? A reed shaken by the wind? A man wearing silk? For those, you must go to kings' palaces.' Jim nodded, approvingly. And not to kings' prisons, thought Johnny, forgetting Herod was only a tetrarch-shmetrarch. 'What was it, then, that you went out to see? A prophet. And something more than a prophet. This is the man of whom it was written in Malachi's prophecy "See where I am sending an angel of mine, to make the way ready for my coming!" I tell you there was no greater than John the Baptizer among all the sons of women; and yet to be least in the kingdom of heaven was to be greater than he.' He stopped, and a sob shook his shoulders, and Johnny suddenly realised Word was speaking in the past tense. Word *knew* something about his cousin, something very different from the question Judas had invented to answer his own doubts whose existence he was trying to conceal. And Word had scarcely finished before a disturbance at the door resolved itself into Peter's mother-in-law ushering in a well-dressed lady who made little effort to conceal her weeping. She walked over to Word, embraced him, and said 'Master, he is dead, the son of your mother's sister is dead, he has died bearing witness against the sin of Herod and Herodias', and big tears rolled down her black cheeks. Johnny had seen Ethiopians among the crowds listening to Word, but this was the first self-confessed follower. She was no stranger to Word, who said quietly 'Joanna is the wife of Herod's steward', and lingered and kissed her as she clung to him. He said:

'I take it he was killed on Herod's orders?' She nodded, and gulped, but said: 'Actually, it was on the orders of a child, Herodias's daughter Salome.'

Word said 'What?' and Johnny was simultaneously interested (in a child having power) and revolted (in it having his mother's name, killing someone of his own name).

Joanna was crying afresh. 'It's probably retarded, with all of that incestuous intermarriage, Salome is the child of Herodias and her half-uncle Philip, why we don't have a law against it I don't know, Moses should have condemned it, what was he doing?'

Though she is African, she knows her Jewish law, thought Johnny, and wondered how many other African Jews there were. She might have been an African princess herself, for her deep sorrow in what she had to tell could not offset her regal dignity. Johnny might have seen many more like her at Temple ceremonies if he had ever seen Jerusalem.

Word said, 'The child –?' with dawning horror on his face.

Joanna wept again. 'I'd have said she never was what you would call a bad child. Spoiled, yes, loaded with costly gifts and toys, Herod slobbering over her one minute and forgetting she existed the next, her mother the coldest shellfish any decent fisherman ever threw back in the sea except when she had to get something else out of Herod, the child wandering through the court like a sleepwalker, polite, I will say, but thanking you as if she didn't know where she was! She was enchanted that night, she was a lunatic, she was obsessed by the moon. And I'll tell you something else – I think that, ten-year-old as she was,' (suddenly Johnny shivered) 'she was beginning to realise the tetrarch's dirty eye was on her. And to do her justice she didn't like it one little bit.'

'Where is she now?' asked Word quickly.

'She's dead', said Joanna, holding out her hands with palms upward and moving them away from one another.

Even with a gesture as natural as that she seems ceremonial, regal, thought Johnny. Whatever Word had feared, and had evidently known, about his cousin, be clearly had not expected the fate of Salome, for he gasped, and said with what Johnny could see was utter misery 'Go on!'

Johnny pulled himself up and took Word's left hand: it was all he felt he could do to say how sorry he was for Word's grief at the death of his cousin, and whatever else it was that so hurt him. Joanna seemed to be a long way from the death of John the Baptizer, but Word made no other effort to hurry her or make sense of what she said before she did.

'I suppose the child was surrounded by sex all her life', sobbed Joanna, 'with her mother turning it on whoever she thought might give her more jewels or power or whatever she wanted, her uncle Philip, her uncle Herod Antipas, next stop Pontius Pilate if she thought it could give her anything more.'

'Is she sex-mad?' asked Judas, a bit greedily, it seemed to Johnny who didn't understand why he had thought it sounded greedy but it did.

'She doesn't give one miserable shekel about sex if you ask me', declared Joanna, hurling her hands far apart as if she was throwing out sex with the day's garbage. 'She has it, she uses it, all men want it, she couldn't care less about it except for what it brings her. But she'll talk about it endlessly whether her unfortunate daughter was listening to her or not: in fact she would catch the child up in her hands as if it were a favourite doll and tell it how by means of her adultery she would get whatever she wants from Herod next which I certainly will not describe to you in front of *this* child!' She nodded fiercely at Johnny.

'Nobody wants you to', said Word, which seemed hardly accurate where Judas was concerned, thought Johnny. It all sounded stupid to Johnny. He had once asked what adultery was, having been told to recite the ten commandments, and was informed by James that it was something adults did, and Johnny assumed it was as boring as accounts, except it happened to women rather than men, since women could be stoned for it and men were stoned for swindling other men over accounts, as Johnny remembered from some story.

Joanna went back to her story. 'It was an ugly, sultry night, the air heavy in the throne-room as Herodias likes to call it, the snob, the moon riding high and cold and silver, Salome sickly and complaining about everything, like the Jews and the Greeks and the Egyptians, and the Romans, whom she specially hated.'

'I see what you mean', said Shimon the ex-Zealot eagerly. 'She was a good child.'

'She was a good child', repeated Joanna, 'even if the work she did that night is cursed for all eternity. You could see how she never thought she wanted the sickness that crawls all over that court! She kept saying that it was wonderful to look at the moon, that she was sure the moon was a virgin, it was so chaste and cold. Your cousin was confined in some kind of a cistern in the forecourt of the palace in the last few days and he can never have known it but the cries of his denunciations of Herod and Herodias must have been upsetting and, I have to say, exciting for the child. She only heard these terrible denunciations. True I am the first to admit it, but frightful for a child to hear about her own mother whatever she may have thought of her. She had never seen the man whose great voice echoed through all the palace, it seemed, and certainly through the forecourt.'

'Was it Herodias who had him put in the forecourt?' asked Nat.

'You tell *me* it was Herodias! I tell *you* it was Herodias! What kind of magician are you, to know what I haven't told you?'

'Why should she want everyone to hear the things he was saying about her?' asked Peter.

'Maybe she wanted to get Herod mad enough with the prophet to have him killed', said Nat.

'Like Jezebel and Elijah', put in Johnny. Word gaxed down on him as if he were about to order him out of the room, but Johnny looked beseechingly, and Word said, half to himself, 'the girl was only ten also'. He held Johnny's hand a touch tighter.

Joanna was true to her word to respect Johnny's tender years, whatever John the Baptizer may have done, contenting herself with 'Jezebel was a virgin if you compare her with that Herodias! Say what you like about her, at least she has the good taste to be dead! Well, the child kept on saying she wanted to see the prophet, exactly like as if she had been asking for the sight of an elephant owned by Pontius Pilate.' Matthew whispered something to Thomas, presumably an enquiry as to how many elephants Pontius Pilate possessed, but Thomas shook his head, perhaps questioning if he had any. Joanna went on:

'She was appealing to the captain of the guard to let her see the prophet, and I don't need to tell you in front of that boy how persistent children can be when they want something.'

102

'You do not', said James, but with a flicker of a smile in Johnny's direction.

'The captain of the guard was a romantic, foolish young Syrian, who always made this cult of saying he was sworn in the service of his princess, so of course the child called his bluff the first chance she got and made him get the prophet out for her to look at or she would never speak to him again but if he would do what she said she would give him a nice smile, maybe, when she was carried past him in her litter. In a woman, it would have been heartless. In a child, it was just playing games. I won't say there wasn't a touch of – of being a little beyond her age in the contrivance but not the slightest idea of what anyone might make of it except that she wanted to see Pontius Pilate's elephant! And the young fool let the child persuade him, and out of the cistern came the prophet, and she was all over him as if he had been an expensive new doll. Saying, look at his eyes, they were like black stains left by torches on Tyrian tapestries, and like black caverns where dragons lived, and like black lakes troubled by fantastic moons. I'll say this for the child, she deserved high marks in poetry. Then she became excited because he was thin, and he certainly was, God knows how much that bitch Herodias was trying to have him starved to death. The child saw him as a silver image, chaste like the moon, like a moonbeam, his flesh like ivory – not that she had one iota of knowledge of what she was talking about.'

'What was she talking about?' asked Peter. Joanna glared at him, quite wrongly thinking he was making a questionable joke, and went on:

'Then she wanted him to talk as if she might want her doll to talk, and he started talking about you, and how you were the person she should seek out.'

'Well, she was right there', said Johnny, though he wondered what Miriam would have made of her.

'Then she wanted to know if you were as beautiful as he was, and he was shocked at a girl of her age talking like that in a sensuous voice, and of course never having been in a court before, he didn't realise that everybody made any ordinary conversation sound like one that shouldn't be repeated in front of children, even if the people having the conversation *were* children! She told him that she loved his body, it was white like the unmowed lilies of the field, and the unmelted snows of the mountain, and the garden roses of the Arabian Queen who was Herod's mother-in-law until he deserted that wife for Heradias. And Salome wanted to touch him. And I tell you it meant nothing more than if she wanted to touch the elephant, I'm an old woman –'

'You're not', said Word, firmly.

She smiled through her tears. 'I will say for your mother, Master, she brought you up well. But I have seen women making advances on every level of impropriety and all that poor child simply saw was a new toy or pet animal and that was all she meant. But to him she was the daughter of a woman whom he told her had filled the earth with the wine of her iniquities and the cry of her sins came up to the ears of God, which was all very well, but that didn't mean Herodias had wasted much time in child-rearing.'

'I don't think he had ever known many little girls', said Word sadly.

'Well, this was no time to start, not where he was, not where she was. His trouble was, he was not only too innocent, he thought Herod was more innocent than Herod is. Herod wasn't just making it with his brother's wife, with his own half-niece, giving him adultery and incest for the price of one. He was going to be the Alexander of the family bed, with more worlds to conquer. That was why Salome suddenly became very powerful, without having the faintest notion of what power was or what she really wanted to do with it. So your cousin thought he was denouncing just the usual family scandal, with Herod's trimmings: If that had been all it was, he might still be alive. Your cousin did suss out one thing: he said he could hear the beat of the wings of the angel of death in the palace, and if we didn't know before, that he was a true prophet we know it now.'

She paused for breath. Johnny drew closer to Word. It seemed colder in the room, somehow.

Joanna hummed for a moment, almost a straight line of music, it seemed to Johnny, and then she went on:

'It became exactly like a child's game. You know, I love my love with an 'H' because he is happy. I hate him with an 'H' because he is hideous? Or maybe riddling to find out what someone is thinking of. She would say she loved his body, then he telling her to be quiet. She saying his body was hideous, she liked his hair, it was like cedars of Lebanon giving shade to lions and robbers, and blacker than moonless nights, then he telling her again to be quiet. She saying his hair was horrible, she loved his mouth, it was like a scarlet band on a river of ivory, or a pomegranate cut with a knife of ivory, or come to think of it it was redder than that, it was redder than winepressers' feet, it was redder than doves' feet, it was redder than a lion-slayer's feet, it was like priceless coral brought from the sea to kings, or the vermilion from the mines of Moab, or like the vermilion-tipped bow of the Persian monarchs, or redder than any of them, and she wanted to kiss it. Like I say, it was a child's game, but he never saw that, and when she claimed her kiss he let out a screech that she might have likened to an eagle seeing an intruder in its nest, if she was stuck on making likes upon likes. And she insisted she was going to kiss him, and the two of them were making so much racket that the captain of the guard, expecting Herod and Herodias would be in on top of them every second, demanding to know who let him out of his prison, maybe putting the captain to the torture for doing it, drew his dagger and killed himself before the eyes of each and every one of us standing there in the forecourt, except the child didn't see it, she kept gazing at your cousin and repeating she wanted to kiss his mouth. Your cousin was horrified and told her she was polluted and only you could save her, and he suddenly seemed very sorry for her, and said she would find you on the sea of Galilee in a boat with your disciples, and she should kneel down on the sea-shore and call your name, and that you would come to her because you come to anyone who calls for your help...'

She stopped. Great sobs were shaking Word. Johnny put his arms around him, and Word picked him up in his arms, and Johnny stroked the tears from his face. At last Word told her told her to go on.

'Then he said she should ask you to forgive her sins, and she hadn't the faintest idea of what he was talking about and said she would kiss his mouth and he cursed her and said she was cursed and went back into the cistern and she kept saying she would kiss his mouth as if it was some forfeit in a game he hadn't paid when he should have. And I remember some soldier saying the body should be removed because the Tetrarch did not like looking at bodies unless he had slain them himself, but that they would be all right because the Tetrarch would not come into the forecourt since he did not want to hear what your cousin was saying about him. And wouldn't you know it, the minute he said it, in came Herod and Herodias and every crawling sycophant in the court, it's the biggest nationality in the place by far and Herod is its king even if he isn't the king of anything else including his own wife. And he wanted Salome, where was she, he had told her to return to the banquet, why did nobody obey his orders, what was he, was he the tetrarch or a nobody? And Herodias told him to stop looking at her daughter which might sound like decent feeling except that in that family they are always wondering will someone else put in for their job and see they get the chop, no matter who is related to who how!' She glared at Johnny, daring him to understand her, but Johnny was honestly bewildered and much more concerned at Word's grief. 'Then *they* started arguing about what the moon was like, except Herod's notion of the moon was tasteless in the extreme, no chastity there, and Herodias said the moon was like the moon, whatever you can say against Herodias she has a head on her shoulders, and she certainly intends to keep it there no matter who doesn't, and then Herod slipped in the blood.'

'And hurt himself?' asked Johnny hopefully.

'Unfortunately not. But being a great tetrarch he wanted to know who was dead and why, he was much too delicate to look at the face, and when he was told the captain had killed himself he got very annoyed because he hadn't told the captain to kill himself, and the Roman envoy who had come in with him I will say he was no sycophant, he owned the place and let you know it – he told Herod that Tiberius Caesar had written a satire against people who kill themselves and everyone was reciting it everywhere.'

'Or else –!' said Shimon the ex-Zealot, somewhat unnecessarily drawing his forefinger across his throat.

'And at once Herod started gibbering about how wonderful Tiberius Caesar was and there was nothing he couldn't do, and clearly expecting the envoy to take a note of this, but the envoy simply sat and sneered whether at suicides or Caesar or Herod I for one neither know nor care. Then Herod wanted the child to drink wine from his glass, once he had caught sight of her, she had been keeping out of his sight as best she could, and she told him, perfectly politely, that she wasn't thirsty, and Herod complained about her lack of discipline, and that he wanted to see her little red lips in the wine, and then he wanted to see her little white teeth on a fruit which he would subsequently eat and she said she wasn't hungry and he got mad again.'

'Is he mad?' asked Johnny.

'Yes', said Word, 'incurably'.

'Then Herod and Herodias argued as to whether she had brought her daughter up properly and she told him he was the son of a camel-driver and a robber and he told Salome he would give her her mother's throne and the child very properly said she wasn't tired. And then your cousin spoke from the cistern, nothing rude, simply saying the day he foretold was at hand, I realise now he meant he was expecting to be killed. But it wasn't all he meant. He said the day of the Lord had come and he heard on the mountains the feet of him who would be Saviour of the world.'

Word had sat down, still holding Johnny, but now he jumped to his feet, leaving Johnny down as he rose and shouting 'John said that!'

'John said that.'

Word threw a look at Judas, more resigned than angry, and sat down, saying quietly, 'Go on.'

And as Joanna resumed, Johnny thought he heard Word mutter 'so it wasn't only his own death he prophesied' but he forgot it in the excitement of the story and it only came back to him much, much later. Joanna went on:

'Herod wanted to know who was the Saviour of the world, and the Roman envoy, I remember his name was Caius Marcius Tigellinus explained it was one of Tiberius Caesar's titles, the cheek of him' (Johnny wondered whether it was Caesar's cheek or Tigellinus's) 'and Herod went mad wondering if Caesar was coming to Judaea and Tigellinus said he didn't think so and Herod thought Caesar's feet weren't up to the trip as he had gout making his feet look like elephant's feet' (which Johnny decided Herod must have seen when he visited Pontius Pilate) 'and then some people in the crowd said you were the Saviour which they said meant you were the Messiah and that you worked miracles and Herodias said she didn't believe in miracles, she had seen too many, and I dare say her maids who prepare her body and face and hair each day would agree with her, and other people said you had changed water to wine, and cleansed lepers, and opened the eyes of the blind, and raised the daughter of Jairus from the dead and Herod said he forbids you to raise anyone from the dead.'

Word recovered his tranquillity and said, raising his eyes to Heaven, 'I'm terrified', and there was a general laugh, in which Judas, having looked this way and that, joined. Johnny's laugh was the loudest but that was largely from relief that Word could still make jokes. It would be horrible if Word didn't make any more jokes.

Joanna nodded at Word approvingly. 'Now I've told you, and you can't say I haven't. As the candid truth I may tell you I'm an envoy from Herod myself because he said people were to find you and give you his instructions so while I simply came here to find you telling nobody but my husband, I can go back and truthfully say I had fulfilled the demands of the mighty tetrarch.'

Word said thoughtfully: 'I don't think you'd better. He may decide anyone who knows me is a security risk and kill you. And I'm very fond of you, Joanna, so I don't want that to happen, do you mind staying alive, to please me?'

Joanna saw the need to keep it light: 'To please you, Master.'

Johnny realised they were talking like that to stop him being frightened, but he felt rather pleased at the thought that he, Johnny, must also be a security risk since, after all, he knew Word. He glanced at the others: he saw a few shoulders being squared, notably Peter's big ones, and Shimon looking belligerent, and Judas smiling a little nervously as though someone had make a joke he knew he must laugh at but couldn't quite see.

Joanna continued: 'Then your cousin began to shout again, calling Herodias a wanton and a harlot and a daughter of Babylon with golden eyes and gilded eyelids which showed that he hadn't exactly kept his own eyes shut, and he said many men should come and stone her, captains should pierce her with swords and crush her with shields, and Herodias demanded action of Herod against him and Herod insisted they must all drink a toast to Caesar.'

'Meaning that nobody else could control Herodias?' inquired Thady.

'One thing I will say for Tiberius Caesar' said Joanna 'you can rely on his name to change any conversation. But now your cousin began to speak again, and it looked as if he was still talking about the day of his death, which was the same day on which he spoke. He said that in that day the son would become black like the sackcloth of hair, and the moon would become like blood, and the stars of heaven would fall upon the earth as figs fall from the fig-tree, and the kings of the earth would be afraid. But he must have been wrong there, because that didn't happen when he was killed.'

'Maybe it wasn't his own death he was speaking about', said Word very quietly. Johnny thought it an odd remark: whoever John had meant, it clearly hadn't been Word, since Word being God could not die. Still, Johnny shivered a bit and climbed on Word's knee sitting with an arm over his shoulder. Word gave him a wonderful smile, and drew an arm around Johnny's waist.

'Then Herod turned on Salome and asked her to dance.'

'That was changing the conversation', remarked Nat.

'Her mother objected, and the girl said she didn't want to dance, and your cousin shouted that someone, he didn't say who, would be seated on a throne and would wear scarlet and purple and would bear a cup of gold full of his blasphemies and that worms would eat him, and Herodias said the prophet was speaking of Herod and Herod said he meant the King of Cappadocia and maybe he was right to denounce their marriage. And then Herod was off again, wanting Salome to dance.'

'What a night!' sympathised Peter.

'What a family!' said Andrew savagely, and looking over at him Johnny could see he had been weeping silently for the death of his former Master. And Judas, for all of his little intrigues and nervous deceptions, looked very close to tears himself. Johnny felt a flicker of good feeling towards him: he might be a liar, but he wasn't a heartless one. Shimon had been heard to say that Roman oppression made liars out of them all.

'Herod really went ape this time, promising the girl half his kingdom – did he mean here? or Peraea where he was? – if she would only dance, and she got him to swear he would give whatever she wanted to her, whatever it might be. And she said she would. I don't know what Tigellinus made of it, and I could hardly see him letting Herod hand over half the tetrarchy he held from the Romans to a girl of ten, but if she had asked for it, Herod probably intended to give it to her and kill her afterwards if he had to, without too much fuss. And he was gazing at her the whole time as if she was a rare and succulent dish cooked for him on a recipe specially devised by Tiberius Caesar, making it at once his duty and his pleasure to consume.'

'The old beast!' said Judas suddenly, his face wrinkling up with disgust. The others seemed to agree with him, Johnny noticed. Would Salome make a better ruler than Herod? He was wondering himself.

'She kicked off her sandals – no, she waited until slaves removed them, because she knew enough to play the game with ceremony. It still was a game for her. John the Baptizer owed her a forfeit, Herod would owe her a forfeit, Herod would make John pay his forfeit. I don't think she was thinking of any forfeit Herod might be wanting her to pay, apart from the dancing. And she danced divinely, and in one way it was no more than a little girl doing her party piece showing she had been conscientious in learning all the steps. And in another way it was absolutely indecent, although to my dying day I will say I don't think she had any such intention. Instinctively she knew what to do, and had seen enough people doing it. Most of all, I suppose it was like a puppet show, but instead of the crudity of a doll it had the delicacy of the most perfect miniature. She really was quite small, she hadn't grown quite as fast as most girls of her age, and she showed no signs of maturity. But she entered into the dance so well that she seemed to have certainty with all the beguiling, seductive, enchantment that any adult would use if they could master the craft as well as she had, and there were few of her ability. There was nothing deceitful about her. She said she would dance, and she did dance. She chose to do the dance of the seven veils, and the way she slipped out of each one was enrapturing all the more because it was purity and innocence themselves. There is something really horrible in the conscription of innocence in the cause of corruption. And the climax of the thing was the child's anarchistic delight in flinging the veils here and there, one of them hitting Tigellinus across the eyes and falling into his wine-goblet, and the leer he gave would have soured the milk of the largest flock of goats in the Roman Empire. If ever I saw a child perfectly in control of her task and hopelessly unaware of what it entailed, that was her. It was sheer beauty sublime and I can't say how glad I was when she finished. And within thirty seconds of her finishing I wished to God she had gone on forever. She asked him for the head of John the Baptist, exactly as if she had got all the rest of him for her collection and only needed the head to round it out. Master, I am sorry, but that is the only way I can describe it. She even said she wanted it on a charger, like a child wanting the wrapping on a toy to enhance its attraction, however perfect a present it might be in its own right. I think she must have gone completely possessed by a demon, she was not human, driven out of her mind by everything from the woman in the moon to the eyes of Herod!'

'And he gave it to her.' Word did not ask, merely spoke it in a dull, dead voice.

'And he gave it to her. Oh, he wriggled, and twisted, and bribed, and bullied, and promised her anything else including the mantle of the high priest and the veil of the sanctuary!'

Everyone exclaimed in horror. Word said bitterly that the child hardly required another veil. Joanna nodded: 'He could have saved himself the blasphemy. She would have nothing but the head of John the Baptizer. She had said she would kiss his red lips which was exactly what she did when the head was delivered. And then Herod killed her, or rather told the soldiers to kill her. They crushed her under their shields. She was still crying that she had kissed his lips. I don't think it took her long to die, the flesh was hardly twitching when the shields were withdrawn.'

'Probably as long as it took John to die', said Word sadly. 'And Herodias?' Andrew's voice was hard.

'Never moved a muscle. He walked out as soon as it was clear Salome was dead. She waited until he was gone, then offered her arm to Tigellinus and walked off in the same direction as Herod. I've seen none of them since, and I hope I can get my husband away and clear without my ever having to lay eyes on any one of them ever again.'

'What did Tigellinus think?' asked Judas.

'Probably found it no different to the family life of the Caesars', suggested Nat. 'When it comes to that kind of thing, there's no place like Rome.'

'Damn right', snarled Shimon.

Johnny said nothing until he was alone with Word. Then Word threw his arms around Johnny, sat on a couch, and sobbed aloud. Johnny still said nothing, only rocked Word to and fro, as the tears fell. When at last Word was quiet, Johnny said, 'Word, would it have been possible to exorcise a devil from Salome?'

Word looked up, with eyes still red. 'If you could have kept her away from that Gehenna, certainly.'

'Do you think I would have liked her, the way I like Miriam?'

'I don't think so. You see, Johnny, she had never learned to think of anyone except herself. Or rather to think *for* them. She knew how to exploit them.' Word smiled faintly. 'Children do, even you. Sometimes, especially you. But your love goes out, Johnny, to me and to so many others. She had little chance to think of anyone else.'

'It seemed so strange, as if she had grown up far too quickly in some ways, and in others as if she hadn't even caught up with her own age.'

Word seemed to look beyond Johnny. 'God in his mercy send her grace. It's all we can pray for.'

'But you're God!'

'I'm not God on duty as judge at the moment. I am *very* sorry for her. Poor child, she never really lived. Be very thankful you were a fisherboy, Johnny, not a prince.'

'Not as thankful as I am to be your disciple', said Johnny, and Word rumpled his hair.

'Let us walk on the shore of the sea, Johnny, and think of the good that was done by my cousin and your namesake.'

The waters were tranquil, and the sky was an innocent blue. Pretty soon they found a level stretch where they could run, keeping up with one another. They tasted salt on their lips and in their ears sounded the gentle pressure of the waves. A few swallows wheeled and chattered among themselves.

EIGHT

PETER

And the life was the light of men

Mary was still staying with Johnny's parents, so that James had taken Joanna back there, wisely leaving Word with Johnny. After their race along the sea-shore (and Johnny noticed that nobody except James seemed to see their races), the two made their way homeward. Mary had heard the full story from Joanna by then. She was very much at one with Johnny's mother, and by now they were calling one another 'Sally' and 'Mary' as if they had been intimates as children, and Word remarked that they seemed to think he and Johnny were not only brothers but twins, with James as a suitable elder. Mary had wept quite a lot herself, remembering John the Baptizer much more vividly from occasional visits in his boyhood than Word seemed to. 'We were all he had left', she said.

'So you are next of kin', reflected Zebedee tapping his right forefinger on the table edge, a gesture Johnny unconsciously imitated throughout his own life. Zebedee's remark wasn't picked up beyond nods from Word and Mary, but Johnny had reason to remember it later. Obviously nobody was going to Herod to ask for John's remaining possessions, still less for his body and head. It turned out that some of his remaining disciples had actually managed to remove the head in the confusion after Salome's being killed, and three of them took it away. Johnny met one of them, long afterwards, and the phrase that stuck in his mind was 'We had to take it in turns to carry it, for it was very heavy'. They buried it beside the Jordan, at the nearest point where John used to preach and baptise.

Johnny's mother insisted on Joanna lying down after they had eaten, and Mary insisted Word must lie down too, Johnny fortunately having tired him in their running. When Johnny was left alone with Mary, she began remembering the young John, running her hand through Johnny's hair as she talked. Johnny had feared to upset her in talking of Nazareth, but Word's grief and then hers made him see that this was worse than their exile from Nazareth, so he drew her out as best he could. Naturally Johnny wanted to know if John had been like him, and then was embarrassed at his own egotism, as he would not have been before he met Word. But it was a natural route for Mary, who reflected silently and then said:

'I don't think so. My son and you are like each other' (Johnny lifted his head in amazement but despite her combing his hair with her fingers Mary didn't seem to notice and her next words punctured his momentary pride), 'since both of you became young apprentices at your father's business, and both of you know a great deal of scripture by heart but not from reading. John was a great reader, and studied his father's collection of scrolls. You would have thought my boy would be the one to preach in the wilderness, being used to the active life, but in fact he preaches to crowds by lakeside and in villages and towns, though he never really likes the towns or feels welcome there. John had much whiter skin because of his scholarly work, but you've heard us say that already.'

'Word didn't know him when they were small children.' Johnny was encouraging her to repeat what she had told him before, knowing that repetition of old stories helps to ease the pain of a death.

'No, we were in Egypt, and we did not dare return until the trouble was cleared up. It was after my son was born, and Daddy-Joe was warned that the king in Jerusalem intended to kill the child whom he had learned had been born and who was to be king of the Jews, since if a newborn child would become king the old king would be unlikely to live much longer than the child's coronation at whatever age. You know my son's kingdom is not of this world, Johnny, but kings seldom think of anything but this world.'

'Which king was that?' asked Johnny. 'King Herod the Great?'

'Do you know, Johnny, I don't know. I usually imagine it must have been Herod the Great, although few enough of the people I knew thought that he was anything great apart from being a great nuisance and from time to time a great scourge. But it could have happened after Herod was dead, with one of the other Herods – whatever else they were called, they all had to be called Herod. It could be that after the great Herod was dead, and before the Romans who really ruled the country decided Jerusalem and Judaea should have a Roman governor, one Herod got control for a time and was all the more ready to murder anyone who seemed a rival. Anyhow, this was what happened, Daddy-Joe took us to safety in Egypt there we lived for several years. My son began life as an African. But back in Judaea all little boys under two years of age were put to death on the orders of that horrible king or would-be king or whatever he was. Whoever it was he made the name of Herod mean cruelty, and it looks as if that can apply to any of the Herods.'

'Why didn't they kill your nephew John, since he was only a few months older than Word?'

'That's one reason why I think it may not have been the great Herod. For one thing, *he* was very efficient, and Daddy-Joe might have had much more trouble getting ourselves, and the donkey, to Egypt if he had been directing the soldiers. And Herod was the King of all the holy patrimony of Jacob, including Peraea and Galilee and Nazareth and Samaria, and Ituraea and Abilena and I don't know what, and his writ, which means his very brutal soldiers, ran across the lot. In the confusion after his death his son Herod Aristobulus might have seized power – no, thinking about it, he might not, because his father the great Herod had killed him already. Maybe it was Herod Archelaus, whom the Romans made ethnarch of Samaria at the time they fixed up the Roman protectorate in Jerusalem. He would have controlled Jerusalem at that point and maybe Samaria as well since he was able to hang on to that later, so maybe it was him. I've heard it said he killed at least 3000 Jews, when he took over, many of them probably children. But when people talk of that time, and they don't talk about it much, they always say it was Herod the Great was the great child-killer. Maybe he didn't kill any children apart from his own, which was bad enough. Anyhow, our cousin John was quite safe, and Zachary and Elizabeth never said anything about him or any other children living near them being in danger. They lived in Ituraea which was far enough away. I suppose John was about six when we came back and he first met his little

Egyptian cousin.'

'Wasn't there danger in Egypt from the Pharaoh?'

'That was thousands of years ago, Johnny, or maybe not thousands, but at least hundreds, well over a thousand years. The Romans ruled in Egypt when we lived there just as they do everywhere else. The last Egyptian ruler of Egypt – thinking about it, I remember them saying she was Greek – was Cleopatra who could have put anyone to death, she had killed quite a few of her own relations, but I doubt if I was born when she died, and the Romans took over.'

'But did Word really seem Egyptian when he returned? Surely he was a good Jew, as he is now.'

'You have many Jews in many countries, and provided they observe the law of God they are good Jews. Actually, my son sounded more like a Greek than anything else. There were many Greeks in Alexandria, which was founded as a Greek city.'

'Why Alexandria? Isn't that far away?'

'It is from here, but less from Bethlehem. We had to take ship from the coast after hiding in a caravan which was going from near Bethlehem, and the boat we got was going to Alexandria, so there we stayed until they told us things were quiet. Mind you, on the way back I remember Daddy-Joe saying we must go nowhere near Samaria.'

'Certainly not', said Johnny, with all the pious parochialism of a good Galilean Jew. Mary laughed.

'I don't think Daddy-Joe was thinking along the same lines as you. I was surprised at the time because no man was less bigoted. But that seems to show the murder of those little innocents was probably ordered by Herod Archelaus. In fact I think I remember news of his death a couple of years after we settled in Nazareth. And I recall Daddy-Joe saying we could go to Jerusalem now, that it was too dangerous earlier, which would have meant that although Herod Archelaus no longer controlled it, he could have had plenty of influence there while he was alive. Not so much after he was dead. There's precious little ancestor-worship among the Herods.'

'Why did Herod kill Salome?'

'Show me a Herod and you show me a horror. They don't need much excuse for killing anyone, especially family. When she started kissing the lips of the head of that poor boy I suppose Herod thought she mightn't be long before she was giving orders for his death. And he may have been right. When she grew up a little more she might have been very dangerous, especially with a mother like that.'

'But women don't rule!'

'Try telling Cleopatra that and I doubt if you would have seen the next inundation from the Nile.'

'Well, women don't rule us Jews.'

'Have you forgotten Deborah who judged Israel and under whose orders Barak defeated Sisera? Her song after the victory is one of the oldest we sing.' Mary looked very much like Word teaching.

Johnny hung his head. 'I remember now.'

'Praise ye the Lord for the avenging of Israel', sang Mary, 'when the people willingly offered themselves.'

Johnny responded: 'Hear, O ye kings: give ear, O ye princes: I, even I, will sing unto the Lord: I will sing praise to the Lord God of Israel.'

'Lord', sang on Mary 'when thou wentest out of Seir, when thou marchest out of the field of Edom, the earth trembled, and the heavens dropped, the clouds also dropped water.'

'The mountains melted from before the Lord' sang back Johnny, 'even that Sinai from before the Lord God of Israel.'

'Women have not only ruled the Jews, Johnny, they also made songs about it.'

'You're forgetting to sing Jael killing Sisera with a tent-peg.'

'No, I am not forgetting to sing Jael killing Sisera with a tent-peg. I just don't want to sing it. Nor do I want to sing that bit at the end about Sisera's unfortunate mother waiting vainly for his return.'

'But she wanted her share of the spoil her son was bringing her', and Johnny sang:

> The mother of Sisera looked out at a window,
> And cried through the lattice,
> Why is his chariot so long in coming
> Why tarry the wheels of his chariots?
> Her wise ladies answered her,
> Yea, she returned answer to herself,
> Have they not sped?

Have they not divided the prey?
To every man a damsel or two:

To Sisera a prey of divers colours,
A prey of divers colours of needlework,
Of divers colours of needlework on both sides,
Meet for the necks of them that take the spoil?
So let all thine enemies perish, O Lord:
But let them that love him be as the sun
When he goeth forth in his might.

Mary half-raised her hand as he began, but let it fall on her lap as the strong unbroken treble voice soared into the heavens, and at least, she reflected, Johnny was still at the age when spoil consisting of a damsel or two was no more than an allocation of presents at a party save that he would believe toy swords or boats would have made a more satisfactory spoil than damsels. Johnny ended, and almost sounded as if he had read her thoughts by saying, 'surely that meant his mother was thinking of the spoil, wanting needlework, and damsels? Sisera wouldn't want needlework and would hardly want damsels tripping him up and getting in the way of the fighting, but of course his mother would want slave girls, the more she had, the bigger the snob she was, like that Herodias.'

Mary's lips twitched at this practical if unexpected reading of the text, but she simply said 'it still doesn't get away from her being a mother facing the prospect of her son's death, and while Deborah couldn't know what Sisera's mother had really been thinking when he didn't come home, her song seems to have captured a mother's anxiety that something terrible had happened to her boy.'

'But he was our enemy!'

'He was still his mother's boy. It's a wonderful birthright to be a Jew, Johnny, but we share human feelings with Gentiles. I'm thankful Elizabeth didn't live to see the day her son was killed. The worst thing I can imagine' (and Mary looked straight in front of her) 'is the death of your child before you die yourself'.

Johnny put an arm around her. 'Well, thank God *you* don't need to worry about that. What was John the Baptizer like as a boy?'

Mary considered. 'Very studious, and talked about it a lot. Used to have great arguments with Thomas, who was always in our house in Nazareth imitating my son and wanting to know the why and the wherefore of everything. My boy – your Word – used to listen to them both, and that silent listening helped make him a good arguer, as early as twelve. But I think Thomas may have lost interest in John later. Did he seem upset by the news of his death?'

'Not very', remembered Johnny. 'Of course we were all greatly shocked by Joanna's account of what happened.'

Mary nodded. 'You may find when you grow older, Johnny, that you don't desert childhood friends but their memory is like something in a dream and the grown-ups they have become may not seem to be the same people. Certainly none of us would have thought that the boy John we knew would one day be telling the tetrarch whom he shouldn't marry, although none of us would be surprised at his courage.'

Johnny looked troubled. 'How could I forget Word when I grow up?'

Mary caught her breath. 'No, Johnny, I don't think there's the slightest chance of that. You will probably remember more than anyone else, your memory is most remarkable. Of course my vision of John was always haunted by the picture in my mind put there by Elizabeth, of his old father Zachary blessing him when naming him John, prophesying the saviour God had promised us, and telling the baby "As for you, little child, you shall be called a prophet of God, the Most High. You shall go ahead of the Lord to prepare his ways before him, to make known to his people their salvation through forgiveness of all their sins, the loving-kindness of the heart of our God, who visits us like the dawn from on high".'

And Word walked into the room as though on cue. Mary looked at him and added to Johnny, 'Zachary ended his prophecy "He will give light to those in darkness, those who dwell in the shadow of death, and guide us into the way of peace."'

Word kissed his mother and tousled Johnny's hair. 'Well, if that's my job', he said, 'I'd better get on with it.'

Johnny looked at him speculatively. 'It must be a wonderful thing to be the Son of God, Word', he said at last, 'but it seems just as wonderful to be Mary's Son.'

Mary's hand flew up to her mouth, as though she might be able to restrain Johnny's utterance by covering her own lips, but Word smiled with pleasure and said 'Quite right, Johnny, it is.' Then he reflected. 'All the same, I don't think you'd better say it in the hearing of our eleven friends when they realise who I am, or you may upset them, and I think one or two are getting near knowing.'

'Peter, for instance', suggested Johnny.

'That's what I was thinking', nodded Word. Being God, he never seemed to mind putting himself on the same level as Johnny.

'But you have taught all of us to call God our father', reflected Johnny. 'Other Jewish prayers don't address him as father.'

'What's the use of having a father if you can't share him around?' asked Word.

'And your mother?'

'Perhaps that will happen too', smiled Word while Johnny hugged Mary before they went out. 'My mother and my brothers are those that hear the word of God and keep it, nobody more than my real mother. Nobody will ever have more of the word of God to keep than she.'

'After all, she kept Word for thirty years', said Johnny cheekily, and dodged a swipe from Word's hand in reply. Then he slipped his own hand into Word's and they made for the seashore. Word had evidently told the others they were to put out across the lake, perhaps because his grief for John made it more of an ordeal to teach and heal so many. But the crowds simply followed him along the sea-shore, and were clearly insistent on forming a congregation and an open-air hospital when they arrived. Word had led the others up a hill, as he often did, when expecting to teach, so that if he was disappointed at not getting a break he made no sign of it. Waiting for the devout pursuers, they prayed themselves, and then Thomas said:

'Funny, the things they call you?'

'What sort of things?' asked Judas, a bit suspiciously, Johnny thought.

'Elijah was the last one I heard.'

'And Elisha', nodded Matthew, 'I've counted at least seventeen mentions of Elisha.'

'Somebody thought you were Joseph the son of Jacob', smiled Thady, who liked Joseph as a failure in the land of Israel who had succeeded in Egypt.

'What made him say that?' asked Thomas.

'He said the Master had an Egyptian accent.'

Thomas whistled. 'I remember your having one, as a boy, Rabbi, but I thought you'd lost it.' Word smiled. 'Clearly a good philologist, your friend of Joseph. Anyone else?'

Andrew's lip trembled for a second. 'John the Baptizer.' Word became solemn. 'Who do you say I am?' Johnny looked across at Peter who tumbled the words out 'The Christ of God', and then James, as if he had been waiting for the command, said 'The Son of God', and Nathaniel nodded his head and said 'God', and Johnny heard and saw all of them saying it then. He was silent himself, since he had told Word what he thought a long time ago, but when all eleven had spoken, including Judas (noted Johnny), Word said 'Johnny?' and Johnny rather to his own surprise fell on one knee and said 'God', and so did the rest, but Word quickly bade them rise and embraced Peter, saying 'Blessed are you, Shimon Bar-Jonah, for flesh and blood did not make you realise this but my Father who is in heaven. You are Peter, and upon this rock I will build my church; and the gates of hell shall not prevail against it.' Peter, seeming confused, looked around his feet: to see a rock?, wondered Johnny, 'And none of you should tell anyone else that I am God, or that I am the Christ, the Messiah who was prophesied.'

To Johnny's surprise James cleared his throat and said, 'I haven't discussed it directly with them but I think Mother and Father know.'

Word smiled and said 'And my mother knows'. Peter said 'And my mother-in-law'. And Philip said 'The women are more likely to know more'.

Johnny said in a soft voice 'Miriam knows'. And Word said, with a touch of sadness in his smile 'So long as Herodias doesn't'.

As they were moving away from one another to take up positions so that the sick and disabled would be made ready for Word, James (who had heard Johnny's remark about Miriam with even more surprise than Johnny had heard his about their parents) pulled his brother aside and said 'you've known for some time?' and Johnny said 'yes, very early on', reporting a scientific fact rather than jeering at his slower brother, and in the same level tone he asked 'and you?' and James, hiding nothing said 'I took much longer, I realised only very recently. It was Peter who made me see, without meaning to: I realised that he had come to that conclusion, and decided he was right. He didn't say anything until now. And then I thought about the way Father and Mother have been looking at the Master recently, very loving, but with a reverence they wouldn't waste on a normal Rabbi. Well, Johnny lad, you have the laugh of me there. This situation really gives one an extraordinary feeling, doesn't it?'

Johnny was touched. James had never made him so much of an equal before. He smiled back, a bit shyly, and said 'But it's such a nice one.'

James laughed, again unusually, and agreed, and then they got down to work. Johnny found himself directing a group of lepers, from whom he would have fled before he knew Word, but whom he now made as comfortable as he could, showing no fear of their foul and stinking wounds. The drill was that he or anyone else of the disciples who attended lepers would report at the end of the teaching and healing to Word, who would touch whatever part of them had touched or been nearest to a leper. Then, addressing the crowd, Word talked of John the Baptizer, quietly, without inflaming the people even if Shimon the ex-Zealot made occasional gestures which might have been inflammatory if anyone had been looking. 'I can of mine own self do nothing', Word startled Johnny by saying, 'as I hear, I judge; and my judgment is just: because I seek not mine own will, but the will of the Father who sent me. If I bear witness of myself, my witness is not true.' Johnny thought how he himself and everyone he knew seemed to talk about themselves more than about anyone else, and yet for all that they talked about themselves, none of them paid serious attention to other people's opinion of *them*selves. Word's voice became gentle, yet it was clear as a bell in the ears of the huge crowd that had assembled, thronging the perimeter of the mound and stretching all the way to the lake shore. 'There was another who bore witness of me, and I know that the witness which he witnessed of me is true.' Word gave a wry little laugh on his repetition. 'You sent unto John, and he bore witness to the truth. He was a burning and a shining light: and you were willing for a season to rejoice in the light.' Did they know John was dead? Word was firmly in the past tense. Word paused: there was a lot of whispering, and then Word raised his hand, and the crowd became silent, and stood mute for minutes, mourning. 'But I have greater witness than that of John', resumed Word 'for the works which the Father has given me to finish, the same works that I do, bear witness of me.' And when he had ended, and Johnny saw him working his way through the crowds of invalids, one after another discovering the sheer beauty of sight, or the glory of sound, or the pride of upright stance, or the majesty of firm legs and gait, or the purity of skin cleansed of leprosy, or the silver of speech, or the grandeur of sanity, there indeed was his witness, the boy told himself. And yet Word had also spoken as if the witness of his works was ignored. He had ended with a wry joke. 'Had you believed Moses, you would have believed me, for he wrote of me, but if you do not believe what he wrote, how can you believe my words?'

The people had followed Word to a place far from a town or even a village since he had meant to go there to grieve for John and to pray with his disciples, but although he seemed to reproach the crowd for its lack of belief, it believed enough to get itself including crippled and blind invalids in front of him, whether on litters or on donkeys, and whatever its other inadequacies Word seemed chiefly concerned about its lack of food. He whispered something to Johnny when he was curing lepers and Johnny was preparing them for his touch and blessing. So Johnny hurried to the sea-shore, desperate to fulfil the command or no request – he no longer knew the difference when they came from Word – but this plea? chore? wish? had been for anything with which to feed this gigantic congregation. As he went, he heard Word say to Philip, the next disciple to them, 'Whence shall we buy the food that these may eat?' and Philip, desperate, 'Two hundred pennyworth of bread is not sufficient for them, that every one may take a little', and Johnny heard no more, moving as rapidly as he could, and at his wits' end to think of Word apparently counting on him, and what could he do? He had no money and there was no place to buy nearby. He saw some boys near the edge of the crowd, apparently facing the same problem as himself, for they had thrown little fishing-lines into the water from a small promontory that jutted into the sea.

'Any luck?' asked Johnny, desperately. The biggest boy – there were three in all – made a face and held up two miserable little tiddlers, of the kind that Johnny no less than James would have thrown back into the water whatever the size of their catch on a normal fishing expedition, but this time no such luxury availed them. Johnny wondered whether to fight the boys for their fish. Word had asked him, no sign of a miracle. Were all of Word's miraculous powers exhausted with the scores of invalids he was curing at that moment? Johnny crushed down the thought, but it left in its place the conviction that Word expected Johnny to rise to the occasion, and his rise would be the size of the tiniest rejects any decent fisherman had ever held beneath contempt, even if he could get them from the three boys. Johnny looked at the fish, then at the boys, then at his own hands which he half-formed as fists then opened again. The boys looked back at him. There was a long pause, and somehow on the air came floating the tones of Word healing some sufferer with appropriate sounds though much too remote for them to comprehend the words. The boys were not much bigger than Johnny. Johnny crunched up his lips, and, suspecting predatory intent, the boys inched closer together, with tiddlers in the biggest one's hand. Once again, Word could be heard if not understood. And then, as if responding to the words he could not make out, Johnny said humbly rather than, as he had half-intended, truculently:

'That's Word, healing the sick. And he wants to feed us all. Can we ask you for your fish?'

And the boy, half-ready to jeer a refusal, or shrug a dismissal of the worthless fish, caught the pleading in Johnny's eye even more than his voice, and said:

'It's nothing, but here it is.'

And the youngest boy said:

'Our mother gave us these five little bread- rolls, but if your Word wants them – ?' he left it unfinished, and then the middle boy said:

'Here they are.'

Johnny thanked them with gratitude which he hoped disguised the misery in his voice. As he wormed his way back through the crowd, holding the ludicrous booty, he reached Andrew, and he felt so inadequate that he stammered:

'W-W-W-W-Word w-w-w-wanted m-m-m-me to g-g-get f-f-f-food for the c-c-c-c rowd and I-I-I-I c-c-c-ould only f-f-f-f-find th-th-th-th-these I-I-I-loaves and f-f-f-f-ishes' and Andrew said coldly:

'Are you trying to make fun of Judas again? and Johnny realised that Judas had reported his bad behaviour to them all when Johnny had been seeing Miriam home, and Andrew clearly resented the insult to his fellow-disciple, all the more united mourning their former Master John the

Baptizer. It hardened Johnny's heart against Judas, miserably inadequate as he felt, and in his own hunger and exhaustion he burst into tears and shoved the loaves and fishes into Andrew's face. Andrew glared at him and shouted at Word:

'There is a lad here' – jerking his thumb at Johnny as though he had never seen him before in his life – 'who has five barley loaves' – and he spat out the word 'barley' as though Johnny had selected the cheapest and least nutritious grain on purpose – 'and two' he paused – '*small* fishes: but what are *they* among so many?' Johnny would have given his life to be under the Sea of Galilee. He had shamed himself and Word before thousands of people. But Word simply said 'let them sit down in groups of fifty' and the disciples shouted instructions to the various segments of the crowd. Then he called over Andrew and took the loaves, blessed them and gave thanks to his heavenly Father for them, and handed them back, as it seemed, yet Andrew found himself held in thrall passing loaf after loaf to the tune of about fifty, and each disciple towards whom he passed them, found himself passing out fifty or so it seemed, and multiples even more extraordinary happened with the fish, still two when Andrew began to pass them, and about twenty thousand by the time they had reached the lips of the hungry. Johnny had pulled himself together by this stage, and ate his fill along with everyone else, and at the end found baskets and filled them up with the remnants, and the twelve baskets were filled, three of which Johnny brought back to the boys whom he hoped had not seen him crying. If they had, they were in much too much awe of what Word had done to bother about it, and the eldest boy said: 'Your Word is a magician', and Johnny said 'My Word is greater than any magician', although wishing greatly to say 'My Word is my God'. Then he had the sense to add. 'But he couldn't have done it without you', and they all said 'Shalom' to one another, and Johnny went back to Word.

But many of the crowd had announced that Word ought to be made King whether he wanted to be or not, and Word had disappeared. Johnny, looking around in alarm, avoided Andrew and Judas, and didn't want to appear like a small boy in front of James just as he had gained status as some kind of grown-up, and with some relief found himself falling over Peter, or Peter falling over him. And to Johnny's surprise Peter said, 'no, he isn't angry with you, but he won't be king here on earth for anyone, so he told me quickly to get you all back to the boat when we can manage to clear our way through the crowd, and he'll follow us across the lake.'

This was a much more decisive Peter than Johnny was used to, but not yet with all the answers, so Johnny asked how Word would get across the lake if they sailed without him, and Peter, looking a bit more like the old Peter, seemed surprised to think of it and said he didn't know. But Johnny, keeping close to him, for want of Word, found Peter awkwardly protective, and much more alert than usual, whispering to him less loudly than was to be expected 'Don't worry about Andrew, he's upset about his old Master, John'. So Johnny followed Peter on to the boat and took up his usual place as ship's boy to James, leaving Andrew, Judas and the rest to enjoy their voyage, with plenty to do in a contrary wind. They took turns on the watch, and there was rowing in the face of the wind, and it was about the fourth watch that Johnny, taking his turn, saw a dim figure on the water behind them. All his frustrations vanished, and he happily told himself it was Word, and wondered if he should run over the sea to join Word as he had run over the shore when first they met, and instead of thinking that he couldn't run on the surface of the waves he simply vetoed the idea on the correct ground that he was the watch and the watch must never desert his boat and his comrades. And then he wondered if he should announce that Word was walking on the water behind them and making better time than they were, and what would be the naval term for such an announcement. Should he say to James 'Word walking on water, sir' or should he remember that the others called Word 'Rabbi' so should he say 'Rabbi on water' which sounded like some sort of code and would Shimon the not so ex-Zealot think this was the signal for a roaming against the risings – suddenly Johnny realised with horror that despite his responsibilities for Peter, however comforting, and Andrew, however censorious, and James, however fraternal, and Judas, however hostile, and Word being on the water in front of his eyes, he was falling asleep on his own watch. So he let out a roar in his best Boanerges bellowing 'Man on Water' leaving it to the rest of them to see that this was literally true instead of a confusion of 'on' with the usual 'in' on such occasions, and slightly to his secret satisfaction this was answered with a screech from Judas that they were being pursued by a spirit whom he identified as the ghost of John the Baptizer (apparently reunited with his head). Judas seemed to

126

think John the Baptizer was determined to punish himself and Andrew for having ceased to be his disciples and having gone over to Word, in spite of Andrew's belief as told to Johnny weeks ago that John encouraged Andrew and Judas to become disciples of Word. Johnny's shouting and Judas's shrieking were now joined by Word's voice, calm and gentle and yet insinuating itself audibly between the shouts and shrieks, and Word said 'Be of good cheer, it is I, be not afraid', an instead of worrying if Word was angry with him Johnny had the sense to kiss his hand to Word, and Word kissed his back to Johnny, and Peter shouted

'Lord, if it be thou, –' '– it is!' roared Johnny, whether as watch or as Word's ward, which Peter evidently accepted, just continuing 'bid me to come to you on the water', and Word said 'Come'. And Peter dropped over the side of the boat, and Andrew half-moved protectively to hold him back from danger, and Johnny remembered how much he had liked Andrew before Judas had arrived, and Word was still walking forward and holding out his hand to Peter, and Peter was actually walking on the water too just like Word. Or not quite like Word because when he had walked seven paces he evidently stopped thinking that this was Word whom he loved and he was going to him, and instead began to think that he was Shimon, and he might drown and the wind was wild, and the water was wet, and he began to sink and as the water reached his shoulders flung out a hand towards Word, crying 'Lord save me', and Word's hand caught Peter's, and Word could be heard saying 'Oh you of little faith, why did you doubt?', and holding Peter by the hand drew him out of the water like taking a stopper from a bottle, and walked with him, or rather walked him, to the boat and waited while he climbed on board, and then vaulted in himself and strolled over to where Johnny was once more fully awake at his watch, and kissed him, and then Word took his sandals from the back of his neck where he had been carrying them tied by cord with one over each shoulder, and put them on his feet. And Johnny said 'Word!' And Word ran his band over Johnny's right and left hands which had been touching the lepers when last they met, and asked 'you didn't touch anyone after the lepers?' and Johnny remembered that he hadn't, and said no, not even the boys who had produced the small share of food. Word had taught him to be very careful of contagion, and staying clear of people who might be infected by invalids to whom Johnny had ministered before

127

Word cured them.

And Word said 'I want you to apologise to Andrew', as if they were talking one minute after Johnny had thrown the loaves and fishes in Andrew's face, and Johnny said miserably, 'Yes, Word', and then didn't feel miserable anymore after he had said it, and Word pushed the hair off Johnny's forehead back over his skull, and Johnny smiled happily, and said. 'Now?' and Word looked across where Andrew was calming Judas and said 'when he is alone, always the best time to apologise', and Johnny said 'And to Judas too?' and Word said 'I'm afraid an apology might make things worse there, now that I've cured his stutter, it's not easy to refer to it without seeming rude again' and Johnny said 'Sorry, Word', and Word said 'it was only one word, Johnny, that stutter at Judas, and yet you see how much damage a moment's surrender to temptation to be cruel can cause?' And Johnny said 'I see now'. And Word said 'Good'. And Johnny said 'I wasn't trying to make fun of Judas when I stammered at Andrew'. And Word said 'I know you weren't', and Johnny put his arms around Word's neck and kissed him in his turn. Johnny found Andrew and apologised before they reached the shore and after his watch was finished. Word had taken the final watch.

Andrew accepted the apology a little stiffly, Johnny thought, and made none of his own, but Johnny knew there was no point in thinking any more about that. It did cross his mind again when a few days later Word took him and James and Peter up a mountain without asking Andrew, although the disciples were enough of a unit now not to need anyone from Word's earliest followers to keep an eye on them in Word's absence. But what happened on the top of the mountain put the whole thing out of Johnny's mind. Word had simply said they were going to climb the mountain and then pray, and when they reached the summit, Word lifted his arms, and prayed, as usual addressing his heavenly Father as 'Abba', and as soon as he said it his clothes, comfortable and unpretentious as they were, suddenly shone with a whiteness Johnny had never seen anywhere in the world, neither on the foam of the sea, nor on the wings of a seagull in sunlight. Word's was the face Johnny loved most in all the world, much though he loved his parents and (more than ever since he met Word) his brother James. But now Word's face became changed while retaining the features Johnny loved so well, as though it were reasserting its own character but that character could now be seen in a reality unknown on earth. We can give no better description, because Peter and James never talked of what they had seen until long afterwards, and Johnny never talked of what he had seen at all, except to Word. Suddenly two other people appeared talking to Word, and Peter, James and Johnny knew that they were Moses and Elijah, neither of whom they had ever seen. Peter and James stood as though transfixed, but Johnny walked forward and took Word's hand, as usual, not thinking Word needed protection from Moses and Elijah, but that it was right they should see someone who loved Word standing by him. Johnny could be conceited enough, but there was no conceit in this, merely love. Merely. Johnny was not frightened, although Moses looked formidable, but Elijah winked at him, and Johnny remembered that Elijah had had a friend who was a boy, the son of the widow in Zarephath, and that Elijah had revived him when he was dead. And Johnny remembered a song his mother Salome would sing:

> Elijah the prophet,
> Elijah the Tishbite,
> Elijah the Gileadite,
> May he come Speedily
> With Messiah,
> The son of David.

Word and Moses and Elijah seemed to speak to one another in what Johnny knew from worship was Hebrew, although a strange and exalted form of Hebrew, which is a language of great dignity in itself. But while their words were not fully clear to Johnny he understood enough to know that they were talking about something which would happen in Jerusalem when Word was there, and Johnny suddenly told them that where Word would go, he would go. Word picked up Johnny and kissed him, and Moses and Elijah raised their hands in blessing, and Word put Johnny down, and made the slightest gesture for him to go back to the others. And when Johnny was back in line with Peter and James, he suddenly realised that they looked as though they were awakening from sleep, and they had not realised Johnny had left their side for a few minutes. And Peter, eagerly, said to Word 'Master, it is good for us to be here', and Word turned round with a face full of love for Peter's sweetness; and for his impulsiveness, which was now blurting out 'and let us make three tents, one for you, one for Moses, and one for Elijah'. Johnny was pleased to see that Elijah beamed with delight, appreciative and not at all derisive, and even Moses melted into a smile. And a cloud now descended, and covered Word, Moses, and Elijah, and from it Johnny heard a voice strangely like Word's, but definitely not Word's, and sounding unlike any earthly sound for all of its kinship to Word's, and he could see Peter and James heard it also, as it said in a tongue they did not know but could fully understand 'This is my beloved son: hear him'. Johnny saw Peter and James throw themselves down and cover their faces. He lifted his own face, his lips parted, and his eyes shone, looking directly at the cloud. He lifted his hands in silent prayer, knowing no words to say and needing none. It was as though the cloud was smiling at him.

So they remained for what might have been a year and might have been a moment, and then the cloud lifted, and only Word was standing there, and Johnny ran over to him and took his hand, and Peter and James lifted their faces from the ground. Johnny looked up at Word's face. It was now once again as he had always known it, but he searched Word's eyes, and in their depth he could see love, and sorrow, and laughter. Then Word said to all three of them not to speak about this until the Son of Man was risen from the dead. Johnny knew that Word seemed to be speaking about himself when he spoke of the Son of Man, but he sensibly decided that whatever this meant would be clear to him in the future, and left Peter and James to ask each other what it might mean. Word hinted strongly that ugly things were going to happen in Jerusalem, particularly to him, and while Johnny disliked the thought of this very much, he was certain that Word would be all right, being God, and therefore when Word spoke of being killed and rising after three days he could be sure this was a parable or story to be explained later. And Peter said Word ought not to talk like this, and Word said to him 'Get behind me, Satan', leaving Peter looking very foolish and ashamed, and Johnny was quick to hug Peter and squeeze his hand, so that Peter walked on still bewildered, but comforted. But when Johnny and Word were alone together, Johnny told Word that he meant what he had said to him and Moses and Elijah, and where Word went, Johnny went. And Word smiled, a funny twisted smile, and said

'Faithful unto death, Johnny?'

And Johnny said 'You know it. All the way to death, Word. And back.' He didn't quite know why he said 'And back' but it seemed vaguely relevant to things he had heard Word say which he could not understand. And Johnny added quickly 'Not that you can die', and laughed. And, after a moment's hesitation which Johnny remembered later, Word laughed too.

NINE

JUDAS

And the light shineth in darkness

Chuza arrived a few days afterwards. He was a very innocuous person himself, Johnny felt, used to ceremony and polite, but somewhat mystified by Word's ease of manner, by the informality of the obvious veneration in which everyone held Word, and by the freedom given to – or taken by – Johnny himself. James came closer to Chuza's style than anyone else, but not nearly far enough, especially now that he had become more human, from Johnny's standpoint. Johnny realised that Chuza was someone of high, wealthy and authoritative situation and it was clear that his days as Herod's steward were over, to his regret as well as relief. But for all the allowances Johnny wanted to make for him, many more than those he probably wanted to make for Johnny, his arrival was the end of what Johnny afterwards remembered as the golden days of Word's ministry. From the coming of Chuza onwards, they were thinking of journeys, or going on journeys, or trying to avoid journeys, all to prevent Word being arrested in the name of Herod before he reached Jerusalem. For it was Chuza who told them of Herod's getting the news of Word's miracles and teaching, and in his guilt and terror concluding that Word was in fact John the Baptizer risen from the dead. Herod might have another attempt at killing John the Baptizer – not that he could succeed in killing Word, thought Johnny scornfully – or he might imprison him, or badly hamper his movements. And since Herod was tetrarch (however shmetrach) of

Galilee, Word needed to avoid it and the other territories he ruled, while journeying to Jerusalem. Chuza had picked up enough news at Herod's court, either officially as steward or unofficially as gossip, to tell Word firmly that sooner or later Herod meant to deal with him. 'He is in two minds', said Chuza, as if he was conducting visitors to twin reception rooms.

'Perhaps he might settle on the more peaceful one', reflected Peter optimistically. Chuza smiled, mirthlessly, but showing white teeth in sudden expanse amid his black flesh.

'Alas, no, my hopeful young man, you will wait longer for peace Herod sends your master than for one of your own fish', and he smiled again. If Peter were as sensitive as he sometimes showed himself he might have thought that the magnificent and punctilious Chuza condescended to him, a mere fisherman, but in fact Chuza had already shown he greatly respected fishermen when in conversation with Zebedee. A good steward consulted experts in all that pertained to the feeding and entertainment of his employer. Johnny noted Chuza's deference to his father as akin to Word sometimes conversing with a man of law or scripture who used his knowledge to find truth rather than to hide it.

'Then what are these two minds?' asked Philip.

'An interesting medical condition for which I have sought to cater for some time', nodded Chuza. 'Let us imagine you have a single mind, rather like this orange, which I now bisect.' He did so with as swift and clean a cut as any executioner could ask. 'In one half', and he waved it before them with a slight flourish, 'you remain the tetrarch, as supreme in your dominions as God' – and he bowed courteously to Word – 'and Tiberius Caesar' he smiled with flickering disdain – 'will permit. You give orders, inspect accounts, dictate letters, tax subjects, digest banquets, employ or' – his smile was briefer, grimmer – 'dismiss servants and give orders for their apprehension.' He then lowered the half-orange and picked up its counterpart. 'In the other half, you live in a state of lust, fury, terror, fear, suspicions of everything including the other half of your own mind – most of all, of that, it may be.' He lowered that half-orange but kept it in his hand. 'The official half-mind is concerned about our true Master' – his bow to Word was more spiritual than formal now – 'whom he learns from Romans or lawyers or priests or spies is the next of kin of the judicially slain

John the Baptizer. The mad half-mind' – he paused as though celebrating his own announcement of the height of the evening's entertainment – 'is at its extreme want of balance, convinced that our Master's miracles and sayings proclaim him the foully murdered and newly risen John the Baptizer. So as a good administrator Herod wishes to seize our Master, and as a mad guilt-ridden voluptuary Herod wishes to seize our Master.' He replaced the second half-orange on the plate, looked at it for a moment as though waiting for it to state who it was, removed its skin with a knife and ate it. 'I would advise departure to Samaria with no further delay.'

Word looked worried, and as usual, Johnny realised, it was not about himself. 'What of you and Joanna? You risk your lives for me.'

Chuza laughed, a rich deep-throated amusement. 'We would save our lives by losing them, if we lost them in your service.'

'You would indeed', smiled Word. 'But that does not mean I want you to lose them.'

Chuza nodded. 'We will go back to Ethiopia by sea, through Alexandria.'

'Are there good travel-routes?' Matthew was suddenly interested.

Chuza raised his eyebrows. 'We are very Egyptian in Ethiopia. You must come and find out how much. We will need workers to bring the message of the Master.'

To Johnny's surprise Matthew nodded, as though his predictable many questions would wait until he had a moment alone with Chuza. It often startled Johnny to see grown-ups, however cocksure, still capable of learning. But as the conversation broke up into small groups, Chuza walked over to Andrew and Judas, and Johnny, careful to stay away from them, could still see him put his arms over the shoulders of each. Johnny realised he was probably bringing last news, and perhaps personal messages, from John the Baptizer, and that seemed certain when Judas wept, and Andrew's Adam's apple moved as though he was swallowing hard once or twice. Judas angrily ran his hand over his eyes and glared self-consciously, unfortunately resulting in a direct look at Johnny, who gravitated quickly to Word, for whom Zebedee was plotting the best route:

'Capernaum – Magdala – we could land you near Magdala if you like, or perhaps at the extreme south before the lake narrows to the Jordan? – if you make it to Magdala you could cut across country to Nazareth –'.

'Not Nazareth', said Word quickly, and Johnny put his hand in Word's left hand equally quickly. Word surreptitiously squeezed Johnny's hand, and Johnny thought he probably wanted to weep as much as Judas.

Zebedee looked up at Word's face. 'Sorry', he said, 'stupid of me.' His eyes rested on Johnny's face, and Johnny realised his father was glad to see Johnny was where he was when he rested his hand on Johnny's shoulder for a moment.

'Not your fault', said Word, unusually taciturn. 'But thanks.'

'Nain', said Zebedee.

'That makes sense', nodded Word.

'And then Samaria', affirmed Zebedee.

Johnny thought it sounded all wrong for Word to be going to Samaria, where the people were heretics worse than infidels, but he had the sense to keep his mouth shut. It was enough to know Word was glad of his silent presence. In the same way Zebedee and Salome had privately told each it was as well to let Johnny go with Word even on this present long journey. 'If he has lost Nazareth, he has found Johnny', said Zebedee, and Salome had answered that she thought Word had the better bargain, which she certainly would not have said in front of Johnny or James. Mary would stay with Salome and Zebedee: any soldiers or spies would not connect an extra woman with the dangerous agent or avatar of John the Baptizer. In fact, Salome and Zebedee called Mary 'cousin' as a simple precaution, which explains the subsequent tradition that James and Johnny were related to Word. Word called all his followers his brothers and sisters in any case.

But that long journey actually began at Capernaum, from where several prominent Jews had sent requests to Word to come heal the servant of a Roman centurion. Even Word's forehead wrinkled at this request, since he was more accustomed to be abused for civility to Romans, (a) because they were not Jews, (b) because they were Romans. But the Jewish elders told Word simply that this centurion loved the Jews, and had built them a synagogue, being a fairly rich Roman plebeian. So Word went toward the centurion's quarters, but was held up by more Jewish friends of the centurion, bearing his assurance to Word that he knew himself to be unworthy of either entering Word's presence or bringing him under his roof, but that Word would only have to speak a word, and the servant would be healed.

'He respects our laws against pollution', acknowledged Word to the centurion's envoys.

'He respects more than that', said one of them. 'He says he knows you only have to say the word because he in his profession also gives orders, and he can understand healing taking place when you direct, just as one man comes when he says, and another goes when he says, and his servant does what he says.'

Word whistled. 'I have not seen faith as great as this in all Israel.'

'Why did you say that?' asked Johnny, when Word had spoken the word of healing, and the envoys had gone back to the centurion. ' Why is our faith not greater than his? We believe in you longer and deeper than any old Roman.'

'Because, Johnny, his faith had to travel a much longer distance than yours.'

'You mean, because Rome is farther away from you than Galilee?'

'I mean, because a Roman soldier is farther away from God than a Jewish fisher-boy. So I expect more from the Jewish fisher-boy', and he chucked Johnny under the chin.

'And you'll get it', said Johnny.

'And I'll keep it', said Word.

They left Capernaum. Johnny had hoped to see Miriam again, but she had gone back to her father's house. They travelled in Zebedee's boats as far as Magdala, from where they meant to start overland for Nain. Johnny was not quite as confident as his words to Word might imply. Before Chuza and Joanna left them, Chuza caught him alone and said 'You're not frightened of meeting Herod's soldiers, little Johnny?'

Johnny, who did not relish this way of addressing him, growled 'No, of course not!'

'You're lucky', smiled Chuza. 'You're very lucky! I would be very frightened. I would be scared stiff!'

Johnny gazed at him. 'But you said to Word that if you were killed in his service you would save your life by losing it, and the same for Joanna!' Chuza laughed again. 'I meant and mean every word. But that doesn't stop my being scared stiff!' He beamed, as though he was announcing the serving of some oriental delicacy of great rarity and price. Johnny looked up at him, wondering. And then Chuza caught him up, raised him above his head, kissed him and said 'So be careful, little Johnny! You have a great man to guard! But don't be afraid of being afraid. It's thinking you can't be afraid that causes trouble in the long run!' Johnny nodded, and hugged Chuza back. In times to come he thought of his words as a kind of blessing. They were to be of great comfort, once he was ready to admit to himself that he might be afraid, and that sometimes he was.

Joanna's parting was much more emotional than Chuza's, but while Chuza's had made him feel small and then strengthened, Joanna's was maternal, adjuring Word, James and anyone else who would listen to keep that boy out of harm's way and make sure he grew up good and strong. When she was saying her goodbye to Johnny she looked at him fondly and said she hoped she would have a son like him when she was settled in Ethiopia. 'I'm getting on', she said, 'and Chuza is no younger, that much is certain, but I'd like a son like you before I die. We will see what Ethiopia can do for us.'

Johnny half-opened his mouth and closed it. But Joanna wasn't a diplomatic steward's wife for nothing.

'Good boy, you have a sensible question and you are too sensible to ask it. Why didn't we have children while we were at Herod's court? I'll tell you straight out why we didn't have children at Herod's court. Herod's court is no place to bring up decent children. Either it would be what some people might make happen to them, or what they might make happen to other people when they began to grow up, like that Salome. And that poor child was anything but the worst, may the good lord be kind to her miserable, muddled soul! Stay away from court, any courts, is my advice to you, little Johnny. I won't deny there's money there. Chuza and I won't starve even if he gets no position in Ethiopia. But it's no place for a child.'

Saying goodbye to Johnny's family had been much simpler in comparison. Mary told Word to look after Johnny, and told Johnny to look after Word. James said firmly *he* would look after them both. Mary nodded, and kissed all three of them, and surprised Johnny by saying she would see them in Jerusalem at Passover. Salome then said that so would she, equally kissing them all. Zebedee placed his hands on Johnny's head, saying in Hebrew:

May the Lord bless you and keep you.

137

May the Lord make his face to shine upon you
and be gracious unto you.
May the Lord turn his face to you
And grant you peace.

James was taller than Zebedee, so he knelt down for the same blessing. Then Word walked in front of Zebedee after James had stood up and moved away, and Word also dropped on his knees. Zebedee bowed deeply to Word, clearly surprised, but asked no question, and placed his hands on Word's head, repeating the same words. Afterwards Johnny asked Word how he, being the Lord, could be blessed with a prayer that the Lord bless him. Word smiled and swung Johnny round to face him:

'Johnny, any person who blesses in the name of the Father, or in the name of the Holy Spirit, or in my name, is doing our work, and reflecting our love back on us. Your father is taking the place of my Father in blessing me. If I share my father with you, you also share your father with me.'

'So if I bless you, Word, I am being your father?'

'Essentially, yes.'

'Bless you, Word,' Johnny was quite solemn.

'Bless you, Johnny.' Word was as solemn. Then they were outside the house, and Word gripped Johnny by the wrists, and swung him in a circular motion about half a dozen times, catching him after Johnny got his feet on the ground again and his dizziness made him fall.

When they all got started, the journey by boat to Magdala had a strangeness about it, although the lake waters were home to Johnny as much as anything on land. He had been to Magdala before (it embarrassed him that the first time he had thought its fountain-house was a synagogue), and then as now he had voyaged there in his father's high-masted boat with the same feeling that he, Johnny, was the son of Zebedee, than whom no man had a greater right to call himself ruler of the Sea of Galilee (always excepting Word), and yet this time it was as though Johnny would never again be able to call the waters his home. It was not a sad feeling, particularly, because he had Word, and Word filled up the world, and the stars above them, and the dust and plants in the land, and the waters of every sea; but it was as though Johnny had to turn away from a bed which had been his from his earliest days, and now must seek his sleep where he could find it. He didn't even look back across the water after the boat had slipped out of its protective cove and they had all waved to Mary, and Johnny's mother Salome, as well as Chuza and Joanna whom they could hardly expect to see again. But now, as Johnny stood in the bows of the boat with Word sitting beside him, he was coming to a place he knew well, and yet suddenly unfamiliar in which dark and doubtful mysteries hid themselves. Johnny was not afraid, and with Word beside him he was not likely to be afraid, but he almost felt that he was about to become another Johnny, a Johnny of dusty roads and long hard miles in place of the old Johnny of lakeside villages and long, cool boat-journeys, and even the familiarity of awkward sails and reluctant fish and gales raging.

But the first thing that hit Johnny's sight when they had come to Magdala and said goodbye to Zebedee was something he knew and hated all too well, an evil spirit, this time in a woman whom he might have thought beautiful if she bad not been twisted in face and body by the pressure coming from the foul things within her. In a mildly dotty sort of way Johnny's first thought on seeing her was that this would make much more sense if it were happening in the nearby city, Tiberias, built a few years ago by Herod Antipas in the usual belly-crawling, slavering, nauseating worship of Tiberius Caesar. That was a city fit for Romans, and demons, and Herodians, and slaves, polluting Johnny's beloved lake-shore. Word and the disciples were very careful to avoid Tiberias, it being the place where Herod's desires would have the best chance of fulfilment anywhere in Galilee. Magdala was also too big to be home, but it was a traditional part of their lake, and if Johnny was always going to prefer a lakeshore village or hamlet to a lakeshore town, a lakeshore town with beginnings deep in Jewish history would always be better than some Roman monstrosity, all the worse in the case of Tiberias because Herod had deliberately built it over ancient tombs, desecrating them and violating the reverence and the memory which should always shroud dead people deserving honour. Before Johnny had met Word, and learned that his heavenly Father intended such dead people to be taken in spirit to Heaven and there dwell with God, after Word, in some way Johnny didn't yet understand, had made it possible – before that, Johnny had understood the souls of dead people lived as long as their names were remembered, and Herod had decreed oblivion to many who had a right to their souls' survival. Johnny might not believe in the sacred function of tombs in perpetuating souls' existence, but the shade of his former belief angered him still against Herod. And the nasty new city Tiberias had blasphemous idols of animal origin, like Egyptian bird-heads and dog-heads. So that it was a fit place for people taken by devils. But this woman was here, in Magdala, twisting and turning herself as she spat hatred at Word.

Johnny had not seen a woman suffering from demons before: men, yes, even before he met Word he saw several, who went their way still screaming and shouting with no prospect of release until death.

But sick women stayed, were kept, in their homes. Johnny's religion might seem to give a superior place to men, but in Johnny's own life, women received greater respect, being weaker in the body and stronger in the mind than men, as a rule anyway. It seemed doubly unnatural that a woman should be taken by devils, using horrible words, getting herself dirty and looking awful, matted and bloody hair, torn clothes, and a face made brutish by her tragedy. Like the man whose devils entered the pigs, she seemed to hold several fighting demons within her, and not all of them spoke, at least one very powerful one sounded like a savage dog, yelping and snarling, and when it could be heard the white flecks of foam on her lips became almost like paint for her mouth. Then her lips would go back in a dreadful, mocking grin, stretched round to show gleaming, murderous teeth. Johnny had the thought that if she bit anyone (as in fighting he sometimes did) if they were not Word, they would surely die.

But he never discovered what would happen, because Word swung round on James, Andrew and Judas and said 'Go find Zebedee's fish-seller in Magdala, and discover what lodgings we can get. We must stay here tonight and we may have to pay. Judas, take our purse', and then, as though in an afterthought, 'Johnny, go with them, you may find the man quicker than James can'. Put like that, Johnny felt on his honour to outstrip James in the quest, and headed off into the narrow streets, away from the commotion with James in hot pursuit, and the other two following more slowly. Johnny's zeal for any work Word might give him got them well away from the woman who was afterwards known as Mary Magdalen, and it was many seasons before he would realise that Word was getting him out of earshot of things the demons might force the woman to say, and that Word had given him his task in that apparent afterthought so as to prevent his having any suspicion that his innocence was being protected. Equally, Johnny's hunting through the town, depending on half-memory instead of stopping to think his information out, vying with James instead of pooling their recollection, drew the four farther away. James probably realised Word's main intent was to shield Johnny: at all events he played up, and kept Johnny arguing the merits of different directions for Zebedee's man in Magdala, whom they had never seen away from the landing-place, and whose name James seemed to have difficulty in recalling save to feel sure that whatever Johnny imagined it to be, must be wrong. Neither of them got too far away from Andrew and Judas, but neither were near enough to hear their conversation, on which Word may also have counted.

'Why does the Master waste our time with that brat?' demanded Judas, as they watched James and Johnny enter false trails, argue, head back on their tracks but away once more rather than return to Andrew and Judas, still arguing incessantly at every stage.

Andrew shrugged. 'He likes him. He likes children, you know.'

'Some do, I suppose. Never could, myself.' Andrew raised an eyebrow.

'Not even when you were a child?'

Judas shuddered. 'I hated being a child.'

'Didn't you have any friends among other children?'

'One. Once. I thought we were friends. Then a bigger boy got him to say he would never be friends with me, and never had been. That was that.'

Andrew eyed him with a dash of pity. 'No siblings?'

'None. Not even one like Peter.'

'I'm very fond of Peter', said Andrew stiffly.

'I'm getting very fond of him. I wish I'd known a boy like him when I was a child.'

'More than like me?' Andrew was grinning.

'Much more than like you', and to Andrew's satisfaction Judas grinned back. 'You would have been far too adventurous for me. I wanted a quiet life.'

'I agree you may not have a quiet one with Johnny around', this being delayed in Andrew's speech until some argument Johnny was making against James had somewhat subsided after rising to deafen the heavens for all that it was a street and a half away. Judas sniffed.

'Why this brat in particular?'

Andrew tilted his head to one side. 'Well, he is God – I mean, the Master is', hastily before Judas could indignantly dissociate himself from any question of the divinity of Johnny.

'Yes, I agree with that now. And I think it is what our old Master thought.'

'Blessing on his name.'

'Blessing on his name.'

'Which is also Johnny's name.' Judas smiled sardonically. 'My name is that of the hero Judas Maccabaeus, but nobody expects me to lead a revolt against our oppressors.'

'We have enough to do as it is. But my thinking is this. Our Master talks of God his Father, and teaches us to call his Father our Father.'

'Blessed be his name.'

'Blessed be his name. But it means that the one thing we know about him which sounds like our own lives is the idea of Fatherhood. To be a Father, God has to have a son. And in human form, God may feel he wants a son.' Andrew enunciated it slowly.

'But the boy John has a perfectly good father of his own. Our Master has no word of criticism for him.' Nor did Judas sound as though he himself had, whatever his doubts about Zebedee's younger son.

'No, I would never expect him to have. But boys can do with many fathers.'

'And even many mothers?' Judas sparred, but only mildly.

'Especially many mothers. Have you ever known a woman to refrain from telling off someone else's child when she felt it needed it?'

They had little chance to develop these ideas in the next few minutes, for Johnny had rushed back, having decided he remembered the name of the missing man and the narrow street in which his house had a foothold, or else James had decided they had confused themselves long enough. When they had got what they wanted from the man (and it turned out that he was waiting for them, having been alerted by a messenger from Zebedee), they hurried back to Word to say that they all had accommodation and Judas didn't need to pay anything to anyone, and they found Word and the others waiting, but the woman was gone. Word simply said that she was well, and that seven devils had been driven out of her, but Peter told Johnny afterwards that it was as nasty a business as he had seen up to now,

142

although he would not repeat one word to Johnny which had been uttered by the demons through the woman's mouth. Johnny saw that Word's hair and beard were rumpled, as though someone had been tugging and tearing at them, and there seemed to be spittal on his cheekbone. Before they went back to Zebedee's business friend, Johnny dragged Word into a nearby bath-house, and carefully washed his face and beard, and combed his hair, and when Word protested mildly, Johnny said firmly that he had promised Mary to look after Word, and Word agreed that he, too, had promised Mary to look after Johnny, and both of them had been doing what they had promised. Johnny did not quite see how Word had been specifically carrying out his part of the bargain, but he remembered their talk and when the time came he realised how carefully Word had looked after him from the moment it became clear what kind of horrors Mary Magdalen was screaming. A lot of Johnny's future remembering had to mix itself with new realisations. As for Mary Magdalen herself, Word said she was now cured of the devils which had possessed her, and that she would never again be troubled by them or by other demons. Philip and Nathaniel had taken her to a woman Philip knew, who would help her in the early days of her convalescence. For some reason Johnny asked Word whether they would ever meet Mary Magdalen again, and Word looked a little startled, but said they would. It occurred to Johnny that he himself might not recognise her when her face was at peace, but clearly Word would and that was what mattered.

They left Magdala by road, cautiously, working their way between Nazareth and Mount Tabor. Thomas was rather on the look-out for any acquaintances from Nazareth, and Johnny felt fairly sure that Word would be very thankful not to meet any Nazarenes. But they did encounter many people who had heard of Word, and followed the thirteen of them down the road, most saying nothing to Word or his disciples, but simply waiting for something to happen which on their arrival outside the gate of Nain, did. A funeral was going through the gate, with much loud ululation of mourners, and the crowd around the corpse quick with their story, that the body was of a young, able-bodied man, his widowed mother's only son, and never a day's illness behind him until he was suddenly stricken and left dead after the shortest possible time. But the story almost faded from earshot in Johnny's mind when he caught sight of the widow herself.

It was a face still crawling with the shock still hardly capable of knowing that its future had been annihilated, yet a face half-eaten with grief. The natural colour had left it, and what took its place was grey. Johnny had seen mothers of dead sons once or twice in the past – inevitably, the Sea of Galilee had taken an occasional toll, and his father would be called on to comfort and compensate parents or widows of fishermen in his employ, and Johnny might be required to attend funeral ceremonies or accompany his own parents for mourning visits. But he had never seen grief equal to this. Miriam's parents had been shattered when they thought they had lost her forever, but they were live people by comparison to the widow of Nain. She was a woman literally infected by death. Johnny never saw anything her until Word's mother looked into his own face while Word was dying, and yet Mary's ravaged features still found love for Johnny amid her own suffering. The widow of Nain seemed robbed of any emotion with a spark of hope or faith or love left in it.

Word took one look at her, gave a clipped 'Weep Not', touched the bier being carried before her, and in a tone which made the mother the son's first responsibility rather than the other way round said 'Youngster, up you get!', and the lad jumped up, off the bier, and threw his arms around his mother, crying 'I'm all right, Ma!, I'm all right!' He needed to hold her, too, and Word was quickly at her other side, and Johnny swore she lost thirty years as the thing became clear to her. Her eyes turned on Word, with no doubt as to what she owed him, and the depth of her thanks sang like the beauty of dawn, and Johnny seemed to hear rather than remember the words of God to Job of how the morning stars sang together and all the sons of God shouted for joy. Behind them the torrent of amazement broke like a sudden squall striking waves against the side of one of Zebedee's boats, and Johnny could feel the battle between fear and wonder in the cries that rippled back to the edges of the funeral crowd. They consolidated their emotions in calls of glory to God, and hailed Word as a great prophet, but at the fringes of the tribute Johnny could hear the wilder cries that God had visited his people. Which, of course, He had, reflected Johnny, and felt that Nain knew its business where Nazareth certainly did not. Word got clear rapidly enough, pointing out to responsible-looking women that mother and son needed food and rest quickly, and were best to go to a house nearby to get them. Several places near at hand were drawn into the work, and Word agreed that his men and himself would take food with the ex-mourners. The disciples were scattered over three or four homes, and Johnny was briefly cut off from Word, whom he could see talking earnestly with the youth and his mother, and yet not so seriously that his laugh didn't ring out, followed more shakily by those of mother and son. When the thirteen had all eaten and regrouped, Word led them through Nain. The young man wanted to go with them, at least to the outskirts of his town, but Word told him to stay with his mother who certainly didn't want him out of her sight. Johnny had one last glimpse of her over standing at her own door with her son's arm over her back and a look of rapture on her face beyond description. Word turned back to her just before they moved out of her sight, and opened the fingers of his right hand, moving it down and then slanting left and upward and finally across.

And then it was tramp, tramp, tramp down roads, and over paths, and across scrubland, and in and out of little byways and even dried river-beds. Just before leaving Galilee they caught sight of what looked like a small defile of troops on the horizon, first glimpsed by Andrew, and Word laid his finger on his lips reminding them that human voices would carry on the still air. The thirteen took the first chance to put hillocks and woods between themselves and the soldiers. When they were out of earshot, Word remarked that this was probably the result of adulation at Nain giving clues to Herod's troops as to the whereabouts and direction of the wonder-working prophet, a term he turned with sardonic relish. And Johnny said that whatever clues they gave Herod's men, he knew that if Word had the chance of playing that part of their journey again, Word would still bring the widow's son back into being. And Word said quietly that he would. Johnny was rather touched that it was Judas who then said, rather like a child who remembered a treat, 'wasn't the widow's face wonderful when you brought her boy back to life?' They generally agreed that it was. And then they were over the border into Samaria which meant safety from the tetrarch's soldiers, but sectarian hostility of a different kind, which Johnny anticipated by eyeing the landscape as though it concealed every known theological abomination. He warned Word of the traditional warfare between Galilean and Samaritan robber bands, and he did it in the traditional Galilean way of blaming the Samaritans for everything. Word picked up, and picked at, a few of his stories, mostly to show him that there was a case for the Samaritans in most arguments as well as for the Galileans, but even Andrew (who thought it his duty to cut a few feathers from Johnny's wings for Johnny's own good) and Thady (who naturally sympathised with the Samaritans as being a lost cause, especially when Galileans or Judaeans controlled the discussion) found themselves agreeing that Word was in physical danger from the Samaritans. If their progress had been circumspect in Galilee to escape from Roman military order, it needed even more discretion in country populated by Samaritan guerrilla disorder. They took care nevertheless to keep to the east, nearer the Jordan than the Mediterranean, on whose coast Roman ports and forts kept control. The faster they travelled, the safer their journey was likely to be, and Johnny was looking forward to finding himself among Jews once more – having yet to discover that Judaeans considered themselves very different from Galileans like himself – when the agreeable and fertile plain brought them to Sychar. Johnny would remember Sychar as a city: no native of Jerusalem would. The disciples were sure of making contact with Jews in Sychar, and told Word that with any luck they would entirely avoid the Samaritans, at which point Word dismayed them by saying he was tired, and the rest of them should go into Sychar to get food. He made it clear that even Johnny was to go on this mission, but after a short journey Johnny took advantage of the twelve splitting their forces into two, and secretly worked his way back to Word. For one thing, Johnny really did not like to leave Word alone, and felt that two of them would be better than one in standing up to Samaritan robbers, and with Word's good nature a robber-band might quite easily kidnap him if he were left alone and take him God knew where although of course they could not hurt him. Also, Word had remained at what was called Jacob's Well and Johnny had some notion that this being holy ground if he came back he might see Word wrestling with an angel, or something. But when he got back within earshot he heard Word talking to a woman, and dropped to the ground, wiggling his way out of her line of vision while enabling himself to hear all they said.

She was a handsome woman, and Johnny made no value judgment in calling her that in his mind. He was used to authoritative men but this woman was authoritarian: she made no pretence of any man running her life, Johnny decided. At first her manner in talking to Word was mocking, and she would probably be so with most men, if not all. Their conversation didn't seem to have started more than a sentence or two by the time Johnny picked it up, and it seemed to have begun with Word asking her to give him some water to drink out of what she had drawn from the well. This surprised Johnny, since normally Word was quicker than most men to avoid bothering working women, and Johnny concluded that for some reason Word wanted to get her into conversation, and being used to Word's thought which seemed able to build on what was in the minds of others Johnny began to suspect that Word had known the woman was corning to the well when he told his disciples he wanted to rest there. Anyhow, she looked at him, tall, broad, strong and matriarchal as she was, and said with a touch of derision:

'And here are you, a Jew, asking me, a Samaritan, for a drink! Is it one of the wonders of the world you are?' (It is, thought Johnny with a grin to himself.)

Word's mouth twisted in a half-smile, turning down on the left-hand side, and, sounding oddly like herself in tone answered: 'If you knew what God is giving you, and who is asking you for a drink of water, it is yourself who would do the asking, and then he would be giving you living water.'

The woman's eyes narrowed, and her habitual questioning grin became more precise: 'The water of life?' Word inclined his head: 'The water of life.'

Her eyebrows – or at least the right eyebrow cocked itself at him:

'And me a Samaritan?' (And well might she say it, thought Johnny.)

Word looked at her as if both of them knew her to have made an irrelevant jest: 'There was a Syro-Phoenician woman who asked me to cure her daughter who was possessed by a demon. I said to her that my sole mission was to the lost sheep of the house of Israel. She besought me to help her. I said that it was not appropriate to take bread meant for the children and cast it to dogs. She said that the dogs eat of the crumbs which fall from their masters' table.' Word was smiling all over his mouth now, and his eyes were brimming with laughter.

The woman said: 'Well, she was a bold lassie, and gave you as good as she got. What did you do?'

Word gave the slightest shrug. 'Her daughter was fully restored to her senses that very hour. Naturally, I was delighted with the way she said it, but it was her great faith which made it happen.'

The woman pondered momentarily. 'But she wasn't a worshipper of our God.'

Word's smile became more sardonic, and retreated to his left side once more. 'But she must have been, mustn't she, at least by the end of our conversation?'

The woman categorised, businesslike: 'But she was hardly a believer in our father Jacob, who gave us this well, and who drank out of it, himself and his sons and his cattle. Are you a greater man than Jacob, to provide living water when you have no bucket, the well is deep and from where would you get living water?' So saying, she handed Word a cup of water.

Word raised the cup in her honour and drank luxuriously from it, then smiled fully and answered: 'Anyone who drinks of this water will be thirsty in the future from time to time, but the water I give creates a spring of water within the drinker to flow forever bringing everlasting life.'

All trace of banter had left the woman by now. 'Give me that water', she said, 'so that I shall never be thirsty or have to come here for water again.'

But the smile still lurked around Word. 'Go home', he said, 'get your husband, and come back here.'

She eyed him grimly. 'I have no husband.'

Word gave her back look for look. 'True enough', he said, 'you have had five husbands, but your present man is not your husband.'

Johnny realised that the woman seemed delighted at what many would have called an accusation. She sounded like his mother Salome when she decided that some man, possibly even her husband or one of her sons, had actually said something sensible. 'I know what you are, you're a prophet. Well, our fathers worshipped on this mountain' – she flung out a hand to what Johnny had heard Judas say was Mount Gerizim – 'although your crowd' – she bowed in a slight return of her earlier manner – 'say that it is in Jerusalem we should worship.' She paused, and Word cut in:

'Believe me, lady, the time is coming when neither to here nor to Jerusalem will you be going to worship the Father.' He sipped the water.

'You don't know what you are worshipping, and we do, because salvation will start from the Jews.' He looked directly at her, and Johnny thought she seemed to realise he meant himself. 'The time is coming, and indeed is here, when true worshippers will worship the Father in spirit and in truth, and the Father will claim such people for his worshippers.' Word held out his arms as though they were a coat that did not always fit him comfortably. 'God is a spirit, and anyone who worships him must do so in spirit and in truth.'

The woman's lips parted, as though she was on the verge of a discovery she only had to enunciate for it to happen: 'I know the Messiah, the Christ, is to come and tell us all things.' And she waited for what she clearly expected to hear. And heard it. 'I, who speak to you now, am Christ', said Word quietly. Johnny heard some of the others returning, and the woman put down her water-pot, heavy as it was with its water, and went back to the outskirts of the town without apparently going as far as her house, to take Samaritans to Word.

Johnny waited until she was out of sight, and then made his own way to Word before any of the others reached him, but Word looked at him with what seemed serious annoyance. Johnny remembered that when he had eavesdropped on Word's talk with Shimon the Zealot and had talked to Word about their conversation later, Word had warned him not to let it out to Shimon or anyone else that he knew Shimon wasn't a Jew, but had not seemed displeased. But now it was different. Word's eyes flashed at Johnny ominously. Johnny did not know fear as he looked into their dark brown depths, but he felt ashamed. Word said:

'You were supposed to be with the others.'

Johnny said: 'Yes, but you might have needed someone else in case of attack.'

Word half-smiled, but became serious again. 'I know I didn't tell you not to eavesdrop when you listened in to Shimon, but this was different. He was talking over the chance of becoming one of you, and although he didn't want you others to listen, it was in some ways your business. This wasn't, and you should have known it wasn't. When a person wants to be alone with me to talk, and the talk is about themselves, not just about the Roman Empire or something, then they have a right to be alone with me.' Then the others came up, and Johnny didn't have time to tell Word he was sorry, or maybe he didn't want to find a tactic which could give him a moment to say it. The woman then arrived bringing many people from the town with her, and they stayed in Sychar for the next couple of days. Johnny and James were told by Word to go to a nearby village south of

Sychar but still north of the Judaean border, and there arrange for Word and the rest to stay overnight. This might have seemed a sort of promotion with Johnny entrusted with a delicate diplomatic mission entirely to himself and his brother. But in fact Johnny was ashamed for what he now saw was sneaking, angry with himself for not apologising to Word, angry with Word for reprimanding him and for being right to do so, angry above all with Samaritans of every shape and kind without whom he would never have been in this trouble and who were taking up Word's attention in time Johnny felt would have been better spent with Johnny. So he went on his mission with James, and his bad temper sent James back into the haughty manner he had directed against Johnny before they had ever met Word. The journey was painful under foot for much of the time and their idea of finding the village by use of a short cut across Mount Garizim took more time than it saved. When they finally reached their destined village – and significantly Johnny could never subsequently remember its name – the mission proved an utter disaster. The villagers denounced them as greedy Jews trying to leech off their betters instead of doing a stroke of work; when James and John said they had been well received in Sychar the Samaritan villagers proved as hostile to their own bigger towns as any Galilean might be about Sephoris or Tiberias; when it came out that James and Johnny had come over Mount Garizim the villagers accused them of blasphemy, and their attempt to explain that Word had come to abolish all pre-existing variations in worship resulted in the villagers screaming abuse against Word. Ultimately James and Johnny fled back to Sychar in tempers that grew worse every minute.

Word was so preoccupied with the Samaritans that when James and Johnny finally reached him it was quite some time before they could win their place in his attention, and the two of them told their story, agreeing in its details but vying with each other to tell it, and as usual ending by shouting rival sentences at the hideously raucous utmost pitch of their voices. Their vehemence of tone incited vehemence of message and in their anxiety to make clear how vicious had been the villagers' hatred of Word, they asked Word to give them powers to burn down the village with fires from heaven.

'And when', demanded Word, mildly but with an edge in his voice, 'did my Heavenly father provide fire from Heaven for the use of his agents?'

'Elijah', said Johnny smartly.

'Confuted the priests of Baal', shot in James.

'Set his sacrifice alight with fire from Heaven', gabbled Johnny.

'After he had first watered it', annotated James.

'And the priests of Baal couldn't make their sacrifices catch fire', intoned Johnny.

'And God was given Glory', slid in James.

'And Jezebel confounded', pronounced Johnny.

'And who was burnt in the fire lit by Elijah?' asked Word, as if he didn't know.

'Well, maybe nobody', said Johnny, 'but your heavenly Father did send fire from Heaven on Sodom.'

'And Gomorrah', contributed James.

The Samaritans were of course listening to all of this and in retrospect Johnny (and James) saw that so public a demand for mass murder needed a very public reply, which they certainly received:

'Ye know not what manner of spirit ye are of', said Word, icily. 'For the Son of Man is not come to destroy men's lives, but to save them.'

Johnny wanted to burst into tears, but held himself in, knowing Word was right and that he and James had imperilled the whole mission to the Samaritans. James and he looked at one another, for a moment hating each other worse than they ever had in the worst of their old days. Then they made their way to the back of the crowd, choosing places well away from one another, James finishing up fairly near Peter, while the only one of the twelve near Johnny was Judas, which summed up the wretchedness of everything. Word began to speak to the crowd, talking of his message of love and forgiveness, and of course Johnny (and James) were calmed in their anger and even their shame as they listened. If they had been near each other they would have embraced and kissed, and vied in making mutual apologies, and they certainly intended to get to Word at the earliest possible point after the speaking was over, but they kept their places now, not wanting to draw further attention to themselves or do anything else disruptive. And sure enough at the end of Word's sermon, James began to work his way back to Word with Peter alongside him and quickly made his apology, rightly blaming himself the most, as the oldest, and then looking around for Johnny, whom he was sure would be making the same pilgrimage back to Word.

But the crowd had been at its farthest from Word where Johnny finally took his stand. He could hear Word perfectly (as all crowds listening to Word, however large they were, managed to do). But he could no longer see him clearly, and he drew back from the Samaritans close at hand. He idly noticed a couple of Roman soldiers not far away, and listened to words spoken to one another from corners of their mouths in case they had any intention against Word, even if they had less official freedom to act in Samaria than in Judaea or Galilee. He had picked up enough Latin from his lessons with Word to be able to follow conversations of Romans, and in any case all Galileans needed some Latin to respond to official Roman enquiries if they wanted to avoid a blow with the flat of a sword, or a kick. He heard the words *'Ecce Puer'* which struck him as an odd description of Word, who was surely not a boy except in knowing how to talk to Johnny when they were by themselves (and the sooner the better, hungered Johnny). Then the other soldier said *'Iste?'* which was a rude way to speak about anyone but which might be expected from such ignorant brutes: declaring 'that one', they had called him, declaring themselves Word's superiors. The next word Johnny caught was *'asprior'* which made no sense at all: why should Word be called rougher or rather rough or too rough, especially when he was preaching gentleness and love? It was the second fellow who said it. The first one answered: *'Tiberius aspros amat'*. Tiberius loves rough people? Were they going to ask Word to convert the Emperor? And then everything dissolved for Johnny in a sheet of flame.

Only Judas saw the soldier club Johnny. He had picked up the failure of James's and Johnny's mission, and had heard Word's censure of their horrible demands. He naturally felt some satisfaction about the disgrace, however temporary, of the child who had once humiliated him and who clearly had no friendly thoughts towards him. He had in fact been looking back at Johnny, mockingly, relishing the boy's shameful isolation, when the blow was struck. Judas hesitated not a moment. However obnoxious Johnny might be, Johnny was one of themselves and above all he was beloved by the Master. Judas's friendlessness, and suspicion of the Samaritans, meant that he made no effort to seek allies, arouse the crowd, find Andrew, call to Word, or anything else. He simply flushed almost as red as his hair, and charged the Roman soldiers who were dragging

Johnny's body away. He succeeded in punching one of them so violently that he fell, dropping Johnny, but the other turned on Judas and drove his sword into the Judaean's throat. Judas, dying, fell forward on the ground, and his blood drenched Johnny's footprints.

EN

TIBERIUS

And the darkness comprehended it not

All Johnny remembered from the early stages of his kidnapping was pain in his head, worse than any he had known, even when Nat had knocked him out in Nazareth; and that had ended with Word's cool bands eradicating the pain so well as to make the memory likeable. Now it was nothing but grinding agony, as though spikes were being driven in at either side of the skull, or occasionally, as though to amuse itself with variations, the pain would drive straight up from above his spine. His arms and legs didn't seem to belong to him, and flopped about helplessly, and he must have had some bad knocks when he was unconscious or half-conscious, because when he finally recovered consciousness he discovered he had several bruises ready to take their turn in making him want to yell or moan. In fact he curbed any outcry when he knew of anyone near him: he dimly realised from his first half-waking that his kidnappers were the Roman soldiers he had heard, and he would not let them think a Jewish boy whimpered at his injuries.

At some point Johnny had been thrown on a camel, and he even heard in his deadened mind the commands for the camel to kneel (*'Ikh'*), to stand (*'Dhai!'*) and to walk (*'Yahh!'*), perhaps because the beast pitched Johnny's body in various directions as it obeyed. He must have been tied on in some way, but that did not register, nor did he ever recall having been held in place by a rider who still had his senses. He probably did have such a companion, because somewhere along the way he was probably struck again or given some opiate forced down his throat or jammed against his nostrils. He had eerie recollections when (years afterwards) he was a more or less willing passenger on a camel, that he had felt the beast skimming over the sands at some remote time. Then there was oblivion again, and when next Johnny came to himself he was lying alone in pain and darkness in what turned out to be a ship, much bigger than any ship he had ever known.

What followed had a dream quality in retrospect, and Johnny could never give a coherent account of it, not even to Word. Word obviously had little difficulty in working out the main details, but he never told Johnny much about his conclusions, and Johnny came to realise Word wanted him to dwell on it as little as possible. So Johnny never told others about it in his later life, not even when he was remembering his life with Word. It is true that the end of the adventure was something he looked back to with utter delight, but it also suited him not to talk about that: one memory was not to be recalled, the other was to be cherished, but cherished alone. There was certainly nothing to be cherished in what he could remember of what it was like when he first began to wake up. He realised fairly soon that he was on the upper deck of a great ship, in a tent. It was dark when he first woke, and he scrabbled about as he dimly drew thoughts around him, his fingers getting and rocking a beaker which slopped water on them so telling him to drink if he felt thirst, as he did. He went back to sleep then and would half-awaken to hear snatches of conversation, from various voices, some in his own Aramaic, some in Latin, some in Greek. One strong Roman voice must have been the captain, in whose keeping Johnny now was. From what Johnny could gather, the captain had bought him from the Roman soldiers who had kidnapped him. The ship had been sailing from Alexandria to Rome, full of grain, and as usual winds were contrary, this time driving it back in foul weather until the captain thankfully made port at Caesarea, on the coast of Samaria, where his captors had brought Johnny. It was north-west of where they had slugged him, but as the main Roman port in those parts they expected it to provide a buyer for Johnny, although not one commanding so magnificent a vessel. (Johnny took the captain's word for it that the vessel was magnificent.) The captain made it clear to those to whom he talked (enquirers about the boy in the tent, Johnny supposed) that he would not normally stoop so low as slave-trading, but it was known that the Emperor's servants would pay high prices for what the Emperor liked, and the captain had lost time and money by being blown off course by winds which the captain cursed in picturesque language. Johnny for some extraordinary reason retained at least one of the curses, with no notion that he had, until he was having an argument with Paul about something quite trivial to do with Roman customs, and Paul smugly stated '*Civis Romanus sum*', never having quite got over his privilege in being a Roman citizen, and Johnny, instinctively hostile to the Romans, suddenly found himself resurrecting a few choice if incomprehensible remarks from the captain. And, equally unconsciously, he did so not in his own voice but in what neither Johnny nor Paul could know was a perfect imitation of the presumably now long-dead captain: harsh, loud, gravelly from many draughts of sub-Falernian wine, trained to throw itself successfully over howling winds, and even when deferential to bully beneath the deference. Paul was horrified, and staggered back, gasping 'Where did you learn language like that? You told me you learned most of your Latin from the Master! He can never have taught you that!' 'Taught me what?' asked Johnny, puzzled. 'What you just said!' 'No, we didn't do those words when doing Latin. I may have heard Roman soldiers saying them. What do they mean, anyway? I just remember them as being something to say to express annoyance with an undesirable phenomenon.' Paul glared. 'Oh, I don't mean you', said Johnny pacifically, 'you're quite useful, one way and another. But I don't much care for Roman citizens, by birth or acquisition. Not that it counts with friends. Some of my best friends', added Johnny thoughtfully, 'are Roman citizens. But we don't talk about it. What do those words actually mean?' Paul went scarlet. Johnny had been looking down while talking, but he swung his eyes directly at Paul now. And before he could stop himself, he grinned one of his widest grins. 'No, on second thoughts, don't tell me. I suppose you had to learn them to qualify as a Roman citizen?' Paul looked so distraught that Johnny gave him a hug to charm his anxiety away and Paul, after a little shudder of embarrassment, squared his jaw and hugged Johnny back. Johnny remembered Word saying that it would take all sorts to make a church.

Johnny never actually saw the captain, another reason why his recollection lacked a visible body with which to associate the curse drifting down his memory (and permanently sunk within it, never to rise again, after Paul's horror). He could recall a tall, malevolent-looking figure coming in to the tent occasionally when he was awake, to bring in fruit or remove empty vessels and slops. Johnny could move around, but was shackled to a large iron ring and the long chain from it ended in another ring snapped above his knee. Even in his bemused and possibly still half-drugged condition Johnny could deduce that if the captain was not normally in the business of kidnapping and enslaving boys, he had expected to carry adult captives from time to time, and the ring would usually be snapped around a grown-up's ankle. At first Johnny had wondered if the attendant was the captain, but it was quickly clear that he was not. He despised Johnny, certainly, and made no answer to Johnny's grunts and moans on the first day, or to his enquiries in three languages on the second. The man was darker than Johnny, not as dark as Chuza, and remembering the boat usually sailed to Rome from Alexandria and back, Johnny decided the man must be an Egyptian slave. Johnny supposed the Egyptians looked down on everyone else. So did the Romans, of course. So did the Greeks. They gave themselves airs of superiority which would only have been justified if they were Jews. And, thought Johnny, Galilean Jews at that. It helped him to face the ugly fact that Galilean Jews would count for very little where he was being taken.

Johnny found the voyage miserable, but he gave himself the satisfaction of calling the Egyptian slave 'Potiphar' in his mind, after the Egyptian who first owned Jacob's son Joseph when his brothers had sold him. This became 'Potty' when Potiphar's duties proved to include getting rid of the results of Johnny's relieving himself, as well as the dirty water, Johnny as a Jewish boy being dutiful about washing frequently. During the daytime – the second daytime, Johnny having been much too ill to notice the first day – Potiphar seemed to give him looks mingling curiosity and resentment. It didn't interest Johnny very much. What filled his whole consciousness when he was conscious was that he had lost Word, maybe forever, and that at their last meeting Word had been very angry with him. He was sure that nobody could have seen him taken prisoner, with the remotely possible exception of Judas, who certainly wasn't likely to do anything to let Word know what had happened and would be glad to have seen the last of Johnny, if he had seen it. Almost every memory of family or friends was hurtful. He could hardly bear to think of his father or mother, or James, especially as he and James had been furious with one another when last they had parted. Of course James would go looking for him, and surely Word would, he was responsible to Zebedee and Salome for Johnny even if he was angry with him, but none of them would find anything. He would never see Mary again, with her generous smile of understanding, or Miriam, endlessly teasing him and yet his friend whenever needed – except now, thought Johnny helplessly – or nice, blundering Peter, or interesting, censorious Andrew, or Philip, or Nat. It was all over. He was a lost cause for Thady to take up, or an oppressed person for Jim to champion, or a betrayed Jew for Shimon to make a cause of revolt, or a quandary for Thomas to doubt, or the remains of ancestors long enough to take Matthew into tomorrow to count.

There couldn't be any world without Word. If only Johnny had managed to get some message to Word that he was sorry, and that he would show his sorrow, being ready to cut Judas's toenails if need be, or empty everyone's slops like Potty, it wouldn't be so bad. As it was, it couldn't be worse. Yes, it could, though. Suppose those soldiers had really been trying to take Word prisoner, or wound or disable him or something, not that they could hurt him because Word was God, but they might take him prisoner, and make it very difficult for him to get back to the others, maybe by their killing all the others. So it was a good thing if Johnny was a prisoner instead of Word being one. Johnny smiled faintly through his tears. The thought really made him feel better. If only he had actually done something to help Word, it would be much better. But even the thought of Word became a way of Johnny feeling stronger. He still managed to sleep, possibly because something had been put in his fruit juice, but the looming horror of what was to happen to him and why the Emperor would want him, and for what, seemed to shadow his dreams, in which at first he found himself fighting with Roman soldiers, and ugly old men in togas, and Potiphar who had suddenly become seven people screaming at him that he would have to eat pork, all of them blocking off any way of Johnny getting out, and when he wasn't fighting he was either hearing voices when he was awake or dreaming them.

He must have been asleep when he first saw Them. He remembered little enough of that dream later, though enough of it lasted for him to know what he had gone through when with the advancement of years he was able to make some sense of it. He felt he was being carried by two winged things, although he did not seem to feel their touch. It was as though some part of him had been pulled out of the rest of him, painlessly but vitally enough for him to feel that what was important was what he could see now, not what might become of the rest of him, lying asleep in the tent on the ship's deck. He seemed to be travelling in sunlight, above an endless sea, but one of brighter blue than he had ever imagined water could have. It was in fact the Mediterranean Sea, but Johnny did not connect it with his later, wakeful, first sight of it in daylight (for he had been unconscious when he was first taken aboard ship, and it had been night-time). He remembered his dream vision of it for the first time many years later, when he was being taken as a prisoner to Rome to be informed by the Emperor Domitian that he was about to die (informed inaccurately as it turned out). His first land-fall in Italy and the sea around the coast brought back the colour of the sea in his dream. So it must have been Italy where the sea ended in his dream on shipboard, he told himself while being hustled down the gangway en route to Domitian. The prospect of that meeting should have concentrated his mind wonderfully, but it did not: he amused himself recalling the long-forgotten dream, as though he was going somewhere he had previously only beheld in pictures or on urns. Johnny had never forgotten Chuza's advice about the need to feel his fear, but the prospect of Domitian did not particularly disturb him. He had, after all, seen rather a lot of things before seeing Domitian, who was going to have to put up a memorable performance to compete with Johnny's memories, which now included that shipboard dream. And Johnny could remember that he had been frightened then.

When did his fear begin in his dream?

Not when he first saw the Emperor. The Emperor Tiberius, that was. Curiously enough, he first realised he had seen him in the shipboard dream when he was being marched through to his audience with Domitian, and he suddenly stopped before a statue and said 'Who is That?', and his guards, not thinking it wise for them to keep an Emperor waiting, wanted to hasten him, but the old man (which Johnny was, by Domitian's time) completely altered his compliant manner and refused to budge until they had answered his question, and after some slight groping of memories the guards agreed among themselves it was the successor of Augustus the Divine, Tiberius, and Johnny raised eyebrows now grey and enquired whether they thought Tiberius was a god, and after some hesitation they doubted it, and he said he agreed with them, and, looking again at the handsome face with its unusually large eyes said that he supposed a sculptor would not find it easy to represent pimples, even if it could have ever been politic so to do. And the oldest guard stopped in his own stride, and asked how Johnny had known about Tiberius's pimples. Had Johnny ever been in Tiberius's presence? And Johnny said no, not physically, but said it lightly and the guard missed any additional meaning in it.

The old guard was silent for a moment and then said that it wasn't a thing to be talked about, and if you were overheard you could have been put to death with some very nasty tortures, but his father had seen Tiberius and in old age had told his children that the Emperor had pimples, bad ones too. He continued to look with some wonder at Johnny as they continued their journey to Domitian, a bit more rapidly than before, Johnny obligingly hastening his own movements now, apparently with little difficulty. And when Domitian had given orders that Johnny was to be put to death by immersion in a vat of boiling oil before the Latin Gate of Rome, and Johnny had been thrust in and showed not the least sign of pain, much less of death, and had to be taken out, the elderly guard was heard to mutter that he was not surprised, and said that this was a holy man who could not be injured, and accompanied him back to the isle of Patmos where Johnny made him a follower of Word, and Johnny remarked that even the pimples of Tiberius could be put to divine use however lacking in divinity Tiberius as a totality might be. No, Johnny was not afraid of Tiberius. Or at least, not of seeing Tiberius. What he was afraid of, was being Tiberius.

Or of becoming some Emperor, being buried in some Caesar. It took a little time for it to be clear that that was a prospect in store for him, in his dream, and first of all when he found his spirit hovering over Tiberius's court at Cumae, he simply gazed in shocked amazement at opulent hangings and carpets and statues far beyond any expression of worldly wealth he had ever imagined, much less had ever seen. He was less surprised by the dress of the Emperor, having seen his court furnishings. He saw it was expensive. He thought he might enjoy flaunting himself in it, annoying James and rousing the envy of the men who had been boys when he was a boy. He doesn't seem to have thought of Word, at this point, and while the dream kept in his sight the thought of himself as an adult becoming Emperor and strutting about, anything else like the boys among whom he had played before becoming a fisher-boy dated from the few years he had lived before meeting Word. Apart from James; and in his dream Tiberius did not have the love for James that had been growing in him since he first met Word: without hating James, his dream-thought of James was someone to be outdone, outsmarted, humiliated. As a little boy Johnny had heard stories of the youngest son becoming the most important, like King David. And now he, Johnny, would be the greatest ruler on earth. He seemed to hover over the Emperor whom he knew to be Tiberius, and could see was an old man (of 72, in fact), with white hair, thinning and greasy (not rich and woolly which Johnny connected with aged piety) and a strong but resentful-looking face, once handsome, perhaps, but now broken out with suppurating pimples. Tiberius was walking up and down, stiffly, with his neck shoving his head forward, dark eyes darting suspiciously at an entourage practically slavering in front of him. Tiberius was swathed in imperial purple and Johnny wondered how he would look in it, when he was old enough to wear it, but wasn't he old enough now, wasn't he a fully-grown man, ready to displace Tiberius and rule the world whenever he felt like it? Tiberius barked out a few commands, and courtiers fell about him reverently, and whipped their way out of sight, as if he had put the dogs on them.

At first Johnny was aware of Tiberius speaking without particularly hearing, much less understanding, what he was saying. But he began to hear and understand, as though the Romans were obligingly speaking in easy Latin, and Tiberius was evidently complaining about things which seemed to relate to somebody called Sejanus. Johnny became interested in working out what the name was, after having first worked out that it was a name. It was clear that Tiberius was angry, or at least complaining petulantly either about things Sejanus had done and ought not have done, or about things he had not done and should have done, or about things that ought or ought not have happened which Sejanus should now be asked or told to rectify. It never became clear whether Tiberius was attacking Sejanus or extolling him, but whatever he was saying turned on what Sejanus had done, or was doing, or would do, or hadn't done, or wasn't doing, or wouldn't do, and it was also clear that Sejanus was in Rome, and Tiberius was in Cumae, or not so much in Cumae as in Caprae, the island in the bay. Again, Johnny did not recall this detail of the dream for many years, not in fact until he was back in Patmos after his inconclusive death sentence from Domitian and was idly chatting with his new friend and former guard and asked him about Tiberius and was told of the tyranny of Sejanus while Tiberius lived on Caprae. He worked it out that he must have heard Sejanus's name on board ship when half-asleep, so that it could feed his mind when in dreams but not when awake, and he supposed that the voyage must have happened when Sejanus's fall was near at hand. But Sejanus played no part in the dream, and Johnny in the dream was evidently satisfied in having worked out that Sejanus was being referred to without discovering anything about him except that Tiberius thought that he was important, but less important than Tiberius himself, of course. Also, while Johnny in old age learned that Sejanus until his overthrow and death had usurped much of Tiberius's own power while nominally always subservient to him, Johnny in the dream had no doubts but that Tiberius was the great emperor with all the power he wanted or needed to rule the world. It never occurred to him at any point that the actions of Pontius Pilate with regard to Word might have been perturbed by the enlargement of Sejanus's power or the imminence of his fall, but such great changes sent rapid ripples as far as Judaea. Certainly if a grainship's crew were talking animatedly about Sejanus one might expect the topic to concern senior officials in the lands whither and whence they sailed.

In Johnny's dream Tiberius ultimately must have dismissed his attendants or else Johnny's focus had narrowed to prevent his seeing them, but he could still hear Tiberius talking, apparently to himself, and this time he seemed preoccupied by the thought of a traitor. This probably related to accusations made against Sejanus which Tiberius was continuing to reject, or was trying to dispel, or was beginning to believe, but Johnny doesn't seem to have made that connection. What he did pick up was the repetition of the name of Marcus Junius Brutus in the context of treachery by a trusted friend and beneficiary, and the name was known to Johnny since it was mentioned in his hearing by Jews who wanted to reassure themselves about the instability and probable destruction of Roman rule. Brutus had murdered his friend and benefactor Gaius Julius Caesar and for a time had ruled in Macedonia while his fellow-assassin Gaius Longinus Cassius had ruled Syria as proconsul with some idea that his province included Galilee and, as Rome was in the hands of his enemies Mark Antony and the future Augustus, his decisions were what counted in Syria until Brutus and himself were defeated and killed at Philippi. It had happened when Johnny's grandfather was a little boy. Later, when the name of Judas Iscariot became synonymous with 'traitor' for Johnny (and everyone else, but most of all for Johnny), there were occasional discussions as to whether Brutus was almost as bad: to Romans, Brutus was worse because Caesar was Caesar unless you secretly cherished the old Republic and Johnny never knowingly met anyone who did; to the followers of Word, Judas Iscariot would be worse than anyone, because he had betrayed Word, and Word was God. But most people didn't want to discuss Judas Iscariot, Johnny especially: the name was regarded as unlucky, and while Word never talked about luck, most Jews did, and Word's disciples naturally did. On the other hand while Jews, including Word's followers, liked to pretend they were indifferent to the squabbles among Gentiles (a pleasing way of thinking of Roman civil wars provided no Romans were listening), they gossiped a lot about Roman politics, most of all when they were around the courts of Herod and his successors, and of Pontius Pilate and his. Johnny had spent little of his young life in the neighborhood of Roman gossip, but he knew who had killed Julius Caesar.

And he knew that the Emperor Augustus had not been Julius Caesar's son, as he was known, but his great-nephew, and that he had killed Caesar's son, Caesarion, whose mother was Cleopatra. Johnny was unlikely to have learned details of that kind from the fisher-folk of Galilee, but any discussion of any prominent family, Jew or Gentile, in the presence of Matthew brought authoritative pronouncements on who begat whom. Equally, Matthew briefed everyone who would listen to him on Tiberius being Augustus's stepson and not his actual son. So Johnny knew that Tiberius's successor might be little or no actual relation to him (although in fact, as Word remarked during his talks with Shimon the Zealot – when Shimon still was a Zealot – the most likely candidate was Gaius Caligula, his actual grandson, and so it proved). But in his dream Johnny did not worry about realities like that. Anyone could succeed Tiberius. He could (ignoring Tiberius's hostility to Jews having extended to exiling them from

Rome, however many he may have brought to Caprae for one reason or another). He would come to Caprae in the grainship. Tiberius would adopt him. Why Tiberius would want to adopt him, the dream did not disclose and Johnny did not ask, beyond the thought that Tiberius seemed to be going to a lot of trouble – or at least causing a lot of trouble – and would have to spend quite a lot of money to get Johnny to Caprae, and so with Johnny as an investment already, he might just as well make a good thing cut of it and adopt Johnny as his son with a view to inheriting the Roman Empire.

Something was nagging at the back of Johnny's mind during this flirtation with the idea of inheritance not to speak of zooming between the ages of 10 and whatever you needed to be to inherit the Roman Empire. (Gaius Caligula would be 25.) His dream self seemed to know it was playing a game and that what he did in the game did not commit him when awake. Yet something was wrong: someone or somewhere he had known was holding him back from becoming the new Tiberius. But before he had time to think it out, or to remember what it was that worried him, Tiberius had stopped mouthing, suddenly threw off his purple cloak, and walked out of the room in the opposite direction from his attendants, tugging at his toga as he went. Johnny assumed that he had gone into a dressing-room, though before seeing Tiberius he had got the impression that that entrance to his room had given on to the adjoining Blue Grotto: remembering that, Johnny concluded he was off to have a swim. That might be satisfactory: a Tiberius who loved the sea, or however much of it got inside the protected Bay of Cumae, might find he had something in common with his future adopted son, fresh from the Sea of Galilee. Anyhow, regardless of the possibility that Tiberius might return and find him (penetrating his invisibility if the dream was keeping him invisible), Johnny somehow got himself on the floor, and wrapped the purple cloak around himself, discovering a full-length mirror in which to view the results. This was something of a shock: Johnny had never seen a mirror. There were several in fashionable Jerusalem, especially in Roman houses, and Sidon had a few, as had Caesarea Maritima, but Johnny had never found them. So he was startled by his first sight of one, all the more because he beheld himself swathed in imperial purple. And as he looked, he began to experience a chill, prickling at the base of his skull, slowly travelling down his spine, the first actual sensation he had felt during the entirety of the dream, so far as he could remember. He began to suspect he was becoming someone else, or that someone else was entering him, possessing his body, darkening his mind. He began to struggle, physically, and suddenly saw that he must throw off the purple robe. It resisted his attempts, but after fighting it for some moments it tore, and Johnny extricated himself. He turned back to the mirror, and the form within it seemed to be him, whereas in the robe his face seemed only a mask of him. He smiled with relief, and his image smiled back. He raised his right hand, half-saluting the mirror-image's reply with its left one. But then he looked at his right hand, and knew it ought to be in the left hand of someone else. And at last he knew who, and why he must not inherit the Roman Empire. It was at that point that he tasted fear, a prickly repulsive fear, a sense of having come to the brink of defilement. Breathing seemed harder, as though he had to draw his breath through what pin-pricks in some fog that his chest could find. Something was forcing his jaws shut, preventing him from saying a word he had to say, a word he could almost but not quite remember, a word short in itself, dear to him, strong somehow. It was as though he was back again in the toils of the purple cloak, which still lay at his feet, crouched in an ugly mess, awaiting his surrender. And then Johnny remembered the word, and yelled: 'Word!'

Then They were back, if They had ever been away, since They had brought him here and presumably had let him land painlessly beside Tiberius's cloak. And They began to speak, with curious titters, as though Their own language consisted of titters into which They managed to get enough sound for Johnny to understand Them. They were apparently talking to each other, but were careful to be sure of his comprehension of all They said.

'Oh, the clever boy!'

'Such a clever boy!'

'He's remembered it.'

'I didn't think he could!'

'But he did!'

'Yes, he did!'

'Wasn't it clever of him?'

'Oh, very clever of him!'

'What happens to him now?'

'He knows what side he's on.'

'He's on the side of his Word.'

'How nice for Word!'

'Yes, isn't it?'

'After all, Word needs a friend like him.'

'A friend who will become Emperor!'

'Won't it be nice for Word!'

'He can decree everything Word wants.'

'Word won't have to do a thing.'

'Everything good will become law.'

'Nobody will be allowed to eat pork.'

'Nobody can do anything wrong.'

'Johnny will execute anyone who does.'

'Execute them with horrible tortures.'

'Make an example of them!'

'Kill them, kill them horribly!'

'Kill them excruciatingly!'

'Watch them writhe!'

'Watch them die!'

'All for Word!'

'All to please Word!'

'Give them the rack!'

'And the boiling oil!'

'Give them the death of a thousand cuts!'

'Give them the hell of a thousand hells!'

'Johnny will be angry!'

'Johnny will do well to be angry!'

Johnny was getting very angry, but not with the imaginary future miscreant. And then he realised his anger was what They wanted. To stop being angry when you feel you do well to be angry, is no easy matter, all the more when the incessant tittering irritated the anger more and more with every titter. Johnny felt wrath rising within him, from his belly, through his lungs, around his throat, in his mouth, all over his tongue. He set his jaw, closed his eyes, clenched his fists. And then he thought that he must think of Word. And his mind flew back to the two of them splashing each other with water in the Sea of Galilee, laughing at each other, loving one another. And he smiled.

'Word does not want me to hurt anyone, least of all in His name. Word would never want *anyone* to hurt anyone in His name!'

The tittering stopped, and before Johnny could say another word he found himself shooting into the sky, with no sense of how he got out of Tiberius's chamber any more than he had had of getting into it. He was no longer enjoying his flight, but he felt no more fear. The fear of becoming something else, something horrible however attractive or noble to an audience, had been big and hurtful and leading to despair. But that went when he cried for Word. With so big and ugly a fear as that out of the way, what happened outside him could never frighten him so much as what might happen inside him. He remembered Word saying when people complained that his disciples did not observe sufficient rules to keep themselves ritually clean: 'it is what comes from inside that can be most unclean, the evil passions and the urge to follow them'. He was being taken higher and higher into the sky, and the sky was becoming black and stormy, rain beginning to lash his face and his hair. And he heard a voice from one of the titterers hissing venomously 'Now you can see if your Word can save you! He cannot even save himself!'

And he was dropped, falling through the dark wind and rain down, down, down. His first reaction was certainly one of terror, though oddly enough it was followed by a curiously hypnotic feeling that this was what had always been the case, Johnny falling through the air forever, and ever, and ever. But he broke the spell and simply said 'Word, I love you with all my heart and soul'.

And then he heard Word's wonderful voice inside his own head saying: 'I love you, Johnny. All is well. Sleep till I speak to you again.' And the falling sensation ended, and Johnny dropped into a deep, dreamless sleep. He woke many hours later, to hear Word's voice saying 'Johnny, I am here.' The voice was still in Johnny's head, and it quickly added 'Don't speak. Just think. I'm reading your thoughts.' 'I'm shackled above the knee', thought Johnny. 'Not any more', replied Word in his head, and the gyve fell from Johnny's thigh. 'Stand up very slowly', came Word's instruction, 'you could fall down and bring them in on you if you fall. Rub your legs, first the leg which was tied, up and down, a bit harder, get your calf muscle loose again, now try the other leg – '*pull* the other leg?' enquired Johnny impudently. He heard Word laughing inside his head. 'You're as bad as ever you were. And they say that travel broadens the mind! All right, don't start giggling or the captain may decide he isn't ill-treating you sufficiently. You should be able to stand up now. *No*, right, wait a minute, try crawling silently on hands and knees to the flap of the tent. Good. Now stay inside the flap. Don't go out until I say. When I tell you to move, make for the prow, starboard side. I'm waiting down below.' 'Well, seeing that you can walk upon the water', thought Johnny, 'it makes sense that you can stand on it.' 'Quite right. So will you. Vault over the side of the ship and I'll catch you as you come down. Can you stand up without feeling your legs don't belong to you?' 'Yes', thought Johnny, still inside the tent, and then to his horror saw a shadow falling directly on the fragment of flickering light at the tent-flap. It must be Potiphar. In an instant he had pulled back the tent-flap, and Johnny, still only half-upright, head-butted the Egyptian in the solar plexus and shot out of the tent, leaving Potiphar gasping for breath followed by horrendous noises. Johnny skittered down the side of the ship, taking a moment to work out where the prow was and where starboard was. Some torches lit up the deck, unfortunately, and some sailor evidently spotted him and realised that he was too small for Potiphar and that the noises in the tent must *be* Potiphar. A yell went up that the prisoner was escaping, and several bodies moved into position cutting Johnny off from the prow. Johnny marked them, thinking descriptions of their placing for Word's benefit. And Word came back to him, still in his head: 'Fall back behind the tent. Check quickly that there's nobody near you at that point. Nobody there? All in front of you?' ' Yes, and Potiphar is crawling out from the tent, still making horrible noises.' 'Poor Potiphar. Thank goodness I never gave you your head, think what might have happened to me!' This time Johnny did giggle quite loudly, which so startled the sailors lined up and moving towards him that one or two of them stopped in their tracks. '*Now*, Johnny', shouted Word's voice in Johnny's head. 'Between those two on your far left' and Johnny whizzed to the left himself, ran straight for the gap, shot between the two sailors, saw another one ahead of him, feinted a further break to the left and whipped across to the right as his new adversary grabbed at where he wasn't, leaped over some obstacle in his path – a loose sack, in all probability, but filled enough to stand up – half-skidded on the deck so that he almost fell within reach of a huge dark figure ahead of him but managed to throw his own body to the right, whizzed between the last two sailors between him and the prow and heard with delight the sound of their skulls crashing together as they bent down to catch him followed by simultaneous roars of rage and pain, and then, with Johnny's heart thumping like a Roman drummer trying to impress Pontius Pilate, he had launched himself at the ship's rail, got his left hand on it, and vaulted over it yelling 'JEREMIAH!' at the pitch of his lungs. Word asked him afterwards why he had chosen Jeremiah, and Johnny said that he had thought he ought to shout something to show where he was about to come down, and Jeremiah was the first thing that came into his head. 'I suppose', said Word, thoughtfully, 'if you had said "Isaiah, Isaiah, Isaiah" they might have thought you were about to tell a joke.' 'Well', said Johnny, a trifle smugly, 'at least I had the last laugh.'

That came later. As it was, Johnny went sailing over the side of the ship, and began to plunge what was in fact something short of 140 feet. As he went down it occurred to him that the side of a grain-ship should surely bulge out half-way to sea-level, but he was nowhere near it, and in fact he could not make out the ship's outline on his downward flight. He was hindered by nothing until he tumbled into Word's outstretched arms, held out to receive him. 'My little eagle', murmured Word, as Johnny crashed down on his forearms. Word was indeed standing on the water, but Johnny's advent necessarily sent the two of them down below the surface of the sea, so that Word himself was immersed as far as his chin and Johnny's back was drenched. But they were up in a moment, and Word had swung Johnny round so that his arms were around Word's neck and his feet stuck out on either side of him, and so they remained, hugging one another, their tears and laughter intermingling, each of them murmuring the other's name. At last Word put Johnny down on the water beside him, and Johnny took up his accustomed stance with his right hand in Word's left, and suddenly said:

'Where is the ship?'

'Did you want it back for something?' enquired Word, politely.

Johnny gurgled delightedly. 'No, not really, but what happened to it?'

'I blew with my breath', recalled Word judiciously, 'while I was waiting for you to join me. It sheered off, and I must have managed to blow another gust in the form of a parabola because the ship sailed away on course for Rome, or possibly Cumae, at a splendid rate of knots, if that is the term I want, you should know, you've had ever so much more experience in sailing than I have.'

'Or than I want', said Johnny fervently. 'At least outside the Sea of Galilee.'

'I did what I could', continued Word, considerately. 'I thought that since I was doing the captain out of the price of a slave, the least I could do was to send him a gallant wind. That was all I had time to think, because the next moment you evidently felt I was in want of a bath, and obligingly provided one.'

'Did I get you very wet?' asked Johnny in a contrite voice.

'Since you mention it, yes. And we'd better do something about drying before we go down with colds.' It was nice of Word to talk as though he was subject to the same ailments that the rest of humanity was, thought Johnny. Meanwhile Word whistled, high, piercing.

ELEVEN

DEIANERA AND DEIPHOBOS

There was a man sent from God, whose name was John

'Why do you do that?' asked Johnny.

'Well, I would have thought you hardly want to walk home', remarked Word, 'even if the water is gentler underfoot than dusty roads or desert sands. You could probably do with sitting down on the return voyage. My arrangements can't compete with the luxurious quarters as provided for the future slaves of Tiberius, I'm afraid, but you may nevertheless enjoy the novelty of my method of Mediterranean transport.' And in front of him surfaced two large objects. It was a clear, starry night and Johnny with difficulty made them out to be two dolphins. They uttered rapidly modulating whistles and, to Johnny's amazement, Word replied in a similar whistle. Then he spoke again to Johnny:

'This is Deianera, Johnny, and that is Deiphobos. They are Greek dolphins but your Greek may not be sufficient to understand Greek at their pitch, and they only speak a little of it. But they are happy to fall in with my suggestions. Deianera will give you a ride, and Deiphobos will look after me. Just climb up on Deianera's back, holding on to her dorsal fin. That's right. Lean forward. It won't matter if you go to sleep, because I've managed so that you won't fall off, and neither will I. We won't be going fast, just about 150 stades an hour, or five parasangs, if you prefer Persian measurements. I suppose I'd better warn Deianera that you may snore, and that it might sound like the arrival of a low-flying harpy', and he whistled

171

another phrase or two to Johnny's dolphin, who clearly went into a fit of dolphin laughter. Johnny was too tired physically and emotionally to do much more than giggle sleepily at this. It was as though Word's nonsense wrapped itself around him like a comfortable blanket and sent him to sleep almost before he had settled on the soft, flexible skin of Deianera. The sun was high in the heavens by the time he woke. We cannot say whether any passing ship saw the man and the boy on the dolphins, but someone must have done, for the tradition of a boy, and of a man, each on a dolphin, first becomes prominent at this time, and thus must have arisen from Word and Johnny. Nobody knew who they were, and so the story is vaguely taken to be Greek mythology. But the Greek part was Deianera and Deiphobos, and none of it was mythology.

Observers' attention would initially have been drawn by singing. The dolphins' high notes were not in themselves loud enough to alert most auditors, but when supported by Johnny's piercing soprano, and Word's pleasant tenor, there was enough to puzzle a historian. Johnny was tactful enough to clear the subject of musical composition with his marine hosts, and the foursome sang their way along the eastern Mediterranean:

> What's the finest road from Rome?
> Dolphin-riding, dolphin-riding.
> What's the finest way to home?
> Riding on a dolphin!
> Way ho! away we go!
> Dolphin-riding, dolphin-riding.
> Way ho! away we go!
> Riding on a dolphin.
>
> Sailing round the isles of Greece,
> Dolphin-riding, dolphin-riding,
> Where the heroes sleep in peace,
> Riding on a dolphin!
> Calm sea for Odyssey!
> Dolphin-riding, dolphin-riding.
> Calm sea for Odyssey!
> Riding on a dolphin!

The verses were Johnny's, so how did he know what an Odyssey was? We cannot do more than speculate, but Galilee was near enough to Asia Minor and the Ionian isles for versions of Homer's epics to circulate among Syro-Phoenician travellers and hence Jewish fishermen. If Pharisees disapproved of listening to Gentile fairy-tales that would be all the more reason for Johnny to learn them. Word contributed something to Johnny's grasp of Odysseus's adventures, and when Johnny asked how he knew, said he heard it from the dolphins. God of course would know automatically but Johnny accepted it that Word did not use his God-power beyond human possibilities, so while God had known Homer, Word on earth had not.

> Now on Alexander's track
> Dolphin-riding, dolphin-riding,
> Till his conquests broke his back –
> We'll sing on our dolphins!
> With world enough and time,
> Dolphin-riding, dolphin-riding,
> With world enough and time,
> Riding on a dolphin!
>
> Word will reach Jerusalem,
> Dolphin-riding, dolphin-riding,
> Word will reach Jerusalem,
> Riding on a dolphin!
> Then all the palms will wave,
> Dolphin-riding, dolphin-riding,
> Then all the palms will wave,
> While we ride on dolphins!

It was only in retrospect, some time later, that Johnny remembered Word had not joined in the singing of the last verse. He had been fairly preoccupied himself in making up verses that scanned as the dolphins swam along. The dolphins did notice Word's silence for they followed the last verse with a song of their own, high and sweet, and faintly sad. It seemed to have come from somewhere a long way away, Johnny reflected. Nevertheless he liked it, and listened attentively until its many verses were over.

And then Word sang a song of his own, and Johnny realised it was meant for him:

> When all the world is young, lad,
> And all the trees are green;
> And every goose a swan, lad,
> And every lass a queen;
> Then hey for boot and horse, lad,
> And round the world away;
> Young blood must have its course, lad,
> And every dog its day.
>
> When all the world is old, lad,
> And all the trees are brown;
> And all the sport is stale, lad,
> And all the wheels run down;
> Creep home, and take your place there,
> The spent and maimed among:
> God grant you find one face there,
> You loved when all was young.

'Will I?', asked Johnny, simply.

'You will', said Word, equally simply.' The last face you see on earth will be one you loved when all the world was young, even though you won't have seen it for a long time.'

'It will be as you say, Word', answered Johnny. 'It will always be as you say', and he stretched out his right hand, as always, for Word's left, although they could not keep holding hands while the dolphins were forging ahead.

Johnny never forgot what they said, and therefore he never forgot the song that led up to it, but he never repeated that song to anyone, because of Word's promise to which the song brought them, so the song would have perished if Word had not remembered it (whatever hymn-writers imagine, Word remembers everything). And eighteen hundred years later Word put it into the mind of a holy man who very fittingly was writing a book about water-babies, though he had to give him the song in English and not in the original Aramaic. The holy man had a greater heart than head, and wrote it into his book.

Then Word sang Johnny another song, which seemed to arise from the great blue waves and white foam along which they wafted, and the sparkling sunlight turning the sea into endless fragments of gold, and it was also something he would put into the mind of a holy man only a few months after nestling the first song in the mind of the other one, and in the intervening months the two holy men had been fighting because each of them were good and noble followers of Word, but neither thought the other one was, and so each of them wrote with great sincerity about how wrong the other one was, and many other people would go on with the argument after they were both dead (although when the first holy man died the second invoked Word's love for his soul, and the first one would have done the same thing – differently, of course, in form but the same in purpose – if the second holy man had been the first to die). And the song was again made into English by Word, and then made the last part the wonderful dream the holy man was making into a poem telling how Gerontius left this life with an angel telling him:

> Softly and gently, dearly-ransom'd soul,
> In my most loving arms I now enfold thee,
> And, o'er the penal waters, as they roll,
> I poise thee, and I lower thee, and hold thee.
>
> And carefully I dip thee in the lake,
> And thou, without a sob or a resistance,
> Dost through the flood thy rapid passage take,
> Sinking deep, deeper, into the dim distance.
>
> Angels, to whom the willing task is given,
> Shall tend, and nurse, and lull thee, as thou liest;
> And Masses on the earth, and prayers in heaven,
> Shall aid thee at the throne of the Most Highest.

Farewell, but not for ever! brother dear,
Be brave and patient on thy bed of sorrow;
Swiftly shall pass thy night of trial here,
And I will come and wake thee on the morrow.

We know more of what Word's singing sounded like, because music can make us hear him clearer than our words can, but how I explain what it seemed to a little boy riding on a dolphin listening to God singing words in music which would be composed to carry the words thirty-five years after they had been written and the music as sublime for words in English as it had been for words in Aramaic, ending perfectly what the composer would begin on his own (or nearly). I don't need to explain it, since all you have to do is to think of the sea, and the dolphins, and the man who was God, and the boy who loved him, and the two holy men nearly two thousand years later understanding each other at last when they had the good fortune to be dead, one with a name like unto a king and the other that of a man reborn, and both of them loving Word and quite unable to see how much the other one did, until good fortune came to them. And we can be equally grateful for what they left us, as wonderful now as when Johnny first heard it on the Mediterranean Sea, except that we cannot see Word singing it, yet.

Johnny would have been very badly sunburnt from the dazzling light on the water but when he woke up on Deianera's back he found he was covered from neck to ankles in silk tunic and trousers, with a wide hood over his head and shoulders. The trousers seemed to shrink and stretch depending on how much of his legs came near the water, but they never got wet. Most of his own clothes had been torn off during his journey before Word rescued him, leaving him only a loin-cloth by the time Word called him to begin the return journey. He noticed Word was dressed much the same as himself, but more so, being a foot taller, but it didn't seem important to ask how their clothes had got on to their bodies or where they had come from. After seeing five thousand people filling their bellies to their utmost satisfaction on five loaves and two fishes what was a silk garment or two? Equally, neither Word nor he went hungry. Fish flew out of the water into Word's hands, were still and apparently dead before reaching them, were held by Word for a minute or two and then passed to

Johnny, or eaten by Word himself, and tasted better than any meal Johnny could remember. They did need to stretch their legs now and again, and the dolphins would stop, while Johnny and Word walked up and down holding hands. They landed on one or two islands, one of which was inhabited, but somehow nobody saw them. Johnny remembered that Word had been able to escape from the lynch-mob in Nazareth simply by denying them the ability to see him any more, and he supposed that he would confer that power on a companion if necessary just as he made it possible for Johnny to walk on the water with him. Johnny only remembered the name of one of the islands afterwards, partly because Word gave him a wry little grin when pronouncing it: 'Patmos'.

Of course Johnny wanted to know how Word knew where Johnny was, and asked how he knew. 'Or would you have known anyway, being God?' he asked.

Rather to his surprise Word said 'No, I didn't know, until I heard from you. You see, I had to empty myself to become one of you, and while faith gives me certain powers anything I can do for anyone else they have to want me to do, for love.'

'For love of you?'

'Not necessarily. That widow's son at Nain had never heard of me, so far as I know, when he died. But he died loving his mother and wanting somehow to save her from the mortal hurt he was giving her when he died. And her love for him was a generous love, wanting to make him grow and radiate goodness in his own surroundings, not a thing of selfishness which only imagines it is love.'

'But I never stopped loving you.'

'But you had been knocked out by the soldiers and were being kept unconscious by drugs, cutting you off from any way of communicating. You hardly knew who you were when I finally got through, although what got me through to you was when in that dream you spoke my name, and then when you showed you had learned the lesson that I would never have anyone injure others in my name – or at all – and most important of all when you cried that you loved me. That is always the way to reach me, and the way I can reach you.'

'But I was in a dream.'

Word smiled, with the left corner of his mouth a little crooked. They were half turned to one another now as they talked while the dolphins rode onward. 'Dreams are strange things, Johnny, and we sometimes have some control of them, especially if we are near wakening. They can express very truly what we really want to do and what we really believe, however strange they are. Once you spoke my name, that opened your mind for me to see and hear and when you called me that you loved me, that gave me the way to you.'

'Those Things – did you know about them? They came from It, I suppose?'

Word's face was dark. 'They came from It.' Then he laughed. 'But you showed you knew how to control a dream with my name. They wanted – It wanted to hurt me through you. And now It knows It can never do that with you. It can hurt me through my love for everyone else, but never again through you, and never through Mother. Thank you, Johnny.'

Johnny's eyes shone. 'I've been able to do something.'

'You've been able to do something.'

'It doesn't seem much.'

'It is everything.'

Johnny rode on in happy silence. Word rode alongside him. They did not even need to touch hands.

'How did you first find out that I was gone?'

'When we found Judas.'

'What did he say?'

'Nothing first of all. He was dead. I revived him. You know he did not like you, and thought I was silly and sentimental to include you among my twelve. He gave his life for you.'

'He what?'

'He gave his life for you, threw himself on the soldiers who had blackjacked you, all by himself instead of rousing others to what was happening, apparently convinced that if he didn't fight for you, you would be kidnapped for good. And he was right. We have to be ready to lay down our lives for people we don't like. Most people would be ready enough to do it for those they do love. Mothers, for instance, do it all the time for their children, when you think about it.'

'And we have to be ready to lay down our lives for people who don't like us', said Johnny, a shade contritely as he remembered why he and Judas had begun to dislike one another.

'You will like him now', reflected Word, not as a command.

'I certainly will', responded Johnny fervently. 'Was he badly hurt?'

'He was killed quickly, as far as I could see, and so would have suffered greatly but briefly. He seems practically to have thrown himself on the sword of one of the soldiers while trying to get your body away from him. It was as though he was careless of what pain might be inflicted on his body in his anxiety to do what is right. He is impulsive. So are you.'

'I'm learning.'

'You will find it easier to learn, at your age. He'll be ready to be friends now, but don't expect too much. After all, you're the one who needs to express gratitude.'

'I will.'

'I know you will. Remember, he's had very little love in his life, and you've had a great deal, from many people.'

'How is James?'

'Nearly out of his mind with worry, initially. I had to make him sleep. But they were all very upset about you, wondering where you were and how we would get you back: Peter, Nat, Andrew, Thomas.'

'Andrew!'

'Andrew was really upset, all the more because you had grown a little apart from one another. He kept on remembering what you were like before I arrived.' Word grinned. 'I was very good, and did not ask if it was all my fault.'

Johnny laughed. 'No, but it's partly mine.'

'And Philip kept on saying "What will Miriam say?"'

'I never realised he even noticed her.'

'Well, he did. Eventually I got them to let me go on alone once we reached the sea. Peter, of course, wanted to go with me, but I pointed out to him that James needed his support and vigilance, and he must take my place in looking after James. Andrew will look after everyone else.'

'Did they realise why I had been kidnapped?'

'Did you?' Word was looking grim.

'Something about Tiberius the Emperor wanting certain kinds of slave, I couldn't quite see what in particular they thought I might be good at. It seems to have been work as a courtier of some kind, and I don't imagine soldiers know much about the work for which courtiers are fitted.'

'They see enough when they are on duty in royal courts. Courts are horrible places, Johnny, as my father remarked to Samuel when the Jews said they wanted a king. Those are places where people spend their time exploiting others instead of producing anything of value themselves. They spend their time flattering people, backbiting people, hurting people, dishonoring people, starving people, killing people. Provinces are reduced to famine so that some courtier can make a splash with his lavish clothes and parties. And people try to own others, body and soul, own every bit of them to do what they like with. Tiberius would have owned you, and your only way of freedom would have been to get ahead yourself by exploiting others in the same way. One of these people will kill Tiberius in the end, finding more chance of advancement with another master.'

'Or trying to become Emperor themselves.'

'Ah, you saw that in your dream. Thank God you said no to it, Johnny. It looks like the ultimate in luxury and power, and it is the abomination of desolation. Judas was absolutely clear in his mind why they wanted to enslave you, to make you an imperial creature. He's learned a little about such places, and he had thought a great deal about the conditions in Herod's court when his first Master, my cousin John, was a prisoner there. No wonder John hated such places so much.'

Johnny shivered violently. This time Word did stretch out his hand and held Johnny's.

'Thank God I have you.'

'Thank God you do. But everyone has me. I only wish they realised it. Even Tiberius, God save us and guard us.'

'Bless you, Word.'

'Bless you, Johnny.'

'I want to sing blessings on you', said Johnny with the eagerness of a ship leaving a storm.

'And so you shall. But it occurs to me, since we were thinking about my cousin John the Baptizer, that you are not yet John the Baptized.' Johnny screwed up his face. 'I never thought about it, but no, I'm not. Are the others?'

'I think all of them.'

'Did you baptise them?'

'No, I've never baptised anyone.'

'Who did, then?'

'Andrew and Judas. Having been trained by my cousin John it was the natural thing for them to do. Naturally the others asked me, and I certainly had no objection.'

'Where did they do it?'

'In our Sea of Galilee.'

'Why didn't they do me?'

Word drew his lips to the left, a little quizzically. 'It's a matter of confidence. My cousin John baptised many people because they had confidence in him, and in what he was saying about the Redeemer coming.' (Johnny looked up, a little startled, never having heard Word refer to himself like that before.) 'You were not on terms of confidence with Judas, or even Andrew, when they began to talk about it, after we heard what happened to my cousin John. Both sides need to have it, and you would no more have been ready to accept baptism from Judas than he would have been to offer it to you. If Andrew had been baptising on his own, he would probably have asked you, and you would probably have said yes. But Judas was there, and so, partly because of loyalty, and partly because of the lack of confidence, you were not asked. The two of them began to get worried about whether it was right to baptise children.'

'Children have as much of a right to be baptized as anyone else', said Johnny indignantly.

'Spoken with all the God-given right of a boy who had never thought about it for a moment until you heard others had been given it and you had not.'

Johnny was about to roar a protest, and then swung round to catch Word laughing at him. That made him laugh at himself.

'No, but seriously, Word. Why shouldn't I have it?'

'Well, why should you?'

'Because the others have.'

'That's not a reason, or at least not a good one.'

Johnny paused, and the dolphins swam on. They seemed to be listening, although Johnny never solved the problem of what they were listening with. Johnny drew back his head and scrunched his skull into his neck. Then he scratched the lower back of his skull.

'Because it's a way of showing we are your people. That's what your cousin John' (Johnny gave great pride in pronouncing John) 'wanted everyone to be.' Word smiled at him. 'You have it now. And of course I want children to be my people. They understand so much about me as it is.'

Johnny wrinkled his nose. 'I've even seen babies looking as if they understand about you.' Word nodded. 'The blessings we receive from babies are wondrous blessings. And they do it so well.'

'But your mother hasn't been baptised. And nobody could be one of your people more than she.'

'Mother has been baptised. She had become one of my people from the moment that she told God she would do as he asked and bear me as her son. But when I went into the desert to pray and fast and repel It, John came to Nazareth to stay with her and baptized her there, at the well.'

'With everyone looking on?'

'Oh, he baptised them too. They were all women, or almost all. Oh, and Thomas, who naturally argued about it in advance and then thought it was a good idea when he heard I had been baptised. He said that if I was one of my people, then he was too. You can't beat Thomas for logic.'

'You can not', said Johnny, who had tried.

'So, you want to be baptized. Well, I haven't done it, but I should be able to manage. Do you reject It?'

'You know I do.'

'I know now you do. And all Its works.'

'And all Its works.' 'And all Its pomps.'

'And all Its pomps. What are pomps, Word?'

Word made a face. 'Imperial purple robes, maybe. And false gods, including emperors. And worship of earthly power. And killings, and stealings, and lies, and stealing other men's wives and husbands.'

Johnny was shocked. 'I wouldn't steal anyone's wife or husband. What would I want them for, anyway?'

'Just as Andrew and Judas have to learn to accept children and try to understand the blessings they can give and the dangers that may await them, you have to understand grown-ups.'

'That doesn't mean I have to behave like them.'

'Certainly not in the bad things they do. You remember that Herod stole his brother's wife, and she stole him from whoever was married to him at the time.'

'But I'd never carry on like Herod.'

'No, but you were tempted to carry on like Tiberius. You were too sensible to yield, but you were tempted.'

'I wasn't sensible', said Johnny firmly. 'I just knew I couldn't become Tiberius, because I love you.'

'That is being sensible', said Word, affectionately. 'Now, I will seal you of the tribe, baptizing you with water.'

'What shall we do for water?' asked Johnny, innocently. Word let out a hoot of laughter, and the dolphins echoed him.

'There's quite a lot of it around', said Word, mildly. 'You are ready to receive baptism?'

'Yes', said Johnny.

'We need a witness.'

'You are the witness', pointed out Johnny.

'Very well. The celebrant can also be the witness. Now, Johnny, I stand with you' (the dolphins stopped, and Word slipped off Deiphobos, on the side nearer to Johnny) 'and I promise with you that you will reject the Prince of this World, and that you wish to be sealed of my tribe. You receive the water.'

At that point Deianera dived into the sea with Johnny still on her back, and came up rapidly with Johnny spluttering and gurgling. He climbed off Deianera and faced Word, who was grinning at him. So Johnny, who had momentarily been furious, laughed.

'It might be as well to have a little salt on your tongue', said Word, thoughtfully.

'I already have', said Johnny forcefully. He spat out some seawater.

'In that case', said Word, 'I suppose you might fall on your knees – on your knees', for Johnny was showing signs of tumbling into a sitting position but managed to twist himself so that he knelt before Word. Word raised his hand and touched Johnny on his head, eyes, and tongue and said 'I baptize you, Johnny, in the name of the Father and of the Son and of the Holy Spirit', and Johnny said 'Amen', and Word hugged Johnny and kissed him, and the two dolphins seemed to echo Johnny's 'Amen', and they climbed on again and the dolphins forged onward.

Johnny said nothing for about five minutes, and then said 'That was wonderful, Word'.

And Word said 'especially when you got the water outside you rather than inside you'.

And Johnny said 'and I am yours for always and always'. And Word said 'and you are mine for always and always'.

Johnny's clothes and his skin seemed to have dried very rapidly, almost without his realising it. Maybe the silk had that property from the first, or maybe Word had told it to dry. Somewhere at the back of his mind Johnny remembered that Peter had little sign of damp on his garments on board ship after he had tried to walk on the water like Word and had lost faith in himself and began to sink. But Johnny thought little about being wet – certainly much less than he would have done if he had stayed wet. He simply felt utter physical happiness inside and out. He was to baptize many people in the course of his life, and always told them there was no happiness equal to baptism, adding silently 'for you' since for Johnny happiness was a permanent condition of being with Word. Baptism had simply found a higher altitude, and on that plateau Johnny stayed, until they reached Jerusalem and the bad things began to happen. But now, as the dolphins thrust forward, and the wind ruffled Johnny's hair and Word's too, and the sky competed with the sea in the beauty of its blue, Johnny began to sing. The sun was not too warm nor the water too wet nor Deianera too hard, but the song Johnny sang was what was sung by Ananias, Azarias and Mizael (NOT to be called Shadrach, Mishach and Abednego except by Word when pulling Johnny's leg) as they walked around inside the fiery furnace into which Nebuchadnezzar had thrust them.

'O all you works of the Lord, O bless the Lord', sang Johnny, and Word gravely replied 'To him be highest glory and praise forever.'

'And you, angels of the Lord, O bless the Lord', continued Johnny, confident rather than impudent in his instruction of angels, and Word responded 'To him be highest glory and praise for ever' but then took up the next line 'And you, the heavens of the Lord, O bless the Lord', and Johnny answered, automatically looking up at the faint white threads at the remote edge of the sky 'And you, clouds of the sky, O bless the Lord', and Word continued, familiarly speaking to invisible people who seemed there when spoken to, 'And you, all armies of the Lord, O bless the Lord', and Johnny: 'To him be highest glory and praise for ever'.

The Mediterranean undulated in its encircling omnipresence but as Johnny looked up the sky seemed to dwarf the watery counterpart, in its centre the pitiless orb no man could face, but –

'And you, sun and moon, O bless the Lord', sang Johnny, and Word, seeming to build on top of the sky Johnny had summoned, called back.

'And you, the stars of the heavens, O bless the Lord', giving Johnny a sense of comradeship with the heavenly bodies which would make it so much worse on the day when the sky turned black. But today Johnny's own discomfort was limited to a faint thirst, if anything quenched by his 'And you, showers and rain, O bless the Lord', and Word drew all together with 'To him be highest glory and praise for ever', and a little, unspeakably welcome, breeze flickered around them as Word went on 'And you, all you breezes and winds, O bless the Lord', and Johnny slipped in his 'And you, fire and heat, O bless the Lord', and Word, seeming again to build with one of Johnny's bricks and one of his own followed: 'And you, cold and heat, O bless the Lord', and Johnny, rejoicing in being so near his target, shot his arrow 'To him be highest glory and praise for ever.'

And now it was for Johnny to lead once more, with a land-line 'And you, showers and dew, O bless the Lord', taken up by Word 'And you, frosts and cold, O bless the Lord', answered by Johnny 'And you, frost and snow, O bless the Lord', and once again Word seemed to weave the blessings into one: 'To him be highest glory and praise for ever.'

'And you, night-time and day', continued Word, 'O bless the Lord', and Johnny had never felt such friendship in the idea of night before, and answered 'And you, darkness and light, O bless the Lord' and Word took it up, apparently asserting its logical follow-up 'And you lightnings and clouds, O bless the Lord', which they must have done so far above as to be out of sight, thought Johnny thankfully while affirming 'To him be highest glory and praise for ever.'

And then both voices in unison thrilled gigantically 'O let the earth bless the Lord', and, above them both Johnny could hear Deianera and Deiphobos in high notes soaring to join the response 'To him be highest glory and praise for ever'. And now it was Johnny once more calling to the heights above and below the water 'And you, mountains and hills, O bless the Lord', and Word almost as though he was making them grow under his gaze came back 'And you, all plants of the earth, O bless the Lord', and Johnny half-wondering if the sea made its mountains and when they were most like land counterparts 'And you, fountains and springs, O bless the Lord', capped by Word 'To him be highest glory and praise for ever'.

Word opened his arms in welcome to the Mediterranean, as he sang 'And you rivers and seas, O bless the Lord', but Johnny paused to let the dolphins cry what was surely 'And you, creatures of the sea, O bless the Lord', to come in himself on 'And you, every bird in the sky, O bless the Lord', and in obedience a great gull came squawking triumphantly as it wheeled over Word whose smile did not impair his 'And you, wild beasts and tame, O bless the Lord' and all four of them united 'To him be highest glory and praise for ever.'

Johnny drew a deep breath, but before he could chip in with his next bit, Word sang it, and Johnny mentally agreed it came better from him:

'And you, children of men, O bless the Lord', since he was both inside and outside them, thought Johnny as he replied 'To him be highest glory and praise for ever', and then himself sang 'O Israel, bless the Lord, O bless the Lord', and Word, with a slightly grim tightness in his face answered

'And you, priests of the Lord, O bless the Lord', and Johnny proudly proclaimed his own status from Khirber Qana onward 'And you, servants of the Lord, O bless the Lord', and Word raised his open palms

'To him be highest glory and praise for ever'.

Word drew his next command in a great sigh, almost expelling the entirety of his lungs, 'And you, spirits and souls of the just, O bless the Lord', and Johnny, comfortably and almost snugly came back 'And you, holy and humble of heart, O bless the Lord', and Word, in all ways word-perfect, addressed 'Ananias, Azarias, Misael, O bless the Lord', as though he had never teased Johnny with Shadrach, Mishach, and Abednego, and Johnny crowned all with 'To him be highest glory and praise for ever', and the four of them raised a great shout of joy ringing out over the Mediterranean.

They went onward in a grateful silence for many minutes, but at last Johnny asked Word for a story, and Word promptly began 'Once upon a time there was a man with two sons', at which Johnny looked a trifle uneasy, all the more when Word continued 'and got on well with both, who worked hard with him in his fields, and he prospered, and had many servants, and one day's work followed another, until the younger suddenly said "I don't want to wait for your inheritance until you are dead",' and Johnny exclaimed in disgust and Word raised his eyebrows and went on, telling how the younger demanded his half of what would come to him when his father died, and his father handed it out without a word. And Johnny said 'there had been no quarrel, nor any hard words between them?: and Word said, no, not at all, and the younger son had been perfectly polite although businesslike. The elder said nothing, continued Word, although he looked as if he could say a great deal if he liked. Anyhow his father made it clear that all that was left belonged to the elder, apart from what the land required, and the servants' wages demanded, and the food they all needed to eat would cost. 'Was it the same?' asked Johnny. 'It looked the same', said Word thoughtfully, 'but when a few days later the younger son translated all his inheritance into money, meaning a part of the land had to be sold, it might seem he had even more than his fair share. Anyhow, he went into a far country.' 'Like Italy?' asked Johnny, 'I shouldn't wonder', answered Word, wryly 'and there he wasted his substance, living riotously.' 'Doing what?' asked Johnny. 'The feasts and banquets he gave to whole cities in the far country, the costs of Persian rarities, and of Egyptian cooks to dress them, the expenses of men and singing women' – 'couldn't he sing for himself, and save money?' asked Johnny indignantly – 'like us', murmured Word demurely, 'no, he couldn't, when people have money they forget the value of what else they have, and there were also the costs of the musical instruments, the flute, the harp, the sackbut, the shrill squealing of the wry-necked fife' – 'what is a fife?' demanded Johnny 'be glad you don't know', said Word, comfortingly, 'it hasn't been invented yet, so you can imagine how expensive that made it'. Johnny spluttered in reproach but Word continued firmly 'all kinds of music, and then he had to dress for these occasions, and favoured the dress of Persian courts, how magnificent! their slaves how numerous – their chariots, their horses, their palaces, their furniture, what immense sums they had devoured! –what expectations from strangers of condition! what exactions! and then he was cheated at Damascus by one of the best men in the world, as he told himself.' 'If he was that good why was he a cheat?' snorted Johnny. 'Because in that world men they call good are those who are the most successful cheats – and he lent a part of his substance to a friend at Nineveh, who had fled off with it to the Ganges' – 'the end of the world?' gasped Johnny – 'certainly a long way from debtpaying', nodded Word, 'and then a wicked lady from Babylon swallowed his best pearl to show how far she was above such things, for wickedness has its austerity no less than virtue. And he had anointed the whole city with his balm of Gilead.' 'Which was the city?' demanded Johnny. 'It doesn't have to be any one city', said Word, 'that's what your imagination is for, it could be Rome, or Damascus, or Nineveh, or Babylon.' 'Or Jerusalem', reflected Johnny. 'That's true', said Word, as if he had only just thought of it. 'It might even have been Jerusalem.'

'And when he had spent all', continued Word, having satiated Johnny with the prodigal's extravaganza, 'there came a mighty famine in that country, and he began to be in want. And he sought service with a local citizen who sent him into his fields to feed swine. And he would fain have filled his belly with the husks that the swine did eat: and no man gave unto him.' 'How appalling!' breathed Johnny. 'The cruelty of the country's people?' asked Word. 'It is what you get in a land which lived only for pleasure and was then faced with hunger.' 'No', said Johnny, 'it was the thought of him living among pigs and wanting to eat what they ate. Unclean animals!' 'There are worse things', said Word, 'and famine and foolishness drive many people to horrible extremities. Eventually he got back some little of his lost balance, and thought how well his father had treated his own servants in comparison to this. "How many hired servants of my father's have bread enough and to spare, and I perish with hunger! I will arise and go to my father and will say unto him 'Father, I have sinned against Heaven and before thee.'"' 'So he was sorry for wanting the pig-feed', nodded Johnny. 'No doubt', grinned Word cheerfully, 'but he was probably thinking of sins he had committed when he had the money to commit them. Expensive sins, in all senses.' 'Sins Tiberius and his court would have the money to commit?' reflected Johnny. 'That kind', said Word. 'So he decided to tell his father "I am no more worthy to be called thy son: make me as one of thy hired servants."' 'His father wouldn't want his servants living among pigs either, or eating their food', insisted Johnny. 'His father might have kept pigs like that man in Gergesa', Word pointed out. 'He wouldn't have kept them long if you were around the place', Johnny pointed back. 'The Gergasa pigs aren't the only things likely to find themselves in deep water', said Word grimly. 'I have every reliance on Deianera's ability to dive whenever I want and if there is one more crack like that, I will want.' Johnny laughed happily and kept quiet while the story went on.

It was one of the marvels of Word's storytelling that his voice seemed to surround his hearers with the landscape or surroundings he described. Now Johnny could see the wretched swineherd padding his half-naked, filthy person through a barren land and its blighted vineyards. The long road mocked its traveller, and the dust befouled him further and settled deep in his lungs. Blisters arose on his heels and dogs barked their passing contempt. All that kept him going was the thought of winning back the thinnest edge of his father's world, and strangely, however thirsty and hungry he became, stealing figs and slurping fugitive streams as his maximum food and drink, he thought more and more of his father and less and less of his comfort. The last stretch of the road came, that white prospect winding its way from his father's door down which he paraded so long ago on an opulent Arab steed, and now it mocked him down its pitiless length, stones bruising any remaining soft parts of his feet. 'But while he was still a long way off', continued the music of Word's voice, 'his father saw him, and *he* had pity, and the footsore reprobate saw the old man running towards him, shouting for servants to follow, galloping the last of the yards separating him from his son so dazed at the sight of his father's approach that his tortured progress was at a standstill. And the father ran up, threw his arms around the son's neck, and kissed him. And the son, stammering through his sobbing, cried "Father, I have sinned against Heaven and before thee, I am not worthy now to be called thy son" to which his father replied with a shout to the servants hurrying up behind him "Bring out the best robe, and clothe him in it, put a ring on his hand, and shoes on his feet, bring out the calf that has been fattened and kill it, let us eat, and make merry, for my son here was dead, and has come to life again, was lost, and is found".' And Word's voice fluctuated magnificently between the snivelling tones of the repentant prodigal and the exultation of the rejoicing old man. But as Word turned the story to the elder son, tired but virtuous, suddenly confronted on his return home after a day's honest toil with sounds of music and dancing, a new tone sounded stronger than his brother or father, yet with a growing petulance from which a child's tears were not far away. "'Think how many years I have lived as thy servant'" – Word managed to endow the elder brother with possession of the status for which his exiled brother yearned, as if he had heard the prodigal's prayer from afar off – '"never transgressing thy commands, and thou has never made me a present of a kid, to make merry with my friends, and now, when this son of thine has come home, one that has swallowed up his share of your money in the company of women selling themselves, thou has killed the fattened calf in his honour"', and Word made his wail of bitterness rise to the skies. And he ended on the blessing of the old man's forgiveness to both his sons, telling the elder '"My son, thou art always at my side, and everything that I have is already thine, but for this merry-making and rejoicing there was good reason, thy brother here was dead, and has come to life again, was lost, and is found."'

Johnny exhaled a long sight of satisfaction. 'It is wonderful to think of that forgiveness awaiting us however low we sink.' 'It is', said Word, 'but that is not the part of the story that is really important for you.' 'Well, what part is?' asked Johnny, puzzled. 'The elder brother, Johnny. Forgiving those whom your father forgives can be the hardest task of all. You have shown there is little danger of your making a fool of yourself like the prodigal son. But I would not want my friends to have hearts harder than mine or my father's. You must embrace those who have risen from the deaths into which they sank themselves. And it will not be easy.' 'I thought you meant I was the Prodigal Son', said Johnny, 'and that I had wasted your patrimony to me when I wanted you to destroy the Samaritan town.' 'I think that would have to be the elder son', said Word. 'The younger brother is self-destructive, the older one is punitive, perhaps self-destructive in that refusing mercy destroys the one who cannot forgive. But the prodigal son betrays his father in turning away from him, and it might be that the elder son finds it hardest to forgive that betrayal. Some day you may have to forgive as many as eleven brothers for betraying me. And be sure you do.' Johnny looked across at him in amazement. Word laughed. The dolphins made shrill sounds of agreement, and as their music ascended to Heaven Johnny wondered if the noise of angels would strike the human ear to seem like that.

WELVE

MARY, MARTHA, LAZARUS

The same came for a witness, to bear witness of the Light

Deianera and Deiphobos, guided by Word, landed them a few miles south of Joppa, not far from a village where the other eleven were waiting. Johnny hated saying goodbye to the dolphins, all the more because they had meant his having Word to himself amid company but without rival humans. He crushed any thought of wanting to delay meetings with the others, above all James, but also Peter, with whom he now held real comradeship, and Andrew, whom he was so anxious to keep as a friend, and Judas, who was to be a new friend, clearly. The dolphins were no substitutes for them, but offered a different kind of friendship, something much more than a bird or beast could do and something with its own integrity. Their confidence in speaking to Word had much to do with it. He was so obviously theirs, and they were his. They seemed ready to be Johnny's, too, older and wiser, perhaps, but generous in affection. He wondered if he would ever see them again. He did, some years later, when a message from Word sent him back to the coast where he had last seen them, and they carried Word's mother Mary and Johnny to Ephesus.

Johnny was still choked by his farewells to the dolphins as Word and he turned their backs on the Mediterranean having seen Deianera and Deiphobos head off to the West. He kept his right band in Word's left as they made their way to the marketplace where they were to meet the others at some point in daytime. The eleven were to take turns making

191

sure two of them were always to be found there while sunlight lasted. As it happened, James and Judas were the two on duty when Word and Johnny reached the village. Johnny realised that James had probably spent all of his waking hours there waiting for his errant brother, and like a sensible lad threw himself into James's arms at once and let himself cry and laugh to their hearts' content. Eventually James, with a rather forced grin, said 'You great nuisance, we will never be rid of you', and Johnny kissed him and said 'Not so long as I have anything to do with it', and Word came up with Judas, so Johnny sensibly jumped at Judas's neck, pulled his head down, kissed him and said 'thank you for giving your life for me, dear Judas', and Judas, blushing red, but looking very glad, said that it was nothing, and managed to add that he wasn't going to let those dirty Romans kidnap a comrade, and the shy smile with which he said it made it easy for Johnny to look forward to a real friendship building between them. James added that nothing must cause argument between them again.

Becoming friends with Judas was easy in some ways, hard in others. Johnny worked at it very openly so that Peter was surprised, Andrew pleased, James approving, Philip inquisitive, Nat philosophical, Matthew auditory, Thomas sceptical, Jim philanthropic, Thady optimistic, Shimon collegial and Word benign. Johnny would draw Judas out on the history and customs of Judaea, where they were going but which few of them apart from Judas really knew. All except Johnny had made visits to the Holy City of Jerusalem, but on the whole they had little sense of it apart from the magnificence of the Temple, and their journeys had been as part of Galilean pilgrimages. Judas had spent several years in the city, had a Judaean accent and would have carried more street credibility if there had been any streets in which to be credible, which there would be in Jerusalem and Jericho but not much between Joppa and the great city. They stopped at Lydda which gave itself urban airs. Johnny didn't much care for it. He heard several derisive reference to their company as Galileans, something Word had evidently expected since he put Judas in charge of the funds and payments which meant their negotiator would be identified with Judaea. The Lyddans probably had inferiority complexes about neither having the maritime perspective of Joppa nor the sacred metropolitanism of Jerusalem or the pride in being gateway to the east as Jericho liked to think of itself, and Judas tried to persuade Johnny that

Lyddan airs and graces were simply self-defence against having so little in themselves. More and more, Judas became identified with Judaea in Johnny's mind. It was a way to make Judaea more palatable, to think of it not as an alien land but as the embodiment of a friend. After all, if you imagine a hostile country has actually saved your life at the cost of its own, you don't mind its snootiness so much. Not that Judas himself was snooty. If anything, he was so grateful for Johnny's gratitude and so pleased to have made his first child friend, that he was in danger of spoiling Johnny rotten. He would try to save enough from his allowance to give Johnny some special sweetmeat, and go hungry himself so that the boy would have small luxuries. He was shy about admitting it, and when Johnny asked him where he got the money to make such gifts would joke that he had stolen it from the common purse he was guarding. He didn't realise that Johnny didn't understand that kind of joke, and felt awkward that Judas was stealing on Johnny's behalf and yet did not want to worry Word about it, or cause trouble when Judas was trying to be so kind. Probably the best thing to do would be to discuss it with Word in a way that would be friendly to Judas, when whatever the trouble Word seemed to be anticipating in Jerusalem was over.

Everybody would have been ready to spoil Johnny after his return from what seemed a hopeless disappearance, but only Judas had funds and so the thought of luxuries didn't cross their minds. Judas knowing so little about children seemed to feel he had to buy Johnny's friendship or at least consolidate it with gifts, so he gave himself a priority in treating Johnny which the Galileans would have thought quite unnecessary. Johnny initially didn't worry too much about it, although later on he realized that Judas's joke – which Johnny thought a confession – should have bothered him more than it did. There was another factor Johnny never realised. What Judas knew about evil conduct in court circles and city self-indulgence made him suspect that Johnny had been worse treated by his kidnappers on land and sea than in fact he was, and he wanted to keep Johnny from brooding about horrible things that might have been done to him or that he might have been threatened with. Judas was very careful never to talk about such things to Johnny, believing that the sooner Johnny could forget or distance himself from any horrors he had suffered, the better. But Judas had known a lot about strange doings in court and city, and had fled to the Jordan and become a disciple of John the Baptizer in his revulsion from them. He was in fact the only one of the twelve who had sought out his spiritual leader because of things which had happened to him, rather than because Word looked at him (as had happened in different ways to Johnny, Peter, James, Phil, Nat, Matt) or because of hearing him (as had happened to Jim, Thady, Shimon), or because he had known him and joined up at disciple-gathering time (Thomas) or simply because of what John the Baptizer had told him (Andrew). Judas had been like Andrew in following Word after listening to John the Baptizer, but Andrew had gone to John the Baptizer from spiritual interest, not because of any rejection of Galilee or even fishing, while Judas's flight to John had been emotional rather than intellectual. Andrew liked enquiry for its own sake, perhaps more objectively than Philip but with the same Greek-style thirst for knowledge and wisdom; Judas was more like a hurt animal trying to find safety. They all loved Word, but Judas's love of Word was more like Johnny's and Peter's than was the love of any of the rest, like a child's whom Word had saved from harm. Of course Thomas had loved Word before any of them, and had loved him as a child, but thought of him with the pleasure of an old companion whose friendship had proved alive and strong after all those years, not as a Saviour. All of them would come to think of Word as Saviour, but only Johnny, Judas and Peter did so now. Judas, the most experienced of the three, was the only one to have worked this out, although Johnny naturally saw that Word must mean more to Judas after bringing him back to life. Johnny didn't think Word could ever mean more to him than he had from the first, but in one vital way he did: Johnny would never again doubt Word's unending love for him after the rescue from the Romans. The logic in Peter was less obvious, but it had a lot to do with fish, and with his mother-in-law.

Johnny enjoyed the stories Judas told about life in Jerusalem, unaware of Judas's care in selecting the right kind to tell, or that Judas had gone into the matter with Word who certainly did not want to add to Judas's anxieties but who agreed with him about the things not to be told to Johnny. Johnny as an audience did Judas good, since Johnny could always see the funny side of things, and Judas was often pleased to find bits of his stories which Johnny showed him were funny. Things that frightened Judas Johnny also thought funny. For instance on the journey from Lydda they were hailed by a group of richly-dressed courtiers who stopped them on the road and evidently recognised Word from descriptions or because he led twelve disciples, one a boy, and their spokesman oiled his way in front of them (as Judas remarked later) and said 'Peace be upon you' in a voice sounding as if he was selling them spikenard, thought Johnny, but Word said imperturbably 'and to you, peace' and the oilman (as Johnny called him, answering Judas) asked if he had the honour to be in the presence of the famous Jesus of Nazareth, managing to make Nazareth sound like a social solecism, and Word said, yes he was, and the oilman said, he brought Word greetings from his master the noble Herod, who would dearly like to meet him at his palace in Machaerus, not a long way from here, and Word without a flicker to show he knew the man spoke of the place where John the Baptizer was killed said he was sure the tetrarch would like to see him there.

'We have all kinds of interesting visitors', went on the oilman.

'And you entertain them in an interesting way', said Word.

'With music', said the oilman.

'And dancing', said Word.

'Yaas, yaas' agreed the oilman. 'Though I am surprised at so holy a man as you taking pleasure in dancing.'

'It may be better to take pleasure in dancing than to take pleasure in the dancer', said Word inflexibly.

'Such pleasures do not last long' and the oilman raised his eyes piously.

'Or live long' agreed Word.

'Nothing', smarmed the oilman as though he was trying to seem hypocritical, 'nothing could give me greater pleasure than to see you in the hospitable hands of Herod.' It was amusing, thought Johnny, that he could sound as if he never meant a word he said while clearly wishing very much indeed that Word was in the hospitable hands of Herod, with the executioner of John the Baptizer front and centre stage. (Johnny did not think in theatrical terms as a rule, but the story of Salome always seemed to him like a play.)

'I have no doubt of it', replied Word, with a faint curl of his upper lip.

'But if we cannot persuade you to give Herod the privilege of your presence presently, do us the profound honour of answering a theological quandary of mine. We know you are true, and teach the way of God in truth, nor do you hold any person in awe not seeing any distinction between man and man, even those of the utmost rank, even Caesar himself' and the oilman swung his hands with open palms upward away from his body. 'Tell us, tell us, should we give tribute to Caesar?' The oilman smiled, fatly. Johnny could see Shimon the ex-Zealot growing tense: Word must either repudiate Caesar, surely a signal for rebellion, or he must disgracefully knuckle under, crawling to the name of Caesar. Jim was quieter, but if anything even more attentive. Word raised an eyebrow, and jerked his head back as though he had seen a snake fork its tongue flickeringly in front of his face.

'Why tempt me, hypocrites?' he murmured.

The hands came back to the oilman again, elbows to his sides, palms brought open facing up once more. 'Hypocrites, Master? We only thirst for knowledge', and now Andrew and Philip began to look a little concerned at Word's hostility to the oilman.

'Show me the tribute money', demanded Word, and a coin was produced from the oilman's inner recesses. Word whose first memories were Egyptian looked Sphinxlike at the face on the coin (and Johnny, near enough to see it, shuddered a moment): 'Whose face is that?' The oilman said that it was Caesar's, trying to sound reverent and rebellious in the same voice. Then Word pointed to the writing on the coin: 'Whose name is there?' Once again the oilman got the name of Caesar out from contrasting sides of his mouth. 'Give back to Caesar what is Caesar's' nodded Word 'and' apparently absent-mindedly throwing his left arm over Johnny's shoulder 'to God what is God's'. The oilman looked at him with all flattery gone and bitter respect in its place, and oozed away. And Johnny laughed. Judas protested: 'peace, Johnny, they could have indicted the Master for stirring up insurrection or proclaim him a coward if he had not been so wise' and Shimon grunted appreciatively. But Johnny simply said 'that's why it's so funny, victory over the nets of the fowler is always funny', and then Judas did begin to laugh, and several of the others followed. Word walked on with a smile a little grimmer than Johnny liked, but it never occurred to him that Word might have been thinking of a victory which would not bring laughter tumbling behind it. He simply squeezed Word's hand, and Word swung around and looked down at him, and then Word's smile was happy again. But Nat, for one, gave thanks that their meeting with the Herodians had not happened when they were within Herod's dominions, and Judas reflected that whatever the shortcomings of Pontius Pilate at least he detested Herod. Andrew thought of the fate of his old Master John, and Thomas remembered Nazareth, proudly when the Herodians had sneered at it, and miserably when he looked at Word driven out of it. It occurred to James that one great advantage of having Johnny there was that the group could not depress themselves by brooding on the surrounding dangers. Peter wondered morosely if he would ever be able to think up answers the way Word came out with them, and Philip decided that Word was more skilful in answering questions by questions than he was. Shimon was at least glad that they were off the hook and sorry to miss the revolution. Jim was confirmed in his conviction that the rich were at their worst in a city or a court which sat well with what Johnny had found, and Thady concluded that Herodians were a cause well lost, for once in a way. Matthew agreed with all of this and pointed out to anyone who would listen that Herod Antipas had been begotten by Herod the Great who had been begotten by Antipater who had been begotten by Herod (Johnny's head was spinning by this time) who had actually been a servant in the temple of Apollo at Ascalon. 'I thought they were followers at Atargatis in Ascalon', said Judas, inquiring rather than contradicting. 'Who is Atargatis?' asked Johnny, needing some way out of the begetting. 'Baal's wife', said Word, blandly. 'Baal?' asked Johnny, more surprised to find the name on Word's lips than in ignorance. 'The chap who didn't know how to light a fire when Elijah was about to light one', said Word, helpfully. 'Well', said Andrew, ready to enter this if only to discourage Matthew's genealogy, 'since she is supposedly a fish-god that may explain why the fires of Baal were too wet to light.' 'But Elijah poured water on the fire he lit', shouted Johnny, anxious to show he had indeed remembered Baal. 'Ah, but fish-gods come from deep water', said Word. 'She forbids the Syrians to eat fish', said Andrew, darkly, 'bad for business.' 'Bitch', said Peter, zoologically challenged. 'She may have been a fish at one point', said Word vaguely, 'so I suppose you wouldn't want her to be a cannibal.' 'I wouldn't want her at all', said Peter indignantly. 'That's a relief', said Word, but Peter saw the glimmer in Word's eye, and laughed. 'In any case he was captured', said Matthew grasping the conversation firmly by the back of the neck. 'By fish?' asked Philip helpfully. 'By Idumaeans', said

Matthew heavily. 'Who is this that cometh from Edom, with dyed garments from Bozrah?' quoted Word. 'Dyed from the blood of our people', said Shimon bitterly. 'What did you say his name was?' asked Nat. 'Herod', said Matthew. 'I thought it was Antipater, like his son', intervened Thomas. 'It was Herod Antipater', said James, firmly ending the argument, which he regretted the next moment because Matthew sailed in promptly.

'Herod Antipater begat Antipater, and Antipater begat Herod, and Herod begat Herod Archelaus of the Samaritan woman Malthace, and Herod also begat Herod Antipas of the Samaritan woman Malthace, but he begat Aristobulus by Mariamme I, and Aristobulus begat Herodias who married Herod Philip and then Herod Antipas...'

Johnny preferred listening to Judas's amusing stories of city life which gave him a hold on the character of Jerusalem before he ever saw it. As Judas remarked, it had lost its Herods to everyone's advantage, and said it without mocking Matthew.

Johnny knew he was pleasing Word by listening to Judas and drawing him out, and he no longer needed to be told what Word wanted, most times. Judas discovered he greatly enjoyed expounding the unknown city to a lively and appreciative boy. He had repudiated the city and city life in general when he fled to John the Baptizer, and he was all too ready to denounce Judaea in general and Jerusalem in particular to patriotic Galileans, feeding their prejudices and hailing them as virtue. But part of him remained Judaean, and below his revulsion from Jerusalem corruption, there remained the magic Jerusalem threw around her dwellers. He managed to convey some of the magic to Johnny without violating Johnny's Galilean patriotism and love of blue water. Word sometimes joined in their talk, and Johnny discovered that Word knew, and was apparently fond of, Jerusalem much more than Johnny had imagined. In fact, Word had first knowingly seen Jerusalem when he was little older than Johnny, but he never told about it, since he was anxious to keep Judas basking in Johnny's limelight, and nowadays when Word spoke in Johnny's presence Johnny hardly saw anybody else. Judas gave an excellent description of the Temple, for instance, which Johnny eagerly drank in, with all kinds of questions about its architecture, furnishings, arrangements for worship, age, dreams of David about it, achievement of Solomon in it, Babylonian destruction of it, Nehemiah's rebuilding of it, Herod's improvements of it (slightly startling Judas by insisting Herod was not to be called the Great but Herod-shmerod). But when alone with Word, Johnny without a moment's hesitation simply said 'Of course the Temple doesn't matter any more, Word, now that you are here', putting up his face to be kissed, and Word lifted him high in his arms. None of the others would have put it quite like that, although they all now spoke of Word as God. Equally, Word prayed in their presence to his father in Heaven, but Johnny was the only one who said 'your father' as he might have spoken of the father of a neighbour's child. Mary's way of treating Word and Johnny as two brothers, or as playmates of the same age, made it easier for Johnny to think of Word's father in the fullest sense.

The meeting with the Herodians led to some discussion between Word and the others as to whether it was wise to go directly to Jerusalem, or to make a roundabout route. Nat pointed out that Word had blocked any chance for the Herodians to charge him with treason against Caesar, or to stir up bad feeling against him from the Zealots, but Thomas morosely remarked that if the Herodians wanted to lie about Word, who would stop them? Judas was fairly sure that the Romans would pay little attention to the Herodians since Pilate disliked Herod and would hardly think much of his toadies, unsupported by evidence, but Matthew scored an unexpected victory by pointing out that Herod Antipas's father and brothers had won many advantages by intrigues with Roman officials, and what Herod the Great could do with a procurator those whom Herod begat could do, always providing, as Peter interjected, that Herod hadn't killed them first. Andrew thought it as well to go to Jericho before going to Jerusalem, and James remembered that his father had one or two business contacts in Jericho. To Jericho they went, not by the most direct route. Shimon was alive to the chance of Word's enemies hiring robbers to murder him, and Jim remarked that if so, such robbers would be more likely to strike from near Jerusalem or Jericho because Word's enemies in Jerusalem would be less able to hire those farther away. The conversation was interrupted by meeting another traveller, this time a wealthy lawyer with a servant and what looked like a pupil or apprentice. Johnny was startled when the man walked up to Word and with nothing beyond the briefest of salutations began 'Master, what shall I do to inherit eternal life?' More and more people seemed to be aware that Word was on his way to Jerusalem, even if they found him on unexpected roads. Peter wondered, not too quietly, who had sent him, and Philip, a little more quietly, whispered that it must be priests or Pharisees, since Sadducees expected nobody to inherit eternal life, not even as a lost cause, chipped in Thady. But Word sized the lawyer up fairly obviously, with a faint quiver at the left-hand corner of his mouth as though he saw more deeply into the lawyer than the lawyer may have seen into himself. And then Word said, with a faint parody of legal consultation, 'what is written in the law? What is your opinion of it?' And the lawyer, slightly showing off before his pupil, and maybe even before his servant, came out with a round charge trailing subordinate clauses: 'Thou shalt love the Lord thy God with all thy heart, and with all thy soul, and with all thy strength, and with all thy mind', and threw in almost as an afterthought 'and thy neighbour as thyself'. Word turned his marvellous eyes on the lawyer's face and said, very directly 'You answer right: do it, and you will live'. The lawyer was clearly shaken by the directness of this, an academic performance suddenly turning into personal moral instruction of a kind he thought himself more appropriate to give than to receive (grinned Johnny to himself) and back he came with another question to edify his pupil and impress his servant. 'Who', he twinkled, 'is my neighbour?'

Word glanced with some amusement at the robber-analysts in his entourage and evidently decided to draw on the fearful imagery they had thrown around. 'A certain man', he reflected, 'went down from Jerusalem to Jericho, and fell among thieves – ' ('told to attack him by wicked men in Jerusalem?' thought Johnny, 'Quiet!' thought Word, back) – 'who surrounded him, struck at him, hurt him, wounded him in fact, tore his clothes off and went away, leaving him half dead on the side of the road.' Johnny could not tell, now, whether it was that Word was letting him see the pictures in Word's mind as he spun the story into existence, creating it, or whether Word simply told it so vividly that Johnny himself conjured up the pictures. He never found out. The dusty, deserted Jerusalem-Jericho road wound its way more definitely than the one under his own nose, the rocky hills divided by it and the rough gravel and sand underfoot occasionally reflecting a cruel sun, more often dark, grey and ominous. Johnny did not see the robbery itself, but his eyes picked out the brown and white flesh of the traveller, the dark bloodstains on his body and on the ground, the utter and seemingly Godless silence and stillness. It is odd to think of seeing silence, but that was what it felt like to Johnny. Word's narrative was spare, but its compassion for what the unhappy traveller was going through charged his tones. It could have been James, or his father Zebedee, thought Johnny, had they entrusted themselves to lone journeys through land in place of their natural habitat, their own Sea. 'And, as luck had it', said Word, his voice slightly more remote, 'a certain priest came down the road on his beast, looked at the body which still showed some signs of movement, and passed by on the other side.' Was it fear of blood-pollution, or of robbers remaining in wait, or simply a comfortable desire to avoid trouble without enquiring too closely what form it might take? On the whole, Johnny inclined to think it was concern for his own comfort, as the donkey picked its way delicately between the stones and the priest wrapped himself more closely in his cloak. 'And likewise a Levite, when he was at the place, looked on the man, and passed by on the other side.' As Johnny saw them, the Levite was leaner than the priest, and not so expensively mounted or his donkey furnished with trappings, but the body he gazed at groaned, and the Levite clashing his heels against the side of his donkey was back across the road and moving rapidly enough to catch the priest around the next two or three bends of the road. When they did would either mention the stricken man they had left to die, wondered Johnny, and whether from Word or from himself the answer came, they would know, they would not need to speak of it, each stood to justify the cruelty of the other. And Word paused, and smiled, and drew in his breath: 'But a certain Samaritan' – and Johnny thought, I knew this was going to happen, and Word's voice answered in his head 'You did' even as Word's voice was saying audibly to the lawyer 'as he journeyed, came where the wounded man lay, and seeing him, took pity on him'. A gasp of – pleasure? – came from where? – lawyer, pupil and servant were all agog, intent, silent, with perhaps a slightly open mouth in the pupil's case – Johnny's eyes flickered from one apostle to another, he having noticed that they were calling themselves 'apostles' since his return from the Mediterranean, perhaps because they felt like emissaries when Word had had to leave them on their own. But which one had been so pleased that the compassionate traveller had been a Samaritan? Suddenly Johnny heard Word's voice in his head 'Shimon' and then

Johnny got it: Shimon, officially unknown to anyone (though presumably he realised that Word knew) a crypto-Canaanite, and Jewish suspicion of Samaritan orthodoxy involved hints that the Sarnaritans were intermingled with the Canaanites (as well as the Philistines, if the Canaanites *weren't* the Philistines), and the Assyrians and God knew who. If a Canaanite was gratified by a favourable allusion to a Samaritan that looked as though the Jews were right in assuming ethnic intermingling between Canaanites and Samaritan, unless, of course, Shimon was Samaritan on his mother's side. All of this – and gratitude to Word for letting Johnny know that much of his own mind, since of course while Word knew the contents of Johnny's mind, neither Johnny nor anyone else could see what was in Word's unless he showed them – all of this raced through Johnny's mind while Word was moving to the next bit of his story without loss of pace.

'The Samaritan went to the injured man, and bound up his wounds, pouring oil and water into them, setting him on his own beast, bringing him to an inn on the outskirts of Jericho where he supervised the man being taken up to a bedroom on the first floor away from the noise and dust, and coaxed him into eating and nursed him through the night, redressing and rebinding the wounds to ease his pain. And the next morning he paid for himself and the injured man, and gave more money to the inn-keeper saying "Take care of him and whatever you spend above this I will repay on my return". Which now of these three, d'you think, proved neighbour to the man who fell among the thieves? Hm?' The pupil said promptly 'the Samaritan'. The servant said after a moment's hesitation, 'the Samaritan'. The lawyer cleared his throat as though entering on a weighty judgment, with perhaps a rebuke to his hasty subordinates, but in fact, avoiding the word 'Samaritan' said 'he that showed mercy on him' and then suddenly began to cry, fell on his knees before Word and bowed his head. Word hugged him, and gave him a kiss saying 'and that's what you will do'. The lawyer held Word tightly for a moment, and then stood back letting Word and the twelve continue towards Jericho, but detaining Judas, as the man carrying the purse, and pressing coins into his hands. The two groups called cries of 'Shalom!' to one another while still within earshot, and the last thing Johnny could see (from his seat on Peter's shoulders, good thoughtful Peter) was the lawyer standing with one arm around his pupil and the other around his servant 'so he has made his first discovery of his neighbour', thought Johnny happily. It was typical of Peter to have noted the slight stumble or two made by Johnny just before the lawyer and his sidekicks met them, and then when they were stopped, and Word had dropped Johnny's hand while telling his story – Word seemed to conduct silent music with his hands when he told stories – Peter grabbed Johnny and swung him aloft. The tired boy was very grateful, but Peter well knew that he would have died before admitting weariness. Word reached up to pat Johnny on the back and give a thankful squeeze to Peter's arm as they strode on. Eventually they reached an inn, Johnny drew his legs back from around Peter's shoulders and slithered down to the ground, going round to the front of Peter to draw his face down to thank him with a kiss before asking Word was this the inn to which the Samaritan had brought the robbers' victim? Word drew back his hand feigning a swipe at Johnny, then looked at the inn, grinned, and said 'it might have been, mightn't it?', and then told the innkeeper what they wanted which duly arrived and for which Judas paid. It was fine weather, and they ate their fruit and vegetables outside, and drank their water, getting into conversation with a traveller returning from Jericho. Their new friend told stories well, laughed a great deal and asked them questions about themselves. He told them his name was Eleazar, the same as Moses's nephew, the son of the priest Aaron, and he lived in Bethany, near Jerusalem, with two sisters Martha and Mary. He pointed out that this left him without any real identity because both of his sisters were more memorable than he was, Mary being the intellectual, and Martha the practical one of the family, so that there was nothing left for Eleazar to be. So Johnny asked him what trade or profession he followed, and James hastily apologised for his brother's rudeness, and Johnny said that it only showed a polite interest in Eleazar, and Eleazar, being used to siblings' arguments, realised they could keep going on like this all day, and quickly told them he was a silversmith. Judas asked him a few professional questions, and Johnny worried a little as to whether Judas was going to try some scam to do with Eleazar's silver, and the communal purse, and hoped Judas wouldn't do anything which might force Johnny to say something to Word (who probably was vaguely aware of what was in Johnny's mind but was hardly alerted to it as it gave no sign of causing conflict). It was Philip who asked why Eleazar had chosen to become a silversmith, and Eleazar startled them all by saying that it seemed the best way to have something in common with the Messiah. The twelve froze, Word laughed, and Johnny wanted to know what silversmiths could have in common with the Messiah. So Eleazar said:

'Have you forgotten the words of the last prophet?'

Word was really enjoying this, but said nothing, though his smile grew wider and wider. Johnny tried to twist his mind into reading what was in Word's, but simply felt as though a veil was blocking the way, a veil through which the fingers of Johnny's mind could make no entry. Andrew said, startled, 'do you mean, John the Baptizer?'

Eleazar frowned, and said, 'John the son of Zachary?'

'The same', said Word.

'I beg your pardon', said Eleazar, 'of course he would have been the last prophet. I was thinking of the prophets whose words we read in the scrolls, but scrolls are only one way of finding the voice of God.'

'So you meant Malachi', nodded Matthew. 'Why?'

Nathaniel laughed, 'Because Malachi prophesied that God would send his messenger, and the Lord whom ye seek would suddenly come, but who may abide the day of his coming? who shall stand when he appeareth? for he is like a refiner's fire, and like fuller's soap –'

And Eleazar joined in unison with Nat 'And he shall sit as a refiner and purifier of silver, and he shall purify the sons of Levi.'

('And God knows they need it', murmured Word, and Johnny thought of the priest and the Levite in Word's story of the Samaritan).

'And purge them as gold and silver', shouted Eleazar and Nat together, Andrew and James joining in, 'that they may offer unto the Lord an offering in righteousness'.

'Well, now is your chance', and Johnny lifted up his chin and looked Eleazar in the eyes. There was a sudden silence, and Eleazar looked at Johnny and said 'What do you mean?' and Johnny stood up, dropped on one knee in front of Word, inclined his head down and then eyed Eleazar, saying 'That's him!'

The innkeeper had left them to themselves after serving them, and none of his other patrons were eating outside the inn. Eleazar said very quietly, in a voice which could mean he might be talking to lunatics or he might be meeting the Messiah 'Him?', nodding his own head at Word.

'Fraid so', and Word smiled his leftward smile. Eleazar sat absolutely still, then stood up, and fell on his knees before Word, who kissed him and raised him up. Eleazar looked like a man who had just seen the most wonderful sight in the world. His brown eyes were watering. Yet his infectious merriment did not disappear for his next words were 'How right I was to become a silversmith!'

'How right you were', said Word solemnly.

'And what a good thing that you go around with a boy who asks impertinent questions' nodded Eleazar.

'I knew there must be some reason for it, if only I could remember what it was', agreed Word, tousling Johnny's hair.

'And this', said Johnny pointing to the inn as though he owned it, 'is the inn of the Good Samaritan.'

'I didn't know there was one', smiled Eleazar.

'An inn?' asked Peter.

'No, a good Samaritan', answered Eleazar.

'Well, there was', said Johnny, reprovingly. 'Or there might have been. Word, you'll have to tell him now.'

Word stood up, stretched his arms, yawned, and waved down any others who had risen as well. 'In that case', he explained, 'Eleazar will have to come with me for a stroll. The rest of you have heard it, and I'd feel a bore in knowing you had heard it. So you wait here.' Johnny looked up at him with beseeching eyes. Word raised his own eyes to Heaven, and sighed. 'Oh, very well. You'll have to put up with him, Eleazar. And, Johnny if you interrupt, or tell me I've got it wrong –' his voice died away as the three passed out of earshot. Judas laughed. To his surprise, so did James, and most of the others chuckled.

Neither Eleazar nor Word said much at the start of the walk, and Johnny, knowing he was there on sufferance, kept quiet. Eventually Eleazar said 'What was Good about the Samaritan?' and Word told him. Johnny had not expected to be bored at the story's retelling: what surprised him was to find it more interesting the second time. If he had been thinking of it as performance, it might have led him to notice Word's emphases, and starts and stops, and rises and falls of tone. But since listening to Word's stories was a matter of seeing them, for Johnny, what happened this time was that the contours of the landscape and its figures were so much sharper, as though Word had stepped back from the pictures he had painted and somehow twitched them into stronger focus. The inn, of course, was much more recognisable to Johnny since it was now the place where they had met Eleazar: it was no different in kind from the inn as first envisaged by Johnny (or by Word) although Johnny had never seen it when he first heard the story. Word did not ask Eleazar to identify the true neighbour to the injured man since it was clear that Eleazar knew perfectly well, and Word had opened the story by saying that it was created to answer a lawyer's question as to who was his neighbour. At the end Eleazar drew a deep breath, and said 'I bet that silenced the lawyer', and Word said 'pretty near', and Eleazar said 'tears?', and Word nodded, and Eleazar swallowed and said 'I'm not surprised. Blessed is he who draws tears from a lawyer, even more blessed than he that draws blood from a stone.' 'Thank you for my blessing', said Word politely, 'I'm glad to have earned it because I'm inclined to leave what blood is in stones to remain in them. Tell me about your sisters.' And by time they had rejoined the others Eleazar was insisting on Word and his disciples not only coming to stay with Eleazar, but making his family's house headquarters for comings and goings to and from Jerusalem. Word murmured that there were too many to sleep there, but Eleazar said Word and Johnny and James could sleep at his house and the rest could sleep in the house of Shimon the leper. 'Who is Shimon the leper?' asked Word, and Eleazar said he was a man who had lived in Bethany until he contracted leprosy after which his neighbours shunned him and he could no longer attend synagogue, and he sold his house and gave most of what he got for it to the poor. Word nodded and said 'for which his sins are forgiven', and Eleazar looked a little startled, but went on to tell them how Shimon took to walking the roads of Judaea until he became too ill, and died, but people thought the house was unlucky, and it could never command a good selling price, and Eleazar and his sisters were able to buy it for very little. 'Martha would make some man a fine wife', said Eleazar thoughtfully, 'or Mary might interest one in her conversation, and a good house isn't a bad dowry.' 'Might not a prospective husband be discouraged by the thought of dwelling in what was once a leper's house?' asked Thomas, but Eleazar said that people should be proud to dwell in the house of Shimon the leper who was a good man, having pity on the poor, and bearing his hardship with the patience of Job, and he wouldn't want any man who despised Shimon or feared the ghost of his leprosy to marry one of his sisters. And Word said he was right, and he would be honoured to stay with Eleazar and his sisters in or out of the house of Shimon the leper. So they all went to Bethany with Eleazar.

Somewhere on the journey Johnny managed to get a little time in silence to talk to Word in his own mind. 'It's about what you will tell the world about me when you are old', said Word's mind. 'You want to make sure you will remember what I say. Well, you will, Johnny, I will see to that, my words will take root in your mind and you will tell the world only what is true when you speak my words. So you will say less about what I did, and more about what I said.' But, as if to compensate, Johnny did not always remember what happened in the right order, or rather he would tell Polycarp, his young disciple who took down much of what Johnny remembered, something as he recalled it, forgetting that his last dictation to Polycarp was about a different time. Since Johnny remembered most of all what Word said after his promise that Johnny would remember his words correctly, Polycarp would find himself taking down Johnny's memories of Word in or near Jerusalem, and was vaguely left under the impression that Word made more journeys to Jerusalem after he had first met Johnny than was really the case. Because Johnny concentrated so much on Word's sayings he paid less attention to making it clear where they were when certain things were said. For instance, Polycarp was left imagining there was always fear of people attempting to kill Word from the time he started preaching, and that the ones wanting to do it were the Temple priests, but in fact not much was said about such a thing until news came of Herod killing John the Baptizer, and after that Herod and his followers and hired emissaries or assassins seemed to be the main danger. It was not until Johnny reached Lydda that he became aware of the snobbishness and enmity to Galileans so rife among the Judaeans, and it was only near the end of Word's life in Jerusalem that Johnny began to think of the Judaeans, or at least some of them, wanting Word's death. Then after Pontius Pilate stopped being governor and was sent home, Caligula as Emperor would give more and more power to Herod Agrippa I in place of Herod Antipas, and the Emperor Claudius, succeeding Caligula, made him king of what had once been Israel, and he killed Johnny's brother James while ruling Jerusalem. As an old man Johnny found himself thinking of Jerusalem and Judaea as killing-places, and it shadowed his memories of Word when talking to Polycarp.

Johnny's memory of Eleazar and his sisters separated itself from the journeys to Jericho and Jerusalem after they had met Word. They became sealed off from the rest of the story because Word very firmly told them to sell up their property in Bethany and go abroad, almost as the very last thing he said to them, before making his last journey to Jerusalem, and Johnny heard later that they had taken ship for Gaul, far to the north of Rome. In any case they were all three such vital people, that they naturally dominated memories of the scenes in which Johnny remembered them, long before life and laughter became so permanently identified with Eleazar as his identity. Eleazar had been waiting for an apprentice to catch him up at the Good Samaritan's inn (as Johnny would permanently remember it), and when he appeared and had got some nourishment and rest, Johnny and he were sent forward to tell Martha and Mary that they had a dozen guests for dinner who would be staying overnight and on various other nights unspecified and that they were all Galileans and that Herod would be glad if at least one of them came to a rapid end. Forth went Johnny and the apprentice, Daniel – Danny to Eleazar, Martha and Mary but Daniel, very much Daniel, as far as Johnny was concerned, and this was no time for starting private hostilities, quite apart from Danny, or rather Daniel, being at least sixteen and in no mood to take backchat from an eleven-year-old. Danny – Daniel – had been given firm instructions from Eleazar as to what he was to say to Martha, and what to Mary (Martha was to be told that they were hungry men in their prime, and Mary that they were intellectuals whose Master was a profound mystic, and Johnny was not to tell either of them that Word was God, or the Messiah, or even that he was the cousin of John the Baptizer who had in fact baptised Eleazar and his sisters). But when they met Martha and Mary Johnny found he had very little time to say anything as Martha overflowed with inquisition and indignation as to what her brother thought he was doing, filling the house with shiftless, homeless, conscienceless Galileans, as if they didn't have enough to do to keep body and soul together among the three of them, not to speak of a worthless, idle, do-nothing apprentice who ate twenty times as much as he worked, to say nothing of Mary's wandering around the house inventing new prayers as if the old ones weren't enough trouble to remember, and who was this little brat whom Daniel (formalised now as a means of reproach) had picked up from God knows where, and not even a boy of his own age but he must be getting the lot of them into trouble by leading children to follow his bad example, and the next thing would be the child's mother storming at the door of the house and accusing the lot of them of having kidnapped her wretched son. Danny was clearly more accustomed than annoyed by this reception but as he had attempted to keep up appearances with Johnny by an oracular silence most of the way to Bethany he gave the smaller boy a dirty look from the corner of his eye, daring him to giggle. As the Jeremiad took its course Johnny kept quiet, knowing that to announce his mother was in Galilee would be no more welcome than to announce that he was a disciple of the Messiah. Eventually Martha grew tired, and finished a splendid likening of the two boys to a couple of wilderness jackals whose mange and menaces she particularised with scientific accuracy, and then grabbed Johnny, threw him over her shoulder, and marched into the kitchen with him, slamming him down on a stool before a place at the table which she filled with a succulent and nourishing meal while her sister Mary, vaguely looking as though she had momentarily broken off a conversation with an angel, did the same for Daniel who had followed Martha into the room with purpose as well as prudence. Martha would not allow Johnny to say one word until he had eaten, and Daniel knew he had said quite enough, so they had a silent meal apart from Martha's blessing the Lord at the outset in a tone which Johnny realised meant however much she might come to believe in Word, she would give him no easier an edge of her tongue, God or no God. Johnny also knew Word well enough to predict that Martha would delight him, and Mary was obviously designed by nature to greet him. But the first greeting Word got on his arrival was Martha's, and even Daniel and Eleazar seemed startled by it: she raised her chin, looked him formidably in the eye, gave him a bow which might almost be deemed a soldierly nod, handed him a cup of water, and said 'I thought you would turn up sooner or later' with a note of what almost seemed like welcome well mixed with grim satisfaction at her own powers of prediction. This changed when Philip went into a splutter of laughter, and Martha asked Word with barely the slightest decibel variation whether he thought she was running a home for the feeble-minded. He agreed that it must look like it, and Johnny, who was by now regarding Martha as an old friend, nonetheless thought better of offering individual characterisations of the other disciples in support of her thesis.

In any case Johnny had no time for any such thing because as soon as he had finished eating, Martha was telling him to bless the Lord, which Johnny did, looking directly at Word, who smiled back at him. Martha paused for a moment, and so did Mary, and then Martha was asking Johnny without leaving a moment in which to reply whether he had done so much as a hand's turn for his unfortunate mother and he needn't think he would get away with that here because there was boy's work to be done, and go over to Shimon the Leper's and get the tables ready for the men who had just come in, and bring that idle loafer who fancied himself as a silversmith's apprentice with him, what good was he at all beyond eating them out of house and home? Johnny skittered down the house to the door, avoiding the sardonic eye of James, and Danny raced after him. Johnny had to wait until Danny caught up with him outside, indicated where they were going and once they had reached Shimon the Leper's pointed out where the table-coverings were. To Johnny's slight surprise Danny seemed a lot friendlier and in fact began by saying 'She likes you. I thought she would.'

'Then she likes you too', reflected Johnny.

'Yes, we're old sparring partners' acknowledged Danny.

'Silent in your case' suggested Johnny.

Danny laughed. 'Certainly.'

Neither of them relaxed for a moment, well knowing that Johnny's new friend would expect everything ready to serve before there was time to draw a breath, as Johnny thought to himself. When he did draw another breath, it was to ask, whether there was anyone Martha didn't bully? Danny nodded approvingly.

'Anyone she doesn't trust', he affirmed.

'How does she stop talking long enough to size them up?' asked Johnny.

'I've often wondered', said Danny, 'but if Eleazar has some business with a new supplier or customer he will often make sure Martha has a look at him. It's most instructive to watch. If she says nothing beyond brief civilities, it's a bad sign. If she smiles at the guy, it's worse. And if she pays a tribute to his wisdom and probity, that's absolute Roman war. Eleazar never bothers to ask her opinion afterwards, he will have discovered it

210

from her manner. Her worst judgment against someone is if she ever says "Forgive me, but –". That's when Mary and I take one look at her and two at the underside of the table. We'd better get back or she'll have the steaming dishes ready to go and your ravenous brood of uncles or whatever they are to you playing leap-frog to get after them and if you think the fact that Martha likes you will prevent her raising blisters on every joint on your body when you slip up – and it's when, not if – you're very, very wrong.'

But when they got back to the first house the vials of wrath were splashing over the brows of Word and Mary. Johnny got within earshot to hear:

'... so unless there's going to be another miracle like the 5000 fed with two fishes and five loaves, or the other way around, who was it I was hearing this from?, Andrew, though even then you'd have had to have all of your idle disciples working hard to get the bread and fish handed out across the multitude, and we here without the smallest miracle in sight getting your dinner and my sister up here putting questions to you instead of putting a plate in front of you, alright, I'm sure you'll be a gentleman and say it was all your fault...'

Word was laughing too hard to speak but at this point he interrupted firmly with 'It's nobody's fault. Fault means wrong. There's nothing wrong in Mary learning about loving our enemies, even the ones who will kill me...'

Johnny frowned. Word ought not to make these jokes, since Johnny knew it was impossible but someone might believe it.

'... so Mary has chosen the better part since Man and Woman should not eat by bread alone but by every word that comes from the mouth of God.'

'Well', nodded Martha triumphantly, 'in that case I'll listen myself, what am I waiting for?' and sat down beside Word, while Mary arose and began to serve.

In the weeks that followed, Johnny had ample opportunity to study the family, particularly in their relations with Word. Johnny had almost put to rest his jealousy if Word gave unusual attention to anyone, but enough of its shadow remained for him to ponder and analyse the links. He was much entertained to see how different was what Martha called their listening. In her case it was one-ear listening, since she would hold a lengthy conversation with Word, frequently interrupting and usually dragging the conversation back to the problems and, it was clear, the fun of ordering daily lives. In the middle of what either Word or she might say, she would hurl out a stream of remarks or (more likely) reproaches as to what someone or someone else was doing or ought to be doing if they weren't, and when her quarry had improved or inaugurated action, she would be back to Word as if there had been no break. She also enjoyed making fun of herself as well as everyone else, as Johnny was realising her reproaches often did. On one occasion he heard her proclaiming to Word 'and you'll have to listen to me carefully now, because when it comes to theology I'm as ignorant as any four High Priests', to which Word crowed with delight but unfortunately Johnny never heard what they were talking about because Martha caught him listening and demanded whether he thought the last task she had given him was going to do itself or he imagined that his Master had nothing better to do than to make signs and wonders to keep Johnny lazy so that his muscles would end by needing a miracle for themselves before they would move at all.

Mary's talks with Word could hardly have differed more from Martha's, and if Johnny had had the time he would have dearly loved to eavesdrop. He remembered the fragments of Word's replies which he overheard and told many of them to Polycarp long afterwards but did not always recall they were spoken to Mary. Mary seems to have realised quite early that Word would die for his people, that the apostles knew that he had prophesied it but were in denial or that at least some of them were – and that Johnny, normally very quick, had never grasped it at all. So while asking Word about it, she was very careful not to do it in any way that would upset or alarm Johnny when within earshot. Nor would she make direct allusion to Word's enemies, some of whom might have spies in Bethany, so it was clear whether she had been thinking of Herod, or Pilate, or the Sadducees or the Pharisees or even the Temple priests headed by the High Priest Caiaphas, when she asked about false shepherds, and when Johnny remembered Word's reply but not to whom he directed it, *he* wasn't clear whom Word meant either in speaking of a false shepherd breaking into the the sheepfold where the true shepherd came in by the right door. Johnny remembered it as sounding like a poem, as Word said it:

The false herd will break in
Like a thief i' th'night,
But the true herd will stand at the door,
The portal will open,
The sheep will all know him,
And follow when he leads before.

I am the true herd,
I am also the door,
Those who enter by me all will live.
The thief comes to steal
Or to slaughter and kill,
The true shepherd his own life will give.

He who lives for the sheep
Knows them all, they know him,
But the false herd loves only his wages.
I have other sheep too
Who do not yet know you
Whom I'll save from the wolf as he rages.

The Father loves me,
For I lay down my life
That the sheep may return to their fold.
I will die first, and then,
I will rise up again,
Leading wanderers in from the cold.

Johnny liked it, but shivered slightly as he first heard it, enjoying its simple grandeur, yet wishing Word would stop talking about his own death which could not happen. When he remembered it long afterwards he knew a lot more about what it meant. Mary seemed to understand it well at the time, and when Johnny looked into her eyes he saw they were full of tears.

If Johnny wanted examples of false shepherds, Judaea had plenty to show him. If Word healed anyone on the Sabbath, Holy Willies seemed to rise up from between the stones or even the very grains of sand along the road, to denounce Word for polluting the Sabbath. Soon after they left Bethany, passing near to Jerusalem they met a man blind from birth, with two sightless pieces of skin where eyes should be. Johnny found it horrible to look at him, much more than if it was a blemish like lameness or the woman bowed down to the ground (whom Word had also cured on the Sabbath for which a Synagogue ruler rebuked him) or even leprosy (which Johnny had seen too often to think unnatural). But Word tightened his hand on Johnny's and Johnny's mind received Word's mind, telling him to look again at the man, and he did with a slight shudder, noticed by Judas who asked, rather tactlessly loud, a little like a teacher giving an exercise to a class or maybe like Zebedee distinguishing between kinds of fish in training his sons:

'Master, was it this man whose sin made him born blind, or his parents?'

Johnny realised Judas was trying to be kind to him, while forgetting about the blind man's feelings, making the blindness more natural to Johnny by integrating it in Word's teaching. That explained why a bright man like Judas could ask such a silly question, since it was obvious that the man could not have sinned in his mother's womb and the nature of the blindness was meant it had been present from his birth. But perhaps, thought Johnny with a little nudge from Word's mind, Judas wanted Word to pronounce judgment on the whole question of injuries as the fruit of the sin of the sufferer. If he did, he certainly got it. Word, ignoring other travellers also stopping and listening, said unsurprisingly that the man had not sinned, and, more surprisingly neither had his parents: the man was suffering so as to testify to God's work.

'You mean', said Johnny, startled, 'that people who are hurt or injured or blemished may be suffering to help the rest of us?'

'Or may suffer because they have already helped the rest of us', nodded Word. 'A soldier's wounds may have been suffered in the cause of his country. And so a soldier in our struggle against evil may have been wounded in some way we do not realise to help us in that battle. But this man is here so that I shall do what he who sent me –'

'Your father', interrupted Johnny, a little loudly, both to glorify Word and to wave a cocky head higher for the passers-by.

'My father', agreed Word, adding, to Johnny's bewilderment and slight alarm, 'while it is day, for the night approaches when no one can work.

While I am in this world, I am the light of the world', and as he began preparations to open the man's eyes to the light, Johnny could easily follow him in this bit of his explanation. Word did what he had to do much more elaborately than was usual. The miracle had two stages. Word spat on the ground, made clay with the moisture from his mouth, took it in his hands like a sculptor (as Johnny had heard one described), plastered it on where the man's eyes should be, and then told the man to enter Jerusalem and wash in the pool at Siloam to which anyone would direct him. It was several days later when he found Word again, having followed him to Jericho with a new rapidity, rejoicing in his power of movement but also because he had been thrown out of Jerusalem for having been given his sight on the Sabbath. (By now Johnny wondered if some people thought women ought not to give birth on the Sabbath, or be helped when they were giving birth, 'or that farmers should not help cows calve on the Sabbath' agreed Word's mind with Johnny's. Word's mind quoted the prophet who rebuked his opponents for saying 'Stand by thyself, come not near me, for I am holier than thou' and Johnny's mind concurred saying that he must never let his love for Word be polluted by thinking of himself as better than anyone else because of that love. 'Or for any other reason' replied Word's mind, and Johnny's said solemnly 'or for any other reason'.)

The man born blind who could see since he washed in Siloam was called Isaac, which Johnny thought appropriate since the first Isaac could see when young but not in his old age and this one was the other way around, just as Word stood so many things on their heads like insisting what you believed was so much more important than how you looked. Isaac was a native of Jerusalem and so was well known when he returned, but since everyone knew him as blind since birth all were confused by his sight, and several people insisted be couldn't be whom he said he was, and made him tell his story to Pharisees some of whom said Word was Godless because he worked miracles on the Sabbath while others said he could not do miracles if he were Godless, and others still blamed Word for dividing the people into those who thought Isaac wasn't Isaac and those who said he was and those who said miracles could not be miracles on the Sabbath and those who said miracles could be on the Sabbath if they were miracles. Isaac's parents were called, and insisted that he had been blind and that he was their son, but they did not know how he could now see and that he was old enough to tell his own story. And now something else came out. The Judaeans had decided that if anyone said Word was Christ, he was to be put out of the synagogue, and this meant a lot to Isaac's parents who were very respectable and were pillars of the synagogue which seemed to exempt them from responsibility for Isaac's blindness by blaming Isaac himself for it, while Isaac himself had drifted outside of Jerusalem for the most part and was hardly in the synagogue often enough for it to matter if he were put out of it. It looked at one point that they might all agree when a sensible Pharisee told Isaac to give God the praise, but then added that they knew the man who healed him was a sinner, and Isaac, insisting that all he knew was that he could now see, asked them why were they questioning him like this, and was it because they wanted to become disciples of the man who had made him see? This seems to have frightened his hearers even more than it angered them, and as Isaac told the story Johnny realised that those Judaeans who attacked anyone calling Word Christ or the Messiah were afraid of bringing the Romans or the Herodians or the rich Sadducees down on them with charges of disruption since Herod thought Word might be John the Baptizer risen from the dead and hence needing to be killed once more and the Romans hated anything new which they had not approved and the Sadducees did not believe in spirits and therefore were frightened of anyone who seemed to know how to get help from spirits. In fact, Johnny was realising that many more people than Herod were enemies of Word, and wanted to do him harm, and while he was sure Word could not be killed, he wondered if Word could be hurt and feel pain, and was afraid that he might feel it before his miraculous powers healed any wound and dissolved any pain as he had done for Johnny when they first met and when he rescued Johnny from the Roman galleon. And Johnny found himself wondering uneasily whether Word would take the same trouble to ease his own pain as he did in healing others. So he was very much in agreement when Judas, Peter, James and Andrew all told Word they had better go beyond the Jordan until this row about Isaac had died down. Isaac himself insisted that nobody had ever heard of the healing of a man born blind since the world began: there had been tales of men cured of blindness but these had once had sight. The very fact that Word had used his own saliva to cure the man had a ring of earlier miracles, though not of similar cases, and Johnny,

216

perhaps prompted by Word's mind, found himself thinking that Isaac was expelled from the synagogue by men convinced that Word was a fraud but also by other men less convinced of that than they wanted to be. For expelled he was, in the end by a mob of worshippers yelling 'you were born in sin, and you have the nerve to try to teach us!' and Isaac may have been lucky to get away alive. Johnny was reminded of what happened to Word in Nazareth, and wondered if there had been men there, too, who had been afraid that they might be persuaded to believe in Word. Oddly enough, Isaac still had no idea who Word might be, even if his persecutors did. Word asked him if he believed in the Son of God and Isaac asked very politely who was that? He would like to know, so that he would believe in him. So he hadn't said Word was Christ, thought Johnny, and had been expelled because those Pharisees jumped to conclusions quite wrongly: however mad it was to call it a crime to think Word was the Messiah Isaac had not committed that crime. Johnny realised that saying any good thing about Word was frightening some people to do very nasty things. Word told Isaac simply that he was the Son of God, Isaac fell down and worshipped Word, Word drew him to his feet, embraced and kissed him, and in the end advised him to make his way to Galilee: James scribbled a note to Zebedee explaining matters so that Isaac might be helped find work, for James had studied to help his father with accounts and legal documents. Word and the twelve made their way beyond the Jordan. Johnny was fascinated by their destination, for it was there that John the Baptizer had done so much of his work, and Andrew, Judas and Word showed him many places where John had spoken and told many things he said, and somehow Johnny always thought of it as the beginning of Word's story, however thrilled he was by what Mary had told him of Word's birth in Bethlehem, and youth in Egypt, and growing up in Nazareth. In later years it sometimes seemed to Johnny that John the Baptizer had spoken the prologue of a play to which he himself would speak the epilogue.

Johnny realized Word sometimes spoke in other minds when one day he looked very grim, and said that Eleazar was very ill. Johnny asked how he knew, and Word said he had heard it from Mary, and gave a wry half-smile and said 'and Martha for a moment or two between her instructions to the others'. They waited for a couple of days, and then Word said they would go back into Judaea. Judas said the Judaeans would stone him, and

Word gave an odd little grin and said that if they walked in the day they would not stumble but that when night came, they would. Judas froze, realizing Word expected trouble, but not yet, and Nat also looked at Word very apprehensively. Word continued that their friend Eleazar was asleep and he was going to waken him up, but Peter said that surely sleep would be the best thing for Eleazar's illness, whatever it was. James was quicker, and Johnny saw his face fall, and was less surprised when Word said quietly that Eleazar was dead. 'And I'm glad for your sakes that we were not there, so that you can believe.' Johnny at once realised Word would raise Eleazar from the dead, and that this time there could be no pretence that the body was anything but dead, whatever the ambiguities about Miriam and the boy at Nain. He swung towards Word, who nodded, and James brightened with the same realisation. Johnny did not hear Thomas's brave words to several of the others – 'Let's go, and let's die with him' – but Andrew told him later on, to explain why Thomas found it so hard to believe Word could return after dying since he blamed himself for not being dead too.

But in the event they met little trouble on their way, although Word took care to eradicate the sufferings of any invalids or cripples he saw. When they got near Bethany, they saw Martha waiting outside the little town, and clearly she had known they were on the road and near at hand. She was a very different Martha, slow, aged, tearless after weeping. As they came up, she surprised Johnny by catching him up in her arms and kissing him, and then Johnny remembered that Eleazar had been younger than Mary and much younger than Martha who must have helped bring him up when he was a boy. He hugged her silently, grateful for a chance to share her sorrow while knowing no words to say. But Martha found words, looking at Word more in grief than in reproach, sadly and factually: 'Lord, if you had been here my brother would not have died.' She paused. Then she spoke with the effort of not telling someone to do something. 'I know well that God will grant whatever *you* ask.' Johnny had a wild hysterical urge to express his wonder at Martha admitting there was one being, God, whom she could not have at her beck and call. In fact he stood beside her, trembling a little, looking at Word who was saying in a dry factual tone very like hers 'Your brother will rise again.' Martha nodded, saying 'I know he will rise again in the resurrection that will happen on the last day.'

Word stood looking at her, and Johnny began to feel the hair prickling at the back of his own neck, knowing from Word's mind that he would speak a wonder. And Word said:

'I am the resurrection and the life, and the person who believes in me even if they are dead will live on, and anyone who believes in me and lives cannot die through all eternity. Do you believe that?'

Johnny felt his own life stood in Martha's shoes, as she replied without the slightest hesitation 'Yes, Lord, I have learned to believe that you are the Messiah, that you are the Son of the living God, that you are the person for whom the world has waited.' And it seemed to Johnny that they had found themselves at the top of a mountain with none of the labour of climbing it. Martha smiled at Word. She never seemed a beautiful woman, dressed simply, and carried more weight in all senses than her siblings: but her face was radiant now, and Johnny was dazzled by her beauty. And then she walked back into the town while Word, making a sign to the others, stood like a statue, and the apostles were silent, and the onlookers seemed infected by them to grow still.

Johnny knew that Martha had gone to tell Mary that Word was here, and soon they saw Mary coming up the road Martha had gone down, and behind her Danny and many local Judaeans who must have thought she was going to pray at Eleazar's tomb for they were obviously startled to see Word and the apostles proving Mary's destination. And as soon as she reached him, Mary knelt down before Word's feet, saying what Martha had said, that if Word had been here Eleazar would not have died. And Danny muttered to Johnny, by way of greeting 'what kept you, anyway?' But before Johnny could think out an answer much less speak one, Word groaned, and was obviously upset, and suddenly Johnny thought that if Word could die (which he couldn't) he would have expected death for bringing Eleazar back to life, for it would induce far more anger than the fight over Isaac, and that had been bad enough. And Johnny saw that Word would have preferred not to be the centre of conflict but since it was the only way to revive Eleazar he would do it, asking where the body had been laid, and Mary bade him come and see. And Word wept. Down the years Johnny came to realise he had wept for several reasons, one being that raising Eleazar definitely ended the open, free lives they had lived until now: another, that bringing back Eleazar would only mean losing him again since it would be far too dangerous for him to remain in Bethany as living proof of the might of Word's work, a third, that Word loved Mary and Martha and hated putting them through the sorrow of Eleazar's death necessary as it was to climax Word's public life as miracle-worker and a fourth, that Word did not want to die, separating himself from his mother and from Johnny and the others whom he loved, and he did not want the physical torture that would now lie ahead of him. But it was all necessary, if Word was to bring the world back from spiritual death, and that greater love no one could have than to lay down his life for his friends, and Eleazar was the first beloved friend for whom he would lay it down. The watching Judaeans were moved by Word's weeping and rightly saw how much Word had loved Eleazar, although none saw beyond that. Johnny could hear murmurs of surprise that Word had not prevented Eleazar's death, Danny's voice among them, and when they reached the grave Word cried aloud, almost to the point of a scream, as though he himself had been wounded to the heart.

It was love, thought Johnny, as he followed Word and Mary to the tomb, somewhat cut off from Word by the mourning Judaeans who encompassed him. It had happened suddenly enough, both the love and the death, though Eleazar could charm Balaam's ass into going where he wanted, not to speak of Jonah's big fish. They had all fallen in love with Eleazar, even Thomas, even Judas; perhaps it was his laughter. Eleazar would still be laughing in – in the tomb, Johnny realised he was thinking. But Word had loved Eleazar both for himself and for his brotherhood with Martha and Mary, and loved each of them for themselves and as sisters to each other and to Eleazar. Word was not so much a family man as a man for a family: how well he and his mother fitted into Johnny's, for instance, and straightened out its leading wrinkle – the anger dividing Johnny and James – from the moment he found it. There was an element of disappointment in it, Johnny realised: Word would have been ready enough to love his own half-brothers if they had ever let him, but they had cold-shouldered Mary from the first, and sneered at Word, mockingly advising him (on the rare times when any of them revisited Galilee) to bring his mission to Jerusalem where (Johnny now knew) Word would actually meet many more enemies than he would encounter in Galilee. It was no thanks to those wicked brothers, thought Johnny, that Word wasn't killed, not that he could be, but they didn't know that. They were every bit as bad as the half-brothers of Joseph who sold him into slavery, as Scripture told. Anyhow Eleazar, Martha and Mary had given Word a way of living among siblings which he hadn't had before, not even in Johnny's family because he didn't think of Johnny as a brother, more (the thought struck itself into Johnny's mind suddenly) like a *son*! James and the others, again, were more like friends of Word who were also business partners, as Peter had been to Johnny's father. May be, thought Johnny, I wasn't supposed to be part of that. I'm glad I am what I am, now.

All of this worked its way through Johnny's mind in much less time than it took him to come to a standstill amongst the others outside Eleazar's tomb where they found Martha had already arrived. Already, Word was telling his disciples and Danny and the other men present, to move the stone and Martha, choking with grief but practical as always said: 'Lord, he bas been dead for four days and by now will stink of the corruption and rotting that is to destroy him' but Word said, putting an arm over her shoulders whose tenseness held back her tears: 'Didn't I tell you that if you believe you will see the glory of God?' and her mouth half-opened with a hope she had been unable to suppress from the moment of Word's arrival, and the men rolled away the stone, and Word cried out a prayer:

'Father!' (my grandfather, I suppose, thought Johnny) 'I thank you for hearing my prayer, as you always do, but today particularly because of these people standing here I say it so that they may believe you sent me.' And he suddenly raised his voice, as though his Father was nearer to him than the dead Eleazar to whom he cried 'Eleazar, come out and stand beside me!' Unlike most of the locals Johnny had expected what now happened, but still he felt the hair rise on the back of his neck, below his own skull as he watched the figure in white gravecloths and a napkin over its face, lurching slowly but firmly towards Word, who said quickly 'Loose him and let him free'. The cloths were wound back, the napkin fell, and there was Eleazar's merry face laughing at them all. And Martha promptly shouted 'Pull some garments around you, you great booby, and don't be standing there in your pelt, disgracing us before all the neighbours and getting your death of cold; Danny, get back to the house and bring your master's finest garment instead of standing there with your jaw dropping off you like a half-wit; and you, Johnny, get along after him and give him

221

a hand carrying them, he's sure to drop them, what do we keep the two of you for?; and let the rest of you come down to the house in the next half-hour with sensible looks on you instead of yawping the way you are now, anyone would think you'd never seen a man raised from the dead before!' Even for Martha this was impressive, and Eleazar laughed helplessly, rather weak in his movements and voice, but gathering strength as he clung to Word whom he had kissed as soon as he reached him, and Mary laughed and sang, and Word hugged Eleazar generously, and Martha at last got her arms around her brother and burst into happy tears, glaring round her with so martial an eye that Danny and Johnny chased one another back to the house as if she was after them already. Oddly enough the last thing Johnny heard as he battled his urgent way through the crowd was Philip's voice, saying to himself rather than to Eleazar (who was hardly near enough to hear him): 'What is it like to be dead?'

HIRTEEN

PHILIP

That all men through him might believe

'When shall the trees cry love?
Not in the spring
But in a season of
God's making.'

Philip had found a lyre in Shimon the Leper's, possibly originally the property of the Leper himself, and was drawing music out of it for Galilean songs, occasionally with a Greek intruder or two. As other evangelists have said, Philip's voice was sweet rather than strong. He happily drew on all kinds of songs, some not so much religious as turning out unexpectedly to have God at their apex, others pretty little love-ditties:

'My love lay across the waters,
Twenty leagues away,
Fairest of fifteen daughters,
So they used to say.
I'll go back to her some day.'

He had found the right day for singing it, for Martha, who might have been inclined to denounce him for time-wasting or worse when ruling her roost, simply smiled and joined one or two choruses, and took the solo part in one song with the greater strength than Philip's which Johnny would have expected, but with its own quite rare sweetness which he certainly did not. There must have been some time when Johnny was asleep or doing some errand and Word had told his story of the prodigal son in her hearing, for she had turned it into a fine ballad on which she must have worked with Mary: as the song went on Mary took the son's part and Martha remained narrator, joining in a perfect unison to end each verse

> 'Oh, the prodigal son!'
> 'Oh, the prodigal son!'

until the time came for the resentful elder son to be heard when Eleazar entered the song, swelling with righteous anger, absurd and mildly contemptible, and yet with an underlying pathos amid the comedy:

> All these years I have been a good son,
> Asking no favour, doing no wrong,
> Never a prodigal son.
>
> Yet never even a kid did you slay
> That my friends and I might eat and laugh.
>
> But my brother, who's thrown his wealth away,
> For him you kill the fatted calf,
> For that prodigal son.

The sisters left each last line to Eleazar alone once he began to sing. Word had taken the verse in which the father welcomed back his prodigal son but there he stayed out of the chorus-line which the sisters held in unison. But Word sang the last verse alone apart from Philip's lyre and Martha's four narrator-words:

> 'Son, son, you are always with me,
> What I have is yours', said his father then
>
> 'But it is right that we shout with glee
> For he that was dead is alive again.

It is right that we dance in a joyous round,
For be that was lost, my son, is found.
Oh, my prodigal son.'

And then Philip led the rest in repeating the last line. Johnny wanted to laugh and cry at the same time, and so did many of the rest, and even Word and Eleazar, while seriously playing their parts, clowned at moments, Word ruffling Eleazar's hair on the line of the dead being alive again.

It was a wonderfully happy evening, free from such as would seem to hover over their next and last visit to Eleazar and his family's, but before James removed an almost sleep-conquered Johnny to bed in the family's home (the impromptu party happened at Shimon the Leper's) there seemed some tenseness in the last words he accidentally heard between Word and Eleazar. Johnny had in fact drifted into sleep and half-woke to hear Word saying 'use the Greek form of your name after you all set forth. It's real, it's true, and like so much that is real and true it's not immediately obvious.'

'Lazarus?' asked Eleazar.

'Lazarus', agreed Word.

'Truth is so confusing', laughed Eleazar, a saying Johnny would suddenly remember when he heard Pontius Pilate intoning grandiloquently 'What is Truth?'

Johnny missed the next bit, and knew little more until James picked him up, put him over his shoulder, swung round to let Word kiss Johnny good-night, and they were out the door. But on their departure from Bethany next day, Word was asked by the crowd waiting outside (still half-shattered by the raising of Eleazar) to tell a story, and for once he gave one of its characters a name: Lazarus. Lazarus in the story was a very good man but also desperately poor, rotten with some skin disease which covered him with sores (Johnny wondered if it was leprosy, or boils like Job, but knew he must not interrupt when the story was being told to a crowd).

It would be a little while before Johnny realized that the people of Bethany would associate the name Lazarus to someone in one of Word's stories and nothing to do with their answers to inquisitive Temple priests, or suspicious Saduccees, or prying Pharisees, or ominous Roman soldiers or officials, or spies from Herod. By that time Eleazar would have gone away with Martha and Mary and Danny, and the name under which he would now lead them to another country would have a completely different connection, all the more because the story Word told fixed itself forcefully in the memory of anyone who heard it, or had it repeated to them. Johnny listened in fascination to the rich, strong, subtle voice which sometimes reminded him of a river, from its profound depths to its happy rapidity depending on where Word was in his story. It was a lovely morning, and the sun shone through Word's hair as he stood above them in a cart which Danny had put in place for him:

'Once upon a time there was a very rich man. He dressed in purple.' ('He might have been Tiberius' said Johnny in his mind. 'He might', replied Word's mind, 'although he wasn't.') 'He feasted sumptuously every day.' And as Word spoke Johnny saw the wealthy man at his table, surrounded by wines and meats, delicacies and staples, fruit and fish, ortolans and breads. Now Johnny was watching the plutocrat, swollen with his gluttony and complacent in his satisfaction, arms thicker than Peter's legs, chins propping one another up, belly almost bursting the luxurious garment clothing him. He was surrounded by figures only slightly less obese than himself, pawing nasty-looking ladies whose lips were larded with lurid light. Ugly musical instruments made noise, fortunately inaudible to Johnny. Servants approaching their master's weight padded in and out with fresh trivialities on request, as well as duly staggering under the next course. The wealthy man sang: that is, he opened his mouth, showing gold-encrusted teeth, and sounds must be coming from his inside. His guests smiled, smirked and sniggered, clapping their hands, and curling their lips on the leeward side. Fat dogs waddled in and out of the hall, slurping and salivating. Then Johnny found his glance following the dogs as they slobbered over to a bundle of rags lying in the gateway: 'a certain beggar named Lazarus' came Word's voice and now Johnny saw Lazarus kicked by the rich man's servants as he besought them, shivering with agony from sores which obviously became agonising as the dogs' tongues fouled them. Lazarus was pitifully lean, and coughing horribly, and even as Johnny watched and Word spoke, a convulsive shudder took Lazarus at the end of which he lay dead. The dogs moved in on the body with teeth open and eyes aflame, but Johnny saw no more of that, and no more, indeed, of anything, by now a most unusual situation when hearing Word's stories. Johnny understood why he was for once deprived of the picture Word's words made when he heard Word saying that Lazarus was carried by the angels to Abraham's bosom, and Johnny knew that no vision of Heaven would be given to him while he remained on Earth. (As it happened, he was wrong about that, but it would not be for many years to come.) Nor would he see Hell, to which the wealthy man was taken after death, according to Word, crying out to Abraham 'have mercy on me, and send Lazarus to dip the tip of his finger into water to cool my tongue, for I am tormented with this flame'. ('So', thought Johnny, 'the rich man knew who Lazarus was, and recognized him in Abraham's bosom, although he had never done anything for him while on Earth: and he knew that Lazarus would go to hell on an errand of mercy for the man who had utterly neglected him, which is one reason for Lazarus being in Heaven.') Word told how Abraham replied that the wealthy man had received his good things, and Lazarus only evil ones in life, and that a great gulf prevented any coming and going between Hell and Heaven. And the rich man begged Abraham to have Lazarus tell the rich man's brothers (who doubtless had been without pity for Lazarus when calling on their brother to share his feasts, and once more Johnny marvelled at the rich man's realisation that Lazarus's charity to those who had left him to rot remained boundless in all senses, and that the rich man was as ready when dead to exploit Lazarus as in life he had been ready to ignore him at all times). But, Word continued, 'Abraham told the rich man that his brothers had Moses and the prophets and could hear them, and when the rich man said that if someone went to them from the dead they would repent, Abraham further answered that if they did not hear Moses or the prophets they would not be persuaded even if someone did rise from the dead', and Johnny remembered without understanding the sad little grim smile with which Word ended his story. It, too, would acquire new meaning for him later.

The crowd became silent, but Philip asked what evil had the rich man done, and Word answered 'Nothing' and when Philip asked why then should he have been condemned, Word said that to do nothing was to assist evil when one should be fighting poverty, disease, misery, and suffering of any kind. 'To let evil flourish all that is necessary is for people to do nothing, and those who do nothing will receive nothing, those who permit hell will obtain hell. It would be as though you, Philip, being able to sing and make music, refused to give us the pleasure of your song.' Philip laughed and promptly started another song, to which they marched out of Bethany. Before long he had worked out a version of the story of Lazarus chorussing:

> And the rich man died,
> And he went down to Hell-y-um,
> Skim-your-milk maluya,
> O Raj-er-um!
> And the poor man died,
> And he went up to Heaven-y-um,
> Glory hallelujah,
> O Raj-er-um!

Johnny hoped such vulgarisation of the story didn't annoy Word, but in fact as they strode onward, hand in hand, Johnny felt Word's mind responding to his own with the words of the prophet 'for the earth shall be full of the knowledge of the Lord, as the waters cover the sea: be of good cheer, Johnny, for we shall hear the word of the Lord in many tunes on many tongues, by many lyres and in every kind of music. We shall yet hear Noah tell that he doesn't care where the water goes if it doesn't get into the wine' and when Johnny thought 'surely, Word, Noah never said that?', Word's mind solemnly answered him 'He will, Johnny, he will' and the two of them thought the same laughter and marched on.

Johnny hardly noticed the wear and tear on his own feet, and as usual Word kept pace with him, the others falling in line all the more readily with Philip's singing and playing (Martha had given him permission to take the lyre, snorting that it would give her more peace out of the house than she would get if it remained in it with the risk of Mary or Eleazar – or, worst of all, Danny – getting hold of it and fancying themselves as musicians, and she supposed she could add that to her causes of gratitude to Word, at whom she grinned firmly). They had tried out various songs and had somehow worked their way back to the parable of the wealthy man and poor Lazarus when their progress was suddenly barred by a young man of obvious wealth, to judge by the number of his attendants, sycophants and camels, and for a moment Johnny wondered if Word had willed him into being as a further illustration, and then wondered why the young man would look different from the way the wealthy man had looked in Johnny's imagination of Word's story. And the young man at first seemed to confirm this suspicion by addressing Word with the same unctuous condescension that Johnny was sure the rich man in Word's story spoke to Abraham, Hell or no Hell. In fact, the mix of the story, the song, and the unctuous address gave Johnny a very creepy feeling, and he knew by the way Word's hand tightened over his that Word was also finding a chilling recognition. 'Nature imitating Art' murmured Word's voice in Johnny's mind as the young man fawned on Word, whom he called 'Good Master' in a tone of voice that Johnny thought made him sound as if 'Good' meant 'half-witted':

'Good master, what good must I do to inherit eternal life?' Put like that, thought Johnny, you'd swear he saw the whole thing as some cash deal, to be gift-wrapped and held in trust for him so that he could buy his way into Heaven the second he was dead. 'Why do you come to me to ask of goodness?' demanded Word (his voice seeming to chill back, Johnny thought); 'God is good and he only.' ('But in that case he's right', argued Johnny to Word in his own mind. 'Word is God and if God only is good, then he sees Word is God.' 'Be quiet, and listen', said Word's mind.) The rest of the disciples glanced curiously at Word, since all of them now acknowledged him as the Messiah, and could see that Word was testing the rich youth. 'If you have a mind' (said Word, as if chatting about what hobby the rich youth might take up) 'to enter into life' (and Johnny for a dazzling moment saw how thin what we call life actually is when compared to real life, as though we thought of a puddle while trying to imagine the Mediterranean) 'then keep the commandments'. And when the wealthy young man asked which commandments he should keep, Johnny thought Word would speak of whole-hearted and whole-souled love of God and love of neighbours as ourselves, but to his surprise Word gave a much drier, more textual response, almost as if he were reading out loud something he had written himself:

'Thou shalt not Kill. Thou shalt not commit Adultery. Thou shalt not steal. Thou shalt not bear false witness. Honour thy father and thy mother.' And at that point, his eyes narrowing slightly, Word added 'Thou shalt love thy neighbour as thyself' and Johnny knew that the self whom the young man must love his neighbour as much as, was higher than any mountain he could imagine. He noticed also that Word had only spoken of commandments about love of our neighbours, and realised that God was altogether outside the young man's imagination. Meanwhile the young man was purring gently as though about to demand his prize. 'All these things I have kept ever since I have grown up', he smirked (and how could he have committed adultery before he grew up? thought Johnny irritably) 'Where is more expected of me?' 'If you want to be perfect', said Word, very simply, 'go home, sell everything you have, and give it to the poor, so your treasure will be in Heaven, and you yourself come back and follow me', and Word smiled, generously but a little tragically. The tragedy was quickly staged. The young man looked at servants, sycophants and camels, looked again at Word as if waiting for some flicker to tell him it had been a joke, found none, looked away from Word, sighed, and wheeled around, taking himself towards Jerusalem. 'Ah' thought Johnny, 'he really is rich.' 'Not at all', thought back Word, 'he is exceedingly poor.' 'And has just bankrupted himself', replied Johnny's mind. 'Pray for him, poor devil', responded Word silently, and to the other eleven he said out loud 'A rich man cannot enter the kingdom of God easily. A camel will find it easier to go through the eye of a needle, than a rich man to enter the kingdom of Heaven when he is rich in the world's goods.' 'So why not say a rich man cannot enter the kingdom of Heaven?' enquired Philip, ever the questioner. ('I was wondering that too', confessed Johnny's mind to Word's.) 'You don't know Jerusalem', said Judas irritably, mildly affronting Philip who on the basis of some annual pilgrimages to the Temple had thought that he did. 'The gate known locally as the Needle's Eye will only admit a camel with the greatest difficulty, which is what the Master meant, is it not so, Master?' 'It is so', acknowledged Word, faintly disappointing Johnny, who had been toying with a daft vision of camels looking in bewilderment at a smug needle held up in front of them.

'But it seems a harsh saying', continued Judas, 'especially now when we could do with friends in high places.' Jim, who had been delighted at Word's refusal to be patronised by the young man and rejection of his riches, snarled back at Judas 'we don't need friends like that! They only take pride in what drags them down, if they only knew it! The rich man passes by like bloom on the grass and the sun also rises, bringing the scorching wind, drying up the grass till its bloom falls and its beauty dies away, and so the rich man and his business enterprises will disappear.' 'That is a good gospel', said Word, mildly. 'But we will need such friends', insisted Judas. 'I know Jim has a noble mind, better than mine.' ('He means it', thought Johnny, 'Judas really is a decent chap.' 'I'm very glad you think that now', answered Word's mind to his.) 'But I know the dirty deceit and destruction men plot in their hearts in Jerusalem. The time may come when we really need friends who count for something there, however rotten the society that worships the golden calf.' 'And it is rotten', affirmed Matthew, his lips trembling slightly, as if a raw memory brought him close to tears ('with never a "begat" to comfort him', thought Johnny, sympathetically). 'You never know when you might need a rich friend, Master', Judas appealed to Word, who raised his eyebrows and gave a wry grin. 'The rich make fine tombs for themselves', Word answered, 'and I may need one sometime, for some time.' ('Stop making those silly jokes!' barked Johnny's mind at Word's, and Word laughed in his own mind back, and messed Johnny's hair sufficiently with his left hand to put Johnny to the trouble of flattening his hair out again with the fingers of both his own hands, forgetting what he had thought was Word's joke.) Thady threw them all back on themselves by remarking with a grim satisfaction 'If salvation is so hard for the rich, who can be saved?' and eyed them with new interest as though they were all so many lost causes. Word replied very seriously that such things were impossible for men to achieve, but not for God, to whom all things are possible. Shimon brightened up and said 'So we have the only friend we need in a high place', and Nat murmured 'and a very high place it is!' But Peter as usual wanted it spelled out. 'What about us, who have said goodbye to all our possessions and loved ones and followed you?' 'I haven't said goodbye to Johnny', mocked James. 'However much you tried', shouted Johnny, and James laughed while Word promised them that everyone who forsook home and lands, wealth and place, social standing and neighbours' admiration for Word's sake and the sake of his gospel, would get a hundred times their value and persecution as part of it, and everlasting life in the world to come. 'But many will be first who were last, and last who were first' he finished, and Jim nodded, 'Damn right.' Word smiled slowly. 'We will soon go up to Jerusalem, where the Son of Man will be given into the hands of the chief priests and scribes, who will condemn him to death, and then give him to the Gentiles who will mock him, spit on him, scourge him and kill him, and on the third day he will rise again.' It sounded like a game to Johnny, but he still couldn't think of it as more than a parable. Word couldn't die, and would live on as fully as Eleazar, thought Johnny, not clear why he thought Eleazar. Nor did it occur to him that he had never seen Eleazar die, or lie dead before him. 'As for the rich', added Word, 'God help them for they make gods of their riches. We must stop owning lands and money, we must hold wealth in common. Work for love, not for money. Give to any who need the means of living. If you let a child starve, you are letting God starve.' Johnny brightened up at this, and Word promptly realised their talk had made Johnny think of his next meal. So they walked on, and after several meal-stops where they met generosity enough to make Johnny think more kindly of Judaeans, they reached Jericho. And as they came to the town a blind man sat begging on the edge of the main highway. Johnny, who was perched on Peter's shoulders, saw the beggar ask who was passing, for the hospitality shown them along the way had produced its plenty of followers for Word, and someone seemed to answer, giving Word's name to the beggar. Yet the beggar knew more than the crowd, for he cried 'Son of David, have pity on me!' Johnny saw Matthew promptly look at the beggar with new respect, and turn to Word who nodded and stopped, asking to speak to the blind man, who was helped forward by Matthew and Judas. In fact, Matthew found a second blind beggar near at hand, and helped him over to Word as well while the first man was telling Word he was the son of Timaeus, and Word asked, what did they want him to do for them? Johnny had seen enough of the world by now to see how sensible this was. The men might simply want alms, and might not want to lose an assured income as blind beggars. But Bar-Timaeus said like a shot 'Lord, give me back my sight', and very quickly the other man said, 'And give back mine also', and Word stretched out his hands to both, saying 'Receive your sight: your belief has made you see again', and the crowd shouted for joy. The first thing each man did was to grab one of Word's hands and kiss it, and Johnny had seldom seen such joy on human faces. Word blessed them, and the lot of them marched on, only for them to stop once more as they came closer still to Jericho, and Word gestured up to a sycamore tree. Johnny could not quite see what he had seen there, but suddenly he distinguished among the branches a small, fat man, holding on but leaning over. The man looked as if he was counting the people, but Johnny could see that like so many before him, he was working out which of them was Word, who gazed up at him, lips quivering with laughter, and said without enquiry to anyone 'Zaccheus!'

The little man shook as though he were in an aspen rather than a sycamore, reflected Johnny, and grabbed a branch more firmly at which Word said 'Come down, quickly, I'm stopping off at your house!', which so much startled the little fat man that he really did come tumbling out of the tree, somersaulting as he landed, Word's hands flying out to catch his arms and set him on his feet, on which the little fat man swayed for a moment before seeming to take root on the highway. Once on the ground he seemed ready at last to let his feet stay where they were and began working his hands circularly one around the other and back, moving with extraordinarily quick gestures, vaguely reminding Johnny of people drawing wools together before spinning garments from them. Sometimes Zaccheus's hands would tire of any association with one another and both would fly upward, fingers whirling round and round while palms seemed to be pushing things over to the other side of a non-existent room. Johnny was still on Peter's shoulders and was thus too far away to make much sense of what Zaccheus was saying to Word, except that his voice shrilled in a few high notes and then dropped into incomprehensibility again. Then he began to smooth imaginary pieces of wool between the thumb and balls of his longest three fingers in each hand, and the hands themselves climbed upwards as far as the top of his head with about a foot separating hands from head. Word seemed to be making soothing gestures, and then Zaccheus suddenly took to his heels and pelted into Jericho looking like a small bear hurtling itself into the city in urgent pursuit of its father bear and mother bear, imagined Johnny to himself happily. Of course bears didn't live in houses even when there were three of them, and Zaccheus certainly did, as Word and the rest of the crowd were able to see when they arrived where he had stopped, to find a large house buzzing with activity. Zaccheus was hard at work directing servants, beseeching friends, instructing relatives, and ordering food and drink, and Word simply waited in front of the house, when suddenly even the noise being made by Zaccheus and his people preparing hospitality was crushed from earshot as sounds of laughter, tears, argument, song, imitations of horses' hoofs, and general indeterminate human noise increased in volume just beyond the next turn of the road and Johnny recognised the approach of his own kind. His first reaction was a flicker of resentment – he was Word's child, what were these others that they should muscle in? – but he had squelched that before Word's mind had to tell him to. On the other hand, Judas showed clearly that having reconciled himself to one child – and indeed saved its liberty at the cost of his own life – enough was enough, Peter's muscles seemed to tighten under Johnny's weight, Thomas's brow knitted in impatience, James pursed his lips and Shimon glared malevolently ahead of him as though Caesar's vilest legions were about to appear. Then about a score of children swept into view, followed by mothers and elder sisters carrying small fry. Matthew had been jumpy and ill-at-ease since Zaccheus fell out of the tree and evidently did not want Word to go to the house of Zaccheus, but his silence on that score now whipped him into a fairly savage snarl to the first arrivals 'Be off with you, and don't trouble the Master!' Several of the others made similar noises, either in words or in grunts. Immediately the mothers now in earshot replied with vehement cries that they wanted the Master to bless their little ones and lay his hands on them. Their combined outcry ended at one go, probably by accident, and Judas's querulous 'Go away, you little beasts!' bellowed hideously into the silence.

Word was furious, and glared at the disciples in general, and at Judas in particular, thundering 'Never prevent a child from coming to me, for it is from them the kingdom of God is made!' whereupon the children yelled with delight, Johnny's yells among theirs, as thunderous as Word himself. Judas flamed to the roots of his red hair, Matthew bit his lip in shame, Peter managed a hug for Johnny sliding down from his shoulders, Thomas kicked himself in the shin as though conscious of having betrayed the childhood he had shared with Word. But the children's yells stopped after that one cheer, and Word spoke again quieter now but clear as the sound of running water when first heard by a traveller in the desert. 'Be it so, and it is so. Whoever does not welcome the kingdom of God like a child shall never enter it.' And there he half-stood, holding the nearest children in his arms until their weight drove him down on one knee. Another small child promptly sat on the other knee. Johnny suddenly shivered, almost coming out in imaginary goose-pimples, as he remembered his own first meeting with Word, and thanked God for having known how to greet Word while not even thinking it out. And these children clearly knew. They crowded around Word, hugging his arms, hands, fingers, climbing on him and kissing him, rubbing their heads on his shoulders, surrounding him so that Johnny could hardly even see a hair of his head. Mothers thronged around that mass of boys and girls. Johnny stood grinning in sympathy at their happiness, but it was Philip who made the best answer from the disciples, moving back to a nearby wall, pulling out his lyre and singing

> Gentle Jesus, meek and mild,
> Look at me, a little child,
> Pity mine, and pity me,
> And suffer me to come to thee.

After some more verses he switched his tune:

> You saved the sons of Abraham,
> And children in the ark,
> Took Johnny from the Roman ship,
> And Miriam from the dark.

And then he started to sing about children:

> Ye are better than all the ballads
> That ever were sung or said:
> For ye are living poems,
> And all the rest are dead.

Word would teach those words in English translation to an American father nearly two thousand years later. The American did not think Word was God, but he knew it. The first verse Word would teach to an English maker of hymns a hundred years before the American. Many people repeated the words, and we cannot be quite sure we have the exact text, and we must always remember that English is a different language from Aramaic.

Eventually Zaccheus came out of his house to tell Word that food was ready for everyone, and since it was a fine day many people including the children were able to eat outside. Johnny got some of the older children to give him a hand serving platefuls to everyone. Zaccheus had not quite expected that everyone of the people following Word, and the mothers and children whom Word had blessed, would be staying to eat with him since however rich he was he was a tax-collector, but he gallantly disbursed funds to get more food and realised that Word had met him half-way, so to speak, since he found much more food in his house than he had imagined. It was only after they had eaten that people began to complain that Word had gone into the house of a sinner and had made them eat the sinner's food even if they themselves had not entered the sinner's house. It was men in the crowd who said this, and the women told them it was no way to speak of the Master, and the children began yelling that Word was their king, and eventually Word and Zaccheus came out of the house and waved their arms for silence, which they got at once from the children and after some delay from the women and, last of all, from the men who had denounced Word (and many men such as the disciples and formerly blind beggars defended Word angrily). And Zaccheus, throwing open his arms and starting the dance of his fingers once again, shouted 'Here and now, Lord, I give half of all I have to the poor, and if I have taken money wrongly from anyone I give back four times the amount', and Word told them 'Today, salvation has been brought to this house, for Zaccheus too is a son of Abraham.' (Philip grinned in gratitude to Word for using his verse so well, although Philip had simply meant the children Ishmael and Isaac, both of whose lives had been saved by God when doomed by their father Abraham, whom they ultimately laid out after his death and buried with honour.) Word stood looking at the crowd after it had shouted itself hoarse in honour of Zaccheus, and then added 'That is what the Son of Man has come for, to search out and to save that which was lost', and he took Zaccheus in his arms. And Johnny saw that Zaccheus was now perfectly still.

Word stayed for some hours with Zaccheus while Johnny played games with some of the children and Philip sat near at hand remembering and inventing songs which liked a lyre's accompaniment. In fact before the end of the evening, Word joined Johnny and the children in a ball-game, inventing its rules and making sure children would outnumber grown-ups.

They decided to play it with feet, but players were allowed to punch the ball away from them. The object seemed to be to kick the ball between two posts which were put up at each end of the field. Word took one team, Andrew the other, Thomas joined Word's forces, James supported Andrew's which included Johnny. Zaccheus acted as arbitrator, partly because he could whistle very loudly, which became the way they signalled a jail, the term used when the ball had definitely been sent through the posts. By the end of it each side had kicked ten jails. Andrew remarked that the game would be well worth teaching people in other countries when telling them the message of Word, and Johnny asked Word if it would be played with as much enjoyment in later times. 'That I can't tell you', said Word, 'but it's like the kingdom of Heaven in one way: people will enjoy it if they don't think the money that can be made from it more important than the game itself.'

They stayed the night in Jericho, with Zaccheus, some of his friends, and some of the parents of the children Word had blessed. Afterwards Word said they had better be getting back to Bethany, as he wanted to stay there before going on to Jerusalem which he must reach five days before Passover. On the way they saw ten men walking together, some needing crutches or sticks, some shuffling horribly, some hideously changed in faces and arms. They did not come too near, but they were near enough for Johnny to feel sick: somehow ten outcast lepers together seemed so much worse than the many Johnny had encountered as part of the people being laid out to be healed by Word back in Galilee. But however foul they looked, and however isolated, they knew Word, and cried 'Jesus, Master, have mercy on us'. Word stood in the highway, placing his hands to make a trumpet round his mouth, and cried 'go show yourselves to the priests', and as he walked on with Johnny's right hand in his left, Johnny's mind received Word's thought that they would be cured as they walked. But the confirmation of this came when about an hour later a solitary man came running up to them from Jerusalem, shouting 'Glory to God, Glory!', and throwing himself on the ground before Word and thanking him almost hysterically, and piteously looking up at Word to get permission to embrace his feet. Word smiled at him, caught a Samaritan accent, and asked where were the other nine while only the stranger had come back to glorify God? Then he raised the ex-leper from the ground, kissed him and said, 'your own faith has healed you'. Johnny knew that the Samaritan's body was now as clear of leprosy as his own, yet he could not avoid mental recoil from the thought of kissing a face which within the last couple of hours had been rotting away before the eyes of the world, the lips grey sponges, the nose disintegrating, the eyes sunken behind yellow matter and suppurating cheeks. In his mind Word spoke 'you, too, must have faith, Johnny, and I must have the greatest faith of all'. 'I'm sorry, Word', said Johnny contritely. 'No need to apologise to me, Johnny. And you will find your faith grows much as your own body will grow.' The Samaritan stood beside the road, waving a perfect hand after them until they were out of his sight. Johnny reflected to Word 'of course he could not have shown himself to the Temple priests, being a Samaritan'. 'Of course he could not', agreed Word in Johnny's mind, 'but he returned to recognise me as the priest to whom he should show himself. And it seems sad, Johnny, that I am apparently a more natural object of reverence to Samaritans rather than to my own people.' 'Well, you have me', thought Johnny quickly. 'For always and always', said Word in Johnny's mind. 'For always and always', answered Johnny's mind, and they walked onward towards Bethany hand in hand. Just for a moment it seemed to Johnny there was nobody in the world but himself and Word. Then Philip began to sing once more with appropriate lyre music, and the world was as it had been. They reached Bethany easily enough and it seemed superficially unchanged. Martha was as usual ready and waiting both to feed them and to belabour them. 'It's all very well bringing back my brother to life', she told Word, 'but you've given him enough energy to fill another boyhood as well as a man's strength. Danny will grow fat and die for want of work, with Eleazar taking on everything I tell the boy to do. I had been keeping some carpentry jobs for you, since you're a professional' (Word bowed, for want of a place to reply since Martha drew neither rein nor breath) 'but he's done each and every one of them, and to make matters worse he's done them so well that I can't even find anything wrong with them which would need you to do it over. Boys can be very aggravating, not that I need to remind you with him around' (she pointed at Johnny who momentarily shut her up by climbing on her knee and kissing her, to her great satisfaction). 'Tarshish?' asked Word, in the single breath she was obliged to take before planking Johnny back on his feet and herself resuming transmission. 'Yes, and going well, but a whale of a job', and Johnny realised Eleazar and his sisters were fleeing from Bethany by ship across the Mediterranean within a few days: Word's allusion to the flight of Jonah was clear enough, all the more because nobody now knew where Tarshish was, not that Jonah ever got there. Martha drew back her head and looked at Word from an angle that gave her a flickering resemblance to a very intelligent eagle (Johnny, who had liked being called an eaglet by Word when be zoomed from the Roman ship, wondered whether to salute her as a distant relative but thought on the whole that he had better not). 'I had an odd dream just after you left', she said, pensively. 'I thought I was trying to shove a camel through the eye of a needle. I can tell you it's very hard work.' 'A needle-eye like the Jerusalem gate?' enquired Word. 'No, the real thing', insisted Martha. 'And they're nasty, dirty things, camels. I had to get out of its way quickly whenever it tried to spit its green cud into my eye. Its breath stinks, and this one stank to the high Heavens, I'm surprised the angels stood it. I tried to put it through the eye of the needle as if I was threading the needle but I could only get its mouth in, and it tried to bite me and would have bitten me if I hadn't been lucky enough to have its muzzle on one side of the needle with its nose on the other.' 'You make me feel quite sorry for the camel', grinned Word. 'Just like a man, clinging to your own. It was a male camel, of course. Then I gave up on trying to thread the needle with the camel and put it into a handbag, and it wouldn't go into that either.' 'Don't worry about it', smiled Word. 'Riches won't stand in your way: you love the rest of us too much ever to let anyone come to harm if you can help it. You'll need any profit you make from the sale of the houses and the silver-smithy, for the costs the lot of you will meet when you get to your destination.' He looked at her with more concern and dropped his voice. 'Massilia is your Tarshish?' She nodded, suddenly silent. 'You'll make a fine country of it, provided you don't make it think it is one.' She smiled, a little sadly: 'I won't change. But I'll miss you – and that pest of yours' (and Johnny ducked her swipe at his head). 'I'll be with you', said Word, 'and you'll see Johnny sometime later, with God's help.' 'And now get over to Shimon the Leper's, the two of you, or not a drop nor a bite will go between the lips of the usual crowd of drop-outs you've brought with you, and they won't thank me for saying you kept me here listening to you which was the better part of the meal they hadn't got. Make sure my brother hasn't lost his burst of energy, or Danny isn't snoring on the supper-table, or my sister hasn't brought everything to a standstill by having one of her visions. She has a much higher class of nightmare. It'll be all right by me if I never see another camel. Get off, the pair of you!' But she suddenly wrapped her hand around Word's, and looked up at him with something very like fear in her eyes. Johnny would have sworn she was afraid for Word and not for herself, but he dismissed the fancy as ridiculous.

Philip was developing what he called a football psalm on the lyre with light-hearted suggestions from Nat and Andrew and even James, when Word and Johnny arrived at Shimon the Leper's. He kept working away on songs about Word and his work, many of which would be of use to people building up oral accounts of Word from which the writers of the Gospel would draw later still. Although Matthew had seen much, he would draw on the songs and folk-stories much as would Mark and Luke, who had never spoken to Word (Luke never even saw him). Johnny's gospel would be much more firmly limited to what its author had seen and heard. On the other hand it contained no reference to football, which apart from anything else would have taken too long to explain, and some of whose rules were in vague dispute. Word had given judgment on one or two matters such as what constituted an erroneous action which gave the other side an uninterrupted kick, but he never had another opportunity to iron out all arguments about it. Johnny never played it again in Judaea – there was too little space in Jerusalem and too many things happened there – but he did get up teams of players in Ephesus, and the game became popular among Christians there. The teams he knew best called themselves the Galatians and the Travellers, and it pleased Johnny greatly that any bad feeling resulting from matches was always dispelled because they recognised in each other believers in the same Christianity.

That supper at Bethany was the last formal meal they would all have with Martha, Mary and Eleazar. It was understood that as the week before Passover went by, members of the group would make their own way back and feed themselves as best they could, each night. Word and Johnny stayed in Jerusalem, how and with whom we will see later. By Thursday Martha, her siblings, and Danny, were to be on the road. Nobody made any public statement of farewell, but as Word reclined at the table with Johnny at his left and Eleazar on his right, Mary stood at Word's feet holding a pound of most expensive ointment of spikenard, and rubbed it into Word's feet, creating an exotic scent throughout Simon the Leper's house, and Johnny saw that she wept as she polished the feet, and, kneeling to kiss them, wiped them clean with her own hair. Johnny was moved by the solemnity of her action, and for once Eleazar looked sorrowful, leaning over to hug Word with an arm over his shoulders. But inevitably after Mary stood up and glided away, tongues were unloosed and Johnny was disgusted at criticism actually coming from the guests, though he realised most people there would not know how quickly Mary's household, and Word's followers, were soon to be sundered, never more to meet save in the remotest improbability. But as talk flowed Johnny was really shocked to hear Judas's tones sharpening among those of other critics: 'I'd put the price of that spikenard at three hundred pence and surely the Master's instructions would be better carried out if it had been sold and the money given to the poor.' Eleazar started up in real anger, but Word's hand shot out of his sleeve, and grasped his host's wrist, and he turned round to face Judas and say 'she has kept this for the day of my burial' – and Johnny realised Mary must have bought the ointment to anoint her brother at his burial a couple of days before Word raised him. Johnny thought it odd she should have bought a double portion with Word in mind, but perhaps she had some idea that he would bring Eleazar back to life and wanted to honour him. Mary had a touch of the prophet, Danny had told him that much. What Word had meant by his own burial must be part of what Johnny insisted were strange riddles or jokes he kept on making about his own 'death', and the focus on Word drew attention away from the imminent flight of the family of Bethany. But Johnny didn't like Judas having spoken like that, in danger of hurting the beloved three (four if you counted Danny, which Johnny sometimes did). And he remembered Judas's joke, which Johnny didn't know was a joke, about stealing from the common purse – if they had taken the spikenard as a gift and sold the ointment, would the poor ever see it? Something was dragging Judas back to the bitterness Johnny remembered in him before they became friends: but Johnny had never realised how much jealousy had lain at the heart of Judas's dislike of himself, and the same spirit of jealousy, looking for another outlet, had found it in Eleazar's family whom Word obviously loved so much. For all of Word's instructions to give to the poor, he continued to defend Mary, again in terms that made Johnny uneasy: 'the poor you always have with you, but me ye have not always'. Still, there was no doubt about it, for Word to put things like that took attention away from the family's future.

Johnny wondered if Danny would go with them, and Danny frankly told him he would, when they talked after supper. 'But I thought you would go back to your people?' asked Johnny. 'These are my people', said Danny. Johnny looked at him in confusion, and Danny shrugged his shoulders: 'either Mary or Martha is my mother, I've no idea which. I don't know who my father was, and I don't care. To have two mothers may be better than having a father.' 'They're lovely people', said Johnny shyly. 'They are', said Danny. 'You're a good kid, Johnny. Bet you can't beat me to the tree at the other end of the village if I let you get to the fig-tree down the road there before I start to run.' They never spoke of the matter again, but when they finally said goodbye to one another next day, Danny gave Johnny a tiny chalice, beautifully worked in silver, casually remarking that it was the best bit of work he had done under Eleazar's direction and that the family were happy to have him give it to Johnny as a keepsake from them all. Johnny gave Danny the football he had been carrying since Jericho. When Johnny was on his own with Word he asked if Word knew whose child Danny was, and Word smiled and said 'yes, and I have forgiven her, and she has forgiven herself. She is a truly good woman, as people who have risen above their sins are. It is the people who are convinced they never sin, that sin all the time.' Johnny never found out which one she was, and never tried to.

By the time Danny and Johnny had gone back to the supper-room Philip was entertaining the company again with some more of Word's stories put into verse:

> Now who was the kindly neighbour here
> In the eyes of that robbed and wretched man
>
> The Levite, to the Lord most dear,
> The priest he had been taught to revere,
> Or the despised Samaritan?

Johnny nodded off, and once again James saw him to a comfortable bed. Before they left Bethany the morning after, Philip proved to have won more lasting attention from his songs than he had expected, and he was approached by some Greeks who wanted to meet the man behind the songs. This looked like getting in the way of the start of their journey, so Philip quickly consulted Andrew as the disciples' organizer, but they agreed it was wrong not to introduce the Greeks to Word. 'And here is the man whose words take root in songs', proclaimed Philip, one eye on the line he had just spoken with a view to future use, only to have his powers of invention thrown on another track by Word's grinning greeting 'Next he'll call me Lord of the Dance'. But when the Greeks asked Word for his philosophy (to the annoyance of Johnny, who didn't know what a philosophy was), Word stood very straight and tall, and it seemed almost as though his hair and beard were bristling. Philip said afterwards 'it was as if he was thinking poetry', and Johnny, who could not reach Word's mind at this point, suspected that this was what Word really was doing, closing the edges of his mind in the act of creation. 'The hour is come', said Word at last, 'that the Son of Man should be glorified.' Johnny let out a cheer, Andrew, anxious but affectionate, gently slipped his hand over Johnny's mouth. Word nodded his head, saying 'be it so, and it shall be so, that unless a grain of wheat falls into the ground and dies, it lives on as itself and nothing else, but that if it dies, it brings to birth fruit in abundance. He who loves his life shall lose it, he who hates his life and what fattens it in this world will keep it in eternal life. Anyone who is to be my servant must follow my way, and so my servant must be where I am.' Once again Johnny had the thought that he and Word were standing absolutely alone, that as always Word's presence gave him happiness beyond all description, but that suddenly a cold wind swept down on them, preventing them from holding hands although not from willing their love to one another. 'If any one serves me, my father will honour him.' And now Johnny, almost blinking as his eyes caught Philip and Andrew and the Greeks, looked again directly at Word who looked back at him saying 'Now is my soul troubled, and what am I to say? Father, save me from undergoing this hour of trial? But I have only reached this hour of trial so that I might undergo it. Father, make your name known.' And a voice Johnny had heard when he stood at the top of the mountain with Peter,

James, Moses, Elijah, and Word, spoke again 'I have made it known, and will yet make it known.'

To Johnny, of course, this was the voice of Word's father, which he greeted as boys of ten usually greet the fathers of their friends, that is, with a slightly timid smile. Since Word obviously loved his father, the smile was not too timid. He could hear other voices at his back saying 'Thunder' (saying it in Greek, but Johnny (being a Son of Thunder) had been taught the word by Word) while still others (and Johnny thought he could hear the voices of Mary, Martha, Eleazar and Danny) were saying 'An angel was speaking to him'. Andrew and Philip, who had heard nothing like this in their lives but who had a better idea who it was, fell on their knees. Johnny lifted his head, nodded, and knelt also. Farther away, alongside the Bethany family, Peter and James were also on their knees, knowing quite well who it was, Nat followed their example, the other disciples remained standing and looked confused. Word looked at Johnny with real pain, and said 'It was for your sakes and not mine that these words were spoken. Judgment is now being given and sentence being passed on the prince of this world who will be cast out. And if I am lifted up from the earth I will draw all men unto me.' Johnny ran over to Word and put his arms around him. He could make little sense of this, but if Word was going anywhere, or being taken anywhere, Johnny was determined he would follow. He did not need to promise. Meanwhile a few local Pharisees were disputing with quotations from the book of Daniel that the Son of Man would be given authority and rule for ever and what did Word mean that the Son of Man was to be lifted up, and what Son of Man was this?, not the real one, surely if he was not the immediate conqueror. Word lifted Johnny in his arms, kissed him, whispered 'tell Eleazar and his sisters that I will be back soon to say goodbye', and set him down, and while Johnny worked his way through the crowd on his errand, Word spoke again: 'The light is still with you, but only for a short time. Walk while you have the light, lest darkness come upon you, for the people who walk in darkness do not know where they are going. While you still have the light, believe in the light, so that you will become children of the light.' And suddenly he could not be seen, and after a few moments' wonder, the people went their different ways. Johnny did not see what became of the Greeks, and assumed they were on their way to Jerusalem for Passover, but in fact they were guides who would start Martha, Mary, Eleazar and Danny on their long journey, and take ship on the Mediterranean with them. They remained out of sight, from good nature, when last farewells were being taken of the Bethany family by Word and Johnny.

Philip got the disciples moving with a new song:

> The Spirit lives to set men free
> Walk, walk in the Light:
> He binds us all in unity
> Walk, walk in the Light.
> Walk in the Light!
> Walk in the Light!
> Walk in the Light!
> Walk in the light of the Lord!

Johnny, walking somewhere in the middle of the group alongside Word, was suddenly struck by the thought that Miriam would probably like Philip and his songs. 'But she'd tell him where he gets off for that line about the Spirit living to set men free, and would insist it implies women will be left as slaves. He'd have to mend his manners if he married her', he thought, and sensed Word's reply in his mind 'especially if their children were all daughters.'

OURTEEN

ANNAS

He was not that Light, but was sent to bear witness of that Light

Thinking and talking about Jerusalem after he had left it and gone to Ephesus, Johnny always seemed to conjure it up as a single picture, though he must have become aware of it first as bits of town thrusting themselves amid the peace of the countryside. But he had a mission to fulfil then, and thought about that before he began to think about Jerusalem. Johnny would live several years in Jerusalem, and the worst thing in his life and in the life of the world happened there, something that was also the best thing for the world, and Jerusalem was inextricable from those terrible and wonderful memories. But the city itself lived, and all the terrible things that had happened to it and would happen, were men's things. Johnny knew that King Saul had lived in Jerusalem where David brought him Goliath's head, and what with blood and flies wasn't that a dainty dish to set before the King? who didn't like it, and didn't like David very much either, although his son Jonathan did. And when they were dead David ruled in Jerusalem having reigned seven years in Hebron. Johnny liked thinking about David before he became king, but not so much afterwards, and Solomon his son made beautiful meditations and proverbs but forsook God for hundreds of nasty pagan women in Jerusalem and even Saul was probably all right until *he* started living in Jerusalem. Johnny asked Word who founded Jerusalem, and who owned it before Saul used it, and David later took it over. Word said he thought the Egyptians founded it, but that there was probably settlement there before them, and that Saul and David

246

took it from the Jebusites.

'And who were the Jebusites?' demanded Johnny.

'Do you remember what Ezekiel was told to tell Jerusalem? "Your root and your nativity is of the land of Canaan."'

'Then – 'Johnny was going on when Word's voice came into his mind 'Don't speak it. Think it.' There was nobody near them but they could have been overheard, especially if they mentioned someone's name.

'They are cousins of Shimon the ex-Zealot', thought Johnny to Word.

'They were', thought back Word. 'There weren't many left after Joshua. No, come to think of it, the Jerusalem Jebusites were one people Joshua didn't murder. There were too few of them, and he mustn't have thought they were important enough to kill. Lucky them. I suppose not too many survived David and Solomon.'

'Didn't you – or your father – tell Joshua to kill?' erupted Johnny's mind.

'Didn't I – and my father – tell everyone not to kill?' replied Word's mind.

'But the sacred words have said it?' spluttered Johnny's mind.

'God cannot do wrong, or say wrong', replied Word's mind. 'God cannot unsay his own commandment. You are to love one another as I love you. My way of loving you isn't to kill you, is it?'

'No', replied Johnny's mind. 'It is to increase my life beyond anything I know.'

'Exactly', and Word swung Johnny's hand in his as they walked along.

One effect of thinking about the Egyptians founding Jerusalem and the Jebusites holding it long after the children of Israel conquered Canaan was that Johnny saw it take a new being in his mind. It was no more alien to him and no less part of him than it bad been: full of Judaeans and therefore not Galilean enough, but containing the Temple which was the centre of Johnny's faith until he met Word. But it took on a solitude he had not imagined before. It was younger than his own world, where the waters of Galilee had been playing their harpstrings before a Jew set foot in Jerusalem – or indeed before anyone did, thought Johnny, but Jews like him must have been fishing in Galilee long before David and Solomon. Yet one thing singled out Jerusalem. Its red rims rose above its hollow centre as though it was a great mouth calling its blessing on God before anyone walked near it. If ever there was a city shouting to God, it was Jerusalem.

It was as if God had made a place on earth so that it would speak to him. When David's hands were on the harp creating psalms instead of on the sword singing death, he chanted that as the mountains are round about Jerusalem, so the Lord is round about his people from henceforth even for ever. It was when the Lord was among his people that the trouble happened, thought Johnny in retrospect. To be encircled by God should mean that God also comes inside the circle, but that was not how people wanted him. And so the worst thing happened.

And yet it all began so happily. Or so it seemed. Word might have seemed faintly overcast, as though a cloud hinted passage over the sunlight to which Johnny so often likened the light of Word's face, yet when he looked at Johnny, or heard him, the light returned. Johnny talked or thought at Word more frequently on this account, whether he had anything to say or not. It was as though he was in a play and all would be well so long as he kept talking, although they had forgotten what lines to tell him to say, or he had forgotten to learn them. And as they drew near to Jerusalem, standing on the Mount of Olives, Word asked Andrew and Judas to get him an ass's colt, as yet unridden, which he would take to ride into Jerusalem, and tell anyone who might object (such as the owner) that the Lord had need of them. Johnny realised that since Word chose Andrew and Judas, the owner of the colt had been baptised by Word's cousin John and should probably be able to identify them as John's disciples. There was some argument about what Word had said, when the two were setting out, Matthew insisting Word had demanded both the colt and its mother the ass, while Judas and Andrew vehemently insisted that even Word was not going to ride on two quadrupeds at once, but as it turned out the colt's mother trotted alongside it, and the owner simply told Andrew he was proud to fulfil the word which his own Baptizer had prophesied. Johnny learned that outcome later. He was off on his own mission, having alerted the children in Bethany drawn by Philip's songs to watch their departure, and having told the children in Jericho to await Word's arrival in Jerusalem if they could and to pass the word via relatives and friends to Jerusalem if they couldn't. Johnny had asked Word how he would enter Jerusalem, and Word, expressing hope that Johnny now knew the prophets from Amos, told him he would find the answer in the end. So Johnny naturally ran over what he could remember of the prophet Zachary (not the father of the Baptizer) and was very pleased with himself when he spotted the verse

> Rejoice greatly, O daughter of Zion:
> shout, O daughter of Jerusalem: behold,
> thy King cometh unto thee: he is just,
> and having salvation; lowly, and riding
> upon an ass, and upon a colt the foal
> of an ass.

And Johnny told Word he thought it was a great example in humility for Word to lower himself to that level, and when Word asked what was low about a colt, Johnny leered and said 'nothing low about a colt, only about a king' and Word hooted with laughter. That conversation had happened before Jericho, so that Johnny had had plenty of time to make his plans, open to Word's inspection in Johnny's mind, but not something they talked about. Once Andrew and Judas started off to find the colt, Johnny skittered off to where children were playing, and shouted 'the Great King who raised Eleazar from the dead is coming, mounted on a colt as the prophet Zachary foretold!' and the children raced off and found other children and their yells as they raced across Jerusalem arose to high heaven, and pretty soon the whole line of Word's obvious progress from the Mount of Olives to the Temple was thronged with children of all ages, waving flags and brightly-coloured cloths, shouting songs, singing psalms and canticles, bellowing instructions at one another, and occasionally being drilled into line by Johnny who raced from one end of the ranks to the other and back, detouring as necessary. To Johnny's delight, Philip entered into the spirit of it by extemporising a fine march on his lyre 'Sing the Return of the King!' and James, of all people, found a drum and strode out in front of Word on the colt, while Johnny skipped away ahead of them.

Along the way Johnny recognised faces if not names from Bethany, and even a few footballers from Jericho: he knew Danny could not be there, because he had to help get his family off on their exile, and to his surprise Johnny found himself missing Miriam even more. But she was far away in Galilee, and Johnny himself was careful to speak with a Judaean accent so as to win and hold street credibility as far as his powers of imitation permitted him. Johnny set the example of shinning up tree trunks and cutting light boughs and slithering down to wave them up and down and ultimately hurl them before the colt (and its mother) while taking up Philip's 'Sing the Return of the King!' and starting various other chants so that Word, smiling and laughing and waving, made a stately progress over the branches and cloaks flung under the hooves of his mount to the sounds of *'Hosanna! Hosanna! Hosanna!' 'Blessed is he who comes in the name of the Lord!' 'Sing the Return of the King!' 'Blessed be the kingdom of our father David that cometh!' 'Hosanna: Blessed be the King of Israel that cometh in the name of the Lord!' 'Peace in Heaven!' 'Glory in the Highest!' 'Who Cares for Pontius Pilate?'* Some sanctimonious bystander shouted 'Master! Rebuke thy disciples!', which unquestionably asked a miracle of no mean order, given James's drum, Philip's lyre, Jim's chanting 'You cannot be serious and worship Tiberius!' Johnny's latest bellow 'WORD WILL MAKE YOU FREE!' (somewhat impeded by giggles induced by Word's voice in his mind 'must you advertise me like a laxative?'). Eventually Word drew abreast of one of the men demanding suppression of noisy disciples and slid an answer into the tiny space when the crowd caught its breath: 'if they shut up, the stones would roll in song!' ('What did he say to you?' asked a companion. The aggrieved Pharisee spat. 'He was taking the Mick.')

By now innumerable fronds of palms were fluttering down before the colt and ass as more and more children shot up and tore the branches away. Roman soldiers were looking with some contemptuous concern at the procession, but they were not formed into any regular body, and the individual troops, while armed for action, made little contact among themselves. Two of them were together when five or six of the jostling, shouting, leaping children managed to destabilise one of the two, and after swaying furiously for two or three moments he toppled over, was rescued by his friend, and peered savagely at the stream processing its miscreants far from him. His companion thrust a wooden stave into the crowd, but children jumped over it, and eventually two or three jumped on it and smashed it. The soldiers mumbled threats but despaired of making a serious capture, and however much they would have liked to kill a child or two, it caused more trouble than it was worth, as they told one another.

But they noted Word, as what they called a ringleader.

At last the colt reached the Eastern Gate, and Word was able to dismount. Johnny knew from the thoughts they had exchanged on the way that Word was more amused than annoyed at the demonstration Johnny had orchestrated, but he was not prepared for Word catching him up in his arms, kissing him heartily, and speaking the words of the other Zachary, John the Baptizer's father, first spoken to his infant son:

> As for you, little child,
> You shall be called a prophet of God, the Most High.
> You shall go ahead of the Lord
> To prepare his ways before him,
> To make known to his people their salvation
> Through forgiveness of all their sins,
> The loving-kindness of the heart of our God
> Who visits us like the dawn from on high.
> He will give light to those in darkness,
> Those who dwell in the shadow of death,
> And guide us into the way of peace.

Johnny threw his arms around Word's neck, a little bewildered, but realizing that Word had known his antics as a wildly expressionist act of love. What he did not expect was that Word would be crying, not violently, but with big tears which furrowed down his cheeks. For no reason that he could understand it made Johnny cry too. So they stood there like that while the procession hooted and cheered, sang and danced, yelled and chanted, all around them, and the other disciples came up. Word had only time to say 'stay on in the Temple when I leave, don't tell anyone you're with me, and go with the people who will ask you to go with them, and then come back to the Garden of Gethsemane', and Johnny to say 'I love you'.

But he thought quite a bit while the others were gathering, and plans were being made where they would stay the night, and who would go back to Bethany, and who knew someone in Bethphage, and what was where and why. He had realised long ago that Word did not like towns and cities, and preferred country roads and blue water, and if he was in a town was happiest in the house of a friend. Nazareth Word never mentioned, if he could help it: the hurt was too great. But even when he liked a town – Capernaum, for instance, or Bethsaida, places where fisherfolk lived – he was hard in what he preached about it. Johnny had asked him why and Word said that towns were places where people thought too much about money and thought about each other in wrong ways, exploiting and swindling one another, domineering and exulting over one another, using the worship of God for ostentation and social advantage. Yet in his grim warnings to the towns, Word always sounded a note begging for their repentance and return to love of God and of one another: if it was possible for Nineveh to repent and atone, it was possible for the towns of Galilee. If he said harsh things, he spoke as a friend. Here Word was in a city which he knew held his bitterest enemies. Yet its welcome had been wonderful. But – it was almost all from children, Johnny realised, with some cheering from women. And virtually no men except some frowning Pharisees and sneering Sadducees and ugly Roman soldiers. So they turned to the others who came up now (James had held them back as he saw Word needed a few moments with Johnny). But as they did, Johnny's mind wondered why Word had wept, and it was as though his own mind was filled with weeping through which he could hear Word crying 'Jerusalem! Jerusalem! you that kill the prophets and stone those sent unto you, how often would I have gathered your children together as a hen gathers her chickens under her wings, and ye would not.' 'The children have come to you', said Johnny's mind. 'And it is the children who will suffer for the actions of their elders and ancestors', answered the mind of Word, 'and give their lives through no fault of their own. But they will die beloved of my father who will give them the justice they will never have here.' And now he was speaking out loud, as they were joining the others, and Judas, with the pardonable pride of a city-dweller was sliding unmistakably if unwittingly into the character of a guide:

'In the fifteenth year of his reign, Herod rebuilt the temple, and encompassed a piece of land about it with a wall, which land was twice as large as that before enclosed. The expenses he laid out upon it were vastly large also, and the riches about it were unspeakable. A sign of which you have in the great cloisters that were erected about the temple, and the citadel which is on its north side. The cloisters he built from the foundation, but the citadel he repaired at a vast expense, nor was it other than a royal palace, which he called Antonia, in honour of Antony.' ('Who was Antony?' flicked Johnny's mind to Word's. 'A Roman general later defeated by Caesar Augustus when he allied with Cleopatra, whom you have heard of.' 'From your mother', said Johnny, and could almost feel warmth returning to Word's mind.) The Galileans began to grow a little restive but Judas continued remorselessly:

'We now approach the south front of the temple, which has indeed itself gates in its middle, as also it has its royal cloisters' ('he's told us this bit!' snarled Johnny's mind and it wasn't alone in its irritation) 'with three walks, which reach in length from the east valley unto that of the west, for it is impossible that it should reach any farther; and this cloister deserves to be mentioned better than any other under the sun' ('Who asked you to mention any of them?' champed Johnny's mind) 'for while the valley is very deep, and its bottom cannot be seen, if you look from above into the depth, this farther vastly high elevation of the cloister stands upon that height, insomuch that if anyone looks down from the top of the battlements, or down both these altitudes, he would be giddy, while his sight cannot reach to such an immense depth.' It was unfortunate that he paused for breath as Matthew was heard to speculate to Thomas 'I wonder how much the tourists paid him for this when he was living here?' answered by Thomas's 'too much!' Judas was rapidly reverting to urban sophistication, one of whose doctrines is that it is always countryfolk who are the bores, so he practically spat at Matthew and Thomas, and Johnny hardly improved matters by giggling, which genuinely hurt Judas. Some of the children were visibly drifting away, Judas's lips tightening as he saw twos and threes hissing a word or two to one another and stealing off. But Word straightened his shoulders and strode towards the Temple gate, leading them into the Outer Court up the grand stairway which Judas was now too furious to discuss or proclaim. The Royal Portico under which they entered also received no guidance, and just as well since when they actually got into the Court the babel of noise would have made Judas incomprehensible apart from adding to its ghastly volume.

The first thing that assailed Johnny was the lowing of cattle, closely harmonising with more insistent sheep-bleats. Behind them the sacrificial birds were making noises anywhere between love-calls and laments, and indeed for the first time Johnny was aware how justifiably the Psalmist had spoken of moaning like a dove. Breaking through the animal and bird sounds was the rattle of coin as money-men disputed the temple-offerings they were ready to trade in exchange for denominations of every known kingdom and imperiate under the sun, or at least under Tiberius. Arguments now made their distinctive way into the chaos and recriminations of various degrees of vituperation added their several colours. Herdsmen occasionally yelled at one another to get their animals under control and not be blocking the traditional movement of whoever they were preventing from moving. Meanwhile the children flocking in after Word and his disciples and followers began to shout at each other, all the louder since they were released from the pretence of listening to Judas.

Johnny was genuinely shocked. He had supposed that his first sight of the Temple would be one of the most profound religious experiences of his life, apart from Word, and anyway much more solemn, and one could have no more solemnity or reverence here than at a bazaar or marketplace anywhere. His mind automatically transmitted his disappointment and disgust to Word, and Word gazed on Johnny's disillusionment for a moment and then whirled round, nearly colliding with a cattle-dealer who was already in three-sided altercation with a rival farmer and his own prize bull which bellowed its answers to him with a spirit as good as his own. The dealer was striking the bull with a whip of cords, thus raising the serious possibility of the bull taking its retaliation to even more ferocious lengths, so that in grasping the whip Word was probably rescuing its indignant owner. Johnny never saw Word seize the whip, and as Word coiled it round his own wrist Johnny somehow got the idea he had made it. Anyhow, he skittered after Word as fast as he could, for by means of the whip Word was cleaving his way through men and menagerie alike and caring very little about which be knocked over, no, he did care, for when a sheep backed away from him and then half fell over with a pathetic wailing bleat, Word reached across and brought it back to its feet. Johnny swore he could see the sheep give a smile of gratitude, and fancied the sheep passing on its pride to a colleague or friend. And now Word had reached the dove-sellers, and struck left and right, not to connect with the flesh of the vendors, but loosing their control of their birds whose cages he opened and strings he broke. Johnny following behind him imitated Word, ducking the occasional fists of the furious custodians. When he got

254

enough space to look around, partly through the vendors getting out of Word's way as he made for the money-changers, Johnny could see several free fights going on. One cattle-dealer (who looked indeed as if he had graduated as a cattle-thief) had actually succeeded in felling Peter with an ugly rabbit punch, only to be sent flying by a beautiful upper-cut from Andrew, roaring with rage. Matthew had evidently made a bee-line for the money-changers straightaway, reaching them before Word, and Johnny could just hear him shrieking 'and then you look down on us publicans!' while he kicked the legs of the nearest table, toppling it over, and then (accidentally, Johnny assumed) kicked the legs of the money-changer behind it. The money-changer grabbed the table and whirled it round so as to crash it down on Matthew's head, but Shimon the ex-Zealot, coming up smartly on Matthew's right, lowered his head and drove it into the stomach of the table-wielder, who lost interest in further hostilities for the moment. Meanwhile a couple of attendants, usually left to keep an eye on the Court with little obligation to interfere at most times, came hurtling across towards Word, having decided he was the root of the trouble, but they never reached him. James squared up against one of them, and when the fellow backed off he went head over heels across Johnny, who had dropped on all fours behind him in response to James's tactics: they had fought with each other at home often enough to anticipate each other's moves, however unusual it was to find themselves fighting on the same side. Jim came racing across to the other attendant, with Thady behind him, and the two of them grabbed him by the shoulders, swinging him clear of the ground: his threshing feet made it easier for Philip and Nathaniel to seize them and rush him to the Portico through which they slung him. He was hurt more in dignity than in person, and he did not return. Word had meanwhile reached the money-changers' tables, and began systematically to upset them: Thomas got behind him, and whenever any money-changer looked like attacking Word, Thomas simply hit him over the head with an earthware pot he had found somewhere. It broke over the skull of the last financier. Meanwhile Judas remained at the Portico, almost frozen with horror.

Word turned towards the Court, and Johnny saw he was about to address them, so Johnny bellowed at his best, perhaps inspired by the bull, and James thunderously took up the cry of silence for Word. Even the children, who had followed the various component parts of the struggle with individual support, stopped their shouts of approval and applause, and the animals showed their customary deference to Word. A pair of turtle-doves took up their stance one on each shoulder, which if anything only added to Word's regal appearance, as he said wholly audibly though very cool and quiet:

'It is written, My house shall be called the house of prayer; but you have made it a den of thieves.' Johnny could remember how the Lord told Jeremiah to tell the people that if what they did was good, God would dwell with them in the Temple, but to have no hope in lying and then thinking all would be well because they were in the Temple. What led up to that anyway? He nodded; he had it:

> Behold, ye trust in lying words, that cannot profit.
>
> Will ye steal, murder, and commit adultery and swear falsely, and burn incense unto Baal, and walk after other gods whom ye know not:
>
> And come and stand before me in this house, which is called by my name, and say, we are delivered to do all these abominations?
>
> Is this house, which is called by my name, become a den of robbers in your eyes? Behold, even I have seen it, says the Lord.

Johnny's excellent memory could probably have supplied that on its own, but he wondered if Word's mind had given his a nudge, because it looked as if many other minds had recaptured the same words. Certainly the money-men were gathering up their coins as quick as they could and not bothering even to fight with one another as to whose denarius this was, or whether he or he owned that shekel, or whether somebody else had so many drachmae or had it been mostly oboloi? At least the shepherds and cowboys knew their own, as could be seen from the speed with which they were moving them through the Portico. Meanwhile the children began to call out again '*Hosanna to the son of David!*' More child voices could be heard taking the cry up outside. The disciples began to clean up the Court as best they could, while worshippers began to stream into the Court both from the Temple itself and from the city outside. Johnny saw blind people being piloted in towards Word, and some lame people, and deaf and dumb persons to judge from the sign language being made to them, and Word touching some and speaking to others. Some attendants appeared, more pacifically than their predecessors, but still belligerent enough in tongue, one snarling at Word as the children continued to hail him son of David. 'Do you hear what they are saying?', and Word, his hands still healing and looks still curing, replying without turning his head 'Have you never read, "Out of the mouths of babes and sucklings hast thou ordained strength"?' And another, heavily, officially: 'What sign do you show us, seeing that you do these things?' Word sent a leper from him with skin pure and holy before he replied 'Destroy this temple, and in three days I will raise it up', and they came back almost counting on their fingers to show that it had taken forty-six years to build the Temple and how could he do it in three days? And they looked nervously around them as though Word might do it while they blinked. Word laughed, a little mirthlessly, Johnny thought, and went back to healing his many petitioners, and Johnny seemed to hear Word's mind within his own saying that his own body was the Temple, and Johnny's mind replied happily that he knew that, without bothering to ask why Word should talk about the destruction of his own body. And still the invalids and disabled flocked before him, and the attendants hung around a little longer, but gave it up and went back to helping in the clear-up.

But there was still a great deal to clean up after all Word's miracles had been worked, and Word walked out of the Court with his disciples, followed by the children. He nodded to Johnny as he left, and Johnny nodded back, saying in his mind 'see you soon, in the Garden of Gethsemane', and Word's mind repeating 'in the Garden of Gethsemane'. Johnny ran around hither and thither, having had to stop to wash himself several times, and getting brushes to remove dirt and waste, and straightening any tables still knocked over after the last departures, and was still plentifully occupied when a very old man entered the Court from the Temple itself, clucking like a hen who mislaid her chickens. He was clearly a priest, though not particularly richly dressed. His beard was long and white, his hair long and grey, his eyebrows long and faintly yellow. Below the eyebrows his eyes were predictably brown, and darted left and right. His shoulders were bowed, and his height can never have been high: at present he was only slightly taller than Johnny. He shuffled rapidly around, muttering to himself. It took Johnny a little while to realise that he was muttering verses of the scriptures, but then at first he was not near Johnny, who went quietly about his own work. But as he washed, and brushed, and cleaned, Johnny realised the little old man was drawing nearer and nearer, and finally Johnny heard clearly what he was saying. The words were the words of the Preacher, the son of David, whom Johnny had been taught to think of as Shlomo, the great King Solomon as the Gentiles called him, but if something was holy Scripture Word must have caused it to be written in his capacity as God. Johnny listened, and now the old man began to sing, in what was a cracked voice and thin, even tinny, where once it might have had sweetness, and yet a voice which had known for seventy years or so what it was now singing, whose intimacy with the verses and the contour of the tune was the love affair of a lifetime, so that in old age the song continued to love the singer, as the singer his song. So the old man sang:

> To every thing there is a season, and a time to every purpose under the heaven:
> A time to be born, and a time to die; a time to plant, and a time to pluck up that which is planted;
> A time to kill, and a time to heal; a time to break down, and a time to build up;
> A time to weep, and a time to laugh; a time to mourn, and a time to dance;
> A time to cast away stones, and a time to gather stones together; a time to embrace, and a time to refrain from embracing;
> A time to get, and a time to lose; a time to keep, and a time to cast away;
> A time to rend, and a time to sew; a time to keep silence, and a time to speak;
> A time to love, and a time to hate –

He stopped, and looked enquiring at Johnny, who promptly sang back:

a time of war, and a time of peace.

The old man smiled, transforming his face into joy, giving it a strange beauty for all of the empty gums it revealed to match the pleated skin. Johnny smiled back, welcoming a new friend, yet being thankful he bad remembered to sing his part of the Preacher's song in a confident, urbane, cultured voice born and bred in Jerusalem. He was sure that Word wanted him to meet the old man, but he could not know whether the old man was a friend or an enemy. Anyhow he was the friend of a song Johnny loved, and that wasn't a bad start.

'You like that song, my boy?' asked the old man,

'I do, Sir', answered Johnny.

'Why do you like it?'

This might seem a little peremptory, but Johnny preferred it to hypocritical pseudo-courtesy such as 'May I ask... ?' or 'May I venture to enquire...'. Some grown-ups went to a lot of trouble to make children seem silly.

'It is music, Sir.'

'You like its sounds?'

'Yes, Sir.'

'Do you like what it says?'

'Well, it seems sensible, Sir.'

'Where is the sense?'

Johnny looked at the old man, looked standing with the broom in his hands and his chin almost on the top of its handle. 'We sow seed in the Spring, and reap the harvest in the Autumn.'

'You have a season in your youth, and I have a different season in my age.'

'I suppose so, Sir.'

'A time to be born, and a time to die.' The old man smiled bitterly.

Johnny smiled back, rejecting the bitterness. 'Not yet, Sir, I hope.'

'Why should you care whether or not it is my season to die? You do not know me.'

'You have honoured me in speaking to me, Sir, and there are not so many men of your age' (he managed to avoid saying 'old men') 'who honour boys of mine.'

259

The old man laughed, but this time there was no bitterness in it. 'So at last someone has found a use for me. It was high time someone did!'

Johnny was doubtful about answering this, but the old man saw his embarrassment and did not want to increase it, as Johnny realised he easily could have done. 'A time to kill, and a time to heal. Do you believe that?'

'There is a time to kill, Sir, certainly, the best time for preparing beasts for sacrifice according to what the priests tell us.'

'And a time to heal, eh? What about that?'

'It is always a time to heal, Sir.'

'So Shlomo – and as a good boy you have to say it was written by Shlomo – Shlomo is wrong when he implies that there are times which are not times for healing?'

'He does not say there are times when it is wrong to heal, Sir.'

'Not even on the Sabbath?'

'He does not say, Sir.'

'Do you think it is wrong to heal on the Sabbath?'

'No, Sir, it is never wrong to heal.' Johnny had no intention of identifying himself with Word unless it was a matter of affirming or denying Word. He knew he would never deny Word, so much so that it no longer would have crossed his mind even as a possibility. He wondered were they nearing a point when he would be affirming Word, and Galilee too, he supposed. But the old man persisted:

'A time to break down?'

Johnny felt as though he were walking on water and could only cry in his mind to Word to keep him afloat:

'Yes, Sir, when things are polluted and abused it is time to break down the causes of their sickness.' ('Is it you, Word, who are making me say this?' 'I do not make you say it, Johnny: I leave it for you to use.')

'Such as – ?' The old man seemed dangerously silky.

'Such as when the Outer Court of God's holy Temple is polluted by beasts and birds, and therefore must be purified.' ('Guide me, Word, this is going faster than a trotting camel.')

'The sacrificial animals have been here by long custom.'

'The children of Israel were in Egypt by long custom, but the Lord told Moses to let them go. Sir.' ('Thank you, Word, I should never have thought of it.' 'But you did, Johnny.')

'But the children went free, not so the sacrificial animals.'

'The doves went free, and the pigeons, and the birds of the air, all flew away none knew whither.' ('You freed them, Word, which is why I can say that.' 'But you are saying it, Johnny.')

'But the animals, my boy, they went the way their masters told them, when their masters were driven from the Temple where they were accustomed to be.'

'The masters, Sir, or the beasts?'

'The beasts would hardly return a second time, before today.'

'So they won some measure of freedom, Sir.'

'Merely a respite, my boy, merely a respite.'

Then Johnny, hardly knowing why, sang:

> Calves are easily bound and slaughtered,
> Never knowing the reason why,
> But whoever treasures freedom,
> Like the swallow, must learn to fly.

He stopped, half-horrified at his own temerity. But the old man let out a cackle of laughter and took up the next verse:

> How the winds are laughing!
> They laugh with all their might,
> Laugh and laugh the whole day through –

He stopped momentarily, and Johnny realised it was an invitation to join in, and united their voices:

'And half the summer's night.'

Then they sang the 'Dona' chorus, and stopped, and looked at one another. The old man began to laugh again, almost as hard as the winds, thought Johnny.

'A time to laugh, my boy?'

'I am glad it is not a time to weep, Sir.'

'It will be', and the old man suddenly was grim once more. 'Should we stone the men who drove out the sacrificial beasts and put the birds to flight – and the money-changers to flight?'

261

'You should not, Sir.' And Johnny was firm and sure standing before him. He did not threaten but anyone could read his answer, that anyone stoning his master must stone him first. The old man read it, and laughed again:

> As arrows are in the hand of a mighty man, so are children of thy youth.
> Happy is the man that hath his quiver full of them: they shall not be ashamed, but they shall speak with the enemies in the gate.

'I do not think of you as an enemy, Sir.'

The old man smiled, and Johnny thought it was his best smile yet. 'Let us say, it is a time to cast away stones, rather than to cast them.' Johnny instinctively put out his arms and embraced the old man:

'A time to embrace, Sir, if you will.'

The old man looked very pleased, and embraced him in return. 'And yet, my boy, the time will come to refrain from embracing.'

'I am glad that time is not now, Sir.'

'It will come soon enough. Put away that broom, and follow me to my house. You need feeding: boys always do. I am the father of five, and should know.'

'You are very kind, Sir.'

'I am very old, boy, but I can remember only one boy who answered as well as you do.'

'Who was that, Sir?'

'I do not know. It was some twenty years ago. I was high priest here at the time.'

'You are not high priest now, Sir?'

'You should know that I could not walk unattended if I were high priest. It is true that the people still call me high priest, save when my son-in-law is present.'

'Why should he make a difference?'

'Because he is the actual high priest.'

'How did that happen?'

They were walking along the streets of Jerusalem now, and the old man remarked that it was better to keep things like that until they were in a house and could not be heard. 'For what I will tell you, my boy, is so well known that nobody is wise to say it.'

Johnny realised it had something to do with the Romans, and indeed Judas had told him enough of Roman interference with the Temple to make it a logical deduction. The old man kept pace with him along the way, and drew his attention to various buildings. Johnny realised that the old man certainly knew he was not from Jerusalem and may have concluded he was Galilean despite his care to retain his best Judaean accent. They had reached the house, and the old man clapped his hands, demanding fruit and juice and strudel, to which Johnny did justice and the old man showed courtesy. When they had spoken blessings on God for the food, the old man began to talk of his life, with a certain amusement rather than resentment.

'We are, like your swallow, free, and our kind Roman masters see to our freedom.' Johnny looked directly at him, and the old man grinned wickedly at him. 'They are very kind, sometimes it might seem too kind, but we must not be unappreciative. We Jews are free to worship as God has taught us, with our own priests, but sometimes we do not really see what priest we ought to have, and then the Romans help us, and it shows you how clever they are that they can know who should be priest without even being Jews themselves. Of course our High priests were appointed by Herod and by his son Archelaus.'

'Herod – shmerod!' said Johnny, momentarily forgetting where he was, which the old man rightly took as a compliment.

'Ah, I see you have heard of our great king, or was your allusion to his son still happily with us?'

Johnny's face was full of fruit at this point, but he managed to say through the fruit 'Tetrarch – shmetrarch!'

'Poets must begin somewhere, I suppose, if they are to begin at all. Well, after the great Herod was dead, and his slightly less great son Archelaus had been removed – you won't think up a rhyme for him in a hurry, the scum.'

Johnny's jaw dropped open, revealing some partly-masticated fruit.

'Scum?'

'Scum', said the old man, deadly serious now. 'He killed my infant son. Did I say I was the father of five sons? I lied. I am the father of six sons but one was murdered by the orders of Archelaus who for his own sport was killing all boys under the age of two.' Just for one moment the old man looked young, and terrible. Johnny put his hand across the table and touched the old man's wrist. The old man looked wildly round, and then seemed to remember that he was old, and looked at Johnny, and smiled, and patted his hand. He was silent for a minute, and then put his head to one side, a little like Andrew. 'He might have grown up to look like you.' His eyes filled with tears.

Johnny, feeling useless, murmured 'I wish he had.'

'I wish it too', and the old man's sigh seemed as though it could have broken the back of his chair. 'God forgive me, it may be because of that I was made High Priest, and what luck could there be with such an office won for such a cause? The new ruler from Rome, Quirinius, looked around for a high priest who would not want to keep Archelaus's influence at the centre of power in Judaea. Maybe Quirinius was not the brightest shekel in the offering, but he was certainly right about that. If I could have squeezed Archelaus as painfully as possible into something the size of a mustard-seed and left it, still alive, forever in the path of all traffic on the main Roman highway, I would have had some faint flicker of my former happiness.' ('A time to love, and a time to hate', thought Johnny, but be did not say it.)

The old man looked beyond Johnny into what seemed a dark and desert past. 'The Lord held the hand of Abraham to spare Isaac, and the Lord made Reuben keep his brothers' hands from Joseph and so Jacob found him again after many years in Egypt, but there was no saving of our own sons from the hand of our own King. Truly said the Lord to Jeremiah, A voice was heard in Ramah, lamentation, and bitter weeping: Rachel weeping for her children refused to be comforted, because they were not.' He shot a look at Johnny, not in enmity but in envy of his existence. 'You remember what the Lord told Shmuel about kings?' 'Shmuel' was Samuel, correctly.

Johnny looked back at him: 'He will take your sons, and appoint them for himself, for his chariots, and to be his horsemen; and some shall run before his chariots.'

'And some he shall kill to slake his lusts and fears. No, if the Lord told that part to Shmuel, Shmuel told it not.' He shook his shoulders deliberately, and leered at Johnny. 'And there may be many things you have not told, my little Shmuel?' Johnny said nothing. The old man's eyes glazed again. 'Shmuel when he was your age or younger was told by the Lord that Eli's sons were wicked men, and that he told Eli. You bring no testimony against my sons?' His voice grew louder.

Johnny shook his head. 'I know only from your mouth that you have sons.' He was sitting very still now. He had stopped eating.

The old man leered again. 'And above all you bring no testimony against my son-in-law, my most worthy and honourable son-in-law, he who knows the Romans so much better than the rest of us, he who can tell when it is expedient that one man should die for the good of the people?'

'None, Sir.'

'None, Sir', mocked the old man. 'None, save that he has too many beeves and sheep and changers of money in the Temple precincts! Can too much money change in the Temple precincts?'

'Yes, Sir', said Johnny, well adrift by now, but knowing that no answer of his must deny or betray Word.

The old man drew in his lips. 'Yes, Sir. You have spoken truly. The Lord said to Amos, I hate, I despise your feast days, and I will not smell in your solemn assemblies. Though ye offer me burnt offerings and your meat offerings, I will not accept them: neither will I regard the peace offerings of your fat beasts.' He grinned at Johnny, half-sympathising with his bewilderment. 'But I am no Eli: my sons are good men. That is my tragedy.'

'How may be it so, Sir?' Johnny peered at him.

'Every one of them has made or will make an excellent High priest.'

'Bless the Lord, Sir.'

'Will the Lord accept my blessing? My sons are excellent High priests to keep order, and deference, and sacrifice, and prayer, so that no Roman has a word to say against them until they tire of them, and then that son is no longer the High priest. But the Romans are no blood foes of our family, oh, oh, no, if one of my sons has tired them, and they remove his High priesthood, they will take another. Or if not a son, a son-in-law. I have given each son such money as will help him bribe the Romans when his turn may come. Judeans use money. Romans love money. Or at any rate they love respectful presents.' The head leaned to on side again. 'Eat some more fruit, my boy. I frighten you with my foolish talk.'

Johnny smiled and bowed at the old man, and took an orange, pushing the bowl back to his host. 'What about the boy who answered questions well, Sir?' he asked, feeling more sure of himself if the talk could turn on someone else's sons.

The old man raised his head, and sniffed, not condescendingly, but as though he was drawing back the scent of a memory. 'Yes, you want to hear about someone like yourself, instead of hearing of my sons, who do everything right. Or, of course, my son-in-law, nowadays the most righteous of us all. It may have been about twenty years ago, as we count years. I had been High priest for ten years or so before that. It was the Passover, but after it, not before it as we are now. These Temple ceremonies can be very exhausting, although' – his gums crunched and he drew the skin of his chin upward – 'the Romans with their usual kindness took away our most sacred vestments which were also our heaviest. I was resting in the Temple, just on the way to the outer Court which you were so obligingly cleaning to-day – cleaning it up after your friends had been cleaning it. They were your friends, weren't they?'

Now it had come. Head up, shoulders back. 'They were. They are, Sir.'

The old man leaned back, luxuriously. He smiled, a little greedily. 'I would give much for a man to say he was my friend, just like that.' Johnny hardly knew how to answer. 'No, don't try. It's too late. And your loyalty to your friends would probably make it impossible for you to be loyal to me – and, more to the point, to mine. But my blessing on God who may not have given me friends of such loyalty, yet he has shown one to me. Have another orange. Your thumb has a good nail for skinning them. We will return to the safety of the past. It is after the Passover, I am High priest, and I am tired. I am talking with other priests of the Temple. And here comes a boy who by the sound of him is Egyptian. And he asked me some questions about the ceremony and then about the Scriptures we had been celebrating.' Suddenly the old man's face seemed almost technical, like Zebedee or James when they were talking about a complex problem in fishing equipment.

'What sort of questions?'

'That was the strange part of it. There were clearly things he wanted to

266

know, and yet when we told him, it seemed almost as if he discovered he knew more about them than he thought he did. Nothing boastful or showing off. It was as if you were teaching a child how to swim and you found – and he found – he could swim far better than you could. Yet he kept asking, as if he needed to know, and we kept on asking him for his opinion on texts and customs, and he sometimes looked on us in a startled way, as though he had no idea of the answer as we asked our questions and yet out he would come with an answer almost surprising himself. This went on for three days. We fed him, of course, and we let him sleep I think probably in my house – and we went back to our discussions, and explanations, and arguments, and questions, and answers. He must have been tired, but he bore up very well, and bored nobody, which must make him well-nigh unique among theological disputants.'

'What became of him?'

'That was strange too. We were still there on the third day, arguing in our usual place in the Outer Court, fortunately still free of its usual traffic which had temporarily exhausted itself after Passover. Suddenly in came a young woman, and a decidedly older man, and looked across, saw us, hurried over, and asked the boy what he thought he was doing, giving them so much anxiety, making them turn back on their journey away from Jerusalem, and he looked at them and said that surely they would have known he would be about his father's business.'

'And what was his father's business?'

'We discovered that, although I never picked up where they lived, something distracted me, some piece of business *I* had to attend to. But his father was a *carpenter* and the boy certainly never talked about carpentry to us or tried to sell us goods for the Temple or our homes. And yet he clearly was a truthful boy. I liked him very much, and often hoped I would see him again. But I never did.'

('You heard all of that?' asked Johnny's mind of Word's. 'I heard it' said Word's. 'Was it you?' 'It was.' 'Shall I tell him?' 'No.' 'Am I right to like him?' 'You are right to like him.')

The old man looked at Johnny with a strange kind of finality. 'That's all. That's my story. And now I need to sleep.'

Johnny rose to his feet and hastily began to thank the old man. His host shook his head. 'No, my boy, the thanks are mine. I haven't enjoyed a conversation as much in twenty years. Yes, of course, I will give you my blessing.'

And after Johnny had got to his feet again, and embraced the old man once more, they walked to the door, where the old man said 'we probably will not meet again. You had better tell your friends to get out of Jerusalem. It's dangerous for you. Just before I found you' – and Johnny realised there was nothing accidental about the finding – 'one of your people came in to my son-in-law and was telling him plenty.' Johnny wondered idly if this was one of the older children, ashamed of joining up with its juniors and anxious to win credentials from the Temple: it could hardly be one of Word's disciples. As they parted, the old man asked 'do you think we became friends enough for me to know your name?' and Johnny giggled, and said 'John, Sir'. And the old man froze and looked at Johnny hungrily: 'it was the name of the son who was taken from me.'

'It's not that usual, is it, Sir?' Johnny liked feeling an element of exclusiveness.

'Not too common, certainly. There was a priest from the country serving in the Temple just before our son was born, and his wife had a child when she seemed much too old to have one, and they called it John. Strange business: he lost the power of speech when he was in the Temple and recovered it after the boy was born. Zachary his name was. I was thinking John could be a lucky name, since Zachary got back his speech after declaring the boy's name as John. But it wasn't lucky for my boy.'

Johnny would not, as a rule, ask an old man his name, but he thought he had better so as not to desert the old man when he was upset. So he came out, and said it: 'And what is your own name, Sir? '

'Annas. Don't get it wrong. Most people do. If I had a gold piece for all the times I have been called Ananus, or Ananias, or Andros, or even Andrew, my sons would be even richer men than they are, and my son-in-law, of course, would have more than anyone. Annas.'

Johnny had just made his bow to Annas, when something else crossed his mind, though he said it more to be polite than thinking it was of any importance: 'May I come back to your house some time?'

It was the right thing to say. Annas gave his best smile of all, and said:

'You will always be welcome in the house of Annas!'

FIFTEEN

NICODEMUS

That was the true Light, which lighteth every man that cometh into the world

Johnny walked away from Annas's house rapidly towards the Temple as the first stage on his way to the Garden of Gethsemane. He was not feeling too pleased with himself. He realised that there was much too much danger in their situation for that but it amused him that here he was only a few hours in Jerusalem and already he had organised a triumph for Word, participated in a riot (but glad it was non-violently, assuming that falling on all fours to make a foe somersault backwards counts as non-violence), cleaned up at least part of a Temple forecourt, and eaten and sung with the high priest, or rather not the high priest but the man whom people call the High priest although the Romans had removed him from his holy office and given it to his son-in-law having tried out at least one of his sons and how many other people first? How would the Romans like it if other people told them who would be their High priest? Suddenly it occurred to Johnny that when Word's mission was fulfilled, that was exactly what would happen, and he laughed and laughed. In his mind he could hear Word laughing too, and then telling him to behave himself. Johnny grinned and longed to eat up the distance between himself and Word. It would be all right if the others were at Gethsemane, but he hoped there would be no strangers. Annas had been fun and he was glad Word said it was all right to like him, because Johnny liked liking him, but it had been a perilous passage, and for all of his liking for Annas, Johnny did not trust him an inch. He knew

Word knew that, too, and he thought Word agreed with him there as well. A High priest carries too much power and wealth, even when the Romans have taken the one away from him, and his children (and, above all, his son-in-law) have taken the other, and so he can never be fully on the side of people with no power or wealth, all the more when they have Word who has so much that the high priest should have, and doesn't. So it would be good to have Word to themselves, and even better if it was to himself.

Hence Johnny was far from pleased as he passed the Temple (South side) to find a tall, opulently-dressed man evidently waiting for him. Johnny knew there was no hope of smiling politely and hastening past, as if he were the priest or the Levite in Word's story about the compassionate Samaritan. The man cleared his throat with considerable difficulty, since it didn't want to be cleared. For one daft moment Johnny thought of hitting him an almighty whack on the back from alleged concern, and then pelting off hell-for-leather leaving him to get over it in his own time, but he knew what Word would want, and would not want, so he slowed down his footsteps and drew level with the man just bringing his throat to a standstill. The man looked at him, and for a ghastly moment Johnny thought he was about to start the throat-clearing again, and wondered if he couldn't persuade Word to let him sidle away, but the man pulled himself together to say in a very stage whisper: 'Are you the boy with the Nazarene?' For a moment Johnny was genuinely bewildered: he never liked to think about Nazareth after its rejection of Word, and to call Word a Nazarene was rather like calling Moses an Egyptian, not that Word had wanted to make an exodus from Nazareth. But he pulled himself together and said 'my master is from Galilee, yes'. The man said 'good', and then looked around carefully to make sure nobody was looking, which Johnny thought was crazy, since anyone looking would be careful not to look as if they were looking. Then the man said 'where will your master be at nightfall?', and Johnny looked at him suspiciously, and said 'with me', and the man said he needed to consult Word, so Johnny said he was now on his way to meet Word in the Garden of Gethsemane, and he supposed night would fall in the next half hour, and if the man wanted them to wait until then, he supposed his master might be ready to wait. He made it fairly clear that if he, Johnny, had been the master, they wouldn't wait, but the man seemed uninterested in this, leaving his reputation in Johnny's eyes as that of a typical grown-up, indeed, worse, a typical Judaean grown-up, maybe a tad superior to a Samaritan or a shade worthier than a Roman, but nothing on which to compliment a cat for bringing in.

Then Johnny noticed that the man kept flicking his fingers against his thumb, as though he was brushing something off, and seeing Johnny's eyebrows rising involuntarily (at least Johnny tried to tell himself it was involuntarily) the man said, with an authority completely lacking up to now, 'Oak'.

'What?' demanded Johnny.

The man gave a lift to his own eyebrows, more authoritatively than Johnny: 'You wanted to know what I was flicking off my fingers. I was flicking off oak.'

This made as much sense as if the man said he was flicking off the veil of the Temple should a single thread adhere to his thumb. Oaks were great, powerful trees, making ships and carried by them. Had the ship from which Word rescued Johnny been carrying oak? Egypt had oak. But so, of course, did Italy, so why take it there? You could make a proverb to illustrate useless traffic: bearing oaks to Italy. But the man's eyebrows were rising higher, if anything, so Johnny tried a touch of civil advancement of the conversation, not so as to make the man think it would be all right to hang round Word for half the night, but enough to keep up the decencies, for Word's sake. ('And I hope you can hear how polite I am trying to be, Word', thought Johnny virtuously. 'I hear as man, not as God', said Word sardonically into Johnny's mind, which was ridiculous since he could hardly know the contents of Johnny's mind if he weren't God but being used to Word now Johnny merely tried to think a giggle in reply. His mind registered a responsive chuckle from Word.)

'Is it permissable to ask' began Johnny (to a stage groan from Word in his mind at this elephantine diplomacy) 'how you got oak on your fingers?'

'It is', said the man, evidently ready to receive this embassy, at least for the moment.

'Which is what?' asked Johnny, cascading from his formality.

'Which is that I was carving oak.'

'Why would you be doing that?'

'To sculpt.'

'Sculpt?'

271

'Yes, to sculpt. To make likenesses of faces and forms. Surely you know what sculpture is?'

'Oh, yes, yes' said Johnny, his mind idiotically tearing through topics which might show that he knew what sculpture was. (Word came up with the idea of asking did the man prefer to sculpt people or things, so Johnny tried it.)

'People', said the man.

'What kind of people?'

'Priests. Rabbis. Scribes. Prophets, if I could find any.'

'Is that why you wanted to see Wo – my master?' Johnny sounded a little like a doorkeeper reluctantly agreeing to open his door another notch.

The man suddenly remembered that he was nervous. 'Partly', he said, with a little shiver, and another look around. Johnny thought it might be polite for him to go, if the man was going to play peekaboo with imaginary spies and would feel easier being nervous if Johnny wasn't there to watch him doing it. ('I suppose so', said Word in his mind, more in resignation than enthusiasm, but Johnny knew the resignation was for the man, pointing out to Word that Word would want to see him, Johnny, first, and Word said he clearly had no alternative). So Johnny told the man that they would meet in the Garden of Gethsemane when the sun had set as it was supposed to be doing (to Word's thankfulness, he confined himself merely to thinking the last bit). And Johnny ran the rest of the way to the Garden, where Word was indeed sitting – or rather kneeling – by himself. Johnny rushed into his arms. Somehow each minute with Word seemed more and more to be treasured, pearls of great price – but wasn't the price of pearls conditioned by rarity? Johnny didn't want to follow that logic, and he began to tell Word his adventures with Annas and then with the sculptor, and Word's eyes began to sparkle with fun as Johnny tried out his imitation of Annas's voice in speech and song. But when he began to try the sculptor's voice, Word pressed his foot softly and Johnny heard feet coming through leaves in their direction. He couldn't see the leaves any more by now, nor the grass which brushed the sculptor's heels. During the day-time the Garden looked a strange colour, like blue pretending to be green or the other way round. The sculptor's feet sounded nervous, and Johnny called out to him in a low voice that they were over here. The sculptor came up to them and evidently saw there were only two of them, and when Word said 'Peace be to you', started and said 'I thought I heard another voice there' and Word told Johnny's mind: 'Fortunately, no man knows what he sounds like', but said to the sculptor: 'We are only two. And it is late, so Johnny must stay with us', anticipating the inevitable demand for privacy. ('He probably wants you to forgive him for sculpting a golden calf', thought Johnny. 'Think something nice and polite for a change', flashed back Word's mind, but Johnny smirked to himself that he could sense Word holding back a laugh.)

'Rabbi', said the sculptor, evidently giving up on the third man who wasn't there, 'we know you are a teacher come from God.'

'Who are we?' asked Word, sounding more curious than censorious.

'I am the Pharisee Nicodemus', said the sculptor.

'You are welcome', said Word.

'You are from God', said Nicodemus forcefully (leaving no room for escape' thought Johnny) 'for no man can do the miracles you do unless God is with him.'

('What if he be God himself?' murmured Johnny's mind. 'If he be God himself', said Word's mind grimly, 'he ought to be better able to keep Johnny's mind more respectful.' 'Or at least respectable', thought Johnny. 'Impossible', flicked back Word's mind. 'Nothing is impossible to God', thought Johnny, piously, and Word's mind grinned – don't ask me how a mind grins in another mind, it can when it is Word's – and told Johnny's mind to pay attention to Nicodemus, it might be important later, and Word might want Johnny to tell or write it. So Johnny's mind behaved itself for the moment, and paid attention.)

Word's voice in reply to Nicodemus was in fact very serious and rather solemn: 'In all truth I tell you, unless someone is born again, they cannot see the kingdom of God.'

'But how can a man be born again when he is old? Can he enter the second time into his mother's womb, and be born?' demanded Nicodemus, with the air of having solved a problem baffling his hearers. Everything taken literally, thought Johnny, better not try with one of Word's stories or we'll be here all night. Oddly enough, Johnny had heard an Egyptian fairy-tale about a man – a prince, anyway, if not a normal man – who was born a second time by re-entering his mother's womb, but this was clearly no time to mention it. ('No, indeed', muttered Word's mind in Johnny's.)

But Johnny realised that a sculptor has to have a model to inspire him or her (it occurred to him that Word's mother might make an admirable model), and Word was very patient in guiding Nicodemus. 'In real truth I am telling you a human being must be reborn of water, and of the Spirit, without which they cannot enter God's kingdom. What is born in Nature's way, is Nature's product; what is born by spiritual birth is the Spirit's creation. Don't be surprised at my saying you must be born anew. The wind breathes where it wants to, and you can hear its sound, but you do not know where it came from or where it will go.' ('Poetry' thought Johnny approvingly.) 'And that is the way' continued Word firmly 'when one is born by the breath of the Spirit.'

This seemed very beautiful to Johnny, as though an invisible baby were being born in the joy of its new creation when the human being was called by Word and rushed into his arms. Nicodemus seemed to find it more difficult. Johnny supposed that a sculptor wanted something more solid. Anyhow, the sculptor demanded how could such things be? At least he is not saying they cannot be, thought Johnny, and it is proper he should be amazed. (Word suddenly put into Johnny's mind the lines a great playwright would think in a thousand six hundred years' time:

> Can such things be,
> And overcome us like a summer's cloud,
> Without our special wonder?)

But for all the future poetry, Word saw no reason for the wonder to be special; 'You are a master in Israel. You teach the young that Sadducees deceive themselves. You tell that there is angel and spirit. You teach them how to think, and how to carve what they think, which sometimes outlasts the thought. So how can these things be strange? All I tell you is what we know and have seen and can witness, and you refuse our witness.' Johnny was pleased about the 'we' and liked to think it referred to his running to Word the moment he saw him, and Word baptising him by having Deianera duck him in the Mediterranean. It had taken a moment or two to see anything when he rose up from the sea, of course. 'If you put no faith in what I tell you about the things of earth' ('and sea', mentally added Johnny) 'how can you put faith in what I tell you about the things of heaven? No man has gone up into heaven, but one has come down from heaven, the Son of Humanity whose being is in heaven.' Johnny liked Word calling himself the Son of Humanity, as if a son were in some way an improvement on what had gone before him. It made sense: becoming a man, he might call himself man's child, and therefore less than man, but being perfection beyond man, therefore more than man. A child, thought Johnny, is both less and more than a grown-up, but does anyone except Word realise it? Certainly Nicodemus didn't seem to. But now Word was speaking again, having given Nicodemus a minute in which to fail to understand.

'And as Moses lifted up the serpent in the desert, the Son of Humanity must be lifted up, so that all who put faith in him will not perish but will have everlasting life. For God so loved the world that he gave up his own Son, so that all who put faith in him will not perish but will have life that never ends. For God sent his own Son into the world, not to condemn the world, but that through him the world might be saved. The person who puts faith in him is not condemned, but the person who puts no faith in him is condemned already, because he has not put faith in the name of the only begotten son of God.' ('That', said Johnny to himself, 'is the real "begat". I hope Matthew has realised it by now.') 'And this is the condemnation, that light came into the world, and that human beings preferred the darkness to light: for their doings were evil. For anyone doing evil hates the light, and will not come into the light in case what they do is shown up for what it is. But the one who makes truth, comes into the light, so that her or his deeds become visible and clear, deeds done in God.'

'If I carved you in wood', said Nicodemus, 'I would be making truth.'

'It would be a deed done in God', smiled Word, 'even if it was done when the Son of Humanity had been lifted up.' And he made a funny sign, like the letter 't' in Greek he had taught Johnny, with a vertical line pointing upwards, and a horizontal line running across it, slightly shorter, and equal on each side of the vertical line. Johnny could make no sense of this, though he meant to ask Word to explain it later. Nicodemus could make perfect sense of it, whatever it meant, his eyes, like Johnny's, having become used to the darkness. His voice trembled in saying to Word 'Not that?' And Word answered 'Even that.' And his voice became softer as he added 'It has to be. And though you come in the darkness, you can do what will help to bring the light.'

'How?' asked Nicodemus, simply.

'I will not expect you, or indeed want you, to speak for me in the council of Temple guardians', reflected Word, 'but it would be useful to tell me what happens there especially since I shall be teaching in the Temple for the next four days.'

'Where will I find you?' asked Nicodemus. 'Where will you stay?'

'Foxes have holes', said Johnny, feeling he had been silent long enough, 'but the Son of Humanity –'

'Not to speak of the son of Zebedee' murmured Word.

'– have nowhere to rest their head.'

'Heads', said Word thoughtfully, 'you should have limits to your self-sacrifice, Johnny. You may keep your head, now that you have learned to.' Johnny thought this might be a little rough on Nicodemus, who had been having enough difficulty understanding Word, without having to put up with the two of them. But to his surprise Nicodemus said, in much the most businesslike voice be had uttered yet, 'You mean you need a place to sleep?'

'He does', said Johnny, before Word might feel the need to be polite.

'I have a studio where I do my sculpture', stated Nicodemus. 'Nobody knows that it is my house apart from my pupils, all of whom have been dismissed until after the Passover. There is food and water there.'

'Nobody knows it is your house?' repeated Word.

'Nobody', confirmed Nicodemus.

'Then, with your permission, we shall call it Johnny's house. You hardly want to draw attention to it or to yourself by using my name for it, and your domicile is known as your house, so we will know what we are talking about if we call it Johnny's. It is very kind of you. Johnny, thank Nicodemus for giving you his nice house.'

Johnny thanked him, a little doubtfully, but to his relief Nicodemus began to laugh, although still looking at Word rather uncertainly, almost as if he feared looking at him too much might cause Word to break like a delicate piece of wood-carving. It was not, felt Johnny, that Word was fragile, or could be hurt or damaged. Still, if Nicodemus's way of showing respect meant looking like that, by all means let him look like that. Johnny had no doubt that he was a friend, albeit a slightly cowardly one: well,

Johnny wasn't going to look down on anyone for feeling afraid, not after what Chuza had told him, and the way he knew he would feel if Word were not with him. As far as moonlight could let Johnny read Nicodemus's face it now seemed a sensitive if still authoritative face. An authoritative face may be useful to conceal your fear when you are frightened, mused Johnny, half-missing what Nicodemus was telling Word, or not so much missing it as registering it without thinking about it, much as Johnny had learned many texts of Scripture without thinking about them before he met Word.

Nicodemus was actually telling Word about some conversation among the priests and Rabbis in the Temple when they were looking for Word or at least had told anyone who knew where he was to report it, having heard of Word raising Eleazar from the dead. Word was interested that they seemed ready enough to believe in his miracles, even the Sadducees, but their reaction was to fear that if people heard of the miracles, they would put faith in Word, and if people put faith in him, the Romans would come and take away our place and our nation. Then the High Priest Caiaphas rounded on the rest and told them they knew nothing at all. 'Did he often say that?' inquired Word. Nicodemus said that he did, and was believed, being someone in constant communication with the Romans, who had, after all, given him his job. But instead of name-dropping about what Pontius Pilate might be saying about Tiberius, Caiaphas intoned 'you don't realise it is expedient for us that one man should die for the people, so that the people will not perish'. Word smiled, a smile which twisted his lips slightly, and said that Caiaphas has had prophesied truly even if he didn't know as much as he thought he did.

Johnny was beginning to listen again, and said, 'will he try to work with Herod, who also wants to kill you?' Nicodemus seemed a little taken aback by Johnny's matter-of-fact docketing of persons anxious to kill Word (not realising that Johnny was confident they would never succeed) but said that Caiaphas usually worked with Pontius Pilate who didn't like Herod. Johnny said that was the best thing he had heard of Pontius Pilate, and Word laughed, and tousled Johnny's hair. But when Nicodemus added that Caiaphas and his friends were talking amongst themselves about how best to have Word killed, Johnny laughed and said they were wasting their time, and didn't notice Nicodemus's sudden silence, nor Word's.

He simply walked on with his hand in Word's occasionally swinging their arms. At length they reached what was to be Johnny's house, and Nicodemus showed them his studio, fixed up where they should sleep, gave them keys and said goodnight. He went on to his own big house to eat but had left enough food for their evening meal and breakfast the next day. They would meet the others outside the Temple, Word explained.

But before Word could enter the Temple and start teaching a group of scholarly looking men arrived, whom Johnny realised must be the doctors of the law, the scribes, and by their faces they were out to make fun of Word and trap him in some way, so Johnny gleefully awaited their fall. In the middle of the group was a woman whom they were driving and hustling, and her face was the picture of utter despair. She was pretty, in rather a wild way, but she had had no time to put her hair or her clothes in order. Before they had quite reached him, one of the scribes called out in a tone of poisonously pretended deference 'Master!' He sounded as if he were trying to imitate a sheep, thought Johnny, and for that at least he was giving a fairly good school try. 'Ma-a-aster! This woman was taken in adultery.' Another one of them joined in, almost dribbling in his satisfaction. 'In the very act!' They seemed very proud of someone's timing. 'Mo-o-o-ses' (now Johnny was struck by the proficiency in imitation of a cow) 'Moses in the law commanded us that such should be stoned.' Johnny vaguely knew of that law but surely Moses had never intended people to be so pleased at the thought of stoning women to death? And in any case Word, who was greater than Moses, would not favour taking anyone's life. But if he opposed them they would say he denied Moses, and defended adultery, and maybe they would try to stone him. Johnny thought of Chuza, fought down the fear his next thought gave him, and told himself that they would have to stone him before they tried to stone Word: for a moment he wasn't thinking that Word couldn't be hurt. Word sent a quick smile to Johnny and bent down, writing something in the dust with no sign of having heard them. And again came the bleat of 'Master!' and the mooing of 'Moses!', getting more obstreperous as now one took them up, and now another. (If they don't watch out, thought Johnny savagely, they'll be driven into the Temple as livestock for sacrifice and Word will have to drive them out.) 'What do you say?'

Word raised himself and gazed at them, suddenly looking magnificently tall. 'He that is without sin among you, let him cast the first stone.' It was as though he had told a crowd attacking a leper that they were all lepers. The bleating and mooing and whinnying suddenly died, first to hear Word, then in the shock of what they heard. One face looked at another, the sanctimoniousness and punitive virtue slobbering off them, a horrified exposure of guilt taking their place. One or two seemed brazen for a moment, profession of innocence unable to assert itself but bluff trying to maintain it. Word bent down and wrote again. One scribe elbowed his way forward, looking at the words Word had written. He literally jumped, threw a look of hatred at Word, and pelted off. His neighbour pushed his way in, perhaps hoping for something against the colleague who was running away. He stifled a shriek and hurried away too, in a different direction. Then another, then another, pushed their way forward, looked, and were gone as fast as they could. As each came up Word was still writing, and when the last had gone, he stopped. Only the woman was left, still utterly bemused. Word looked at her, with the air of a clerk who has mislaid a document, and asked with a touch of a smile 'Lady, where are your accusers? Nobody to condemn you?' She said, in a warm, rich voice still almost amazed at still being able to speak: 'No man, Lord.' Word smiled all over his face and said 'Neither do I condemn you.' Johnny laughed but not out loud because Word was the only man who had never committed a sin, and yet his 'Neither' almost sounded as though he was declaring himself as ineligible as the foiled stone-throwers. The woman threw herself on the ground and kissed his feet. Word raised her up, and said almost in the voice he had used to Jairus when he had raised Miriam from the dead and told her parents to give her something to eat, 'Go, and sin no more'. She stood as happy and grateful as any invalid whose debility he had removed. Word bowed to her, and Johnny made a sketchy little bow behind him. The woman opened her lips, exhaled a sigh of gratitude, and walked away, gathering her mantle around her having straightened her hair. Johnny for the first time was close enough to read where Word had been writing. Word had not rubbed out or cancelled any writing, but when Johnny looked there were no marks to be seen. Word turned towards the Temple gate where the others were standing. Johnny saw that they were all waiting, no not quite all, ah, yes, there was Judas coming from inside the Temple.

Word sat on the Temple steps, talking lightly with people who had come to hear him, but stood up when someone asked 'Rabbi, why did you drive the money-changers, and sacred birds and beasts from the Temple? Was it because Caiaphas and his family are making an illegal profit, and giving favour to certain vendors and farmers and money-men?' Several people in the crowd looked at one another, and Johnny was pretty sure he saw attendants among them who were probably there to hear what Word said and report it to Caiaphas and to Annas, admitted Johnny sadly to himself. He hoped this would not bring on a personal confrontation between Word and the old man. In fact, Word shook his head, and said 'when people think that buying and selling are more important than working for my Father it is time to cleanse the Temple'. His questioner asked what kind of work he spoke of, and Word said that it was the duty of all of God's people to see to the poor, the sick, the imprisoned, the old, the children, who without love would die in their poverty and suffering. 'My Father wants no person to think his love of his neighbour is less important than keeping the Sabbath. And if we are only concerned with showing off as we do our, religious duty, what good are our prayers?'

'Who are you?' cried some tempter, or doubter, or genuine enquirer, from the growing crowd. Word said very quietly 'I am the light of the world'. Johnny thrilled to it. Of course he would record it in his future account of Word, but it charged the wonderful words with which his statement would begin. Word went on: 'He who follows me shall never walk in darkness, but shall own the light of life.' ('And those who hold your hand', thought Johnny firmly. 'Those who hold my hand', thought back Word, 'I shall forever hold in my hand.') Then what looked and sounded like a Pharisee, and a snooty one, sniffed 'you are your only witness, your own witness is not true.' Word set his smile a little more severely and looked him back in the eye: 'Even when I am my only witness, my witness is true. I know from where I have come, and where I will go. You do not know whence I have come or whither I will go. You judge by the flesh' (suddenly Johnny realised that Word's questioner bad been on the edge of the crowd of scribes intent on stoning the woman) 'I judge no human being. Yet if I judge, my judgment is true since I am not alone but it is also that of the Father who sent me.' Johnny realised that Word was thinking of himself as a man when he refused to judge anyone, and as God when he spoke of judging with the Father. For a moment the vastness of the idea frightened him, but looking at Word he won the reward of a quick grin, and all was well. But as Word turned back to his critic, his face hardened, as he said 'It's in your law that the witness of two persons is true, I'm one, and the Father who sent me is the other.' 'Who is your father?' snapped the Pharisee. 'You do not know me' agreed Word grimly 'or my Father. If you had known me, you would have known my Father.' His voice sounded strangely remote. Men were looking nervously this way and that, now anxious to claim his fellowship, now urgent to repudiate him. Word said sadly 'I go away, and you will seek me, and will die amid your fatal flaws, where I go is where you will not be able to come.' Johnny could hear several whispering 'Is he going to kill himself?' 'Is this what he means?' 'Where he goes we can't go, does this mean suicide?' 'No, he doesn't.' 'Yes, he does.' Johnny wanted to yell at them, 'it's the way you live that prevents your going where he will go, Word would never kill himself or you, he makes he doesn't destroy.' But he felt Word's mind hugging his back, telling him this must be for his hearers to decide. And Word told them again 'You are from earth, I am from heaven, you are from this world, I am not. That's why I told you you will die amid the wounds tearing your characters asunder, unless you put faith in me to be the one you seek.' Johnny unconsciously was trying to will the crowd to realise Word could and would save them, and some cried 'Who are you?' Word smiled wanly and said 'I'm what I always was, and I could tell you much and evaluate much but all I tell you are the true things I have learned from Him Who sent me, and Who is Truth.' They still could not understand that he meant the Father.

Johnny had no difficulty understanding Word's having come from the Father, and sorrowed that grown-ups lost so much as they grew. But when Word spoke again Johnny himself lost his way for Word once again talked of himself the Son of Humanity being lifted up, and it seemed to be by the people he was speaking to, or maybe by men in general, 'then', said Word firmly, 'you will see that it is myself you seek and that I do not act by my authority but by the way my Father has taught me to speak'. And then Word smiled, a wonderful, welcoming smile as if he were Johnny looking at Word himself. 'He Who sent me is with me, He has not left me all alone, for I do all those things which please Him best.' And now as Word spoke many of the Judaeans began to put faith in him. It was as though Word were a taper lighting dead candles, Johnny felt.

'If you continue in my word', Word told them 'then you are true disciples. And you will know the truth, and the truth will set you free.' 'We are the children of Abraham' objected one reluctant convert with a high neck and sweeping glance 'and nobody has ever been able to enslave us yet.' ('Tell that to Pontius Pilate', thought Johnny, malevolently. 'Pontius Pilate may yet have something to hear' murmured Word almost a grace-note in Johnny's mind. 'Not from Shimon the ex-Zealot?' worried Johnny. 'Not from Shimon the ex-Zealot' reassured Word so softly at the back of Johnny's mind.) Out loud Word continued to face his potential critics and converts, several now muttering 'you say we shall be made free, how so?' Word told them 'whoever is enslaved to the corruption in their own characters, are imprisoned in that corruption. And those prisoners cannot live in the house of freedom where the Son lives forever. But if the Son makes you free, free you will be.' Then he looked back at the Pharisee whom Johnny had identified as the only remaining botched stone-thrower, and with him some others with similar sneers and snarls. 'You are Abraham's descendants all right', he said bluntly, 'and you seek to kill me, because my word finds no place in you.' ('And you find no place in my Word', responded Johnny's mind, addressing Word's targets however ineffectively.) 'What I speak of I saw with my Father, what you speak of you learned from your parent.' And with half-echoes of one another Word's enemies chorused 'Abraham is our father'. Word's eyes flashed: 'If Abraham were your father in truth, you would do what he would want you to do. But as false children you really mean to kill the Son, who is telling you the truth. That wasn't what Abraham did: when he heard God's truth, he freed his son and dropped the weapon of death. You are following the example of your real parent.' The knot of vipers (as Johnny was now thinking them) hissed 'We are no bastards' and James looked across at Johnny to make sure he wasn't responding favourably to the example of that kind of language. Johnny made a small headshake in understanding. 'God is our Father', shrilled the vipers. Word's smile twisted. 'If God were the father you recognize, you would have recognized me, since I come from God. I did not come unsent: he sent me. Why can't you understand what I am saying? Your ear will not carry my message. You belong to your parent, to the thing, to the negation, to It. You will do what It would do. It was a murderer from the start, and lies outside the truth, with no truth in It.' (Suddenly Johnny saw the light that was Word driving back the darkness trying to menace him. It was as though he had seen for the first time the logic of a word in translation – a Word in translation, he told himself happily.) 'When It speaks lies, It says what is Its, It is all lies, and enabled lying to be born. So if you don't put faith in me, you don't want the truth. Can you prove me false? If not, why don't you believe me when I speak truth? Those whom God owns listen to God's words: it's because you don't belong to God that you don't hear them.' Johnny felt a cold wind beginning to make the roots of the hair at the base of his skull bristle. As he saw them now, those were the faces truly bowing down to It and reverencing the father of falsehood. He swallowed hard. It was all very well to follow and love Word with his whole heart and his whole soul, but he hardly wanted to let his stomach sympathise with Word so much that he would begin to vomit at the enemies of Humanity in his sight.

'Samaritan!' screamed the stone thrower *manqué*.

'Diabolist!' yelled his pal alongside.

'Lunatic!' bellowed another sidekick.

'Possessed!' gibbered a fourth.

'*I* have no devil' said Word, icily. 'I honour my Father, and therefore you won't honour me. Not that I care about my reputation or what becomes of it: there will come the One who seeks and judges. I say to you truly, truly, if a human being keeps faith with *my* word' ('and with Word', thought Johnny) 'he will never know death.'

'Now we know a demon has you', yelped the sons of It.

'Abraham is dead – !'

'The prophets are dead – !'

'You say if someone keeps faith with your word – !'

'He will never know death!'

'Are you greater than our father Abraham?'

'Who is dead –!'

'And the prophets who are dead –!'

('Maybe they will freeze like this' thought Johnny irritably 'and go round and round and round saying their rubbish again and again and again. You'll have to cleanse the Temple again, Word.' For reply, Johnny felt his mind register a chuckle from Word, however grimly Word was facing Its creatures.)

'What do you claim to be?' growled one, at least varying the rain of cliché.

'If I honour myself', said Word simply, 'my honour is nothing. It is my Father who honours me, Whom you say that is your God, although you don't recognise Him. But I know Him, and I am true to His Word.' ('And are His Word', snuggled Johnny's mind happily.) 'If I were to say I don't know Him, I'd be what you are, a liar.' He sounded like a scientist classifying a specimen rather than a mocker 'Your father Abraham was happy to see my day.'

'You have seen Abraham?' snorted Its rabble, or a hemichorus of them.

'You who are less than fifty!' jeered the other hemichorus.

Word smiled with unshakeable finality. 'Truly, truly, before Abraham existed, I am.' Johnny wanted to cheer and applaud: it was a perfect last word.

That certainly was how Its creatures saw it, and rushed out to get stones to hurl them at Word.

Word set Johnny on his shoulders, and led his old disciples – we should say, in deference to Johnny, the rest of his old disciples – across the way so that their route lay through the path of the stone-throwers, but only a cloud gleaming with sunlight seemed visible to the children of It.

And the children of It – more correctly, the spawn of It, thought Johnny – could not comprehend the light. And Word walked on.

Nicodemus came round to his house – or Johnny's house – very late that night, looking very worried. He responded mechanically to their greetings, returned their wish of peace with the air of a wish for a miracle, declined a seat (which meant that Word and Johnny had to remain standing), pawed the ground with one foot while standing on the other, kept moving his fingers and flicking imaginary crumbs of wood from them, scratched the back of his head, refused some of the food and drink they had bought with the offerings the disciples had collected from the more sympathetic of Word's hearers, looked at Word while until his own forehead creased with his concern and his eyebrows arched their way to heaven, and finally bit the little finger of his left hand savagely and said:

'They ordered your arrest today.'

'Did they now?' remarked Word, with the air of a polite reply to unwanted information about Tiberius's new clothes. 'And who are they –?'

'– when they're at home?' grinned Johnny, once again surprising Nicodemus by his imperturbable response to the likelihood of Word's danger.

'The chief priests', muttered Nicodemus. 'The Pharisees. The Sadducees. The Herodians.'

'Not Pontius Pilate?' Word's eyebrows were scarcely elevated by comparison to Nicodemus's.

'Not yet', whimpered Nicodemus.

'Poor fellow', reflected Word. 'At this rate he may be in danger of missing the show. Tiberius will be wondering what he pays him for – I assume he does pay him, and doesn't simply expect Pilate to wring his salary from the Emperor's subjects in Judaea.'

'It's bad enough as it is' snapped Nicodemus. 'They sent Roman soldiers as well as officers of the Temple guards to take you.' Johnny thought Nicodemus was being a bit rude, but Word promptly walked forward and took the sculptor in his arms and kissed him.

'Poor old fellow', murmured Word. 'I'm being a tiresome nuisance to you. I'm sorry.'

Nicodemus burst into tears, and Johnny felt bad for having thought him rude. He realised now that Nicodemus was in fact terrified, even before he began sobbing 'I'm so frightened. I'm so frightened!'

'We can go', offered Word.

'Oh, no' answered Nicodemus. 'What's the use of being afraid if I'm left with nothing to be afraid for? Anyhow, I've burnt my boats. They say I'm a Galilean.'

'Galileans don't burn their boats' interrupted Johnny with more surprise than indignation, seeing that this was one of the very few anti-Galilean jokes he would not have expected from a Judaean, especially from one of the few he thought of as friendly.

'Put down your feathers, my little eagle', smiled Word as poor Nicodemus reeled a pace back from this flank attack. 'Time enough for them later, more as pens than porcupines.'

'It was only', stammered Nicodemus piteously, 'that the officers said they refused to command the soldiers to arrest him, or, I suppose, ask them, since the soldiers were Roman, and when the priests and Pharisees reproached them, said no man had ever spoke as you did, and Scribes said the only people who believed in you were those who did not know the law.'

'And I suppose they would know to whom they had taught the law and to whom they had failed to teach it', nodded Word.

'And I said', whimpered Nicodemus, 'did our law judge someone without hearing him and finding out his real actions and intentions? And they asked me if I was a Galilean and that I should search and look in the holy scriptures and never once would I find that a prophet had come from Galilee.'

'Oh, poor Nicodemus!' said Johnny, anxious to apologise for thinking he had been racist about Galilee, and pulled Nicodemus's shoulders down so as to kiss him too.

'Well done, Nicodemus!' applauded Word, slapping him on the shoulder-blade when Johnny was finished with it. 'That took real courage!' Nicodemus looked at the two of them in surprise, and began to smile through his tears.

'What did happen today?' he asked.

'Dear me', Word wrinkled his forehead. 'Johnny, tell Nicodemus what happened today.' Johnny realised that Word was actually training Johnny himself in describing things that had happened, so that he would have laid the foundations of his craft when his time came to tell all of Word's story that he was supposed to tell. So he began with the woman taken in adultery (translating it into Greek as an exercise for Word the following day before going out), worked his way on to the first confrontation in the Temple, and finished more or less triumphantly on Word's departure invisibly to the would-be stone-throwers; after which he caught his breath. Nicodemus caught his, too, and Word nodded, not having interrupted. 'I think that's the essence of it', he told Nicodemus. 'Any questions for Johnny?'

'What had the Master written in the sand which frightened the accusers of the woman?' asked Nicodemus, and Word waited for Johnny's answer with a little smile on his curved red lips.

'I saw nothing', said Johnny simply, 'and so we shall never know.'

He looked wisely at Nicodemus as though he had rigidly followed the formula for telling an old nursery legend.

'Unless some of the people who wanted to throw stones come back to say what they saw', said Word solemnly, almost concealing a glimmer in his eyes.

'And I don't think they will', said Johnny, considering the matter. 'In any case it looked as if they were seeing different things, one man something about *him*self, his neighbour about *him*self, and so on. I suppose Word wrote so that one would read things *he* had done or thought or said, and another things he had done or thought or said.' Johnny looked a little owlishly at Nicodemus, who had the sense to reply with comparable owlishness that he imagined Johnny was right. Johnny nodded with the air of a teacher pleased with a problematic pupil's unexpectedly good performance. 'In any case I wouldn't have known what the things they had done were.'

'Why not?' asked Nicodemus, startled

'Because they would have been stupid things stupid grown-ups do', and Johnny dismissed the matter as unworthy of a sensible child's further attention.

'So there you have it', and Word turned to Nicodemus with a sigh he tried to make sound relieved.

'So there I don't', and Nicodemus managed a watery smile.

'Or, as you say, so there you don't' nodded Word. 'After we left the Temple we had some lunch with the others strolling around the Mount of Olives very good olives they are, too – and then we wandered back to the Temple where for some reason the nastier questioners of the morning didn't seem to have found their way once more.'

'I think one or two of them found their way to my meeting', replied Nicodemus, rather gloomily.

'Scribes?' asked Word.

'One was. Another was a rich Sadducee. I didn't see any fellow-Pharisees.'

'Are Annas and Caiaphas Sadducees?' asked Johnny.

'Caiaphas is. He makes much of doing things and thinking things as they had been thought and taught in the old days.'

'Does he think Moses and David were Roman proconsular appointments?' enquired Word, amused. He was sitting down now, Johnny having correctly diagnosed that Nicodemus had relaxed enough to sink down on a couch if one was pushed around into availability, after which Word could relax as well, and Johnny found a stool for himself.

'I think it's his being a Roman appointment that makes Caiaphas so quick to talk tradition' reflected Nicodemus. 'And it's convenient. We are told to believe in the Pentateuch, but given no encouragement to read later scriptures which might instruct us on resistance against alien rulers in our own land. We are allowed to dislike Egyptians keeping us in Egypt.'

'What about Annas?' asked Johnny, a little anxiously.

'I don't know. It's so long since he was High Priest, and since he was removed as well as installed by the Romans, he doesn't have the same need to worry about our reading anti-foreign Scriptures, or at least he doesn't turn every disputation into veneration for Genesis and Exodus and practically nothing else.'

'Is he polite about angels?' asked Word, a little as though he wanted to find friends for his friends.

Nicodemus shook his head. 'Annas doesn't *say* things like that, especially with Caiaphas present.' (Johnny grinned to himself – and therefore to Word – secretly.) 'But once or twice he sounded – no, properly, he failed to sound contemptuous of a future existence after death. I have spoken of the light of the spirit when he was there, and – I don't know why – I had the odd feeling that his silence wasn't a hostile silence. Because when he doesn't agree with you he can cut up arguments like a Damascus sword dismembering a rotten orange. His sons are Sadducees right enough, but then several of them will probably be High Priests when Pontius Pilate feels that in the interest of his health Caiaphas should demit office.'

'Soon?' Word sounded indifferent.

'I don't think so. Caiaphas may well see Pilate off. But that could sink him. The friend of one Governor seldom finds another friend in the next.'

'They are friends now.' Word might have been talking about their capacity for team-work in a chariot-race, with Caiaphas as the horse, contemplated Johnny.

'They certainly are. I'd swear Caiaphas would love to be a guest at one of Pilate's banquets. But the Temple priests really would revolt if he polluted the Temple by such antics with a Gentile.'

'Poor Caiaphas', smiled Word. 'So annoying, to have to make sacrifices for rituals in which you don't believe. Or perhaps I wrong him. Maybe he does, and is encouraging this vigilance where I am concerned to prevent pollution of the Temple by the scum of Galilee.' Johnny bubbled over with laughter at this self-description.

'What happened after lunch?' Nicodemus had calmed down almost entirely by now, and was peeling an orange from Johnny's fruit-bowl.

'Oh, we became intellectual. People wanted to know, how I could write without having studied? I said my teaching was not mine, but from Him who sent me, and if anyone followed *His* teaching he would know fast enough whether it was God's or something concocted by an earth-bound me. I pointed out that people who speak about themselves and derive from themselves, only seek their own glory, but those seeking the glory of him Who sent them, show they are true – and truth, and no wrong is in them. At this point I realised we had, at length, been joined by the happy stone-throwers once more so to welcome them I remarked that Moses gave them the law and none of them kept it, so why were they trying to kill me?'

'And they said?' demanded Nicodemus from the depths of his orange.

'The usual. I had a devil. Notwithstanding this, whom did I imagine was going about trying to kill me?'

'And then?'

Word thought back. 'I singled out one of my actions which had astounded them all. Moses had given us circumcision, I said (though I added it actually came from the patriarchs), and so on the Sabbath they circumcise men, and Moses's law is not broken, so why object when I restore people to full health on the Sabbath?

'Fair enough', said Nicodemus thoughtfully.

'You also told them to judge by the truth, not by what things look like', reminded Johnny.

'A fine old row developed at that point', recalled Word. 'One group wanted me identified as the person the authorities sought to kill, yet kept asking why when I spoke out nobody said anything to me.'

'I thought you said they were saying rude things to you', reproached Nicodemus.

'It was probably their way of asking why I had not been arrested. "Do the rulers really know that this is Christ?" they chorussed. Then still others said they knew where I came from but when Christ comes nobody will know whence he comes.'

'You come from Nazareth, don't you?' Nicodemus wanted to be sure.

'Galilee', murmured Johnny, considerately.

'As a matter of fact', said Word, 'I am a Judaean. I was born in Bethlehem.'

'But we don't hold it against him', explained Johnny.

'Isn't that nice of him?' grinned Word.

Nicodemus laughed, and said he felt better. Word strolled to the door with him, Johnny a pace or two behind him. As Nicodemus raised his hand in blessing before turning away, Johnny thought he heard Word say to him 'you'll see to the burial when it's over' to which Nicodemus nodded rather apprehensively, but as to what they meant Johnny had no idea. He was beginning to find things on which he didn't want to ask questions.

IXTEEN

EUCHARIST

He was in the world, and the world was made by him

Next day, Johnny had finished writing about Word saving the woman taken in adultery and had put it into Greek, and Word had complimented him on his progress and exactitude. 'Some day, Johnny', he said seriously, 'you may write the most sublime Greek that has ever been written.'

'Then it will be about you', said Johnny automatically. Word hugged him, but instead of their going out as Johnny expected, Word sat him down on the couch beside him and swung round, looking at him.

'Do you remember a time, Johnny, when we were in Capernaum?' began Word. 'I told a crowd that I am the bread of life, the bread that came down from Heaven, and people could eat of it and not die.'

'You said that if any person ate of this bread they would live for ever, and the bread you would give was your flesh, which you would give for the life of the world', nodded Johnny. 'Then they argued among themselves, asking how could you give them your flesh to eat, and you said "Truly, truly I tell you unless you eat the flesh of the Son of Humanity and drink his blood you will have no life in you." Whoever eats your flesh and drinks your blood has eternal life, lives in you and you in him, you said. And this shocked quite a number of your crowd and many of them drifted away, the sillies.'

'The sillies?' Word's eyebrows shot up. 'Why sillies?'

'Well, you'd think they could work it out for themselves', said Johnny in disgust. 'It's quite obvious. If someone *really* loves someone, they want to be full of that person for ever and ever. We kiss each other, but that's only the beginning of it. And we want God to swallow us up completely, we don't want to be apart from Him in the slightest, and since He isn't visibly there except being here as you, we swallow up you, and we live for ever because you live for ever. It's no problem at all. I think it's a lovely idea, and I can't see why everyone doesn't realise that.' Johnny opened his eyes wide and smiled at Word.

'And how does this happen?' Word's voice was full of love as always, but strangely quiet as though he were waiting for something to happen.

'You'll tell us. I've no idea. You don't announce your miracles in advance.' Johnny was quite business-like. He might have been waiting for James or Zebedee to tell him they were about to go back to the sea, having noted signs of a good draught of fish.

'I will have to announce this one', and Word gave a little sigh.

Johnny's eyes sparkled.

'Will this happen during Passover?' Johnny was looking for Passover, the Seder which would be his first one with Word. He knew that he, Johnny, would have the crucial obligation of asking the questions as to why the Seder is eaten and why it takes the form that it does, for the youngest person would have that duty and everyone knew who that was.

But Word smiled wanly, and said 'In a way. But it will also have happened before it.' Johnny did not push Word for more explanation at this point: but where such restraint in the past would have been because he knew Word was tired, or that he knew one of Word's stories would soon be coming up and he wouldn't want to pre-empt it, this time he knew he would prefer to let things take their course, and see them in their own time. He never claimed to have had a premonition as to what would happen in the next days, but he felt conscious of something like an invisible shadow ahead of him which be did not intend to penetrate before its time. They walked out now and were joined by most of the apostles. Judas had not arrived yet, nor Matthew. Word must have read Johnny's mind, as usual, and seen his perception of a shadow ahead, and so Word himself began to speak of signs of what is to come, taking the example of the fig-tree and all other trees whose early shoots proclaim that Summer, or at least Spring, is at hand. He stopped underneath a fig-tree to demonstrate what be meant, but Peter thought he was trying to eat a fig, and was annoyed at not finding one. And when Word decided to use the barren fig-tree as a parable, and tell the apostles and the other disciples around them that those who looked well and appropriate and promising of fine fruit but never produced any would be cut off in their time or their prime and cursed for their non-productivity, Peter evidently got it firmly into his head that Word had cursed the actual fig-tree, and he repeated it to Matthew. Word never cursed anything.

It was particularly silly because soon after this Word told one of his stories again turning on just this point. He was back in his accustomed place in the Temple with a good crowd around him and leaned luxuriously back, shaking out his hair and briskly stroking his beard. Johnny stood beside him, as he usually did these days, to be alert for trouble and the rest stood near at hand. Word started curiously, as though he had begun the story in the middle though Johnny knew he had been silent from their arrival at the Temple. 'Likewise', said Word, 'there was a man about to travel to a far country who called his slaves and handed them some of his wealth, and to this one gave five talents, and to that one two, and to that one one. He favoured every man in proportion to his ability, and off he went. The slave with five talents earned the same again, and thus "made" another five. In the same way the man given two obtained another two. But he with one dug in the earth, and hid the silver of his lord. Much time elapsed, and the lord of these slaves came, and worked out their accounts. And the one with five, showed five more, and his lord said he would make him ruler over many things, and the same in proportion for the one who had made two, but the one who had buried his one talent came and said "you're the hard man, reaping where you have not sown, harvesting where you have not strewn, and I was afraid, and hid your talent in the earth, and here is what is yours". His lord answered him, "you bad and hesitant slave, you knew I reap where I have not sown, and harvested where I have not strewn, you should have left my money with the financiers when at my return I would collect my talent with usury. Take the talent from him, give it to the slave with ten talents for who has much will receive more, and who has not will have taken from him what he has. And send the unprofitable servant into outer darkness where there is weeping and tooth-gnashing.' And Johnny said in Word's mind 'what a horrible Lord' and Word said in Johnny's mind that the lord was horrible indeed, but that Johnny must listen to what the story meant.

And sure enough one of the crowd asked what the story meant, and Word said that the Son of Humanity would come with the angels to give judgment on Humankind, separating them like sheep and goats, and those who had put their talents to good use would be those who fed the hungry, and watered the thirsty, and housed the stranger, and clothed the naked, and visited the sick and the imprisoned, but he would put it that they had fed and watered and housed and clothed and visited him himself and so 'Come ye blessed of my Father and inherit the kingdom prepared for you from the making of the world' and when he was asked when they had done these things would say that what they had done for the least important of his brothers and creatures they had done to him. And those who had refused good works or put their talents to no use for their neighbours had refused their true Lord, and should be sent to everlasting punishment and those who did good should be given eternal life. And Johnny realised Word had told the same story whether about the talents or about the fig-tree.

But Word certainly did not mean to say that those with the most talents were the most favoured of God, and as he watched rich men throwing fat purses into the treasury he saw a poor widow throwing the thinnest possible offering, and pointed out that the widow had given more than all the rich men put together. 'For all these have thrown from their heaps of wealth and she has given all she has in the world.' 'And what about you?' sneered a Sadducee. 'I also will give all I have in the world', said Word, adding, to Johnny's horror 'after two days is Passover when the Son of Humanity has been betrayed to be crucified.' But before Johnny could demand from Word something to explain, or, better, to explain away this revolting metaphor – it must be a metaphor, surely, a symbol, a way of talking, a parable again – Jim came up and said seriously to Word 'you can't expect the fig-tree to produce olive berries?'. Word said you couldn't, and that he wanted people to use the talents they had, not to pretend use of talents they lacked. While they were discussing it, Word looked over his shoulder to Peter and Johnny, and told them to prepare the night's meal for them to eat on the eve of Passover. Peter said 'Where?' and Johnny spoke in Word's mind 'Nicodemus's?' to which Word said they mustn't risk disclosure of Nicodemus's secret studio which might then be attacked by crowds if it got out he was sheltering the scum of Galilee, which made Johnny laugh again, while Word said out loud to Peter that near the closest gate of entry into Jerusalem they would find a man carrying a pitcher of water whom they were to follow into a house, and inside that house they were to ask the owner on behalf of their Master ('or Word' said Johnny's mind to Word's) 'Where is the guest-chamber where he is to eat the meal on Passover eve with his disciples?' And the master of the house would show them a large upper room where there would be plenty of space, and where there was sufficient furniture, and where Word would have room enough to wash the feet of the disciples at dinner with him, with Johnny as attendant following him to dry the feet and any slopped water.

Johnny shivered without fully knowing why at Word's remark that he would be washing their feet. It was just like Word to do such a thing and show his love for them all by acting as their lowly servant which also meant showing that they too had to conduct themselves as servants to other people when necessary. What bothered Johnny was that it seemed an oddly final gesture, as though Word was setting a seal on their love, not in repudiation, but implying that it was going to take a different form. Johnny had always crushed down the thought that Word might go back to his Father some day although he knew perfectly well this must happen, and it might be quite soon. He had found supreme happiness with Word, and he realised that people could not hope to continue so happily on earth for any length of time, and Word was older than Johnny and in the normal usages of life must go first, and all that. But he kept such realisation in the uttermost depths of his mind. And now here was a goodbye sign, perhaps, with some awful joke of Word's about crucifixion having been made earlier. But what surprised Johnny was that Peter was greatly displeased about Word's proposing to undertake the work of a servant, and said as much to Johnny as they made their way to the nearest gate of entry to the city.

'I mean to say', said Peter, 'he's got his dignity to think of.'

Johnny had become very fond of Peter, but not for stuffiness like this. 'But Word doesn't think about his dignity', he said.

'Then he should think about it', barked Peter, 'when we have half the country looking at us with a third of a million people in Jerusalem itself.

Andrew was talking to some of the Temple guards and that was the figure they put on it.'

'Do a third of a million people live in Jerusalem?' gasped Johnny, who had never quite believed the world contained so many.

'Not all the time, but coming in for the Passover, yes. And since he's God, he should be acting like God.' Johnny seemed to see Peter handing Word a list of rules for being God.

'If Word started acting like God', said Johnny thoughtfully, 'none of us could bear to appear alongside him.'

'You mean, he'd look so much finer than us', said Peter approvingly.

'No, I mean we'd feel so unworthy of his company', answered Johnny. 'One way we know how much be loves us is that he has become like us while he is with us.'

'Yes, but he must show he isn't like us', argued Peter firmly. 'He's letting himself down if he washes our feet. As I told him once, I am a sinful man.'

'Not more sinful than any of the rest of us', urged Johnny.

'You wouldn't know', sniffed Peter loftily. Johnny kept the thought to himself how like grown-ups it was to be snobbish about their sins. Actually Peter was trying to say that Johnny's innocence was superior to what was in the souls of the adults, but unfortunately it came out as condescension.

'Matthew is a publican', suggested Johnny, trying to share the sinfulness around, but unintentionally stiffening Peter's rebellion.

'That's what I mean. It's one thing to admit a publican to our number, and I will say for Matthew he's certainly shown me how easy it is to like a publican which I never thought I could do, once he's stopped telling you whose father was who. But washing a publican's feet – there may well be something in the Torah forbidding it.' Peter pursed his lips into indignant shelves rather like a duck's beak.

'But surely Moses couldn't have told publicans not to wash their feet?' Johnny was genuinely puzzled.

'Nothing against them washing their feet', snapped Peter. 'I dare say nobody needs it more. It's someone else washing publicans' feet that would have worried Moses.'

'But why should Moses object to their wives washing their feet?' persisted Johnny. 'And their mothers must have washed their feet when they were babies.'

'They wouldn't have been publicans when they were babies!' shouted Peter.

'You don't think it would have been a family business, making them Father Publican, Mother Publican, and all the little Publicans?'

'I do not think it would have been a family business' shouted Peter, and then saw Johnny grinning at him. He grinned back in spite of himself. 'You young reprobate, I should have realised you were thinking of your own family. You'll be in trouble with James if I tell him you likened your family to publicans.'

'I didn't', replied Johnny with dignity.

'You did, you little story-teller', hooted Peter.

'I didn't', leered Johnny, 'I likened publicans to my family.' And he shot down the road laughing, as Peter lumbered after him to fetch him a clip on the side of the head, and thus they progressed, in and out of the increasing crowds, Johnny now making Peter chase him round a pillar, now falling back to be on the verge of being caught, and finally with the city gate in sight they thundered down the last lap and Johnny was just ahead of Peter when he realised that he was about to bump into a man carrying a pitcher of water, and the man hastily moved to one side to be charged full tilt by Peter, let go of the pitcher, and was about to see it shattered before his eyes when Johnny got to it, grasped the handle, and held it up with practically none of the water lost. The man thanked Johnny after taking a deep breath with a clear suggestion that he would have liked to say several other things to him first, gave a withering glare to Peter, who was grunting out what little breath he had left, and resumed his course with a dignity sadly lacking in Peter and Johnny. In Johnny's mind he could hear Word's voice with scarcely concealed amusement: 'You abominable brat! What would you have done if I hadn't made sure you held the jug?' 'Prayed to you to mend it, of course' replied Johnny's mind demurely, 'I'm a carpenter, not a long-distance potter', reproached Word severely, 'and if you don't keep your eye on that man he'll be in his master's house, and you'll be left looking at Peter, who won't simply be looking at you.' 'Yes, Word' responded Johnny's mind in a tone of respect which fooled neither of them, and moved rapidly before Peter having caught his breath could now catch up with him, so that the man set foot in his master's house only a second before Johnny made a flying entrance followed by the thudding of Peter's pursuit, and Johnny was gasping at the door-porter 'Canlseeyourmasterwithamessagefrommymaster?' to which the door-porter, not unreasonably, replied that he didn't know Greek, and would Johnny mind repeating his message in Aramaic which was in fact the language Johnny had been trying to utter. Peter's arrival set back further progress since Peter tried to achieve instant dignity and succeeded in sounding like a camel disapproving of its latest passenger. Johnny resumed a diplomatic offensive but slower (eyeing Peter suspiciously since it was quite possible that Peter would give dignity a further rest and resume hostilities regardless of the door sentinel). The porter muttered a clear instruction to the water-carrier to tell the houseowner that someone had allegedly brought a message and they (with emphasis) couldn't be left alone in the hall, which suited Johnny as insurance against Peter. Peter breathed stertorously and balefully. Johnny recovered his breath more rapidly, but his attempt to sidle towards the door by which the seigneur might be expected to enter was firmly blocked by the porter who told him truculently to stay where he was. Peter grinned wolfishly and Johnny turned up his nose, sticking out his tongue as an after-thought. The owner appeared at that moment, a tall, thin, sardonic-looking figure, who mistook Johnny's gesture as impudence in his own direction, and glared, until Peter, still breathing heavily, said that the Master had said to ask where was the guest-chamber where he might eat with his disciples. At that the houseowner pursed his lips and whistled, adding rather unkindly 'I've been expecting messengers but messengers with –' he stopped and Johnny asked helpfully 'rather more dignity?' Neither this nor the necessary good behaviour improved Peter's temper, nor did the stairs to the upper room, where there was, as Johnny pointed out with supreme tactlessness, plenty of room for Word to wash the feet of his disciples. The houseowner nodded, thus incurring his share of Peter's disapproval, and said 'Anything he wants. Eleazar was a very good friend of mine', which explained why Word could be confident of getting the room when he asked for it. The owner added 'Tonight isn't it? I thought it might be for tomorrow night but he said no, when I saw him last, not the Passover meal itself, I suppose he'll be going to the house of some relative for that.' Johnny said that he supposed so, thinking that the four elder sons of Daddy-Joe were about the last people likely to want to see Word among the three or four hundred thousand on offer in Jerusalem at that moment. (Johnny never did see any of them.) Peter pulled himself together to thank the houseowner, and Johnny gave some sort of bow, on which the houseowner smiled and pulled Johnny's hair, bowing to Peter. Johnny thought it as well not to mention that Eleazar and his sisters were by now well on their way to Gaul, and managed to get Peter out of the house before he remembered some version of their departure. Peter gave him a grim look as they left, but made no attempt to start their shenanigans again so when they were out of sight of the house Johnny pulled down Peter's shoulders and kissed him, and Peter gave Johnny a suitably smothering bear-hug, after which they made their way back as friends.

But, however much of a casualty his own dignity might be. Peter had not given up on Word's, as he showed when they were all assembled in the upper room. When all were seated except himself and Johnny, Word took off his robe, Johnny took off his, and they put towels around their waists, Word having evidently asked the houseowner to leave them in readiness, as he also left clean water in the pitcher Johnny and Peter had nearly broken between them, together with a jug, a basin and a large receptacle into which Johnny would have to empty the basin, each time someone's feet had been washed in it. Johnny was pleased to see that Word had ensured there also would be a small towel, and evidently intended Johnny to be his acolyte from the time he made the arrangements in Bethany (either after Eleazar's return to life, or during the last party, when he must have met Eleazar's friend the houseowner). There was nothing odd in such a request: all Jews knew that they probably washed themselves more often than any other people on earth, while seldom affording or desiring the luxurious Roman bath-houses. The supper was to be eaten at a long table, with Word in the centre, Johnny at his left as always, Peter at his right for some reason, James beyond Peter, then Matthew and Thomas at the short breadth of the table, Shimon the ex-Zealot perpendicular to Thomas, then Judas and Thady (both facing Word directly), Jim after Thady at the corner with Nathaniel at right angles to him, then Philip, with Andrew round the corner beside Johnny. The place at Word's right was by tradition the one of most honour in Jewish and most other societies, and Word clearly wanted to establish Peter symbolised as a future leader, but just as he was now presenting himself as the servant, indeed the slave, of all of them, so he inverted the place of honour in relation to the order of foot-washing, and Peter would be the last to be approached. Johnny liked the idea of mingling ceremony and diplomacy: this way, Peter would be asked to have his feet washed when everyone else except Johnny and Word had had theirs done, and there would be ten precedents, Andrew first.

Would Andrew react as Peter was threatening to do? Then Johnny looked at Andrew's tall form, with head cocked to one side, and a welcoming grin in Word's direction as Word knelt down, unlatched Andrew's right shoe, poured water from the pitcher Johnny handed him, and Andrew leaned forward to Word with the whisper 'Like old times in the Jordan!' (Johnny could see that for all of Andrew's smile tears stood above his lower eyelids, and he suddenly realised Andrew was thinking of John the Baptizer pouring water on Andrew's head, and, later, on Word's, the Baptizer having previously told his own disciples and hearers 'I baptise you with water but one stands among you whom you do not know, he comes after me but will rank above me, and I am not worthy to unlatch his shoe!') Word said gently 'Thanks, Andrew!' and a tear fell from his own eye with a slight splash into the basin, and after Word had washed and dried both of Andrew's feet he hugged Andrew's knees before kissing him. He kissed them all, as the turn of each was finished, but that little embrace of the knees was specially for Andrew.

When Word had latched Andrew's shoes Andrew stood up, stretched his arms and legs so that for one moment he looked like a Greek Chi (or like our letter X), thus giving more room for Word and Johnny in their ministrations. Andrew strolled to the side of the room where Philip joined him when his turn was over, and Nathaniel after that. They didn't speak to one another but were very much at ease together: as a rule Philip automatically checked with Andrew before taking up some point with Word, and Phil was Nat's closest friend. Jim followed Nat, which brought Andrew back to the table, and the self-regulating ebb and flow of the group kept that order, three away from the table giving room to the next foot-washing. Thomas seemed to remember some game he had played with Word as a boy, and whispered some recollection of it, and Word grinned, flicking a drop of water from his right thumb-ball with his long finger so that it landed on Thomas's nose, when he had dried Thomas's feet and latched his footwear. Johnny had of course been kept very busy moving back and forth between the foot-washing and the large vessel for dirty water, keeping up a supply of clean towels for Word (they had been given four big ones as well as Johnny's little one) and having his jug ready each time Word needed to fill the basin again. He hadn't much time to look at the other apostles when each one's turn came, but he fetched a smile for Judas, feeling sorry that they had seen less of each other in the last few days, yet Judas did not seem to see Johnny, or indeed to want to see him, but kept staring at Word as though he had never seen him before.

To Johnny's irritation, Peter still insisted on climbing his high horse again regardless of everyone's compliance with Word's wish, headed by his own brother. Word had fallen on his knees before Peter, James having austerely risen to his feet after Word had washed and dried them and refastened his shoes and kissed James, and Johnny had removed the water (James softening his austerity and delighting Johnny by pulling a spectacular face at him as Johnny straightened up with the basin). As Johnny returned with basin and water, Peter demanded of Word 'do you wash my feet?' Johnny savagely thought that even Peter should have come to that conclusion by now, but Word said softly 'What I do, you do not know now, but you will know after these things'. Again, a little shiver caught Johnny: what were these 'things' and why would Peter not understand them until afterwards (if he was ever to understand them at all)? Wasn't it clear that Word was teaching them the importance of being servants as he had rather too successfully taught Johnny before the Qana wedding-feast? Yet Peter was firing up 'You will not wash my feet while I am alive' which Johnny thought invited the answer 'How soon after you're dead?' But Word's answer was deadly serious. 'If I do not wash you, you will have no heritage from me.' And his look was infinitely sad even to think of such a possibility. It gave Johnny a terrible sense of loneliness at the thought of a friendship without a future after all they had shared, and Peter, directly confronted by it, felt it so much more powerfully that he let out a yell which caused Shimon, returning to his seat, to miss it and tumble on the floor, and Judas, who had been skinning an orange, sent it rolling out of his hands along the floor only to be stopped by the far corner of the room. Word's face had melted into sympathy even before Peter bawled 'Lord, not my feet only but my hands and my head!' and started to tear off his robe while Johnny wondered if Peter ever would realise there was space between A and Z (he actually thought 'Alpha and Omega' with some elation at how naturally a Greek analogy came to him after Word's teaching). Word smiled faintly as he said 'He who is washed need only have the feet washed, he is clean in all his flesh, and you are clean, but not every one of you' which Johnny took to mean that he himself had to have his turn, which he did when Peter had had his feet very thoroughly washed, sticking his ankles below as much water as he could get for them. Word finished Johnny, who marvelled as he always did at Word the carpenter having the gentlest hands in the world, and then Johnny firmly pushed Word back on his own seat and washed his feet, kissing each one as he dried them and put them into their shoes. Peter fortunately missed this, Johnny thankfully realised, suspecting he might have demanded it for himself from Word had he noticed it. Then Johnny brought the basin and jug back to the foul-water receptacle for the last time, and Word followed him to wash his hands while Johnny washed his, since their hands now did require it, but fortunately Peter also missed this, having started an argument with Matthew on whether Jonah needed to wash himself while in the belly of the big fish. It suddenly occurred to Johnny that Peter's exceptionally argumentative mood that day was as if he, like Johnny, felt some shadow of a dark future which Peter's method of staving off was to get wildly excited about trivialities in the present, naturally inflating them far above trivialities. When they had put on their robes and got back to the table, Johnny drew even closer to Word than he usually would, at a meal, drew his own feet upon the couch (they were clean, after all), and worked his head around so that it half-lay on Word's shoulder and breast – near his heart, in fact. Word seemed to understand and made no move to put Johnny in a more convenient posture and even James, looking across from beyond Peter, only nodded as if to say Johnny was best where he was, for his sake and perhaps for Word's.

They started to eat, and Word after a short while smiled at them and said 'You know what I have done to you? You call me teacher or master and Lord' (and Word, thought Johnny) 'and you speak with beauty in so doing, for so I am' ('and I am Word, too' his mind accorded happily to Johnny's, and Johnny thought how elegantly Word showed that beauty was truth). 'If I then, Lord and Master' ('and Word') have washed your feet, you also have the duty to wash one another's feet' (Johnny was hoping desperately that Peter wouldn't suddenly insist on washing all their feet now). 'I have led you to do as I have done. Truly, truly I tell you the slave is not greater than his lord, nor the apostle greater than the one who has sent him. If you know these things, you are happy if you do them. I am not speaking of all of you. I know whom I have put to the test. The Psalmist tells "Mine own familiar friend in whom I trusted, who did eat of my bread, has lifted his heel to trip me up". I am telling you this now before it happens, so that when it does, you can have faith in its identity with me. And truly, truly I tell you, they who give hospitality to those whom I send, give hospitality to me, they who give hospitality to me, receive him who sent me.' Johnny suddenly saw the houseowner standing for a moment at the door of the upper room, Word bowing to him, and him bowing back with a rapturous smile for once softening his sardonic features; and then he left. Had Word put it into his mind to look in just at that moment? wondered Johnny, and Word in Johnny mind said he had, it being a good way of saying thanks and celebrating gratitude.

Then Word took bread, and lifted it up in his right hand, and gave thanks, and broke it, and gave a portion to each disciple, and said: 'Take, eat, this is my body' and he took his wine-cup, and gave thanks, and gave it to them, pouring into the wine-cup of each. Johnny and the others saw that all the wine-cups were of the same size, yet each of the twelve wine- cups into which Word poured the wine from his was filled like it had been as near to the brim as was possible with safety. Andrew looked at Philip and then at Johnny, as they remembered Word turning five loaves and two fishes into food for five thousand. Johnny gulped, feeling his eyes smarting slightly. Word saw their observation rather than surprise at the fullness of their cups, and said 'Drink all of it, for this is my blood of the new Covenant, which will be poured out for many to be set free from sins.' He himself now poured water into his own cup, saying he would not drink wine again until God's kingdom was come. Johnny automatically murmured in his mind 'not even water becoming wine this time, Word?' and Word laughed in Johnny's mind and said 'the smaller miracle is unnecessary when all is brought into the greatest miracle of all'. Johnny ate and drank knowing that he was at last receiving Word's promise and taking Word within himself in the fullness of love and the forgiveness it brings, and while he himself was consumed in the glory and wonder of the moment he did not think at first what this meant would happen to Word.

And then Word spoke to them all: 'Truly, truly, I say to you, one of you is ready to deliver me up.' It was a very ugly moment. Even Johnny for a split second found himself wondering if Word meant this was the result of Johnny making friends with Annas, but Word promptly, indeed almost violently, shouted in Johnny's mind 'No! NO! You are true to me, Johnny, and I will never think of you as anything else', and Johnny nuzzled his head on Word's breast. Word put an arm around him for the brief moment it needed, and all the other disciples looked fearfully into one another's faces. Then Peter leaned across Word, gesturing to Johnny to ask Word whom he meant, Johnny nodded quickly, thankful that Peter wasn't inaugurating an inquisition of the entire table, and Word, seeing Johnny's mental record of Peter's question, said so quietly that only Peter and Johnny heard 'It is he to whom I shall give the piece of bread dipped in the dish by me now' and handed it to Judas, with the words 'What you are about to do, do quickly'. Judas looked wildly at him, and got up, and hurried out into the night. Matthew said cheerfully 'oh, yes, the Passover meal, sensible to start buying for it now', and Jim wondered to Thady if it wasn't an errand to make sure any extra money in the communal purse was going to help the poor to eat the Seder. Nobody asked Word.

Johnny's mind was swimming wildly through utterly unknown seas. To whom would Judas deliver Word up? And how would he trip him up, or try to? Word seemed to be talking as though he wouldn't be eating again, or was it only wine that he would not drink again, or did it mean that the kingdom of God was about to arrive, as he had taught them to ask in the prayer he taught Johnny which Johnny had spoken to the crowds on the Mount in Galilee? What was going to happen to Word, and what could happen, he being God? That horrible joke about crucifixion could only have been a joke, and all those allusions to the Son of Humanity being lifted up couldn't have anything to do with crucifixion although its victims were lifted up. But Word was speaking again:

'Now is the Son of Humanity glorified, and God is glorified in him!' ('Thank God', thought Johnny, 'that's all right, then, all will be well. Perhaps the world is about to end, and Word will take us all to his Father.')

'If God is glorified in him, God will glorify him in himself, and will glorify him immediately.' ('That's glorious', warbled Johnny's mind, 'and all things are well. How does one greet God the Father anyway? "I'm a friend of your Son, Sir", no, "Lord", no, perhaps I call him "Father" too, after all. I already have, in that prayer. Anyhow, he's God and Word is God so he is really Word. But what is Word saying now?') 'Little children' ('that's good, he's lumping them all with me') 'I am with you for a very small time.' ('But then we are with him forever?') 'You will look for me, and as I told the Judaeans, where I go you will not be able to go.' ('But that was the Judaeans: can't we Galileans go with you, you are one of us!') 'I am giving you a new command: to love one another. As I have loved you, so you love one another.' ('But I can't love anyone as I love you, Word.' And at last Word's voice came to Johnny's mind: 'I'm not asking that. But you must love the others.' 'But what's happening to you?') 'In this way all men will know you for my disciples, that you have love for one another.'

Peter stammered out what they were all thinking: 'Lord, where are you going?' Word said simply 'I am going where you cannot follow now'. Johnny's jaw set. Word went on: 'But you must follow me later.' Peter said 'Lord, why can I not follow you now? I will discharge my life for your sake.' Word raised his eyebrows: 'You will discharge your life for my sake? Truly, truly I tell you, the cock will not crow until you have denied me utterly, three times.' Johnny, his elation vanished, froze alongside Word, thinking again and again 'I have no life without you now, I could not live if I denied you', and Word's mind ended his repetition by saying 'hold on, Johnny, all will be well, but not in the way you think now. But you must be true not only to me, but to them. You will be true, but you must love Peter and all those who are untrue. You will be true to me tenfold when you are true to them. And even when I do not seem to be there, I will always be with you.' Johnny wedged his body as close to Word's as he could, and took his hand underneath the table. 'You will?' asked Word's mind. 'I will do as you command, always', answered Johnny's mind. 'I will love them all, but never as much as I love you.' Johnny could almost see Word smiling in his mind. 'I know, Johnny. And I love you even more than you love me.' So Johnny let his mind feed on what was happening out loud.

Word smiled at them all, if a little more remotely than he had smiled in Johnny's mind. 'Don't sorrow, have faith in me as you have faith in God. There are many dwelling-places in my father's house, otherwise would I have said I am going to prepare a home for you? And if I go away to make a home for you, I will return to take you to myself so that you also may be where I am. And now you know where I am going, and you know the road.'

Thomas spoke to him: 'Lord, we do not know where you are going, and how can we know the road?'

Word said: 'I am the road, and the truth, and the life. No person can come to my Father except through me. If you had known me, you had known my Father also. From now on in, you know Him, you have seen Him.'

Philip spoke to him: 'Lord, show us the Father, that will satisfy us.' Word laughed, and it was a memory Johnny cherished down the years, remembering what subsequently happened which Word knew would happen: 'Have I been so long a time with you, Philip, and you have not known me? He who has seen me, has seen the Father. And how can you then say, show us the Father? Do you not put faith in my being in the Father, and the Father in me? The words I speak are not my own words, and the Father who lives in me does my work. Put faith in me, that I am in the Father, and the Father in me. If not, put faith in the work. Truly, truly, I tell you, the one who puts faith in me will be able to do what I do also, and more besides. I go to my father, and what you ask of the Father in my name I will do that the Father gain glory in the Son. What you ask in my name I will do.'

There was a beauty in all of this founded on truth beyond anything anyone had ever known, thought Johnny. He had half-known for some time what Word was now saying, but its movement from what Johnny had deduced, to what Word said, was like seeing a ghost become wonderful flesh and blood. Johnny wanted this moment to last forever, and he realised that ultimately it would, but that so many other things had to happen first. He would have to think about them very soon, above all to confront the shock of Judas from which his mind was still retreating even as it basked in Word's new message. And if Word was now making words of what Johnny had always instinctively known, it was still the old companionship of their journeyings. Some things did not change, however terrific the changes in the worlds through which they moved. Word had to be patient with Peter, tactful, but if need be, brutally direct. Word was direct with Thomas from the first, partly for old times' sake, the simplicity and frankness of boys talking together or shooting drops of water at one another. Word could play with Philip, somewhere between Philip's love of music and verse, and his endless questioning, with the questions rolled around and returned wrapped in the knowledge that they carried their own answers. Johnny nestled alongside Word, very easily following his command of loving them all, James the most (after Word), but then big, big-footed, big-hugging, big-mouthed, big-hearted Peter, then Andrew who had begun the whole thing with his restless quest for spiritual leadership, then Nat who knocked Johnny out in Nazareth and Philip who would one day be a song without end and Thomas whose boyhood friendship with Word had helped make Word so perfect a friend for a boy, and then all of them, Jim with his marvellous hunger for justice for all the people but especially the poor, and Matthew with his hilarious but utterly honest tabulation of evidence, and Shimon slowly coming to terms with a future for the children of Israel and himself which did not depend on mass slaughter, and Thady with a perpetual eye of love for those beyond hope.

And –

Johnny knew that in this time of supreme happiness there could be no running away. Above all in this time there could not be.

Judas.

What on earth had happened? What was happening? Even now with Judas marked as about to deliver up Word to the priests, or to the Herodians, or to the Romans, or whoever, Johnny still could not eliminate the memory of his kindness, his interesting stories of Jerusalem, his courage – Johnny of all people knew that Judas had courage. Nor did Johnny want to forget those things. In any case Peter, whom he could never reject from friendship, would apparently reject Word in some way, perhaps even that very night. For the shadows had silently moved up much closer to Johnny, and he was all too aware that this night, now so sublime, could yet contain something horrible. Word's quiet testament of love for them all, and firm acceptance of what was to come which in some way would cut him off from them for a time, foretold it in one way, Peter's boast and its dreadful prophetic demolition, Judas's look at Word and refusal to look at Johnny and flight into the night foretold in another.

'If you love me', Word was saying to them all, 'guard my commandments.' Johnny knew that the commandments had been given to Moses by God. It seemed to him that for the first time Word was almost casually talking as God, not simply as Word who had told them he was God. Perhaps he had done so earlier, but Johnny had never been so forcefully aware of it as now. Johnny shivered involuntarily: was Word talking like this because he was about to unite with God once more, leaving his earthly body behind him like a snake losing its skin? And that word 'guard', as if the twelve of them – now the eleven – were not only to follow the ten laws God had told Moses, and the two Word had made of them (loving God above all and all Humanity as much as themselves), but were somehow to make sure they were honoured, fulfilled, and not diminished by people's denial of them. And were the eleven to do this alone, without Word? Word answered Johnny's mind in his next words to the group: 'I will ask the Father' ('good', thought Johnny, 'he is speaking as earth-born Word again') and he will give you another helper, who will remain with you for ever' ('but I don't want anyone else' whimpered Johnny's mind 'I want *you*', and Word's mind said 'he will be me, in a different way, but he won't be a one as I am now'). 'It is the Spirit who gives Truth, Whom the world cannot conceive because it cannot behold Him, cannot know Him. But you will know Him for He remains with you, He will be in you. I will not leave you orphaned, I will come to you. In a very small time from now the world will behold me no more' (Johnny shuddered) 'but you will see me. Because I live, you will live.' Johnny drew a deep breath. 'When that day comes you shall know that I am in the Father, and you in me, and I in you.' ('For which eating you as is our earthly way', reflected Johnny silently. 'That's it', answered Word's mind.) 'The person who loves me, will be dearly loved by my Father' (Johnny drew a deep breath) 'and I will love him and will show all that I am to him.' ('Or her', thought Johnny. 'Or her', echoed the thought from Word.)

Johnny was still grapping this as Word became silent, but Thady, his face creasing with concern, intervened: 'How come that you show all that you are to us, and not to the world?' Johnny nodded his head: Thady had found the ultimate lost cause – the rest of Humanity. Word's smile was a trifle ironic, though Johnny would not realise either the irony or its reasons for some time, not knowing what was about to happen to Word and how much it has to do with Humanity being a lost cause no longer. For the present, Word answered Thady gently 'if any one loves me, he will guard my commandments, and then the Father will love him and we will both come to him and be one with him. The one who loves me not, does not guard my words. And this word which you hear is not my creation but that of the Father who sent me.'

Word paused and spoke the old greeting giving peace to the hearers, adding 'Peace I send to you, my peace I give to you, not as the world gives do I give it to you' (and several sets of lips tightened, reflecting the endless deaths by which the Romans proclaimed their peace). 'Do not let your hearts be troubled, or be afraid. You heard my word to you that I go away and come again to you. If you love me, you will be happy that I pass over to my Father for my Father is greater than I. Now I have told you this before it happens, so that when it happens, you may have faith in it.' (Suddenly Johnny felt Word grasp his right hand below the table's surface. Word was telling him especially, knowing Johnny's special love for him. Very faintly, Johnny had a glimmering that there might be another reason: the next hours would tell.) 'I cannot speak much more to you now, because the Thing spawned by the world's evil is coming, and has no part of me.' Johnny's mouth went dry. He swallowed, feeling the constriction of a rope around his throat. Word's hold on his hand tightened, and Johnny relaxed, but his eyes still rounded in apprehension. 'But so that the world will know that I love the Father who gave me instructions, I will do as He has said.' He stopped. Johnny managed to hold back an uncomprehending sob, and probably wasn't the only one. Word rose. He smiled with welcome. 'Here we go!'

Word continued talking with them as they walked towards the Garden of Gethsemane and Johnny let what he was saying wash around him, luxuriating hungrily in the sound of Word's voice. He knew he would recall exactly what Word had said: it was fixed between them that whatever mistakes Johnny might make in order, dating or detail of happenings in what he would record about Word, all that Word said would be in Johnny's mind as Word had said it. Johnny would not record what Word had said in Johnny's mind: that was their business. But Word's speech was for the world to hear, as far as the confines of a book could make it. So now Johnny walked along, hearing and half-listening to Word, and telling himself this would not be their last walk together, Word's left hand in Johnny's right. In spite of what he was saying, Word answered that fear in Johnny's mind, and said it would not be their last walk together. He did not say there would be many more, or when. The others intervened many times, and their progress was conversation not monologue, but at this point it was only what Word said that Johnny would docket and make part of what he would call his Reward of Good Tidings. Quite a lot of what Word said went over what he had already told the others, but they needed hearing it again. He returned to his metaphor of the fig-tree, or grape-vine:

'I am the true vine, and my Father is the farmer. All twigs in me that carry no fruit, he takes away, and all twigs that bear fruit he will make pure, so that it will bear much fruit. Now you are made pure through the word I have spoken in you.' ('And Word within us, yourself eaten by us as bread and wine' thought Johnny. 'Truly, truly' smiled Word in Johnny's mind.)

'Abide in me, and I will abide in you', Word told them. 'The twig cannot bear fruit by itself unless it abides in the vine, no more can you unless you abide in me.' Peter marched along with even greater resolution, shoulders raised, elbows swinging. Andrew raised his tall head more far-seeingly. James looked more responsible, Philip more certain, Nat more visionary. Johnny had no additional reaction: he shared such ideas with Word automatically by now. He could not see the others behind him, although Matthew could be heard making some point about the vine's ancestry; indeed he was only aware of the others as impressionistic silhouettes in the darkness as they strode. He picked up Word's voice again: 'As the Father has loved me, so I have loved you: keep yourselves in my love. If you guard my commandments, you will abide in my love, even as I guard the Father's commandments, and abide in his love.' ('Separately the Father's and Word's' thought Johnny 'and together.') 'I have spoken these things to you so that my joy may abide in you, and that your joy may be full. This is my commandment, that you love one another as I have loved you. No man has greater love than this, to lay down one's life for his friends.' Johnny nodded: it might be necessary for him – Johnny – to lay down his life for any or all of them. James in the darkness smiled grimly: he expected to. James looked at the shadows walking with him: they were worth dying for, every one of them, Johnny and of course Word, most of all. Probably most of the others responded the same way, without James's certainty of martyrdom. None of them thought that Word was speaking of himself. Equally, they were not thinking – not even Thady – how vast the number of Word's friends, in past, present, and future, or by what strange names those friends would know and love him.

SEVENTEEN

PONTIUS PILATE

And the world knew him not

Word turned to the others as they arrived at the garden, and told them to sit down where they were under Andrew's guidance as usual, and said he did not expect to be long in the garden, but to call him if they saw anyone coming, and then took Peter, James and what seemed the inseparable Johnny, inside with him. When they were inside, Word asked the three to wait, disengaging his hand from Johnny's and telling him inside his mind not to hang on, but any possibility of Johnny's feelings being hurt or anxieties being alerted he squelched with 'bless you, my beloved', leaving Johnny so elated that he scarcely took in Word's explanation to the other two 'my soul sorrows' as he walked away as far as Johnny would have thrown a stone, and knelt. Because Johnny had been beside him before he walked forward, Peter and James remained a pace or two behind, and Johnny did not turn back to them. He could faintly hear Word's voice as it spoke to his Father in Hebrew '*Abba*', asking that this chalice be allowed to pass away from him. It may only have taken a minute, but to Johnny it seemed endless. Word's sorrow radiated in Johnny's mind strong enough almost to touch, and all Johnny could do was to repeat 'I love you', hoping that somehow it might be of some help. Eventually, Word rose and walked back, found Johnny and kissed him with a long hug, and discovered the other two asleep. They sounded sleepily contrite when Word awoke them with a sigh of mild reproach. Johnny stayed in the background and neither then nor later told either of them that he alone had stayed awake; it would be one of many things that night and next day that he would never tell them.

Word went back to the inner garden and Johnny stayed where he had been, pretty soon hearing a snore from Peter and deep breathing from James, colliding with the faint sound of Word's 'Abba, if this chalice may not pass away, and I must drink it, Thy will be done', which made Johnny wonder, since Word had said he would drink no more wine after he had drunk with them all the wine that was himself. Again, Word returned, found the other two asleep and roused them with good-humoured protest. They came to, still half-slumbering. Johnny only realised later that Peter was exhausted by the day and all the energy he had thrown into fighting off the fears that surrounded him, while James was tired out from nerving himself for possible death. Word waited but clearly felt the need to return to his prayers, and when he finally stood up, Johnny rushed over to him and threw his arms around him. But as Word kissed him Johnny found for the first time ever that he tasted the salt of sweat from Word (who was in such perfect physical condition that he had never seemed to perspire at all), and mingled with the sweat was something bitter which it took Johnny some seconds to realise was blood.

Johnny asked no questions, nor allowed himself to think any, only hugging Word and repeating how much he loved him, with Word hugging and kissing him in return. Then Word woke the others, who scrambled up ruefully, still thinking Johnny had slept along with themselves, and the four made their way out of the garden where Andrew rose and stood at the head of the other apostles. Lanterns and torches were waving down the path and were evidently held by a large group in fairly disciplined order. The lights and what moonlight there was enabled Johnny to see the flash of metal in armour, in several places over several forms. Soldiers. He tightened his hold on Word's hand. Word stood, impassive, and any questions framed in Johnny's mind now were simply answered by Word with words of love. Word's disciples stood in dismay, which became close to panic when the many men came up, headed by Judas, who promptly put his arms around Word's neck and kissed him. Simultaneously Word let go of Johnny's hand, put his arms around Judas and ordered Johnny in his mind 'climb the nearest tree, hide inside it, and don't come out until we've gone' and Johnny obeyed automatically. He missed Word's reply to Judas's half-bleat 'Master! Master!', 'Judas, do you betray the Son of Humanity with a kiss?' which Peter and most of the others heard, and Word's lower whisper to Judas 'when the worst moment comes, Judas, call my name!', which only Judas heard. Then Johnny saw Word standing upright, facing soldiers, officers, Temple guards, Roman troops, Pharisees, Sadducees, scribes, priests, camp-followers and (thought Johnny bitterly) It, the master of all evil, knew what else. As this horrible ambush took up their stand in front of Word, there was a sudden silence, and Johnny could actually hear the brook Kedron below them, splashing over stones.

Then Word said quietly but clearly 'Whom do you seek?' The priests shouted 'Jesus of Nazareth!' which Word promptly answered 'I am he!' Then an officer gave a signal, and Roman soldiers with what looked like some Temple servants moved forward to seize Word. The next second every man who had moved fell back on the ground, several of them yelling. Judas raised his hands with what Johnny took to be encouragement to his shattered followers, but which those followers may have suspected was more like a hopeless attempt at dissuasion. Word said again 'Whom do you seek?' Once again, the intruders, now little more than a mob, some of them picking themselves off the ground, answered 'Jesus of Nazareth!' some voices rising close to screams especially if their owners had been among the fallen. 'I have told you that I am he', asserted Word, 'if therefore you seek me let those with me go free.' At this point Peter grabbed a sword which had fallen from one of the invisibly smitten soldiers, and whirled it over his head as though he were casting a fish-hook, to be answered by a scream of pain and rage. A cascade of confused shouts followed. First of all a Roman soldier bellowed some question in Latin, which received incomprehensible answers apart from 'Iste!' which Johnny managed to distinguish and which presumably identified Peter, rudely. Then Judaean voices could be heard in Aramaic, identifying Peter's victim as 'Malchos' who in turn was identified to others as the servant of the High priest. Then Word strode forward, grabbed the yelling man, ran his hand over the man's ear, and stood back as the howls of pain suddenly ceased. Word could be heard saying to Peter 'take that sword away and bury it; the cup that my Father has given to me, shall I not drink it?'

Then Johnny saw Shimon the ex-Zealot breaking free from the apostles and beginning to run, followed by Matthew, Thomas and Thady. James began shouting for Johnny, who stayed very still within the tree. Judas seemed to have moved off, and Johnny never saw what became of him. Andrew shouted at the running disciples, and started after them, apparently to round them up, James had gone back into the inner garden, and Jim, Nat and Philip evidently joined what seemed to them a general panic, pelting down the path. Meanwhile Word's arms had been caught hold of by the soldiers, and were fastened behind him. The procession moved off, leaving Peter standing with the sword which he belatedly took back into the outer garden. Suddenly the road was empty in front of the garden, and the crowd was away with their prisoner. Johnny very quietly got himself out of the tree, and followed the crowd.

He felt very small, and very much alone. He didn't even try to communicate to Word because if Word had told Peter not to use the sword he might well tell Johnny to go home, or to do what James told him, or otherwise to leave Word to his fate. It was true that Johnny felt very vulnerable, and rather frightened, but thanks to Chuza the fear helped to strengthen him, and his love for Word drove him inflexibly on. The creator of Evil, It, must have been doing dirty work among Word's friends that night, beginning with Judas, and scattering them for who knew what reasons they might give themselves. Johnny would follow on, and when a thought crept into his mind as to how could he be of any use, after all, he mentally snarled at it as though he could bite it in two and spit out the pieces. He kept on walking, and as the mob made their way through city streets realised they were probably bound for the house of Annas. Johnny smiled: that was the first stroke of luck. Then he heard heavy wheezing and big footfalls behind him, and realised Peter was on the road. Johnny slowed down without stopping and thought wistfully of this morning's chase, which seemed centuries away now. Peter caught up with him, and said: 'Where are they going?'

Johnny said 'Annas the high priest's house.'

'Well, we can't get in there!'

'I can', said Johnny, with some shade of smug satisfaction.

'You'll be arrested.'

'Annas told me I would always be admitted.'

'Annas told you! Have you been cosying up to the priests like Judas?'

Johnny turned on Peter with a release of the hatred for Judas which had been building up in his heart. 'Don't you *dare* to compare me to that swine!' So great was his fury that Peter drew back slightly.

'Alright, I didn't mean anything. How do you know Annas, anyway?'

'He met me when I was cleaning up in the Temple at Word's instructions after Word had driven out the money-men.'

'Why didn't he tell you to go to hell?'

'Because I'm a nice, well-behaved boy' (for a flickering moment he wished Peter was Miriam) 'and because I was careful to make my voice sound like a Judaean.'

'I couldn't do that.'

'And don't try. Leave it to me to get you in, in case there's trouble. Look, they are turning off into Annas's place now.'

'But he isn't the high priest now.'

'And he knows it. They're probably making a brief stop before going to Caiaphas's. Annas wouldn't have done this on his own.' Peter was just beginning to realise he had to deal with a new, rapidly ageing Johnny, when they reached Annas's door. As Johnny had predicted he himself had little trouble getting in. Johnny tactfully announced that the high priest Annas had bade him return at will, and he was promptly admitted. It was to the old man's credit both in charity and in cunning that he made himself accessible to those who might want him, and even on a wild night like this with soldiers and prisoners arriving at ungodly hours it was as well to remember his rules. Apart from not wanting to risk loss of well-paid jobs with high Judaean status, Annas's door-keeper was aware that his courtesy to her gender could easily equip itself with a fine cutting edge in sarcasm. And Johnny's voice was impeccably that of a sophisticated young Judaean, so much so that Peter for a bewildered moment looked around to see who was speaking. So great was Johnny's urgency for Word that he hurried through the outer court without waiting for Peter while the door-keeper was telling Peter that he must wait until she could take up his case with a priest when someone came to relieve her, but as he chafed silently and she eyed him suspiciously, Johnny came racing back as though he owned the place and told the door-keeper that it was all right for Peter to wait in the outer court where a fire was invitingly burning. The door-keeper bowed to Johnny, evidently feeling that if he was so favoured by Annas, a smile in his direction did nobody any harm, and he seemed a nice, well-behaved boy. It's hardly necessary to state that Johnny had gone nowhere near Annas, whom he hoped would not notice him, although if the old man did, Johnny would face him and do his utmost to charm him. He had been perfectly truthful in saying it was all right for Peter to wait in the outer court: it was all right by him, Johnny. It would not have been all right in the interior apartments where Word was being questioned: Peter would probably run amok and they would all be killed, putting Word to the trouble of bringing them back to life while dealing with this ugly arrest. Johnny – like Peter, as it happened – thought that the two of them were in much more serious danger than was Word, since Johnny and Word had both seen the way Word's arrest had been resisted, not by Word, but by Heavenly forces. Johnny didn't want to be killed, since it might be fairly painful. Of course Judas had faced and endured a painful death, for Johnny, but that was the last thing Johnny wanted to think of, with every kind sentiment he had ever felt for Judas turning to bitterest herb-taste in his mouth. But Johnny was quite clear that he was going to risk death rather than see Word blasphemed and back he went to the room where Word stood, being harangued by Annas about the cleansing of the Temple and the rout of the bankers, the birdmen, and the cowboys. Peter went out of Johnny's mind as soon as he found himself within earshot of Annas and Word. Peter himself stayed by the fire, waiting till this unpredictably adult Johnny came out to tell him what to do next. What he got next was the door-keeper strolling after him when her relief arrived, asking 'Are you another of *his* disciples?', jerking her head towards the inner court. Peter rightly assumed she meant Word by '*him*', not Annas (or Johnny): in his agitation he failed to pick up what she meant by 'another'. Whatever Johnny's standing personally with Annas, even Johnny was hardly likely to expect admission on the strength of being the prisoner's child disciple, and her 'another' meant that she had seen Judas in Annas's house. In fact, her concern was to see if Peter was there to give evidence against Word, as Judas apparently had done a day of so earlier and if so, to work out at what stage she should let Annas know he was there to begin grassing. Judas's absence from the house, she may have felt, meant that more evidence would be needed: like Johnny, she didn't know to what place Judas had gone. (Judas at that moment was standing in front of the real high priest,

Caiaphas, shrieking 'STUFF IT UNDER PONTIUS PILATE!' as he hurled thirty pieces of silver in Caiaphas's face, and hurled himself out the door.) Anyhow, Peter indignantly denied being Word's disciple. He could have claimed, later, that he did so to avoid any attempt to conscript him as an informer against Word, but he never did any such thing. The girl shrugged her shoulders and joined them in the circle around the charcoal fire. She eyed him nevertheless. It was well-known that potential informers lost their nerve while on the verge of confessing their knowledge of some associate under arrest. She whispered a word to an officer standing by, one in whose respect she was happy to stand, and he raised a languid eyebrow at Peter: 'are you not also one of that fellow's followers?' Once again Peter missed the implication he was there to grass, as he became increasingly Galilean in his rejection of any acquaintance with Word. By now his denials had thoroughly convinced the group round the fire that he must be Word's man, and a servant among them pointed at him, accusing: 'you cut off the ear of my cousin Malchos, I saw you in the garden!' This was all too likely: everyone in these clerical courts was probably someone else's cousin. Peter roared 'I'm damned if I had anything to do with him!' And outside, ringing like an exultant victor, came a cock's crow. Peter's jaw dropped, he gazed blindly at their derisive faces, and blundered wildly towards the door, sobbing in heartbreak. A guard moved to stop him, but another intervened: 'Hysterical. They would get nothing out of him now. He'd admit everything one minute, deny it the next, and probably swear he and not the prisoner was guilty of whatever charge they make.'

'What were you saying to them in the Temple, anyway?' Annas was demanding of Word. 'Who are these disciples of yours?' Word looked at him, and suddenly saw, near the door, the youngest of the said disciples, and stalled, not knowing if Johnny was under arrest or otherwise identified (although quite sure Johnny was not there to grass). He replied courteously but firmly 'I spoke in the open to the world, in the synagogue, in the Temple, wherever Jews gather together; I said nothing in secret. I am no conspirator. Why ask me? Ask those who listened to me what I said, they know well enough what I said' while simultaneously telling Johnny's mind to get out of there and go back to Nicodemus's house, all the more as he didn't want Johnny made part of this inquisition however certain Word was of Johnny's bravery. Johnny for the first time in his life said no to Word, in his mind's answer. Before Word could answer that a temple guard whirled his right hand around, striking Word across the face with the open palm, and spitting 'that will teach you how to answer the high priest!' Word stood his ground, despite the red mark leaping across his face, and answered quietly 'if I have spoken evil, show where is the evil, but if well, why cudgel me?' Meanwhile Johnny came racing across the room with head down to butt the Temple guard in the bread-basket, the Temple guard whipped out his short sword, and both Word and Annas shouted in unison 'No, John, NO!' and looked at one another. Johnny froze to a stand-still. The Temple guard glared, and stumped out of the room. Word said out loud 'Go home, Johnny!' Annas looked at Word and then swung back at Johnny. His face crunched into anger: 'Take them both to Caiaphas', he ordered, and turned away, choking. Johnny thought it was with rage, but Word felt it was more like shame. As usual, Word was right. In fact, when they arrived at Caiaphas's house, Annas told the guards to release Johnny, who thanked him but slipped out of reach before orders could be given to exclude him from the building. The group went into an inner chamber in which attendants were setting up chairs, screens and stools. Johnny got access to the chamber on the heels of an attendant and then whipped behind a screen, out of sight of Word and Annas. The room was filling up: Johnny actually recognised a money merchant whom Word had driven out of the Temple, but it was certainly not a full assembly of the Sanhedrin, and Johnny never made the mistake of saying it was. If it had been, Nicodemus would have been there, and he was not. Nor did dress suggest there were any Pharisees present at all, unless Annas could possibly be one. Annas himself was very visible, bowing low to Caiaphas with a sneer doing duty as a respectful smile. Caiaphas bowed back, losing no love in the process. Caiaphas then sat back on an ornate throne, with the air of an ambassador between God and Tiberius.

On the whole Johnny had never seen a person of more self-assurance than Caiaphas. It was impossible to imagine him losing his cool. Johnny had known far greater people than Caiaphas in knowing Word, or his mother, or Johnny's parents, or Chuza: being a child his judgments were extremely logical, and their standards had much more to do with integrity than appearance. For that matter Johnny far preferred the angry or sardonic or playful speech of Annas: there was a real and likeable human being there, even if he had been ready to sentence Johnny for some sort of trial before Caiaphas. And in that, Annas was simply like Zebedee or like James in deciding Johnny needed punishment and then, after consideration, letting him off (not that they always let him off). Johnny had not realised, though he might have deduced without realising, that Annas ordered his arrest from affection, having taken a liking to him and wanting to get him out of the clutch of what Annas regarded as dangerous and destructive Galileans. And when they reached Caiaphas's house Annas, knowing his coldly procedural son-in-law, realised that once formally indicted before Caiaphas, whatever the outcome, Johnny's future life in Jerusalem would be that of a Temple police suspect. Nevertheless Annas hoped to get Johnny away from the Galileans, first from Word and then, when he saw Johnny again many weeks later, from Peter.

Caiaphas was in fact looking far more self-assured than he felt. Firstly, he was annoyed that the capture of Word had been followed by the guards reporting to Annas and not him. Even after all these years far too many people insisted on treating Annas as if he were the real High priest, regardless of Caiaphas being in office. Something to do with the Romans having dismissed Annas, and having later installed Caiaphas. Miserable superstition! As though Annas had not himself been made High priest by the Romans! But Annas had been installed more than a quarter-century ago and Caiaphas, although already a high priest for longer than Annas had been allowed to serve, ruled a Temple whose guards had been educated (insofar, he curled his lip, as they had been educated) when Annas was still enthroned. He was contemptuously aware that some people (including his own wife, Annas's daughter) regarded Annas as more pleasing to God than Caiaphas. As if they knew! Caiaphas worshipped a God who had the highest opinion of Caiaphas. It had actually been just as well that the guards had brought the Galilean Temple-wrecker to Annas first, all the same, since that disgruntled follower, Judas, proved as impulsively unreliable to Caiaphas as he had to the Galileans, and made a wretched scene in Caiaphas's house, culminating in his flinging the far too generous bribe already given to him, into the high priest's face. Caiaphas was still internally raging at the blasphemy, the discomfort, the sheer inconvenience of it. He had had to get attendants to disrobe him to prevent pollution on the eve of Passover by any of the money touching him, and it had ultimately entailed them having to strip him naked since one piece of silver insisted on adhering to an innermost garment – in fact, touching his skin, and thus polluting him if he could be polluted but he saw no reason to admit that to anyone else. He would rule over Passover as he always did. Priestly performance always meant 'rule' to Caiaphas. He had no doubt that Tiberius could have taken lessons from him with profit.

Judas had come to him when the riot was happening in the outer court of the Temple, and Caiaphas was ready to make the most of him. These Galileans were impugning Temple sovereignty, depriving his valued clients to whom he had granted money-changing rights, and drawing support away from him with possible alarm and reprisals from the Romans. It was expedient indeed that their leader should die for the good of the people, and Caiaphas knew only one authority on what constituted the good of the people: himself, and certainly not Annas. He had been careful to make sure Annas interviewed this Judas the day after he himself had done so, not because he wanted Annas's opinion, but that if anything went wrong, Annas would be the scapegoat. Annas even looked like a scapegoat, Caiaphas told himself, although a bad-tempered and cynical scapegoat, one still with many good butts in him. This Judas business might yet have awkward repercussions. Caiaphas had sent a guard after him. Initially the fool had lost him, but just before the prisoner had been brought from Annas's house, Caiaphas had the report. The guard had found Judas hanging himself. Admittedly, Caiaphas wanted as little public knowledge as possible of his having trapped the Nazarene personally, save for those priests and Romans and politic Temple elders who would profit by awareness of Caiaphas's political skills. Of course the guard would now be prohibited from celebrating Passover, and would probably lose his job. He was polluted by the sight of Judas's dead body. By now Judas was actually dead, Caiaphas got confirmation of that, since Judas had made a mess of hanging himself and the body had actually fallen from the tree on which it was trying to kill itself and burst its guts out far below. The guts were still there. That was at least that, and no more than the wretch deserved for insulting the high priest. Possibly the realisation of the depravity of such behaviour induced the suicide.

(Judas had of course killed himself in self-hatred for his betrayal of Word, and realisation that Word's hatred of unjustly acquired and hoarded wealth and contempt for those who profited from poverty were absolutely right, and not an unjustifiable challenge to Jewish social structures and attitudes. He had let Word down. He had let Johnny down. He had brought his true God – and Judas was now once more convinced Word was his true God – into the hands of his enemies, to face pain and a dreadful death. He could never face any of his former mates again. He condemned himself. Moreover, he saw his death as a pragmatic expiation. He was directly responsible for Word's arrest at the garden, but any number of people could have told the Temple priests that Word might be expected to show up in the garden, sooner or later. Where Judas's treachery was required, and for which he was paid, would have been testimony at Word's trial before Caiaphas, and maybe before Pilate and perhaps Herod (now on visit to Jerusalem) as well. And Judas suspected that if he withheld any adverse witness against Word, Pilate's torturers might make him tell not just what he knew (which was innocuous) but what he did not know and would not be true. And so the rope, the tree, the awful gulf below, the break, the fall – and the last cry of Word's name.)

Caiaphas had developed certain theatrical talents combining the judicial and the theological. He knew perfectly well that as well as any man could be, he was the modern representative of Jewish history, of Abraham, Isaac and Jacob, of Moses, Aaron and Joshua, of Gideon, Samson and Shmuel, of Elijah, Elisha and Isaiah, and (while for various reasons less ready to claim it out aloud) of King Saul, King David and King Shlomo. When any man spoke of history, Caiaphas always assumed a proprietorial air and all but began his reply 'History speaks'. He knew history gives another dimension, and walked as though his shadow had thickness as well as length and breadth. And he had learned cheap lessons from history as to men's rise and fall, as to diplomacy and directness, as to babying and bullying. He was uninterested in the casualties of history among whom he included his father-in-law Annas, and had no intention of becoming one himself.

Meanwhile Word had reached Johnny's mind and was telling him to go back to Nicodemus's, and Johnny was telling Word he was not going to betray him by going home, and Word said that was not betrayal, and Johnny said it would be because Word had spoken about disciples betraying him and Johnny was not going to be one of the ones who did (he thought that Andrew and James had not betrayed Word, and while knowing Peter was predicted to do so, had no knowledge of its having happened, nor would he know of it until Peter told him when next they met). Finally in his mind Johnny said that he had promised Word to drink of the cup that Word would drink of, and that James would do it in the future, but Johnny would do it now. Word tried to stall Johnny by saying Johnny had already drunk from the cup whence Word drank, and drank Word himself in the cup, but Johnny said that the cup Word and the apostles had drunk was the cup of love, and what Johnny was talking about now and what Word had talked of so long ago was the cup Word in the garden begged his Father to let him avoid if possible but if not he would take it, and Johnny said that if Word was now taking it, Johnny must take it too. Word in the midst of his guards could not see Johnny behind his screen, although of course Johnny by opening his mind to Word showed him where he was. But Word knew the loving brown eyes were now hard with determination, and he told Johnny that it would be terrible, but that Johnny would drink of the dreaded cup.

Johnny's mental conversation with Word meant that he never recorded a strong picture of what trial Word was receiving in front of Caiaphas. He noticed with approval that Annas said practically nothing, and with Word's assistance began to suspect that Annas was far from easy in his mind while politically committed to agreeing to what Caiaphas might decide. There was some calling of witnesses, people whom Johnny had no recollection of ever having seen before, and suddenly on one of his peeps outside the screen Johnny began to notice that while Caiaphas seemed certain and suave in his body and his speech, his eyes were roving less easily. Annas for some reason flickered a sour smile from time to time. What had actually happened was that Caiaphas had carefully built up the trial that would be staged, and then Judas who was of course to be the chief witness, had disappeared and would not return. Annas, without telling Caiaphas, had thought of using Johnny but once he had let Johnny go free his mind recoiled from the thought of tempting that young idealist to betray his master. Also, Annas's mind luxuriated in the thought that Johnny would probably refuse to do anything of the kind, and Annas liked him for it. Caiaphas would probably try to force testimony out of Johnny by torture and that, for Annas, was another reason to keep his own mouth shut while enjoying Caiaphas's attempts to make evidential bricks out of rotten straw. Annas did not know where Johnny had got to, and since Caiaphas did not know about Johnny at all, Annas saw no reason to mention him. Suddenly, turning around for a moment, Annas did see Johnny peeping from behind his screen. As he turned back he noticed the prisoner looking closer at him than at the miserable perjured witnesses. For one split second Annas nodded at Word, with a grim little smile, settled back in his chair and said nothing. He was satisfied that Word would know his intentions and saw no need to add anxiety to the rest of his sufferings. The boy would have to take care of himself, and if he could, Annas might see what could be done for him afterwards, but now was no time to reveal young John and throw him on the mercy of Caiaphas.

The witnesses were indeed a miserable lot, self-contradictory and frequently leaving Johnny (and Annas) with the impression they had never actually seen Word at all, or certainly not close up. Bright young priests, anxious to catch Caiaphas's eye, caught it all right by efforts to elicit evidence which inevitably exposed flat disagreements between one witness and the next. Johnny did hear one witness say Word had said 'I will destroy this temple that is made with hands, and within three days I will build another made without hands' (to which Annas sniggered 'look, Ma, no hands!'), eliciting a glare from Caiaphas momentarily interrupting his habitual suavity. Johnny remembered that when Word was cleansing the Temple someone homicidally demanded a sign from him to justify doing what he was doing, and Word had paused long enough to say, as they threatened him, 'Destroy this Temple and in three days I raise it up', and his audience were bemused, yelling 'they took 46 years to build this flipping building and you and who else will raise it up in three days?' but by that stage Word had moved on, and the pressure of departing sheep and cattle made the bullies move off. Johnny had assumed this was a metaphor by which Word meant his own body, although he wondered why Word had said three days. Now the phrase haunted him: surely Word could not mean these people were going to destroy him now, and that he would show his immortality after a lapse of three days? He sent an urgent plea to Word's mind on the question, but Word was now facing questions from Caiaphas.

Caiaphas remained smooth, while inwardly raging. At the very end of this house of testimony built on sand someone testifies to intentions of the prisoner to demolish the Temple, perhaps meaning to start another cult outwith the Temple with loss of the jobs and status of everyone connected with the Temple, or perhaps meaning to attack it physically, the evidence given too stupidly to convince the most pig-ignorant hayseed on the Sanhedrin, and that vicious old monster Annas is leering in satisfaction through his withered gums. Caiaphas had fully intended to remain aloof while the evidence did its worst, after which it would only remain for him to pronounce sentence and remit the prisoner to Pontius Pilate, whereas now the only way out was from one of his, Caiaphas's, forensic *coups*. He had shut them all up with his 'It is expedient for one man to die for the good of the people' and he would do that one man in by the same blow to the heart. They weren't going to condemn the Nazarene over the Temple, however much of a danger he posed either to its existence or to that of the money-men in its outer court. But the Temple had to be protected from Jewish alternatives or from controversies which would bring in the Romans and perhaps sack the Temple once again. Caiaphas initially was curt. As he rose, threw a glance at the prisoner, and addressed him, he gave one brief rag of respectability to the witnesses:

'You say nothing to answer the evidence given against you?'

Word was silent, and Caiaphas half-caught an approving nod from Annas out of the corner of his eye. For one moment rage threatened to overwhelm him, but it never had, and it never would. Instead his voice became honey itself. Caiaphas knew all about vanity and how to appeal to it. He became almost reverent in addressing Word:

'I adjure you by the living God to tell us if you are Christ, the Son of God.' He sounded as though Word had only to give the signal and Caiaphas would be on his knees.

Johnny knew there could be but one answer for Word to give, should he speak at all. Word looked at Caiaphas without a trace of vanity, almost like a scholar asked to disclose unalterable conclusions reached by his research:

'I am, and you will see the Son of Humanity sitting on the right hand of power, and coming in the clouds of heaven.'

Johnny just managed to restrain himself from applause, and noticed Annas sitting bolt upright, giving Word a very strange look. But it was

Caiaphas's moment, and he was not to be denied it. He first raised his hands to his hair as though about to tear it from his head, having first torn off his head-covering; but Johnny noticed that his hands never in fact touched what looked a decidedly costly coiffure. Then he tore his mantle from his shoulders and with one magnificent gesture rent it in half so dramatically that Johnny realised operations had already been commenced on the mantle in undress rehearsal: in other words, Caiaphas had always intended matters to end thus, by whatever road he must take to get there. He raised his voice to what he clearly regarded as a wholly sympathetic Heaven 'You have heard the blasphemy! What need do we have of further witnesses?' Cries of 'None!' 'Yea!' 'Blasphemer!' swept the chamber, drowning Annas's 'didn't need the first witnesses either!'

'Your verdict?' demanded Caiaphas, apparently still asking Heaven, for whose failure to reply the audience substituted 'he is guilty of death' leaving Caiaphas to make the most of their confusion of verdict and sentence. The result was in fact chaos, since several of them surrounded Word, hitting at him, spitting on him, and asking him to say who had struck him, and Johnny tore out from behind the screen clawing at the clerics, hitting and scratching, until he got up to Word, throwing his body in the way of the blows. Annas was on his feet shouting 'Leave that boy alone!' while Caiaphas was yelling about taking him to Pontius Pilate, 'him' being Word, though he probably would have been glad if it could have covered Johnny and Annas as well. Johnny, driving each elbow into the stomachs of the bullying clerics and servants surrounding Word, got close enough to give Word a kiss, and Word apparently surrounded Johnny with something of the force which had initially prevented his own arrest in Gethsemane. Eventually Word was taken by them to the court of Pontius Pilate, and Johnny, protected by Word and by Annas, went along beside Word. Since Word's hands were still bound it would only make his path more difficult were Johnny to place his hand upon them, so he could only hope that his company proclaimed his love, and Word told him through their minds that indeed it did. With Passover to prepare, Annas and Caiaphas remained behind. But Annas left Caiaphas's house as soon as the crowd of guards, servants and prisoner had gone.

'Decent of Annas to save you', projected Word into Johnny's mind as they were marched towards the Governor's palace.

'Pity he's on the wrong side', answered Johnny's mind.

'People don't always stay on the same side', reflected Word.

'Who are you telling?' snorted Johnny's mind, with sulphurous anger against Judas. Word must not have wished to answer it at that point, because he changed topic:

'Caiaphas must have told Pilate what would be sent to him from the trial.'

'But it's an inconclusive verdict for all of their blithering about death which you will prove impossible – and it's about Jewish questions and no business for the Roman governor.'

'Romans often find it useful to review what isn't their business', and Word gave a slightly hollow laugh in Johnny's mind.

'How so?' asked Johnny, puzzled.

Word sounded a little anxious to shield Johnny as his mind answered:

'Pilate likes to scourge people who come before him whether he believes them guilty of anything or not. I have to warn you it may be nasty. Some of the prisoners die under the lash.'

'But you can't let them do that!'

'That's just what I have to let them do. I have to take on myself the punishment for ordinary people across all time. The Son of Humanity has to expiate the Sin of Humanity.'

'But that's not fair!'

'If I don't do it, none of you can get to Heaven. Not our friends, not your family, not you, not even Mother.'

'But your mother hasn't done any thing to keep her out of Heaven!'

'Nobody can get in unless I go through this.'

'But why on Earth –?'

'That's the whole point. Men have poisoned Earth so that nothing from it can get to Heaven unless I take all the poison on myself. You know what to do when a snake bites you?'

'Call to you.'

Word laughed, quietly. 'Suppose I'm not there?'

Johnny thought harder, and the thought said 'bite the wound and suck out the poison.'

Word nodded, a little bleakly. 'That's it, if you multiply the wound by the size of the Earth and all the time from Earth's first humans to its last.

That's why they need the biggest sacrifice.'

'One man?'

'A man who is God.'

'But we can't let you suffer like that for us!'

'You'll have to.'

'I don't want you to do it for me!'

'You don't know what you're saying, although I'm grateful for it. But don't you want to see my mother saved, and your parents, and James, and the others? You do, you know, even if you won't say it for fear of agreeing to what I must go through.'

'Word, couldn't I suffer it instead of you?'

'Johnny, I would give nearly any thing to kiss you for that. I was going to tell you again to go back to Nicodemus's –

'I won't go.'

'I know you won't go. A fine disciple you are, saying no to your Word.' (In the middle of the horror getting bigger with every step, Johnny giggled.)

'So I'm not going to ask you, merely to say that I would have asked if there were the slightest chance of obedience from you.'

'There isn't.'

'You're going to see bad things tonight.'

'We will go together.'

'And since you won't leave, I'll admit I'm very glad you're here. I'll hate the thought of what you will suffer from what you see, but you will give me strength from your love. And you will be my witness. It is fitting that what I began with one John as my witness, I should end with another.'

'End?' Johnny felt as though his guts had been drawn out of him in one horrible blast of wind, leaving him an empty husk.

'End and begin. It will be a terrible voyage but it wins a new world for all, if they will take it.'

Johnny stared. 'They'll be mad if they don't, after what you'll have done for them.'

'Most of them won't know what I have done for them, and many who do will be too proud to accept it.'

'Like who?'

'Well, Caiaphas, for instance.'

'Maybe Annas won't be too proud.'

'Maybe Annas won't. You may have something there, Johnny, and you may be the boy who will help it to happen some day. But I doubt if either of us will have much success with Pontius Pilate.'

'But he's a Roman! They don't count!'

'Wonderful, Johnny, Shimon our ex-Zealot could never equal your contempt for an Empire! After all you did renounce it, whether or not you were ever near getting it. But if what I am doing is to be real, it doesn't mean simply dying for ourselves and our fellow-Jews. It means for everyone, even Pontius Pilate, whose judgment we now await regardless of his probably having made it before the trial begins.'

'How you do know?'

'Look at the soldiers guarding us. Some are Temple police, but many are Pilate's own legionaries. They weren't sent out as a guard of honour for Passover. Caiaphas and Pilate worked this out between them over the last day or so.'

'Why do you think that?'

'The huge crowds in town for the Passover mean that Pilate will be stretched to make use of every soldier he's got and must be bringing in more. He won't be providing them for Caiaphas to repress, or even to stone, some ordinary breaker of the laws of Moses. He'll have been told that I'm a threat to the Roman Empire.'

'The liars –' and then Johnny caught himself. 'That is –'

'Quite right, Johnny' (and Johnny could hear Word laughing inside Johnny's head). 'I *am* a threat to the Roman Empire. But not in the way Caiaphas and Pilate mean.'

'But how can Caiaphas sentence people to be stoned to death? Surely it isn't lawful for us Jews to kill anyone, as far as Roman rulers are concerned?'

'It isn't, but most of the time they would simply let Pilate know they intend to kill this person or that, provided Pilate has no objection. Most of these Romans insist they are bored by Jewish religious arguments. Pilate doesn't interfere with Caiaphas. Caiaphas doesn't interfere with Pilate.'

'Do you know that he doesn't?'

'You remember that time we were told of the Galileans whose blood Pilate mingled with their sacrifices? Someone asked me if those Galileans were the worst sinners in Galilee and therefore they suffered?'

'You said of course not.'

329

'You might as well say that what I am about to suffer in my body and what you are about to suffer in your mind are punishment for our sins. I told the questioners that they might suffer the same fate if they didn't repent of theirs.'

'And you said the same about those killed when the tower fell in Siloam, the same place where you told a blind man whom you cured to wash himself in its pool.'

'Your memory is good.'

'You made it good for anything you would teach.'

'No wonder you're doing well with your languages. Sounds as if one or the other of us was cheating.'

'You couldn't cheat, and since I am yours to command, I wouldn't dare.'

'But you would dare to stay with me in spite of me.'

'I would. I do. What were you going to tell me about the Galileans Pilate murdered?'

'Pilate seized the Temple treasure to pay for his aqueduct. He could not have done that without approval from Caiaphas and the captain of the Treasury.'

'And of Annas?'

'I like the way you stick up for Annas.'

'He liked the way I stuck up for you.'

'And it will not be forgotten to him. I doubt if they needed his approval, or if he could have opposed it without injuring his own family.'

'He might have opposed it on principle.'

'When you are given your priesthood by the Romans you lose the ability to oppose them on principle. Not the power. The ability.'

'No wonder he's bitter.'

'With a bitterness chiefly against himself, as most bitterness is. Anyhow when Pilate took the money built up from Temple taxes, so that Jerusalem might have better water, it annoyed Galileans much more than Judaeans, and Pilate had those Galilean pilgrims to Jerusalem who objected clubbed down after they had left the Temple. I doubt if Caiaphas said anything about that either.'

'They're a couple of crooks.'

'Oh, no, Johnny, I'm quite sure Caiaphas tries to do his best for Judaea, while making sure it is also the best for himself. Obviously I don't think he does his best for God, and he knows I don't, so he wants me to go the same way as the Galileans.'

'The other Galileans.'

'Don't deny me Bethlehem. Or Egypt.'

'Do you think Pilate is crooked?'

'He probably has to be, in his job. But unlike Caiaphas I doubt if he is really for anyone. Rome, nominally, but who is Rome? Tiberius? Caligula? Sejanus? It's like loyalty to the gladiator on whom you have wagered.'

'Maybe the Roman Emperors will be chosen from the gladiators in the end.' Johnny had never seen a gladiatorial show, and therefore it had its attractions for him.

Word checked himself from answering that as of now gladiator attempts to gain self-rule had only resulted in appalling numbers of gladiators' crucifixions. Johnny was beginning to assimilate the danger that Word might die, and even to see the way it would hurt Johnny himself, but he was not yet ready to discover the way in which Word was going to die. In any case there was no time, since they were already crossing the tassellated pavement in front of the Praetorium of the Roman Governor in the western, elevated part of the city. They came to a halt before the Hall of Judgment, and a long haggle broke out between the leader of the Temple police and the Roman centurion, in which the Temple guards' commander pointed out that the Temple troops had to be on duty over Passover in which they might not take part and whose Seder they might not eat if they were defiled as they would be if they entered the hall whence a prisoner might be sent to death, and the centurion belligerently enquired if that was the only reason, and the commander said that he didn't want to give offence, and the centurion said he was giving it by not telling the whole truth, and the commander said be would not allow any man to call him a liar, and the centurion said this amounted to treason.

It had, after all, been a long night. Johnny began to get hopeful that the guards and the legionaries might start fighting and he would be able to get Word away, but Word became very sad and said in Johnny's mind that kind of conflict, erupting from virtually nothing, could arise in the future and end in the Romans' destruction of the Temple on which would be left not a stone upon a stone. Eventually the Temple commander yelled that he would be polluted if he entered the hall of Pontius Pilate, and the centurion asked whether the fact it had previously belonged to Herod the Great made it easier to filter out the pollution, and the commander said that Herod was a polluter, and Johnny was thinking that in that very building Herod the Great or Herod Archelaus, or one Herod or another, had given orders that all the children under two should be killed, and his soldiers went out and did it. And a Roman captain came out of the hall bellowing commands at the centurion to the effect that he was disturbing the sleep of Pilate's wife and that Pilate was eating his breakfast and what in the name of Jupiter Capitolinus was the row about and couldn't the centurion keep those blasted Jews quiet? And the Temple commander said that he was polluted by listening to the name of a false god, and the captain wanted to know how dare he imply that a Roman god was a false god, and the centurion yelled that the captain must see how impossible it was to deal with these people and nothing but the sword could be understood by them, and Johnny wondered if he and James could have made as much noise during one of their arguments before they became disciples.

And out came Pontius Pilate.

Pilate more or less slunk out of the front door of the Praetorium, but any implication that this betokened humility on his part was dashed, not so much by the trumpet-peal hastily following him, as by the shiver running through the centurion's troops. The captain said deferentially 'Sir!' and the centurion said furiously 'Sir!' and the Temple commander said obsequiously 'Sir!' and there followed a silence Johnny thought thick enough to trisect. Pilate, dressed in a Roman toga of some opulence over quieter garments, walked down the steps and drew up in front of Word and looked at him from very cold blue eyes (Johnny remembered the rumour Pilate was originally German, and the blue eyes supported that, but Johnny had heard that Sulla, the greatest tyrant of the Roman Republic, had had very cold blue eyes and an old Roman pedigree). Pilate took about ten minutes to look at Word without saying anything: he looked Word in the eye, and looked away rather quickly, and walked around Word, and looked down at Johnny with a brown eyebrow raised in the direction of his shaven scalp, and raised a lip curling over his small and rather unpleasant upper row of teeth, sneering at Word 'Are you the king of the Jews?', actually 'Rex Iudaeorum?'. Johnny assumed that he wanted to begin by humiliating Word for his ignorance of Latin, because he looked decidedly annoyed when Word said quietly *'Dices'* meaning Pilate was saying it, not necessarily that is was so, and Johnny knew that agreement would have to be signified by 'Ita' or some such construction. (Johnny had not been surprised to learn from Word that there was no word in Latin for 'Yes'.) Then the Temple commander began to bawl that Word was not the King of the Jews but said he was, and Pilate's sneer began to grow again as he swung in serpentine swivel on the Temple commander. He waited until the Temple commander began to decline to a growl, then a mutter, and finally silence. Then he said:

'Pr-r-ray forgive me, but I do not think I evinced a desire to hear you at the immediate moment? It is, of course, *always* a privilege to listen to a Jew – how fortunate am I to endure, I mean, enjoy, such privileges every day of my command! – you do know it is my command, do you? – how fortunate! – but I think I can dispense with your pearls of utterance for the nonce if you are indeed capable of suspending the blessing of your conversation – you are? – how fortunate!' As he spoke he slid his hands around, palms up, palms down, ending in a slight chopping gesture. Johnny's mind clamoured to Word: 'How could your Father let you fall into the hands of this horrible creature?'

Word replied with equanimity. 'The Father shows his love for us all by letting me fall into those hands. I have told you that what will happen to me is in its way as ugly for you as it is for me. It will be as ugly for my Father as it will be for Mother, maybe worse. I am in the Father and the Father suffers when I suffer. I was in my mother, but I am always in my Father. My Father and I know it is the only way, and he hates the prospect of it as much as I do, even as much as my horror at what you will go through and Mother will go through.'

'Is your mother coming here?'

'We will see her later today. Let us listen now to the serpentine Pontius Pilatus Prefectus. Oh, he's on to you. Steady, now, don't fear, and even more important, don't laugh.'

Pilate was coiling in Johnny's direction. 'And what have we here? A page for the King of the Jews? *Servus servi Dei?* You see I know your monotheistic superstitions! And you will even be able to serve me! Do not feel obliged to conceal your obvious delight! You will be a witness'(at this point Johnny gazed at him open-jawed and Pilate salivated with blue eyes agleam) 'to my treatment of your King. Then you can tell the world about it. How exquisitely fortunate!'

Pilate paused, to allow a simper a moment in which to hover, and then swung round once more on the commander of the Temple police; drawing his hands together so that the palms met and the fingers folded crosswise over the other palm of each hand: 'And now the moment we have awaited with such bated breath and effervescent expectations is at last among us. Our gallant commander, for a few golden hours giving us the boon of his utterance instead of leading the legions of the Temple God in his neverending struggle against whatever it is! Fortunate, thrice fortunate, am I to give him audience if unable to grant it with quite the speed his military manners and sacerdotal significance required of me in the first instance. All is now resolved! Friends, Romans, countrymen, lend him your ears!'

Johnny never expected to feel sympathy with Caiaphas's leading thug, but even he felt a pang as he looked on the misery charging the wretched commander: 'most noble Pilate', he got out, in Aramaic. A tasteful shudder denoted Pilate's acknowledgement of constraint to hear the language of the country whose wealth he wrung for Rome.

'Must we?' and Pilate threw a glance over the features of the commander whose broad face made no concessions either to intellect or to spirit. 'I fear we must! Alack, our good fortune has deserted us! Temporarily, I trust. Question this man in his barbarous language, someone, and yield me the result. Who shall interpret? Does the prisoner know Aramaic? Why, he must, must he not, how can he rule the Jews without knowledge of their exceedingly vulgar tongue? And as we have seen, he knows one word of Latin. Fortune returns to her throne! Interpret, prisoner!' Pilate paused, his hands apart, palms facing upward, thumbs slightly raised. He elevated his eyebrows in mock-expectation. There was a further silence. Then Pilate smiled with even greater malevolence:

'Ah, yes, the King of the Jews needs to hear a word before he interprets it. How remiss of me! Ask the brave commander and be sure to address him as a brave commander, look at all those dangers he so gallantly puts to flight in the service of our dear friend Caiaphas – I should say, our most holy and dear friend Caiaphas – ask him – ask him – prisoner, what shall I tell you to ask him? Let us have royal inspiration!'

'What accusation do you bring against this man?' said Word, as though it were his own question.

Pilate's eyes sparkled and he clapped his hands. He evidently had no intention of disguising his knowledge of Aramaic, however much he deemed it beneath his contempt to speak it. 'Succinct and to the point! What a wise king! A Daniel, as you Jews like to say, a Daniel come to judgment! And in the lions' den, too! Speak, brave commander, the King awaits your reply.'

The commander swallowed thickly, grunted twice, glared at Word to avoid glaring at Pilate, and snarled 'If he were not an evil-doer, we would not have handed him over to you.' Word translated this into Latin, regardless of Pilate's obvious understanding of it. Johnny realised that Pilate knew quite well that the commander had no instructions to explain Word because Caiaphas had told Pilate what he knew about him. On the other hand, Pilate might have expected some report of the questions Caiaphas had put to Word, if proof of treason against Tiberius had been given; and it had not. From Caiaphas's point of view Word deserved death for calling himself God; from Pilate's he probably did not, because he had not called himself King. So Pilate's nastiness to the wretched commander may not simply have come from Pilate being nasty, though he was, so much as Pilate's prodding to work out what to do next. Pilate twisted his open hands away from one another, thumbs up. He leered at the commander:

'Take him, and judge him according to your own law.' Word quickly translated.

The commander looked around wildly, and half-relying on his nearest soldiers to back him up, bellowed 'we have no power to put any person to death', which they echoed, and Pilate's eyebrows shot up, and Johnny thought of the woman taken in adultery. Word translated, unnecessarily.

Pilate smiled snakily: in fact Johnny was wondering how any human being could be so much like a snake without becoming one. Pilate went a stage farther by swinging his head and shoulders to and fro, narrowing his eyes till they became slits. Suddenly he stopped, turned away from the Judaean troops, and snapped at Word and, apparently, Johnny, 'Follow!' He walked back into the Palace without checking to see whether they kept up. They did. Johnny's mind was whirling back to one night a few days ago when Word was talking to the other eleven and Johnny had fallen asleep, but in his sleep he heard something which now came back, Word saying 'The Son of Humanity will be betrayed to the chief priests and the scribes, and they shall condemn him to death, and shall deliver him to the Gentiles to be mocked and scourged and crucified: and the third day he shall rise again'. Surely he had dreamed the last part, despite all coming true so far? Johnny looked at Word, and Word's voice came clearly into Johnny's mind as they entered the Praetorium behind Pilate: 'It is all true.'

And before Johnny could grapple with this farther, Pilate had whipped round and barked at Word, no play-acting now: '*Are* you the King of the Jews?'

Word faced him squarely: 'Are you saying this yourself, or did others say it of me to you?' Johnny could see that he was bringing out the conspiracy of Pilate and Caiaphas, almost in a scientific demonstration for Johnny's benefit.

Pilate rocked back, almost as from a blow, whirled around to check on eavesdroppers, and improved on his serpentine imitations with a hiss dripping with venom: 'Am I a Jew?' And Johnny realised he had never heard such hatred for Johnny's people in anyone's lips. Pilate's chin and mouth narrowed, an ugly frown gathered across his forehead, and he practically spat out a futher reply to distance himself from Caiaphas:

'Your own nation and the chief priests have sent you to me: what have you done?'

Word looked at Pilate, with the faintest flicker of amusement, but he spoke straight and clear: 'My kingdom is not of this world.' (Johnny felt the prickles rising on his back hair, climbing to the top of his head and down each side towards his ears.) 'If my kingdom were of this world, my young officers would fight to prevent my delivery to the Judaeans; but my kingdom is not from where we are now.'

Pilate jumped on what he hoped was an admission: 'So you are a king, are you?'

Word very deliberately replied: 'You say that I am a king. I was born and came into the world to testify to the truth. All who are of the truth hear my voice.' Pilate leaned back, sniggering 'What is truth?' He rolled it around his mouth, savoured it, almost tried it like a wine for taste, spat it out, and went to the door.

IGHTEEN

BARABBAS

He came unto his own, and his own received him not

Johnny wondered whether he and Word were supposed to follow Pilate out on the Palace forefront, but Word did not move and as soon as Pilate had slithered through the door, two hard Roman legionaries marched in and took up suspicious places in the room. Word and Johnny remained where they were, with their guards' arms at the ready, and their guards' eyes glaring at them. Pilate could be heard through the open door speaking to the Judaean troops while his Roman soldiers stood impassively awaiting command to keep someone in order, preferably as ruthlessly as possible. It was still early morning, and no civilians were visible. The Passover made it unlikely any devout Jew (and the city and its visitors largely consisted of devout, or at least observant, Jews) would want to risk polluting themselves by straying into the grounds of the heathen Roman Palace. Jews would be theoretically safe if they stayed outside the house, but a bullying guard might decide they required a security check inside it, thus excluding them from the festival they loved. Pilate's Jewish audience must have been made up of the Temple guards alone, give or take the odd servant or messenger. Pilate's voice rose high, and at first it gave Johnny new heart. 'I find no fault in him!' Johnny's face lit up, and he beamed on Word, whose affectionate smile in reply twisted in irony, and then Johnny saw what was happening. Pilate was deliberately infuriating the Temple guards, like a bear-baiter tormenting a shackled bear. 'I find no fault in this man! Are you not proud of the virtue of your king? Or do you know more than me, poor heathen Roman that I am?' He taunted them into muttering, and the muttering into grumbling, and the grumbling into an angry roar like the Sea of Galilee frightening land-lubbers. 'He stirs up the people!' 'He makes them irreverent!' 'That s why we let him go so long!' 'The people are led into sedition by him!' 'The people are deceived by him!' 'He causes unrest throughout all Jewish lands!' 'He raises rebellion!' 'He opposes Caesar!' 'Here!' 'And in Galilee!' 'He began in Galilee!' 'From Galilee to here!' Pilate was in his element. 'Ah! you make a plea for your king against my jurisdiction, do you? I must concede that it may be a weighty plea! How ably you plead for your king!' The Temple guards (fearful lest rumours that they really had defended Word might get back to Caiaphas and cost them their jobs and wages) bellowed that they had no King, and one or two had the wit to add 'No king but Caesar!' And Pilate sniggered again. 'Ah! You speak of a King! But if this man be of Galilee, is he not under the rule of the King who is no King, the son of the great Herod! How fortunate! The lesser Herod is in Jerusalem this very day! Send your king to Herod and let us see if Herod will judge him, or if falling down he will adore him! And his lovely wife! Will she adore him too? What a day we are having! Whoever would have thought Jew temple guards would argue so well! Take him to Herod!'

Pilate said nothing about Johnny but when the Roman soldiers were leading Word away, Johnny marched as near alongside as he could get, and when a legionary queried his presence Pilate purred with pleasure, oiling out his gratification: 'Oh, but of course, the great King of the Jews must have his little Jew page. Otherwise we would have to provide one – some master of grace and charm like you, for instance!', and he pointed a derisive finger at a hulking brute of a Temple guard with a face reminding Johnny of some mythical monster, pictured in the eloquent lies of a returned traveller. 'Indeed, perhaps we might make a substitution!' Johnny's heart plummeted but before he could cry to Word's mind for instructions, and work out how best to disobey them if Word took advantage of the situation to order him back to Nicodemus's house again (and anyway Word, reading all of this in Johnny's mind, had his own mind reassure Johnny that he wouldn't), Pilate withdrew this last contemptuous lampoon. 'But no, leave the King of the Jews his actual Jew page, so fortunately with us! We would not have the King attended by some lesser breed, however elegant! We must have the Jewish king at his most regal when paying a state visit to the Jewish prince, even if the prince is but a quarter prince' ('tetrarch – shmetrarch' murmured Johnny's mind) 'and the King perhaps lacks some of the sacred revelations of his power and wealth. March the King on, soldiers!'

Since the Romans confiscated Herod's father's palace, it might have been a graceful act to let Herod and Herodias use it during their visits to Jerusalem, and Johnny, who was getting to know Pontius Pilate, realised that such a thought was enough in itself to make sure Pilate would not do it – at least not without some hard assurances of rich returns from Herod. The Roman and Temple guards marched Word and Johnny to what had probably once been a dwelling for one of the ministers of Herod the Great, small, mean, with ugly attempts at pretension in its throne-room, a converted dining-room. Johnny was expecting to see a fairly horrible specimen of humanity, whose father had been Herod the Great, whose brother had been Archelaus the mass murderer, and who himself had executed Word's cousin John. Johnny could sense Word's anger at being judged by his cousin's killer, as though he would be faced with some creature repugnant to Nature itself. What happened startled the two of them. The guards marched them into the throne room, placed Word and therefore Johnny in front of their own ranks, bawled some unintelligibility into the air signifying delivery of prisoner all present and correct, and then became silent. Word and Johnny gazed at the empty throne. Then they heard shambling footsteps, and a large, loose-lipped creature with wine-bibber's skin came slowly, apparently reluctantly, within eyeshot of Word, and promptly dropped his jaw, saying 'But you're not him!' and then dropping the jaw again. Johnny could even see a purple tongue partly escaping from the blue-veined lips. Simultaneously Word's voice cut curtly into Johnny's mind 'He thought I was John, risen from the dead, as he had said when he heard of my preaching and miracles after his murder of John. Now he's decided I'm not cousin John, but I'm me. We'll see what he expects me to be.'

The Temple guards could make no sense of Herod's cry (the Roman legionaries did not even try) and for reply Herod Antipas was greeted by shouts about Word which the guards thought appropriate speech to a

Jewish dignitary. 'He's going to knock down the Temple!' several yelled to be followed by others 'He'll put us all out of work!' 'He's dishonouring your father's benefits to the Jewish nation!' 'He's a blasphemer!' 'He's an idolator!' 'He's a Samaritan!' Herod was now sitting down on the modest throne, playing with its ornate and opulent trappings. He leaned forward, dropping his jaw yet again, and tapping his half-purple teeth with a fan. Several guards continued to demand death for Word on the ground that Word intended death for Herod, but Herod made no reply and probably had not heard them. Eventually his tongue flickered all the way out, licked dry lips, retreated, and then said: 'Work a miracle, and I'll get you off! Work a miracle for me! Come on, you know how! Command that these stones be made bread' and he gestured at some curiously shaped stones at the foot of his chair. The stones looked like large snail-shells. 'Command that my throne-room have hangings made from the skins of tigers! Command a tiger-skin under your own feet! Command that all these Temple guards become statues! Command gold to fall in place of rain! Command Pilate to be transformed into an asp, that should be easy, he's practically one already!'

Word said nothing. The commander of the Roman soldiers shouted something about honour to Caesar's deputy, which apparently included prefects under imperial appointment. Johnny's main thought was that here were the two most important people he ever met (as the world counts importance) and they were faced by God, who was here to save the world past, present, and future, or as much of it as would let itself be saved, and all they could do was to play mad games and think they were clever. If Word met Tiberius, would Tiberius want him to discuss improvements in a pleasure-grotto, or to advise on the most effective tax-system, or to turn Tiberius's hair purple? If you were important as the world counts important, did that mean that you were unable to understand or contemplate anything really important? What good sense the fisher-folk of Galilee had!

By now some of Herod's entourage had arrived and taken up positions around the throne. Johnny had wondered what a tetrarch, even though only a quarter of a king, was doing without a page, and thought that Pilate would presumably regard it as a breach of regal protocol. But the pages were among the arrivals, all two of them, pale, sickly boys waving fans rather inefficiently with looks as though they wanted to be somewhere else. The attendants had entered the room walking, so Johnny realised they came late on Herod's orders. Johnny suspected that Herod didn't want any of his people to see his reaction if Word really turned out to be the risen John the Baptizer, and that signals were picked up when it became clear all Herod was going to get was a magic-show, if that. And in fact he wasn't going to get much of that. Word's hands were still tied behind him at the wrists (which Johnny feared must be cramped and painful by now, but Word's mind transmitted nothing of that). Herod continued to demand that Word produce miracles, Word continued to say nothing, the Temple guards continued to demand Word's death, and the Roman soldiers waited with utter indifference. Johnny even noticed one scratching himself with his short sword. Eventually Herod screamed 'I can put you to death, for your crimes in Galilee! Where are the witnesses?', to which, the Roman commander replied in a bored voice that the witnesses were useless, and had been dismissed.

'What's he doing here, then?' snapped Herod.

'He was taken into custody on the information of one of his followers.'

'A follower from his days in Galilee! Where is he?'

'We don't know.'

'You don't know? Why wasn't his evidence deemed satisfactory?'

'Because he never gave it.'

'You mean this man enchanted him?'

'I mean he didn't go to the house of the high priest Caiaphas.'

'You arrested this man without holding the man who informed against him?'

'The man Judas took us to the garden of Gethsemane where he said the prisoner would be praying.'

'And was he?'

'Not when we arrived. He seemed to be waiting for us.'

'And –?'

'We took him captive.'

'Anyone with him?'

'Some Galileans. They ran away – but this boy must have followed us from the garden.'

For the first time Herod turned his eyes on Johnny. His eyes glittered. A trace of spittle appeared on his lips. 'And whither did you lead him?'

'We led him nowhere, leading him being no part of my duties on assignment to keep watch on the Temple and its priests.'

'Troops for Caiaphas, spies for Pilate', thought Johnny. 'Economical, at all events', replied Word's mind, with a hint of laughter. Johnny's eyes travelled over to Word with new wonder. He would have loved to hug him for that laughter, but it was vital to give no ammunition to Herod, who was quite nasty enough without it. Herod's lip curled at the Roman centurion.

'And your duties didn't extent to holding witnesses against dangerous criminals?'

'Our duties required backup for the Temple guards on that expedition, should they require it. They did not require it. One of the prisoner's sidekicks abstracted a sword which a Temple guard had let fall, and cut off the ear of a servant of a priest.'

'Was the servant badly wounded? Why was not the prisoner's sidekick taken prisoner?'

The centurion paused, uneasily. 'The servant was not wounded at all.'

'Are you insane, man? How could his ear be cut off without any wound?' The centurion's mouth turned down at the corners. His eyes glittered with hatred for Herod. 'The prisoner touched the servant, and his ear was restored unharmed. I saw it.'

'I can't believe it!'

'I couldn't believe it', said the centurion in (very) temporary accord with Herod. 'But I saw it.'

'So you are a magician!' hissed Herod at Word. 'Centurion, cut the ear off that boy so that we can see the magician restoring it!'

'Not my place', said the centurion.

'I order it', snapped Herod.

'Our duties assigned to us by the imperial Roman prefect are to support any legitimate exercise by the party to whom we are assigned. I'm not assigned to you.'

Johnny was not altogether surprised at this, since the centurion's failure to address Herod by any mark of respect was all too obvious. The thought of having his ear cut off made very little impression on him, since all his anxieties now centred around Word. Afterwards he was surprised at this, when he looked back, but he was glad.

'I'll report you to the imperial Roman prefect', spat Herod.

'And when I'm questioned by him, I'll inform him that you told the prisoner to turn the imperial Roman prefect into an asp, contrary to the statutes of the Roman Senate', and the centurion closed his mouth with a finality boding no good to Herod.

Herod radiated poison, but said nothing more to the centurion. To the captain of the Temple guards he addressed a curt order to cut off Johnny's ear. The captain drew his sword and stepped towards Johnny, who looked at Word. When the captain was almost a sword's thrust away from Johnny, he was hurled back on the ground. Herod gazed open-mouthed. The captain retrieved his sword, which he had dropped, and walked back to his place with lowered eyes. Word had not moved or spoken, but Johnny transmitted in his mind 'Thank you, Word' and Word's mind answered 'My pleasure, Johnny, and for the rest of the day nobody will be able to injure you.' 'I wasn't thinking of myself', replied Johnny's mind, unnecessarily. 'I know you weren't, bless you', came back Word's mind.

Herod had had his miracle, but he seemed not to want it. His fingers drummed uneasily on the arms of his thronelet. 'What happened to the witness Judas?' he rapped.

'He greeted the prisoner before his arrest, and then we were distracted by our guards' inability to approach the prisoner, in the manner you have just witnessed. 'The centurion was ready to admit that now, since Herod had seen for himself how it could happen.

'And you didn't see the witness Judas again?' demanded Herod.

'No', acknowledged the centurion.

'Utter incompetence!' sniffed Herod.

'Not under our orders' bit back the centurion.

'And this fellow Judas made no appearance before Caiaphas?'

'Or before Annas, to whose house we went first.'

'They must have been delighted!' Herod's voice sounded like the bubbling of an acid bath.

He clearly intended this to elicit no comment, and was annoyed when the centurion on reflection gave it one. 'Don't think Annas noticed. Caiaphas was quite annoyed about it.'

'Yes', flashed back Herod, 'that makes sense. Annas wasn't there when Caiaphas and I – ' his eyes suddenly became round, and his jaw shut.

'And Pilate, he was going to say', Word's mind told Johnny's.

Herod smouldered another look in Word's direction. 'Why cannot I put you to death here and now?'

'Because', said the centurion gratuitously but malevolently, 'prisoner is reported popular with natives and they might make a disturbance, especially since morning has broken.' Morning had, although Johnny bad scarcely noticed it. The centurion reflected for a moment. And we haven't orders to prevent Jews killing you, if they want to.'

Herod went white, then purple, and half-screamed 'Take the prisoner back to His Excellency Lucius Pontius Pilate, prefect of the Empire! Or stay, he is insufficiently garbed. Get my father's robe of state, the one he left here on a visit'. His pages ran to execute his command since he was sounding extremely irate. 'Why should Herod the Great go home without a robe of state he had been wearing?' asked Johnny's mind of Word's. But Word did not answer, and Johnny forgot the question when the pages returned, dragging a golden garment once opulent and now moth-eaten. Herod venomously ordered that the Temple guards put it on Word, over his head, covering his own clothes and fitting on over his arms still bound behind him. The Temple guards approached Word very gingerly, but nothing stopped their craven advance, and they managed to get the thing over him. Word neither aided nor prevented them, and his mind ordered Johnny not to interfere. The robe tore in the process, and Word's own clothes might have looked ridiculous emerging through the holes; in fact some of the Temple guards shouted, a trifle artificially, and a few Roman soldiers guffawed while Herod belched with satisfaction. But Johnny thought Word looked dignified and benign as ever, and in his mind Word thanked him, again with a ghost of a laugh. Then they were marched away, leaving Herod looking disappointed. But when they reached the Praetorium, Pilate came out and went into a fit of sniggers when he saw Word (sounding like an asthmatic hen, Johnny thought) and proclaimed his eternal friendship with the tetrarch. Nobody mentioned Herod's attempt to have Word turn Pilate into an asp, and Johnny supposed nobody ever would, provided Herod did not start witch-hunts against the candid centurion.

But when Johnny stood again on the tasselated pavement in front of the Praetorium he found himself among more people than the Temple guards and the Roman legionaries. Since their departure some Jewish civilians and even a few priests had made their way into the courtyard, and Johnny's first sight of them told him if they were evidently waiting for someone or something. Johnny had hopes that the crowd might consist of some of Word's former audience, but none were. Johnny had never seen any of these before, that he knew of, although a few of them reminded him of Shimon the ex-Zealot before he was 'ex'. For one thing many flourished some scarf, or flag, mostly yellow in colour. They were all men, of course, and they looked a fairly tough bunch. They paid little attention to Word, although they had no goodwill for him, and one or two hissed at him. Johnny would have liked to exact retribution, but Word's voice in his mind, sharper than its wont, stabbed his fleeting thought, telling him not to *dream* of going anywhere near this new crowd. It looked as though Word knew what they were there for, although he did not tell Johnny and ignored a broad hint that he should do so. They seemed to amuse Pilate, but so bizarre were the sources of his amusement that Johnny could make nothing as to the relevance of that. Then Pilate began to speak, and it was clear that whatever the differences dividing the Temple guards and the ominous crowd, their hatred of Word could be relied on; so naturally Pilate went out of his way to praise Word, while the guards glowered and the mob moaned like a stormy wind.

'We have some further products of Jewish grace and civility before us', he leered. 'Fortunate are we! I must be agile in the extreme to contend with the wisdom of so many Jewish theologians! Alas that my poor Roman training has to pick its timorous way amid the profundities I see carved on your faces! I crave indulgence!' He tittered. The growl of the Jewish laity increased. Pilate smirked 'Well, let us take our decision! As to the prisoner, your own King' (roar from the laity, rumble from the Temple guards). 'You brought him to me, as one who was driving the people from their true allegiance to Caesar (for whom your solicitude unmans me!) and of course to your famous god whose name eludes me.' (Real snarl of protest from the Temple guards; odd silence, apart from distant bellyaches, from the new crowd.) 'I examined him' (eyebrows arched, mouth curved like a crouching cat) 'and Herod examined him, and I find no fault in him and so sent him to Herod, and Herod finds no fault in him and therefore sends him to me! So – what shall we do? Shall I release him?' (Angry bee-buzzing and horse-whinnying from the mob, growls from the Temple guards.) 'Ah,

345

yes, I take your profoundly intellectual points. Fortunate your presence! You would like me to observe your ancient custom that a prisoner must be released at the Passover!' Suddenly deafening yells of assent came from the new crowd. 'I will do it! I am but the servant of Caesar, but Caesar, as you know, is as wise as he is merciful! Fortunate, a thousand times fortunate, are we in our Emperor! By the power of my authority from the Emperor I decree that your prisoner shall be released! The King of the Jews is set free among the Jews! Is not that a happy resolution of all our little difficulties?' Pilate was hardly audible, because all the new crowd were screaming at the pitch of their lungs: 'BARABBAS!!! BARABBAS! We want Barabbas! We want Barabbas! Release our Barabbas! Nobody but Barabbas! Freedom and Barabbas! Triumph with Barabbas! Barabbas means Freedom! Freedom for Barabbas! Barabbas our Saviour! Barabbas our chief of men! Barabbas the conqueror! Barabbas! Barabbas! Barabbas!!!'

Pilate entertained himself by fluttering around, here soft-mouthing toughs, there deferring hypocritically to very minor priests and even legionaries. When the crowd had shouted themselves hoarse, Pilate leered afresh and said 'So you will that I release the King of the Jews!' The screaming reached so many levels that Pilate was left mouthing inaudibly. He made little effort to shout, and simply twittered to the annoyance of all. In the midst of the yells, Johnny sent a thought into Word's mind: 'Have you ever heard of an ancient custom that a prisoner is released at Passover?' Word's mind laughed. 'No, Johnny.' Johnny persisted: 'Or any Roman usage so deferential to the Passover that it releases a prisoner?' Word's mind was still smiling: 'No, Johnny.' Johnny was troubled: 'I had thought this was a way of getting you off.' Word's mind continued to smile: 'No, Johnny.' 'Then why is Pilate making so much fuss about a privilege which doesn't exist?' 'Because', thought Word, 'he wants to annoy the Temple priests by pretending he is about to free me, but he will let it be determined by the crowd whom he has actually called here, the friends of Barabbas.' '*He* called them here?' yelped Johnny's mind. 'That ravening mob who seem only just stopping short of assassinating him!' 'That ravening mob' smiled Word's mind. 'Naturally they don't know he called them here. He would have had one of his spies spread rumours that there was a chance of Barabbas's release if his friends come and shout loudly enough. Then he releases Barabbas, and tells the Temple priests that sedition is evidently popular. Barabbas might well prove Pilate right, if he returns to his former trade of patriotic murders. A war against the Jews might be quite popular in Rome – a foreign war often strengthens an unpopular government – and Pilate's friend Sejanus has no love of the Jews.'

Suddenly Pilate made a signal, taken up by legionaries whose gestures resulted in the booming of a gong from inside the palace. This startled the demonstrators into silence, promptly followed by a roar of '*Silentia*!' from all the Roman soldiers. To Johnny's horror, Pilate now proclaimed: 'To give us a little entertainment, I shall have the King of the Jews scourged at the pillar inside the Praetorium by my master of the whip! It will be so helpful for you, you will be able to see how brave he is, and how much dignity he can retain by the end of it! Then you can measure Barabbas's claims for release against his! Are you not fortunate! And the King, too, how fortunate is he to have this opportunity to show his endurance and royalty! I fear he will have to endure the lash without the protection of that unmatched model of fashion in which our beloved tetrarch has piously clad him! Do be careful when removing it, my soldiers, lest so sacred a garment take any additional injury! Take him inside, and downstairs to the chamber of correction! Oh, *is* not this exciting? We might *all* like to attend the King's performance at the pillar, but the chamber has no room for spectators! Possess your souls in patience, good people, until they can feast on the return of the King!' And with Pilate almost dancing with delight at the top of the steps, the Roman soldiers pulled Word up the steps and inside the Praetorium. Johnny rushed after them, watchful for any sign of someone intercepting him, but all he got was a shriek of satisfaction from Pilate: 'So the little page wants to see the ordeal of his King! What could be better instruction in the manners and customs which lie in wait for any claimant for the Jewish throne? Let the boy pass! Our ban on spectators must not apply to him! Ah, such a good boy, anxious to learn all available lessons!' He was still reeking his hypocrisies when the pace of the soldiers drew Johnny out of earshot.

When they had gone down a couple of floors, Word was pushed into a long room and the door changed behind Johnny, the last to enter. The room was badly lit, by flaming torches, which was (as Pilate might say) fortunate, since several instruments of torture were never seen by Johnny, who in any case had his eyes fixed on Word and the captors immediately around

347

him. They stopped at a tall oaken pillar, Herod's garment was drawn over Word's head, his hands were untied, his other garments removed, and his wrists drawn up so as to be held above his head tied to the top of the pillar. Johnny had of course seen Word's body many times, but as it stood there facing the pillar, for the first time the thought came into Johnny's mind that it was beautiful. It had never occurred to him before that anyone's body was particularly beautiful. A sculptor might, for instance, have called James's body beautiful when at its most dignified, and a poet might have seen him, even when fishing, to be cold and passionless as the dawn in his dignity but Johnny believed James's dignity usually meant trouble for Johnny, at lease he believed it until Word arrived. But now, lit up in the cold, flickering darkness, Word's brown back and shoulders had a glory which for some reason made Johnny think of a golden sunrise, or of a boundless, gentle sea. The next minute a huge Roman brute swaggered up behind Word, drew back his own right arm, and sent several cords of the whip it wielded whistling through the air.

But they did not reach Word's back. Mention has been made in this history of Johnny's talent for biting, although we have not yet witnessed it in action, and he had never used that skill since becoming Word's disciple. Now he whizzed through the military ranks loosely spread out around the torture-chamber, paused for a second as he drew level with the whipmaster, turned at right angles, stood on the balls of his feet, projected himself upwards with hands reaching out, grabbed the whipmaster's hand, and luxuriously sank his teeth into the flesh above and below hand beneath the knuckle. Johnny's teeth were in excellent health, and they had never bitten deeper or harder in any conflict. The master of the whip dropped his weapon and flung his arms back, lost his balance, and rolled shrieking on the ground, blood dripping from his bitten hand. Johnny glared down at him, his lower lip drawn back from his teeth in a purely animal snarl.

Several soldiers laughed. They might not have done so had one of their own comrades been injured, but the whip master had been separately trained in his grisly skill, and proudly held himself aloof from the ranks. A few attempted to seize Johnny, but he was still supernaturally protected and they were hurled back. Then Word's voice came, quietly but audible to everyone. It spoke in Latin. 'Whipmaster, bring your injured hand to my right shoulder and place your wound on my flesh.' Scarcely without knowing what they did, two soldiers took pity on the whipmaster's efforts to rise, helped him up, and moved him behind Word. The whipmaster raised his bleeding hand. He brought it to Word's flesh as gently as he knew how. 'The pain has stopped', he said, in a voice those who knew him well could hardly recognise. He looked at his hand. 'The blood has stopped too.' 'Very well', snapped the centurion. 'Get on with it.' The whipmaster glared at him. 'If you think I'm raising my hand to this man, you're out of your mind! I know what kind of bastard I am, and I'm not that kind!' And he stalked towards the door, walked through it, and slammed it behind him. Neither his fellow-soldiers nor Pontius Pilate ever recognised him again, although years later he became a friend of a man called Mark, and helped him in collecting and writing the story of Word. He never told Mark about Johnny, or about the whip, or his own wound, but he seems to have seen what happened to Word after he was brought back to Pilate.

Word now spoke to Johnny through their minds. 'Johnny', came the beloved voice in thought, and though Johnny knew Word would tell him he should not have bitten anyone, Word's tones had never been more charged with love, 'our way is never the cruel way, no matter what others do or threaten. I know with what love you did it, but reliance even once on such methods makes you their slave. We have to suffer, you and I, if humankind is to be saved. Go now, sit outside the door, and wait. At least I can stop you from seeing, but what you feel will be worse.' Johnny stood on his toes to plant one kiss between Word's shoulder-blades, and then walked to the door. He walked through, after one look back at Word, around whom the soldiers were beginning to form. He closed the door, and sank down on the last marble step of the stairs. Herod had evidently kept the approaches to his torture-chamber in irreproachable elegance for the benefit of his victims and their tormenters.

He heard nothing from the room he had just left, and would hear nothing till the door was opened and the Romans led Word out. Herod had seen to proofing the sound. He would not have wanted his banquets interrupted and perhaps even upset by shrieks of anguish from below. But Johnny was sure he would have heard Word cry out, in his own mind, if Word ever did. Nothing like that happened. What did, was that Johnny, without suffering pain himself, knew when each blow fell on Word. Word must have had tears in his own eyes, even if he did not visibly weep as the whip fell. Johnny wept, cruelly, heartbreakingly, even loudly. His shoulders shook; his hands clenched in hopeless anger, and beat against the marble stairs. It was as though everything he loved in the world, his parents, James, Word's mother, their friends, his own body, were all burning before his eyes, chief among them Word. He did not feel ashamed at his own helplessness. His love for Word had now liberated him from any consideration of himself at all. He did not even hate the men who were plunging and replunging Word into such agony. He hated the follies and stupidities, the mean betrayals and rotten pride, the brutal oppressions and the endless exploitations, which had united from their despicable places throughout history into the utmost pain on the beautiful God come to save the makers of his misery. All that was good, ever had been, ever would be, was behind that door, and all that was evil was deluging it in all possible extremities of pain. Johnny wept for his Word, but he knew now no prayer could come between Word and the terrible price he was paying for his people. The only prayer Johnny could utter was one of thanks, and to Word himself, as Johnny almost drew Word's gasps of pain in with his own breath, Johnny projected again and again the repetition of his love. It was pitifully little, but he knew however mouselike his strength, it was something for Word in agony also to feel he was not alone.

Fortunately (there is no escaping from Pilate) Johnny did not realise that Word's sorrow for what Johnny was suffering was part of his sorrows for the endless tragedies and transgressions of all humankind, for which he was trying to atone. And these sorrows had no part in the physical pain which he underwent: they were, like Johnny's grief, mental but no less cruel. The very last tragedies before the soldiers began to tear Word's flesh with their whip, were part of the sorrows he tholed as well as the price that he paid: Judas's despair, Peter's bitter self-reproach, the shame of the fleeing disciples, the deeper self-doubts of Annas below his irritation, the final loss of the idealistic worshipper who had disappeared long long ago into the complacency and supremely professional politics of Caiaphas, the hollow mockery and nauseous wit now covering and stifling the love of beauty and laughter once animating Pontius Pilate, the knowledge that must be tearing Word's mother to pieces as she hurried south for the fulfilment of the horror so long ago prophesied to her, the momentary pain of Malchos's ear and the whipmaster's hand. These several last things were the most immediate and urgent in the human mind of Word, but to it was added (as far as we can judge) the divine knowledge of all for which Word's human body was suffering. Johnny did not know these things, but because he was a child he could envisage the bigness of what Word was fighting, and for which he was suffering, without the confusing qualifications and sophistications with which grown-ups lumber themselves.

Johnny could not have said how long it was before his mind stopped recording Word's reception of each lashing. He himself had varied his bruising blows against the marble with savage gnawing of his own nails: the thought hit him, probably not from Word, that since Word had forbidden him to bite anyone else he could only find solace in starting on himself. But it was a little like one of Word's jokes, and a wan excuse for a smile flickered for a moment over Johnny. When the regular bouts of pain stopped their impact on Johnny's mind, he waited, and a slow signal came from Word. Characteristically, it apologised to Johnny for the suffering it must have been for Johnny to record. Johnny cried back to Word's mind that he was glad to do anything, but how badly had they hurt Word? To Johnny's amazement the answer came back, slowly but firmly: 'Johnny, we are going to win. All will be well.' Then followed many minutes until the door opened, the soldiers – almost all of them – first, and then, half-supported by two or three soldiers, Word himself. It tells us what Word had gone through that Johnny was convinced, then and ever afterwords, that the soldiers had found a purple robe in the torture-chamber, and forced Word into it. It was simply Herod's moth-eaten golden robe thrown over Word's naked body: his own clothes were carried contemptuously by another soldier. But Herod's garment seemed purple in the torch-light because so much of Word's blood had stained it, and continued to well up from the open wounds on his back, sides, shoulders and arms. The soldiers were forced to move slower because Word now walked like an old man. Johnny shot over to Word's side, and kissed the blood-spotted face, while knowing he must balance on toes without touching Word, to whom any fresh impact must be agony. Word's chin was blood-spattered worse than his upper face: he must have bitten his lower lip in his pain. Some blows had landed on Word's scalp, and bloody drops cascaded down his forehead: for the moment Word was almost blind, and in utter need of Johnny's left shoulder (as always Johnny had surfaced on Word's left side, but not for hand-holding this time). Slowly Johnny managed to work them both back up the stairs while the soldiers waited impatiently, several snarling 'Keep moving, Jews!' 'Trust Jews to crumple with a little pain!' 'If the Jews' King is as weak as that, we'll polish off the rest in a week!' Word was suffering for the whole human race, but especially he suffered as the representative of the Jewish people. Johnny was proud to know they were persecuted for being Jews – there was nothing better than to be a Jew, though of course Galilean Jews were the best of all. Word's hand was heavier on Johnny's shoulder than Word would have wanted, but they got higher and higher. To be a Jew serving Word was better than best.

Johnny had cherished some forlorn hope of Pilate so horrified on seeing Word that he would order his release on the spot. In fact, Pilate clapped his hands, as though hailing the entrance of an internationally famous actor. 'The Return of the King! How privileged we are! Fortunate above the fortunate! What a performance he gives us! All we need is a crown!' He caught Word's eye as he said it, and evidently Word could now see, and also look, so that Pilate turned away avoiding Word's eyes, and fussily squawked fresh demands for a crown.

Designed to be set well back from the common street, the Herodian Palace was now used only when Pilate had to come down from Cesaria, and so a tiny wilderness of wild plants sprouted at the very gate of the imperial Roman Praetorium. Some thorny bushes ran outside the tassellated pavements, and some soldiers caught enough reeds and branches to weave a crown of sorts into which large thorns could be worked. They came back to the platform outside the Palace where Pilate was exhibiting Word, and Johnny stayed where Word could lean on him. Soldiers handed one another the crown, and the one nearest Word slammed it on his bedraggled and bloodstained hair, forcing it over his ears, and adding scratches to the other wounds and lacerations. Pilate clapped his hands at the sight and gestured the soldiers to further efforts, so that they cried 'Hail to the King of the Jews!' 'Royal greeting to the King of the Jews!' 'Convene your court, O King of the Jews!' And Pilate waved his hands in the air shouting exultantly 'There is your King, in whom I find no fault! Who could fail to be impressed by his regal demeanour?'

Barabbas's followers assumed that this was the moment of decision, or thought they did, and yelled 'Crucify *him*! Crucify *him*! Release to us Barabbas!' The Temple guards joined in. The Roman soldiers sneered. Jews yelling for the death of Jews was just what an imperial army wanted to hear. Once Word was dead, his followers might make a cult of him, thickening blood-feud against the other Jews. That would simplify Roman rule over Judaea. In fact, Pilate had determined on putting Word to death when Caiaphas and Herod had talked the case over with him, and all subsequent talk of release was pure pantomime, throwing in a little crowd-pleasing, and taking an opportunity to insult the Jews with picturesque variations. Meanwhile, Word staggered as he stood, and Pilate realised there was a danger Word would die before he could be crucified. Scourging was the first stage of crucifixion, but the soldiers' thought of scourging the Jewish King was hungrier for ornament than they would give most prisoners. So the soldiers had laid on more savagery towards Word than even they were accustomed to administer. Pilate frowned, and gave instructions to attendants to steer Word and Johnny back into the throne-room, and put them in adjoining chairs. Word sank back at the first chance he got to sit, and Johnny arranged him as best he could, pulled round the other chair for himself, and brought his own arm around Word's shoulders. But even his gentle touch was too much, and Word flinched, drawing forward away from him, so all Johnny could do was as usual to hold Word's hand for moral support. Blood dripped on Johnny's hand from Word's lacerated wrist, torn by twisting in agony against the hard ropes binding his arms to the pillar. There was no need for ropes around the wounded wrists now.

Far in the distance Johnny could heard the bleat of young lambs in the early morning destined for passover and he suddenly remembered it was for the day at whose Seder he had expected to ask the questions. It meant nothing to him now. Even the lambs whom he normally knew simply as creatures to be slain for the Seder, now seemed sorrowful signs of victimhood, creatures innocent and beautiful, like Word. Johnny did not yet complete the analogy by thinking of Word as marked down for slaying; in fact he scarcely thought beyond Word's broken body in its virtually open wounds alongside him. Word needed healing and sleep – and the best method of healing was of course the touch of Word himself, which could not happen here, if humankind was to be saved. Johnny saw none of the humiliation which had been thrust on Word: whatever they might do to him, Word was and always would be the most wonderful person wherever he was. Johnny had never loved and revered Word more. The horrors of bodily wounds were a hero's honours, all the more since Word had suffered them for everyone, even the debased and despicable wretches who inflicted them on him. It occurred to Johnny that nothing could be more absurd than to think of soldiers as heroes: their victims were the heroes.

Suddenly Johnny heard the sound of lighter feet than any he had heard this day and he swung round to see a young woman, dressed in dark simple Roman garments, hurrying towards them. She was carrying some message, he realised, and it must be for Pilate. But she saw Word, and let out a half-cry of horror, and backed away as though she was in danger even by looking at him. The thought added another bitterness to Johnny's misery. Meanwhile, out of doors, Pilate's teasing questions flowed on, tempting and tantalising the Barabbites (so Johnny had mentally named them) as they whined their endless demand that Pilate crucify Word.

'Take him, and crucify him yourselves, for I find no fault in him!' (If you find none, thought Johnny furiously, how dare you half-kill him by scourging?)

'Release Barabbas!' The Barabbites might want Word dead rather than Barabbas, but there was no use in their killing Word, or trying to – Johnny still clung to his conviction that Word, being God, could not die – since that still meant Pilate would kill Barabbas.

'Why doesn't he let Word go since he can kill Barabbas?' thought Johnny. 'I will not have my life saved by another man's life being taken instead', gasped Word's mind back to him.

Then a priest, who seemed to have come in with the Barabbites, could be heard: Johnny had fleetingly noticed him by his dress, setting him off among them, and his formal, legal, even prayerful tone, coming from outside, confirmed which of them he was: 'We have a law, and under that law he is fit to die, because he made himself the son of God.'

Suddenly Pilate's voice ceased, and the maid-servant must have given him her message in a written note, because he re-entered the hall turning it over in his hand, and looking for the first time both serious and worried. He glared apprehensively at Word, as though he feared what Word might do, and yet at the same time was obviously puzzled, wondering why if

Word was what he had said he was, he hadn't already done it. Johnny felt a vindictive satisfaction at the thought that at last Pilate was being made to suffer some tiny fragment of the suffering he had caused to Word, and to God knew how many other Jews, good, bad, and indifferent. Pilate frowned, and suddenly barked out, almost confidingly, 'my wife –' and then stopped, pulling around him the memory of patrician reserve. Then he said to Word, sharply but with respectful note never audible before: 'Where do you come from?' and actually shivered as he said it. Word may even have been too badly injured to speak at that moment: at all events, he stayed silent. He did look at Pilate, and Pilate backed away slightly, with another slight shiver. Meanwhile the maidservant had re-entered the hall in Pilate's wake, and moved sideways looking at Word and Johnny, and taking no notice of Pilate, incredibly, and when she had circumnavigated the prisoners, Johnny could hear her running madly away.

Pilate ignored the fleeing girl. Instead, his blue eyes smouldered as he looked on Word, and Johnny's conviction that the prefect was afraid grew stronger. Johnny allowed himself to think, rather than have his mind ask Word's, 'is he afraid? He must have been a soldier once, and he looks like a soldier suspecting an ambush may lurk behind the next hill.' And to Johnny's rapture, Word, although weak, came back to his mind clearly 'well watched, Johnny. He is afraid he may be ambushed by God.' 'But he doesn't believe in God!' 'No, he thinks he believes in nothing but Fortune, like most of these Romans when they gave up seriously worshipping the gods they stole from the Greeks. But he is worried there is something or someone else.' Even more to Johnny's delight, Word's mind gave a clear, if shaky, laugh, as it added 'He's right about that.'

Pilate continued in a very different voice from his posturing, play-acting performance up to now: 'You have no word for me?' which brought Johnny, not Word, to his feet in amazement, but Pilate ignored him where previously he would have tried to make fun of Johnny's surprise, and sought to divide him from Word, or annoy Word with him. 'Do you not know', he snapped at Word edgily, 'that I have power to crucify you, and that I have power to set you free?' But he looked at Word as though he suspected Word knew a lot more than that.

Word gasped 'You have no power over me, save that you got it from above. Therefore' – Word stopped, drawing in his breath and shaking a little in voice and hands – 'he who handed me over to you has the greater flaw. Word's language made Johnny, rather dottily, think of Word's training as a carpenter, and a very soft laugh from Word's mind into Johnny's agreed. Pilate looked at Word as though he half-rejected the evidence of his own bejewelled ears, and hurried out.

Johnny stood up and stroked Word's face, and kissed it, and Word put an arm around him, moving it very slowly. Johnny did not want to tire Word in the slightest degree more than he had been exhausted already, so he thought his next question although nobody was there to overhear it. 'Was that Caiaphas you meant?' Word nodded, winced, and thought back 'Yes', and after a moment added 'a priest will always have greater responsibility than a mere governor or prefect'. 'Or a mere Emperor', reflected Johnny. 'Yes', thought back Word, 'those people do not know how much they have to follow God and God's laws. A priest should, and as God's servant wrong doing should be impossible for him.' 'Evil Caiaphas!' glowered Johnny's mind. 'Oh, no', came back Word's mind, a little more easily. 'Caiaphas is not a bad man, save that he thinks of priests as an order in themselves without thinking much about why they are there. Priests are nothing without God: Caiaphas might agree with that, but he tells himself God is in full agreement with his deals with the Romans and his financial profit from the Temple. In any case, Caiaphas spoke more truly than he knew when he said one man had to die to save the people.' It was now Johnny's turn to gasp, but before he could say anything else, an appalling row broke out from outside where Pilate had apparently been cajoling the Temple guards and the Barabbites that Word was to go free.

The brighter Barabbites must have realised they had worked up Pilate into fear of an unknown God (theirs) and had hastily changed their pressure into one of Roman loyalties. 'If you release this man you are no friend of Caesar', could be distinguished, as could its repetition several times. Johnny wondered how any person in their senses could imagine that releasing the mad murderous malodorous Barabbas (fleetingly, he savoured his adjectives) was an act of friendship to Tiberius, but Pilate was panicking fast between God and Caesar. The Governor re-entered the hall, gestured at Word to come out, and once more Johnny stood beside Word and himself took Word's hand, put it on his own left shoulder, and told Word's mind from his own to lean on him as much as he could. Of course Word did not, but he did have to lean to some extent. Then Pilate shouted to have Barabbas brought in, and Barabbas was placed on his right side, Word on his left, with Johnny still on Word's left. Barabbas was still manacled. But he was smiling.

Barabbas had rather a nice smile, as murderous smiles go, and he was in general a fine figure of a man, muscular, brown and broad-chested, with strong thighs and good legs. Much of his flesh was visible, since his clothes appeared to have been badly torn in whatever struggle had been caused by his arrest. He waved his chained hands into the air, getting a great cheer from his followers, some mutters of support from the Temple guards, and sour looks from the Roman soldiers. Johnny could see a couple of priests among the Barabbites now, and they were looking as if they personally had created Barabbas on the orders of God, and were expecting high fees for it. The contrast between Barabbas's obvious fitness and Word's broken body under the ghastly Herodian dress, was horrible. But Johnny, however much he mourned for Word's injuries, thought Word cast every other person into insignificance. Word was the king of the sun, moon and starts and however badly he had been hurt, he could never look anything else. His gaze on Pilate, Barabbas, the soldiers who had half-murdered him, the guards who had betrayed him, the Barabbites who wanted to kill him, was calm, unreproachful, acceptant, generous, Johnny thought. Word sent his thanks to Johnny's mind. There was even a faint smile around the well-loved lips. Johnny would have given his life without the slightest hesitation to restore Word's well-being and end the pain he must still be tholing all over him; but apart from the effects of the soldiers' brutality, the crown of thorns and the robe from Herod, Johnny wouldn't want any change in Word. Barabbas could get himself sold for a piece of Greek statuary at the highest money going, for all Johnny cared, and even if they judged him a wonder of the world equal to the hanging gardens of Babylon, he could never remotely begin to approach the glory of Word. If the official purpose of what had been inflicted on Word had been to turn away his followers, no formula had ever worked worse. The only follower present could not have looked on his leader with greater pride.

The Barabbites bellowed on: 'whoever makes himself a king, speaks against Caesar!' as Pilate gestured at Word crying 'Behold your King!' 'I'm not a king', smirked Barabbas, waving his chains as if he was about to parade in a pageant, thought Johnny savagely. 'Away with the Galilean!', spat the Barabbites with some aid from the Temple guards. 'Kill the Nazarene!' 'Crucify! Crucify! Crucify!' Pontius Pilate made one last attempt, giving in by the very way he phrased it: 'shall I crucify your king?' The Barabbite priests were ready for him: 'we have no king but Caesar!' In their zeal for Barabbas, Johnny realised, they were repudiating not only Word, but God, their official king, as well. The cause of Barabbas was a cause for which priests gave up their souls.

Some priests, Johnny knew, did not believe they had souls, being Sadducees, but Pilate, who presumably believed in his own soul even less, if possible, now looked as if he was using every chance he could get to save it. He was calling for water, he had an attendant pour it into a basin, he washed his hands with every display of his zeal to show himself clean. He shouted that he himself was innocent of the blood of Word, which, Johnny knew, was a flat lie, since it had already been shed in great quantity at Pilate's orders. Johnny wanted to say that, but Word thundered in Johnny's mind that he must remain silent. The Barabbite priests shouted back to Pilate 'His blood be on us, and on our children' and when they had said it, the Barabbites in general and the Temple guards with them shouted the same thing. Johnny remembered Word having said when on the road to Jerusalem and warned that people were trying to kill him, 'O Jerusalem, Jerusalem, killer of the prophets, and stoner of those sent to you, how willingly I would have gathered your children together, as a hen gathers her chickens under her wings, and you would not. Your house will be left desolate'. They had made Barabbas leader, and they gave themselves over to the rule of murder and violence. They had put pride of priesthood before pride in what the priesthood served. The fathers had eaten sour grapes and the children's teeth would be set on edge. Johnny would live to hear of the destruction of Jerusalem by the Romans, and their dismembering of the Temple, when the Barabbites led their innocent fellow-citizens in suicidal rebellion forty years after. It was only a handful who said it, but they spoke as if for the beautiful city, for the laughing and loving children who had welcomed Word, for the country behind it, for the world behind that, Judaean and Galilean, Jew and Gentile, man and woman, past and future, who were told the way of Barabbas was the road to freedom and the way of Word, however admirable, was irrelevant. Barabbas himself, now released, went swaggering down the steps of the Praetorium, yodelling something incomprehensible that sounded like *Tiocfaidh Ár Lá!* Johnny saw that as he joined his followers, a glittering dagger was handed to him, and several more were flourished as they took themselves off the tessellated pavement. Pilate vanished inside the building, and Johnny heard a woman's voice speaking to him in angry Latin.

But these things no longer mattered to Johnny. Word was being brought down the steps and told to carry a long plank of wood, and a short one. Johnny at once hurried up, and said Word could not possibly carry either and that he would carry them. Word said Johnny couldn't, Johnny said he could, and the centurion told them the rules: Word must carry the planks but Johnny could take the shorter one. Johnny wanted to protest over them moving Word anywhere but Word's mind gently silenced him.

NINETEEN

MARY MAGDALEN

But as many as received him, to them gave he power to become the sons of God, even
to them that believe on his name

Johnny could never fully remember his own thoughts as they made their
way to Calvary or Golgotha, the place of crucifixion. He still was certain
in one layer of his mind that Word, being God, could not die. Yet Word
talked as though he could, and would, and these words blended in with
all sorts of other words earlier, which Johnny had dismissed as jokes or
symbols or things for grown-ups to understand. It looked as though the
other disciples – or at least most of them, apart from James, Andrew, and
Peter (and what had happened to Peter?) – had concluded that Word was
going to be killed, in the most shameful of all deaths, crucifixion, and that
was one reason why they fled: seeing Judas guiding soldiers to arrest Word
convinced some of them all was lost, while their flight convinced others.
Johnny smiled grimly at the thought that he was more courageous because
he was sure Word could not die. But even as fears that Word would be
killed grew greater and darker in Johnny's mind, his determination to stand
by Word whatever would happen grew stronger still. He was different
from the others: he was a child. In any case he had no time to think at all,
virtually, apart from thinking messages of love to Word, who, whatever he
was going through, kept sending his messages of love back. Each knew
the other most urgently needed every loving thought as they struggled
on. The shorter beam was heavy enough for Johnny to bear, and he had

had no sleep for many hours – and no food since their last supper. Word explained the easiest way to carry wood for a long distance, and joked that Johnny should respect his advice because he was a carpenter to trade. But Word himself was in dreadful condition to carry his own beam.

The soldiers had produced Word's garments, jeering at their poverty, although Word's cloak, woven for him by his mother and her friends, won open admiration, coupled with several greedy hopes of stealing it when Word was dead. These callous jibes were part of the soldiers' garments of speech, as it were. They lived with death, and to fight off fear they were forever making jokes about their own possible deaths and everyone else's. Johnny was close to screaming at them, but Word held his mind firm, telling Johnny they would dishonour themselves if they reacted to this rubbish, and that the soldiers had no idea of what they were actually doing, and no sense of what they were really saying. But the soldiers' hardness about human suffering was all too evident in thought, word, and deed. They tore Herod's ghastly robe from Word's back, making the blood run afresh where the robe had congealed with the open wounds. Johnny forced them away from Word, snatched the hateful robe, and used it to staunch the welling blood as best he could. The soldiers would have liked to strike Johnny and kick him out of the way, but found, to their own secret fear, that they could not lay hand or foot on him. They insisted on Word dressing as soon as they could, after Johnny had managed to soak up the worst bleeding. Eventually Johnny and Word had all Word's garments on him again, and they kissed each other quickly before Word was handed his wooden beam. The soldiers never made jokes about the affection Word and Johnny showed one another: some had children, all had been children, and would want to think of women and children wishing them safe when they had to go into battle. But they never seemed to stop making horrible remarks about Jews.

It was a long, back-breaking journey, probably less than a mile, but feeling as though it had been ten miles by the end of it. Johnny's own weariness and pain in carrying his share grew steadily worse, and while Word tried to conceal his exhaustion and agony from Johnny's mind, it was all too easy for Johnny to realize what he was going through. The soldiers struck Word once to make him go faster, and he promptly fell down, putting Johnny in momentary terror that he was dead. Johnny dropped his beam and wept over Word's prone form so loudly that the soldiers became concerned that dead bodies polluting the streets on the day on which the Seder was to be eaten and rendering those who saw them ineligible to eat it, could mean very nasty complaints against the army to Pilate, probably from persons not connected with Word's arrest. Pilate was by now uneasy enough about the whole business to be on the look-out for a scapegoat, and with Annas and Caiaphas having stayed away from the Praetorium, and Judas dead, these were in short supply: if need be, the centurion in command of the crucifixion party would have to do. The centurion realized this, and he had shown Herod that he knew how to contend with unscrupulous politicians. He dropped his former legalism. Word must be got to Calvary alive at all costs: so the first able-bodied male passer-by was conscripted to carry the heavier beam while Johnny carried on as best he could with the smaller one. Johnny did so the more readily because he had managed to get to his feet, and on finding the conscript had taken over Word's beam Word wanted to take Johnny's from him and carry that. But for once Johnny and the soldiers were in solid alliance. Word was left to stagger on with nothing to carry. The conscript was good-natured as well as powerful, and felt sorry for Word: what had he done? Word was too exhausted to speak, and the soldiers could hardly have cared less – in any case the conscript was a Jew, and as such contemptible. But Johnny talked readily enough partly because he was seething with rage, and partly because he liked the conscript, who was black and reminded him of Chuza, provided Chuza was twenty years younger and had been for some months on a punishing diet. The conscript was called Shimon, he came fom Cyrene in north Africa on the Mediterranean coast, he had three children, Alexander, Rufus and Sara. Johnny reminded him of Rufus, except that Rufus had red hair, which you didn't find many Jews having, had Johnny ever seen a red-haired Jew? Johnny shuddered and said he had, and at that point Word entered the conversation and very simply told Shimon why he was being crucified, how he had acknowledged that he was the Son of God. Shimon actually stopped at that point and began to laugh: the Romans hit him next, and he glared at them but resumed his heavily laden walk at Word's side (Johnny had slipped over to Shimon's other side, fearing Word would try again to take over Johnny's beam). 'You mean', said Shimon, 'that when you said you were the Son of God, the chief priest felt you were bound to fire him from his job if you were. And the Romans agreed to have you killed in order to oblige the High Priest? They must like us Jews a lot better than I thought they did.' Johnny said that the priest had told Pilate Word was trying to make himself King of the Jews and therefore anyone who did not denounce him must be an enemy to Caesar who was the real King of the Jews. 'I hope Tiberius will be grateful to them', grinned Shimon. 'I thought God was the real King of the Jews. I suppose they had to drop him once they decided to kill his son.' Word smiled, a little wanly and said Shimon reasoned well. Johnny asked, would Shimon not like to become one of Word's disciples? Shimon thought it was a bit sudden, and looked as if it would be over too soon to count, but Johnny said no, that if you decided to follow Word you were to be his disciple for ever and ever, and love Word for ever and ever, and Word would love you for ever and ever. Shimon asked Word, did he approve of Johnny's invitation, and Word said he did. He also said it would be a pleasure to have more African disciples, he had two who by now must be in Ethiopia and he himself had lived in Egypt for several years in his infancy. And then Word laughed, a strange, frail, little laugh and said Shimon might as well join them, there could be no better time than this, nor no better occupation than for him to carry Word's cross. Shimon must have felt the warmth and love radiating from Word just as Johnny was doing, for all of Word's exhaustion; he beamed at them both and told them he would become one of them, and would start a movement of Christians in Cyrene. He was sure that when he told Alexander, Rufus and Sara that he had been converted by the son of God and by a ten-year-old boy, they would want to become disciples immediately. Word visibly grew happier under their eyes.

As Johnny walked, trying not to think of the wood he was carrying with its weight apparently increasing, his mind spun back memories of words whose antiquity mocked his attempts to close his mind to any danger of Word's dying:

> Who hath believed our reports? and to whom is the arm
> of the Lord revealed?
> For he shall grow up before him as a tender plant, and as

a root out of a dry ground: he hath no form or comeliness:
('And *that's* a lie', Johnny thought scornfully to himself)

> and when we shall see him, there is no beauty that we
> should desire him,
> He is despised and rejected of men: a man of sorrows, and
> acquainted with grief: and we hid as it were our faces from
> him: he was despised, and we esteemed him not.

('speak for yourself' snarled Johnny to Isaiah yet he was chillingly aware that if the Scripture had failed to prophesy how he would feel, it foretold the grown-ups of his own generation. He hardly noticed that he was making no exceptions, neither Peter nor Andrew nor James: but something made him amend his thought to the 'adult males' of his own generation. Perhaps it was a memory of Mary, or of his mother Salome, or of Miriam, or of Joanna or Martha or Martha's sister Mary.)

> Surely he hath borne our griefs, and carried our sorrows:
> yet we did esteem him stricken, smitten of God, and afflicted.

('Well, if we did, we were idiots', growled Johnny. 'How could God strike and afflict himself?')

> But he was wounded for our transgressions, he was
> bruised for our iniquities: the chastisement of our peace was
> upon him; and with his stripes we are healed.

Suddenly Johnny seemed to feel an invisible cold wind (for a sailor can see visibility in a wind, all too much of it sometimes). Lines which he had chanted unthinkingly from his first ready learning of them now came to life, almost shouting at him that for this had they been conceived:

> All we like sheep have gone astray; we have turned over
> every one to his own way; and the Lord hath laid on him the
> iniquity of us all.

Johnny then recalled Word saying something about a shepherd, a story but not a story with a plot, a shepherd whose voice the sheep know and would follow. Or had the story a plot which Word had not filled in? Word had gone on to say he was the good shepherd, and he defined the good shepherd – Johnny was now shivering – as one who lays down his life for his sheep. That was a good definition, certainly, but Word had not left it there. Johnny forced his mind to remember what it wanted passionately to forget, Word saying 'And for these sheep I am laying down my life'. It had been easy to see this as a wild metaphor, as a way of stressing how deeply Word loved disciples, followers, everyone he could, but it came back now, however hard Johnny tried to stop it, no metaphor in this cold grey morning with bits of wood heavily hauled alongside Word who was nearly half-dead.

And now Johnny began to dwell on what he himself had seen and heard. Like the earlier verses from Isaiah, they first forced themselves on his unwilling mind, for it was hard to reject the memory while fighting to retain control of a lump of wood at least three feet tall, nothing as heavy or as awkward as Word had been forced to carry and Shimon the Cyrenean had taken over, that was at least six feet in height, but bad enough, especially since any sign of weariness from Johnny, meant that Word, eternally watchful, would be leaping to take it from him as fast as a badly crippled man can leap. Johnny's mind was forced back to the time Johnny and Shimon Peter, and James, had been on the top of the mountain with Word, and Word's father whom Word called Abba was there inside a cloud to whom Johnny had prayed without words, and Moses had been there, severe, and Elijah, winking at Johnny, all of which was very nice to remember but what wasn't was that they had evidently talked amongst themselves about something bad to happen to Word in Jerusalem, and Word had told Johnny, James and Peter not to speak about it until the Son of Man was risen from the dead. Johnny knew no more now than then what that meant, but he feared it now whereas then he had simply set it aside as some grown-up way of talking. Then Word had had some curious argument with Peter, who complained about Word saying in public that the Son of Man must suffer many things, and be rejected by elders and chief priests and scribes, and be killed and after three days rise again. Johnny had wanted to seal all that out of his own mind, but Peter became upset about it, and whispered to Word that he shouldn't talk like that (as though Word had been telling a dirty joke in front of Peter's mother-in-law, Johnny had thought irritably). And Word told Peter 'Get me behind me, Satan, for that was not God's thought but men's. (Word returned to this later, telling Peter in front of the twelve that he was a devil to be counselling departure from Word's mission in the name of caution: but when Johnny remembered that incident decades later, he took it that Word had been addressing Judas, not Peter.) Word spoke to the disciples, and to any of his earlier crowd of listeners who could still hear him, that his followers must deny themselves, take up their cross, and walk in Word's steps, and that anyone wanting to save their own lives would lose them and those who would lose their lives for Word's sake and the Gospel's sake would save them. That didn't matter, thought Johnny at the time: he would be glad to die for Word, and even though Chuza would later teach Johnny a lesson about fear, Johnny would remain less concerned about losing his own life than of making the slightest concession to the idea that Word might lose his. Today it would be a relief to die for Word instead of having to see Word die, inconceivable horror from which Johnny still yearned to recoil. And there had been other times when Word had told them all that a man could not be his disciple unless he took up his own cross and followed Word. Johnny had taken that to mean that people must face any difficulties and dangers in their particular path, but there was an ugly sound about taking up that cross, as though it were the example Word himself would give. Well, he was giving it now. And at the same time he had spoken of the need to hate one's own life or life-style in order to follow him. (He had got Johnny to stop fighting with James.) Did this mean he, Word, had to hate the prospect of continuing his own life, so as to prove by death that he was himself?

All this was impossible. God could not die.

But stronger and stronger in Johnny's mind, like some weed which had eluded the hand of the gardener and now was thicker and deeper than ever, grew the fear that it was going to be true.

In his fear Johnny called out to Word in his own mind, but Word simply smiled at him as they walked, and in his mind told Johnny he loved him.

But was it Word who set off in Johnny's mind the memory of Johnny himself promising to follow Word to death and back? Johnny was ready to do it, now as then, and now as then without knowing what he meant by it, or even why he said it. But, obscurely, he was very thankful he had said it.

Johnny had noticed, almost without reflection, that they met very few people, no doubt because the way they were going was well known as the short route from Pontius Pilate to Death, and to behold passengers to Death would pollute the Passover. Most folk who saw them turned their faces away, if they did not turn back from their paths and seek another street. A few rough-looking men had yelled things at Word which Johnny hardly took in: something about Word saving others and being unable to save himself. Barabbites, roaring to quiet their own dirty consciences that their vaunted leader walked his murderous way free, courtesy of Pontius Pilate, and another man was to die in his place. Brave leader! Even by their own homicidal standards the Barabbites looked mean with Barabbas crawling his way to freedom by the courage of one whom even *his* followers now knew to be the better man. Interesting that the Barrabites seemed unconcerned about their own pollution from seeing Word supposedly on his way to death: they were zealous Zealots for Jewish freedom, and the Jewish faith held a very low place in their list of priorities. How would they pray? O God, whose duty it is to get yourself killed while we cut the throats of whomsoever we like so that we can free your chosen people, get on with it? But here Word's mind cut in on Johnny's, slower than normally, to head off Johnny's mind from danger: 'No bitterness, Johnny! This *must* happen. None of these people know what they are doing!'

Johnny had hardly noticed any women on their line of march, but suddenly one appeared and Word fell again as she came close. At once the woman hastened across to him, dropped on one knee, raised his head, pulled off her headscarf and softly kneaded it over his bleeding, sweating face. Johnny dropped his own short plank and raced across to cushion World's nearer shoulder. The centurion spat something which Johnny found meaningless (though the captain of his prison-ship would have known what it meant). Word was clearly much weaker now, and seemed even heavier to Johnny despite the aid of Shimon the Cyrenean who had also dropped his much heavier beam and like-wise sank on one knee to help Word. The soldiers took time off to spit individually, non-verbally, although turning away from the woman: one had to take any signs of delicacy one could get from Roman civilization, and be thankful.

Word's breath was now coming with greater gasps, even wheezes, as though some great stringed instrument were badly wrenched out of tune. The woman had drawn the scarf away quickly enough after saturating it in Word's blood and sweat – and tears, Johnny realised – and she murmured 'Blessed be God!' and Word's voice revived in Johnny's mind with a little joke about the good Samaritan come to life. 'She *does* know what she is doing', thought back Johnny. 'Women know, as a rule', came back Word's thought, faintly. 'Since women give life, they know.' The woman rose to her feet, folding the scarf with what seemed extreme veneration. Johnny never found out how much she knew.

Yet he mentioned the woman a few times in retelling the story of Word, many years later, unlike what happened next, which he never discussed with anyone except his mother and Word's. They were making their dreadful, miserable way when they heard voices cry after them to stop, and turning round saw a litter carried by slaves and bearing a lady most opulently dressed. She herself was making authoritative gestures, and the slaves were calling, so Shimon and Johnny dropped their wood, and Word thankfully leaned on the shoulder Johnny was quick to place awaiting Word's left hand. The slaves had made good progress from the Citadel where Word had been tried by Pilate. Eventually they drew level and lowered the litter, and a female attendant who had been walking along-side them aided the great lady to arise. The lady glared at the soldiers, who cowered before her. Then she turned to Word, and fell on one knee. Word stepped forward, placed his grimy hands on her beautifully coiffured head and ornate head-dress, and asked God to bless her. The female attendant also fell on one knee, and her, too, Word blessed. The great lady rose, and was turning back to her litter, when Johnny, realising who she must be, fell on one knee himself and asked her in Latin could not Word go free? Word gently raised Johnny, shaking his head, and the great lady shook hers, saying in a choking voice '*Quod dixit, dixit*' which Johnny knew from Word's teaching meant 'What he has spoken, he has spoken'. She turned back to Word, who said 'I forgive him', in Latin, and she gave a terrible smile, answering 'and you have more to forgive even than I'. Then the litter was made ready for her and the slaves took her away.

From this point the soldiers looked very uneasily at Word, conducting him roughly but no longer brutally. Clearly they had never expected resistance from Word's disciples, or supporters, after the apostles' flight from Gethsemane, and the want of any public opinion at Pilate's court (other than the Temple guards and the Barabbites), made it even clearer: few of them had been assigned to detail as crucifixion party for Word, but that few of them had been considered a sufficiency, with almost all other Roman soldiers on the usual alert for Passover. Interventions by women were something else, especially when the second had been from Claudia Procla, wife to the imperial Governor. But now a fresh female menace presented itself, not in quality, but in quantity. These women were not following from Jerusalem: they had been waiting in something very like an ambush. As soon as Word, the soldiers, Shimon of Cyrene, and Johnny, came within earshot, the waiting women started crying lamentations from Isaiah:

> Rise up, ye women that are at ease: hear my voice, ye careless daughters; give ear unto my speech.
>
> Many days and years shall ye be troubled, ye careless women: for the vintage shall fail, the gathering shall not come.
>
> Tremble, ye women that are at ease;
>
> be troubled, ye careless ones; strip you, and make you bare, and gird sackcloth upon your loins.
>
> They shall lament for the teats, for the pleasant fields, for the fruitful vine.
>
> Upon the land of my people shall come up thorns and briers; yea, upon all the houses of joy in the joyous city.
>
> Because the palaces shall be forsaken; the multitude of the city shall be left: the forts and towers shall be for dens for ever, a joy of wild asses, a pasture of flocks.

Johnny naturally made more sense of this than did the Roman soldiers: he knew it for the Hebrew of the prophet Isaiah, they knew it for gobbledygook, black magic, or warning of peasant uprising – depending on the contextual atmosphere. The women were all covered, cloaked and muffled, according to strict Jewish convention, but there was nothing conventional in their presence almost on the verge of a crucifixion-field, on the very day of the Passover itself. Incredibly, they now continued the later text that had coursed through Johnny's mind only a few paces ago:

> He was oppressed, and he was afflicted, yet he opened not his mouth: he is brought as a lamb to the slaughter, and as a sheep before her shearers is dumb, so he openeth not his mouth.
>
> He was taken from prison and from judgment: and who shall declare his generation? for he was cut off out of the land of the living: for the transgression of my people was he stricken.

Johnny gazed at them, and at last he realised what had happened. Word's mission to his fellow-creatures had not failed, as it had seemed to fail.

The men had betrayed him, tormented him, turned away from him. The women had not.

And in Johnny himself alone, the children had not, either.

Or was it himself alone? One of the waiting women, smaller than the rest, broke ranks and walked up to him, and a voice behind her veil whose tones he remembered all too well hissed 'I told you what men were like!' Automatically, Johnny answered Miriam by argument 'I'm a man! And *I'm here*, if nobody else is!'

'You're a child! And be thankful you are! Word, as you call him, is the only man worth anything! And he's God! And now they're going to kill him!'

'They can't! God can't die!'

'He can if those bastards of men have anything to do with it! We women can't hold the road indefinitely! We've taken them by surprise at the moment, but they'll force through to Calvary!'

'How did you get here?'

'Mary of Magdala. That tall woman at the head of our people.'

'But she's mad! Or she was. Word drove seven devils out of her.'

'Well, he put seven angels in. She mobilised women from Galilee, Samaria, Peraea, Judaea, Idumaea. Somehow, we don't quite know how, she discovered his life was in danger, and sent messengers – all women, needless to say – mostly to places where he'd been; to women among whom he'd worked, women whose children he'd saved, and whose illnesses he'd cured, and whose sins he'd forgiven, and whose future he'd made! Syro-Phoenician women, Samaritan women, Syrians, Lebanese, Greeks, Jews. He's the only man who ever treated women as if they were as good as men!'

'He's the only grown-up who treated children as if they were humans', agreed Johnny, 'not just as parents being kind but someone bringing us our freedom.'

'Is it any wonder the men want to silence him, destroy him, finish him?'

'Are there any other children here with you?'

'I'm not a child', snorted Miriam. 'I'm Mary of Cleopas, Word's aunt.'

'What? What on earth are you talking about?'

'I wasn't going to be kept out of this. I was one of his greatest miracles, don't forget.'

'As if you'd let me forget it', and Johnny grinned, despite himself.

'Give men a moment and they'll forget anything to do with women!'

'And we agreed I wasn't a man', added Johnny, pacifically. Miriam looked as though she was eyeing him narrowly behind her hood, but she continued:

'It was his mother who said I should be let come. She's here, of course. She told me to be her sister. And you're not to tell anyone Mary of Cleophas was me! Anyone! Ever!'

Johnny respected this now and later, but he wanted to see Word's mother and his own, if she too was there as seemed pretty certain. The women had stopped reciting and were wailing in high voices, when Word painfully turned to them and said: 'daughters of Jerusalem, do not weep for me. Weep for yourselves and for your children. Days will come which people will ask whether the barren are not happier, and the wombs that never gave birth, and the breasts that never suckled. It is then that they will begin to say to the mountains "Fall on us!" and to the hills "cover us up!" If it goes so hard with the tree that is still green, what will happen to the tree already dry?' Johnny would remember this forty years later when he heard that Jerusalem had been destroyed by the future Emperor Titus Flavius Sabinus Vespasianus: Jerusalem women listening to Word now would be old and no longer child-bearing when that would happen, and it would kill many of them. Did Word realise many women in front of him were not from Jerusalem? If not, he found it out quickly, for Mary Magdalen threw off her head-covering, and to her right Word's mother threw off hers, while Johnny's own mother twisted hers off as she ran across hers to Johnny himself and took him in her arms. But their eyes, and Miriam's, and Mary Magdalen's, were riveted on Word and his mother, who gazed at one another, she with welling eyes as she saw the additional suffering on his face from his sight of the horror on hers. Johnny felt his mother's grasp tightening around him as they looked on Word's mother, and for all her own fury Miriam clearly felt the cosmic grief and inched her way closer to Johnny and Salome. Word stretched out his hands to his mother Mary, and seemed about to go to her when he suddenly crashed full-length on the ground. In a moment Mary was at his side, her hands running over the stricken shoulders. Johnny kissed Salome and wriggled out of her arms to get to Word. The centurion raised his hand to command Word's rise, but lowered it irresolutely: that last fall looked too much like the last fall ever. If Word was not dead, he had fainted.

Johnny hardly saw what happened next above him while he burrowed under Word's armpit to raise the body and help it breathe, if yet it could. Mary was gently raising the head. It is doubtful if they heard Mary Magdalen's crisp command, to the centurion, telling him he could not take Word farther, the women would bar the way. Salome and Miriam added their voices, followed by those of countless women from Word's life. There was the Syro-Phoenician who had held Word in debate to get him to heal her daughter, and the woman whose issue of blood he had cured while on his way to heal Miriam, and the woman bowed almost double for eighteen years whose cure by Word on the Sabbath was so bitterly attacked, and the widow of Nain whose son Word had raised. Johnny did not identify all the women's voices, though the differences in their accents helped him greatly, especially in such cases as the Samaritan woman with whom Word talked so long after first asking her for water (which in retrospect Johnny realised had been a splendid way to begin with her, by showing that Word valued speech with women and men equally, and that despite the Jewish prejudice against Samaritans he was happy to drink water from her cup).

As Johnny and Mary were managing to raise Word's head and shoulders from the ground, they could hear more of the dialogue between the Roman soldiers and the women. By now Mary Magdalen was calling 'We are many, you are few; we bear no arms, but we will stand between you and Calvary, and we will bear our master from hence to live in freedom and go on teaching us' and the women crying 'Amen! Amen!' and the centurion yelling 'you treasonous hags! We will crush you to powder!' 'You do not deal with cowardly men now' mocked Mary Magdalen. 'Who cares for you?' snarled the centurion. 'No man will even take up your cause, apart from the brat!' 'Don't you dare call him a brat!' screamed Miriam, firmly disguised behind the head-covering of Mary of Cleophas. 'And you do have one man in your path', thundered Shimon of Cyrene. 'You!' and the centurion vented his rage in contempt for the conscript. 'You are here as our slave, carrying this criminal's gibbet by our orders!' 'You have taught me to love your victim', retorted Shimon, dipping his answer in gall. He had dropped his great cross-beam shortly after Johnny had dropped his in springing to Word's aid. Now Shimon respectfully fell back a pace or two behind Mary of Magdala, facing the Romans. Salome took her place alongside him, Miriam alongside her. The centurion's jaw set at an ugly angle, and he ordered his men to draw their swords.

But Word had managed to summon life back into his torn and bloody frame, and heavily weighting his mother and Johnny, pushed his body upright, first raising his head and shoulders, and then gazing on the confrontation while still kneeling. Hastily he scrambled to his feet, gasping to the women 'you must not die for me – at least, not now. It is I who must die for you. All of you here are the most faithful of my disciples, but if I risked your lives I would not be faithful to you. And I must do the work the Father asks of me. Mother, tell them it must be so!' With a note of the most terrible sorrow Johnny had ever heard in a human voice Word's mother took up his demand without a pause. 'Sisters, you have vindicated the name of woman, but it must now be as my son says. Stand not in the way of his butchers, but help him make the sacrifice to save us all!' She kept her voice level.

Slowly the women divided, and Word, with his mother on one side and Salome now on the other, staggered forward, followed by Shimon with the cross-beam, and Johnny with the smaller one. The centurion's eyes smouldered, but he said nothing more and his men shamefully got in line. Johnny's heart and soul were utterly revolted by what the soldiers had done, were doing, and would do, but however he abominated the cruelty they practised, and the people in whose name they practised it, Johnny thought it utterly ineffectual. Word walked wounded, but with every sign of glory. Johnny despised earthly Kings remembering what the Lord had said to Shmuel, but if a man was to be measured by his kingliness, Word was the greatest King the world had ever known and would ever know. And, being God, he was the greatest man. And nothing men might do to him could touch his perfection. Johnny was more miserable and more proud than he could have imagined possible. He knew that Word would not let others fight on his behalf, but Johnny really thought the best thing that could have happened would have been for himself to be killed by the soldiers while Word was got away. But as he thought it he felt Word's thought in reply: 'Johnny I could not have lived had I been the cause of your death. Stay with me, and you make a much greater sacrifice than your death could be. Your martyrdom will be to live!' So Johnny hauled his wood onward with strange comfort.

If it was bad for him, it must be infinitely worse for Word's mother. Johnny could not imagine how bad, only that it was bad beyond his power to imagine. He realised that his own mother, Salome, would understand more than he could. But with a child's belief in fair-mindedness, Johnny squared his shoulders as best he could, and thought it fair that he should suffer in seeing Word suffer. He had chosen to follow Word, however little thought he gave it at the moment he saw him and ran to him or when, having recovered breath, he insisted on being Word's disciple. He had made a bargain, for what he had realised would be the most wonderful love anyone could have, and now he was going to pay the bitter price of that bargain, the forfeit, the penalty. To follow Word meant to be part of his Kingdom, however small a part; but conquest demands payment. Word was asking more of him than death: it would be hard, but Johnny would give it. But Mother Mary had not chosen to bear her Son: she had simply agreed to bear him. Johnny supposed she must have known from the first that it would bring tragedy: the innocent infants, killed by some Herod, drenched her story in tragedy: almost before it started. She must have been told by Word as well as by the angel who first alerted her, that Word would ultimately be sacrificed. Many a mother had mourned for many a son, killed before her own death, but no mother, whatever she might imagine, had had a Son like Word.

All of these things were locked up in the three forms that walked, or shuffled, ahead of Johnny. Behind him, he knew, were the Romans, followed by Mary Magdalen's legion, Jairus's twelve-year-old daughter at its head subordinate only to the commander from Magdala, herself subject only to Word, and, it seemed, to Mary his mother. Since Mary Magdalen's forces had been volunteers from the time they got her message, it made sense that their discipline put even the Romans to shame, which in any case was where the Romans were. They were all by now outside the walls of Jerusalem, and very near one of the main highways running into it. Johnny would learn later about the Roman preference for crucifixions on or near public thoroughfares, as examples to passers-by, and as expressions of Roman taste. If it was possible for them to expose Word to shame, they would ensure it. The place to which they were going, Golgotha (Skull Hill) or Calvary, was standard, although the proximity to the Passover meant that very few would meet their deaths at it on this day, if any Jews had any control over the situations. When Word and the rest, homicidal or otherwise, reached Golgotha, only two victims were in place awaiting them. Johnny was almost sick at the sight of them, and the place itself bore out its ugly title: the plateau lay before them like a leering, rotten skull. The centurion indicated a vacant post.

The blood under the crosses on either side of it was fresh. The torn and agonising bodies that hung on them were alive, and the occupants screaming. Great nails had been driven through their wrists and their legs held in profile together to let another nail transfix foot over foot. The faces surrounding the screaming mouths were dark and dangerous when free: now they were simply personifications of pain. The bodies hung naked, fighting for breath amid their own screams. 'God's curse lies on the man who hangs from a tree', sang Deuteronomy in Johnny's mind, and surely God's curse must lie on the act of hanging him on it. What were the crimes of these wretches? Behind their yells, the soldiers guarding them (that is, the soldiers who had butchered them) were shouting to their newly-arrived comrades, and Johnny could distinguish enough to realise the crucified were Barabbites, seconds-in-command, left by their liberated leader to rot, and by his followers who had howled for Word's blood so that their master might thrive. In a horrible parody of Philip's folksongs, invented or inherited, Johnny's mind swung into half-anticipation of tear-stricken laments for the Barabbite martyrs to Roman tyranny, their deaths eked out in verse after tragic verse by poets who had neither exerted nor risked their own precious bodies to see their heroes die. Not even women or children had come to lament their suffering (Johnny had a flicker of guilt-ridden wince for that 'even').

Johnny's mind ticked away thus while he automatically went up towards the middle post, following Shimon, and thankfully dropped his block of wood where the Cyrenean had dropped his cross-beam. Then he fell back, turning to where his mother and Word's were easing Word to the ground. Gently Mary drew the robe she had woven from the body of her son, and Salome held Word's head. Salome would have liked to take away the ugly, painful, contemptuous remnants of the thorny crown the soldiers had driven into Word's head, Johnny could see, but Word stopped her. It would probably have given additional pain to withdraw any thorns still in place, but Johnny realised also that Word intended to keep that mocking, vicious crown or what was left of it, and give it the pride of place this hideous enthronement invited. Now two soldiers dragged Shimon's cross-beam behind Word's head, and another drew his sword and carelessly cut the clothes remaining on Word so that they fell away from him. Mary looked on the naked body which she and Daddy-Joe had swaddled in its first clothes so many years ago. It was almost a chequer-board of blood and flesh, but to Johnny it was still the strong, loving human cover in which the Son of God had lived and worked, and he fell on his knees to grasp and kiss Word's left hand he had held so often and so long on land and on sea. A moment later, and a soldier had snatched it away from Johnny, grinding it against the wood.

The hand whose touch had cleansed and closed Johnny's bleeding scratches when first be ran to Word, the hand that had caught him as he plummeted from the Roman ship, the hand that had broken bread to be called Word's body, was now left to curl in agony as a huge nail was hammered into the wrist or forearm beyond it, and the same done for its fellow. Salome drew Johnny back from the savage soldiers, whispering 'I would never have let you go to Jerusalem if I had known you would witness this, and yet I thank God that you have been entrusted to be its witness'. Johnny almost without thinking slid his right hand into her left.

She kept it firmly.

In retrospect Johnny was very grateful for this. At the time he hardly noticed, being paralysed with horror at what was happening to Word, whose exhaustion was obvious but whose self-control was endless. Even as the first nail went in and his mouth automatically constricted into a dreadful grin, the veins in his neck standing out like taut fishing-lines, he worked his lips back into a painful but loving smile for Johnny. Even as the leap of Word's heart drove its impact into Johnny's mind, Word's eyes were still clear and kind. Mother Mary stood alone, a monument of stoical grief. Mary Magdalen led the other women in a shout of rage and reproach, with no effect on the soldiers who now began to drag Word's cross-beam to the post, whereupon Shimon of Cyrene placed his arms under Word's knees and lower spine, and carried him with amazing concord to the cross-beam movers until they reached the foot of the post. As the sole representative of adult men, thought Johnny, Word couldn't have found better than this Shimon in mind or body. Now the great black shoulders moved into a gigantic, final thrust as the brown, blood-drenched body above him was raised on high so that other soldiers on ladders against the great post could bend down and pull the cross-beam into the slot that awaited it. Word's beautiful, battered, bramble-crowned head towered above all until the short plank Johnny had carried was handed up, and a legend firmly affixed to it, so that it projected above Word's hair while the plank in its turn found its slot. Word's mind kept murmuring words of love and blessings for bravery to Johnny's, which Johnny answered in desperate attempts to stifle his own horror.

At the foot of the cross, other soldiers drove Word's legs upward, together, parallel, so that the knees stuck out to the right, and when they could go no higher a beam the width of the cross was hammered in immediately under the trunk of Word's body, while Word's feet were pulled back flush with the cross and another beam hammered over them so that the nail would go through, pierce both of Word's feet and then penetrate the wood of the cross behind. When Johnny was an old man he would see occasional attempts by wood sculptors to recreate an idea of what the crucified Word resembled, but all broke down when it came to realising the sheer brutality. The images would have a peaceful symmetry which was worlds removed from reality. (Nicodemus is believed to have sculpted a wooden image of the crucified Word based on his sight of the original, but Johnny never saw it: Nicodemus had more sense than to offer the sight of it to the boy, or indeed to any of the other witnesses apart from the man who came with him to help move Word's dead body from cross to tomb, Joseph of Arimathea. It was quite dark before they arrived.)

The Barabbites had stopped yelling by now, and Word let out one cry when his feet were nailed, a wordless cry for which his mind apologised to Johnny's, and Johnny's wept back. But then Word's mother went forward and kissed the pinioned feet, followed by Johnny and Salome, and then by Shimon of Cyrene smiling awkwardly but walking resolutely enough, and then by Mary Magdalen and all of the other women one by one, each one letting their facial coverings fall and then resuming them when they had kissed the feet. The soldiers looked at them uneasily, but had the decency to refrain from shouting any insults. Johnny and Salome stood near the cross beside Mother Mary, with enough room for the procession of Mary Magdalen and her followers. Johnny heard some talk among the soldiers, chiefly about the legend now inscribed over Word's head. What it said was quite legible from the ground, and the broad and Latin letters were Greek and Latin capitals, as well as Hebrew symbols. Word even asked Johnny through the communion of their minds whether the translations were correct, and Johnny, gasping, did his best to say. The words should have simply read 'JESUS THE NAZARENE THE KING OF THE JEWS' but the last word was the same for 'Jews', 'Judaeans', and 'tribe of Judah'. The soldiers at least seemed to be clear as to what was meant: their problem was more why it was meant. Johnny easily followed their Latin. He neither understood nor assimilated the many obscene adjectives, exclamations and participles they used in irritable support of their remarks, and so these have not come down to us.

'Pilate's orders: wrote it himself.'

'Well, he has to do something, can't simply sit around looking pretty.'

'But it's an odd thing to say. This fellow isn't king of the Jews.'

'Herod's the king of the Jews.'

'No, he isn't, neither. His dad was. *He's* tetrarch of the lands north and east.'

'Well, this man is no Herod.'

'That's one thing to be said for him.'

'So why call him King?'

''Cos he said he was King, told Pilate he was.'

'Makes sense that way, you tell the Roman Governor you're king, and he'll call you king on the bit of wood he's sticking you up. Can't do fairer nor that.'

'The Jews say you can.'

'What Jews?'

'That high priest, Caiaphas, the one who likes paradin' round 'is temple in fancy clothes. 'E didn't like it, doesn't like it, said so.'

'Well, we own *him*, can't change his undies without Pilate's OK. Why should Pilate get *his* knickers in a twist because of old Caiaphas?'

'Bein' wot 'e is, Pilate maybe did it to wind up Caiaphas. What did Caiaphas want 'im to write?'

'Wanted him to say this bloke said he was king of the Jews, mustn't give the impression he was, really, tried to tell Pilate it was high treason for Pilate to say anyone but Caesar was king of the Jews.'

'Wot did Pilate say?'

'Became *very* silky, told Caiaphas if Caiaphas wanted to tell him how to do his job it would keep Caiaphas so busy that Pilate would have to get someone else to do Caiaphas's job. That was the last we heard out of Caiaphas.'

'Went away then, did 'e?'

'Oh, no, he'd never been there. This was all messages up and down from Temple to Praetorium and back wearin' out everyone else's feet while his holiness and his excellence were sittin' on their thrones.'

'And that was why you couldn't get up here until now?'

'Right. We all knew Pilate's way of endin' an argument, *Quod scripsi scripsi*, bastard's afraid if he changes anythin' he writes, folks will think he doesn't really know how to write. So we had the palaver so that Caiaphas can say he remonstrated, and Pilate can say he consulted, and each of them can show how they respected local religious customs by only speakin' to each other by long-distance runner. Makes me sick, the hypocrisy of it. And I missed all the fun by only getting here after the crucifixions.'

'Take it from me, Lucius, when you've seen one crucifixion you've seen the whole bleedin' lot.'

But Johnny knew that there was more to it than that. Pilate could annoy very many Jews at one stroke. Judaeans would be annoyed at his implication that a Nazarene was really king of the Judaeans. Johnny was slowly beginning to realise that in a job like that most of the time officials get their kicks by fighting with other officials just enough to annoy them but not enough to give them a good case to protest. It was as if they were all children, thought Johnny, and then was startled by Word's thought coming into his mind 'that's not fair to children!' Startled, Johnny agreed that it wasn't, and was left in admiration of Word at work keeping Johnny fair-minded while himself in extreme agony. Word answered in his mind 'always look on the bright side!'

It was so like Word. There he hung on what his murderers intended to be the most infamous and despicable form of death a human could suffer, his hands and feet split open with literally God alone knowing how much agony filled his every conscious moment, and him trying to cheer Johnny up. It was certainly a wonderful doctrine, looking on the bright side, and Johnny thought of those words decades later amidst the opening of his evangel, 'And the light shines in the darkness, and the darkness comprehended it not'. Nearly two thousand years later Word inspired comic young men making a funny movie to end with a chorus of crucified people singing 'always look on the bright side of life': in the darkest hour in the history of the world the message from the crucified God was one of faith, hope, love – and therefore the brightness of life. And Word kept insisting in Johnny's mind it was the bright side he should think of: Word was going to die, that the people of the world should live if only they were ready to live.

Then Word told Johnny to look at the compliment the soldiers were paying Mother Mary, throwing dice to see which of them would get the robe she had woven for Word. He was evidently saying the same to his mother's mind – it was at this point that Johnny realised Word had always talked to his mother's mind the way he began to do in Johnny's on the Roman ship when Johnny had opened his mind and Word could enter it. Johnny could see Mother Mary's left cheek go up in a very weak smile as she looked on the soldiers fondling the robe and hazarding throw upon throw for it. Then both Johnny and herself were drawn back to the crosses by a row breaking out between the two Barabbites, one suddenly turning bitterly on Word to ask why he didn't save himself and them, clearly to mask the shame of Barabbas having left his followers to perish in agony. But then the other said that the two of them were being put to death for good reasons.

'Like what?'

'Like slitting the throats of anyone we liked. Or that we disliked!'

'Provided they were traitors!'

'Everyone was a traitor if their purse was big enough to slit their throat for.'

'Serve them right!'

'As you say, but serve us right too. We dished it out, we must take it. This man did nothing except bring people to life, and cure them, and tell them to live lives to help other people.'

'How do you know that?'

'The same way you know it.'

'Gossip.'

'Well-confirmed reports.'

'No more than that.'

'Yes, there was, and you know that, too. We were counting on his arrest to beg Barabbas off. We got our people in the Temple guards to cry out against this man.'

'And much good it did us.'

'We can't blame him because they all forgot us.'

'And wanted to forget us.'

'They didn't like your bad temper.'

'They didn't like your inconvenient truths.'

'They just didn't like us'

'They'll like us well enough when we're dead.'

'I'd prefer this man now we've found him. Lord, remember me when you come into your kingdom.'

And then Johnny heard Word's voice 'I say truly to you that today you will be with me in Paradise.'

It hit Johnny like a mortal wound. Every particle of reasonable logic he owned told him Word must die, but only now was he forced to admit Word would, and in a matter of hours if not minutes. So he missed the cry of rapture from the truth-teller, and of course he never knew what happened in the mind of the ill-tempered patriot, who responded to the gift of mercy to his mate with a mental snarl, and then the unspoken admission 'Dismas *is* right, he always is, blast him. Well, I'm asking no favours. I'm sorry for abusing this chap and I wish I hadn't. But I'm not saying that' and then in the depths of his own mind he heard the gentle 'you don't need to. If our killers do not know what they do, neither did you.' We can take their communion no farther except to hope Word brought two from Golgotha to Paradise.

But if Word had brought hope amid the uttermost despair on the crosses, he had to face the misery amongst his followers on the ground, many of whom must be tempted to abandon their belief in his relationship to God, however they had seen it. He could be sure of his mother, and also of Johnny who was now learning the meaning of his own promise to follow Word to death and back. So Word thrust his head forward, calling the words 'My God, my God, why hast thou forsaken me?' And immediately Mary Magdalen realised what he was doing and swung all her followers into action for the next words from the Psalm known to some as 21 and to others as 22:

> why are thou so far from helping me, and from the words
> of my roaring?
> O my God, I cry in the daytime, but thou hearest not; and
> in the night season, and am not silent.

Word had done it again, thought Johnny gratefully, smiling through his tears. He had given all of them a chorus to chant together and so to take comfort in their solidarity, and he had chosen one which perfectly prophesied the despair that seemed inevitable at this moment and which would end by declaring hope for the future, all the more comforting since it was part of everyone's memory.

The women's voices rang out, drowning the disputes of the gambling soldiers:

> But thou art holy, O thou that inhabitest the praises
> of Israel.
> Our fathers trusted in thee: they trusted, and thou
> didst deliver them.

They cried unto thee, and were delivered; they
trusted in thee and were not confounded.

Mary Magdalen raised her hand, and the crowd promptly fell silent,
leaving her to cry out alone:

But I am a worm, and no man; a reproach of men,
and despised of the people.

She had been magnificent, thought Johnny, when she had defied the
soldiers with the cry that they faced women who rejoiced in greater
courage than coward men dared to show. She was even greater now, in
the tragic notes proclaiming the psalmist's prophesy that Word (how clear
it was now, at last, that the psalmist had been prophesying Word) would
be made to seem lower than men. The women answered:

All they that see me laugh me to scorn:
they shoot out the lip, they shake the head, saying,
He trusted on the Lord that he would deliver him:
let him deliver him, seeing he delighted in him.

Mary Magdalen raised her hand again, and went on alone:

But thou art he that took me out of the womb: thou
didst make me hope when I was upon my mother's breasts.
I was cast upon thee from the womb: thou art my
God from my mother's belly.

And again the women replied:

Be not far from me; for trouble is near; for there is
none to help.
Many bulls have compassed me: strong bulls of
Bashan have beset me round.
They gaped upon me with their mouths, as a
ravening and a roaring lion.

Instinctively Johnny swung round to look at the soldiers, some of whom were indeed gawping now at Word, now at the women. The centurion so far detached himself from his gambling responsibilities to yell at the women 'SILENCE!', quite uselessly. Mary Magdalen's hand went up once more, but the silence she commanded, successfully as usual, was to clear the air for her solitary voice:

> I am poured out like water, and all my bones are out of joint: my heart is like wax; it is melted in the midst of my bowels.
>
> My strength is dried up like a potsherd; and my tongue cleaveth to my jaws; and thou hast brought me into the dust of death.

The centurion began to yell 'SILENCE!!'once again, and so Johnny joined his thundrous cadences to the chorus of women. It had taken a few minutes for him to recollect the exact words of the psalm, but he had it flowing well now:

> For dogs have compassed me: the assembly of the wicked have inclosed me: they pierced my hands and my feet.
>
> I may tell all my bones: they look and stare upon me.

Automatically Johnny turned back to look on Word, and nearly abandoned his part in the chorus at the sight of some of Word's bones actually partly visible through flesh and skin where the whips ending in jagged edges had torn. Johnny's throat seemed to rush into his mouth, but in a miserable gasp be swallowed it back as Mary Magdalen resumed alone:

> They part my garments among them, and cast lots upon my vesture.
>
> But be not thou far from me, O Lord: O my strength, haste thee to help me.

It had made perfect sense to Johnny to think that prophets and psalmists bad spoken in the scriptures about Word, and indeed he thought it so obvious that Matthew's perpetual stitching scriptures to Word's sayings and actions often appeared funny. There was nothing funny about this, but it made Johnny feel that if he hadn't known Word was God and the Messiah long awaited, he would have known it now. The very things meant to degrade Word uplifted him: as he had said, men would lift him up like Moses lifted up the serpent in the desert. Johnny hadn't understood that or spent much time trying to, when he had heard Word say it to Nicodemus, but now he could see it himself, and seeing, came back again and again to his love of Word as Word and as God. He cried out amongst the women's voices:

> Deliver my soul from the sword; my darling from the power of the dog.
> Save me from the lion's mouth: for thou hast heard me from the horns of the unicorns.
> I will declare thy name unto my brethren: in the midst of the congregation will I praise thee.

Mary Magdalen in solitary voice cried to them all:

> Ye that fear the Lord, praise him; all ye the seed of Jacob, glorify him; and fear him, all ye the seed of Israel.
> For he hath not despised nor abhorred the affliction of the afflicted; neither hath he hid his face from him; but when he cried unto him, he heard.
> My praise shall be of thee in the great congregation: I will pay my vows before them that fear him.

And now for the first time Johnny saw Mother Mary and Miriam and his own mother Salome add their voices:

> The meek shall eat and be satisfied: they shall praise the Lord that seek him: your heart shall live for ever.
> All the ends of the world shall remember and turn unto the Lord: and all the kindreds of the nations shall worship before thee.

385

For the kingdom is the Lord's: and he is the governor among the nations.

All they that be fat upon earth shall eat and worship: all they that go down to the dust shall bow before him: and none can keep alive his own soul.

A seed shall serve him; it shall be accounted to the Lord for a generation.

They shall come, and shall declare his righteousness unto a people that shall be born, that he hath done this.

And every chanter raised their right hand to salute Word.

A loud cry of exultation came from the centurion, who had returned to the dice and won Word's robe.

WENTY

DADDY-JOE

Which were born, not of blood, nor of the will of the flesh,
nor of the will of man, but of God

Word would be dead very soon: even Johnny knew that now. His breath was becoming harder and harder to draw. Johnny's mind no longer recorded thoughts from Word's. Johnny himself almost wept in sheer agonising as to whether it was more selfish to want Word to live with all his suffering, or to want him to die so that his ordeal and therefore everyone else's would have an end. It was only one of a thousand causes for Johnny to weep, yet he managed to keep almost dry-eyed for the sake of his mother, and Mother Mary, and Miriam. Word was now drawing up his knees as far as he could, in a last effort at speech. It was now that he managed to get out the verb 'I thirst', and it was Shimon of Cyrene who took a sponge, filled it with vinegar belonging to one of the women, found a straw or reed growing on the verge of the plateau, stuck it in the sponge, and hurried across to Word, leaning on Word's cross so he could stand on his toes and put the reed to Word's lips. It gave Word just enough additional strength through the shock of the vinegar's bitterness, and Word drew his head down again over his lacerated neck. As though on a signal, his mother looked up into his dying eyes. Johnny, unprompted, found himself moving beside her.

'Woman!' Why did Word address his Mother like that? Then the next words 'See – your – son' and as if moved by a silent instruction from his mind to hers, Mother Mary swung round to Johnny and threw her arms round him. Then Johnny knew the next command was to him:

'See – your – mother', and into his mind came 'she will be to you what I was', and so Johnny knew why Word said 'woman', for she was to be his parent – suddenly Johnny thought of the word 'god-parent' or perhaps Word put it in his mind, wordlessly in so many senses. Salome kissed them both, and Johnny hugged the two women back. All knew Salome was as much Johnny's mother as always, and that Mother Mary would strengthen the love of Salome and Johnny, as Word had done. It occurred to Johnny touchingly if absurdly, that as son of Salome and Mary he must take them to his house, since that was what Word had agreed they would call Nicodemus's studio. It was so like Word to make the most dreadful moment of Johnny's life the most wonderful, dying himself to give Johnny to Mother Mary and her to Johnny with his next to last breath. For some reason Johnny wanted to think of it as an unassisted breath, and ever afterwards imagined Word's cry of thirst had taken place after and not before that giving. But it was not so, and the moment of giving was followed by Word's almost inaudible 'It is finished', and the dear, beloved head slumped forward. Yet Johnny's mind recorded one last message from Word, almost resting there for a breath before going on its journey forth: 'Father, into your hands I commend my spirit.'

It was long afterwards that Johnny was told how at that moment the veil of the temple was rent from top to bottom. Annas, who saw it, sank on his knees. Caiaphas, who was told of it, said that the material had evidently been of inferior quality, and that he would hold the Temple spinners severely to account. But they and everyone else had other concerns. The sun vanished. But nothing came in its place. Throughout the previous night Johnny had been faintly irritated by the gorgeous silver circle of the moon, bathing in its enchanted silver radiance the horrors of Word's suffering and arrest in the garden of Gethsemane, and all that had followed until daybreak. Now the moon might have been plucked from the sky, and every single star whipped away as though (thought Johnny with a lunatic savagery) the stars were God's daisy-chain. Behind him, Johnny could hear the centurion yelling for a light, which nobody could provide. The man's fury increased, a fury whipped up by fear, culminating in a wordless 'Aw-w-w!' and a bitter yell 'In truth this must have been the son of God!' though Johnny never found out whether this was indeed a profession of faith or the ultimate in contemptuous and disgusted sarcasm. Johnny had no time to think about it. He could still descry the living Barabbites on their crosses, and the dead Word in front of his own eyes, and at his arms' length Mother Mary, and Miriam, and Salome, and beyond them Shimon of Cyrene, and –. Something or someone was coming closer and closer, although no trace of a shadowy form was visible. Something had come between Mother Mary and the others, something that blocked off parts of her shape. And then to Jonny's utter amazement, Mother Mary began to laugh, a rich, powerful, profound laugh, far too sane for her amazed hearers to put down to her sufferings having driven her mad. Salome said quickly 'Mary, what –?' And Mary replied 'Sally! Johnny! Miriam! Mary of Magdala! He's won! He's won! My son is victorious! He has vanquished sin, and the adversary is thrown down, and death must die!' And Salome said 'How do you know?' And Mary answered 'Because my husband has come to tell me. Thanks be to God, it's Daddy-Joe, come to bring us the news that the struggle is over and my son is the conqueror.' And Johnny suddenly knew the meaning of 'It is finished'.

Johnny knew little of what followed, for with Mary's declaration of victory the inhuman strength that had kept him going snapped, and he fell forward, more or less asleep. Daddy-Joe reached him before he fell, caught him and held him sleeping in his arms. It should have been very cold with no sunlight, but warmth seemed to radiate from Daddy-Joe, although nobody except Mary ever saw him. Later, when Mary was telling Johnny about it, she reflected that it must have turned on dead people being brought to those they had most loved, while entering Heaven to which Word's death had admitted them. They never heard of anyone else being visited by a dead beloved one, although there were stories of dead people being seen at that time. People kept quiet about specific instances known to themselves, and Matthew, while carefully noting the existence of such stories, was silent about his own experience, which was a joyful visitation from his parents somewhat marred by the realisation they brought him that he should not have run away. But they simply told him to be ashamed but not afraid and go back to Word's people. Shimon Peter was implacable afterwards in accusing himself of cowardice, and making sure every account of Word's life that was written included Peter's boast to Word and his betrayal before the cock crew. But he never said that the person who made him take his remorse to Word's mother was Peter's own dead wife. Not even Johnny was prepared to include Daddy-Joe's return in what he wrote and dictated about Word: it was Mary's privilege, and he would not intrude himself in it, even if he had slept in Daddy-Joe's arms without ever seeing him.

It was not until the light returned and the Seder was being eaten in most households, that Johnny awoke to find many of the women gone, and his mothers, as he now thought of them both, sitting on either side of him with Miriam and Mary Magdalen huddled together just beyond them. None of them felt cold, although the soldiers had complained of it. Straight in front of them was the dead, lacerated body of Word, still torn open by wounds, and marked with blood from head to heel (although his back was much more brutally injured): yet Word's face gazed at them with a wonderful serenity, as though he was about to greet them. Johnny realised that he had been awakened by the sound of military footsteps, exchange of passwords and the clash of feet in salutation. He slowly pulled himself upward as he made out the Latin speech of the soldiers, half-looking at Word to correct his mental translation where it might be faulty.

'OK, we get them off the gibbets.'

'Smartish.'

'Smartish.'

'Anyone know why?'

'They're irreligious.'

'Well, that's why they said they wanted them killed, wannit?'

'They're irreligious to be before the public gaze on a holy day.'

'Wot's an 'oly day?'

'This is.'

'You coulda fooled me.'

'Why does Pilate give a brass monkey for a Jew's holy day?'

''E's very solicitous when it doesn't matter and doesn't mean work for 'imself.'

'I'm new on this job. How do we go?'

'Well, you want your body dead, by way of a start.'

'You get your body dead by brikin' its legs.'

'Wot good does that do?'

'Well, the way they stays alive on these crosses is raisin' their legs an' pumpin' air into thesselves.'

'So if your legs is broke you can't pump no air, see?'

'So let's 'ave a look.   Let's take the middle lad first, proper treatment, 'e's king of the Jews, give 'im royal precedence.'

'Well, you can't, 'cos he's dead, see?'

Johnny and the four women moved a little back, and the soldiers on duty came up to Word, gaping.

"S right, 'e's 'ad it.'

'Best be sure.'

'OK, up with the spear. Nice and straight, get it right in, near the heart as you can get, IN!'

And out from where the spear had entered Word came blood and water showing be was already dead. Johnny felt as if he was about to vomit, but he had had no food for many hours, and now he simply but noisily retched and heaved. Miriam was little better. Mary said 'Thank God that was one pain he never felt'. They turned away from where the soldiers were breaking the legs of the Barabbites, but the screaming followed them. Then two figures came up, and to Johnny's amazement one was Nicodemus, who by rights should have been digesting the Passover Seder, and remaining in seclusion for the ensuing Sabbath, He walked up to Johnny, who said 'Mother Mary, this is Nicodemus, who owns my house; to which I shall be taking you', and left them to make sense of it as best they might. Salome knew the grief behind the sickness and confusion, and took him in her arms, and now Johnny really wept. He set Miriam off, and Mary Magdalen embraced her, more awkwardly, but with the warmth and comfort so urgently needed. Miriam said later that she had never felt so bad since she was dead, but she liked Mary Magdalen.

Johnny remembered the Passover meal he had not eaten, whose questions he would have asked if he had had it, and how the Lord had told Moses and Aaron that no bone of the Paschal Lamb must be broken. Word had told them they had eaten his flesh and drunk his blood on the night he was betrayed, and that they must eat and drink them again in memory of him, and now Johnny could see that Word had himself become the Lamb to be sacrificed with none of his bones broken. It was as though Word himself were the coping-stone of what it meant to be a Jew, all the more fitting because he himself was God.

But now Johnny was slowly coming to listen to the outside world again, from which he had thankfully taken refuge in Salome's arms. Dimly he could hear Nicodemus's companion talking rather self-importantly to Mother Mary:

'So that you understand it was simply an investment in case of emergency. No disrespect to your son, of course, ahem, I would hardly be doing this and breaking the great Sabbath to do it if I didn't respect him, would I?, but what with house-prices climbing in Jerusalem, everybody wanting to live in the district Caiaphas has made fashionable, bit risky at the time, I remember thinking, doesn't mean he's going to make a go of it just because he is High Priest, after all he was appointed by the Romans, no getting away from that however long he was in power, and what the Romans give, the Romans can take away, but it worked, I will say for Caiaphas he made it work, people are flocking to the place now, beginning with his brothers-in-law the sons of Annas, not that Annas would move his dwelling by so much as a cubit, says he's too old a dog to learn new ways, and Caiaphas said he oughtn't to be calling himself a dog, by doing so he was risking disrespect being brought on the office of the High Priest, by dogs one rightly meant Samaritans, and Gentiles, and Annas said he was too old to learn any better, in any case more and more properties are being bought up and the recent rumour that Pontius Pilate is going to live here for half the year sent properties going sky-high around the Praetorium as well, and all that meant there was less room for people to be buried in and so I decided to lash out on a grave for myself, after all I'm in perfectly good health as you can see, putting on a little weight maybe, no point in pretending I'm not, you can see it for yourself, and nobody's getting any younger though from the way they dress themselves and disport themselves they seem to think they can fool anyone I always say that to a shepherd who knows sheep mutton isn't lamb and never will be but there you are, but if I live out my time threescore years and ten as we all know except when it isn't like your Son ma'am sorry about that so I'll have plenty of time to choose a better grave, this one is far too near the place of the Skull for any comfort, but I worried about being squeezed out if the property boom went on, I dare say it'll be clear soon that Pilate won't live longer than he can help in Jerusalem, can't stand Jews, you can see it in his eyes, wrong of me I know but I always enjoy dragging out a conversation with him to have the fun of watching him trying to conclude it so I throw in a few compliments to Tiberius, nasty old creature, there's a dog if you like, and fleas of a kind I won't mention in front of you ladies and the child what's it doing there of course you ladies know your own business best some kind of relative was he? well of course you can't learn too young and it's hard for you all... ' and suddenly to Johnny's amazement Nicodemus's friend cut off his ludicrous cascade of conventionalities and sobbed aloud, waving his hands and wringing them. Mary put her hand on his shoulder, and he slowly dried for as much as two minutes clearly in genuine grief and not simply a mark of respect, though Johnny felt that for him to shut off his eloquence must be a very considerable mark. It was only later Johnny realised that the conversational torrent was hysteria. What do you say to the mother of God whose son has just been crucified and then has died before her eyes?

And what do you not say? Mary went to the heart of what the man was not saying. 'What you are doing surpasses all bounds of human charity, sir. The Temple, the Empire and the world will unite in condemning my son as accursed of God, consigned to the worst death appropriately followed by the vilest burial. You give him your own tomb, just as Nicodemus here lent him his own house. You open your grave as publicly as if you opened your arms to him in the Temple itself when all men spurn him, torture him and turn away from him. Whence are you?' And the man said, very direct now, and uncluttered in his talk: 'I am from Arimathea, lady.' And Mary said: 'a place sanctified by the prophet Shmuel's dying there. And what is your name?' And the man said 'Joseph, lady'. And Mary said: 'your name will be second only to my late husband among those of the name of Joseph revered among future people for their love of my son. And what drew you to my son?' Joseph answered: 'His integrity under trial before the high priests. I became his disciple, but he never knew.' Mary smiled:

'He knew all right. I thank you in his name as well as mine. Bring him down and take him to the tomb. It may be that he will not use it long.'

All of them, including Johnny, made little sense of her last sentence, but he felt it to ring in harmony with things Word had said, such as rebuilding the temple within three days if it were to be destroyed.

Mary was now in command as naturally as Word used to be. She pointed out to the centurion that Joseph and Nicodemus had gained the permission of Pontius Pilate for burial of her son, once Joseph had got that out of himself. The soldiers found themselves bringing ladders and swarming up the cross, and between them Shimon and Joseph and Nicodemus helped take Word's body down. Once it lay on the ground, his mother dropped on her knees and kissed the dead lips, and so did Johnny, and Salome, and Miriam, and Mary Magdalen. Nobody thought of proprieties. Nicodemus with an artist's foresight had brought myrrh and aloes, and was indeed staggering under their weight, since he had brought nigh on a hundred pounds of them, as befitted a king. The production of myrrh proved the one point when Mary herself nearly broke down: Johnny asked her about it when they were alone, and she explained that it took her back to the visit of the *Magi* just after Word's birth, one bringing gold for his kingship, one frankincense for his godhead, and the third myrrh for his death. For the first time she knew in her body what would happen, although God's messenger had warned her: she first felt as though a sword had entered her heart and, as she said to Johnny and Salome, it was a life story from heart to heart, from a spiritual sword-wound, to an actual spear-thrust. But she quickly recovered at Golgotha, and helped Nicodemus prepare Word in grave-clothes as she had initially laid Word out in swaddling-clothes. Shimon, Joseph, Nicodemus and Johnny carried Word to the tomb, Mary, Salome, Mary Magdalen, Miriam and other women still remaining followed. When they had laid him in the tomb, Mary asked Johnny to recite the prayer Word had taught him, and for the first time in history a funeral stood around a corpse speaking the Lord's Prayer. Johnny spoke each line, and the others repeated it, until the conclusion. Then Mary asked Johnny to speak the words of blessing with which Word so often began his talks to crowds, and Johnny once more spoke each line to be repeated by the others:

> Blessed are the poor in spirit: for theirs is the kingdom of Heaven.
> Blessed are they that mourn: for they shall be comforted.
> Blessed are the meek: for they shall inherit the earth.
> Blessed are they which do hunger and thirst after righteousness: for
>   they shall be filled.
> Blessed are the merciful: for they shall obtain mercy.
> Blessed are the pure in heart: for they shall see God.

> Blessed are the peacemakers: for they shall be called the children of God.
>
> Blessed are they which are persecuted for righteousness's sake: for theirs is the kingdom of heaven.
>
> Blessed are ye, when men shall revile you, and persecute you, and shall say all manner of evil against you falsely for my sake.
>
> Rejoice, and be exceeding glad: for great is your reward in heaven: for so persecuted they the prophets which were before you.

'He died the most degraded death known to the men of his time', said Mary. 'Let us now gird ourselves with the sign of that death, to proclaim our gratitude to him with pride.' And after her example, they all placed right-hand fingers on forehead, then on breast, then on each shoulder, then folding hands.

Mary smiled on them all. 'In his name, and in my own, I thank you. He died for us. Let us live for him.' And all answered: 'Amen'. Then Mary turned back to the centurion, who had come up during these proceedings and, surprisingly, remained silent until they were finished. 'Yes?'

'Governor's orders, ma'am. This tomb is to be sealed up with a stone, and Temple Guards placed in front of it so that nobody can steal the body and say it has been brought to life again, as deceased allegedly threatened.' The embalmers had already finished.

'Very well', said Mary quietly. 'We have done what we ought to do, and now will withdraw.' As they departed, they saw a huge stone being rolled towards the entrance to the tomb, but they walked rapidly back to the city without looking at it further.

Their footsteps first traversed the path of blood made by Word on his way to Golgotha. They did not look for traces, but saw a few. Johnny told everything he had seen from the time of their arrival in Jerusalem, but only Mary, Salome, and Miriam would have heard it all, with no more room to walk abreast.

A group of sour-looking Temple Guards were making their way towards Golgotha just as they re-entered the city. Then Mary stopped and spoke to her companions.

'Nicodemus', she asked, 'is it with your blessing that Johnny and I, and Johnny's mother Salome, go back to your studio?'

'I shall be proud and happy if you would, ma'am', answered Nicodemus. Mary Magdalen said she would go back to the tomb in thirty-six hours' time, after the Sabbath. Mary kissed her warmly, and was turning away, when she stopped, tapped her foot on the ground for a moment, and then turned back, looking directly at Mary Magdalen and said: 'come back to where we rest afterwards, and –'

'– and what, Mother?'

Mary hugged her in response to the compliment, so genuine and so automatic. 'Do not be frightened at anything. My son would want me to tell you that all will be well. Come with us now, and see where we stay.' So they took leave of Shimon, Joseph and the other women, and Mary Magdalen walked with them to the studio, and then Nicodemus escorted her to the place where she was staying.

As soon as they were inside the door, Mary, Salome and Miriam took off their outer garments and started to clean the place, leaving Johnny as usual bemused at women's ability to discover dirt where men thought everything was all right. He wanted to help, but all three of them told him firmly to go to bed, Miriam the loudest. But when he had kissed them goodnight, Mary stopped him for a moment. She gestured to the other two to sit down, took bold of the back of a chair and said:

'Johnny, things may happen suddenly, and people arrive here unexpectedly, Sabbath or no Sabbath. Above all, your brothers –'

'James is my only brother', worried Johnny, confused.

'The others are also your brothers', Salome interjected quickly.

'And my son's brothers', added Mary.

'And Mary Magdalen and I are your sisters', Miriam capped them.

'Be it so', replied Johnny, bewildered but obedient.

'So my son said of you when he gave you and me to one another', nodded Mary. 'I know you are special, and you showed it by standing by him. But we don't want to tell them that.'

'They will be very much ashamed of themselves when they come back here, or go to the tomb, or congregate at the Temple, or the garden, or Mount Olivet.' Salome opened her hands and waved their palms upward.

'They will want my forgiveness', and Mary smiled, wanly. 'And of course they must get it.'

'But it will be impossible for them to return to brotherhood if they know that you, a boy, were true to your Word when they all ran away', and Salome's face was dark with sorrow.

'James didn't run away', rapped Johnny quickly. 'He was looking for me while I hid in the tree at Gethsemane.'

'You are a good brother', agreed Salome, 'and James is a good brother to you. But – well, the best thing is to say, whatever the reason, he never came back. But he will come back. And he is the one exception. We will conceal nothing from him. He is big enough to take it, and to face death when his turn comes.'

'He wouldn't have been afraid', urged Johnny, hardly realising he was saying the rest of them were.

'I agree, Johnny', and Salome smiled, even more wanly than Mary. 'But James, as I hardly need to tell you, is naturally very respectable.'

'And this was the death destitute of all respect', and Mary choked for a moment. Salome patted her hand.

'Remember', pronounced Miriam solemnly, 'he's only a man. You can't expect anything else.' Johnny thought it as well to say nothing, especially since both his mothers were grinning as tactfully as they could.

'We tell James', dictated Salome. 'And we tell him to tell nobody else. Of course you will be very understanding with him when he asks you about what happened, and you will tell him everything.'

'Never tell anyone else you were there', and Mary shuddered involuntarily. 'Never until all the rest are dead. My son – ' she corrected herself with a little laugh' – my *other* son – I will only have two, even if the rest of you are brothers, but I may be more successful as a stepmother this time, as far as the rest of them are concerned – my son has told you he wants you to testify to what you saw and heard when you were with him, where others have not spoken, or spoken fully accurately. So when all the rest are dead, and only then, tell your story.'

'I wrote some of it for Word as a Greek exercise', hesitated Johnny.

'Keep that', decided Mary, 'but don't tell any of the others about it, not even James. I'd like to see it, of course, and when I do you and I and Sally will talk about what you will say when the time arrives to say it.'

'But you must *never* say I was Mary of Cleophas', insisted Miriam, to the gratification of Mary and Salome, whose smiles were better controlled this time.

'What about Peter?' asked Johnny. 'He was with me as far as the house of Annas. I don't know what happened to him afterwards.'

'Peter?' asked Mary, momentarily fogged.

'Shimon bar-Jonah', explained Salome.

'Oh, yes, of course', recollected Mary.

Miriam looked grim. 'Well, he didn't follow the trail either, so it's pretty clear what happened to him. The whole thing must have been getting frightening by that stage.'

'No, it wasn't', said Johnny. 'I wasn't afraid, and I've often been afraid.'

Mary ran her hand through his hair. 'You were carried by your love of my son and his love for you. That would carry anyone anywhere, if they had only the sense to know it.' Johnny nodded. He wanted to cry, but he held it back. Other eyes were watering as well.

'And now go to bed', ordered Miriam, 'and leave us women to get on with the house-cleaning', and Johnny kissed them quickly, and then went to the room he had shared with Word. That really did set him off weeping. But he pulled himself together by praying to Word 'wherever you are now'. The prayer he uttered was in fact a memory of his last walk with Word on their way to Gethsemane:

'Dear Word, you are the true vine, and your Father is the vine-dresser. Every branch in you that bears not fruit, he will take away, but let not those who failed to follow you at the Garden or at the house of Annas be held to account for it, for they all love you and will want to have followed you. So let us welcome them back and let them show themselves branches bearing fruit. All of them, dearest Word, James and Shimon Peter and Andrew and Philip and Nathaniel and Thomas and Matthew and Jim and Thady and Shimon.' He stopped, and a terrible shivering convulsed him. For a moment he thought he was going to vomit, but he held himself together. Like the women, he had nibbled figs and dates while talking. He did not mention Judas, as he knew Word would never want him to ask for the damnation of another person. He would have liked to curse Judas. But another thought entered his mind. 'And give Annas a chance to bear good fruit, Word. And you told the others they were clean, even though they went away afterwards. May we all abide in you, as you said, for without you we can do nothing.' Here he really gave way.

But when Mary and Salome looked into the room he was asleep, and they did not bring a light lest they waken him, and so did not see the furrows made by many tears down the brown cheeks. He sighed in his sleep, a sound of sorrow, but he did not groan, or show any sign of waking. The women waited for a moment or two, but it seemed a healthy sleep, likely to do him good. They went back out, closing the door very quietly behind them, and Johnny did not waken until the Sabbath was far advanced. Mary and Salome had not disturbed him when saying morning prayers, but he had prayed himself to Word before they came out. Since he believed Word to be God, Word must be able to hear prayers regardless of having died, and although Johnny could no longer hear Word speaking in his own mind, Word would hear his love in Word's mind, whatever and wherever that might be. Johnny remembered that he must keep his mind open to Word by assurances of love so that Word would be able to communicate with him when it would be possible and right to do so. Johnny remembered how on the last night as they walked from supper to the garden, Word had spoken his own commandment, that the disciples love one another as he had loved them, and he realised that Word had spoken of his love as what had been, their mutual love as what would be, and should be. Now it was for Johnny to show each one of the disciples that he still loved them, even if they had turned away from Word in the stress of flight.

His first sense of resuming contact with Word happened when he walked from what they had made a bedroom into the main room, and for a second he thought he saw Word's face in the light. Then he realised it was Mary at whom he was staring. Salome was looking closely at him, saw the lips parted and eyes shining in ecstatic unbelief, and then the cloud of knowing supervened. But he quickly hurried over to them, threw an arm around each neck, and kissed the lips of each. They were about to draw his attention to the fruit on the table when he startled them by saying 'None of the others shown up yet?' Salome shrugged 'Nicodemus said he wouldn't trouble us on the Sabbath' but Mary saw another meaning: 'None of the other eleven, yet.' 'The ten', warned Johnny, quickly, and Mary nodded 'The ten'. The next moment Miriam, once more veiled in outdoor costume, came in through the front door, and said: 'Shimon Peter is on the road towards us, and he's reeling like a drunken man', and Mary said quickly 'go into Johnny's room, both of you, leave the door slightly open, and don't come in until he has reached some kind of peace within himself – and, I suppose, with me', and they were in the bedroom before Mary had opened the front door. She stepped out into the roadway in front of Peter, who let out a yell which drew Sabbath observers to their windows in indignant protest. Mary grabbed Peter by the right wrist, and drew him into the studio where he seemed partly relieved and partly confused to see Salome.

But this opened up a fresh guilt within him, and he promptly stammered 'Where is your son?', sending Mary white with pain before she realised he was addressing Salome. Salome recognised that unless this line of investigation were disposed of, they were in for appalling confusions and concealments, so having exchanged a quick look with Mary, she called 'come in here!' and Johnny and Miriam entered. Mary took in Miriam's covering and murmured to Peter 'you know my sister?' which was specific enough to nominate Mary of Cleophas and vague enough to embrace the hidden Miriam, who bowed stiffly. But Johnny ran over to Peter, put his arms around his neck, and kissed him, and with a glance of gratitude to Johnny Mary followed, kissing Peter also. Of course Peter promptly bawled 'Away from me, all of you, I am unworthy to be admitted to decent society! I have betrayed your son!' he glared at Mary.

'So have we all', said Johnny, promptly, and Mary's eyes shone. Johnny thought of James's and his own dreadful conduct in calling for fire and brimstone on the unwelcoming Samarian city, and Word's anger at it, and knew that to be his betrayal of Word, but naturally Peter thought he meant some turning away from Word on his own part yesterday or the day before. Not that Peter had the slightest intention of taking refuge from his own betrayal by hiding behind Johnny's guilt, whatever it might be. But he whirled round on Johnny:

'That girl at the door wanted to make me out as one of the Master's disciples, and I said no, and then she whispered to some soldier or guard whom she was ogling and he asked, and I said no, and then –' he fell on the ground before Mary and would have rubbed his forehead in the dust if Mary, Salome, and Miriam had left any dust there '– then a cousin of the servant of the high priest whose ear I had cut off –'

'You cut off the high priest's ear!' Mary hazarded, dizzily: she was expecting Peter's repentance, and had anticipated what it would be for, but this additional self-accusation was unexpected. Salome was also bemused, and looked with anxiety at Johnny: if this was rumoured around, he might be in danger as an accomplice and would certainly be outlawed from the Temple. Miriam took a more cheerful view:

'Well, Caiaphas was never going to listen to anyone else, anyway, being a man.' Johnny sneaked a useless sidelong glance at her: if she kept this up, Mary of Cleophas (if any) would have quite a reputation to live down.

'Oh, no', insisted Peter, shocked. 'It was only his servant's ear.'

'Word healed it', explained Johnny.

'My son, my son' murmured Mary.

'And his cousin said I had cut off the ear and I said I was damned if I knew the Master. And damned I am!' and he burst into horrible, lacerating, heaving sobs.

'You are not!' thundered Mary, who had risen above him. 'I absolve you in the name of my Son and of his Father.' And she made the sign of the cross in the air above Peter's grovelling form. Peter sat up and gaped.

'*You* absolve me!' he said, with his usual tact. 'You – a woman.'

'And who is better to absolve you of your sin against him than his own mother?' demanded Miriam, unanswerably.

'She has to forgive me too', added Johnny, helpfully if vaguely.

'And that will take her all her time', added Salome, pulling Johnny's ear. 'I should know.'

Peter raised his streaming eyes to Mary's face, and was clearly as dazzled as Johnny had been a few moments before: the forgiveness that shone there could have been in Word's face. He held out his huge hand and drew her smaller one to his lips. She smiled at him.

'Peter, if my son were here, he would only ask that you love him.'

'And I do!' stammered poor Peter, beginning to weep afresh. Mary dried his eyes on a kerchief, raised his head and kissed his forehead. He scrambled to his feet.

'I don't know anything that happened after that', he gasped. 'What did you do, Johnny?'

Johnny, taking himself to be licensed for once to invent stories, drew a deep breath. He used to be quite a proficient liar before he met Word, especially when he needed to wriggle his way out of some just indignation of James. Then Salome caught his eye, and he exhaled the breath and took another, milder one. He would have to keep his story as near to fact as possible. He would have liked to have shown Miriam how impressive a liar he could be, while knowing that her only spoken reaction would be to proclaim all men (except Word) as liars and what was the point in boasting about it? It was not to be. 'I got into the tribunal', he explained, 'but they stopped it and went on to Caiaphas's. I managed to tag along, but when they finished there and went on to the Roman praetorium, I was frightened of the soldiers.' So he had been.

Peter took a deep breath. 'So you ran away. Well, nobody will hold that against you. Why, you held out much longer than I did!' And he looked at Johnny with amazement. Johnny wouldn't have minded having a spurious reputation for being braver than Peter, since he could not have, and did not want, the genuine reputation he deserved. But there must be not the slightest suspicion of his having put any other disciple to shame, apart from the one he hated.

'It was nothing, it was really nothing. The old high priest, Annas, whose house it was, had said I could go there at any time, so I was never in any danger. You were, all the time, so you were heaps braver than I was, in going in there', and Johnny's brown eyes looked up at Peter's. It took Peter a moment or two to assimilate, then he shook his head and said 'I suppose you're right. But I should have stuck it out. I didn't.' Then his momentary return of spirit abandoned him, and he said: 'I couldn't live with myself if it hadn't been for what Mother Mary said now.'

'Well, she said it', replied Mary firmly. 'Now you're back with us, so sit down and have some fruit.'

Peter kissed her hand again, and she pressed his head to her breast, and made him sit down. Then he turned to Johnny: 'What did happen at those hearings before the high priests, anyway?'

Johnny told him, and then said: 'There's one thing I didn't think of at the time. They kept on saying the case against Word had been made, and was unanswerable, but for all that, they seemed to be waiting for someone or something who never arrived. I wonder what it was.' It would take him some seventy years to find out, but a strange light dawned in Mary's eyes.

They spent the rest of the day talking, and praying, and the women wanted Johnny and Peter to tell them of their lives with Word. Johnny noticed that what he had to say interested them all, but he quickly confirmed his belief that Word's mind kept Mary in perpetual touch until his death. Mary did not say that she already knew things, but her way of putting questions made it clear to him (though not to Peter) that she did, and she said so when he asked at one point with the two of them alone. Salome had not known of Johnny's exact adventures when he was kidnapped, and hugged him very hard when he first spoke of it, as though she could never let him out of her sight again. Peter was about to tell of Judas's self-sacrifice in trying to prevent Johnny's abduction, but Johnny kicked him enough so that he remembered Johnny's fury about Judas after Peter caught up with him between Gethsemane and the house of Annas. Miriam saw that something was being suppressed, and first intended to tease it out of Johnny, but a look at his set, hard face and glittering eyes changed her mind: she did not like him to grow old in front of her. They all roared with laughter about the dolphins, and Peter had to be discouraged from starting a mission to them. Many years after, when Paul had been speaking somewhat contemptuously of Peter to Johnny, and saying how much slower Peter had been than him, Paul, in seeing the need to welcome the Gentiles, Johnny remembered Peter's wish to evangelise the dolphins, and told Paul of it, adding that of course Word had converted at least two dolphins already. Paul's recovery of speech was not assisted by Johnny's kind reflection that his portfolio would be greatly enhanced by an Epistle to the Dolphins, although it was only fair to warn him that the Dolphins were likely to reply, and it wouldn't be rubbish like 'Great is Artemis of the Ephesians', either.

Peter had been tramping the streets of Jerusalem all night and all day and much of the next night and needed to get to sleep early. When he had gone to bed, Johnny remembered how just before they reached the garden of Gethsemane, all the eleven had told they all believed he knew all things, and came from God (Johnny had of course added in his mind for Word's benefit that Word was God). Word had then told them that every man of them would be scattered, leaving him alone ("man" nodded Miriam, 'not "woman", and not "child"', she added kindly). But Word had added that he had spoken these things to them so that in him they would have peace while in the world they would have oppression, but to rejoice because, Johnny remembered Word exactly, 'I have conquered the world'. 'And that was just before he led us into the garden from which he was brought away as a prisoner.' They said nothing for a space. 'Well, he was right in saying he had conquered it', said Mary.

The next day Mary Magdalen arrived early to go up to Word's tomb. Peter was still asleep, and Mary said Johnny must wait until Peter was awake because he needed Johnny's moral support. Salome and Miriam went off with Mary Magdalen. Nicodemus came to the studio to bring them food, and also made some sketches, one of which Johnny was slightly shocked to realise was an impression of Word on the cross. In fairness to Nicodemus, he kept it away from Mary's eyes, but had realised that very little could be kept from Johnny's. They prayed and ate together when Peter had woken up, and then were brought to their feet when Mary Magdalen, Salome and Miriam came practically flying from the tomb, to announce the stone had been rolled away, and the guards were nowhere in sight, and they had been told by a young man in a long white garment not to be afraid because Word had risen, and of course the young man had terrified the three of them since they had never seen anything quite like him. Johnny looked at Mary and saw her eyes were like stars, and her lips were parted in a great smile, as though she were welcoming the universe, but all she said was 'Johnny, let you and Peter go back to the tomb with Mary. Sally and Miriam, you may as well stay here' and something in her voice brought a flash of recognition from Salome. Miriam muttered something to Johnny about not having been afraid which meant she had been. The three went off.

Mary of Magdala and Peter argued almost all of the way to the tomb. Johnny was silent most of the time. It was clear that Mother Mary was much more delighted than surprised at a report that her son had risen again, and Johnny remembered dimly that she had given a cry of joy just after Word's death, and that the last thing he remembered from then was being held in the arms of someone he could not see, or even feel, and yet in whose keeping he had felt so confident that he had fallen asleep promptly with no misgivings whatsoever, and that Mary had said it was Daddy-Joe. Whatever it was had long gone when Johnny woke up, but Mary could hardly have been wrong. She was too like Word to be wrong, for any length of time anyway. And she had told Johnny's mother and the rest of them that her son had won because only that could have enabled Daddy-Joe to be there. When you thought about it, if Word was going to free all those imprisoned by death, the first one he would go to was the man he had loved more than all other men, his earth-father.

And Johnny remembered that as he plummeted into sleep he had really *liked* whoever or whatever had caught him in his arms. It was a wonderful thing to like someone you only knew when he was dead.

WENTY-ONE

THOMAS

And the Word was made flesh, and dwelt amongst us, (and we beheld his glory, the glory as of the only begotten of the Father), full of grace and truth

Peter was becoming increasingly vehement as they made their way along the route he was following for the first time and Johnny remembered all too well. He kept on telling Mary Magdalen that there must be some mistake, that the stone hadn't been properly sealed or had never been put in place, that there could have been an earthquake or anything – hadn't the weather been extraordinary the previous day with an eclipse of the sun and moon? She pointed out that the eclipse and the earthquake were all the work of God when His son died, as far as the eclipse went, and therefore also when his son returned to life in the case of the earthquake – if it was an earthquake. It was like Peter, thought Johnny, to take as evidence for his case what was probably one of the best arguments against it.

Why was Peter arguing? Well, Peter was of course born to argue as the sparks to fly upward, recalled Johnny in the language of Eliphaz the Themanite to Job about Man being born to trouble. Not that Peter was as wrong as Eliphaz seems to have been: he had been very right in the quickness with which he had seen that Word was God, which hadn't been easy for him, not having the advantage of being a child. But here there seemed to be something very personal in Peter's insistence that Word must still be dead. He had been so happy when Mary had absolved him. And then Johnny got it. He, Johnny, had no difficulty in seeing Mary speak for Word. It made perfect sense that she should. After all, Word had once been part of her body, just as he was part of his father, God. Mary was not God, and would be horrified at the idea of anyone imagining she was. But she had known more of Word's mind for a longer time than anyone else, both when they lived together and when Word's mind talked to hers when they were apart. It simply was not possible to imagine Mary opposing Word's definite decision. But she was quite good as changing his mind before it became definite, Johnny remembered from the wedding-feast at Qana. There was a perfect understanding between those two, and since Word was God as well as human, Mary was his guide when he needed a purely human perspective. They would never disagree.

But Peter had not realised that. And while Johnny was certain Word would endorse everything Mary had done and would do, Peter wasn't. He could not be sure Word would pardon him, as Mary had. So with one part of his mind he was afraid of Word's return. He probably would not admit to anyone that this was really what drove him to argue so violently, but that must be it. Johnny could have made a few points in support of Mary of Magdala but after what his mothers had told him he didn't want to do anything which looked like ganging up on Peter. So he let them argue their way onward and, as Miriam would put it, behaved like a nice little boy. Anyhow he admitted to himself he was not the best person to discuss what Word might have hinted about his rising again, because Johnny had always tried to sweep aside anything that sounded like Word prophesying his own death. He had been in denial of even the possibility of Word dying, almost to the moment he died. So he had seriously tried not to listen to anything like talk of Word rising again. It came back to haunt him now. Even on the night of the supper Peter had made that silly boast about never deserting Word, and Word said something like 'Tonight you will all lose courage over me, for so it has been written, I will smite the shepherd, and the sheep will be scattered.' And wasn't it then that Peter had said he was ready to be killed for Word, and would never lose courage over him, and Word had told him he would disown him before cock-crow? But that followed Word having said something Johnny didn't want to listen to, like 'But I will go before you into Galilee, when I have risen from the dead'. No wonder Peter was afraid of that. The two prophesies – Word's resurrection and Peter's denial – must be interlocked in Peter's mind. Was he dizzily wondering if a risen Word would shame him before everyone in Galilee?

Well, Word would not shame him, nor refuse his repentance. Johnny knew that from what Mary had done, as much as if Word himself had told him. Word would receive the penitent, as he had always received a repentant Johnny and everyone else, and said in story or straight speech that he always would. But it wasn't going to be possible to interrupt Peter and Mary Magdalen to tell Peter that. Peter would be horrified at any such thing. Best go in silence. And then Johnny found an unwanted thought of his own beginning to plague him. If Word forgave the penitent, what if Judas proved penitent? But he couldn't have done. Nicodemus had brought them news of Judas's suicide, and suicide was a final unrepented sin, a last rejection of God. Judas must be damned. Johnny hated thinking about any of this, especially as it brought up moments of Judas's kindness to him, and he suddenly turned on the others interrupting Peter's fifth reiteration to Mary Magdalen that she was only a woman, and shouted 'we're nearly there, race you to the tomb', and took off, which was hardly fair, considering Peter had never seen the place and wasn't likely to have been invited by Joseph of Arimathea (whom he had never met) to view the new tomb he had built for himself. But, fair or not, Johnny ran with all the speed he had shown on the day of the last supper with Peter behind him, then as now. Mary Magdalen, wearing a woman's protective clothing for journeys out of doors, only walked rapidly.

Johnny thought she might be happy enough to be spared immediate necessities of teaching feminism to Peter, who had a genius for fighting over old ground from which he had been driven time after time.

But when Johnny reached the tomb he stopped, saw it was open, bent down and saw linen clothes lying on the ground. And it occurred to him that if Word was inside there, it would be kinder to let Peter go in first, for he needed Word more, whatever he might think. Johnny knew now that nobody, apart from their Mother Mary, loved Word as much as Johnny did, but that was all the more reason to give place and honour to Peter. And up Peter came, grunting and wheezing, and looked uncomprehendingly at Johnny standing outside the entrance, and barged in with what Johnny realised was real courage. Partly to keep up his spirits, Johnny suspected, Peter provided a running commentary – more of a wheezing commentary, felt Johnny, while staying as respectful as he could. Peter sounded something like:

'Nobody here.'

'There are white cloths.'

'More like white clothing.'

'His mother would have put those on him.'

'Not the sort of attention the Roman soldiers give.'

'They hardly look as though they had been on anyone.'

'Not that a corpse wears clothes the way we do.'

'But it might, if it came to life.'

'Those don't look as if anyone in them had come to life.'

'But they do look as if someone folded them, quite neatly.' Then suddenly Peter began to sob:

'Someone who had been taught by his mother to fold clothes neatly.'

'What's this over here?' (Gruffly, trying to disguise his burst of grief.)

'It's a napkin, wrapped round and round, by itself. That would have been on his head. That's what we did for Sara.'

Then Johnny remembered that Peter's wife had been called Sara, and decided he had better enter the tomb himself, before Peter went into mourning on two fronts. Peter looked at him and said 'Well, you see what it looks like'.

Johnny cried: 'He's back. He's done it! He's alive again! Oh, Peter, laugh, dance, sing, it's happened! He's with us once more!'

He capered around the empty tomb doing handsprings and cartwheels. Eventually he ran out of breath, and Mary Magdalen came up. Johnny shouted in his best Son-of-Thunder voice: 'HE'S ALIVE! HE'S WON!! HE'S OURS AGAIN!!!' The yells bounced off the walls echoing horribly through the deserted plateau of Golgotha. 'Oh, Mary, Mary, you were right, he's back, he's with us, he must be with Mother Mary now! I must reach him! Come On!' And he shot out of the tomb, pelting from Golgotha, racing down the hill, arms out, eyes blazing, heart thumping, legs flailing.

Peter looked after him morosely. 'I suppose he's right. That's what it looks like.' Then he turned to Mary of Magdalen and said with simple dignity 'you were right and I was wrong.' Then, to her relief, he laughed: 'I suppose a woman does know best, after all. Well, I'd better go down and take my medicine.'

Mary Magdalen looked at him very tenderly: 'He doesn't use medicine for his miracles. I know.'

'I'll need a special miracle', grunted Peter heavily.

'We all do', said Mary. And then, as Peter, with an awkward gallantry offered his arm (for it was a rocky earth-surface, however few its restraints on Johnny) 'no, you go down to Mary's house. I want to stay here for the moment.' Peter looked at her uncomprehendingly and then began to lurch out of the tomb and down the path Johnny had taken. But he did not follow Johnny all the way home. He went looking for some other disciple with whom he could come to greet Word, someone who had run away even earlier than he had. Mary watched him go, and then turned back to the tomb, which she suspected had more secrets to yield than had been seen by either Johnny or Peter.

She may have been right, but it's not clear whether she saw young men in white at this point, as well as on her earlier visit. Johnny, discussing it with her some time later, was sure she meant now, despite his having seen nobody in the tomb when he was there, apart from Peter and Mary Magdalen herself when she caught up with them. If Mary did see the white robed man again, single or accompanied, he was not much more helpful than he had been on previous appearance, since he would only ask, why was she weeping? Now she returned to tears, perhaps in reaction to Johnny's wild joy and Peter's morose capitulation. In fact, she had been more logical than either: the single concrete fact was that Word's body was gone, and apart from these unearthly figures whom now you saw and now you didn't, was there more to know than that the body had been taken away? Anyhow, whether she saw at this point anyone in the tomb or not, she turned away from it and confronted a human being with relief, since he seemed neither an indeterminately present and numbered angel, nor a hysterically joyful or sorrowful disciple, just a gardener.

But she was so far gone in her weeping that she could no longer see faces clearly, nor even know voices familiar to her, and, hearing what was in fact the answer to her prayers – 'Woman, why weep? Whom do you seek?', which was to say, her sorrow and search were over – she sobbed unknowingly 'If you have removed him, tell me, where, and I will give him suitable resting-place'. Word said very gently 'Mary!'

Mary of Magdala felt her head swimming, but at last she knew her anxieties were over, and grabbed Word with frenzied joy, her arms nearly encircling him and leaving him no means of moving his own. 'Teacher from God!' she cried, half-falling on her knees, thus holding him even more inextricably. And he smiled: 'Don't imprison me! I have not yet begun my journey back to my Father. But go to our brothers and say I am going on that journey to my Father and your Father, to my God and your God.' His voice was even sweeter and softer than she remembered it, and its laughter was even more delightfully infectious. That was as much as Mary Magdalen would tell Johnny about that talk. In fact, Word told her much about what would happen in the future, and how essential would be the wisdom of women to counter the folly of men. Or it may have been that she heard this from him at a later meeting. For while she did make her way down to the city and found some of the disciples, one already needed no telling. Johnny had come down to the house of Nicodemus without mishap though at much greater speed even than that shown by Mary Magdalen, Salome and Miriam, and when he staggered in, met Mother Mary at the door grinning at him as though she were the age of Miriam: 'we have a visitor!' He needed no telling who it was, but when inside the house and looking at the man before him free from all wounds, scars, suffering; Johnny could get out only a rapturous 'Word!', exactly as when they first met, for all of the eternity that lay between the two meetings. Word held out his arms and Johnny rushed into them like a homing pigeon.

When Johnny was making his Gospel he let Mary Magdalen's account of her reunion with Word stand as his signifier for Word's individual meetings with friends when he had defeated death. Johnny was particularly anxious to show the vital part women had played in Word's triumph, so much greater than what men had done, and he thought the story of the man she thought was the gardener was beautiful. But there was another reason for him to do what he so seldom did, letting his Gospel speak of something he had not personally witnessed. His own first meeting with Word after the resurrection was something for themselves alone. Mary, Salome and Miriam went to the room they had made their bedroom and Nicodemus had already returned to his main house. And we will go away from where we are not wanted.

The Resurrection Day was glorious in its reunions, each of which demands its own privacy, but when Johnny looked back on it, Word covered an extraordinary amount of territory, even when you allow for his glorified body moving from place to place without touching ground or being obstructed by walls. Johnny did not remember Word travelling across time and through barriers before: he walked on water but at an ordinary speed, for instance. Now it almost seemed as though time had moved backwards, for Word personally reached most of his twelve disciples that day, apart from Judas who was dead, and Thomas, who had vanished. He appeared among the ten that evening, but during the day eight of them had already met him. Talking to Miriam during one of Word's absences from the studio later that day, Johnny remembered that Eleazar had seemed lethargic enough in his first hours after resurrection, although he was lively enough at the last party in Bethany. They didn't know about the Widow's son at Nain, but Miriam, not now to be contradicted on how dead she herself had been, recalled being a little tired when she came to life although hungry more than anything else, as Word had foreseen at the time. Lethargy didn't apply to Word. After his reunion with Johnny he ate with the four of them and then sent Johnny to find his father's agent in Jerusalem, someone whom neither Johnny nor Salome had thought of pursuing. Johnny even said so, and Word smiled and said that Zebedee no doubt had a very respectable agent, and Salome sighed, and said yes, that Reuben was utterly reliable, absolutely dependable and talked about nothing but fish.

Johnny wanted to know why Reuben's respectability should be important, and Word said that no respectable person would want to have anything to do with a crucifixion, still less with a crucified person, unless other things mattered more in their eyes than respectability. More than that he did not say, but sent Johnny on his way, and the same time he told Miriam to go in the opposite direction, listening for the sound of a folksinger with a Galilee accent, and that when she met him she would know what to do. Nicodemus, who had come back, was asked to go to the Temple and seek a man praying at the back of the building. Mother Mary Word asked to go with himself to where they would find Nathaniel, Salome he asked to remain, to greet anyone and detain them if she thought it advisable. When she asked who might call, Word thought that Joseph of Arimathea might look in, in which case he wanted to thank him for the use of his nice tomb. They looked at him speechlessly, apart from his mother, who spluttered with laughter, and said Death clearly had no power over

412

Word's joy, and Word said, how could it with a mother like his?

Johnny thought there was more behind Word's pursuit of Reuben than he had said, and realised that he would have to be very careful as regards reference to Word himself. It would not be easy. Johnny would have liked to talk to everyone about Word and keep them up far into the night when he did it. But when he got to Reuben's house, whose address Salome had told him, Reuben gave him no time to conceal the topic of Word, or to feign interest in the price of fish, simply saying when Johnny introduced himself 'Master Johnny! You will have come to see your brother. Come in, come in! I have set this room aside for Mr James. Here is a visitor for you, Mr James! Master Johnny has been playing truant! Ah, well, he has come to no harm so perhaps we do not need to be too severe! I will leave you young gentlemen together' and fortunately went out without waiting to sense the atmosphere, which was thick as a cloud with lightning at its edges. Johnny looked at James, whose face was as grim as Johnny could remember, standing behind a table like a judge about to sentence a particularly deplorable criminal. In a flash Johnny realised why Word had talked about the respectability of Reuben: he had known whom Johnny would find when he visited the respectability of Reuben. And he had wanted Johnny to fight this corner on his own.

Johnny eyed James tactically. If things went back to what they were like in Galilee before the arrival of Word, James might proceed to punishment very rapidly, wasting little time on speech, and they had not seen each other over three days, the last link having been broken by Johnny when he failed to answer James's cries for him in the garden of Gethsemane. Fortunately James was behind that table and if need be Johnny would draw him out of the house in chase all the way back to the studio, provided some officious fool did not capture Johnny and hand him over to James regretting the sparing of children and consequent spoiling of rods. Or the other way round. Johnny himself looked like what he was, a boy determined to hold on to something his elders did not want him to continue having. Or this particular elder.

'Where have you been?' demanded James through gritted teeth.

Good, it was talk, at least for the moment, but with an eye needing to watch for sudden jumps and lunges.

'Watching Word being crucified', answered Johnny as grimly.

'Are you raving mad? Don't you know that pollutes you?'

'Word died to save us all.'

'Word – as you call him in your stupid, childish babble – was no more than a blasphemous criminal whom you are to forget you ever knew.'

'Word is God.'

'Don't add your blasphemy to his!'

'Word and our mother have just been having lunch with me, and his mother.'

'I might have expected you to tell lies, but pay me the compliment of lying with the faintest shade of credibility. Next you will inform me that they will dine with Pontius Pilate tonight – or why not make it Tiberius Caesar?'

Johnny was fleetingly tempted to show what he actually knew of Tiberius, but this scene was quite bad enough without making it worse. James repudiating Word made Johnny feel physically sick. 'I tell you Word has died and risen again.'

'I tell you you're a stupid, arrogant, spoiled brat who doesn't know what he's talking about.'

'You betrayed him!' realised Johnny with tactless insight. 'Therefore you want to believe he betrayed you.'

James's face turned an ugly dark. 'I betrayed myself in ever believing in him.'

Johnny tried again. 'Do you really feel better now you have stopped believing in him?'

'Yes – no – mind your own business!'

'Well, you don't mind yours.'

'That's different. I'm older.'

'Mother is older still and she still believes in Word.'

James, who had been looking speculatively at each side of the table to see how he could best make a rush and catch Johnny, frowned and looked directly at him. 'Mother isn't here, what's the point in pretending she is?'

'Because she is. She came here with Mother Mary.'

'She's been imposed upon. We've all been imposed upon, by that smooth-talking carpenter, and that mother of his we left leeching off our parents.'

And then Johnny stopped even pretending to plan his own retreat. His jaw set. 'Attack Word if you must, James, you'll be sorry enough later regardless of anything I may say. But if you insult his mother we're finished, you and I. Just before Word died on the Cross he asked her to make me her son, and told me she would be my mother. He said it in front of our mother Salome, who put her arms around us and speaks of my two mothers ever since. If you attack Word's mother, you attack my mother, you attack our mother. Make up your mind!'

James in his fury was about to leap the table when Johnny made what at another time would have been a ludicrous gesture. He folded his arms. It might have seemed like a boy fooling himself he could look like a man, but it was in fact the gesture of a former soldier signifying his refusal to fight. James could jump across the table, the folded arms said, and could beat the living daylights out of Johnny, with no fear of kicks, blows or bites in retaliation. It was the translation into his own life of how he had seen Word meet scourging, insult and murder. His brown eyes looked up at James. After a hard minute, James looked away. Johnny stayed where he was.

And at that point Word walked in the door. James fell on his knees. Word crossed to the other side of the table and raised James up. He looked across at Johnny, who nodded and walked out of the door and the house, leaving James and Word together. We have no further business there either.

The next time Johnny saw James he got a bearlike hug and kiss, hugged and kissed back as best he could, and then put his finger on his lips. James nodded, and they turned back to the rest of the company and never mentioned it among themselves again. But James did speak of it to somebody else. Paul's first letter to the Corinthians which has survived, speaks of Word's resurrection with the characteristic assertiveness which Paul sometimes showed about events where he had not been present. Then he said Word was seen by Peter, then by the twelve (forgetting one was both Judas and dead). Then he had Word being seen by 'above five hundred brethren' most of whom were still alive at the time of writing.

'Then he was seen by James.' For James's sight of the risen Word to have made so strong an impact on Paul means that James told him the tragic story of his loss of faith, and we can guess why. The passage ended with Paul's self-accusation:

> For I am the least of the apostles, that am not to be called an apostle because I persecuted the church of God.

He must have said this or something like it to James, and James then told him that he, Paul, had only been a homicidal enemy of Word, whereas James himself had been a traitor. What James did, he did big. He was killed by Herod Agrippa at least six years before Paul wrote to the Corinthians, and so would have been included by Paul among those who 'are fallen asleep'. Johnny would not have told that story to Paul or anyone else, but Paul's knowing it from James was another matter. The letter was written from Ephesus, and Johnny was probably there at the time: the passage on charity or love may show his influence.

On the other hand, Johnny would have argued long and loud against Paul's belief that women should not speak in church and should be content to learn religion from their husbands at home, and it may be that Paul obstinately hung on to absurd extremes originally asserted in debate against Johnny. Johnny probably learned most of his practical feminism from his mothers, but in argumentative form it came from the inspiration of Miriam, another chapter in whose saga he saw very soon after leaving Reuben's house. He was walking fairly rapidly back to the studio when he heard the twanging of a musical instrument and a voice yodelling musically if abrasively

> M-I-R-I-A-M – is – Miriam!
> She is the apostle to the throstle.
> She has more spark than the lark.
> Her genius could outcarry the strongest dromedary.
> She is the fire in any good musician's lyre.
> She is M-I-R-I-A-M – Miriam!

And there was Philip capering alongside the diminutive figure supposed to be Mary Cleophas. Johnny shrugged his shoulders: it was the same name, anyway, but it looked as though Miriam had made an exception to her blanket prohibition on the revelation of her identity. He accompanied them to the studio, Philip loudly hailing him with some verse asserting Johnny's boundless admiration for Miriam, a verse Johnny was thankful to forget. But on meeting Mother Mary and Salome, Philip moved into much more solemn if cheerful odes to them, and celebrations of Word's resurrection. By the time Word returned, Philip was all ready with a song in self-reproach for having run away which Word charmingly concluded with a verse of loving welcome back. This also proved efficacious in quietening Peter and Andrew who had arrived in passionate argument as to which of them had behaved worse in letting Word down, each insisting he was infinitely viler than his brother.

Nathaniel arrived with Mary, and James with Word, who had left them to go to Reuben's house. Johnny was much more conscious of Word's knowing what was actually happening, anywhere, than he ever had been before. He knew that Word had been guided by love for him in individual minds, but now seemed to know who was where regardless of whether they were loving him or not. Of course he was guided to Reuben's place by Johnny if not by James.

They had found Nat at the pool near the Sheep Gate, known as Bethesda, with five collonades. It was there that Word had healed a paralysed man brought down to the pool so that he might be the first in, and hence healed, after the local angel had troubled the waters, but for thirty-eight years unable to gain assistance to put him in the pool before someone else took the cure. Word's miracle had produced the usual row about healing on the Sabbath, although the Pharisees never seemed to criticise the angel when he or she healed on the Sabbath (the Sadducees denied there was any angel). Johnny could see the logic of Word's concluding Nat would be there to commune with the angel after letting down Word, and since Nat had been their companion in Nazareth, Mary was the ideal symbol of forgiveness to bring him back. Word had told Nat he would see heaven open, and the angels of God ascending and descending upon the Son of man, so Nat had sought out the nearest place known for angelic epiphany, which also had housed a miracle by Word. It was good to see Nat again, and Johnny signified as much by hitting him on the back of his neck in memory of Nat's removal of Johnny from the Nazareth synagogue. Nat affected to sink under this, but as he rose again, he enveloped Johnny in a thankful hug.

Matthew arrived with Nicodemus who had found him where Word had said a tax-collector had knelt unlike the exhibitionist Pharisee in the front of the Temple. Naturally Matthew would follow Word's parable and decide it was a prophecy even when he himself had run away from Word. He flung himself at Word's feet, perfectly on cue, kissed them and asked Word to be merciful to him, a sinner, exactly as Word had specified in the story. Word raised him up, and Matthew then began recollecting all the allusions in scripture to resurrection which would now prove to have been about Word. Various others tried to compete with him, including a reasonably adept Johnny, a very well-versed Salome from whom Johnny had learned so many of the Scriptures and their songs to recite, a belligerently erudite Miriam who had clearly rehearsed many a quotation with her father Jairus, and an indulgent Mary who took care not to win too often, but in the end Matthew outdistanced them all. James was now seated on the floor alongside Johnny: Word had slipped out once more, and when Johnny resumed conversation in their minds, told him that he was taking the road to Emmaus and to ask no more questions but enjoy discovering whom Word would meet there.

Joseph of Arimathea came bustling in, disappointed at not seeing Word, but full of news of what Caiaphas said when news of Word's resurrection was brought, and how money was given to the soldiers to say that Word's disciples had stolen the body.

Nicodemus remarked that the Temple taxes would be higher than ever this year, and Matthew enjoyed working out for them where Caiaphas would sink the expenses of bribery. A lot might be concealed under the head of refurbishment arising from cleaning the Temple which literally was correct from Word's point of view, and metaphorically from Caiaphas's. Annas had promised to doublecheck the accounts for which Caiaphas's gratitude was more formal than fervent. There was news, also, of a controversy over a vacant position of keeper of the Temple gate. In order to accommodate visiting Jews from Africa, that particular office had been intended for a Cyrenean, who mysteriously failed to appear on the eve of Passover, when he was to be noticed, if not fully vetted, by Caiaphas and others, and had now sent a curt message withdrawing his application for the job. Johnny was pleased to hear his name was Shimon.

Other stories of that day filtered back to Johnny later. There were too many of them in the studio now, and Johnny, happily conscripting James, Peter and Andrew, got the others down to the Mount of Olives to wait for Word, whom he told mind to mind as usual. Miriam, Mary and Salome remained in the studio. Nicodemus and Joseph went with the men. It seemed doubtful if Philip could be stopped accompanying himself in salutation of Miriam instead of accompanying the other disciples but Johnny had no trouble in getting Miriam to send him along with the rest. He realised that Miriam had told Philip where she had been as well as who she was, and that it was with Word's approval, perhaps by his orders, that she did so, but that Philip would never be told about his own presence at Golgotha. Johnny's mothers had been so wise in prohibiting any diffusion of that. He could never have returned to old friendship with the adult disciples if they had known. With James it was different. Johnny having remained faithful to Word when James had defected had been an initial and additional barrier to his return: and when by the aid of Johnny and Word he had conquered that barrier, his mutual secret with Johnny sealed his devotion to Word all the way to his death.

The gathering on Mount Olivet took some time to assemble, and neither Jim nor Thady reached it for some time. Thady had run as far as Ephraim, about ten miles north of Jerusalem, where Word and his disciples had stopped and Word had taught and healed, in the days before that last journey to Jerusalem. Thady, replete with fear and shame, thought nobody would know where he had gone, and none where he had gone would know who he was; and Mary Magdalen had the exact details of his identity, location, disposition, means, and mood within about half an hour of his arrival. Her female network was virtually infallible.

She left him to his self-reproaches during the sufferings, death and resurrection of Word, but when the male disciples began to crawl out of their retreats, the female disciples shook the blanket of their landscape to instruct them on their way. Thady, in an ecstacy of self-contempt, had put himself as the utmost lost cause, only to discover now that he was less lost than Pontius Pilate, in any sense of the term. He found himself hastening south, with women's voices telling him his road lay there, and he had better not wait for food yet, and water would be in better supply a little later, and what to eat was handed to him as he was moved inexorably onward from oasis to oasis, and a lift on a camel or on a donkey was given him before he asked for it, and vessels of water eased their way into his hands with their contents into his grateful mouth, and he was at the Mount of Olives with a tall, formidable woman helping him down and reminding him that his place would be across there, and so he found himself standing beside an equally bemused and beblubbered Jim. (Like Philip, Thady would marry, and like Philip the decision would be taken by his wife.)

Mary Magdalen found Jim herself, through her endless web. Jim had not left Jerusalem however much he wanted to. He was badly shaken by the speed of the disciples' disintegration, Johnny's disappearance, Peter's ham-handed ear-chopping, Judas's presence at the head of an obviously hostile police force, the flight of Thady, Matthew and Thomas, who seemed scared out of their wits, Andrew's cry to the fugitives to come back followed by his cry to Judas as to what was happening and then a rally from Andrew turning into his own flight as Philip rushed forth weeping something about song having been strangled, and then Nathaniel turned and ran and his voice echoed back lamenting that Word had not vanished from the midst of his opponents. Jim was if anything taken by surprise to discover himself running after them but before he could stop, pull himself together and at least work out what was happening to Word, he was knocked over by a running man who promptly fell on top of him. At that point Jim exploded. His rage, chiefly against himself (disguised as anger against Romans, Temple priests, Temple guards, his fellow-disciples, and Word for making no resistance to his capture and therefore probable death), boiled over against the blunderer whose foot appeared to be firmly lodged in Jim's mouth. Savagely removing the foot as soon as he could, he shouted:

'You rich swine running roughshod over the poor, as always!' The young man wailed: 'I'm not shod, I'm naked!' which on inspection was undeniable.

'So you're celebrating the eve of Passover with the latest example of plutocratic depravity!' snarled Jim.

'I'm not depraved, and I'm not a plutocrat, I'm just trying to get home, and you got in my way!'

'I did not! You were tearing along like a mad pig – come to think of it, are you mad?'

'I'm not mad, and I'm not a pig, and your horrible shoes kicked me, and I want to go home', and the young man burst into tears afresh.

'What are you running around without any clothes on for, then?' demanded Jim a little incoherently as he permitted curiosity outweigh generous wrath.

'I was wearing a linen robe given me by my mother', wept the youth, 'and I saw them taking the Messiah prisoner, and I tried to rescue him, and they made me prisoner too, and I only managed to escape by wriggling out of the robe my mother made, and ran away, and goodness only knows what Mother will say, I feel awful!' And he moaned like a dove, as the psalmist sang, thought James, who then had another thought:

'*What* did you call the prisoner?'

'The Messiah! That's what my mother calls him, he's been preaching in the Temple all week and because he's so good they're arresting him and taking him away, jealous old cats! Do you think Mother will say I should have got myself killed?' He contemplated his own demise mournfully until Jim irritably told him his mother certainly wanted no such thing. It should have cheered him up but it didn't seem to. Meanwhile twilight had sunk into dark, and a wind was beginning to tickle Jim's ankles. He rose, virtually without thought, removed his outer robe, and threw it on the young man who said 'Oh, I *say*, do you think this will make Mother better pleased with me?' and then, after a few minutes of possible thought, added 'Very good of you. You must tell me your address, because Mother will want me to return it when it is laundered properly.'

Somehow Jim had been concluding that if Mother gave the orders in that house, she probably did almost all the work. He eyed his new acquaintance speculatively. 'And what is your name?'

'Oh, haven't I told you? I'm called Mark, John Mark really, but I like being called Mark, it's such a *manly* name. More of a Roman name, I suppose, though I think of it as a surname, *cognomen* they would call it, whereas Marcus is a first name, *praenomen*. I wouldn't mind being called Leo. My mother used to call me her little lion, when I was young.'

'And what age are you now?' enquired Jim, with as straight a face as he could manage, not that the dark gave much facial expression away.

John Mark hesitated, and Jim reflected that if he made it a guessing game, he might be firmly dropped once for all, but he ultimately came out with 'Sixteen'. Suddenly Jim thought of Johnny, who seemed years older by comparison. Then Mark wanted to know what Jim's name was, and

Jim, sneezing in the absence of his outer robe, said something like 'Shem' and Mark wanted to know what sort of a name was that, and James, still battling with the sneeze, said 'Shem is short for Jim as James is Jokey for Jacob', and Mark said he supposed so, but he wasn't very good at Greek yet. Jim let it ride.

Then Mark began to witter on about what his mother had told him about Word, and Jim began by being bored and irritated. Mark was a nincompoop, his mother was a busybody, Word was doomed, his movement would obviously collapse (to judge by the speed with which all of them fled at the first threat) and Jim felt he hardly knew who he was himself, now. And then he realised he was actually listening to it more than he had admitted to himself. Mark – or his mother – had managed to find out a great deal, and he had not simply parroted anything she said, though she had almost certainly made up his mind for him on any question of value. But one or other of them had got hold of people who had heard John the Baptizer both before and after Word had been baptized by him. The Baptizer had gone up and down the Jordan from what Jim had heard, and Mark didn't seem to realise much of his work had been in Galilee because he talked as though Word had come into Galilee only after the Baptizer's arrest instead of always being there after his family returned with him from Egypt. But once Mark got his story into Galilee you would have sworn he had interviewed Shimon Peter or Andrew or James or Johnny or all four of them. Jim cross-examined him skilfully and found, as he should have guessed, that the initial source was Peter's mother-in-law picked up from some grapevine by Mark's mother, though it was unclear whether they had ever met directly. In spite of himself, Jim was impelled to think of action. If Jim were ever to meet Peter again, this might be just the lad to harvest his story for posterity. Jim was still assuming Word and his movement were finished, but he was almost unconsciously feeling that some account of Word's career should be saved for the people of the future. And while Peter could supply the bulk of the story, Mark (and his mother) could draw on the testimony of many more participants and bystanders in the public life of Word. It would be important to have a start made on the whole thing before much time had elapsed, since witnesses would die and memories would get rusty or cluttered. So instead of letting Mark and the robe drift out of his life, Jim surprised himself by making a definite date for its (laundered) return, three days' time.

No sooner had this been done than instead of taking leave, Mark wanted to take Jim, ostensibly to meet his mother, actually (Jim realised) to protect himself against her. Jim's own reaction was to leave him to her wrath – she was, after all, hardly likely to murder him however taxing he might be to her patience. But the idea of an editor of witnesses to Word seemed important to follow up, and more for its sake than for Mark's, Jim followed his way homeward. He rather regretted it when they got home, and a small dark woman, at least a head smaller than Mark, assailed the two of them with impressive vehemence:

'Where have you been? What have you been doing? Who is this layabout? Where are your clothes? What is this garment? Have you no consideration for your mother's feelings? What sort of a fool have I brought up?'

Jim hoped they could duck the last question, and thought for a moment that Mark would try to placate his terrifying parent by bursting into tears again, but this evidently would do him no favours as experience had presumably shown. Mark showed another qualification as a historian by giving a clear statement of events to which his mother listened impassively: she had evidently trained him hard and well in reporting, and no self-indulgence would pave any way with her. Then she swung gimlet eyes on Jim:

'You're instinctively generous. You were running away when my son fell over you. You were in a bad temper, not just in response to his clumsiness. You were a short distance from the garden of Gethsemane and had probably just come from there. You were one of the Messiah's disciples. You turned your back on him when his enemies took him.'

Jim was speechless, a condition not aided by Mark adding complacently 'I knew it would be better for you to meet Mother' for which she snapped 'Don't be giving yourself airs for merely making a fool of yourself, as usual'. She swung back on Jim.

'Have you eaten?'

Jim stammered something about the supper and then told the rest of the story, with occasional ill-fated attempts to break free of it. Mark's mother allowed him to sit down while he was telling it, and more or less forced fruit on him to punctuate his narrative. At the end she glared at him:

'Feeling proud of yourself?'

Jim was not, and admitted he was not.

'I should think so, too. But you men are all the same. Full of old talk in easy times and useless in a crisis.' Mark was nodding his head but whether in self-protective agreement or in a helpful attempt to supply himself as the prime example of her disparagement Jim could not decide. Mark's mother, talking more to herself than to them, muttered:

'They'll take him to the Romans and the Romans will kill him. Of course if he were like you two – she glared afresh – 'he might argue his way out of it, but he'll probably argue his way deeper and deeper into it, refusing all escape. He's the one man who could be trusted to do that.' She saw the pain in Jim's face, and barked:

'Oh, what could you have done even if you'd stuck by him? You might as well be here. You're to stay here for the Passover and the Sabbath, and then we'll see what's to be done with you. I was going to send this fool to be a disciple: just as well I didn't, he'd probably have disgraced me before everyone by forgetting to put his clothes on!' Mark went scarlet. His mother looked at his colour with satisfaction. 'Do you know Mary of Magdalen?'

Jim, startled, said that Word had cured her of insanity. The mother grunted, and asked if he had seen her since. He said no, and she said it was just like a man. She added, again more to herself: 'Mary will know what to do, if anything can be done.' She sent Jim and Mark off to bed fairly shortly, telling them that she might be gone when they woke up the next day, and they were to stay indoors. Jim slept very well and long, and realised from the condition of his head when he woke that the drink his hostess had given him probably knocked him out, an intention Mark confirmed. Mark had been up for some time, but it had not been necessary for his mother to enforce obedience on him by an artificial soporific.

They waited the day there, and Jim drew Mark out on what more he knew about Word, and Mark cross-questioned Jim on what corrections he would advise, and what else he could tell which Mark did not know. Jim kept quiet about the kidnap of Johnny and the use of the dolphins, a decision his fellow-disciples would make the same way on their own, but he largely gave Mark what he knew. When the sun darkened and the celestial lights vanished, Mark screamed, and Jim had to pacify

424

him, somewhat irritably: eventually he quietened him quite rapidly by threatening to report him to his mother. When she came back, however, she looked so tired and ill that Mark showed sudden mastery, made her sit down, brewed her a restorative, took off her shoes and washed her feet (which made Jim gulp rather sadly). She even called him a good boy, which made it clear she was upset. Eventually she drew herself together and told them she had come from Golgotha where she had been one of Mary Magdalen's followers, and that she had stayed until Word's death. At that point Jim wept bitterly, and both Mark and his mother were very gentle with him. It suddenly seemed as though all that Jim had believed in had died with Word, never to be reborn. He cursed himself for turning away from Word, but Mark's mother simply held his shoulders in her hands, and swayed him to and fro, saying he could not have prevented Word's death.

Throughout the Sabbath Jim continued to agonise. Just as Johnny had thought Word could not die because Word was God, Jim concluded that since Word had died, God was dead. Word was dead, the movement had fallen apart, there was no more God. Jim was beginning to hate the idea of seeing any of the other eleven disciples, ever again. They might have shame in common, but it made bitter enemies of them, one to the other. His whole devotion to the idea of loving your neighbour as yourself fell to pieces without Word and without God: if he still believed in love of neighbour, why had he been so hostile to Mark at their first meeting? It was all the more dismaying that Mark's mother didn't seem to see any of this. To her Word was dead, but the end was not yet: a Messiah should not be killed, and those who killed him were accursed, but because Word was the Messiah there would be some fresh development. What still remained (Mark's mother remarked early in the third day, pausing amid brushing the floor) was the love of the women devotees for one another. Mary Magdalen, Word's mother, her sisters, the large scattering of women whether on Golgotha or in their homes but still devoted to Word – all of these had been raised from their subjection by Word. (Jim tried to think of any man subjecting Mark's mother, and failed.) They would not sink back to be bullied, dismissed or marginalised by Romans, priests or any other men. They would keep Word's memory alive. She was training Mark to make himself as useful as his limited talents would allow, in getting evidence of Word's life. Now, she turned on Jim:

'Did you ever hear mention of resurrection?'

Jim said, yes, but that was all to be forgotten now. Mark's mother looked at him hard enough to make him uneasy, and then muttered: 'Love'.

'What?' spluttered the amazed Jim.

'Love', she repeated. 'If anything could bring him back it would be love. We'd better start somewhere.' She glared at Jim again. 'You'll have to start loving that crowd of demented sheep who were with you when the Temple guards and Pilate's legionaries took the Messiah away. It may be hard, but it's got to be done. MARK!' Her son jumped from his chair.

'You'll have to love Jim, even if he does make you feel inferior.' Jim and Mark looked at one another with horror, each one knowing the other's alienation from him. 'Oh, stop being fools for one split second, even you must be capable of that! Try to find something in each other to respect! Jim, respect Mark's historicism! And try and do something to make me respect your minds, if any!' Jim awkwardly shambled across to her and gave her a kiss: to his surprise she kissed him heartily in return. Mark followed and kissed and hugged her, and made an effort to embrace Jim, who dutifully pecked him back. Mark's mother sighed. 'Don't you see, we must love one another to be worthy of his Resurrection, or at least somewhat less un-worthy of it?' Jim and Mark eyed one another and decided at least to like one another. It was useless to argue. Once Jim began to think like that, he began faintly hearing his old beliefs on which Word had built love for his neighbour. Mark's mother turned to Mark: 'Jim has good ideas about loving one another, or he will have when he seeks forgiveness for betraying his Messiah. Listen to him then!'

All in all, it was a great relief when Mary Magdalen arrived and told Jim he was to join the others at Mount Olivet. Mark was told to remain at home, and look after his mother, who leered with satisfaction at this assumption of her vulnerability, but as they walked away, Jim looked back to wave, and he saw her weeping on what seemed a broad shoulder Mark had managed to find somewhere. Mary Magdalen said little on the journey apart from suddenly looking reflectively at Jim, and saying 'Our master gave me back my life. I think he is about to give you back yours. In a slightly different way, no doubt. You're not possessed by obvious devils at the moment.'

Jim said, startled: 'But he's dead!'

'Ah, you *are* possessed by devils', answered Mary Magdalen with obvious satisfaction as she strode on. For some reason, Jim was feeling very sad as he reached Olivet, as though he had been unable to find something very dear to him which he had lost. He was even weeping silently when Thady crossed over to him, equally bewildered and lachrymose. Then Johnny and James bellowed for silence, and told them that Joseph of Arimathea had kindly offered them the use of the upper room in one of his houses, and as they walked there Jim and Thady were joined by a very excited Shimon the ex-Zealot (had he stayed ex-Zealot? Jim wondered) who introduced a friend called Cleophas (whose name startled Johnny, but he said nothing). Jim said something about its being a sad occasion, whereupon Cleophas flatly contradicted him, announcing that Word had appeared to Shimon. Jim looked at him speechlessly, and Shimon added ecumenically 'and to Cleophas too!'

'In the name of God!!', gasped Jim.

'I believed in him', remembered Cleophas, with the clear accents of a Galilean who has long lived in Jerusalem and prefers to be thought Judaean. 'He was related to me, or to be specific about it, he wasn't, but his mother Mary had a sister whom I loved and to whom I was betrothed but who died before I could marry her.' This meant nothing to Jim, but to Johnny, eavesdropping since he heard the name of Cleophas, it meant a lot: and a prickle of tears tugged unavailingly at his eyelids as he swallowed them back. Mother Mary had clothed Miriam in a secret sorrow from long ago, skilfully and sentimentally. He lingered.

'I had heard something of his doings', continued Cleophas, 'but had put it down to the usual wild stories from Galilee, where all their mustard-seeds are burning bushes.' Johnny liked this, and looked forward to repeating it to Word, if indeed he was not hearing it now. 'But I took myself to the Temple when he was speaking in it, and I believed in him.' The man of the world smiled at his own simplicity. 'Then I heard he had been arrested, and was told it had been at the garden of Gethsemane, and on my way there I saw men running, and caught one, and Shimon was him I had caught.'

'I was running in despair and in shame', continued Shimon, adding somewhat tactlessly to Jim, Thady and Johnny 'as you were'. None of them contradicted him. 'Cleophas took me to his own house and made me tell

427

him all that had happened since first I was called by the Master. He kept me with him through the Passover meal and the Sabbath, and then having business in Emmaus invited my company.' 'Your friend had despaired of his Master', nodded Cleophas, 'and had decided what we needed was to kill Pontius Pilate in order to free the country. I managed to persuade him that if entering Pilate's house would pollute the Sabbath, murdering him would pollute it even more. To everything there is a season, and one must not kill even Romans out of season.'

Shimon grinned a trifle self-consciously. 'That's why he discovered business in Emmaus when the Sabbath was past.'

'The road is long', pronounced Cleophas, 'over eight miles. The exercise would do him good.'

'And there are robbers', murmured Johnny, catching Jim's eye.

'And an absence of good Samaritans' agreed Jim, mentally thanking Johnny for making a memory of Word a reason to smile.

'And two might walk more easily than one', asserted Shimon.

'Amos asks, can two walk together except they be agreed?' enquired Johnny, with a salt-shake of malice. Jim swung a reproving fist in his direction.

'I'm happy to say we didn't agree at all', and Cleophas ditched Amos firmly. 'He kept on urging violent revolution, and I kept assuring him that the followers of Barabbas were far more likely to cut his throat for love of their country than to make him their general. I'm happy to say that they must have been rejoicing so hard at Barabbas's release that none were found to assassinate or to adopt travellers to Emmaus. In fact, we never encountered a soul until suddenly there was a third man keeping step with us.'

'And we became a lot vaguer', Shimon recollected, 'and confined ourselves to agreeing that the Master's death was a tragedy, whatever our individual sequels. In fact we became so vague that the third man asked us what on earth we were talking about.'

'I suppose we became irritated', reflected Cleophas. 'He looked like a pilgrim who could ponder the scriptures, yet he walked from Jerusalem as though nothing had happened within its walls since king Herod was gathered to his fathers, if any.'

'So Cleophas asked him was he the only person in Jerusalem who had not heard about Jesus of Nazareth', continued Shimon, 'a prophet whose words and deeds were powerful with God –'

'– and with the people his audiences' broke in Cleophas, 'and how the Temple priests handed him over to be sentenced to death –'

'– and so the Romans crucified him', Shimon grabbed it back, 'and for ourselves we had hoped he would deliver Israel, but he had now been dead for three days.'

'I hadn't yet told Shimon because I didn't want him to endanger himself by rioting against the Romans', added Cleophas, 'but I'd heard from a maidservant that women had gone to the tomb and found it empty, and had seen angels saying he was alive, and then some of his men had gone to the tomb and found it empty –'

Here Johnny let himself down by a noisy snigger, and Shimon swung round on him, suddenly understanding: 'You little horror, one of them was you, I might have known. Anyhow that was what sent us on the way to Emmaus, though I didn't realise it at the time.'

And Cleophas resumed: 'This other chap, our third man, said, rather unfairly, I thought, "O unthinking ones and slow in heart to put faith in all that the prophets had spoken" – Oh *shut* up!', for Johnny had begun to giggle, and hardly kept the peace by answering:

'Well, you weren't very fast thinking in recognising him, were you?'

'Why, who was he?' asked Thady, and Johnny had to bite his lower lip, hard, as no doubt it deserved.

'Anyhow', continued Shimon, in a hopeless attempt to wither Johnny, 'the man kept at us, insisting the Master must have found it necessary to suffer these things so he could enter his glory –'

'And he chased us through the sacred scriptures from Moses down', acknowledged Cleophas.

'– interpreting text after text from all the prophets', gulped Shimon, 'all concerning himself, if you only realised it' and he shook his head gloomily.

'And up to then you didn't know they were about him, any more than you knew now you were talking to him', nodded Johnny, feeling it was kinder to take Thady out of his suspense, which it clearly did as he breathed a thankful. 'Oh, so *that's* who it was' and in the rapture of his face Johnny saw the Lost Cause had come home to roost.

And Jim felt an elation so great as to seem lighter than air, while Cleophas survived the loss of his punch-line with a rapid 'And we were in Emmaus before he had reached Isaiah, and he seemed to be travelling onward but we begged him to stay, and we went in ---'

'– to the inn', relayed Shimon.

'– and ordered food –'

'– and when it came –'

'– he took the bread –'

'– and gave a blessing –'

'– and broke it –'

'– and gave it to us –'

'– and then Shimon knew him.'

'It was exactly the way he had done it at our last supper three days before', and Shimon burst into tears. Johnny turned to him, raising his hands, and Shimon took him in his arms and kissed him gratefully. They had stopped walking by now, having reached Joseph's second-best house, and climbed its stairs to the upper room. Cleophas finished:

'And he smiled on us, and was gone.'

'Through the roof?' asked Johnny, and Shimon laughed happily, shaking him.

Cleophas smiled and said 'I suppose so'.

Jim looked at the far wall, and said, 'But this time he comes through the walls', and so Word may have done, because he was suddenly among them. Glorious and immortal, thought Johnny, and was about to run forward to take up his usual place at Word's left hand, when he realised that several of those who had not already seen Word since his death (however much they had welcomed accounts of his return), were obviously shaken, Jim and Thady falling on their knees, Joseph following their example, Peter and Andrew looking decidedly uneasy for all of having been in Word's presence in the studio. Word smiled, the left side of his mouth twisting up as Johnny lovingly remembered it, and, raising his hands, said: 'Peace be to you'.

And everyone there from Mary Magdalen to Johnny felt a calm beyond anything they had ever known. Mary Magdalen and Johnny, and the other women present, could greet Word without shame: despite the good humour of earlier meetings, the guilty men who deserted from Gethsemane on whatever excuse now bowed their heads, yet the calm descended on them no less than on the innocent women and child. A lesser shame enveloped Cleophas, Joseph and Nicodemus: they had done what they could after Word was dead, but they had made no protest while he suffered. Word raised his hands in blessing, and Johnny and the other, including Shimon and Cleophas – saw with horror what had not been obvious to any of them earlier, the marks where the nails had gone through his wrists. Word's smile was by now a little more grim, and he twitched aside his robe to reveal the wound he had sustained after death, the track of the spear that had entered his left side and penetrated his heart. So Johnny realised he should stay where he was while Word was teaching them, with his own body as visual aid in the lesson of his resurrection.

But Joseph of Arimathea had no such scruples, and galloped up to Word with a cry of 'may I serve you refreshments, light refreshments?', and Word, deliberately breaking the tension, took Joseph in his arms, kissed him, thanked him for the use of his tomb, and said he would be very grateful for something to eat. When food arrived in abundance, not a soul touched anything until Word himself had consumed a couple of mouthfuls under their eyes. Johnny remarked in his mind to Word's mind that it must be like feeding-time at some exotic zoo of Tiberius Caesar's, and Word's mind replied that he was a lucky Johnny not to have been fed to Tiberius's zoo himself. Johnny's mind answered that he wanted to be in nobody's zoo but Word's. Meanwhile Jim and Thady drew near to Word, and fell on their knees to ask pardon for having despaired in him. Word raised them to their feet, kissed them, and told them they were his brothers, as were all of his twelve still living. This public profession of their eminence clung to their names, so that subsequently Jim was often singled out as 'the Lord's brother', and Thady humbly designated himself as Jim's brother.

Meanwhile, where was Thomas? Johnny asked Word as they walked back to the studio together at the end of the evening, and Word said that Thomas had returned to Galilee, and would soon be back with them once more. Johnny asked whether he knew of Word's return to life, and Word said he was sure Thomas did not. A week later Thomas was back to Jerusalem, more or less expected on information supplied by Mary Magdalen, who also told Word and Johnny where he was lodging. Word asked or told Johnny (it scarcely mattered which) to look in on Thomas on

431

the morning of the next day, the second day of the Jewish week. Johnny went down early enough to insure against Thomas having gone out, and was admitted. Thomas was looking dreadful. He had clearly been beaten up, his clothes were ragged and dirty – and he used to be as fastidious as anyone in Word's company was likely to be. He welcomed Johnny kindly but mournfully, and his whole aspect was one of despair. It was never Johnny's way to conceal good news, and he promptly told Thomas that Word had risen from the dead and had met the others on the first day of last week. Word had asked Johnny to say nothing to Thomas about Nicodemus's studio, as he wanted to greet him that night before all of the others in the upper room once more lent by Joseph of Arimathea. Johnny knew, without Word saying more, that this was not going to be an easy interview, although he was touched by Thomas's obvious if miserable pleasure in seeing him. But Thomas shook his head when Word's return to life was mentioned. 'You're a good boy, Johnny', he said, 'but you are deceived. He is dead, he cannot come back. I wish to God he could. He is my oldest friend, and in every meaning of the word, he is the best. But it is over. And so, I fear, are we. Galilee is over for us all. It is worse than Nazareth. They are driving out anyone who had anything to do with him. Crucifixion is the lowest form of death, and the friends of the crucified are the lowest form of life.'

'But my father and his fishermen are still respected figures on the lake and on the coastlands', insisted Johnny.

'Your father has sold all of his boats, has wound up his affairs in Galilee, and is probably already in Joppa, disposing of matters there. Jairus has been driven out of his own synagogue. Any man cured by my friend is as well to sell up and get out if they have not already done so. Any woman he cured will be lucky if her husband has not repudiated her, or if her neighbours have not driven her out. The Nazarenes, my former friends and neighbours, are *so* furious about the lowering of the name of their town, especially since he was constantly called Jesus of Nazareth by those who wished to vilify him, headed by Pontius Pilate! They say that anyone speaking of him is to be stoned, or hurled down the cliff they wanted to throw him down. His name may not be uttered in Herod's Court – Herod's Court, where all the filth of the East are congregated and invited! Peter's mother-in-law has sold her property. Magdala would like to stone its Mary, but she had sold all her real estate for good profit, fine businesswoman, and she well knew to say nothing of where she banks her cash, which is certainly not in Magdala. I'm told they wanted to stone that poor lunatic in Gadara but he had had the sense to get out with no news of his next residence. There was even some feeling they should close the synagogue that had been given them by the centurion whose servant was later healed by my beloved old friend. Fortunately for himself, he had been recalled to Rome, otherwise he might have been targeted by Barabbas and his merry men; apart from their pleasure in murdering Romans, and Jewish outcasts, they would be really glad to kill a Roman whom Jews liked and who had liked them. It's not simply the degradation of crucifixion. Herod wrings more and more from Galilee to pay for Tiberias, the city he built as belly crawl to the Emperor, and local resentment is vilified as loyalty to our Master. And the Pharisees were always bitching about Galilee failing to conform to Jerusalem rules of worship, so now any religious dissident is damned as a follower of the crucified and meat for the cross. I don't see how he could hold Galilean support. Anyone who can be shown to have won benefits from the kindness of my oldest friend, is doomed to exile if not to death.'

It was impossible for Johnny to stop Thomas's flow, but at the first real pause he gasped 'if I can show you Word tonight, will you believe he is alive?' Thomas looked at him with utter incredulity, smiled very wanly, and shook his head.

'Johnny, unless I see in his wrists the place where the nails were driven –' he stopped, and a terrible shudder shook him '– and push my finger into the mark of the nails, and push my hand into his side, I will not believe.'

And suddenly Johnny replied 'You saw him when he was dead.'

And Thomas, weeping, shivering, gasped 'I did'.

'How?' asked Johnny.

Thomas pulled himself together a little, and looked past Johnny into what seemed a remote and faraway time. 'You remember he said he would go to Bethany where Lazarus had died, and I said to the rest of you that we should go with him, and be killed with him? And then when I saw Judas leading the Temple guards and Roman soldiers to arrest him, I realised he had been trapped in a deep-laid conspiracy, and if one of his closest followers was going to testify against him, how many more of them would?, and any casual remarks by any of us amongst ourselves would be evidence to have us put to death, and I knew the death would be crucifixion, and the sheer shame of it drove my legs to run away. And I ran, and then I walked, and that night and the next day I walked around, hardly knowing where or who I was, and finally I told myself I was a coward when I had promised to be killed with him. So I found where they had taken him, and made my way up to Golgotha. By the time I got there the sun had fallen out of the heavens and the sky was blacker than I have ever seen it. I saw nobody I knew, except him, crucified, for some reason the blackness could not envelop him.' (Johnny looked at him strangely, perhaps sensing that the words would echo in his mind for many decades to come.) 'So I stood there until light began slowly to return to the sky. I felt as dead as he did, it seemed to me. I might have asked the Roman soldiers to kill me while they were at it, but at that point it didn't seem worth the trouble. I stayed until I thought I might be recognised by any friends of his who were there, (his mother I have since heard was there), and then I moved a fair distance away, but I could still see his beautiful, dead body.' (Johnny remembered the cruel mutilation and bleeding all over Word's corpse, and gazed with something like reverence on Thomas). 'And I saw the soldiers being joined by additional recruits, one of whom then drove a spear into his side. And I blundered away, and walked I didn't know where. I was twenty good miles down the road before I realised I was walking in the general direction of Galilee. So I went there, I suppose feeling I might as well pick up the empty husks of what life remained for me there. None did, as it turned out. Clever of you to realise I must have seen him. You're lucky you didn't.'

For answer Johnny simply kissed him, but got his iron guarantee to join them in the upper room of the second-best house of Joseph of Arimathea, and there he stood beside Thomas, looking at the wall through which Word had come the last time, and there among them all was Word. Johnny swung round to watch Thomas, whose face should presumably have expressed incredulity. It did nothing of the sort. The eyes widened, the lips parted into a sort of schoolboy grin, the kind showing pleasure at the arrival of a friend without wanting to seem sentimental. It struck Johnny that, of them all, Thomas was the only one who had a time-dimension to his witness, the Word he knew having been many years growing under his eyes. (Mary, like Miriam and Salome, remained at the studio where Nicodemus had begged them to stay until Zebedee reached Jerusalem and could buy a house for them all, apart from Word, who was returning to his Father.)

Word stood directly in front of Thomas, though speaking to them all in his 'Peace be to you'. It seemed to Johnny that Word, too, had a schoolboy's expression, as though he had fulfilled some dare for which a friend had wished him goodwill but was sure he could not accomplish. Word almost sang: 'Bring your finger here,' (he might have been demanding the payment of a forfeit in a schoolyard game), 'look at my wrists, let me have your hand and push it into my side', and the open wound flared before them: Thomas simply sank on his knees, and he, who had grown up with Word as his equal, cried out 'My Lord and my God!' The others repeated it. Word raised Thomas, kissed him, hugged him and said 'Because you have seen me, Thomas, you believe. Blessed are they who have not seen, and have believed.' Thomas clung to Word's hand, not in an attempt to measure the wrist's wound, but simply with a hunger for what he thought gone from him forever. Johnny noticed the emphasis Word had put on Thomas having seen. He never asked Word whether, being dead at the time, he had known of Thomas's sojourn before the cross, but he certainly knew it from what Thomas told Johnny. Once Word had arisen from the dead, Johnny did not need to report anything that subsequently happened in his absence.

When Johnny was ending his Gospel, he seemed to do so here, remarking that he would not include the many other things Word had said and done in front of his disciples after he had arisen, and before he left them. As he said, he was writing so that we, also, should believe that Word was the Son of God, and that, believing, we might have life through his name. (He did not add, but he might have added, that Word had always taught the importance of children.) But there was one more memory of Word in those days which Johnny decided we should know. What we don't know is how it happened.

It was in the night, and yet Johnny felt no tiredness or need for sleep. He seemed to be in a group to which Shimon Peter was speaking. Thomas was standing beside him, a happy Thomas, boyish, clad well and trim.

Alongside him was Nathaniel and on Johnny's right was James. There were two others whom Johnny could not quite see, and never fully brought into focus, but he was sure afterwards that they must have been Andrew and Philip.

Shimon Peter was announcing with his usual force: 'I will lead you fishing.'

The others more or less chorused: 'And we will go with you.' It seemed natural that Nathaniel and Thomas, who had never been fishermen by profession, went with the rest as part of the crew.

They got on board a floating vessel, which seemed bigger than what Johnny had been used to in his fishing days. Once they were well into the water it was clear to Johnny that if the boat was different, the sea was the same, his own Sea of Galilee, or as the people of Jerusalem used to call it, 'Lake Tiberias', in allusion to Herod's town. It was like them to want to reduce Johnny's own sea to mere lakedom. Johnny was conscious of considerable passage of time in which nothing happened, the net they had thrown into the water caught nothing, nobody said anything for fear of scaring the uncaught fish, not even the landsmen. And then it was suddenly grey morning, not a surprise, but there seemed no delay between darkness and visible water and shoreline. And Word stood on the shore. Johnny was aware of knowing it was Word, yet he only knew this as a pair of eyes taking in everything, while as one of the group on board the boat, he not know it; he seemed to lack language in which to think it or say it. Then Word spoke, not calling or shouting but perfectly easy to hear although the boat stood well out from land. Johnny knew the voice perfectly well, but Johnny in the boat showed no sign of doing so.

'Children, have you anything to eat?' Johnny as the watcher thought how nice it was of Word to make them all children, although Johnny in the boat was still showing no sign of recognition.

The fishermen cried 'No!' It wasn't clear to Johnny whether his own voice had been among theirs, though he could easily identify Peter's and Thomas's.

Word answered 'Cast the net on the right of the ship and you shall find'. They did what he told them, and then could not draw the net back since so many fish were in it. And now Johnny the fisherman could say what Johnny the observer had known from the first, that it was Word. It was as

436

though having returned to fishing he could only talk fishing, and when Word acted with effect on fishing, he could then speak of Word. Shimon Peter then stood up and threw his fisherman's coat around him. He had been naked while fishing, as was the custom on the Sea of Galilee much of the time; although Johnny hadn't been conscious of his wearing no clothes up till then, and never remembered if the rest of them were wearing any clothes or not. Anyhow Peter put on his coat and swam ashore in it, which Johnny would have found very odd in other circumstances but made perfect sense at the time. Peter seemed to swim more rapidly than the boat could make its way but they arrived pretty close in time to one another, with the net swarming with fish behind them.

And then they saw what it was odd they had not seen from the boat: a coal fire burning briskly, with fish cooking on it, and bread awaiting the hungry fisherman. Word was cooking the fish, certainly. Johnny was not surprised, although at any other time the presence of fish on shore uncaught by any visible fisherman, would have impressed him. Nor did Johnny himself rush up to Word, as he always would do, unless Word had told him otherwise. It was as though his duty just now was to be one of the group, watching and waiting – though also eating, and getting warm without having felt cold earlier. Word told them to bring some of the fish they had caught. Peter drew the net in, unbroken, and reported 153 fish in total: the computation was lightning, most unlike Peter, but nobody seemed surprised. Word told them to come and dine, and gave them plenty of bread and fish, and everyone thanked him, and everyone seemed to know who he was, and yet nobody addressed him as Master, or Rabbi, or Rabboni, or Word. But then Word broke the spell, turning to Peter:

'Simon son of Jonah, are you more fond of me than of all these others?'

Johnny was listening to this with no particular anxiety or unease. In fact he thought the bread and fish had tasted better than any he remembered having had in his life, and was pleased he had taken the precaution of helping himself to the ones Word had been cooking rather than those they had just caught. He would have preferred to sit alongside Word with Word's arm around him, or holding Word's left hand, but no doubt they would have closer communion shortly when whatever Word wanted done, had been done. Nor was Johnny taken aback by the implication that Shimon should be fonder of Word than of Andrew: he assumed that neither Andrew nor Shimon would see anything odd about that, any more than James would think it odd for Johnny to love Word more than anyone, as everyone knew he did. Johnny did not even bother to see Andrew's reaction, if Andrew was one of the two men slightly out of sight, as surely he was. He was a shade surprised that Word was calling Shimon by his original name and patronymic, instead of the name 'Peter' which he had given him, but he didn't agonise about it. Nor, apparently, did Shimon, who simply said 'Of course, you know that I love you, Lord'.

And Word said 'Nourish my lambs'. Again, there was nothing odd about this. Johnny had once asked Word why he liked to compare himself to a shepherd, and Word had said that he supposed it came from the first people to visit him after his birth being shepherds. Mother Mary told Johnny much later that it had been a very touching and therapeutic visit, and that the shepherds, crowding into the manger, had gone on their knees to the little newborn baby, and insisted on putting a twist of sheep's wool between his fingers, drawing on some old ceremony to consecrate a child as a good shepherd. She herself was exhausted with the pangs of childbirth, but she never found herself resenting the shepherds, so genuine and generous they seemed, rather like the kind of shepherd they wanted to make Word.

And now in some curious way Johnny lost eye-contact with the others and stayed only watching Word and Peter. Word was saying again 'Shimon, son of Jonah, are you fond of me?', dropping all allusions to the others just as they had dropped out of Johnny's vision, and Shimon repeated 'Of course, Lord, you know that I love you'. And Word said: 'Tend my flock of sheep'.

Then Word said, speaking to Peter the third time, 'Simon son of Jonah, do you love me?' Johnny perceived that three different questions had been asked. Peter was upset because he thought he was being asked for the third time, do you love me, although it was actually the first time Word had said 'love'. And his answer went deeper just as the affection for which Word enquired now went deeper:

'Lord, you know all things. You know that I love you.'

'Feed my sheep', replied Word. 'Truly, truly I say to you that when you were young, you got yourself going, and went where you wanted, but when you are old, you will stretch out your hands, and another will get you going, and carry you where you do not want to go, not where you do.' It seemed to Johnny that that could well be the fate of many old people, including himself, if he lived long, but this had another meaning. If Peter fed the sheep, he would end giving his life for them, as Word had given his. But Johnny saw that it also meant Peter's death would bear witness to the glory of God and enhance it.

Then Word smiled and said 'Follow me.'

Instinctively Peter turned. Word had not necessarily meant to follow him now, but Peter promptly looked at the way be was not being asked to go, should he follow Word now. What he saw behind him was Johnny; his immediate reaction was to forget himself and ask:

'What of him, Lord?'

Word could have asked no better proof of Peter's contrition than his anxiety, not for his own death, but for Johnny's well-being. Word laughed affectionately and said:

'If I will that he remains until I return, that won't affect you. Follow me.'

Peter cheered up, but as Johnny walked over to Word and slipped his right hand in Word's left, he suspected (rightly as it turned out) that others would think it meant Johnny was immortal. Johnny himself thought no such thing. There was more than one meaning to the return of Word.

TWENTY-TWO

POLYCARP

John bare witness of him

The toothless old man smiled, from his seat on the floor with his back to the wall, the way he preferred most of all to sit.

'He hasn't come for me yet, but it should be soon. If he had remained on Earth he would be over a hundred years of age by now.'

'You've hardly told us how he left Earth', objected the young man, looking up from his writing desk, having taken down the Gospel's last sentences. 'You haven't really finished that story about Lake Tiberias.'

'You *would* call it Lake Tiberias, like all the rest of them', complained Johnny.

'Well, that's what you call it in your account. Or rather, you say "Sea" of Tiberias.'

'Had to. Nobody here in Ephesus or Smyrna or Miletus would know what I meant by the Sea of Galilee. Most of them probably imagine the Sea of Galilee is the Dead Sea, and wouldn't understand why our land-lubbers were afraid of drowning in it. They have heard of the Dead Sea: death is always so much more fashionable than life.'

'People here think of a sea as a lot of water, like the Mediterranean that washes our shores and goes on past Rome to the ends of the earth.'

'The Sea of Galilee was big enough for me – and for Word', said Johnny softly.

'Small is beautiful. And I made it "Sea of Tiberias" so that the ignorant would know. Elementary my dear Polycarp.'

'Why not finish your story about your last voyage on it?'

'Because I don't know how it ended. I don't even know whether it happened, whether I ever saw Galilee again after leaving it for the journey to Jerusalem with Word.'

'But what happened after you took his hand?'

'I don't remember anything more. I don't remember how we got there, or when we went there, or how we left. I think I know why we were there.'

'Why?'

'Because Word wanted Peter to be on his own ground, to remake his discipleship, from his catching more fish than he wanted, to standing beside a fire denying Word. It was all done with those three repetitions of love. Actually the whole Resurrection was caused by love. What would be the point of Word's coming back to Earth if nobody who had known him loved him? Mother Mary could have brought him back on her own, I dare say. So could Mary of Magdala.'

'So could you.'

Johnny laughed. 'I was a child. I didn't count.'

'You did, with him.'

The old man grew serious. 'Yes, I did. He would have come back just for me. He would have come back just for anyone. There needs be only one person. He's like that. But about that last visit or non-visit to Galilee: my next memory is being back in the studio in Jerusalem with Mother Salome telling me to wake up.'

'It was just a dream?'

'Not contemptible, if that's what you mean by just. And maybe not a dream. I took the precaution of asking Peter the next day if we had been on the Sea of Galilee together the previous night. He beamed at me, and said he was sure we had been, but he couldn't remember anything more about how we got there or how we left than I could. I tried James, who by now wasn't going simply to jeer at me as a superstitious kid. He looked at me very strangely and said, yes, that Word must have taken us there to affirm Peter's return to leadership. He said Word had put him through a similar catechism, on his own, so that he would be able to take over in Jerusalem until he was killed, while Peter would rule from Rome, in the end.'

'Who was to succeed James?'

'Jim. Word said if Jim followed James that it would constructively confuse people. And it certainly has. Also, Jim wrote that wonderful letter embodying so many of Word's ideas and principles. Word must have known he would. I remember the beginning: "Consider yourselves happy indeed, my brothers, when you encounter trials of every sort, as men who know well enough that the testing of their faith breeds endurance." He knew all about that, from the way his own was tested during Word's time of suffering and death, and in the end, from his time of it. He put the time of Word's death to good use, too, turning young Mark into an official historian. A fine lad, that. Thrown to the lions in Alexandria the other day. I'm told he faced his death with a grin practically embracing the lion who bit his head off. He'd also faced unflinching being dragged through the roughly-stoned streets at the end of a chariot. He never met Word, only saw him, but he bore witness to him all right.'

Polycarp looked suspiciously at the old man. 'How do you know all this?'

Johnny let out a squawk of laughter. 'When I first met Miriam, Jairus's daughter who married Philip and gave him four daughters, she would have answered questions like that by telling me little boys shouldn't ask big questions. You're much bigger than I was then, and than I am now, but I'm afraid I have to tell you to be a good little Polycarp. I notice how patient you are for the way that everyone seems to imagine themselves appropriate people to give you advice.'

'But I like your advice.'

'That's because, being older than the rest of them, I don't give you much. I guarantee that when you are seventy, you'll still be thanking people politely for advice they heap on you. But my advice here is, listen to those whose advice is worth getting. They are very few. And listen to children, who give excellent advice without knowing it.'

'I thought Paul of Tarsus thought Mark a coward.'

'Mark knew he was afraid. That was the first thing Jim noticed about him. A thing I was told long ago, by Herod's steward Chuza, was to be glad to be afraid. Mark learned that lesson.'

'From you?'

'Probably from Jim. I didn't know him well. I'm not sure Paul learned it. Paul was very brave, personally, but when his time came to bear his last witness for Word he insisted on the clean death of a Roman citizen, no fires, no lions, no crucifixions, just a single sword-cut, over and out. Mark doesn't seem to have opted for more humane methods. Still, we mustn't be hard on Paul. He had to learn so much so quickly, and he was very valuable to us even if he learned it at the top of his voice. What we would have done without him I don't know. He was almost as useful as he thought he was.'

'Was Mark a good historian of Word – I mean, of the Lord?'

Johnny nodded approvingly. 'Yes, Word was my name for him, or, if you prefer, his name for my name for him, and it belongs to us. Mark as historian? Well, he had the right sources landed in his lap, which is a fine start. His mother would have squeezed every available source for him until it was bone dry or perishing for want of air, or both. Peter hammered every detail into him that he could, especially those which Peter thought discreditable to himself. They weren't always as discreditable as he thought, and it was greatly to his credit he insisted on getting them into the record. And Peter had to have everything explained both ways which was invaluable to a historian. Anyone who wants people to make use of their history must know that they must say everything twice, but not in the same words because the greater the stupidity the greater the snobbery. And Mark asked and asked and asked. Jim gave him as much as he could, and told him who would know more about some things. His mother saw he heard the women's stories, and women always know more than men do, as they will tell you if you really win their confidence. Oh, and they will also be generous with their advice.'

'What do you think of his Gospel?'

'I never had a chance to read it. There were no copies where I was, or if there were, nobody told me. I heard long extracts quoted from it, of course, and I admired it, apart from its Greek, which was bad. But then', said Johnny virtuously, 'he wasn't taught by Word.'

'And Matthew's?'

'The same. I suppose their account of Word's conscription of Matthew was correct, but it may have taken longer. The interview I remember was Matthew seeking conscription from Word, but the final stage may have been executed the next day, and certainly Word must have started him off on the impulse to volunteer. He certainly started me off, just by looking at me, and many of the others may have joined up for the same cause.'

'And Luke?'

'Ah, that's another story – and another gospel. You have seen all of them, I know. Anything strike you about Luke?'

'Its rich proliferation of beauty.'

'Yes, he had that all right', agreed Johnny. 'In a way he had to compensate because, of the four of us, he alone never saw, let alone spoke to or heard Word. Anything else?'

Polycarp thought, and then smiled with the joy of a person who usually had little luck in solving riddles. 'He has great detail on the Lord's birth, both before and after. But he was much younger than our Lord's generation, he must have been younger than even you. Mother Mary must have been dead when he came round finding what new facts he could.'

'Mother Mary didn't die, as we understand the process.' Polycarp's jaw dropped. 'But how –?'

'Her son stood beside her bed at the moment she stopped breathing, gathered her in his arms, kissed me, and vanished with her. *That's* the last time I saw him.'

'But I've seen her tomb!'

'And didn't they make her a nice one?'

'But how –?'

'Doesn't it make sense? He was a good son. Wouldn't a good son take his mother home when she was tired?'

'But you had been her son for so long.' Johnny hiccupped with laughter.

'I tried to be a good son to her and to my first parents, but I could hardly compete with Word. He was the best of all Jewish sons, and she was the best of all Jewish mothers, and I can pay no higher compliment.' He smiled widely, and toothlessly. He had learned over many years that tears can be less visible when you smile.

'So where did Luke get his information?'

'Where do you think? My parents died while we were all living still in Jerusalem, I'm glad they didn't have to witness James's death. Herod Agrippa, the first to link those ugly names, killed James. He arrested Peter, who got out of prison by a miracle from Word and was then smuggled out of the city by routes organised by Mark's mother. But Word made it clear to me that his own mother was in danger, once Herod Agrippa realised she was the centre of all our movement, and that any major decision was privately cleared with her. She didn't work in the open. So I took her here.'

'How?'

'Dolphins. The same two whom you will never tell anyone about. They liked her very much and she them. Since nobody heard anything to suggest we left aboard ship, the rumour travelled that both of us died in Jerusalem, I was killed, she wasn't. I found it quite useful to be dead at that time. It's time I died again. Mother Mary and I lived several years here, and either here or in Jerusalem she told me a great deal about Word's childhood, including his being lost for three days in the Temple, when he first met Annas, who really was High Priest then. Yes, Luke was very useful to me. I gave him any thing I didn't want to reserve for my own Gospel, and he saved me the trouble of writing some sort of life-story of Word. So I could concentrate on what Word said, and told you what I hadn't already written down. I was so anxious to do some bits that they are probably in the wrong order in some places.'

'Shouldn't we –?'

'Not now. I'm enjoying talking. Give me some more water, old throats get dry.'

'Annas?'

'Thanks. I'm a trouble to you, being unable to stand up and get it for myself.'

For answer Polycarp kissed the old man on his bald head, and Johnny crowed with pleasure. 'I'll tell you about Annas. He had been quite annoyed with Word and the other disciples for involving me in their movement, because he had become fond of me. After Word had left us in body, about forty days following his death, he sent his holy spirit to fortify us, and Peter and I healed a lame man, and we were haled before Annas, Caiaphas and the Temple big shots. They kept on telling us not to preach in Word's name, and we kept on preaching in Word's name, and on at least one occasion the lot of us were beaten by sacerdotal command. It was mild enough, nothing like what Word suffered, and I suspect Annas fixed up for us to get the mildest treatment allowed, for he told Caiaphas and the others in a nasty, vicious voice that he'd see to our punishment and gave orders to the Temple guards, and then when they started in, I was the first one strung up, and I waited for the lash, and something practically tickled me, and Annas winked at me, and then told the guards to leave me alone and do the others, but made very benign gestures. Nobody was really hurt. Then he pulled my ear and told me I was a disreputable ruffian and I was to come to him for further instruction. So I would go into the Temple, and pray, and call on Annas, who would give me fruit and tell me I was a hopeless case, and ask me all sorts of things about Word. And even I could see he argued less and less, and asked more and more. He also told me many things the Temple priests and officials had said among themselves when getting more and more afraid of Word. I had learned quite a few details from Nicodemus, but thanks to Annas I could put things into my Gospel which even Nicodemus had not known. In the end he was taken ill quite suddenly and asked for me, and I went to his house, and ill as he was he told his sons and Caiaphas to leave the room while he talked to me. And he simply said he was sorry for having had anything to do with putting Word to death, and what could I do about it? And I said that if he repented, Word would forgive him, for before Word left us he had told us that what sins we remitted would be remitted, and whose sins we retained would be retained, and Annas thanked me, and I kissed him, and he drifted into sleep, and died the next day. I was very happy about that, as I had always liked Annas. I did tell him that he had known Word long ago, having heard it by then from Mother Mary. You should have seen his face.'

'Why did Annas like you?'

Johnny shrugged his fleshless shoulders. 'Who knows? Maybe I reminded him of the believer he had once been, and wished he had remained. He *may* have liked me because I reminded him of Word.'

Polycarp was speechless for a moment, slightly aghast. Johnny smiled, a little crookedly on the left side of his mouth, and murmured 'Don't be afraid, Word won't kill me for saying that, or you for listening to it. Word taught me at a very formative age. I lived in his company for months. I loved him so much I could practically have devoured the air in which he moved, and still do, except now I must devour eternity. I learned my languages from him. If my writing has any merit, it comes from what he inspired and what from him I learned to imitate.'

Polycarp forced a smile. 'It was just that I know how you thought the ceiling of the bath-house might fall on the heads of the bathers because the heretic Cerinthus was there.'

Johnny bit back a gale of laughter. Polycarp was an admirable disciple, and a very good amanuensis, much more reliable than Papias, for instance, but his reliability robbed him of humour. Johnny could never tell him what had really happened, when he saw that posturing idiot in the bath-house, pontificating that Word was not God but only an ordinary man into whom Christ came when he was baptised only to desert him at Gethsemane, and that Christ was not God, and that God was not God. Johnny, on an impulse, had shrieked in his loudest voice – still powerful enough then, at 70, that the ceiling of the bath-house would fall in because Cerinthus, the enemy of truth, was inside it, and rushed thunderously through as many of the various chambers as possible before hurtling out of doors, more or less dressed, followed by an increasing crowd more or less undressed, responding to Johnny's chant

> Run, run, the ceiling's falling
> While Cerinthus has a bath,
> Fly, fly, your fate's appalling,
> They will tell it soon in Gath.
> Don't waste time caterwauling,
> Let your terror find you wings,
> When Cerinthus' bath is calling,
> Death brings on his choicest stings.

And the entire bath-house streamed out on the street with Cerinthus at the end (as Johnny had anticipated) shouting 'I'm here, and it's quite safe!' to be surrounded by a yelling crowd who answered him by insisting the sky was falling and they must tell the emperor. It did for Cerinthus in Ephesus, for he could hardly open his mouth in public thereafter without having some buffoon shout that he would bring down the house. It looked for a time as if it would also do for Johnny, who was sent to Rome to be interviewed by Domitian and plunged harmlessly into boiling oil, after which he was exiled to Patmos until Nerva became emperor. Cerinthus was gone by the time of Johnny's return to Ephesus. Nobody knew what had become of him, though Polycarp heard rumours of a rich widow.

'Y-y-yes', resumed Johnny, hoping he sounded above such a coarse topic, 'Annas must have found me in some ways reminiscent of the boy to whom he had talked for three days twenty years or so before he met me. I would have been nowhere as learned, could not hope to be. And I didn't model myself on Word, which would just have been silly: he was Word, and I was me. But I may have argued like Word. Thinking over that Gospel, I suspect I sometimes sound like him. I'm delighted if I do, but I don't want to try to. He always wants us to be ourselves, and who could be him, but him?'

'As the Psalmist says, what god is as great as our God?', responded Polycarp.

'Exactly.' Johnny scratched the back of his head, patting one or two remaining hairs affectionately.

'But we are to be like him in being one another's servants?' Polycarp was dutiful rather than doubtful.

'Certainly. In fact we should try to be like him, not excessive, not overdoing it.' The marriage-feast passed before Johnny's memory and he grinned surreptitiously.

'It is a great thing to be his servant.' Polycarp squared his shoulders.

'It is the most wonderful thing in the world.'

'Tell me, Master –'

'Now, you know perfectly well, that I'll tell you nothing if you call me that. I'm Johnny, or John if you want. I'd call you Polly if it didn't interfere with your dignity as Bishop of Smyrna, of which I expect you to enter into possession when I am no longer here. You will find a ring in my room. Take it, and wear it. Mother Mary gave it to me, and if anyone is entitled to make someone a bishop, she is. Don't speak any suitable response now, just ask me what you were going to ask.'

Polycarp gulped. 'I will try to be worthy of you.'

'That's easy.'

'And of Mother Mary.'

'That's difficult.'

'And of her son.'

'That's impossible. Serve him all the days of your life, that's all he asks.'

'I will. I hope I will never betray him.'

Johnny leaned forward. 'Good man. I was afraid you would say you would never betray him. That's dangerous. Remember poor old Peter.

Now, I believe you will be true to the end, however horrible it may be.

'What was your question back then?' 'I wondered why you never mention your name in your Gospel.'

Johnny's eyes widened. 'But I do. It's the first thing I mention, after Word and God:

> There was a man sent from God, whose name was John.
> The same came for a witness, to bear witness of the Light,
> that all men through him might believe.
> He was not that Light, but was sent to bear witness of that
> Light.'

'But that's John the Baptizer!' gabbled Polycarp. 'That's not you!'

'It's John the Baptizer', agreed Johnny, 'but it's also me. How ends my Gospel?'

Polycarp read, hesitantly:

> This is the disciple who bears witness of these things, and
> we know that his witness is true.
> And there are also many other things which Jesus did, the
> which, if they should be written every one, I suppose that
> even the world itself could not contain the books that should
> be written.

'That's it', grinned Johnny. 'John the Baptizer was sent to bear witness, *but he could only begin the witness, because he was killed!* John's witness had to be continued, and I was the John who continued it. There are two kinds of witness: the witness who gives its life, and the witness who lives its life. The second could be the harder. Those of us who saw Word die knew pain as bad as death can be. Yet I remember Mother Mary, whose agony must have been worse than mine, standing strong and firm, fulfilling her son's word.' He smiled faintly. 'Word's word. But her work from the beginning had been far greater than witness: it had been to enable Word to be made flesh. Equally her work at the end was to enable Word to be made ready for his spirit to return to that flesh. Mine was the simpler task: to see, and to tell, as the other John's had been. But this Gospel is to complete my witness, a witness also made in part in my other writings. Yet to show it was true, it had to end by saying it was not telling all, and that witness to Word could never be complete.'

'Yet you never met the other John?'

'No. Yet I have a strange feeling we communicated. Word and our Mother Mary both told me a lot about him, and so did Andrew, and Ju – some of John's other disciples. But read that early passage where I give his words about Word, still a portion written by me before my eyes grew weak and I started to have it taken down by Papias and then by you. It begins:

A man can receive nothing, except it be given him from heaven.

Ye yourselves bear me witness,
that I said, I am not the Christ, but
that I am sent before him.

He that hath the bride is the
bridegroom: but the friend of the
bridegroom, which standeth and heareth
him, rejoiceth greatly because of the
bridegroom's voice: this my joy there
fore is fulfilled.

He must increase, but I must decrease.

He that cometh from above is above
all: he that is of the earth is earthly,
and speaketh of the earth: he that
cometh from heaven is above all.

And what he hath seen and heard,
that he testifieth: and no man receiveth
his testimony.

He that hath received his testimony
hath set to his seal that God is true.

For he whom God hath sent speaketh
the words of God: for God giveth not the
Spirit by measure unto him.

The Father loveth the Son, and hath
given all things into his hand.

He that believeth on the Son hath

everlasting life: and he that believeth
not the Son shall not see life: but
the wrath of God abideth on him.

Now, I know that is what the other John said. I did not hear his voice
speaking it, but I am certain he spoke through me. It may be that Word, or
Mother Mary, or Andrew, or – some other disciple – or someone else who
was present when John the Baptizer said it. It may have been that such a
person or people told me the words and I forget the telling. In any case I
know Word would not allow me to speak it in my Gospel if it be not true.'

'Who's "we"?' Polycarp was back to an earlier puzzlement.

'We what?'

'We know that his witness is true.'

'Oh, that!' Johnny laughed. 'Word and me. You, if you like, as well.'

'I do like', and Polycarp blushed. 'It just sounds a little odd to have you
say that you know what you testify is true.'

'It's rather an important point', nodded Johnny, impishly. 'I wouldn't
want anyone thinking I wrote what I didn't know to be true. It's also
important that you, without whom I couldn't say it, think that. And it's
most important of all that Word thinks it.'

'And you think he does.'

Johnny's mouth set in a firm though not hostile line. 'I know he does.'

'Why do you call yourself the Beloved Disciple?'

Johnny stared through sightless eyes. 'Because I was. Because I am. It's
the only thing about me that is of any importance other than my witness to
Word. You are a Bishop, my dear Polycarp, and Peter the Rock on which
Word's Church is built, and my brother James is truly called Great, and Jim
is truly called the Just, and Mary is the Mother of God, as well as of me,
and so of us all. I am the Beloved Disciple. Why should I not glory in it?'

Polycarp's head bowed reverently towards the old man, regardless of
Johnny's inability to see.

'And now, tell the other little children –' began Johnny.

'Why do you always call us little children?' expostulated Polycarp.

'Because Word taught me it is the greatest compliment that can be paid.
So tell the other little children, as always, to love one another, for love is
of God, and let them open their purses, and if need be lay down their lives

for love of one another, for God so loves us that he sent his only begotten son into the world, that we might live through him. God is love, and they that live in love, live in God, and God in them. We love him because he first loved us. And our message is of that son, who is life, our Word.'

The old man's head seemed to fall over as he finished speaking, and Polycarp tiptoed out that he could have his sleep.

But when he returned he heard Johnny speaking to someone else.' Polycarp hesitated near the door. Johnny's voice said clearly:

'I have to forgive Judas?' with a note of horror. Then there was a pause, as though someone else was speaking. But Polycarp heard no sound. Then came Johnny's voice again. It sounded reluctant but firm:

'Very well, Word, I forgive Judas. Now, please, will you take me home?' Polycarp fell on his knees and prayed for the old man, for himself, and for the world. He took some time at it.

Then he rose, knocked, and went in.

There were garments on the floor near where Johnny had been sitting. They had been folded neatly, as they might have been folded by someone trained by a loving but strong-minded mother, and as Johnny could not now have folded them.

The room was empty.

ACKNOWLEDGMENTS

When I was working on my *British Children's Fiction During the Second World War* it seemed a good idea to my editors and colleagues at the University of Edinburgh Department of History, Paul Addison and Jeremy Crang, to have a seminar discussion arising out of it, in which we talked about Children's History. Authors discussed in that book had in several instances written books for children based on the life of Jesus, notably Enid Blyton, Malcolm Saville, and the general editor of Puffin Books, Eleanor Graham, although the two who had influenced me most from childhood – Joyce Lancaster Brisley of *Milly-Molly-Mandy* celebrity (*My Bible Book*) and the pacifist Theodora Wilson Wilson (*Through the Bible*) – did not have starring roles in my World War II book. Elinor M. Brent-Dyer's *The Chalet School and Jo* (1930) contains first-class chapters on witnessing the Oberammergau Passion Play (which seems in real life to have been the event determining the author's conversion to Roman Catholicism). The most influential treatment of the Passion for Jesus for twentieth-century children is C. S. Lewis's *The Lion, the Witch, and the Wardrobe* (1950) whose children derived from World War II evacuees: its portrait of Jesus, the Lion Aslan, is the stronger for having apparently been born in the book half-way through.

I found myself asking the question 'Who in the Bible liked Children?' (meaning what humans: the very beautiful relationship between God and Samuel is thus excluded). Jesus Christ alone seemed fond of children.

This invited the question, well, if he liked them so well, why did not one of them write about him, followed by its obvious rejoinder 'How do you know one didn't?' There is only one candidate. Matthew was an adult when Jesus met him; Luke never knew him; Mark was a youth, not a child if, as seems most likely, the boy running away from Jesus's arrest was Mark, but that seems to have been his only recorded moment with Jesus. What we know of John argues youthful career competence as a fisher-boy but, as Enid Blyton's *Adventurous Four* series indicates, this quasi-adult professionalism could serve to weaken class barriers and strengthen child solidarity. I have tried to show here that John's known actions as apostle of Jesus and as his 'Beloved Disciple' (still the most obvious identity for that title) make sense for a ten-year-old as well as for an adult, if not more so. The tradition that John was young is very old, and some artists made him very young.

The narrative in my book owed something to the traditions in writers for children, particularly the anti-heroic figure of Richmal Crompton's William. The convention of an approachable youth through whom we can see an otherwise remote hero was established by Scott, professionalised by Conan Doyle, and brought to boyhood's eyes by Stevenson, and its linkage to a mystical, vulnerable, supremely holy adult is realised in Rudyard Kipling's *Kim*, the best work in the genre, and the best work of its author.

The hospitality of the University of Haifa in 1985, as part of the celebrations of Conor Cruise O'Brien's *The Siege*, enabled me to visit many of the sites for this story. O'Brien's artistic and intellectual guidance then and at all other times was invaluable to me, as was that of the former Chief Rabbi of Ireland, David Rosen, in whose synagogue I was privileged to worship, of Professor David Daiches, son of an Edinburgh Rabbi, and of the then President of Israel, President Chaim Herzog, whose father had been Chief Rabbi of Ireland, and whose perception (in a rich Dublin accent) that the Irish and the Jews had so much in common leads some of the character analyses of this book. I had thought about aspects of the book without realising it from my days growing up in Dublin and learning the story of Jesus from my parents, relatives, priests and schoolmasters. Looking back I remember at age 10 suspecting that there was more to discover about Annas than the Gospel tells. On the other hand, almost all the book's research and writing happened in the twenty-first century, and its ideas are sometimes very recent. I thought of the explanation for Thomas's doubts of the Resurrection while writing the sentence immediately before that which asserts it.

Anthony Burgess in his writings and during our long walk together taught me much that proved of great value, and his *Man of Nazareth* was a splendid inspiration: my idea of Philip builds on his.

The book has been read by several friends, including Very Revd Timothy Calvert OP, Mr Thomas McGrath, Dr Joseph Stuart and Mr Richard Wood, as well as by Professor Declan Kiberd and his family. I owe much to their wisdom and even more to their kindness. My debts to the National Library of Scotland continue endlessly. Since writing the book I have derived much from the preaching and writing of the Revd Alex MacDonald of the Free Church of Scotland whose dramatic realisations of so many of the witnesses to Jesus, *Tell Me the Story*, are masterly studies. My children Leila and Michael and their children have been invaluable in all sorts of ways; my daughter Sara and her husband Dr Paul Parvis, both of our School of Divinity, have given me endless valuable scholarly insights, including Paul's perception that each of the four Gospels have unified linguistic identities. My former student Dr Jeffrey Nelson was a heartwarming enthusiast for this book, and I am deeply grateful to the late Dr Stratford Caldecott for his critical scrutiny of the text. My Godson Christopher Green is the book's legal representative. My wife Bonnie has been a triumphant encouragement to it.

It also owes endless thanks to innumerable persons living and dead of all kinds of religious, irreligious, and anti-religious outlook. Its greatest debts are to Word and Johnny.

O.D.E.
School of History, Classics and Archaeology
The University of Edinburgh, 2015